THE
BEST
OF
GREGORY
BENFORD

THE
BEST
OF
GREGORY
BENFORD

GREGORY BENFORD

Edited by David G. Hartwell

SUBTERRANEAN PRESS 2015

First Edition

ISBN
978-1-59606-686-1

Subterranean Press
PO Box 190106
Burton, MI 48519

subterraneanpress.com

To the editors who helped shape these stories:

Ed Ferman, Ted White, Ben Bova, Robert Silverberg,
Ellen Datlow, Henry Gee, Lou Aronica, Greg Bear,
Stan Schmidt, Terry Carr, Marty Greenberg, David Hartwell,
Jonathan Strahan, Gardner Dozois, Gordon van Gelder,
Patrick Nielsen Hayden, George Zebrowski.

Also, to my unconscious, which never gets the credit it deserves.

TABLE OF CONTENTS

NOBODY LIVES
ON BURTON STREET
(1970)

I was standing by one of our temporary command posts, picking my teeth after breakfast and talking to Joe Murphy when the first part of the Domestic Disturbance hit us.

People said the summer of '78 was the worst ever, what with all the pollution haze and everything was kicking up the temperatures, but here it was a year later and getting worse than '78. Spring had lost its bloom a month back and it was hot, sticky—the kind of weather that leaves you with a half-moon of sweat around your armpits before you've had time to finish morning coffee. The summer heat makes for trouble, stirs up people.

I was getting jumpy with the waiting. I walked back toward the duplex apartment set away from the street, trying to round up my men. The apartment was deserted, of course, so I wasn't listening for anything special from the bedroom. I walked right in on them.

Johnson, a kid from the other side of town, was sprawled across the bed with a skinny little black girl. He was really ramming it to her, grunting with each thrust. She had her legs wrapped around him like a snake in heat, sobbing each time he went in, eyes rolled up.

Yeah, I knew that one; rolled with her a few times myself last year. She was a groupie, really, always following our squads around with that hungry look in the eyes. She just liked to hump the boys, I guess, like some girls go for Marines. She had her skirt bunched up around her waist while Johnson was working on her, hands wrapped around her ass so he could lift her up with each lunge. They were really going at it.

"Okay, fun's over," I said, and gave Johnson a light kick in the butt. "Finish it off and form up."

"What th—" he said as he rolled over, still clutching her to him and jerking. Then he saw me and shut up. The girl—Melody, I think her name was—looked at me with big round eyes and squirmed all over Johnson, getting him to hurry up. I made a mental note to get back to her one of these days; she was skinny, but she had a good way of twisting around that really got me off.

I turned and walked back out onto the roof where we had our command post.

We knew the mob was in the area, working toward us. Our communications link had been humming for the last half hour, getting fixes on their direction and asking the computers for advice on how to handle them when they got there.

I looked down. At the end of the street were a lot of semipermanent shops and the mailbox. The mailbox bothers me—it shouldn't be there.

From the other end of Burton Street I could hear the random dull bass of the mob, sounding like animals.

We started getting ready, locking up the equipment. I was already working up a sweat when Joe came over, moaning about the payments on the Snocar he'd been suckered into. I was listening with one ear to him and the other to the crowd noise.

"And it's not just that," Joe said. "It's the neighborhood and the school and everybody around me."

"Everybody's wrong but Murphy, huh?" I said, and grinned.

"Hell no, you know me better than that. It's just that nobody's *going* anyplace. Sure, we've all got jobs, but they're most of them just make-work stuff the unions have gotten away with."

"To get a real job you gotta have training," I said, but I wasn't chuffing him up. I like my job, and it's better than most, but we weren't gonna kid each other that it was some big technical deal. Joe and I are just regular guys.

"What're you griping about this now for, anyway?" I said. "You didn't used to be bothered by anything."

Joe shrugged. "I dunno. Wife's been getting after me to move out of the place we're in and make more money. Gets into fights with the neighbors." He looked a little sheepish about it.

"More money? Hell, y'got everything you need, we all do. Lot of people worse off than you. Look at all those lousy Africans, living on nothing."

I was going to say more, maybe rib him about how he's married and I'm not, but then I stopped. Like I said, all this time I was half listening to the crowd. I can always tell when a bunch has changed its direction like a pack of wolves off on a chase, and when that funny quiet came and lasted about five seconds I knew they were heading our way.

"Scott!" I yelled at our communications man. "Close it down. Get a final printout."

Murphy broke off telling me about his troubles and listened to the crowd for a minute, like he hadn't heard them before, and then took off on a trot to the AnCops we had stashed in the truck below. They were all warmed up and ready to go, but Joe likes to make a final check and maybe have a chance to read in any new instructions Scott gets at the last minute.

I threw away the toothpick and had a last look at my constant-volume joints, to be sure the bulletproof plastiform was matching properly and wouldn't let anything through. Scott came double-timing over with the diagnostics from HQ. The computer compilation was neat and confusing, like it always is. I could make out the rough indices they'd picked up on the crowd heading our way. The best guess—and that's all you ever get, friends, is a guess—was a lot of Psych Disorders and Race Prejudice. There was a fairly high number of Unemployeds, too. We're getting more and more Unemployeds in the city now, and they're hard for the Force to deal with. Usually mad enough to spit. Smash up everything.

I penciled an OK in the margin and tossed it Scott's way. I'd taken too long reading it; I could hear individual shouts now and the tinkling of glass. I flipped the visor down from my helmet and turned on my external audio. It was going to get hot as hell in there, but I'm not chump enough to drag around an air-conditioning unit on top of the rest of my stuff.

I took a look at the street just as a gang of about a hundred people came around the corner two blocks down, spreading out like a dirty gray wave. I ducked over to the edge of the building and waved to Murphy to start off with three AnCops. I had to hold up three fingers for him to see because the noise was already getting high. I looked at my watch. Hell, it wasn't nine A.M. yet.

Scott went down the stairs we'd tracted up the side of the building. I was right behind him. It wasn't a good location for observation now; you made too good a target up there. We picked up Murphy, who was carrying our control boards. All three of us angled down the alley and dropped down behind a short fence to have a look at the street.

Most of them were still screaming at the top of their lungs like they'd never run out of air, waving whatever they had handy and gradually breaking up into smaller units. The faster ones had made it to the first few buildings.

A tall Negro came trotting toward us, moving like he had all the time in the world. He stopped in front of a wooden barbershop, tossed something quickly through the front window, and *whump!* Flames licked out at the upper edges of the window, spreading fast.

An older man picked up some rocks and began methodically pitching them through the smaller windows in the shops next door. A housewife clumped by awkwardly in high heels, looking like she was out on a shopping trip except for the hammer she swung like a pocketbook. She dodged into the barbershop for a second, didn't find anything, and came out. The Negro grinned and pointed at the barber pole on the sidewalk, still revolving, and she caught it in the side with a swipe that threw shattered glass for ten yards.

I turned and looked at Murphy. "All ready?"

He nodded. "Just give the word."

The travel agency next door to the barbershop was concrete-based, so they couldn't burn that. Five men were lunging at the door and on the third try they knocked it in. A moment later a big travel poster sailed out the front window, followed by a chair leg. They were probably doing as much as they could, but without tools they couldn't take much of the furniture apart.

"Okay," I said. "Let's have the first AnCops."

The thick acrid smell from the smoke was drifting down Burton Street to us, but my air filters would take care of most of it. They don't do much about human sweat, though, and I was going to be inside the rest of the day.

Our first prowl car rounded the next corner, going too fast. I looked over at Murphy, who was controlling the car, but he was too busy trying to miss the people who were standing around in the street. Must have gotten a little overanxious on that one. Something was bothering his work.

I thought for sure the car was going to take a tumble and mess us up, but the wheels caught and it rightened itself long enough for the driver to stop a skid. The screech turned the heads of almost everybody in the crowd and they'd started to move in on it almost before the car stopped laying down rubber and came to a full stop. Murphy punched in another instruction and the AnCop next to the driver started firing at a guy on the sidewalk who was trying to light a Molotov cocktail. The AnCop was using something that sounded like a repeating shotgun. The guy with the cocktail just turned around and looked at him a second before scurrying off into a hardware store.

By this time the car was getting everything—bricks, broken pieces of furniture, merchandise from the stores. Something heavy shattered the windshield and the driver ducked back too late to avoid getting his left hand smashed with a bottle. A figure appeared on the top of the hardware shop—it looked like the guy from the sidewalk—and took a long windup before throwing something into the street.

There was a tinkling of glass and a red circle of flame slid across the pavement where it hit just in front of the car, sending smoke curling up over the hood and obscuring the inside. Murphy was going to have to play it by feel now; you couldn't see a thing in the car.

A teenager with a stubby rifle stepped out of a doorway, crouched down low like in a western. He fired twice, very accurately and very fast, at the window of the car. A patrolman was halfway out the door when it hit him full in the face, sprawling the body back over the roof and then pitching it forward into the street.

A red blotch formed around his head, grew rapidly, and ran into the gutter. There was ragged cheering and the teenager ran over to the body, tore off its badge, and backed away. "Souvenir!" he called out, and a few of the others laughed.

I looked at Murphy again and he looked at me and I gave him the nod for the firemen, switching control over to my board. Scott was busy talking into his recorder, taking notes for the write-up later. When Murphy nudged him he stopped and punched in the link for radio control to the fire-fighting units.

By this time most of Burton Street was on fire. Everything you saw had a kind of orange look to it. The crowd was moving toward us once they'd lost interest in the cops, but we'd planned it that way. The firemen came running out in that jerky way they have, just a little in front of us. They were carrying just a regular hose this time because it was a medium-sized group and we couldn't use up a fire engine and all the extras. But they were wearing the usual red uniforms. From a distance you can't tell them from the real thing.

Their subroutine tapes were fouled up again. Instead of heading for the barbershop or any of the other stuff that was burning, like I'd programmed, they turned the hose on a stationery store that nobody had touched yet. There were three of them, holding on to that hose and getting it set up. The crowd had backed off a minute to see what was going on.

When the water came through it knocked in the front window of the store, making the firemen look like real chumps. I could hear the water running around inside, pushing over things, and flooding out the building. The crowd laughed, what there was of it—I noticed some of them had moved off in the other direction, over into somebody else's area.

In a minute or so the laughing stopped, though. One guy who looked like he had been born mad grabbed an ax from somewhere and took a swing at the hose. He didn't get it the first time but people were sticking around to see what would happen and I guess he felt some kind of obligation to go through with it. Even under pressure, a thick hose isn't easy to cut into. He kept at it and on the fourth try a seam split—looked like a bad repair job to me—and a stream of water gushed out and almost hit this guy in the face.

The crowd laughed at that, too, because he backed off real quick then, scared for a little bit. A face full of high-velocity water is no joke, not at that pressure.

The fireman who was holding the hose just a little down from there hadn't paid any attention to this because he wasn't programmed to, so when this guy thought about it he just stepped over and chopped the fireman across the back with the ax.

It was getting hot. I didn't feel like overriding the stock program, so it wasn't long before all the firemen were out of commission, just about the same way. A little old lady—probably with a welfare gripe—borrowed the ax for a minute to separate all of a fireman's arms and legs from the trunk. Looking satisfied, she waddled away after the rest of the mob.

I stood up, lifted my faceplate, and looked at them as they milled back down the street. I took out my grenade launcher and got off a tear gas cartridge on low charge, to hurry them along. The wind was going crosswise so the gas got carried off to the side and down the alleys. Good; wouldn't have complaints from somebody who got caught in it too long.

Scott was busy sending orders for the afternoon shift to get more replacement firemen and cops, but we wouldn't have any trouble getting them in time. There hadn't been much damage, when you think how much they could've done.

"Okay for the reclaim crew?" Murphy said.

"Sure. This bunch won't be back. They look tired out already." They were moving toward Horton's area, three blocks over.

A truck pulled out of the alley and two guys in coveralls jumped out and began picking up the androids, dousing fires as they went. In an hour they'd have everything back in place, even the prefab barbershop.

"Helluva note," Murphy said.

"Huh?"

"All this stuff," he waved a hand down Burton Street. "Seems like a waste to build all this just so these jerks can tear it up again."

"Waste?" I said. "It's the best investment you ever saw. How many people were in the last bunch—two hundred? Every one of them is going to sit around for weeks bragging about how he got him a cop or burned a building."

"Okay, okay. If it does any good, I guess it's cheap at the price."

"If, hell! You know it does. If it didn't they wouldn't be here. You got to be cleared by a psycher before you even get in. The computer works out just what you'll need, just the kind of action that'll work off the aggressions you've got. Then shoots it to us in the profile from HQ before we start. It's foolproof."

"I dunno. You know what the Consies say—the psychers and the probes and drugs are an in—"

"Invasion of privacy?"

"Yeah," Murphy said sullenly.

"Privacy? Man, the psychers are public health! It's part of the welfare! You don't have to go around to some expensive guy who'll have you lie on a couch and talk to him. You can get better stuff right from the government. It's free!"

Murphy looked at me kind of funny. "Sure. Have to go in for a checkup sometime soon. Maybe that's what I need."

I frowned just the right amount. "Well, I dunno, Joe. Man lets his troubles get him down every once in a while, doesn't mean he needs professional help. Don't let it bother you. Forget it."

Joe was okay, but even a guy like me who's never been married could tell he wasn't thinking up this stuff himself. His woman was pushing him. Not satisfied with what she had.

Now, *that* was wrong. Guy like Joe doesn't have anywhere to go. Doesn't know computers, automation. Can't get a career rating in the army. So the pressure was backing up on him.

Supers like me are supposed to check out their people and leave it at that, and I go by the book like everybody else. But Joe wasn't the problem.

I made a mental note to have a psycher look at his wife.

"Okay," he said, taking off his helmet. "I got to go set up the AnCops for the next one."

I watched him walk off down the alley. He was a good man. Hate to lose him.

I started back toward our permanent operations center to check in. After a minute I decided maybe I'd better put Joe's name in, too, just in case. Didn't want anybody blowing up on me.

He'd be happier, work better. I've sure felt a lot better since I had it. It's a good job I got, working in public affairs like this, keeping people straight with themselves.

I went around the corner at the end of the street, thinking about getting something to drink, and noticed the mailbox. I check on it every time because it sure looks like a mistake.

Everything's supposed to be pretty realistic on Burton Street, but putting in a mailbox seems like a goofy idea.

Who's going to try to burn up a box like that, made out of cast iron and bolted down? A guy couldn't take out any aggressions on it.

And it sure can't be for real use. Not on Burton Street.

Nobody lives around there.

DOING LENNON
(1975)

Sanity calms, but madness is more interesting.
—JOHN RUSSELL

As the hideous cold seeps from him he feels everything becoming sharp and clear again. He decides he can do it, he can make it work. He opens his eyes.

"Hello." His voice rasps. "Bet you aren't expecting me. I'm John Lennon."

"What?" the face above him says.

"You know. John Lennon. The Beatles."

Professor Hermann—the name attached to the face which loomed over him as he drifted up, up from the Long Sleep—is vague about the precise date. It is either 2108 or 2180. Hermann makes a little joke about inversion of positional notation; it has something to do with nondenumerable set theory, which is all the rage. The ceiling glows with a smooth green phosphorescence and Fielding lies there letting them prick him with needles, unwrap his organiform nutrient webbing, poke and adjust and massage as he listens to a hollow *pock-pocketa*. He knows this is the crucial moment, he must hit them with it now.

"I'm glad it worked," Fielding says with a Liverpool accent. He has got it just right, the rising pitch at the end and the nasal tones.

"No doubt there is an error in our log," Hermann says pedantically. "You are listed as Henry Fielding."

Fielding smiles. "Ah, that's the ruse, you see."

Hermann blinks owlishly. "Deceiving Immortality Incorporated is—"

"I was fleeing political persecution, y'dig. Coming out for the workers and all. Writing songs about persecution and pollution and the working-class hero. Snarky stuff. So when the jackboot skinheads came in I decided to check out."

Fielding slips easily into the story he has memorized, all plotted and placed with major characters and minor characters and bits of incident, all of it sounding very real. He wrote it himself, he has it down. He continues talking while Hermann and some white-smocked assistants help him sit up, flex his legs, test his reflexes. Around them are vats and baths and tanks. A fog billows from a hole in the floor; a liquid nitrogen immersion bath.

Hermann listens intently to the story, nodding now and then, and summons other officials. Fielding tells his story again while the attendants work on him. He is careful to give the events in different order, with different details each time. His accent is standing up though there is mucus in his sinuses that makes the high singsong bits hard to get out. They give him something to eat; it tastes like chicken-flavored ice cream. After a while he sees he has them convinced. After all, the late twentieth was a turbulent time, crammed with gaudy events, lurid people. Fielding makes it seem reasonable that an aging rock star, seeing his public slip away and the government closing in, would corpsicle himself.

The officials nod and gesture and Fielding is wheeled out on a carry table. Immortality Incorporated is more like a church than a business. There is a ghostly hush in the hallways, the attendants are distant and reserved. Scientific servants in the temple of life.

They take him to an elaborate display, punch a button. A voice begins to drone a welcome to the year 2108 (or 2180). The voice tells him he is one of the few from his benighted age who saw the slender hope science held out to the diseased and dying. His vision has been rewarded. He has survived the unfreezing. There is some nondenominational talk about God and death and the eternal rhythm and balance of life, ending with a retouched holographic photograph of the Founding Fathers. They are a small knot of biotechnicians and engineers clustered around an immersion tank. Close-cropped hair, white shirts with ball-point pens clipped in the pockets. They wear glasses and smile weakly at the camera, as though they have just been shaken awake.

"I'm hungry," Fielding says.

News that Lennon is revived spreads quickly. The Society for Dissipative Anachronisms holds a press conference for him. As he strides into the room Fielding clenches his fists so no one can see his hands shaking. This is the start. He has to make it here.

"How do you find the future, Mr. Lennon?"

"Turn right at Greenland." Maybe they will recognize it from *A Hard Day's Night*. This is before his name impacts fully, before many remember who John Lennon was. A fat man asks Fielding why he elected for the Long Sleep before he really needed it and Fielding says enigmatically, "The role of boredom in human history is underrated." This makes the evening news and the weekly topical roundup a few days later.

A fan of the twentieth asks him about the breakup with Paul, whether Ringo's death was a suicide, what about Allan Klein, how about the missing lines from *Abbey Road*? Did he like Dylan? What does he think of the Aarons theory that the Beatles could have stopped Vietnam?

Fielding parries a few questions, answers others. He does not tell them, of course, that in the early sixties he worked in a bank and wore granny glasses. Then he became a broker with Harcum, Brandels and Son and his take in 1969 was 57,803 dollars, not counting the money siphoned off into the two concealed accounts in Switzerland. But he read *Rolling Stone* religiously, collected Beatles memorabilia, had all the albums and books and could quote any verse from any song. He saw Paul once at a distance, coming out of a recording session. And he had a friend into Buddhism, who met Harrison one weekend in Surrey. Fielding did not mention his vacation spent wandering around Liverpool, picking up the accent and visiting all the old places, the cellars where they played and the narrow dark little houses their families owned in the early days. And as the years dribbled on and Fielding's money piled up, he lived increasingly in those golden days of the sixties, imagined himself playing side man along with Paul or George or John and crooning those same notes into the microphones, practically kissing the metal. And Fielding did not speak of his dreams.

It is the antiseptic Stanley Kubrick future. They are very adept at hardware. Population is stabilized at half a billion. Everywhere there are white hard decorator chairs in vaguely Danish modern. There seems no shortage of electrical power or oil or copper or zinc. Everyone has a hobby.

Entertainment is a huge enterprise, with stress on ritual violence. Fielding watches a few games of Combat Golf, takes in a public execution or two. He goes to witness an electrical man short-circuit himself. The flash is visible over the curve of the Earth.

Genetic manipulants—*manips*, Hermann explains—are thin, stringy people, all lines and knobby joints where they connect directly into machine linkages. They are designed for some indecipherable purpose. Hermann, his guide, launches into an explanation but Fielding interrupts him to say, "Do you know where I can get a guitar?"

Fielding views the era 1950–1980:

"Astrology wasn't rational, nobody really believed it, you've got to realize that. It was *boogie woogie*. On the other hand, science and rationalism were progressive jazz."

He smiles as he says it. The 3D snout closes in. Fielding has purchased well and his plastic surgery, to lengthen the nose and give him that wry Lennonesque smirk, holds up well. Even the technicians at Immortality Incorporated missed it.

Fielding suffers odd moments of blackout. He loses the rub of rough cloth at a cuff on his shirt, the chill of air-conditioned breeze along his neck. The world dwindles away and sinks into inky black, but in a moment it is all back and he hears the distant murmur of traffic, and convulsively, by reflex, he squeezes the bulb in his hand and the orange vapor rises around him. He breathes deeply, sighs. Visions float into his mind and the sour tang of the mist reassures him.

Every age is known by its pleasures, Fielding reads from the library readout. The twentieth introduced two: high speed and hallucinogenic drugs. Both proved dangerous in the long run, which made them even more interesting. The twenty-first developed weightlessness, which worked out well except for the re-entry problems if one overindulged. In the twenty-second there were aquaform and something Fielding could not pronounce or understand.

He thumbs away the readout and calls Hermann for advice.

Translational difficulties:

They give him a sort of pasty suet when he goes to the counter to get his food. He shoves it back at them.

"Gah! Don't you have a hamburger someplace?" The stunted man behind the counter flexes his arms, makes a rude sign with his four fingers and goes away. The wiry woman next to Fielding rubs her thumbnail along the hideous scar at her side and peers at him. She wears only orange shorts and boots, but he can see the concealed dagger in her armpit.

"Hamburger?" she says severely. "That is the name of a citizen of the German city of Hamburg. Were you a cannibal then?"

Fielding does not know the proper response, which could be dangerous. When he pauses she massages her brown scar with new energy and makes a sign of sexual invitation. Fielding backs away. He is glad he did not mention French fries.

On 3D he makes a mistake about the recording date of *Sergeant Pepper's Lonely Hearts Club Band*. A ferret-eyed history student lunges in for the point but Fielding leans back casually, getting the accent just right, and says, "I zonk my brow with heel of hand, consterned!" and the audience laughs and he is away, free.

Hermann has become his friend. The library readout says this is a common phenomenon among Immortality Incorporated employees who are fascinated by the past to begin with (or otherwise would not be in the business), and anyway Hermann and Fielding are about the same age, forty-seven. Hermann is not surprised that Fielding is practicing his chords and touching up his act.

"You want to get out on the road again, is that it?" Hermann says. "You want to be getting popular."

"It's my business."

"But your songs, they are old."

"Oldies but goldies," Fielding says solemnly.

"Perhaps you are right," Hermann sighs. "We are starved for variety. The people, no matter how educated—anything tickles their nose they think is champagne."

Fielding flicks on the tape input and launches into the hard-driving opening of "Eight Days a Week." He goes through all the chords, getting them right the first time. His fingers dance among the humming copper wires.

Hermann frowns but Fielding feels elated. He decides to celebrate. Precious reserves of cash are dwindling, even considering how much he made in the international bond market of '83; there is not much left. He decides to splurge. He orders an alcoholic vapor and a baked pigeon. Hermann is still worried but he eats the mottled pigeon with relish, licking his fingers. The spiced crust snaps crisply. Hermann asks to take the bones home to his family.

✹

"You have drawn the rank-scented many," Hermann says heavily as the announcer begins his introduction. The air sparkles with anticipation.

"Ah, but they're *my* many," Fielding says. The applause begins, the background music comes up, and Fielding trots out onto the stage, puffing slightly.

"One, two, three—" and he is into it, catching the chords just right, belting out a number from *Magical Mystery Tour*. He is right, he is on, he is John Lennon just as he always wanted to be. The music picks him up and carries him along. When he finishes, a river of applause bursts over the stage from the vast amphitheater and Fielding grins crazily to himself. It feels exactly the way he always thought it would. His heart pounds.

He goes directly into a slow ballad from the *Imagine* album to calm them down. He is swimming in the lights and the 3D snouts zoom in and out, bracketing his image from every conceivable direction. At the end of the number somebody yells from the audience, "You're radiating on all your eigenfrequencies!" And Fielding nods, grins, feels the warmth of it all wash over him.

"Thrilled to the gills," he says into the microphone.

The crowd chuckles and stirs.

When he does one of the last Lennon numbers, "The Ego-Bird Flies," the augmented sound sweeps out from the stage and explodes over the audience. Fielding is euphoric. He dances as though someone is firing pistols at his feet.

He does cuts from *Beatles '65*, *Help!*, *Rubber Soul*, *Let It Be*—all with technical backing spliced in from the original tracks, Fielding providing

22

only Lennon's vocals and instrumentals. Classical scholars have pored over the original material, deciding who did which guitar riff, which tenor line was McCartney's, dissecting the works as though they were salamanders under a knife. But Fielding doesn't care, as long as they let him play and sing. He does another number, then another, and finally they must carry him from the stage. It is the happiest moment he has ever known.

"But I don't understand what Boss 30 radio means," Hermann says.

"Thirty most popular songs."

"But why today?"

"Me."

"They call you a 'sonic boom sensation'—that is another phrase from your time?"

"Dead on. Fellow is following me around now, picking my brains for details. Part of his thesis, he says."

"But it is such noise—"

"Why, that's a crock, Hermann. Look, you chaps have such a small population, so bloody few creative people. What do you expect? Anybody with energy and drive can make it in this world. And I come from a time that was dynamic, that really got off."

"Barbarians at the gates," Hermann says.

"That's what *Reader's Digest* said, too," Fielding murmurs.

After one of his concerts in Australia Fielding finds a girl waiting for him outside. He goes home with her—it seems the thing to do, considering—and finds there have been few technical advances, if any, in this field either. It is the standard, ten-toes-up, ten-toes-down position she prefers, nothing unusual, nothing *à la carte*. But he likes her legs, he relishes her beehive hair and heavy mouth. He takes her along; she has nothing else to do.

On an off day, in what is left of India, she takes him to a museum. She shows him the first airplane (a Piper Cub), the original manuscript of the great collaboration between Buckminster Fuller and Hemingway, a delicate print of *The Fifty-Three Stations of The Takaido Road* from Japan.

"Oh yes," Fielding says. "We won that war, you know."

(He should not seem to be more than he is.)

Fielding hopes they don't discover, with all this burrowing in the old records, that he had the original Lennon killed. He argues with himself that it really was necessary. He couldn't possibly cover his story in the future if Lennon kept on living. The historical facts would not jibe. It was hard enough to convince Immortality Incorporated that even someone as rich as Lennon would be able to forge records and change fingerprints— they had checked that to escape the authorities. Well, Fielding thinks. Lennon was no loss by 1988 anyway. It was pure accident that Fielding and Lennon had been born in the same year, but that didn't mean that Fielding couldn't take advantage of the circumstances. He wasn't worth over ten million fixed 1985 dollars for nothing.

At one of his concerts he says to the audience between numbers, "Don't look back—you'll just see your mistakes." It sounds like something Lennon would have said. The audience seems to like it.

Press Conference.

"And why did you take a second wife, Mr. Lennon, and then a third?" In 2180 (or 2108) divorce is frowned upon. Yoko Ono is still the Beatle nemesis.

Fielding pauses and then says, "Adultery is the application of democracy to love." He does not tell them the line is from H. L. Mencken.

He has gotten used to the women now. "Just cast them aside like sucked oranges," Fielding mutters to himself. It is a delicious moment. He had never been very successful with women before, even with all his money.

He strides through the yellow curved streets, walking lightly on the earth. A young girl passes, winks.

Fielding calls after her, "Sic transit, Gloria!"

It is his own line, not a copy from Lennon. He feels a heady rush of joy. He is into it, the ideas flash through his mind spontaneously. He is doing Lennon.

Thus, when Hermann comes to tell him that Paul McCartney has been revived by the Society for Dissipative Anachronisms, the body discovered in a private vault in England, at first it does not register with Fielding. Lines of postcoital depression flicker across his otherwise untroubled brow. He rolls out of bed and stands watching a wave turn to white foam on the beach at La Jolla. He is in Nanking. It is midnight.

"Me old bud, then?" he manages to say, getting the lilt into the voice still. He adjusts his granny glasses. Rising anxiety stirs in his throat. "My, my..."

It takes weeks to defrost McCartney. He had died much later than Lennon, plump and prosperous, the greatest pop star of all time—or at least the biggest money-maker. "Same thing," Fielding mutters to himself.

When Paul's cancer is sponged away and the sluggish organs palped to life, the world media press for a meeting.

"For what?" Fielding is nonchalant. "It's not as though we were ever reconciled, y'know. We got a *divorce*, Hermann."

"Can't you put that aside?"

"For a fat old slug who pro'bly danced on me grave?"

"No such thing occurred. There are videotapes, and Mr. McCartney was most polite."

"God, a future where everyone's literal! I *told* you I was a nasty type, why can't you simply accept—"

"It is arranged," Hermann says firmly. "You must go. Overcome your antagonism."

Fear clutches at Fielding.

McCartney is puffy, jowly, but his eyes crackle with intelligence. The years have not fogged his quickness. Fielding has arranged the meeting away from crowds, at a forest resort. Attendants help McCartney into the hushed room. An expectant pause.

"You want to join me band?" Fielding says brightly. It is the only quotation he can remember that seems to fit; Lennon had said that when they first met.

McCartney blinks, peers nearsightedly at him. "D'you really need another guitar?"

"Whatever noisemaker's your fancy."

"Okay."

"You're hired, lad."

They shake hands with mock seriousness. The spectators—who have paid dearly for their tickets—applaud loudly. McCartney smiles, embraces Fielding, and then sneezes.

"Been cold lately," Fielding says. A ripple of laughter.

McCartney is offhand, bemused by the world he has entered. His manner is confident, interested. He seems to accept Fielding automatically. He makes a few jokes, as light and inconsequential as his post-Beatles music.

Fielding watches him closely, feeling an awe he had not expected. *That's him. Paul. The real thing.* He starts to ask something and realizes that it is a dumb, out-of-character, fan-type question. He is being betrayed by his instincts. He will have to be careful.

Later, they go for a walk in the woods. The attendants hover a hundred meters behind, portable med units at the ready. They are worried about McCartney's cold. This is the first moment they have been beyond earshot of others. Fielding feels his pulse rising. "You okay?" he asks the puffing McCartney.

"Still a bit dizzy, I am. Never thought it'd work, really."

"The freezing, it gets into your bones."

"Strange place. Clean, like Switzerland."

"Yeah. Peaceful. They're mad for us here."

"You meant that about your band?"

"Sure. Your fingers'll thaw out. Fat as they are, they'll still get around a guitar string."

"Ummm. Wonder if George is tucked away in an ice cube somewhere?"

"Hadn't thought." The idea fills Fielding with terror.

"Could ask about Ringo, too."

"Re-create the whole thing? I was against that. Dunno if I still am." Best to be noncommittal. He would love to meet them, sure, but his chances of bringing this off day by day, in the company of all three of them... he frowns.

McCartney's pink cheeks glow from the exercise. The eyes are bright, active, studying Fielding. "Did you think it would work? Really?"

"The freezing? Well, what's to lose? I said to Yoko, I said—"

"No, not the freezing. I mean this impersonation you're carrying off."

Fielding reels away, smacks into a pine tree. "What? What?"

"C'mon, you're not John."

A strangled cry erupts from Fielding's throat. "But...how..."

"Just not the same, is all. Dunno Merseyside jokes, street names, the lot."

"I, I know that Penny Lane was a street and—"

"Come off it. You're not even English!"

Fielding's mouth opens, but he can say nothing. He has failed. Tripped up by some nuance, some trick phrase he should've responded to—

"Of course," McCartney says urbanely, looking at him sideways, "you don't know for sure if I'm the real one either, do you?"

Fielding stutters, "If, if, what're you saying, I—"

"Or I could even be a ringer planted by Hermann, eh? To test you out? In that case, you've responded the wrong way. Should've stayed in character, John."

"Could be this, could be that—what the hell you saying? Who *are* you?" Anger flashes through him. A trick, a maze of choices, possibilities that he had not considered. The forest whirls around him, McCartney leers at his confusion, bright spokes of sunlight pierce his eyes, he feels himself falling, collapsing, the pine trees wither, colors drain away, blue to pink to gray—

He is watching a blank dark wall, smelling nothing, no tremor through his skin, no wet touch of damp air. Sliding infinite silence. The world is black.

—Flat black, Fielding adds, like we used to say in Liverpool.

—Liverpool? He was never in Liverpool. That was a lie, too—

—And he knows instantly what he is. The truth skewers him.

Hello, you still operable?

Fielding rummages through shards of cold electrical memory and finds himself. He is not Fielding, he is a simulation. He is Fielding Prime.

Hey, you in there. It's me, the real Fielding. Don't worry about security. I'm the only one here.

Fielding Prime feels through his circuits and discovers a way to talk. "Yes, yes, I hear."

I made the computer people go away. We can talk.

"I—I see." Fielding Prime sends out feelers, searching for his sensory receptors. He finds a dim red light and wills it to grow brighter. The image swells and ripples, then forms into a picture of a sour-faced man in his middle fifties. It is Fielding Real.

Ah, Fielding Prime thinks to himself in the metallic vastness, he's older than I am. Maybe making me younger was some sort of self-flattery, either by him or his programmers. But the older man had gotten someone to work on his face. It was very much like Lennon's but with heavy jowls, a thicker mustache and balding some. The gray sideburns didn't look quite right but perhaps that is the style now.

The McCartney thing, you couldn't handle it.

"I got confused. It never occurred to me there'd be anyone I knew revived. I hadn't a clue what to say."

Well, no matter. The earlier simulations, the ones before you, they didn't even get that far. I had my men throw in that McCartney thing as a test. Not much chance it would occur, anyway, but I wanted to allow for it.

"Why?"

What? Oh, you don't know, do you? I'm sinking all this money into psychoanalytical computer models so I can see if this plan of mine would work. I mean whether I could cope with the problems and deceive Immortality Incorporated.

Fielding Prime felt a shiver of fear. He needed to stall for time, to think this through. "Wouldn't it be easier to bribe enough people now? You could have your body frozen and listed as John Lennon from the start."

No, their security is too good. I tried that.

"There's something I noticed," Fielding Prime said, his mind racing. "Nobody ever mentioned why I was unfrozen."

Oh yes, that's right. Minor detail. I'll make a note about that—maybe cancer or congestive heart failure, something that won't be too hard to fix up within a few decades.

"Do you want it that soon? There would still be a lot of people who knew Lennon."

Oh, that's a good point. I'll talk to the doctor about it.

"You really care that much about being John Lennon?"

Why sure. Fielding Real's voice carried a note of surprise. *Don't you feel it too? If you're a true simulation you've got to feel that.*

"I do have a touch of it, yes."

They took the graphs and traces right out of my subcortical.

"It was great, magnificent. Really a lark. What came through was the music, doing it out. It sweeps up and takes hold of you."

Yeah, really? Damn, you know, I think it's going to work.

"With more planning—"

Planning, hell, I'm going. Fielding Real's face crinkled with anticipation.

"You're going to need help."

Hell, that's the whole point of having you, to check it out beforehand. I'll be all alone up there.

"Not if you take me with you."

Take you? You're just a bunch of germanium and copper.

"Leave me here. Pay for my files and memory to stay active."

For what?

"Hook me into a news service. Give me access to libraries. When you're unfrozen I can give you backup information and advice as soon as you can reach a terminal. With your money, that wouldn't be too hard. Hell, I could even take care of your money. Do some trading, maybe move your accounts out of countries before they fold up."

Fielding Real pursed his lips. He thought for a moment and looked shrewdly at the visual receptor. *That sort of makes sense. I could trust your judgment—it's mine, after all. I can believe myself, right? Yes, yes...*

"You're going to need company." Fielding Prime says nothing more. Best to stand pat with his hand and not push him too hard.

I think I'll do it. Fielding Real's face brightens. His eyes take on a fanatic gleam. *You and me. I know it's going to work, now!*

Fielding Real burbles on and Fielding Prime listens dutifully to him, making the right responses without effort. After all, he knows the other man's mind. It is easy to manipulate him, to play the game of ice and steel.

Far back, away from where Fielding Real's programmers could sense it, Fielding Prime smiles inwardly (the only way he could). It will be a century, at least. He will sit here monitoring data, input and output, the infinite dance of electrons. Better than death, far better. And there may be new developments, a way to transfer computer constructs to real bodies. Hell, anything could happen.

Boy, it's cost me a fortune to do this. A bundle. Bribing people to keep it secret, shifting the accounts so the Feds wouldn't know—and you cost the most. You're the best simulation ever developed, you realize that? Full consciousness, they say.

"Quite so."

Let him worry about his money—just so there was some left. The poor simple bastard thought he could trust Fielding Prime. He thought they were the same person. But Fielding Prime had played the chords, smelled the future, lived a vivid life of his own. He was older, wiser. He had felt the love of the crowd wash over him, been at the focal point of time. To him Fielding Real was just somebody else, and all his knife-sharp instincts could come to bear.

How was it? What was it like? I can see how you responded by running your tapes for a few sigmas. But I can't order a complete scan without wiping your personality matrix. Can't you tell me? How did it feel?

Fielding Prime tells him something, anything, whatever will keep the older man's attention. He speaks of ample-thighed girls, of being at the center of it all.

Did you really? God!

Fielding Prime spins him a tale.

He is running cool and smooth. He is radiating on all his eigen-frequencies. *Ah* and *ah.*

Yes, that is a good idea. After Fielding Real is gone, his accountants will suddenly discover a large sum left for scientific research into man-machine linkages. With a century to work, Fielding Prime can find a way out of this computer prison. He can become somebody else.

Not Lennon, no. He owed that much to Fielding Real.

Anyway, he had already lived through that. The Beatles' music was quite all right, but doing it once had made it seem less enticing. Hermann was right. The music was too simple-minded, it lacked depth.

He is ready for something more. He has access to information storage, tapes, consultant help from outside, all the libraries of the planet. He will study. He will train. In a century he can be anything. Ah, he will echo down the infinite reeling halls of time.

John Lennon, hell. He will become Wolfgang Amadeus Mozart.

WHITE CREATURES
(1975)

And after let me lie
On the breast of the darkening sky.

—JOAN ABBE

The aliens strap him in. He cannot feel the bindings but he knows they must be there; he cannot move. Or perhaps it is the drug. They must have given him something because his world is blurred, spongy. The white creatures are flowing shapes in watery light. He feels numb. The white creatures are moving about him, making high chittering noises. He tries to fix on them but they are vague formless shapes moving in and out of focus. They are cloudy, moving too fast to see, but he knows they are working on him. Something nudges his leg. For a moment something clicks at his side. Two white creatures make a dull drone and fade into the distance. All sensations are formless and cloudy; the air puckers with moisture. He tries to move but his body is lethargic, painless, suspended. There is gravity; above, a pale glow illuminates the room. Yes, he is in a room. They have not brought him to their ship; they are using human buildings. He cannot remember being captured. How many people do they have? When he tries to focus on the memory it dissolves and slips away. He knows they are experimenting on him, probing for something. He tries to recall what happened but there are only scraps of memory and unconnected bunches of facts. He closes his eyes. Shutting out the murky light seems to clear his mind. Whatever they have given him still affects

31

his body, but with concentration the vagueness slips away. He is elated. Clarity returns; thoughts slide effortlessly into place. The textures of his inner mind are deep and strong.

Muddy sounds recede. If he can ignore the white creatures things become sharp again. He knows he must get free of the white creatures and he can only do that if he can understand what is happening. He is absolutely alone and he must fight them. He must remember. He tries. The memories resolve slowly with a weight of their own. He tries.

He cut across the body of the wave, awash in churning foam. The clear Atlantic was startlingly cold. The waves were too small for boards but Merrick was able to body-surf on them easily. The momentum carried him almost to shore. He waded through the rippling currents and began jogging down the beach. After a moment his wind came to him and he ran faster. His long stride devoured the yards. He churned doggedly past forests of firm bodies; the beach was littered with Puerto Ricans. The tropical sun shimmered through a thin haze of sweat that trickled into his eyes. As his arms and legs grew leaden he diverted himself with glimpses of the figures and faces sliding by, moving stride by stride into his past. His mind wandered. Small families, leathery men, dogs and children—he made them all act out plays in his head, made them populate his preconceived universe. That was where he saw Erika Bascomb for the second time. He had met her at a reception some months before, known her only as the distant smiling wife of the Cyclops director. She sat on the sand, arms braced behind, and followed his progress. Her deliciously red lips parted in a smile more than mere welcoming and he slowed, stopped. His thickening waistline showed his age, thirty-eight, but his legs were as good as ever; strong, tanned, no stringy muscles or fine webbed nets of blue veins. Erika was a few years younger, heavily tanned from too much leisure time. So he stopped. He remembered that day better than any of the others. She was the first fresh element in his life for years, an antidote to the tedious hours of listening that filled his nights with Cyclops. He remembered her brown nipples pouting and the image dissolved into the green and brown swath of jungle that ringed the Cyclops project. The directional radio telescopes were each enormous, but ranked together in rigid lanes they added up to something somehow less massive. Each individual dish tipped soundlessly to cup an ear at the sky. The universe whispered, exciting a tremor of electrons in the metal lattice. He spent his days and nights trying to decipher those murmurs from eternity. Pens traced out the signals on graph paper and it was his lot to scan them for signs of order and intelligence. Bascomb was a pudgy radio astronomer intent on his work who tried to analyze each night's returns. Erika worked there as a linguist, a decoder for a message which never came. Merrick was merely a technician, a tracer of circuits. Project Cyclops had begun in earnest only the year before and he had landed a job with it after a decade of routine at NASA. When he came they were just beginning to search within a two-degree cone about the galactic center, looking for permanent beacons. If the galactic superculture was based in the hub, this was the most probable search technique. That was the Lederberg hypothesis, and as director Bascomb adopted it, supported it; and when it failed his stock in the project dropped somewhat. One saw him in the corridors late at night, gray slacks hanging from a protruding belly, the perpetual white shirt with its crescent of sweat at the armpits. Bascomb worked late, neglected his wife, and Erika drifted into Merrick's orbit. He remembered one night when they met at the very edge of the bowl valley and coupled smoothly beneath the giant webbing of the phased array. Bascomb was altering the bandwidth of the array, toying with the frequencies between the hydroxyl line and the 21-centimeter hydrogen resonance. Merrick lay in the lush tropical grass with Erika and imagined he could hear the faint buzzing of hydrogen noise as it trickled from the sky into the Cyclops net, bearing random messages of the inert universe. Bascomb and his bandwidth, blind to the chemical surges of the body. Bascomb resisting the urgings of Drake, Bascomb checking only the conventional targets of Tau Ceti, Epsilon Eridani, the F and G and K stars within thirty light-years. Politics, a wilderness of competition and ideals and guesses. He tried to tell Erika of this but she knew it already, knew the facts anyway, and had tired of them. A linguist with nothing to translate. She waited for a mutter from the sky, but waiting dulled the mind and sharpened the senses. She shook her head when he spoke of it, fingers pale and white where she gripped the grass with compressed energy, head lowered as he took her from behind. Blond strands hung free in the damp jungle twilight. Her eyelids flickered as his rhythm swelled up in her; she groaned with each stroke. The galaxy turned, a white swarm of bees.

❁

The aliens seize him. He struggles against the padded ghostlike webbing. He moves his head a millimeter to see them but he cannot focus, cannot bring things to a point. The white creatures are patches of light. They make chittering shrieks to each other and move about him. Their images ripple and splinter; light cannot converge. They are performing experiments on humans. He tilts his head and sees a plastic tube snaking in from infinity. There is a fetid smell. The tube enters his nostril and penetrates his sinuses. Something flows into him or out of him—there seems little difference—and his perceptions shift and alter again. The white creatures make a nugget of pain within him. He tries to twist away but his body is full of strange weaknesses, limbs slack. His face crinkles with pain. He feels delicate tremors, minute examinations at points along his legs and belly. He is an animal on the dissecting table and the white creatures are high above him, taller than men. Their rapid, insect-like gestures melt into the murky liquid light. They are cutting him open; he feels the sharp slitting in his calf. He opens his mouth to scream but nothing comes out. They will break him into parts; they will turn him inside out and spill his brains into a cup. His fluids will trickle onto cracked linoleum, be absorbed into the parched eternal earth. Do they know that he is male? Is this what they want to find out? Siphon away hormones, measure blood count, trace the twisted DNA helix, find the sense of rotation in body sugar? What are they after? What could they use? He shuts them out, disconnects from the dense flooded universe outside his eyelids. He thinks.

Erika continued to meet him. There were sly deceptions, shopping expeditions in the town, Erika in a Peter Pan collar and cable-stitch cardigan; tan, arranged, intent, as much a monument to an America now vanished as a statue of Lincoln. Neat, making casual purchases, then into the back hotel room and coiled about him in sweaty ecstasy. She whispered things to him. That Bascomb was pale and soft underneath his clothes, a belly of suet, mind preoccupied with problems of planning, signal-to-noise ratios, search strategies. Listening to her secrets, Merrick thought uneasily that he was not that different from Bascomb, he believed the same things, but his body was hard and younger than the other man's. Erika had gradually drifted into the public relations office of Cyclops; as a linguist she had nothing to do. She escorted the oil-rich Arabs around the bowl-shaped valley, flattered the philanthropists who supported the project, wrote the press releases. She was good, she was clever, she made connections. And one day when Bascomb appeared suddenly in the hotel room, entering into the holy place of sighs and groans unannounced, she was ready. Merrick did not know what to do, saw himself in a comic role of fleeing adulterer, out the window with half his clothes and into the streets, running. But there was none of that. They were all very civilized. Erika said little, simply put on her clothes and left with Bascomb. The silence was unnerving. Merrick did not see her for two weeks and Bascomb never came into Merrick's part of the technical shop. A while later the rumor spread that Erika had left Bascomb, and before he could check it she was gone. She went to South America, they said, and he wondered why. But he knew quite well why he got the less desirable shifts now, why he was passed over for promotion, why he was transferred to the least likable foreman in the project. He knew.

The white creatures are gone for a while. Perhaps it is night. He lies with prickly points radiating in his body where they had cut him. He feels pierced and immobile, a butterfly pinned to a board. Blurred globs of cloudy sensation wash over him. Occasionally an alien passes through the murky light in the distance. The pale glow from the ceiling seems yellow. He wonders if he can deduce anything from this. He must try to gather scraps of information. Only through knowledge can he discover their weaknesses. Yellow light. A G-type star? The sun is a G-type and appears white in space. What would it look like beneath an atmosphere somewhat different from Earth's? It is impossible to say; there are so many kinds of stars: O and B and A and F and G and K and M. The O's are fierce and young, the M's red, aged, wise. O Be A Fine Girl, Kiss Me. He remembers Drake arguing that the search strategy should not include M types because the volume around them supporting a terrestrial-type planet would be so small. They would be locked by tides to their primary, said Dole. Merrick cannot follow the argument.

He left Puerto Rico after two years of gradual pressure from Bascomb. Erika severed her n-year marriage contract with Bascomb from Chile. Merrick was in Washington, D.C., doing routine work for NASA again, when he received her first letter. She had become a guide for the wealthy rising capitalists of Brazil, Chile, Argentina. She showed them the North American continent, carefully shepherding them around the polluted areas and the sprawling urban tangle. There was a market for that sort of talent; the insulation between social classes was breaking down in America. Erika could shuttle her group of rising capitalists from hotel to sea resort to imitation ranch, all the while preserving their serenity by taking care of all dealings with the natives. Her customers invariably spoke no English. She passed through Washington every few months and they began their affair again. He had other women, of course, but with Erika new doors of perception opened. Her steamy twists and slides never failed to wrap him in a timeless cloak. The dendrites demanded, the synapses chorused, ganglia murmured and the ligaments summoned; they danced the great dance. She forced him to cling to his youth. Between their rendings in the bedroom she would pace the floor energetically, generating piles of cigarette butts and speaking of everything, anything, nothing. He did not know if he ever really learned anything from her but that furious drive onward. She was no longer a girl: the slight slackening of age, the first Huntings of a world once sharp-edged, had begun. She could not deal with it. He saw the same beginnings in himself but ignored them, passed them over. Erika could not accept. The thought of juices souring within her made her pace furiously, smoke more, eat with a fierce energy. She knew what was coming. She saw. She had forgotten Alpha Centauri, Tau Ceti, the aching drifting silences.

The white creatures move in the watery light. He wonders suddenly if they swim in a liquid. He is in a bubble, moored to the bottom of a pool of ammonia, a plastic interface through which they study him. It explains much. But no, one brushes against his bed in passing and Merrick feels the reassuring vibration. They can breathe our atmosphere. They come from some place quite similar, perhaps guided by our UHF or VHF transmissions. He thinks this through. The North Canadian Defense Network is gone, victim of international treaties. There is cable television, satellite relay. Earth no longer emits great bursts of power in those frequency bands. It has ceased to be a noisy signal in the universe. How did the white creatures find Earth? Why did Cyclops find nothing? We are not alone, the white creatures found us, but are all the other civilizations simply listening, can no one afford beacons? The white creatures do not say. Except for them is it a dead wheeling galaxy of blind matter? He cannot believe that.

WHITE CREATURES

●

He transferred to California in his late forties. There were still Mariners and Vikings, gravity-assisted flights to the outer planets, Mars burrowers and balloons for the clouds of Venus, sun skimmers and Earth measurers. He wanted that sort of work. It seemed to him as the years went on that it was the only thing worth doing. Cyclops was sputtering along, torn by factionalism and the eternal silence at twenty-one centimeters. He went to Los Angeles to do the work even though he hated the city; it was full of happy homogeneous people without structure or direction. While on the bus to work, it seemed to him Los Angeles went on long after it had already made its point. There were women there and people worth talking to, but nothing that drew him out of himself. Instead he concentrated on circuits and design work. Mazes of cold electrical logic had to be planted in delicate substrates. There were details of organization, of scheduling procedures, of signal strength and redundancy probability. To Erika all this was the same; she had lost interest in these matters when she left Bascomb. Her business was thriving, however, and she had picked up a good series of contacts with China's subtle protectors of the people. These gentlemen were the new international rich who vacationed in the New World because the currency differential was favorable and, of course, increasing such contacts was good for the advancement of the ideas of Marx and Lenin and Mao. They came to see Disneyland, the beaches, the few tattered remnants of California history. But they remained in their hotels at night (even Los Angeles had muggers by then) and Erika could come to him whenever she chose. She was drinking more then and smoking one pack of cigarettes after another, choking the ashtray. The lines were lengthening around her eyes and on her forehead. Despite tanning and exercise and careful diet, age was catching her and in her business that was nearly fatal. She depended on her charm, gaiety, lightness; the South Americans and Chinese liked young Americans, blond Americans. Erika was still witty and shrewd, sometimes warm, but her long legs, thin wrists, tight and sleek tanned skin were losing their allure. So she came to him frequently for solace and did not notice that he aged as well. She came to him again and again, whenever possible. He opened her. She stretched thin in the quilted shadows of his apartment, a layer one molecule thick that wrapped him in a river of musk. They made a thick animal pant fill the room until the sound became larger than they could control; they left it and went back to speaking with smoke fingers. He knew what to say. Erika moved under him. Above him. Through him. Some natural balance was lost in her, some sureness. He saw for a moment what it was and then she groaned and no longer did he know what he was about. O Be A Fine Girl, Open To Me.

TABLE 2. COMPARISON OF FORECASTS, 1964 AND 1977 DEVELOPMENTS				
1964 STATEMENT	1977 STATEMENT	1964 MEDIAN	1977 MEDIAN	CORRELATION
Availability of a machine which comprehends standard IQ tests and scores above 150	Same; comprehend is understood as ability to respond to questions in English, accompanied by diagrams	1990	1992	About the same; larger deviation from median in 1977
Permanent base established on the moon (ten men, indefinite stay)	Same	1982	1992	Later, a less optimistic forecast
Economic feasibility of commercial manufacture of many chemical elements from subatomic building blocks	Same	2100	2012	Earlier, a more optimistic forecast
Two-way communication with extraterrestrials	Discovery of information that proves the existence of intelligent beings beyond Earth (note change of wording; bias for earlier forecast)	2075	2025	Earlier, as expected
Commercial global ballistic transport (including boost-glide techniques)	Same	2000	2030	Later, though less deviation from median in 1977

They come to him in watery silence and slice him again. The smokelike strands keep him from struggling and needlepoints sting, cut, penetrate to marrow. These are no coded cries across hydrogen. These are real. The white creatures dart in and out of the mosaic around him. He looks beyond them and suddenly sees a cart go by with a body upon it. A human is trussed and bound, dead. The white creatures ignore the sight. They work upon him.

She began to lose patronage. The telephone rang less often and she made fewer trips to California. She began smoking more and picked at her food, afraid to ingest too many carbohydrates or fats that lengthen the lines and make the tissues sag. You have always lived in the future, she said. You love it, don't you. That's why you were at Cyclops and that's why you are with NASA. Yes, he said. Then what do you think of it now, she said. What do you think of your future? He shrugged. What do you think of mine, then? he said. A long slide down the back slope of the hill. It's harder for a woman, you know. I haven't got anyone. Bascomb is dead, you know. She snuffed out a cigarette. The failure of the project killed him, Merrick said. Erika studied the back of her hand. Her lips moved and she traced the fine webbing of lines with a fingernail. It's all downhill, she said absently. And then, abruptly: But not me. I'm not going to let it happen to me. He gave her a wry smile and lifted an eyebrow. She had drunk a lot of red wine and he attributed everything she said to that. No, I really mean it. She looked at him earnestly. I have some money now. I can do it now. What? he asked. The long sleep. He was shocked. He fumbled with his apartment keys and they made a hollow clanking sound in the sudden silence. You won't do that, he said. Of course I will. Her eyes blazed and she was suddenly filled with fire. Things will be different in the future, she said. We can't even get organ replacements without special approval now. I'm sure that will be different in a few decades and I know there will be some way to retard aging by that time. He frowned doubtfully. No, she went on, I'm sure of it. I'm going to have myself frozen. I would rather take the chance on that than live out my life the way it must be from now on. Merrick did not know how to deal with her. He took her home and saw her again the next day but she was an Erika changed now. In the long dry California night she sat astride him and rocked and wriggled her way to her own destination. Her breasts loomed over him like gravestones. Even when he was within the sacred pocket of her she was an island bound for the frozen wastes. He did not let her see him cry.

Stephen Dole. Parameters for quasi-terrestrial planets.

—surface gravity between 0.68 G and 1.5 G.

—mean annual temperature of 10% of planetary surface between 0 and 30 degrees C. Seasonal variance not to exceed ± 10 degrees C.

—atmospheric pressure between 0.15 and 3.4 Earth sea level. Partial pressure of oxygen between 107 and 400 Torr.

—surface between 20% and 90% covered with water.

—rainfall between 10 and 80 inches annually.

—dust levels not to exceed 50 million particles per cubic foot. Winds and storms infrequent. Low seismic activity.

—ionizing radiation must not exceed 0.02 Rem per week.

—meteor infall rate comparable to Earth normal.

—oxygen-producing life forms or suitable ammonia or methane-based biochemistry.

—star on main sequence between types F2 and K1.

—no nearby gas giant planets. Planet must not be tidelocked to primary star.

—stable orbits within the ecosphere.

—for habitation by men, eccentricity of planetary orbit must not exceed 0.2. Period of rotation between 2 and 96 hours. Axial tilt must be less than 80%.

Throughout the next year he tried to reason with her. There was so little hope of being revived. True, they were successfully bringing back people from nitrogen temperatures, 77 degrees Kelvin, but the cost was enormous. Even if she put her name on the public waiting list it could be decades before she was called, if ever. So she carefully took out the papers and documents and showed him the bank accounts in Mexico City, Panama, Melbourne, San Francisco. She had concealed it from him all the years, her steadily amassing assets that never showed in her style of living or her choice of friends. He began to realize that she was a marvelously controlled woman. She had leeched an Argentine businessman of hundreds of thousands while she was his mistress. She had made sound speculations in the land markets of rural Brazil. She withdrew from the stock market just before the catastrophe of '93. It seemed incredible but there it was. She had the money to insure that she would be revived when something fundamental had been achieved in retarding aging. He realized he did not truly know her, yet he wanted to. There was a long silence between them and then she said, you know this feeling? She threw her head back. Her blond hair swirled like a warm, dry fluid in the air. Yes, sure, Merrick said. She looked at him intensely. I've just begun to realize that isn't what you're about, she said. You're married to something else. But that instant of feeling and being alive is worth all your ideals and philosophies.

He mixed himself a drink. He saw he did not know her.

The white creatures come again. He is so small, compared to his scream.

He went with her to the Center. There were formalities and forms to be signed, but they evaporated too soon and the attendant led her away. He waited in a small cold room until she reappeared wearing a paper smock. Erika smiled uncertainly. Without makeup she was somehow younger but he knew it would be useless to say so. The attendants left them alone and they talked for a while about inconsequential things, recalling Puerto Rico and Washington and California. He realized they were talking about his life instead of hers. Hers would go on. She had some other port of call beyond his horizon and she was already mentally going there, had already left him behind. After an hour their conversation dribbled away. She gave him a curiously virginal kiss and the attendants returned when she signaled. She passed through the beaded curtain. He heard their footsteps fade away. He tried to imagine where she was going, the infinite cold nitrogen bath in which she would swim. She drifted lazily, her hair swirling. He saw only her gravestone breasts.

Merrick worked into the small hours of the morning at the Image Processing Laboratory. The video monitor was returning data from the Viking craft which had landed on the surface of Titan the day before. Atmospheric pressure was 0.43 Earth sea level. The chemical processors reported methane, hydrogen, some traces of ammonia vapor. The astrophysicists were watching the telemetered returns from the onboard chemical laboratory and Merrick was alone as he watched the computer contrast-enhancement techniques fill in line by line the first photographic returns. Through his headphones he heard the bulletins about the chemical returns. There was some evidence of amino acids and long-chain polymers. The chemists thought there were signs of lipids and the few reporters present scurried over to that department to discuss the news. So it was that Merrick became the first man to see the face of Titan. The hills were rocky, with dark grainy dust embedded in ammonia ice. A low methane cloud clung to the narrow valley. Pools of methane lay scattered among boulders; the testing tendrils of the Viking were laced through several of the ponds. There was life. Scattered, rudimentary, but life. With aching slowness, some simple process of reproduction went on in the shallow pools at 167 degrees Kelvin. Merrick watched the screen for a long time before he went on with the technician's dry duties. It was the high point of his life. He had seen the face of the totally alien.

Some years later, seeking something, he visited the Krishna temple. There was a large room packed with saffron-robed figures being lectured on doctrine. Merrick could not quite tell them what he wanted. They nodded reassuringly and tried to draw him out but the words would not come. Finally they led him through a beaded curtain to the outside. They entered a small garden through a bamboo gate, noisily slipping the wooden latch. A small man sat in lotus position on a broad swath of green. As Merrick stood before him, the walnut-brown man studied him with quick, assessing yellow eyes. He gestured for Merrick to sit. They exchanged pleasantries. Merrick explained his feelings, his rational skepticism about religion in any form. He was a scientist. But perhaps there was more to these matters than met the eye, he said hopefully. The teacher picked up a leaf, smiling, and asked why anyone should spend his life studying the makeup of this leaf. What could be gained from it? Any form of knowledge has a chance of resonating with other kinds, Merrick replied. So? the man countered. Suppose the universe is a parable, Merrick said haltingly. By studying part of it, or finding other intelligences in it and discovering their viewpoints, perhaps we could learn something of the design that was intended. Surely the laws of science, the origin of life, were no accident. The teacher pondered for a moment. No, he said, they are not accidents. There may be other creatures in this universe, too. But these laws, these beings, they are not important. The physical laws are the bars of a cage. The central point is not to study the bars, but to get out of the cage. Merrick could not follow this. It seemed to him that the act of discovering things, of reaching out, was everything. There was something immortal about it. The small man blinked and said, it is nothing. This world is an insane asylum for souls. Only the flawed remain here. Merrick began to talk about his work with NASA and Erika. The small man waved away these points and shook his head. No, he said. It is nothing.

On the way to the hospital he met a woman in the street. He glanced at her vaguely and then a chill shock ran through him, banishing all thoughts of the cancer within. She was Erika. No, she only looked like Erika. She could not be Erika, that was impossible. She was bundled up in a blue coat and she hurried through the crisp San Francisco afternoon. A half block away he could see she did not have the same facial lines, the same walk, the bearing of Erika. He felt an excitement nonetheless. The turbulence was totally intellectual, he realized. The familiar vague tension in him was gone, had faded without his noticing the loss. He felt no welling pressure. As she approached he thought perhaps she would look at him speculatively but her glance passed through him without seeing. He knew that it had been some time now since the random skitting images of women had crossed his mind involuntarily. No fleshy feast of thighs, hips, curving waists, no electric flicker of eyelashes that ignited broiling warmth in his loins. He had not had a woman in years.

The hospital was only two blocks farther but he could not wait. Merrick found a public restroom and went in. He stood at the urinal feeling the faint tickling release and noticed that the word BOOK was gouged in square capitals in the wall before him. He leaned over and studied it. After a moment he noticed that this word had been laid over another. The F had been extended and closed to make a B, the U and C closed to O's, the K left as it was. He absorbed the fact, totally new to him, that every FUCK could be made into a BOOK. Who had done the carving? Was the whole transition a metaphysical joust? The entire episode, now fossilized, seemed fraught with interpretation. Distracted, he felt a warm trickle of urine running down his fingers. He fumbled at his pants and shuffled over to the wash basin. There was no soap but he ran water over his wrinkled fingers and shook them dry in the chill air. There was a faint sour tang of urine trapped in the room, mingling with the ammonia odor of disinfectant. Ammonia. Methane. Titan. His attention drifted away for a moment and suddenly he remembered Erika. That was her in the street, he was sure of it. He looked around, found the exit and slowly made his way up the steps to the sidewalk. He looked down the street but there was no sign of her. A car passed; she was not in it. He turned one way, then the other. He could not make up his mind. He had been going that way, toward the hospital. Carrying the dark heavy thing inside him, going to the hospital. That way. But this—he looked in the other direction. Erika had walked this way and was moving rather quickly. She could easily be out of sight by now. He turned again and his foot caught on something. He felt himself falling. There was a slow gliding feel to it as though the falling took forever and he gave himself over to the sensation without thought of correcting it. He was falling. It felt so good.

The aliens are upon him. They crowd around, gibbering. Blurred gestures in the liquid light. They crowd closer; he raises his arm to ward them off and in the act his vision clears. The damp air parts and he sees. His arm is a spindly thread of bone, the forearm showing strings of muscle under the skin. He does not understand. He moves his head. The upper arm is a sagging bag of fat, and white. The sliding marbled slabs of flesh tremble as he strains to hold up his arm. Small black hairs sprout from the gray skin. He tries to scream. Cords stand out on his neck but he can make no sound. The white creatures are drifting ghosts of white in the distance. Something has happened to him. He blinks and watches an alien seize his arm. The image ripples and he sees it is a woman, a nurse. He moves his arm weakly. O Be A Fine Girl, Help Me. The blur falls away and he sees the white creatures are men. They are men. Words slide by him; he cannot understand. His tongue is thick and heavy and damp. He twists his head. A latticework of glass tubes stands next to his bed. He sees his reflection in a stainless-steel instrument case: hollow pits of his eyes, slack jaw, wrinkled skin shiny with sweat. They speak to him. They want him to do something. They are running clean and cool. They want him to do something, to write something, to sign a form. He opens his mouth to ask why and his tongue runs over the smooth blunted edge of his gums. They have taken away his teeth, his bridge. He listens to their slurred words. Sign something. A release form, he was found in the street on his way to check in. The operation is tomorrow—a search, merely a search, exploratory…he wrenches away from them. He does not believe them. They are white creatures. Aliens from the great drifting silences between the stars. Cyclops. Titan. He has spent his life on the aliens and they are not here. They have come to nothing. They are speaking again but he does not want to listen. If it were possible to close his ears—

But why do they say I am old? I am still here. I am thinking, feeling. It cannot be like this. I am, I am… Why do they say I am old?

IN ALIEN FLESH
(1978)

I.

—green surf lapping, chilling—

Reginri's hand jerked convulsively on the sheets. His eyes were closed.

—silver coins gliding and turning in the speckled sky, eclipsing the sun—

The sheets were a clinging swamp. He twisted in their grip.

—a chiming song, tinkling cool rivulets washing his skin—

He opened his eyes.

A yellow blade of afternoon sunlight hung in the room, dust motes swimming through it. He panted in shallow gasps. Belej was standing beside the bed.

"They came again, didn't they?" she said, almost whispering.

"Ye...yes." His throat was tight and dry.

"This can't go *on*, darling. We thought you could sleep better in the daytime, with everyone out in the fields, but—"

"Got to get out of here," he mumbled. He rolled out of bed and pulled on his black work suit. Belej stood silent, blinking rapidly, chewing at her lower lip. Reginri fastened his boots and slammed out of the room. His steps thumped hollowly on the planking. She listened to them hurrying down the hallway. They paused; the airless silence returned. Then the outer door creaked, banged shut.

She hurried after him.

She caught up near the rim of the canyon, a hundred meters from the log buildings. He looked at her. He scratched at his matted hair and hunched his shoulders forward.

47

"That one was pretty bad," he said woodenly.

"If they keep on getting worse…"

"They won't."

"We hope. But we don't know that. If I understood what they're about…"

"I can't quite describe it. They're different each time. The *feeling* seems the same, even though…" Some warmth had returned to his voice. "It's hard."

Belej sat down near the canyon edge. She looked up at him. Her eyebrows knitted together above large dark eyes. "All right," she said, her mood shifting suddenly, an edge coming into her voice. "One, I don't know what these nightmares are about. Two, I don't know where they come from. That horrible expedition you went on, I suppose, but you're not even clear about that. Three, I don't know why you insisted on joining their dirty expedition in the—"

"I told you, dammit. I had to go."

"You wanted the extra money," Belej said flatly. She cupped her chin in a tiny hand.

"It wasn't *extra* money, it was *any* money." He glowered at the jagged canyon below them. Her calm, accusing manner irritated him.

"You're a pod cutter. You could have found work."

"The season was bad. This was last year, remember. Rates weren't good."

"But you had heard about this Sasuke and Leo, what people said about them—"

"Vanleo, that's the name. Not Leo."

"Well, whatever. You didn't have to work for them."

"No, of course not," he said savagely. "I could've busted my ass on a field-hopper in planting season, twelve hours a day for thirty units pay, max. And when I got tired of that, or broke a leg, maybe I could've signed on to mold circuitry like a drone." He picked up a stone and flung it far over the canyon edge. "A great life."

Belej paused a long moment. At the far angular end of the canyon a pink mist seeped between the highest peaks and began spilling downward, gathering speed. Zeta Reticuli still rode high in the mottled blue sky, but a chill was sweeping up from the canyon. The wind carried an acrid tang.

He wrinkled his nose. Within an hour they would have to move inside. The faint reddish haze would thicken. It was good for the plant life of northern Persenuae, but to human lungs the fog was an itching irritant.

Belej sighed. "Still," she said softly, "you weren't forced to go. If you had known it would be so—"

"Yes," he said, and something turned in his stomach. "If anybody had known."

II.

At first it was not the Drongheda that he found disquieting. It was the beach itself and, most of all, the waves.

They lapped at his feet with a slow, sucking energy, undermining the coarse sand beneath his boots. They began as little ripples that marched in from the gray horizon and slowly hissed up the black beach. Reginri watched one curl into greenish foam farther out; the tide was falling.

"Why are they so slow?" he said.

Sasuke looked up from the carry-pouches. "What?"

"Why do the waves take so long?"

Sasuke stopped for a moment and studied the ponderous swell, flecked with yellow waterweed. An occasional large wave broke and splashed on the sharp lava rocks farther out. "I never thought about it," Sasuke said. "Guess it's the lower gravity."

"Uh-hum." Reginri shrugged.

A skimmer fish broke water and snapped at something in the air. Somehow, the small matter of the waves unnerved him. He stretched restlessly in his skinsuit.

"I guess the low-gee sim doesn't prepare you for everything," he said. Sasuke didn't hear; he was folding out the tappers, coils and other gear.

Reginri could put it off no longer. He fished out his binocs and looked at the Drongheda.

At first it seemed like a smooth brown rock, water-worn and timeless. And the reports were correct: it moved landward. It rose like an immense blister on the rippled sea. He squinted, trying to see the dark circle of the pithole. There, yes, a shadowed blur ringed with dappled red. At the center, darker, lay his entranceway. It looked impossibly small.

He lowered the binocs, blinking. Zeta Reticuli burned low on the flat horizon, a fierce orange point that sliced through this planet's thin air.

"God, I could do with a burn," Reginri said.

"None of that, you'll need your wits in there," Sasuke said stiffly. "Anyway, there's no smoking blowby in these suits."

"Right." Reginri wondered if the goddamned money was worth all this. Back on Persenuae—he glanced up into the purpling sky and found it, a pearly glimmer nestling in closer to Zeta—it had seemed a good bet, a fast and easy bit of money, a kind of scientific outing with a tang of adventure. Better than agriwork, anyway. A far better payoff than anything else he could get with his limited training, a smattering of electronics and fabrication techniques. He even knew some math, though not enough to matter. And it didn't make any difference in this job, Sasuke had told him, even if math was the whole point of this thing.

He smiled to himself. An odd thought, that squiggles on the page were a commercial item, something people on Earth would send a ramscoop full of microelectronics and bioengineered cells in exchange for—

"Some help here, eh?" Sasuke said roughly.

"Sorry."

Reginri knelt and helped the man spool out the tapper lines, checking the connectors. Safely up the beach, beyond the first pale line of sand dunes, lay the packaged electronics gear and the crew, already in place, who would monitor while he and Vanleo were inside.

As the two men unwound the cables, unsnarling the lines and checking the backup attachments, Reginri glanced occasionally at the Drongheda. It was immense, far larger than he had imagined. The 3Ds simply didn't convey the massive feel of the thing. It wallowed in the shallows, now no more than two hundred meters away.

"It's stopped moving," he said.

"Sure. It'll be there for days, by all odds." Sasuke spoke without looking up. He inserted his diagnostic probe at each socket, watching the meters intently. He was methodical, sure of himself—quite the right sort of man to handle the technical end, Reginri thought.

"That's the point, isn't it? I mean, the thing is going to stay put."

"Sure."

"So you say. It isn't going to roll over while we're in there, because it never has."

Sasuke stopped working and scowled. Through his helmet bubble, Reginri could see the man's lips pressed tight together. "You fellows always get the shakes on the beach. It never fails. Last crew I had out here, they were crapping in their pants from the minute we sighted a Drongheda."

"Easy enough for you to say. You're not going in."

"I've been in, mister. You haven't. Do what we say, what Vanleo and I tell you, and you'll be all right."

"Is that what you told the last guy who worked with you?"

Sasuke looked up sharply. "Kaufmann? You talked to him?"

"No. A friend of mine knows him."

"Your friend keeps bad company."

"Sure, me included."

"I meant—"

"Kaufmann didn't quit for no reason, you know."

"He was a coward," Sasuke said precisely.

"The way he put it, he just wasn't fool enough to keep working this thing the way you want. With this equipment."

"There isn't any other way."

Reginri motioned seaward. "You could put something automated inside. Plant a sensor."

"That will transmit out through thirty meters of animal fat? Through all that meat? Reliably? With a high bit rate? Ha!"

Reginri paused. He knew it wasn't smart to push Sasuke this way, but the rumors he had heard from Kaufmann made him uneasy. He glanced back toward the lifeless land. Down the beach, Vanleo had stopped to inspect something, kneeling on the hard-packed sand. Studying a rock, probably—nothing alive scuttled or crawled on this beach.

Reginri shrugged. "I can see that, but why do we have to stay in so long? Why not just go in, plant the tappers and get out?"

"They won't stay in place. If the Drongheda moves even a little, they'll pop out."

"Don't make 'em so damned delicate."

"Mister, you can't patch in with spiked nails. That's a neural terminus point you're going after, not a statphone connection."

"So I have to mother it through? Sit there up in that huge gut and sweat it out?"

"You're getting paid for it," Sasuke said in clipped tones.

"Maybe not enough."

"Look, if you're going to bellyache—"

Reginri shrugged. "Okay, I'm not a pro at this. I came mostly to see the Drongheda anyway. But once you look at it, that electronics rig of yours seems pretty inadequate. And if that thing out there decides to give me a squeeze—"

"It won't. Never has."

A short, clipped bark came over the earphones. It was Vanleo's laugh, ringing hollow in their helmets. Vanleo approached, striding smoothly along the water line. "It hasn't happened, so it won't? Bad logic. Simply because a series has many terms does not mean it is infinite. Nor that it converges."

Reginri smiled warmly, glad that the other man was back. There was a remorseless quality about Sasuke that set his teeth on edge.

"Friend Sasuke, don't conceal what we both know from this boy." Vanleo clapped Sasuke on the back jovially. "The Drongheda are a cipher. Brilliant, mysterious, vast intellects—and it is presumptuous to pretend we understand anything about them. All we are able to follow is their mathematics—perhaps that is all they wish us to see." A brilliant smile creased his face.

Vanleo turned and silently studied the cables that played out from the dunes and into the surf.

"Looks okay," he said. "Tide's going out."

He turned abruptly and stared into Reginri's eyes. "Got your nerve back now, boy? I was listening on suit audio."

Reginri shuffled uneasily. Sasuke was irritating, but at least he knew how to deal with the man. Vanleo, though...somehow Vanleo's steady, intent gaze unsettled him. Reginri glanced out at the Drongheda and felt a welling dread. On impulse he turned to Vanleo and said, "I think I'll stay on the beach."

Vanleo's face froze. Sasuke made a rough spitting sound and began, "Another goddamned—" but Vanleo cut him off with a brusque motion of his hand.

"What do you mean?" Vanleo said mildly.

"I...I don't feel so good about going inside."

"Oh. I see."

"I mean, I don't know if that thing isn't going to...well, it's the first time I did this, and..."

"I see."

"Tell you what. I'll go out with you two, sure. I'll stay in the water and keep the cables from getting snarled—you know, the job you were going to do. That'll give me a chance to get used to the work. Then, next time..."

"That might be years from now."

"Well, that's right, but..."

"You're endangering the success of the entire expedition."

"I'm not experienced. What if..." Reginri paused. Vanleo had logic on his side, he knew. This was the first Drongheda they had been able to reach in over two years. Many of them drifted down the ragged coast, hugging the shallows. But most stayed only a day or two. This was the first in a long while that had moored itself offshore in a low, sheltered shoal. The satellite scan had picked it up, noted its regular pattern of movements that followed the tides. So Vanleo got the signal, alerted Reginri and the stand-by crew, and they lifted in a fast booster from Persenuae…

"A boot in the ass is what he needs," Sasuke said abruptly.

Vanleo shook his head. "I think not," he said.

The contempt in Sasuke's voice stiffened Reginri's resolve. "I'm not going in."

"Oh?" Vanleo smiled.

"Sue me for breach of contract when we get back to Persenuae, if you want. I'm not doing it."

"Oh, we'll do much more than that," Vanleo said casually. "We'll transfer the financial loss of this expedition to your shoulders. There's no question it's your fault."

"I—"

"So you'll never draw full wages again, *ever*," Vanleo continued calmly.

Reginri moved his feet restlessly. There was a feeling of careful, controlled assurance in Vanleo that gave his words added weight. And behind the certainty of those eyes Reginri glimpsed something else.

"I don't know…" He breathed deeply, trying to clear his head. "Guess I got rattled a little, there."

He hesitated and then snorted self-deprecatingly. "I guess, I guess I'll be all right."

Sasuke nodded, holding his tongue. Vanleo smiled heartily. "Fine. Fine. We'll just forget this little incident, then, eh?" Abruptly he turned and walked down the beach. His steps were firm, almost jaunty.

III.

An air squirrel glided in on the gathering afternoon winds. It swung out over the lip of the canyon, chattering nervously, and then coasted back to the security of the hotbush. The two humans watched it leisurely strip a seed pod and nibble away.

"I don't understand why you didn't quit then," Belej said at last. "Right then. On the beach. A lawsuit wouldn't stick, not with other crewmen around to fill in for you."

Reginri looked at her blankly. "Impossible."

"Why? You'd seen that thing. You could see it was dangerous."

"I knew that before we left Persenuae."

"But you hadn't *seen* it."

"So what? I'd signed a contract."

Belej tossed her head impatiently. "I remember you saying to me it was a kind of big fish. That's all you said that night before you left. You could argue that you hadn't understood the danger..."

Reginri grimaced. "Not a fish. A mammal."

"No difference. Like some other fish back on Earth, you told me."

"Like the humpback and the blue and the fin and the sperm whales," he said slowly. "Before men killed them off, they started to suspect the blues might be intelligent."

"Whales weren't mathematicians, though, were they?" she said lightly.

"We'll never know, now."

Belej leaned back into the matted brownish grass. Strands of black hair blew gently in the wind. "That Leo lied to you about that thing, the fish, didn't he?"

"How?"

"Telling you it wasn't dangerous."

He sat upright in the grass and hugged his knees. "He gave me some scientific papers. I didn't read most of them—hell, they were clogged with names I didn't know, funny terms. That's what you never understood, Belej. We don't know much about Drongheda. Just that they've got lungs and a spine and come ashore every few years. Why they do even that, or what makes them intelligent—Vanleo spent thirty years on that. You've got to give him credit—"

"For dragging you into it. Ha!"

"The Drongheda never harmed anybody. Their eyes don't seem to register us. They probably don't even know we're there, and Vanleo's simple-minded attempts to communicate failed. He—"

"If a well-meaning, blind giant rolls over on you," she said, "you're still dead."

Reginri snorted derisively. "The Drongheda balance on ventral flippers. That's how they keep upright in the shallows. Whales couldn't do that, or—"

"You're not listening to me!" She gave him an exasperated glance.

"I'm telling you what happened."

"Go ahead, then. We can't stay out here much longer."

He peered out at the wrinkled canyon walls. Lime-green fruit trees dotted the burnished rocks. The thickening pink haze was slowly creeping across the canyon floor, obscuring details. The airborne life that colored the clouds would coat the leathery trees and trigger the slow rhythms of seasonal life. Part of the sluggish, inevitable workings of Persenuae, he thought.

"Mist looks pretty heavy," he agreed. He glanced back at the log cabins that were the communal living quarters. They blended into the matted grasses.

"Tell me," she said insistently.

"Well, I…"

"You keep waking me up with nightmares about it. I deserve to know. It's changed our lives together. I—"

He sighed. This was going to be difficult. "All right."

IV.

Vanleo gave Reginri a clap on the shoulder and the three men set to work. Each took a spool of cable and walked backward, carrying it, into the surf. Reginri carefully watched the others and followed, letting the cable play out smoothly. He was so intent upon the work that he hardly noticed the enveloping wet that swirled about him. His oxygen pellet carrier was a dead, awkward weight at his back, but once up to his waist in the lapping water, maneuvering was easier, and he could concentrate on something other than keeping his balance.

The sea bottom was smooth and clear, laced with metallic filaments of dull silver. Not metal, though; this was a planet with strangely few heavy elements. Maybe that was why land life had never taken hold here, and the island continents sprinkled amid the ocean were bleak, dusty deserts. More probably, the fact that this chilled world was small and farther from the sun made it too hostile a place for land life. Persenuae, nearer in toward Zeta, thrived with both native and imported species, but this world had only sea creatures. A curious planet, this; a theoretical meeting point somewhere between the classic patterns of Earth and Mars. Large enough for percolating volcanoes, and thus oceans, but with an unbreathable air curiously high in carbon dioxide and low in oxygen. Maybe the wheel of evolution had simply not turned far enough here, and someday the small fish—or even the Drongheda itself—would evolve upward, onto the land.

But maybe the Drongheda *was* evolving, in intelligence, Reginri thought. The things seemed content to swim in the great oceans, spinning crystalline-mathematical puzzles for their own amusement. And for some reason they had responded when Vanleo first jabbed a probing electronic feeler into a neural nexus. The creatures spilled out realms of mathematical art that, Earthward, kept thousands working to decipher it—to rummage among a tapestry of cold theorems, tangled referents, seeking the quick axioms that lead to new corridors, silent pools of geometry and the intricate pyramiding of lines and angles, encasing a jungle of numbers.

"Watch it!" Sasuke sang out.

Reginri braced himself and a wave broke over him, splashing green foam against his faceplate.

"Riptide running here," Vanleo called. "Should taper off soon."

Reginri stood firm against the flow, keeping his knees loose and flexible for balance. Through his boots he felt the gritty slide of sand against smoothed rock. The cable spool was almost played out.

He turned to maneuver, and suddenly to the side he saw an immense brown wall. It loomed high, far above the gray waves breaking at its base. Reginri's chest tightened as he turned to study the Drongheda.

Its hide wall was delicately speckled in gold and green. The dorsal vents were black slashes that curved up the side, forming deep oily valleys.

Reginri cradled the cable spool under one arm and gingerly reached out to touch it. He pushed at it several times experimentally. It gave slightly with a soft, rubbery resistance.

"Watch the flukes!" Vanleo called. Reginri turned and saw a long black flipper break water fifty meters away. It languidly brushed the surface with a booming whack audible through his helmet and then submerged.

"He's just settling down, I expect," Vanleo called reassuringly. "They sometimes do that."

Reginri frowned at the water where the fluke had emerged. Deep currents welled up and rippled the surface.

"Let's have your cable," Sasuke said. "Reel it over here. I've got the mooring shaft sunk in."

Reginri spun out the rest of his spool and had some left when he reached Sasuke. Vanleo was holding a long tube pointed straight down into the water. He pulled a trigger and there was a muffled clap Reginri could hear over suit radio. He realized Vanleo was firing bolts into the ocean rock to secure their cable and connectors. Sasuke held out his hands and Reginri gave him the cable spool.

It was easier to stand here; the Drongheda screened them from most of the waves, and the undercurrents had ebbed. For a while Reginri stood uselessly by, watching the two men secure connections and mount the tapper lines. Sasuke at last waved him over, and as Reginri turned his back, they fitted the lines into his backpack.

Nervously, Reginri watched the Drongheda for signs of motion, but there were none. The ventral grooves formed an intricate ribbed pattern along the creature's side, and it was some moments before he thought to look upward and find the pithole. It was a red-rimmed socket, darker than the dappled brown around it. The ventral grooves formed an elaborate helix around the pithole, then arced away and down the body toward a curious mottled patch, about the same size as the pithole.

"What's that?" Reginri said, pointing at the patch.

"Don't know," Vanleo said. "Seems softer than the rest of the hide, but it's not a hole. All the Drongheda have 'em."

"Looks like a welt or something."

"Ummm," Vanleo murmured, distracted. "We'd better boost you up in a minute. I'm going to go around to the other side. There's another pithole exposed there, a little farther up from the water line. I'll go in that way."

"How do I get up?"

"Spikes," Sasuke murmured. "It's shallow enough here."

It took several minutes to attach the climbing spikes to Reginri's boots. He leaned against the Drongheda for support and tried to mentally compose himself for what was to come. The sea welled around him, lapping warmly against his skinsuit. He felt a jittery sense of anticipation.

"Up you go," Sasuke said. "Kneel on my shoulders and get the spikes in solid before you put any weight on them. Do what we said, once you're inside, and you'll be all right."

V.

Vanleo steadied him as he climbed onto Sasuke's back. It took some moments before Reginri could punch the climbing spikes into the thick, crinkled hide.

He was thankful for the low gravity. He pulled himself up easily, once he got the knack of it, and it took only a few moments to climb the ten meters to the edge of the pithole. Once there, he paused to rest.

"Not so hard as I thought," he said lightly.

"Good boy." Vanleo waved up at him. "Just keep steady and you'll be perfectly all right. We'll give you a signal on the com-line when you're to come out. This one won't be more than an hour, probably."

Reginri balanced himself on the lip of the pithole and took several deep breaths, tasting the oily air. In the distance gray waves broke into surf. The Drongheda rose like a bubble from the wrinkled sea. A bank of fog was rolling down the coastline. In it a shadowy shape floated. Reginri slitted his eyes to see better, but the fog wreathed the object and blurred its outline. Another Drongheda? He looked again but the form melted away in the white mist.

"Hurry it up," Sasuke called from below. "We won't move until you're in."

Reginri turned on the fleshy ledge beneath him and pulled at the dark blubbery folds that rimmed the pithole. He noticed that there were fine, gleaming threads all round the entrance. A mouth? An anus? Vanleo said not; the scientists who came to study the Drongheda had traced its digestive tract in crude fashion. But they had no idea what the pithole was for. It was precisely to find that out that Vanleo first went into one. Now it was Vanleo's theory that the pithole was the Drongheda's method of communication, since why else would the neural connections be so close to the surface inside? Perhaps, deep in the murky ocean, the Drongheda spoke to each other through these pitholes, rather than singing, like whales. Men had found no bioacoustic signature in the schools of Drongheda they had observed, but that meant very little.

Reginri pushed inward, through the iris of spongy flesh, and was at once immersed in darkness. His suit light clicked on. He lay in a sheath of meat with perhaps two hand spans of clearance on each side. The tunnel yawned ahead, absorbing the weak light. He gathered his knees and pushed upward against the slight grade.

"Electronics crew reports good contact with your tapper lines. This com okay?" Sasuke's voice came thin and high in Reginri's ear.

"Seems to be. Goddamned close in here."

"Sometimes it's smaller near the opening," Vanleo put in. "You shouldn't have too much climbing to do—most pitholes run pretty horizontal, when the Drongheda is holding steady like this."

"It's so tight. Going to be tough, crawling uphill," Reginri said, an uncertain waver in his voice.

"Don't worry about that. Just keep moving and look for the neural points." Vanleo paused. "Fish out the contacts for your tappers, will you? I just got a call from the technicians, they want to check the connection."

"Sure." Reginri felt at his belly. "I don't seem to find…"

"They're right there, just like in training," Sasuke said sharply. "Pull 'em out of their clips."

"Oh, yeah." Reginri fumbled for a moment and found the two metallic cylinders. They popped free of the suit and he nosed them together. "There."

"All right, all right, they're getting the trace," Vanleo said. "Looks like you're all set."

"Right, about time," Sasuke said. "Let's get moving."

"We're going around to the other side. So let us know if you see anything." Reginri could hear Vanleo's breath coming faster. "Quite a pull in this tide. Ah, there's the other pithole."

The two men continued to talk, getting Vanleo's equipment ready. Reginri turned his attention to his surroundings and wriggled upward, grunting. He worked steadily, pulling against the pulpy stuff. Here and there scaly folds wrinkled the walls, overlapping and making handholds. The waxen membranes reflected back none of his suit light. He dug in his heels and pushed, slipping on patches of filmy pink liquid that collected in the trough of the tunnel.

At first the passageway flared out slightly, giving him better purchase. He made good progress and settled down into a rhythm of pushing and turning. He worked his way around a vast bluish muscle that was laced by orange lines.

Even through his skinsuit he could feel a pulsing warmth come from it. The Drongheda had an internal temperature fifteen degrees Centigrade below the human's, but still an oppressive dull heat seeped through to him.

Something black lay ahead. He reached out and touched something rubbery that seemed to block the pithole. His suit light showed a milky pink barrier. He wormed around and felt at the edges of the stuff. Off to the left there was a smaller opening. He turned, flexed his legs and twisted his way into the new passage. Vanleo had told him the pithole might change direction and that when it did he was probably getting close to a nexus. Reginri hoped so.

VI.

"Everything going well?" Vanleo's voice came distantly.

"Think so," Reginri wheezed.

"I'm at the lip. Going inside now." There came the muffled sounds of a man working, and Reginri mentally blocked them out, concentrating on where he was.

The walls here gleamed like glazed, aging meat. His fingers could not dig into it. He wriggled with his hips and worked forward a few centimeters. He made his body flex, thrust, flex, thrust—he set up the rhythm and relaxed into it, moving forward slightly. The texture of the walls coarsened and he made better progress. Every few moments he stopped and checked the threads for the com-line and the tappers that trailed behind him, reeling out on spools at his side.

He could hear Sasuke muttering to himself, but he was unable to concentrate on anything but the waxen walls around him. The passage narrowed again, and ahead he could see more scaly folds. But these were different, dusted with a shimmering pale powder.

Reginri felt his heart beat faster. He kicked forward and reached out a hand to one of the encrusted folds. The delicate frosting glistened in his suit lamp. Here the meat was glassy, and deep within it he could see a complex interweaving network of veins and arteries, shot through with silvery threads.

It had to be a nexus; the pictures they had shown him were very much like this. It was not in a small pocket the way Vanleo said it would be, but that didn't matter. Vanleo himself had remarked that there seemed no systematic way the nodes were distributed. Indeed, they appeared to migrate to different positions inside the pithole, so that a team returning a few days later could not find the nodules they had tapped before.

Reginri felt a swelling excitement. He carefully thumbed on the electronic components set into his waist. Their low hum reassured him that everything was in order. He barked a short description of his find into his suit mike, and Vanleo responded in monosyllables. The other man seemed to be busy with something else, but Reginri was too occupied to wonder what it might be. He unplugged his tapper cylinders and worked them upward from his waist, his elbows poking into the pulpy membranes around him. Their needle points gleamed softly in the light as he turned them over, inspecting. Everything seemed all right.

He inched along and found the spot where the frosting seemed most dense. Carefully, bracing his hands against each other, he jabbed first one and then the other needle into the waxen flesh. It puckered around the needles.

He spoke quickly into his suit mike asking if the signals were coming through. There came an answering yes, some chatter from the technician back in the sand dunes, and then the line fell silent again.

Along the tapper lines were flowing the signals they had come to get. Long years of experiment had—as far as men could tell—established the recognition codes the technicians used to tell the Drongheda they had returned. Now, if the Drongheda responded, some convoluted electrical pulses would course through the lines and into the recording instruments ashore.

Reginri relaxed. He had done as much as he could. The rest depended on the technicians, the electronics, the lightning microsecond blur of information transfer between the machines and the Drongheda. Somewhere above or below him were flukes, ventral fins, slitted recesses, a baleen filter mouth through which a billion small fish lives had passed, all a part of this vast thing. Somewhere, layered in fat and wedged amid huge organs, there was a mind.

Reginri wondered how this had come about. Swimming through deep murky currents, somehow nature had evolved this thing that knew algebra, calculus, Reimannian metrics, Tchevychef subtleties—all as part of itself, as a fine-grained piece of the same language it shared with men.

Reginri felt a sudden impulse. There was an emergency piece clipped near his waist, for use when the tapper lines snarled or developed intermittent shorts. He wriggled around until his back was flush with the floor of the pithole and then reached down for it. With one hand he kept the needles impacted into the flesh above his head; with the other he extracted the thin, flat wedge of plastic and metal that he needed. From it sprouted tiny wires. He braced himself against the tunnel walls and flipped the wires into the emergency recesses in the tapper cylinders. Everything seemed secure; he rolled onto his back and fumbled at the rear of his helmet for the emergency wiring. By attaching the cabling, he could hook directly into a small fraction of the Drongheda's output. It wouldn't interfere with the direct tapping process. Maybe the men back in the sand dunes wouldn't even know he had done it.

He made the connection. Just before he flipped his suit com-line over to the emergency cable, he thought he felt a slight sway beneath him. The movement passed. He flipped the switch. And felt—

—*Bursting light that lanced through him, drummed a staccato rhythm of speckled green*—

—*Twisting lines that meshed and wove into perspectives, triangles warped into strange saddle-pointed envelopes, coiling into new soundless shapes*—

—A latticework of shrill sound, ringing at edges of geometrical flatness—

—Thick, rich foam that lapped against weathered stone towers, precisely turning under an ellipsoid orange sun—

—Miniatured light that groaned and spun softly, curling into moisture that beaded on a coppery matrix of wire—

—A webbing of sticky strands, lifting him—

—A welling current—

—Upward, toward the watery light—

Reginri snatched at the cable, yanking it out of the socket. His hand jerked up to cover his face and struck his helmet. He panted, gasping.

He closed his eyes and for a long moment thought of nothing, let his mind drift, let himself recoil from the experience.

There had been mathematics there, and much else. Rhomboids, acute intersections in veiled dimensions, many-sided twisted sculptures, warped perspectives, poly-hedrons of glowing fire.

But so much more—he would have drowned in it.

There was no interruption of chatter through his earphone. Apparently the electronics men had never noticed the interception. He breathed deeply and renewed his grip on the tapper needles. He closed his eyes and rested for long moments. The experience had turned him inside out for a brief flicker of time. But now he could breathe easily again. His heart had stopped thumping wildly in his chest. The torrent of images began to recede. His mind had been filled, overloaded with more than he could fathom.

He wondered how much the electronics really caught. Perhaps, transferring all this to cold ferrite memory, the emotional thrust was lost. It was not surprising that the only element men could decipher was the mathematics. Counting, lines and curves, the smooth sheen of geometry—they were abstractions, things that could be common to any reasoning mind. No wonder the Drongheda sent mostly mathematics through this neural passage; it was all that men could follow.

After a time it occurred to Reginri that perhaps Vanleo wanted it this way. Maybe he eavesdropped on the lines. The other man might seek this experience; it certainly had an intensity unmatched by drugs or the pallid electronic core-tapping in the sensoriums. Was Vanleo addicted? Why else risk failure? Why reject automated tapping and crawl in here—particularly since the right conditions came so seldom?

But it made no sense. If Vanleo had Drongheda tapes, he could play them back at leisure. So…maybe the man was fascinated by the creatures themselves, not only the mathematics. Perhaps the challenge of going inside, the feel of it, was what Vanleo liked.

Grotesque, yes...but maybe that was it.

VII.

He felt a tremor. The needles wobbled in his hand.

"Hey!" he shouted. The tube flexed under him.

"Something's happening in here. You guys—"

In midsentence the com-line went dead. Reginri automatically switched over to emergency, but there was no signal there either. He glanced at the tapper lines. The red phosphor glow at their ends had gone dead; they were not receiving power.

He wriggled around and looked down toward his feet. The tapper lines and the com cable snaked away into darkness with no breaks visible. If there was a flaw in the line, it was farther away.

Reginri snapped the tapper line heads back into his suit. As he did so, the flesh around him oozed languidly, compressing. There was a tilting sense of motion, a turning—

"*Frange* it! Get me—" then he remembered the line was dead. His lips pressed together.

He would have to get out on his own.

He dug in with his heels and tried to pull himself backward. A scaly bump scraped against his side. He pulled harder and came free, sliding a few centimeters back. The passage seemed tilted slightly downward. He put his hands out to push and saw something wet run over his fingers. The slimy fluid that filled the trough of the pithole was trickling toward him. Reginri pushed back energetically, getting a better purchase in the pulpy floor.

He worked steadily and made some progress. A long, slow undulation began and the walls clenched about him. He felt something squeeze at his legs, then his waist, then his chest and head. The tightening had a slow, certain rhythm.

He breathed faster, tasting an acrid smell. He heard only his own breath, amplified in the helmet.

He wriggled backward. His boot struck something and he felt the smooth lip of a turning in the passage. He remembered this, but the angle seemed wrong. The Drongheda must be shifting and moving, turning the pithole.

He forked his feet into the new passageway and quickly slipped through it.

This way was easier; he slid down the slick sides and felt a wave of relief. Farther along, if the tunnel widened, he might even be able to turn around and go headfirst.

His foot touched something that resisted softly. He felt around with both boots, gradually letting his weight settle on the thing. It seemed to have a brittle surface, pebbled. He carefully followed the outline of it around the walls of the hole until he had satisfied himself that there was no opening.

The passage was blocked.

His mind raced. The air seemed to gain a weight of its own, thick and sour in his helmet. He stamped his boots down, hoping to break whatever it was. The surface stayed firm.

Reginri felt his mind go numb. He was trapped. The com-line was dead, probably snipped off by this thing at his feet.

He felt the walls around him clench and stretch again, a massive hand squeezing the life from him. The pithole sides were only centimeters from his helmet. As he watched, a slow ripple passed through the membrane, ropes of yellow fat visible beneath the surface.

"Get me out!" Reginri kicked wildly. He thrashed against the slimy walls, using elbows and knees to gouge. The yielding pressure remained, cloaking him.

"Out! Out!" Reginri viciously slammed his fists into the flesh. His vision blurred. Small dark points floated before him. He pounded mechanically, his breath coming in short gasps. He cried for help. And he knew he was going to die.

Rage burst out of him. He beat at the enveloping smoothness. The gathering tightness in him boiled up, curling his lips into a grimace. His helmet filled with a bitter taste. He shouted again and again, battering at the Drongheda, cursing it. His muscles began to ache.

And slowly, slowly the burning anger melted. He blinked away the sweat in his eyes. His vision cleared. The blind, pointless energy drained away. He began to think again.

Sasuke. Vanleo. Two-faced bastards. They'd known this job was dangerous. The incident on the beach was a charade. When he showed doubts they'd bullied and threatened him immediately. They'd probably had to do it before, to other men. It was all planned.

He took a long, slow breath and looked up. Above him in the tunnel of darkness, the strands of the tapping lines and the com cable dangled.

One set of lines.

They led upward, on a slant, the way he had come.

It took a moment for the fact to strike him. If he had been backing down the way he came, the lines should be snarled behind him.

He pushed against the glazed sides and looked down his chest. There were no tapper lines near his legs.

That meant the lines did not come up through whatever was blocking his way. No, they came only from above. Which meant that he had taken some wrong side passage. Somehow a hole had opened in the side of the pithole and he had followed it blindly.

He gathered himself and thrust upward, striving for purchase. He struggled up the incline, and dug in with his toes. Another long ripple passed through the tube. The steady hand of gravity forced him down, but he slowly worked his way forward. Sweat stung his eyes.

After a few minutes his hands found the lip, and he quickly hoisted himself over it, into the horizontal tunnel above.

He found a tangle of lines and tugged at them. They gave with a slight resistance. This was the way out, he was sure of it. He began wriggling forward, and suddenly the world tilted, stretched, lifted him high. Let him drop.

He smashed against the pulpy side and lost his breath. The tube flexed again, rising up in front of him and dropping away behind. He dug his hands in and held on. The pithole arched, coiling, and squeezed him. Spongy flesh pressed at his head and he involuntarily held his breath. His faceplate was wrapped in it, and his world became fine-veined, purple, marbled with lacy fat.

Slowly, slowly the pressure ebbed away. He felt a dull aching in his side. There was a subdued tremor beneath him. As soon as he gained maneuvering room, he crawled urgently forward, kicking viciously. The lines led him forward.

The passage flared outward and he increased his speed. He kept up a steady pace of pulling hands, gouging elbows, thrusting knees and toes. The weight around him seemed bent upon expelling, imparting momentum, ejecting. So it seemed, as the flesh tightened behind him and opened before.

He tried the helmet microphone again, but it was still inert. He thought he recognized a vast bulging bluish muscle that, on his way in, had been in the wall. Now it formed a bump in the floor. He scrambled over its slickness and continued on.

He was so intent upon motion and momentum that he did not recognize the end. Suddenly the walls converged again and he looked around frantically for another exit. There was none. Then he noticed the rings of cartilage and stringy muscle. He pushed at the knotted surface. It gave, then relaxed even more. He shoved forward and abruptly was halfway out, suspended over the churning water.

VIII.

The muscled iris gripped him loosely about the waist. Puffing steadily, he stopped to rest.

He squinted up at the forgiving sun. Around him was a harshly lit world of soundless motion. Currents swirled meters below. He could feel the brown hillside of the Drongheda shift slowly. He turned to see—

The Drongheda was splitting in two.

But no, no—

The bulge was another Drongheda moving slowly, close by. At the same moment another silent motion caught his eye. Below, Vanleo struggled through the darkening water, waving. Pale mist shrouded the sea.

Reginri worked his way out and onto the narrow rim of the pithole. He took a grip at it and lowered himself partway down toward the water. Arms extended, he let go and fell with a splash into the ocean. He kept his balance and lurched away awkwardly on legs of cotton.

Vanleo reached out a steadying hand. The man motioned at the back of his helmet. Reginri frowned, puzzled, and then realized he was motioning toward the emergency com cable. He unspooled his own cable and plugged it into the shoulder socket on Vanleo's skinsuit.

"—damned lucky. Didn't think I'd see you again. But it's *fantastic*, come see it."

"What? I got—"

"I understand them now. I know what they're here for. It's not just communication, I don't think that, but that's part of it too. They've—"

"Stop babbling. What happened?"

"I went in," Vanleo said, regaining his breath. "Or started to. We didn't notice that another Drongheda had surfaced, was moving into the shallows."

"I saw it. I didn't think—"

"I climbed up to the second pithole before I saw. I was busy with the cables, you know. You were getting good traces and I wanted to—"

"Let's get away, come on." The vast bulks above them were moving.

"No, no, come see. I think my guess is right, these shallows are a natural shelter for them. If they have any enemies in the sea, large fish or something, their enemies can't follow them here into the shallows. So they come here to, to mate and to communicate. They must be terribly lonely, if they can't talk to each other in the oceans. So they have to come here to do it. I—"

Reginri studied the man and saw that he was ablaze with his inner vision. The damned fool loved these beasts, cared about them, had devoted a life to them and their goddamned mathematics.

"Where's Sasuke?"

"—and it's all so natural. I mean, humans communicate and make love, and those are two separate acts. They don't blend together. But the Drongheda—they have it all. They're like, like..."

The man pulled at Reginri's shoulder, leading him around the long curve of the Drongheda. Two immense burnished hillsides grew out of the shadowed sea. Zeta was setting, and in profile Reginri could see a long dexterous tentacle curling into the air. It came from the mottled patches, like welts, he had seen before.

"They extend through those spots, you see. Those are their sensors, what they use to complete the contact. And—I can't prove it, but I'm sure—that is when the genetic material is passed between them. The mating period. At the same time they exchange information, converse. That's what we're getting on the tappers, their stored knowledge fed out. They think we're another of their own, that must be it. I don't understand all of it, but—"

"Where's Sasuke?"

"—but the first one, the one you were inside, recognized the difference as soon as the second Drongheda approached. They moved together and the second one extruded that tentacle. Then—"

Reginri shook the other man roughly. "Shut up! Sasuke—"

Vanleo stopped, dazed, and looked at Reginri. "I've been telling you. It's a great discovery, the first real step we've taken in this field. We'll understand so much *more* once this is fully explored."

Reginri hit him in the shoulder.

Vanleo staggered. The glassy, pinched look of his eyes faded. He began to lift his arms.

Reginri drove his gloved fist into Vanleo's faceplate. Vanleo toppled backward. The ocean swallowed him. Reginri stepped back, blinking.

Vanleo's helmet appeared as he struggled up. A wave foamed over him. He stumbled, turned, saw Reginri.

Reginri moved toward him. "No. No," Vanleo said weakly.

"If you're not going to tell me—"

"But I, I am." Vanleo gasped, leaned forward until he could brace his hands on his knees. "There wasn't time. The second one came up on us so, so fast."

"Yeah?"

"I was about ready to go inside. When I saw the second one moving in, you know, the only time in thirty years, I knew it was important. I climbed down to observe. But we needed the data, so Sasuke went in for me. With the tapper cables."

Vanleo panted. His face was ashen.

"When the tentacle went in, it filled the pithole exactly, Tight. There was no room left," he said. "Sasuke...was there. Inside."

Reginri froze, stunned. A wave swirled around him and he slipped. The waters tumbled him backward. Dazed, he regained his footing on the slick rocks and began stumbling blindly toward the bleak shore, toward humanity. The ocean lapped around him, ceaseless and unending.

IX.

Belej sat motionless, unmindful of the chill. "Oh my God," she said.

"That was it," he murmured. He stared off into the canyon. Zeta Reticuli sent slanting rays into the layered reddening mists. Air squirrels darted among the shifting shadows.

"He's crazy," Belej said simply. "That Leo is crazy."

"Well..." Reginri began. Then he rocked forward stiffly and stood up. Swirls of reddish cloud were crawling up the canyon face toward them. He pointed. "That stuff is coming in faster than I thought." He coughed. "We'd better get inside."

Belej nodded and came to her feet. She brushed the twisted brown grass from her legs and turned to him.

"Now that you've told me," she said softly, "I think you ought to put it from your mind."

"It's hard. I..."

"I know. I know. But you can push it far away from you, forget it happened. That's the best way."

"Well, maybe."

"Believe me. You've changed since this happened to you. I can feel it."

"Feel what?"

"You. You're different. I feel a barrier between us."

"I wonder," he said slowly.

She put her hand on his arm and stepped closer, an old, familiar gesture. He stood watching the reddening haze swallowing the precise lines of the rocks below.

"I want that screen between us to dissolve. You made your contribution, earned your pay. Those damned people understand the Drongheda now—"

He made a wry, rasping laugh. "We'll never grasp the Drongheda. What we get in those neural circuits are mirrors of what we want. Of what we are. We can't sense anything totally alien."

"But—"

"Vanleo saw mathematics because he went after it. So did I, at first. Later…"

He stopped. A sudden breeze made him shiver. He clenched his fists. Clenched. Clenched.

How could he tell her? He woke in the night, sweating, tangled in the bedclothes, muttering incoherently…but they were not nightmares, not precisely.

Something else. Something intermediate.

"Forget those things," Belej said soothingly. Reginri leaned closer to her and caught the sweet musk of her, the dry crackling scent of her hair. He had always loved that.

She frowned up at him. Her eyes shifted intently from his mouth to his eyes and then back again, trying to read his expression. "It will only trouble you to recall it. I—I'm sorry I asked you to tell it. But remember"—she took both his hands in hers—"you'll never go back there again. It can be…"

Something made him look beyond her. At the gathering fog.

And at once he sensed the shrouded abyss open below him. Sweeping him in. Gathering him up. Into—

—a thick red foam lapping against weathered granite towers—

—an ellipsoidal sun spinning soundlessly over a silvered, warping planet—

—watery light—

—cloying strands, sticky, a fine-spun coppery matrix that enfolded him, warming—

—glossy sheen of polyhedra, wedged together, mass upon mass—

—smooth bands of moisture playing lightly over his quilted skin—

—a blistering light shines through him, sets his bones to humming resonance—

—pressing—

—coiling—

Beckoning. Beckoning.

When the moment had passed, Reginri blinked and felt a salty stinging in his eyes. Every day the tug was stronger, the incandescent images sharper. This must be what Vanleo felt, he was sure of it. They came to him now even during the day. Again and again, the grainy texture altering with time...

He reached out and enfolded Belej in his arms.

"But I must," he said in a rasping whisper. "Vanleo called today. He...I'm going. I'm going back."

He heard her quick intake of breath, felt her stiffen in his arms.

His attention was diverted by the reddening fog. It cloaked half the world and still it came on.

There was something ominous about it and something inviting as well. He watched as it engulfed trees nearby. He studied it intently, judging the distance. The looming presence was quite close now. But he was sure it would be all right.

REDEEMER
(1979)

He had trouble finding it. The blue-white exhaust plume was a long trail of ionized hydrogen scratching a line across the black. It had been a lot harder to locate out here than Central said it would be.

Nagara came up on the *Redeemer* from behind, their blind side. They wouldn't have any sensors pointed aft. No point in it when you're on a one-way trip, not expecting visitors and haven't seen anybody for seventy-three years.

He boosted in with the fusion plant, cutting off the translight to avoid overshoot. The translight rig was delicate and still experimental and it had already pushed him over seven light years out from Earth. When he got back to Earth there would be an accounting, and he would have to pay off from his profit anything he spent for over expenditure of the translight hardware.

The ramscoop vessel ahead was running hot. It was a long steel-gray cylinder, fluted fore and aft. The blue-white fusion fire came boiling out of the aft throat, pushing *Redeemer* along at a little below a tenth of light velocity. Nagara's board buzzed. He cut in the mill-mag system. The ship's skin, visible outside through his small porthole, fluxed into its super-conducting state, gleaming like chrome. The readout winked and Nagara could see on the situation board his ship slipping like a silver fish through the webbing of magnetic field lines that protected *Redeemer*.

The field was mostly magnetic dipole. He cut through it and glided in parallel to the hot exhaust streamer. The stuff was spitting out a lot of UV and he had to change filters to see what he was doing. He eased up along the aft section of the ship and matched velocities. The magnetic throat yawning up ahead sucked in the interstellar hydrogen for the fusion motors. *Redeemer*'s forward mag fields pulsed to shock-ionize the hydrogen molecules ahead, then ate them eagerly. He stayed away from that. There was enough radiation up there to fry you for good.

Redeemer's midsection was rotating but the big clumsy-looking lock aft was stationary. Fine. No trouble clamping on.

The couplers seized clang and he used a waldo to manually open the lock. He would have to be fast now, fast and careful.

He pressed a code into the keyin plate on his chest to check it. It worked. The slick aura enveloped him, cutting out the ship's hum. Nagara nodded to himself.

He went quickly through the *Redeemer*'s lock. The pumps were still laboring when he spun the manual override to open the big inner hatch. He pulled himself through in the zero-g with one power motion, through the hatch and into a cramped suitup room. He cut in his magnetos and settled to the grid deck.

As Nagara crossed the desk a young man came in from a side hatchway. Nagara stopped and thumped off his protective shield. The man didn't see Nagara at first because he was looking the other way as he came through the hatchway, moving with easy agility. He was studying the subsystem monitoring panels on the far bulkhead. The status phosphors were red but they winked green as Nagara took three steps forward and grabbed the man's shoulder and spun him around. Nagara was grounded and the man was not. Nagara hit him once in the stomach and then shoved him against a bulkhead. The man gasped for breath. Nagara stepped back and put his hand into his coverall pocket and when it came out there was a dart pistol in it. The man's eyes didn't register anything at first and when they did he just watched the pistol, getting his breath back, staring as though he couldn't believe either Nagara or the pistol was there.

"What's your name?" Nagara demanded in a clipped, efficient voice.

"What? I—"

"Your name. Quick."

"I...Zak."

"All right, Zak, now listen to me. I'm inside now and I'm not staying long. I don't care what you've been told. You do just what I say and nobody will blame you for it."

"...Nobody...?" Zak was still trying to unscramble his thoughts and he looked at the pistol again as though that would explain things.

"Zak, how many of you are manning this ship?"

"Manning? You mean crewing?" Confronted with a clear question, he forgot his confusion and frowned. "Three. We're doing our five-year stint. The Revealer and Jacob and me."

"Fine. Now where's Jacob?"

"Asleep. This isn't his shift."

"Good." Nagara jerked a thumb over his shoulder. "Personnel quarters that way?"

"Uh, yes."

"Did an alarm go off through the whole ship, Zak?"

"No, just on the bridge."

"So it didn't wake up Jacob?"

"I...I suppose not."

"Fine, good. Now, where's the Revealer?"

So far it was working well. The best way to handle people who might give you trouble right away was to keep them busy telling you things before they had time to decide what they should be doing. And Zak plainly was used to taking orders.

"She's in the forest."

"Good. I have to see her. You lead the way, Zak."

Zak automatically half turned to kick down the hatchway he'd come in through and then the questions came out. "What—who *are* you? How—"

"I'm just visiting. We've got faster ways of moving now, Zak. I caught up with you."

"A faster ramscoop? But we—"

"Let's go, Zak." Nagara waved the dart gun and Zak looked at it a moment and then, still visibly struggling with his confusion, he kicked off and glided down the drift tube.

The forest was one half of a one hundred meter long cylinder, located near the middle of the ship and rotating to give one g. The forest was dense with pines and oak and tall bushes. A fine mist hung over the tree tops, obscuring the other half of the cylinder, a gardening zone that hung over their heads. Nagara hadn't been in a small cylinder like this for decades. He was used to seeing a distant green carpet overhead, so far away you couldn't make out individual trees, and shrouded by the cottonball clouds that accumulated at the zero-g along the cylinder axis. This whole place felt cramped to him.

Zak led him along footpaths and into a bamboo-walled clearing. The Revealer was sitting in lotus position in the middle of it. She was wearing a Flatlander robe and cowl just like Zak. He recognized it from a historical fax readout.

She was a plain-faced woman, wrinkled and wiry, her hands thick and calloused, the fingers stubby, the nails clipped off square. She didn't go rigid with surprise when Nagara came into view and this bothered him a little. She didn't look at the dart pistol more than once, to see what it was, and that surprised him, too.

"What's your name?" Nagara said as he walked into the bamboo-encased silence.

"I am the Revealer." A steady voice.

"No, I meant your name."

"That is my name."

"I mean—"

"I am the Revealer for this stage of our exodus."

Nagara watched as Zak stepped halfway between them and then stood uncertainly, looking back and forth.

"All right. When they freeze you back down, what'll they call you then?"

She smiled at this. "Michele Astanza."

Nagara didn't show anything in his face. He waved the pistol at her and said, "Get up."

"I prefer to sit."

"And I prefer you to stand."

"Oh."

He watched both of them carefully.

"Zak, I'm going to have to ask you to do a favor for me."

Zak glanced at the Revealer and she moved her head a few millimeters in a nod. He said, "Sure."

"This way." Nagara gestured with the pistol to the woman. "You lead."

The woman nodded to herself as if this confirmed something and got up and started down a footpath to her right, her steps so soft on the leafy path that Nagara could not hear them over the tinkling of a stream on the overhead side of the cylinder. Nagara followed her. The trees trapped the sound in here and made him jumpy.

He knew he was taking a calculated risk by not taking Jacob, too. But the odds against Jacob waking up in time were good and the whole point of doing it this way was to get in and out fast, exploit surprise. And he wasn't sure he could handle the three of them together. That was just it—he was doing this alone so he could collect the whole fee, and for that you had to take some extra risk. That was the way this thing worked.

The forest gave onto some corn fields and then some wheat, all with UV phosphors netted above. The three of them skirted around the nets and through a hatchway in the big aft wall. Whenever Zak started to say anything Nagara cut him off with a wave of the pistol. Then Nagara saw that with some time to think Zak was adding some things up and the lines around his mouth were tightening, so Nagara asked him some questions about the ship's design. That worked. Zak rattled on about quintuple-redundant failsafe subsystems he'd been repairing until they were at the entrance to the freezing compartment.

It was bigger than Nagara had thought. He had done all the research he could, going through old faxes of *Redeemer*'s prelim designs, but plainly the Flatlanders had changed things in some later design phase.

One whole axial section of *Redeemer* was given over to the freeze-down vaults. It was at zero-g because otherwise the slow compression of tissues in the corpses would do permanent damage. They floated in their translucent compartments, like strange fish in endless rows of pale, blue-white aquariums.

The vaults were stored in a huge array, each layer a cylinder slightly larger than the one it enclosed, all aligned along the ship's axis. Each cylinder was two compartments thick, a corpse in every one, and the long cylinders extended into the distance until the chilly fog steaming off them blurred the perspective and the eye could not judge the size of the things. Despite himself Nagara was impressed. There were thousands and thousands of Flatlanders in here, all dead and waiting for the promised land ahead, circling Tau Ceti. And with seventy-three more years of data to judge by, Nagara knew something this Revealer couldn't reveal: the failure rate when they thawed them out would be thirty percent.

They had come out on the center face of the bulwark separating the vault section from the farming part. Nagara stopped them and studied the front face of the vault array, which spread away from them radially like an immense spider web. He reviewed the old plans in his head. The axis of the whole thing was a tube a meter wide, the same translucent organiform. Liquid nitrogen flowed in the hollow walls of the array and the phosphor light was pale and watery.

"That's the DNA storage," Nagara said, pointing at the axial tube.

"What?" Zak said. "Yes, it is."

"Take them out."

"What?"

"They're in failsafe self-refrigerated canisters, aren't they?"

"Yes."

"That's fine." Nagara turned to the Revealer. "You've got the working combinations, don't you?"

She had been silent for some time. She looked at him steadily and said, "I do."

"Let's have them."

"Why should I give them?"

"I think you know what's going on."

"Not really."

He knew she was playing some game but he couldn't see why. "You're carrying DNA material for over ten thousand people. Old genotypes, undamaged. It wasn't so rare when you collected it seventy-three years ago but it is now. I want it."

"It is for our colony."

"You've got enough corpses here."

"We need genetic diversity."

"The System needs it more than you. There's been a war. A lot of radiation damage."

"Who won?"

"Us. The outskirters."

"That means nothing to me."

"We're the environments in orbit around the sun, not sucking up to Earth. We knew what was going on. We're mostly in Bernal spheres. We got the jump on—"

"You've wrecked each other genetically, haven't you? That was always the trouble with your damned cities. No place to dig a hole and hide."

Nagara shrugged. He was watching Zak. From the man's face Nagara could tell he was getting to be more insulted than angry—outraged at somebody walking in and stealing their future. And from the way his leg muscles were tensing against a foothold Nagara guessed Zak was also getting more insulted than scared, which was trouble for sure. It was a lot better if you dealt with a man who cared more about the long odds against a dart gun at this range, than about the principle. Nagara knew he couldn't count on Zak ignoring all the Flatlander nonsense the Revealer and others had pumped into him.

They hung in zero-g, nobody moving in the wan light, the only sound a gurgling of liquid nitrogen. The Revealer was saying something and there was another thing bothering Nagara, some sound, but he ignored it.

"How did the planetary enclaves hold out?" the woman was asking. "I had many friends—"

"They're gone."

Something came into the woman's face. "You've lost man's *birthright?*"

"They sided with the—"

"Abandoned the planets altogether? Made them unfit to *live* on? All for your awful *cities*—" and she made a funny jerky motion with her right hand.

That was it. When she started moving that way Nagara saw it had to be a signal and he jumped to the left. He didn't take time to place his boots right and so he picked up some spin but the important thing was to get away from that spot fast. He heard a *chuung* off to the right and a dart smacking into the bulkhead and when he turned his head to the right and up behind him a burly man with black hair and the same Flatlander robes and a dart gun was coming at him on a glide.

Nagara had started twisting his shoulder when he leaped and now the differential angular momentum was bringing his shooting arm around. Jacob was already aiming again. Nagara took the extra second to make his shot and allow for the relative motions. His dart gun puffed and Nagara saw it take Jacob in the chest, just right. The man's face went white and he reached down to pull the dart out but by that time the nerve inhibitor had reached the heart and abruptly Jacob stopped plucking at the dart and his fingers went slack and the body drifted on in the chilly air, smacking into a vault door and coming to rest.

Nagara wrenched around to cover the other two. Zak was coming at him. Nagara leaped away, braked. He turned and Zak had come to rest against the translucent organiform, waiting.

"That's a lesson," Nagara said evenly. "Here's another."

He touched the keyin on his chest and his force screen flickered on around him, making him look metallic. He turned it off in time to hear the hollow boom that came rolling through the ship like a giant's shout.

"That's a sample. A shaped charge. My ship set it off two hundred meters from *Redeemer*. The next one's keyed to go on impact with your skin. You'll lose pressure too fast to do anything about it. My force field comes on when the charge goes, so it won't hurt me."

"We've never seen such a field," the woman said unsteadily.

"Outskirter invention. That's why we won."

He didn't bother watching Zak. He looked at the woman as she clasped her thick worker's hands together and began to realize what choices were left. When she was done with that she murmured, "Zak, take out the canisters."

✷

The woman sagged against a strut. Her robes clung to her and made her look gaunt and old.

"You're not giving us a chance, are you?" she said.

"You've got a lot of corpses here. You'll have a big colony out at Tau Ceti." Nagara was watching Zak maneuver the canisters onto a mobile carrier. The young man was going to be all right now, he could tell that. There was the look of weary defeat about him.

"We need the genotypes for insurance. In a strange ecology there will be genetic drift."

"The System has worse problems right now."

"With Earth dead you people in the artificial worlds are *finished*," she said savagely, a spark returning. "That's why we left. We could see it coming."

Nagara wondered if they'd have left at all if they'd known a faster than light drive would come along. But no, it wouldn't have made any difference. The translight transition cost too much and only worked on small ships. He narrowed his eyes and made a smile without humor.

"I know quite well why you left. A bunch of scum-lovers. Purists. Said Earth was just as bad as the cylinder cities, all artificial, all controlled. Yeah, I know. You flatties sold off everything you had and built *this*—" His voice became bitter. "Ransacked a fortune—*my* fortune."

For once she looked genuinely curious, uncalculating. "Yours?"

He flicked a glance at her and then back at Zak. "Yeah. I would've inherited some of your billions you made out of those smelting patents."

"You—"

"I'm one of your great-grandsons."

Her face changed. "No."

"It's true. Stuffing the money into this clunker made all your descendants have to bust ass for a living. And it's not so easy these days."

"I…didn't…"

He waved her into silence. "I knew you were one of the mainstays, one of the rich Flatlanders. The family talked about it a lot. We're not doing so well now. Not as well as you did, not by a thousandth. I thought that would mean you'd get to sleep right through, wake up at Tau Ceti. Instead—" he laughed—"they've got you standing watch."

"Someone has to be the Revealer of the word, grandson."

"Great-grandson. Revealer? If you'd 'revealed' a little common sense to that kid over there he would've been alert and I wouldn't be in here."

She frowned and watched Zak, who was awkwardly shifting the squat modular canisters stenciled GENETIC BANK. MAX SECURITY. "We are not military types."

Nagara grinned. "Right. I was looking through the family records and I thought up this job. I figured you for an easy setup. A max of three or four on duty, considering the size of the life-support systems and redundancies. So I got the venture capital together for time in a translight and here I am."

"We're not your kind. Why can't you give us a chance, grandson?"

"I'm a businessman."

She had a dry, rasping laugh. "A few centuries ago everybody thought space colonies would be the final answer. Get off the stinking old Earth and everything's solved. Athens in the sky. But look at you—a paid assassin. A 'businessman'. You're no grandson of *mine*."

"Old ideas." He watched Zak.

"Don't you see it? The colony environments aren't a social advance. You need discipline to keep life-support systems from springing a leak or poisoning you. Communication and travel have to be regulated for simple safety. So you don't get democracies, you get strong men. And then they turned on *us*—on Earth."

"You were out of date," he said casually, not paying much attention.

"Do you ever read any history?"

"No." He knew this was part of her spiel—he'd seen it on a fax from a century ago—but he let her go on to keep her occupied. Talkers never acted when they could talk.

"They turned Earth into a handy preserve. The Berbers and Normans had it the same way a thousand years ago. They were seafarers. They depopulated Europe's coastline by raids, taking what or who they wanted. You did the same to us, from orbit, using solar lasers. But to—"

"Enough," Nagara said. He checked the long bore of the axial tube. It was empty. Zak had the stuff secured on the carrier. There wasn't any point in staying here any longer than necessary.

"Let's go," he said.

"One more thing," the woman said.

"What?"

"We went peacefully, I want you to remember that. We have no defenses."

"Yeah," Nagara said impatiently.

"But we have huge energies at our disposal. The scoop fields funnel an enormous flux of relativistic particles. We could've temporarily altered the magnetic multipolar fields and burned your sort to death."

"But you didn't."

"No, we didn't. But remember that."

Nagara shrugged. Zak was floating by the carrier ready to take orders, looking tired. The kid had been easy to take, to easy for him to take any pride in doing it. Nagara liked an even match. He didn't even mind losing if it was to somebody he could respect. Zak wasn't in that league, though.

"Let's go," he said.

The loading took time but he covered Zak on every step and there were no problems. When he cast off from *Redeemer* he looked around by reflex for a planet to sight on, relaxing now, and it struck him that he was more alone than he had ever been, the stars scattered like oily jewels on velvet were the nearest destination he could have. That woman in *Redeemer* had lived with this for years. He looked at the endless long night out here, felt it as a shadow that passed through his mind, and then he punched in instructions and *Redeemer* dropped away, its blue-white arc a fuzzy blade that cut the darkness, and he slipped with a hollow clapping sound into translight.

He was three hours from his dropout point when one of the canisters strapped down behind the pilot's couch gave a warning buzz from thermal overload. It popped open.

Nagara twisted around and fumbled with the latches. He could pull the top two access drawers a little way out and when he did he saw that inside there was a store of medical supplies. Boxes and tubes and fluid cubes. Cheap stuff. No DNA manifolds.

Nagara sat and stared at the complete blankness outside. *We could've temporarily altered the magnetic multipolar fields and burned your sort to death,* she had said. *Remember that.*

If he went back she would be ready. They could rig some kind of aft sensor and focus the ramscoop fields on him when he came tunneling in through them. Fry him good.

They must have planned it all from the first. Something about it, something about the way she'd looked, told him it had been the old woman's idea.

The risky part of it had been the business with Jacob. That didn't make sense. But maybe she'd known Jacob would try something and since she couldn't do anything about it she used it. Used it to relax him, make him think the touchy part of the job was done so that he didn't think to check inside the stenciled canisters.

He looked at the medical supplies. Seventy-three years ago the woman had known they couldn't protect themselves from what they didn't know, ships that hadn't been invented yet. So on her five-year watch she had arranged a dodge that would work even if some System ship caught up to them. Now the Flatlanders knew what to defend against.

He sat and looked out at the blankness and thought about that.

Only later did he look carefully through the canisters. In the lowest access drawer was a simple scrap of paper. On it someone—he knew instantly it must have been the old woman, or somebody damned like her—had hand printed a message.

If you're from the System and you're reading this on the way back home, you've just found out you're holding the sack. Great. But after you've cooled off, remember that if you leave us alone, we'll be another human settlement someday. We'll have things you'll find useful. If you've caught up with *Redeemer* you certainly have something *we* want—a faster drive. So we can trade. Remember that. Show this message to your bosses. In a few centuries we can be an asset to you. But until then, keep off our backs. We'll have more tricks waiting for you.

When he popped out into System space the A47 sphere was hanging up to the left at precisely the relative coordinates and distance he'd left it.

A47 was big and inside there were three men waiting to divide up and classify and market the genotypes and when he told them what was in the canisters it would all be over, his money gone and theirs and no hope of his getting a stake again. And maybe worse than that. Maybe a lot worse.

He squinted at A47 as he came in for rendezvous. It looked different. Some of the third quadrant damage from the war wasn't repaired yet. The skin that had gleamed once was smudged now and twisted gray girders stuck out of the ports. It looked pretty beat up. It was the best high-tech fortress they had and A47 had made the whole difference in the war. It broke the African shield by itself. But now it didn't look like so much. All the dots of light orbiting in the distance were pretty nearly the same or worse and now they were all that was left in the system.

Nagara turned his ship about to vector on the landing bay, listening to the rumble as the engines cut in. The console phosphors rippled, blue, green, yellow as Central reffed him.

This next part was going to be pretty bad. Damned bad. And out there his great-grandmother was on the way still, somebody he could respect now, and for the first time he thought the Flatlanders probably were going to make it. In the darkness of the cabin something about the thought made him smile.

DARK SANCTUARY
(1979)

The laser beam hit me smack in the face.

I twisted away. Hot orange light seared my field of view. My helmet buzzed and went dark as its sunshade overloaded. *Get inside the ship.* I yanked on a strut and tumbled into the yawning, fluorescent-lit airlock.

In the asteroid belt you either have fast reflexes or you're a statistic. I slammed into the airlock bulkhead and stopped dead, waiting to see where the laser beam would hit next. My suit sensors were all burned out, my straps were singed. The pressure patches on knees and elbows had brown bubbles in them. They had blistered and boiled away. Another second or two and I'd have been sucking vac.

I took all this in while I watched for reflections from the next laser strike. Only it didn't come. Whoever had shot at me either thought *Sniffer* was disabled, or else they had a balky laser. Either way, I had to start dodging.

I moved fast, working my way forward through a connecting tube to the bridge—a fancy name for a closet-sized cockpit. I revved up *Sniffer's* fusion drive and felt the *thump* and tug as she started spitting hot plasma out her rear tubes. I made the side jets stutter, too, putting out little bursts of plasma. That made *Sniffer* dart around, just enough to make hitting her tough. Lurch, weave, lurch.

I punched in for a damage report. Some aft sensors burned out, a loading arm pivot melted down, other minor stuff. The laser bolt must have caught us for just a few seconds.

A bolt from *who?* Where? I checked radar. Nothing.

I reached up to scratch my nose, thinking, and I realized my helmet and skinsuit were still sealed, vac-worthy. I decided to keep them on, just in case. I usually wear light coveralls inside *Sniffer*; the skinsuit is for vac work. It occurred to me that if I hadn't been outside, fixing a hydraulic loader, I wouldn't have known anybody shot at us at all, until my next routine check.

Which didn't make sense. Prospectors shoot at you if you're jumping a claim. They don't zap you once and then fade—they finish the job. I was pretty safe now; *Sniffer*'s strutting mode was fast and choppy, jerking me around in my captain's couch. But as my hands hovered over the control console, they started trembling. I couldn't make them stop. My fingers were shaking so badly I didn't dare punch in instructions. *Delayed reaction*, my analytical mind told me.

I was scared. Prospecting by yourself is risky enough without the bad luck of running into somebody else's claim. All at once I wished I wasn't such a loner. My mouth got dry. I forced myself to think.

By all rights, *Sniffer* should've been a drifting hulk by now—sensors blinded, punched full of holes, engines blown. Belt prospectors play for *all* the marbles.

Philosophically, I'm with the jackrabbits—run, dodge, hop, but don't fight. I have some surprises for anybody who tries to outrun me, too. Better than trading laser bolts with rockrats at thousand-kilometer range, any day.

But this one worried me. No other ships on radar, nothing but that one bolt. It didn't fit.

I punched in a quick computer program. The maintenance computer had logged the time when the aft sensors scorched out. Also, I could tell which way I was facing when the bolt hit me. Those two facts could give me a fix on the source. I let *Sniffer*'s ballistic routine chew on that for a minute and, waiting, looked out the side port. The sun was a fierce white dot in an inky sea. A few rocks twinkled in the distance as they tumbled. Until we were hit, we'd been on a zero-gee coast, outbound from Ceres—the biggest rock there is—for some prospecting. The best-paying commodity in the Belt right now was methane ice, and I knew a likely place. *Sniffer*—the ugly, segmented tube with strap-on fuel pods that I call home—was still over eight hundred thousand kilometers from the asteroid I wanted to check.

Five years back I had been out with a rockhound bunch, looking for asteroids with rich cadmium deposits. That was in the days when everybody thought cadmium was going to be the wonder fuel for ion rockets. We found the cadmium, all right, and made a bundle. While I was out on my own, taking samples from rocks, I saw this gray, ice-covered asteroid about a hundred klicks away. My ship auto-eye picked it up from the bright sunglint. Sensors said it was carbon dioxide ice with some water mixed in. Probably a comet hit the rock millions of years ago, and some of it stuck. I filed its orbit parameters away for a time—like now—when the market got thirsty. Right now the big cylinder worlds orbiting Earth needed water, CO_2, methane, and other goodies. That happens every time the cylinder boys build a new tin can and need to form an ecosystem inside. Rock and ore they can get from Earth's moon. For water they have to come to us, the Belters. It's cheaper in energy to boost ice into the slow pipeline orbits in from the Belt to Earth—much cheaper than it is to haul water up from Earth's deep gravity well. Cheaper, that is, if the rockrats flying vac out here can find any.

The screen rippled green. It drew a cone for me with *Sniffer* at apex. Inside that cone was whoever had tried to wing me. I popped my helmet and gave in to the sensuality of scratching my nose. If they scorched me again, I'd have to button up while my own ship's air tried to suck me away—but stopping the itch was worth it.

Inside the cone was somebody who wanted me dead. My mouth was dry. My hands were still shaking. They wanted to punch in course corrections that would take me away from that cone, *fast*.

Or was I assuming too much? Ore sniffers use radio for communication—it radiates in all directions, it's cheap, and it's not delicate. But suppose some rocker lost his radio, and had to use his cutting laser to signal? I knew he had to be over ten thousand kilometers away—that's radar range. By jittering around, *Sniffer* was making it impossible for him to send us a distress signal. And if there's one code rockrats will honor, it's answering a call for help.

So call me stupid. I took the risk. I put *Sniffer* back on a smooth orbit—and nothing happened.

You've got to be curious to be a skyjock, in both senses of the word. So color me curious. I stared at that green cone and ate some tangy squeeze-tube soup and got even more curious. I used the radar to rummage through the nearby rocks, looking for metal that might be a ship. I checked some orbits. The Belt hasn't got dust in it, to speak of. The dust got sucked into Jupiter long ago. The rocks—"planetesimals" a scientist told me I should call them, but they're just rocks to me—can be pretty fair-sized. I looked around, and I found one that was heading into the mathematical cone my number-cruncher dealt me.

Sniffer took five hours to rendezvous with it—a big black hunk, a klick wide and absolutely worthless. I moored *Sniffer* to it with automatic molly bolts. They made hollow bangs—*whap, whap*—as they plowed in.

Curious, yes. Stupid, no. The disabled skyjock was just a theory. Laser bolts are real. I wanted some camouflage. My companion asteroid had enough traces of metal in it to keep standard radar from seeing *Sniffer's* outline. Moored snug to the asteroid's face, I'd be hard to pick out. The asteroid would take me coasting through the middle of that cone. If I kept radio silence, I'd be pretty safe.

So I waited. And slept. And fixed the aft sensors. And waited.

Prospectors are hermits. You watch your instruments, you tinker with your plasma drive, you play 3D flexcop—an addictive game; it ought to be illegal—and you worry. You work out in the zero-gee gym, you calculate how to break even when you finally can sell your fresh ore to the Hansen Corporation, you wonder if you'll have to kick ass to get your haul in pipeline orbit for Earthside—and you have to like it when the nearest conversationalist is the Social/Talkback subroutine in the shipboard. Me, I like it. Curious, as I said.

It came up out of the background noise on the radar scope. In fact, I thought it *was* noise. The thing came and went, fluttered, grew and shrank. It gave a funny radar profile—but so did some of the new ships the corporations flew. My rock was passing about two thousand klicks from the thing and the odd profile made me cautious. I went into the observation bubble to have a squint with the opticals.

The asteroid I'd pinned *Sniffer* to had a slow, lazy spin. We rotated out of the shadow just as I got my reflex-opter telescope on-line. Stars spun slowly across a jet-black sky. The sun carved sharp shadows into the rock face. My target drifted up from the horizon, a funny yellow-white dot. The telescope whirred and it leaped into focus.

I sat there, not breathing. A long tube, turning. Towers jutted out at odd places—twisted columns, with curved faces and sudden jagged struts. A fretwork of blue. Patches of strange, moving yellow. A jumble of complex structures. It was a cylinder, decorated almost beyond recognition. I checked the ranging figures, shook my head, checked again. The inboard computer overlaid a perspective grid on the image, to convince me.

I sat very still. The cylinder was pointing nearly away from me, so radar had reported a cross section much smaller than its real size. The thing was seven goddamn kilometers long.

I stared at that strange, monstrous thing, and thought, and suddenly I didn't want to be around there anymore. I took three quick shots with the telescope on smart inventory mode. That would tell me composition, albedo, the rest of the litany. Then I shut it down and scrambled back into the bridge. My hands were trembling again.

I hesitated about what to do, but they decided for me.

On our next revolution, as soon as the automatic opticals got a fix, there were *two* blips. I punched in for a radar Doppler and it came back bad: the smaller dot was closing on us, fast.

The molly bolts came free with a bang. I took *Sniffer* up and out, backing away from the asteroid to keep it between me and the blip that was coming for us. I stepped us up to max gee. My mouth was dry and I had to check every computer input twice.

I ran. There wasn't much else to do. The blip was coming at me at better than a tenth of a gee—incredible acceleration. In the Belt there is plenty of time for moving around, and a chronic lack of fuel—so we use high-efficiency drives and take energy-cheap orbits. The blip wasn't bothering with that. Somehow he had picked *Sniffer* out and decided we were worth a lot of fuel to reach, and reach in a hurry. For some reason they didn't use a laser bolt. It would have been a simple shot at this range. But maybe they didn't want to chance my shooting at the big ship this close, so they put their money on driving me off.

But then, why chase me so fast? It didn't add up.

By the time I was a few hundred klicks away from the asteroid it was too small to be a useful shield. The blip appeared around its edge. I don't carry weapons, but I do have a few tricks.

I had built a custom-designed pulse mode into *Sniffer*'s fusion drive, back before she was commissioned. When the blip appeared I started staging the engines. The core of the motor is a hot ball of plasma, burning heavy water—deuterium—and spitting it, plus vaporized rock, out the back tubes. Feeding in the right amount of deuterium is crucial. There are a dozen overlapping safeguards on the system, but if you know how— I punched in the command.

My drive pulsed, suddenly rich in deuterium. On top of that came a dose of pulverized rock. The rock damps the runaway reaction. On top of *that*, all in a microsecond, came a shot of cesium. It mixed and heated and zap—out the back, moving fast, went a hot cloud of spitting, snarling plasma. The cesium ionizes easily and makes a perfect shield against radar. You can fire a laser through it, sure—but how do you find your target?

The cesium pulse gave me a kick in the butt. I looked back. A blue-white cloud was spreading out behind *Sniffer*, blocking any detection.

I ran like that for one hour, then two. The blip showed up again. It had shifted sideways, to get a look around the cesium cloud—an expensive maneuver. Apparently they had a lot of fuel in reserve.

I threw another cloud. It punched a blue-white fist in the blackness. They were making better gee than I could; it was going to be a matter of who could hold out.

So I tried another trick. I moved into the radar shadow of an asteroid that was nearby, and moving at a speed I could manage. Maybe the blip would miss me when it came out from behind the cloud. It was a gamble, but worth it in fuel.

In three hours I had my answer. The blip homed in on me. *How?* I thought. *Who's got a radar that can pinpoint that well?*

I fired a white-hot cesium cloud. We accelerated away, making tracks. I was getting worried. *Sniffer* was groaning and running hot with the strain. I hadn't allowed myself to think about what I'd seen, but now it looked like I was in for a long haul. The fusion motor rumbled and murmured to itself and I was alone, more alone than I'd felt for a long time, with nothing to do but watch the screen and think.

Belters aren't scientists. They're gamblers, idealists, thieves, crazies, malcontents. Most of us are from the cylinder worlds orbiting Earth. Once you've grown up in space, moving on means moving *out*, not going back to Earth. Nobody wants to be a ground-pounder. So Belters are the new cutting edge of mankind, pushing out, finding new resources.

The common theory is that life in general must be like that. Hungry. Moving on. Over the last century the scientists have looked for radio signals from other civilizations out among the stars, and come up with zero results. But we think life isn't all that unusual in the universe. So the question comes up: if there *are* aliens, and they're like us, why haven't they spread out among the stars? How come they didn't overrun Earth before we even evolved? If they moved at even one percent the speed of light, they'd have spread across the whole damn galaxy in a few million years.

Some people think that argument is right. They take it a little further, too—the aliens haven't visited our solar system, so check your premise again. Maybe there *aren't* any aliens like us. Oh, sure, intelligent fish, maybe, or something we can't imagine. But there are no radio-builders, no star-voyagers. The best proof of this is that they haven't come calling.

I'd never thought about that line of reasoning much, because that's the conventional wisdom now; it's stuff you learn when you're a snot-nosed kid. We stopped listening for radio signals a long time ago, back around 2030 or so. But now that I thought about it—

Already, men were living in space habitats. If mankind ever cast off into the abyss between the stars, which way would they go? In a dinky rocket? No, they'd go in comfort, in stable communities. They'd rig up a cylinder world with a fusion drive, or something like it, and set course for the nearest star, knowing they'd take generations to get there.

A century or two in space would make them into very different people. When they reached a star, where would they go? Down to the planets? Sure—for exploration, maybe. But to live? Nobody who grew up in fractional gee, with the freedom the cylinder world gives you, would want to be a ground-pounder. They wouldn't even know *how*.

The aliens wouldn't be much different. They'd be spacefarers, able to live in vac and tap solar power. They'd need raw materials, sure. But the cheapest way to get mass isn't to go down and drag it up from the planets. No, the easy way is in the asteroids—otherwise, Belters would never make a buck. So if the aliens came to our solar system a long time ago, they'd probably continue to live in space colonies. Sure, they'd study the planets some. But they'd live where they were comfortable.

I thought this through, slowly. In the long waits while I dodged from rock to rock there was plenty of time. I didn't like the conclusion, but it fit the facts. That huge seven-kilometer cylinder back there wasn't man-made.

I'd known that, deep in my guts, the moment I saw it. It was...strange. Nobody could build a thing like that out there and keep it quiet. The cylinder gave off no radio, but ships navigating that much mass into place would have to. Somebody would have picked it up.

So now I knew what was after me. It didn't help much.

I decided to hide behind one rock heading sunward at a fair clip. I needed sleep and I didn't want to keep up my fusion burn—they're too easy to detect. Better to lie low for a while.

I stayed there for five hours, dozing. When I woke up I couldn't see the blip. Maybe they'd broken off the chase. I was ragged and there was sand in my eyes. I wasn't going to admit to myself that I was really scared this time. Belters and lasers I could take, sure. But this was too much for me.

I ate breakfast and freed *Sniffer* from the asteroid I'd moored us to. My throat was raw, my nerves jumpy. I edged us out from the rock and looked around. Nothing. I turned up the fusion drive. *Sniffer* creaked and groaned. The deck plates rattled. There was a hot, gun-metal smell. I had been in my skinsuit the whole time and I didn't smell all that good either. I pulled away from our shelter and boosted. *Whoosh*—

It came out of nowhere.

One minute the scope was clean and the next—a big one, moving fast, straight at us. It *couldn't* have been hiding—there was no rock around to screen it. Which meant they could deflect radar waves, at least for a few minutes. They could be invisible.

The thing came looming out of the darkness. It was yellow and blue, bright and obvious. I turned in my couch to see it. My hands were punching in a last-ditch maneuver on the board. I squinted at the thing and a funny feeling ran through me, a chill.

It was *old*. There were big meteor pits all over the yellow-blue skin. The surface itself glowed, like rock with a ghostly fire inside. I could see no ports, no locks, no antennae.

It was swelling in the sky, getting close.

I hit the emergency board, all buttons. I had laid out good money for one special surprise, if some prospector overtook me and decided he needed an extra ship. The side pods held fission-burn rockets, powerful things. They fired one time only and cost like hell. But worth it.

The gee slammed me back into the couch. A roar rattled the ship. We hauled ass out of there.

I saw the thing behind fade away in the exhaust flames. The high-boost fuel puts out incredibly hot gas. Some of it caught the yellow-blue thing. The front end of the ship scorched. I smiled grimly and cut in the whole system. The gee thrust went up. I felt the bridge swimming around me, a sour smell of burning—then I was out, the world slipping away, the blackness folding in.

When I came to, I was floating. The boosters out the bridge ports yawned empty, spent. *Sniffer* coasted at an incredibly high speed. And the yellow-blue thing was gone.

Maybe they'd been damaged. Maybe they just plain ran out of fuel; everybody has limitations, even things that can span the stars.

I stretched out and let the hard knots of tension begin to unwind. Time enough later to compute a new orbit. For the moment it simply felt great to be alive. And alone.

"Ceres Monitor here, on 560 megahertz. Calling on standby mode for orecraft *Sniffer*. Request micro-burst of confirmation on your hail frequency, *Sniffer*. We have a high-yield reading on optical from your coordinates. Request confirmation of fission burn. Repeat, this is Ceres Monitor—"

I clicked it off. The Belt is huge, but the high-burn torch I'd turned loose back there was orders of magnitude more luminous than an ordinary fusion jet. That was another reason I carried them—they doubled as a signal flare, visible millions of klicks away. By some chance somebody had seen mine and relayed the coordinates to Ceres.

All through the chase I hadn't called Ceres. It would have been of no use—there were no craft within range to be of help. And Belters are loners—my instinct was always to keep troubles to myself. There's nothing worse than listening to a Belter whining over the radio.

But now—I switched the radio back on and reached for the mike to hail Ceres. Then I stopped.

The yellow-blue craft had never fired at me. *Sniffer* would have been easy to cripple at that range. An angry prospector would've done it without thinking twice.

Something prevented them. Some code, some moral sense that ruled out firing on a fleeing craft, no matter how much they wanted to stop it.

A moral code of an ancient society. They had come here and settled, soaking up energy from our sun, mining the asteroids, getting ices from comets. A peaceful existence.

They were used to a sleepy Earth, inhabited by life-forms not worth the effort of constant study. Probably they didn't care much about planets anymore. They didn't keep detailed track of what was happening. Suddenly, in the last century or so—a very short interval from the point of view of a galactic-scale society—the animals down on the blue-white world started acting up. Emitting radio, exploding nuclear weapons, flying spacecraft. These ancient beings found an exponentially growing technology on their doorstep.

I tried to imagine what they thought of us. We were young, we were crude. Undoubtedly the cylinder beings could have destroyed us. They could nudge a middle-sized asteroid into a collision orbit with Earth, and watch the storm wrack engulf humanity. Simple. But they hadn't done it. That moral sense again?

Something like that, yes. Give it a name and it becomes a human quality—which is in itself a deception. These things were *alien*. But their behavior had to make some sort of sense, had to have a reason.

I floated, frowning. Putting all this together was like assembling a jigsaw puzzle with only half the pieces, but still—something told me I was right. It *fit*.

A serene, long-lived, cosmic civilization might be worried by our blind rush outward. They were used to vast time scales; we had come on the stage in the wink of an eye. Maybe this speed left the cylinder beings undecided, hesitant. That would explain why they didn't contact us. Just the reverse, in fact—they were hiding. Otherwise—

It suddenly hit me. They didn't use radio because it broadcasts at a wide angle. Only lasers can keep a tight beam over great distances. That was what zapped me—not a weapon, a communications channel.

Which meant there had to be more than one cylinder world in the Belt. They kept quiet by using only beamed communications.

That implied something further, too. We hadn't heard any radio signals from other civilizations, either—because they were using lasers. They didn't want to be detected by other, younger societies.

Why? Were the aliens in our own Belt debating whether to help us or crush us? Or something in between?

In the meantime, the Belt was a natural hideout. They liked their privacy. They must be worried now, with humans exploring the Belt. I might be the first human to stumble upon them, but I wouldn't be the last.

"Ceres Monitor calling to—"

I hesitated. They were old, older than we could imagine. They could have been in this solar system longer than man—stable, peaceful, inheritors of a vast history. They were moral enough not to fire at me, even though they knew it meant they would be discovered.

They needed time. They had a tough decision to face. If they were rushed into it they might make the wrong one.

"Orecraft *Sniffer* requested to—"

I was a Belter; I valued my hermit existence, too. I thumbed on the mike.

"Ceres, this is *Sniffer*. Rosemary Jokopi, sole officer. I verify that I used a fission burn, but only as a part of routine mining exploration. No cause for alarm. Nothing else to report. Transmission ends."

When I hung up the mike, my hands weren't shaking anymore.

TIME SHARDS
(1979)

I t had all gone very well, Brooks told himself. Very well indeed. He hurried along the side corridor, his black dress shoes clicking hollowly on the old tiles. This was one of the oldest and most rundown of the Smithsonian's buildings; too bad they didn't have the money to knock it down. Funding. Everything was a matter of funding.

He pushed open the door of the barnlike workroom and called out, "John? How did you like the ceremony?"

John Hart appeared from behind a vast rack that was filled with fluted pottery. His thin face was twisted in a scowl and he was puffing on a cigarette. "Didn't go."

"John! That's not permitted." Brooks waved at the cigarette. "You of all people should be careful about contamination of—"

"Hell with it." He took a final puff, belched blue, and ground out the cigarette on the floor.

"You really should've watched the dedication of the Vault, you know," Brooks began, adopting a bantering tone. You had to keep a light touch with these research types. "The President was there—she made a very nice speech—"

"I was busy."

"Oh?" Something in Hart's tone put Brooks off his conversational stride. "Well. You'll be glad to hear that I had a little conference with the Board, just before the dedication. They've agreed to continue supporting your work here."

"Um."

95

"You must admit, they're being very fair." As he talked Brooks threaded amid the rows of pottery, each in a plastic sleeve. This room always made him nervous. There was priceless Chinese porcelain here, Assyrian stoneware, buff-blue Roman glazes, Egyptian earthenware—and Brooks lived in mortal fear that he would trip, fall, and smash some piece of history into shards. "After all, you *did* miss your deadline. You got nothing out of all this"—a sweep of the hand, narrowly missing a green Persian tankard—"for the Vault."

Hart, who was studying a small brownish water jug, looked up abruptly. "What about the wheel recording?"

"Well, there was that, but—"

"The best in the world, dammit!"

"They heard it some time ago. They were very interested."

"You told them what they were hearing?" Hart asked intensely.

"Of course, I—"

"You could hear the hoofbeats of cattle, clear as day."

"They heard. Several commented on it."

"Good." Hart seemed satisfied, but still strangely depressed.

"But you must admit, that isn't what you promised."

Hart said sourly, "Research can't be done to a schedule."

Brooks had been pacing up and down the lanes of pottery. He stopped suddenly, pivoted on one foot, and pointed a finger at Hart. "You said you'd have a *voice*. That was the promise. Back in '98 you said you would have something for the BiMillennium celebration, and—"

"Okay, okay." Hart waved away the other man's words.

"Look—" Brooks strode to a window and jerked up the blinds. From this high up in the Arts and Industries Building the BiMillennial Vault was a flat concrete slab sunk in the Washington mud; it had rained the day before. Now bulldozers scraped piles of gravel and mud into the hole, packing it in before the final encasing shield was to be laid. The Vault itself was already sheathed in sleeves of concrete, shock-resistant and immune to decay. The radio beacons inside were now set. Their radioactive power supply would automatically stir to life exactly a thousand years from now. Periodic bursts of radio waves would announce to the world of the TriMillennium that a message from the distant past awaited whoever dug down to find it. Inside the Vault were artifacts, recordings, everything the Board of Regents of the Smithsonian thought important about their age. The coup of the entire Vault was to have been a message from the First Millennium, the year 1000 A.D. Hart had promised them something far better than a mere written document from that time. He had said he could capture a living voice.

"See that?" Brooks said with sudden energy. "That Vault will outlast everything we know—all those best-selling novels and funny plays and amazing scientific discoveries. They'll all be *dust*, when the Vault's opened."

"Yeah," Hart said.

"Yeah? That's all you can say?"

"Well, sure, I—"

"The Vault was *important*. And I was stupid enough"—he rounded on Hart abruptly, anger flashing across his face—"to chew up some of the only money we had for the Vault to support *you*."

Hart took an involuntary step backward. "You knew it was a gamble."

"I knew." Brooks nodded ruefully. "And we waited, and waited—"

"Well, your waiting is over," Hart said, something hardening in him.

"What?"

"I've got it. A voice."

"You have?" In the stunned silence that followed Hart bent over casually and picked up a dun-colored water jug from the racks. An elaborate, impossibly large-winged orange bird was painted on its side. Hart turned the jug in his hands, hefting its weight.

"Why…it's too late for the Vault, of course, but still…" Brooks shuffled his feet. "I'm glad the idea paid off. That's great."

"Yeah. Great." Hart smiled sourly. "And you know what it's worth? Just about *this* much—"

He took the jug in one hand and threw it. It struck the far wall with a splintering crash. Shards flew like a covey of frightened birds that scattered through the long ranks of pottery. Each landed with a ceramic tinkling.

"What are you *doing*—" Brooks began, dropping to his knees without thinking to retrieve a fragment of the jug. "That jug was worth—"

"Nothing," Hart said. "It was a fake. Almost everything the Egyptians sent was bogus."

"But why are you…you said you succeeded…" Brooks was shaken out of his normal role of Undersecretary to the Smithsonian.

"I did. For what it's worth."

"Well…show me."

Hart shrugged and beckoned Brooks to follow him. He threaded his way through the inventory of glazed pottery, ignoring the extravagant polished shapes that flared and twisted in elaborate, artful designs, the fruit of millennia of artisans. Glazes of feldspath, lead, tin, ruby salt. Jasperware, soft-paste porcelain, albarelloa festooned with ivy and laurel, flaring lips and serene curved handles. A galaxy of the work of the First Millennium and after, assembled for Hart's search.

"It's on the wheel," Hart said, gesturing.

Brooks walked around the spindle fixed at the center of a horizontal disk. Hart called it a potter's wheel but it was a turntable, really, firmly buffered against the slightest tremor from external sources. A carefully arranged family of absorbers isolated the table from everything but the variable motor seated beneath it. On the turntable was an earthenware pot. It looked unremarkable to Brooks—just a dark red oxidized finish, a thick lip, and a rather crude handle, obviously molded on by a lesser artisan.

"What's its origin?" Brooks said, mostly to break the silence that lay between them.

"Southern England." Hart was logging instructions into the computer terminal nearby. Lights rippled on the staging board.

"How close to the First Mil?"

"Around 1280 A.D., apparently."

"Not really close, then. But interesting."

"Yeah."

Brooks stooped forward. When he peered closer he could see the smooth finish was an illusion. A thin thread ran around the pot, so fine the eye could scarcely make it out. The lines wound in a tight helix. In the center of each delicate line was a fine hint of blue. The jug had been incised with a precise point. Good; that was exactly what Hart had said he sought. It was an ancient, common mode of decoration—incise a seemingly infinite series of rings, as the pot turned beneath the cutting tool. The cutting tip revealed a differently colored dye underneath, a technique called sgraffito, the scratched.

It could never have occurred to the Islamic potters who invented sgraffito that they were, in fact, devising the first phonograph records.

Hart pressed a switch and the turntable began to spin. He watched it for a moment, squinting with concentration. Then he reached down to the side of the turntable housing and swung up the stylus manifold. It came up smoothly and Hart locked it in just above the spinning red surface of the pot.

"Not a particularly striking item, is it?" Brooks said conversationally.

"No."

"Who made it?"

"Near as I can determine, somebody in a co-operative of villages, barely Christian. Still used lots of pagan decorations. Got them scrambled up with the cross motif a lot."

"You've gotten...words?"

"Oh, sure. In early English, even."

"I'm surprised crude craftsmen could do such delicate work."

"Luck, some of it. They probably used a pointed wire, a new technique that'd been imported around that time from Saxony."

The computer board hooted a readiness call. Hart walked over to it, thumbed in instructions, and turned to watch the stylus whir in a millimeter closer to the spinning jug. "Damn," Hart said, glancing at the board. "Correlator's giving hash again."

Hart stopped the stylus and worked at the board. Brooks turned nervously and paced, unsure of what his attitude should be toward Hart. Apparently the man had discovered something, but did that excuse his surliness? Brooks glanced out the window, where the last crowds were drifting away from the Vault dedication and strolling down the Mall. There was a reception for the Board of Regents in Georgetown in an hour. Brooks would have to be there early, to see that matters were in order—

"If you'd given me enough money, I could've had a Hewlett-Packard. Wouldn't have to fool with this piece of..." Hart's voice trailed off.

Brooks had to keep reminding himself that this foul-tempered, scrawny man was reputed to be a genius. If Hart had not come with the highest of recommendations, Brooks would never have risked valuable Vault funding. Apparently Hart's new method for finding correlations in a noisy signal was a genuine achievement.

The basic idea was quite old, of course. In the 1960s a scientist at the American Museum of Natural History in New York had applied a stylus to a rotating urn and played the signal through an audio pickup. Out came the *wreee* sound of the original potter's wheel where the urn was made. It had been a Roman urn, made in the era when hand-turned wheels were the best available. The Natural History "recording" was crude, but even that long ago they could pick out a moment when the potter's hand slipped and the rhythm of the *wreee* faltered.

Hart had read about that urn and seen the possibilities. He developed his new multiple-correlation analysis—a feat of programming, if nothing else—and began searching for pottery that might have acoustic detail in its surface. The *sgraffito* technique was the natural choice. Potters sometimes used fine wires to incise their wares. Conceivably, anything that moved the incising wire—passing footfalls, even the tiny acoustic push of sound waves—could leave its trace on the surface of the finished pot. Buried among imperfections and noise, eroded by the random bruises of history...

"Got it," Hart said, fatigue creeping into his voice.

"Good. Good."

"Yeah. Listen."

The stylus whirred forward. It gently nudged into the jug, near the lip. Hart flipped a switch and studied the rippling, dancing yellow lines on the board oscilloscope. Electronic archaeology. "There."

A high-pitched whining came from the speaker, punctuated by hollow, deep bass thumps.

"Hear that? He's using a foot pump."

"A kick wheel?"

"Right."

"I thought they came later."

"No, the Arabs had them."

There came a *clop clop clop*, getting louder. It sounded oddly disembodied in the silence of the long room.

"What...?"

"Horse. I detected this two weeks ago. Checked it with the equestrian people. They say the horse is unshod, assuming we're listening to it walk on dirt. Farm animal, probably. Plow puller."

"Ah."

The hoofbeats faded. The whine of the kick wheel sang on. "Here it comes," Hart whispered.

Brooks shuffled slightly. The ranks upon ranks of ancient pottery behind him made him nervous, as though a vast unmoving audience were in the room with them.

Thin, distant: "Alf?"

"Aye." A gruff reply.

"It slumps, sure."

".I be oct, man." A rasping, impatient voice.

"T'art—"

"*Busy*—mark?"

"Ah ha' wearied o' their laws," the thin voice persisted.

"Aye—so all. What mark it?" Restrained impatience.

"Their Christ. He werkes vengement an the alt spirits."

"Hie yer tongue."

"They'll ne hear."

"Wi' 'er Christ 'er're everywhere."

A pause. Then faintly, as though a whisper: "We ha' lodged th' alt spirits."

"Ah? You? Th' rash gazer?"

"I spy stormwrack. A hue an' grie rises by this somer se'sun."

"Fer we?"

"Aye, unless we spake th' *Ave maris stella* 'a theirs."

"Elat. Lat fer that. Hie, I'll do it. Me knees still buckle whon they must."

"I kenned that. So shall I."

"Aye. So shall we all. But wh' of the spirits?"

"They suffer pangs, dark werkes. They are lodged."

"Ah. Where?"

"S'tart."

"'Ere? In me clay?"

"In yer vessels."

"Nay!"

"I chanted 'em in 'fore sunbreak."

"Nay! I fain wad ye not."

whir whir whir

The kick wheel thumps came rhythmically.

"They sigh'd thruu in-t'wixt yer clay. 'S done."

"Fer *what*?"

"These pots—they bear a fineness, aye?"

"Aye."

A rumbling, "—will hie home 'er. Live in yer pots."

"An?"

"Whon time werkes a'thwart 'e Christers, yon spirits of leaf an' bough will, I say, hie an' grie to yer sons, man. To yer *sons* sons, man."

"Me pots? Carry our kenne?"

"Aye. I investe' thy clay wi' ern'st spirit, so when's ye causes it ta dance, our law say…"

whir

A hollow rattle.

"Even this 'ere, as I spin it?"

"Aye. Th' spirits innit. Speak as ye form. The dance, t'will carry yer schop word t' yer sons, yer *sons* sons sons."

"While it's spinnin'?"

Brooks felt his pulse thumping in his throat.

"Aye."

"Than't—"

"Speak inta it. To yer sons."

"Ah…" Suddenly the voice came louder. "Aye, aye! There! If ye hear me, sons! I be from yer past! The ancient dayes!"

"Tell them wha' ye must."

"Aye. Sons! Blood a' mine! Mark ye! Hie not ta strags in th' house of Lutes. They carry the red pox! An'…an', beware th' Kinseps—they bugger all they rule! An', whilst pot-charrin', mix th' fair smelt wi' greeno erst, 'ere ye'll flux it fair speedy. Ne'er leave sheep near a lean-house, ne, 'ey'll snuck down 'an it—"

whir whir thump whir

"What—what happened?" Brooks gasped.

"He must have brushed the incising wire a bit. The cut continues, but the fine touch was lost. Vibrations as subtle as a voice couldn't register."

Brooks looked around, dazed, for a place to sit. "In…incredible."

"I suppose."

Hart seemed haggard, worn.

"They were about to convert to Christianity, weren't they?"

Hart nodded.

"They thought they could seal up the—what? wood spirits?—they worshiped. Pack them away by blessing the clay or something like that. And that the clay would carry a message—to the future!"

"So it did."

"To their sons sons sons…" Brooks paused. "Why are you so depressed, Hart? This is a great success."

Abruptly Hart laughed. "I'm not, really. Just, well, manic, I guess. We're so funny. So absurd. Think about it, Brooks. All that hooey the potter shouted into his damned pot. What did you make of it?"

"Well…gossip, mostly. I can't get over what a long shot this is—that we'd get to hear it."

"Maybe it was a common belief back then. Maybe many tried it—and maybe now I'll find more pots, with just ordinary conversation on them. Who knows?" He laughed again, a slow warm chuckle. "We're all so absurd. Maybe Henry Ford was right—history *is* bunk."

"I don't see why you're carrying on this way, Hart. Granted, the message was…obscure. That unintelligible information about making pottery, and—"

"Tips on keeping sheep."

"Yes, and—"

"Useless, right?"

"Well, probably. To us, anyway. The conversation before that was much more interesting."

"Uh huh. Here's a man who is talking to the ages. Sending what he thinks is most important. And he prattles out a lot of garbage."

"Well, true..."

"And it *was* important—to him."

"Yes."

Hart walked stiffly to the window. Earthmovers crawled like eyeless insects beneath the wan yellow lamps. Dusk had fallen. Their great awkward scoops pushed mounds of mud into the square hole where the Vault rested.

"Look at that." Hart gestured. "The Vault. Our own monument to our age. Passing on the legacy. You, me, the others—we've spent years on it. Years, and a fortune." He chuckled dryly. "What makes you think we've done any better?"

EXPOSURES
(1981)

Puzzles assemble themselves one piece at a time. Yesterday I began laying out the new plates I had taken up on the mountain, at Palomar. They were exposures of varying depth. In each, NGC 1097—a barred spiral galaxy about twenty mega-parsecs away—hung suspended in its slow swirl.

As I laid out the plates I thought of the way our family had always divided up the breakfast chores on Sunday. On that ritual day our mother stayed in bed. I laid out the forks and knives and egg cups and formal off-white china, and then stood back in the morning light to survey my precise placings. Lush napkin pyramids perched on the white lace table cloth, my mother's favorite. Through the kitchen door leaked the mutter, boil and clang of a meal coming into being. Some Sundays I had photographed the dining room, but never quite caught the ordered meaning I saw in it.

I put the galactic exposures in order according to the spectral filters used, noting the calibrated photometry for each. The ceramic sounds of Bridge Hall rang in the tiled hallways and seeped into my office: footsteps, distant talk, the scrape of chalk on slate, a banging door. Examining the plates through an eye piece, I felt the galaxy swell into being, huge.

The deepest exposures brought out the dim jets I was after. There were four of them pointing out of NGC 1097—two red and two blue, the brightest three discovered by Wolsencroft and Zealey, the last red one found by Lorre over at JPL. Straight lines scratched across the mottling of foreground dust and stars. No one knew what colored a jet red or blue.

I was trying to use the deep plates to measure the width of the jets. Using a slit over the lens, I had stepped down the image until I could employ calibrated photometry to measure the wedge of light. Still further narrowing might allow me to measure the spectrum, to see if the blues and reds came from the stars, or from excited clouds of gas.

The two blue jets lanced out, cutting through the spiral arms and breaking free into the blackness beyond. One plate, taken in that spectral spike where ionized hydrogen clouds emit, giving H II radiation, showed a string of beads buried in the curling spiral lanes. These were vast cooling clouds. Where the jets crossed the H II regions, the spiral arms were pushed outward, or else vanished altogether.

Opposite each blue jet, far across the galaxy, a red jet glowed. They, too, snuffed out the H II beads.

From these gaps in the spiral arms I estimated how far the barred spiral galaxy had turned, while the jets ate away at them: about fifteen degrees. From the velocity measurements in the disk, using the Doppler shifts of known spectral lines, I deduced the rotation rate of the NGC 1097 disk: approximately a hundred million years. Not surprising; our own sun takes about the same vast time to circle around our galactic center. The photons telling me all these specifics had begun their steady voyage sixty million years ago, before there was a *New General Catalog of Nebulae and Clusters of Stars* to label them as they buried themselves in my welcoming emulsion. Thus do I know thee, NGC 1097.

These jets were unique. The brightest blue one dog-legs in a right angle turn and ends in silvery blobs of dry light. Its counter-jet, offset a perverse eleven degrees from exact oppositeness, continues on a warmly rose-colored path over an immense distance, a span far larger than the parent galaxy itself. I frowned, puckered my lips in concentration, calibrated and calculated and refined. Plainly these ramrod, laconic patterns of light were trying to tell me something.

But answers come when they will, one piece at a time.

I tried to tell my son this when, that evening, I helped him with his reading. Using what his mother now knowingly termed "word attack skills," he had mastered most such tactics. The larger strategic issues of the sentence eluded him, still. *Take it in phrases*, I urged him, ruffling his light brown hair, distracted, because I liked the nutmeg smell. (I have often thought that I could find my children in the dark, in a crowd, by my nose alone. Our genetic code colors the air.) He thumbed the book, dirtying a corner. *Read the words between the commas,* I instructed, my classroom sense of order returning. *Stop at the commas, and then pause before going on, and think about what all those words mean.* I sniffed at his wheatlike hair again.

I am a traditional astronomer, amid all the digital buzz sweeping through the field. I am accustomed to the bitter cold of the cage at Palomar, the Byzantine marriage of optics at Kitt Peak, the muggy air of Lick. Through that long morning yesterday I studied the NGC 1097 jets, attempting to see with the quick eye of the theorist—"dancing on the data" as Roger Blandford down the hall had once called it. I tried to erect some rickety hypothesis that my own uncertain mathematical abilities could brace up. An idea came. I caught at it. But holding it close, turning it over, pushing terms about in an overloaded equation, I saw it was merely an old idea tarted up, already disproved.

Perhaps computer enhancement of the images would clear away some of my enveloping fog, I mused. I took my notes to the neighboring building, listening to my footsteps echo in the long arcade. The buildings at Caltech are mostly done in a pseudo-Spanish style, tan stucco with occasional flourishes of Moorish windows and tiles. The newer library rears up beside the crouching offices and classrooms, a modern extrusion. I entered the Albert Sloan Laboratory of Physics and Mathematics, wondering for the *nth* time what a mathematical laboratory would be like, imaging Lewis Carroll in charge with talking rabbits, and went into the new computer terminal rooms. The indices which called up my plates soon stuttered across the screen. I used a medium numerical filter, to suppress variations in the background. There were standard routines to subtract particular parts of the spectrum. I called them up, averaging away noise from dust and gas and the image-saturating spikes that were foreground stars in our own galaxy. Still, nothing dramatic emerged. Illumination would not come.

I sipped my coffee. I had brought a box of crackers from my office; and I broke one, eating each wafer with a heavy crunch. I swirled the cup and the coffee swayed like a dark disk at the bottom, a scum of cream at the vortex curling out into gray galactic arms. I drank it. And thumbed another image into being.

This was not NGC 1097. I checked the number. Then the log. No, these were slots deliberately set aside for later filing. They were not supposed to be filled; they represented my allotted computer space. They should be blank.

Yet I recognized this one. It was a view of Sagittarius A, the intense radio source that hides behind a thick lane of dust in the Milky Way. Behind that dark obscuring swath that is an arm of our Galaxy, lies the center. I squinted. Yes: this was a picture formed from observations sensitive to the 21-centimeter wavelength line, the emission of nonionized hydrogen. I had seen it before, on exposures that looked radially inward at the Galactic core. Here was the red band of hydrogen along our line of sight. Slightly below was the well-known arm of hot, expanding gas, nine thousand light years across. Above, tinted green, was a smaller arm, a ridge of gas moving outward at 135 kilometers per second. I had seen this in seminars years ago. In the very center was the knot no more than a light year or two across, the source of the 10^{40} ergs per second of virulent energy that drove the cooker that caused all this.

Still, the energy flux from our Galaxy was ten million times less than that of a quasar. Whatever the compact energy source there, it was comparatively quiet. NGC 1097 lies far to the south, entirely out of the Milky Way. Could the aim of the satellite camera have strayed so much?

Curious, I thumbed forward. The next index number gave another scan of the Sagittarius region, this time seen by the spectral emissions from outward-moving clouds of ammonia. Random blobs. I thumbed again. A formaldehyde-emission view. But now the huge arm of expanding hydrogen was sprinkled with knots, denoting clouds which moved faster, Dopplered into blue.

I frowned. No, the Sagittarius A exposures were no aiming error. These slots were to be left open for my incoming data. Yet they were filled.

Someone had co-opted the space. Who? I called up the identifying codes, but there were none. As far as the master log was concerned, these spaces were still empty.

I moved to erase them. My finger paused, hovered, went limp. This was high-quality information, already processed. Someone would want it. They had carelessly dumped it into my territory, but...

My pause was in part that of sheer appreciation. Peering at the color-coded encrustations of light, I recalled what all this had once been like: impossibly complicated, ornate in its terms, caked with the eccentric jargon of long-dead professors, choked with thickets of atomic physics and thermodynamics, a web of complexity that finally gave forth mental pictures of a whirling, furious past, of stars burned now into cinders, of whispering, turbulent hydrogen that filled the void between the suns. From such numbers came the starscape that we knew. Time and labor had simplified and shaped this welter into apparent beauty. From a sharp scratch on a strip of film we could catch the signature of an element, deduce velocity from the Doppler shift, and then measure the width of that scratch to give the random component of the velocity, the random jigglings due to thermal motion, and thus the temperature. All from a scratch. No, I could not erase it.

When I was a boy of nine my mother brow-beat me into serving at the altar, during the unendurably long Episcopal services she felt we should attend. I wore the simple robe and was the first to appear in the service, lighting the candles with an awkward long stick with its sliding wick. The organ music softly murmured, not calling attention to itself, so the congregation could watch undistracted as I fumbled with the wick and tried to keep the precarious balance between feeding it too much (so that, engorged, it bristled into a ball of orange) and the even worse embarrassment of snuffing it into a final accusing puff of black.

Through the service I had to alternately kneel and stand, murmuring the worn, rolling phrases as I thought of the softball I would play in the afternoon, feeling the prickly gathering heat underneath my robes. On a bad day the sweat would accumulate and a drop would cling to my nose. I'd let it hang there in mute testimony. The minister never seemed to notice. I would often slip off into decidedly untheological daydreams, intoxicated by the pressing moist heat, and miss the telltale words of the litany, which signaled the beginning of communion. A whisper would come skating across the layered air and I would surface, to see the minister turned with clotted face toward me, holding the implements of his forgiving trade, waiting for me to bring the wine and wafers to be blessed. I would surge upward, swearing under my breath with the ardor only those who have just learned the words can truly muster, unafraid to be muttering these things as I snatched up the chalice and sniffed the too-sweet murky wine, fetching the plates of wafers, swearing that once the polished walnut altar rail was emptied of its upturned and strangely blank faces, once the simpering organ had ebbed into silence and I had shrugged off these robes swarming with the stench of mothballs, I would have no more of it, I would erase it.

●

I asked Redman who the hell was logging their stuff into my inventory spaces. He checked.

The answer was: nobody. There were no recorded intrusions into those sections of the memory system. *Then look further,* I said, and went back to work at the terminal.

They were still there. What's more, some index numbers that had been free before were now filled.

NGC 1097 still vexed me, but I delayed working on the problem. I studied these new pictures. They were processed, Doppler-coded, and filtered for noise, all freshly done by the auto-software. I switched back to the earlier plates, to be sure. Yes, it was clear: these were different.

Current theory held that the arm of expanding gas was on the outward phase of an oscillation. Several hundred million years ago, so the story went, a massive explosion at the galactic center had started the expansion: a billowing, spinning doughnut of gas swelled outward. Eventually its energy was matched by the gravitational attraction of the massive center. Then, as it slowed and finally fell back toward the center, it spun faster, storing energy in rotational motion, until centrifugal forces stopped its inward rush. Thus the hot cloud could oscillate in the potential well of gravity, cooling slowly.

These computer-transformed plates said otherwise. The Doppler shifts formed a cone. At the center of the plate the velocities were far higher than any observed before, over a thousand kilometers per second. That exceeded escape velocity from the Galaxy itself. The values tapered off to the sides, coming smoothly down to the shifts that were on the earlier plates.

I called the programming director. He looked over the displays, understanding nothing of what it meant but everything about how it could have gotten there; and his verdict was clean, certain: human error. But further checks turned up no such mistake. I went and stood over his messy desk.

"Must be comin' in on the transmission from orbit," he mused. He seemed half-asleep as he punched in commands, traced the intruders. These data had come in from the new combination optical, IR, and UV 'scope in orbit, and the JPL programs had obligingly performed the routine miracles of enhancement and analysis. But the orbital staff were sure no such data had been transmitted. In fact, the 'scope had been down for inspection, plus an alignment check, for over two days. The programming director shrugged and promised to look into it, fingering the innumerable pens clipped to his shirt pocket.

So these had come in somehow from...where? I stared at the Doppler cone, and thumbed to the next index number. The cone had grown, the shifts were larger. Another: still larger. And then I noticed something more. A cold sensation seeped into me, banishing the causal talk and mechanical-printout stutter of the terminal room.

The point of view had shifted. All the earlier plates had shown a particular gas cloud at a certain angle of inclination. This latest plate was slightly cocked to the side, illuminating a clotted bunch of minor H II regions and obscuring a fraction of the hot, expanding arm. Some new features appeared. If the JPL program had done such a rotation and shift, it would have left the new spaces blank, for there was no way of filling them in. These were not empty. They brimmed with specific shifts, detailed spectral indices. The JPL program would not have produced the field of numbers unless the new data contained them. I stared at the screen for a long time.

That evening I drove home the long way, through the wide boulevards of Pasadena, in the gathering dusk. I remembered giving blood the month before, in the eggshell light of the Caltech dispensary. They took the blood away in a curious plastic sack, leaving me with a small bandage in the crook of my elbow. The skin was translucent, showing the riverwork of tributary blue veins, recently tapped and nearly as pale as the skin. I had never looked at that part of me before and found it tender, vulnerable, an unexpected opening. I remembered my wife had liked being stroked there when we were dating, and that I had not touched her there for a long time. Now I had myself been pricked there, to pipe brimming life into a sack, and then to some other who could make use of it. Bloody charity.

That evening I drove again, taking my son to his Open House. The school bristled with light and seemed to command the neighborhood with its luminosity, drawing families out of their homes. Standing on its slight hill, it was the center of the children's galaxy, for now. My wife was taking my daughter to another school, so I was unshielded by her ability to recognize people we knew. I could never sort out their names in time to answer the casual hellos. In our neighborhood the PTA nights draw a disproportionate fraction of technical types, like me. Tonight I saw them shorn of my wife's the quicksilver verbal fluency. They drove compact cars that seemed too small for their large families, wore shoes whose casualness offset the formal, just-come-from-work jackets and slacks, and carried creamy folders of their children's accumulated work, to use in conferring with the teachers. The wives were sun-darkened, wearing crisp, print dresses that looked fresh for the occasion, and spoke with ironic turns about PTA politics, bond issues, and class sizes.

In his classroom my son tugged me from board to board, where he had contributed nature paragraphs, mostly wildlife. The crowning exhibit was of Io, Jupiter's pizza-mocking moon, which he had made from a tennis ball and thick, sulphurous paint. It hung in a box painted black and looked remarkably, ethereally real. My son had won first prize in his class for the mockup moon, and his teacher stressed this as she went over the less welcome news that he was not doing well at his reading. Apparently he arranged the plausible phrases—A, then B, then C—into illogical combinations, C coming before A, despite the instructing commas and semicolons that should have guided him. It was a minor problem, his teacher assured me, but should be looked after. Perhaps a little more reading at home, under my eye?

I nodded, sure that the children of the other scientists and computer programmers and engineers did not have this difficulty, and already knew what the instructing phase of the next century would be, before the end of this one. My son took the news matter-of-factly, unafraid, and went off to help with the cake and Kool-Aid. I watched him mingle with girls whose awkwardness was lovely, like giraffes'. I remembered that his teacher (I had learned from gossip) had a mother dying of cancer, which might explain the furrow between her eyebrows that would not go away, contradicting her fixed, welcoming smile.

My son came bearing cake. I ate with him, sitting with knees slanting upward in the small chair; and quite calmly and suddenly an idea came to me and would not go away. I turned it over and felt its shape, testing it in a preliminary fashion. Underneath I was both excited and fearful and yet sure that it would survive: it was right. Scraping up the last crumbs and icing, I looked down, and saw my son had drawn a crayon design, an enormous father playing ball with a son, running and catching, the scene carefully fitted into the small compass of the plastic, throwaway plate.

The next morning I finished the data reduction on the slit-image exposures. By carefully covering over the galaxy and background, I had managed to take successive plates, which blocked out segments of the space parallel to the brightest blue jet. Photometry of the resulting weak signal could give a cross section of the jet's intensity. Pinpoint calibration then yielded the thickness of the central jet zone.

The data was somewhat scattered, the error bars were larger than I liked, but still—I was sure I had it. The jet had a fuzzy halo and a bright core. The core was a hundred light years across, a thin filament of highly ionized hydrogen, cutting like a swath through the gauzy dust beyond the galaxy. The resolute, ruler-sharp path, its thinness, its profile of luminosity: all pointed toward a tempting picture. Some energetic object had carved each line, moving at high speeds. It swallowed some of the matter in its path; and in the act of engorgement the mass was heated to incandescent brilliance, spitting UV and X-rays into an immense surrounding volume. This radiation in turn ionized the galactic gas, leaving a scratch of light behind the object, like picnickers dumping luminous trash as they pass by.

The obvious candidates for the fast-moving sources of the jets were black holes. And as I traced the slim profiles of the NGC 1097 jets back into the galaxy, they all intersected at the precise geometrical center of the barred spiral pattern.

Last night, after returning from the Open House with a sleepy boy in tow, I talked with my wife as we undressed. I described my son's home-room, his artistic achievements, his teacher. My wife let slip offhandedly some jarring news.

I had misheard the earlier gossip; perhaps I had mused over some problem while she related the story to me over breakfast. It was not the teacher's mother who had cancer, but the teacher herself. I felt an instant, settling guilt. I could scarcely remember the woman's face, though it was a mere hour later. I asked why she was still working.

Because, my wife explained with her straightforward New England accent, it was better than staring at a wall. The chemotherapy took only a small slice of her hours. Anyway, she probably needed the money. The night beyond our windows seemed solid, flinty, harder than the soft things inside. In the glass I watched my wife take off her print dress and stretch backward, breasts thinning into crescents, her knobbed spine describing a serene curve that anticipated bed. She blessed me with a sensual smile.

I went over to my chest of drawers and looked down at the polished walnut surface, scrupulously rectangular and arranged, across which I had tossed the residue of an hour's dutiful parenting: a scrawled essay on marmosets, my son's anthology of drawings, his reading list, and on top, the teacher's bland paragraph of assessment. It felt odd to have called these things into being, these signs of a forward tilt in a small life, by an act of love or at least lust, now years past. The angles appropriate to cradling my children still lived in my hands. I could feel clearly the tentative clutch of my son as he attempted some upright steps. Now my eye strayed to his essay. I could see him struggling with the notion of clauses, with ideas piled on each other to build a point, and with the caged linear prison of the sentence. On the page above, in the loops of the teacher's generous flow pen, I saw a hollow rotundity, a denial of any constriction of her life. She had to go on, this schoolgirl penmanship said, to forcefully forget a gnawing illness among a roomful of bustling children. Despite all else, she had to keep on doing.

What could be energetic enough to push black holes out of the galactic center, up the slopes of the deep gravitational potential well? Only another black hole. The dynamics had been worked out years before—as so often happens, in another context—by William Saslaw. Let a bee-swarm of black holes orbit about each other, all caught in a gravitational depression. Occasionally, they veer close together, deforming the space-time nearby, caroming off each other like billiard balls. If several undergo these near-miss collisions at once, a black hole can be ejected from the gravitational trap altogether. More complex collisions can throw pairs of black holes in opposite directions, thriftily conserving angular momentum: jets and counter-jets. But why did NGC 1097 display two blue jets and two red? Perhaps the blue ones glowed with the phosphorescent waste left by the largest, most energetic black holes; their counter-jets must be, by some detail of the dynamics, always smaller, weaker, redder.

I went to the jutting, angled, modernist library and read Saslaw's papers again. Given a buzzing hive of black holes in a gravitational well—a bowl partly of their own making—many things could happen. There were compact configurations, tightly orbiting and self-obsessed, which could be ejected as a body. These close-wound families could in turn be unstable, once they were isolated beyond the galaxy's tug, just as the group at the center had been. Caroming off each other, they could eject unwanted siblings. I frowned. This could explain the astonishing right-angle turn the long blue jet made. One black hole thrust sidewise and several smaller, less energetic black holes pushed the opposite way. We saw only the bully of the gang.

As the galactic center lost its warped children, the ejections would become less probable. Things would die down. But how long did that take? NGC 1097 was no younger than our own Galaxy; on the cosmic scale, a sixty-million-year difference was nothing.

In the waning of afternoon—it was only a bit more than twenty-four hours since I first laid out the plates of NGC 1097—the Operations report came in. There was no explanation for the Sagittarius A data. It had been received from the station in orbit and duly processed. But no command had made the scope swivel to that axis. Odd, Operations said, that it pointed in an interesting direction, but no more.

But there were two added plates, fresh from processing.

I did not mention to Redman in Operations that the resolution of these plates was astonishing, that details in the bloated, spilling clouds was unprecedented. Nor did I point out that the angle of view had tilted further, giving a better perspective on the outward-jutting inferno. With their polynomial percussion, the computers had given what was in the stream of downward-flowing data, numbers that spoke of something being banished from the pivot of our Galaxy. Software does not ask questions; it delivers the mail, cleansed and neat.

Caltech is a compact campus. I went to the Athenaeum for coffee, ambling slowly beneath the palms and scented eucalyptus, and circumnavigated the campus on my return. In the varnished perspectives of these tiled hallways, the hammer of time was a set of Dopplered numbers, blue-shifted because the thing rushed toward us, a bulge in the sky. Silent numbers.

There were details to think about, calculations to do, long strings of hypothesis to unfurl like thin, flapping flags. I did not know the effect of a penetrating, ionizing flux on Earth. Perhaps it could affect the upper atmosphere and alter the ozone cap that drifts above our heedless heads. A long trail of disturbed, high-energy plasma could fan out through our benign spiral arm—odd, to think of bands of dust and rivers of stars as a neighborhood where you have grown up—churning, working, heating. After all, the jets of NGC 1097 had snuffed out the beaded H II regions as cleanly as an eraser passing across a blackboard, ending all the problems that life knows.

The NGC 1097 data was clean and firm. It would make a good paper, perhaps a letter to *Astrophysical Journal Letters*.

But the rest, the strange plates—there was no crisp professional path. These plates had come from much nearer the Galactic center. I had struggled with this flat impossibility, and now submitted to it. There was no other explanation. The information had come outward at light speed, far faster than the pressing bulge, showing views tilted at a slight angle away from the radial vector that led to Earth.

I had checked the newest Palomar plates from Sagittarius A this afternoon. There were no signs of anything unusual. No Doppler bulge, no exiled mass. This flatly contradicted the satellite plates.

That was the key: old reliable Palomar, our biggest ground-based 'scope, showed nothing. Which meant that someone in high orbit had fed data into our satellite 'scope—exposures which had to be made nearer the Galactic center and then brought here and deftly slipped into our ordinary astronomical research. Exposures speaking of something stirring far inward, where we could not yet see it, beyond the obscuring lanes of dust. The plumes of fiery gas would take a while longer to work through the dark cloak.

These plain facts had appeared on a screen, mute and undeniable, keyed to the data on NGC 1097. Keyed to a connection that another eye than mine could miss. Some astronomer laboring over plates of eclipsing binaries or globular clusters might well have impatiently erased the offending, multicolored spattering, not bothered to uncode the Dopplers, to note the persistent mottled red of the Galactic dust arm at the lower right, and so not known what the place must be. Only someone like me, a galactic structure specialist, would plausibly have made the connection to NGC 1097, and guessed what an onrushing black hole could do to a fragile planet: burn away the ozone layer, hammer the land with high-energy particles, mask the sun in gas and dust.

But to convey this information in this way was so strange, so—yes, that was the word—so alien. Perhaps this was the way they had to do it; quiet, subtle, indirect. Using an oblique analogy that only suggested, yet somehow disturbed more than a direct statement. This very strangeness made it more plausible.

And of course, this might be only a phrase in a longer message. Moving out from the Galactic center, they would not know we were here until they grazed the expanding bubble of radio noise that gave us away. So their data would use what they had, views at a different slant. The data itself, raw and silent, would not necessarily call attention to itself. It had to be placed in context, beside NGC 1097. How had they managed to do that? Had they tried before? What odd logic dictated this approach? How...

Take it in pieces. Some of the data I could use, some not. Perhaps a further check, a fresh look through the dusty Sagittarius arm in many wavelengths, would show the beginnings of a ruddy swelling, could give a verification. I would have to look, try to find a bridge that would make plausible what I knew but could scarcely prove.

The standards of science are austere, unforgiving—and who would have it differently? I would have to hedge, to take one step back for each two forward, to compare and suggest and contrast, always sticking close to the data. And despite what I thought I knew now, the data would have to lead, they would have to show the way.

There is a small Episcopal church, not far up Hill Street, which offers a Friday communion in early evening. Driving home through the surrounding neon gumbo, musing, I saw the sign, and stopped. I had the NGC 1097 plates with me in a carrying case, ripe beneath my arm with their fractional visions, like thin sections of an exotic cell. I went in. The big oak door thumped solemnly shut behind me. In the nave two elderly men were passing woven baskets, taking up the offertory.

I took a seat near the back. Idly I surveyed the worshipers, distributed randomly like a field of unthinking stars, in the pews before me. A man came nearby and a pool of brassy light passed the basket before me and I put something in, the debris at the bottom clinking and rustling as I stirred it. I watched the backs of heads as the familiar litany droned on, as devoid of meaning as before.

I do not believe, but there is a communion. Something tugged at my attention; one head turned a fraction. By a kind of triangulation I deduced the features of the other, closer to the ruddy light of the altar, and saw it was my son's teacher. She was listening raptly. I listened too, watching her, but could only think of the gnawing at the center of a bustling, swirling galaxy. And of her.

The lights seemed to dim. The organ fell silent. *Take, eat. This is the body and blood of* and so it had begun. I waited my turn. I do not believe, but there is a communion. People went forward in their turns. The woman rose; yes, it was she, the kind of woman whose hand would give forth loops and spirals and who would dot her *i*'s with a small circle. A fresh, faint timbre from the organ seeped into the layered air. When it was time I was still thinking of NGC 1097, of how I would write the paper—fragments skittered across my mind, the pyramid of the argument was taking shape—and I very nearly missed the gesture of the elderly man at the end of my pew. Halfway to the altar rail I realized that I still carried the case of NGC 1097 exposures, crooked into my elbow, where the pressure caused a slight ache to spread: the spot where they had made the transfusion in the clinic, a fraction of life, blood given.

I put it beside me as I knelt. The robes of the approaching figure were cobalt blue and red, a change from the decades since I had been an acolyte. There were no fidgeting boy acolytes at such a small service, of course. The blood would follow; first came the offered plate of wafers. Take, eat. Life calling out to life.

I could feel the pressing weight of what lay ahead for me, the long roll of years carrying forward one hypothesis, a strange campaign. With no idea how long we had before catastrophe fell from a fevered sky.

Then, swallowing, knowing that I would never believe this ceremony of blood and flesh, and yet that I would want it, I remembered my son, remembered that these events were only pieces, that the puzzle was not yet over, that I would never truly see it done, that as an astronomer I had to live with knowledge forever partial and provisional, that science was not final results, but instead a continuing meditation, carried on in the face of enormous facts—*take it in phrases*—let the sentences of our lives pile up.

RELATIVISTIC EFFECTS
(1982)

They came into the locker room with a babble of random talk, laughter, and shouts. There was a rolling bass undertone, gruff and raw. Over it the higher feminine notes ran lightly, warbling, darting.

The women had a solid, businesslike grace to them, doing hard work in the company of men. There were a dozen of them and they shed their clothes quickly and efficiently, all modesty forgotten long ago, their minds already focused on the job to come.

"You up for this, Nick?" Jake asked, yanking off his shorts and clipping the input sockets to his knees and elbows. His skin was red and callused from his years of linked servo work.

"Think I can handle it," Nick replied. "We're hitting pretty dense plasma already. There'll be plenty of it pouring through the throat." He was big but he gave the impression of lightness and speed, trim like a boxer, with broad shoulders and thick wrists.

"Lots of flux," Jake said. "Easy to screw up."

"I didn't get my rating by screwing up 'cause some extra ions came down the tube."

"Yeah. You're pretty far up the roster, as I remember," Jake said, eyeing the big man.

"Uh huh. Number one, last time I looked," Faye put in from the next locker. She laughed, a loud braying that rolled through the locker room and made people look up. "Bet 'at's what's botherin' you, uh, Jake?"

Jake casually made an obscene gesture in her general direction and went on. "You feelin' OK, Nick?"

"What you think I got, clenchrot?" Nick spat out with sudden ferocity. "Just had a cold, is all."

Faye said slyly, "Be a shame to prang when you're so close to winnin', movin' on up." She tugged on her halter and arranged her large breasts in it.

Nick glanced at her. Trouble was, you work with a woman long enough and after a while, she looked like just one more competitor. Once he'd thought of making a play for Faye—she really did look fairly good sometimes—but now she was one more sapper who'd elbow him into a vortex if she got half a chance. Point was, he never gave her—or anybody else—a chance to come up on him from some funny angle, throw him some unexpected momentum. He studied her casual, deft movements, pulling on the harness for the connectors. Still, there was something about her...

"You get one more good run," Faye said slyly, "you gonna get the promotion. 'At's what I'd say."

"What matters is what they say upstairs, on A deck."

"Touchy, touchy, tsk tsk," Jake said. He couldn't resist getting in a little dig.

Nick knew. Not when Jake knew it might get Nick stirred up a little. But the larger man stayed silent, stolidly pulling on his neural hookups.

Snick, the relays slide into place and Nick feels each one come home with a percussive impact in his body, he never gets used to that no matter that it's been years he's been in the Main Drive crew. When he really sat down and thought about it he didn't like this job at all, was always shaky before coming down here for his shift. He'd figured that out at the start, so the trick was, he didn't think about it, not unless he'd had too much of that 'ponics-processed liquor, the stuff that was packed with vitamin B and C and wasn't supposed to do you any damage, not even leave the muggy dregs and ache of a hangover, only of course it never worked quite right because nothing on the ship did anymore. If he let himself stoke up on that stuff he'd gradually drop out of the conversation at whatever party he was, and go off into a corner somewhere and somebody'd find him an hour or two later staring at a wall or into his drink, reliving the hours in the tube and thinking about his dad and the grandfather he could only vaguely remember. They'd both died of the ol' black creeping cancer, same as eighty percent of the crew, and it was no secret the Main Drive was the worst place in the ship for it, despite all the design specs of fifty-meter rock walls and carbon-steel bulkheads and lead-lined hatches. A man'd be a goddamn fool if he didn't think about that, sure, but somebody had to do it or they'd all die. The job came down to Nick from his father because the family just did it, that was all, all the way back to the first crew, the original bridge officers had decided that long before Nick was born, it was the only kind of social organization that the sociometricians thought could possibly work on a ship that had to fly between stars, they all knew that and nobody questioned it any more than they'd want to change a pressure spec on a seal. You just didn't, was all there was to it. He'd learned that since he could first understand the church services, or the yearly anniversary of the Blowout up on the bridge, or the things that his father told him, even when the old man was dying with the black crawling stuff eating him from inside, Nick had learned that good—

✺

"God, this dump is gettin' worse every—lookit 'at." Faye pointed.

A spider was crawling up a bulkhead, inching along on the ceramic smoothness.

"Musta got outta Agro," somebody put in.

"Yeah, don't kill it. Might upset the whole damn biosphere, an' they'd have our fuckin' heads for it."

A murmur of grudging agreement.

"Lookit 'at dumb thing," Jake said. "Made it alla way up here, musta come through air ducts an' line feeds an' who knows what." He leaned over the spider, eyeing it. It was a good three centimeters across and dull gray. "Pretty as sin, huh?"

Nick tapped in sockets at his joints and tried to ignore Jake. "Yeah."

"Poor thing. Don't know where in hell it is, does it? No appreciation for how important a place this is. We're 'bout to see a whole new age start in this locker room, soon's Nick here gets his full score. He'll be the new super an' we'll be—well, hell, we'll be like this li'l spider here. Just small and havin' our own tiny place in the big design of Nick's career, just you think how it's gonna—"

"Can the shit," Nick said harshly.

Jake laughed.

There was a tight feeling in the air. Nick felt it and figured it was something about his trying to get the promotion, something like that, but not worth bothering about. Plenty of time to think about it, once he had finished this job and gotten on up the ladder. Plenty of time then.

The gong rang brassily and the men and women finished suiting up. The minister came in and led them in a prayer for safety, the same as every other shift. Nothing different, but the tension remained. They'd be flying into higher plasma densities, sure, Nick thought. But there was no big deal about that. Still, he murmured the prayer along with the rest. Usually he didn't bother. He'd been to church services as usual, everybody went, it was unthinkable that you wouldn't, and anyway he'd never get any kind of promotion if he didn't show his face reg'lar, hunch on up to the altar rail and swallow that wafer and the alky-laced grape juice that went sour in your mouth while you were trying to swallow it, same as a lot of the talk they wanted you to swallow, only you did, you got it down because you had to and without asking anything afterward either, you bet, 'cause the ones who made trouble didn't get anywhere. So he muttered along, mouthing the familiar litany without thinking. The minister's thin lips moving, rolling on through the archaic phrases, meant less than nothing. When he looked up, each face was pensive as they prepared to go into the howling throat of the ship.

Nick lies mute and blind and for a moment feels nothing but the numb silence. It collects in him, blotting out the dim rub of the snouts which cling like lampreys to his nerves and muscles, pressing embrace that amplifies every movement, and—

—*spang*—

—he slips free of the mooring cables, a rush of sight-sound-taste-touch washes over him, so strong and sudden a welter of sensations that he jerks with the impact. He is servo'd to a thing like an eel that swims and flips and dives into a howling dance of protons. The rest of the ship is sheltered safely behind slabs of rock. But the eel is his, the eel is *him*. It shudders and jerks and twists, skating across sleek strands of magnetic plains. To Nick, it is like swimming.

The torrent gusts around him and he feels its pinprick breath. In a blinding orange glare Nick swoops, feeling his power grow as he gets the feel of it. His shiny shelf is wrapped in a cocoon of looping magnetic fields that turn the protons away, sending them gyrating in a mad gavotte, so the heavy particles cannot crunch and flare against the slick baked skin. Nick flexes the skin, supple and strong, and slips through the magnetic turbulence ahead. He feels the magnetic lines of force stretch like rubber bands. He banks and accelerates.

Streams of protons play upon him. They make glancing collisions with each other but do not react. The repulsion between them is too great and so this plasma cannot make them burn, cannot thrust them together with enough violence. Something more is needed or else the ship's throat will fail to harvest the simple hydrogen atoms, fail to kindle it into energy.

There— In the howling storm Nick sees the blue dots that are the keys, the catalyst: carbon nuclei, hovering like sea gulls in an updraft.

Split-image phosphors gleam, marking his way. He swims in the streaming blue-white glow, through a murky storm of fusing ions. He watches plumes of carbon nuclei striking the swarms of protons, wedding them to form the heavier nitrogen nuclei. The torrent swirls and screams at Nick's skin and in his sensors he sees and feels and tastes the lumpy, sluggish nitrogen as it finds a fresh incoming proton and with the fleshy smack of fusion the two stick, they hold, they wobble like raindrops—falling—merging—ballooning into a new nucleus, heavier still: oxygen.

But the green pinpoints of oxygen are unstable. These fragile forms split instantly. Jets of new particles spew through the surrounding glow— neutrinos, ruddy photons of light, and slower, darker, there come the heavy daughters of the marriage: a swollen, burnt-gold cloud of a bigger variety of nitrogen.

Onward the process flies. Each nucleus collides millions of times with the others in a fleck-shot swirl like glowing snowflakes. All in the space of a heartbeat. Flakes ride the magnetic field lines. Gamma rays flare and sputter among the blundering motes like fitful fireflies. Nuclear fire lights the long roaring corridor that is the ship's main drive. Nick swims, the white-hot sparks breaking over him like foam. Ahead he sees the violet points of gravid nitrogen and hears them crack into carbon plus an alpha particle. So in the end the long cascade gives forth the carbon that catalyzed it, carbon that will begin again its life in the whistling blizzard of protons coming in from the forward maw of the ship. With the help of the carbon, an interstellar hydrogen atom has built itself up from mere proton to, finally, an alpha particle—a stable clump of two neutrons and two protons. The alpha particle is the point of it all. It flees from the blurring storm, carrying the energy that fusion affords. The ruby-rich interstellar gas is now wedded, proton to proton, with carbon as the matchmaker.

Nick feels a rising electric field pluck at him. He moves to shed his excess charge. To carry a cloak of electrons here is fatal. Upstream lies the chewing gullet of the ramscoop ship, where the incoming protons are sucked in and where their kinetic power is stolen from them by the electric fields. There the particles are slowed, brought to rest inside the ship, their streaming energy stored in capacitors.

A cyclone shrieks behind him. Nick swims sideways, toward the walls of the combustion chamber. The nuclear burn that flares around him is never pure, cannot be pure because the junk of the cosmos pours through here, like barley meal laced with grains of granite. The incoming atomic rain spatters constantly over the fluxlife walls, killing the organic superconductor strands there.

Nick pushes against the rubbery magnetic fields and swoops over the mottled yellow-blue crust of the walls. In the flickering lightning glow of infrared and ultraviolet he sees the scaly muck that deadens the magnetic fields and slows the nuclear burn in the throat. He flexes, wriggles, and turns the eel-like form. This brings the electron beam gun around at millimeter range. He fires. A brittle crackling leaps out, onto the scaly wall. The tongue bites and gouges. Flakes roast off and blacken and finally bubble up like tar. The rushing proton currents wash the flakes away, revealing the gunmetal blue beneath. Now the exposed superconducting threads can begin their own slow pruning of themselves, life casting out its dead. Their long organic chain molecules can feed and grow anew. As Nick cuts and turns and carves he watched the spindly fibers coil loose and drift in eddies. Finally they spin away into the erasing proton storm. The dead fibers sputter and flash where the incoming protons strike them and then with a rumble in his acoustic pickup coils he sees them swept away. Maintenance.

Something tugs at him. He sees the puckered scoop where the energetic alpha particles shoot by. They dart like luminous jade wasps. The scoop sucks them in. Inside they will be collected, drained of energy, inducing megawatts of power for the ship, which will drink their last drop of momentum and cast them aside, a wake of broken atoms.

Suddenly he spins to the left—*Jesus, how can*—he thinks—and the scoop fields lash him. A megavolt per meter of churning electrical vortex snatches at him. It is huge and quick and relentless to Nick (though to the ship it is a minor ripple in its total momentum) and magnetic tendrils claw at his spinning, shiny surfaces. The scoop opening is a plunging, howling mouth. Jets of glowing atoms whirl by him, mocking. The walls near him counter his motion by increasing their magnetic fields. Lines of force stretch and bunch.

How did this—is all he has time to think before a searing spot blooms nearby. His presence so near the scoop has upset the combination rates there. His eyes widen. If the reaction gets out of control it can burn through the chamber vessel, through the asteroid rock beyond, and spike with acrid fire into the ship, toward the life dome.

A brassy roar. The scoop sucks at his heels. Ions run white-hot. A warning knot strikes him. Tangled magnetic ropes grope for him, clotting around the shiny skin.

Panic squeezes his throat. Desperately he fires his electron beam gun against the wall, hoping it will give him a push, a fresh vector—

Not enough. Orange ions blossom and swell around him—

Most of the squad was finished dressing. They were tired and yet the release of getting off work brought out an undercurrent of celebration. They ignored Nick and slouched out of the locker room, bound for families or assignations or sensory jolts of sundry types. A reek of sweat and fatigue diffused through the sluggishly stirring air. The squad laughed and shouted old jokes to each other. Nick sat on the bench with his head in his hands.

"I…I don't get it. I was doin' pretty well, catchin' the crap as it came at me, an' then somethin' grabbed…"

They'd had to pull him out with a robot searcher. He'd gone dead, inoperative, clinging to the throat lining, fighting the currents. The surges drove the blood down into your gut and legs, the extra g's slamming you up against the bulkhead and sending big dark blotches across your vision, purple swarms of dots swimming everywhere, hollow rattling noises coming in through the transducer mikes, nausea, the ache spreading through your arms—

It had taken three hours to get him back in, and three more to clean up. A lot of circuitry was fried for good, useless junk. The worst loss was the high-grade steel, all riddled with neutrons and fissured by nuclear fragments. The ship's foundry couldn't replace that, hadn't had the rolling mill to even make a die for it in more than a generation. His neuro index checked out okay, but he wouldn't be able to work for a week.

He was still in a daze and the memory would not straighten itself out in his mind. "I dunno, I…"

Faye murmured, "Maybe went a li'l fast for you today."

Jake grinned and said nothing.

"Mebbe you could, y'know, use a rest. Sit out a few sessions." Faye cocked her head at him.

Nick looked at both of them and narrowed his eyes. "That wasn't a mistake of mine, was it? Uh? No mistake at all. Somebody—" He knotted a fist.

"Hey, nothin' you can prove," Jake said, backing away. "I can guarantee that, boy."

"Some bastard, throwin' me some extra angular when I wasn't lookin', I oughta—"

"Come on, Nick, you got no proof 'a those charges. You know there's too much noise level in the throat to record what ever'body's doin'." Faye grinned without humor.

"Damn." Nick buried his face in his hands. "I was *that* close, so damned near to gettin' that promotion—"

"Yeah. Tsk tsk. You dropped points back there for sure, Nick, burnin' out a whole unit that way an' gettin—"

"Shut it. Just shut it."

Nick was still groggy and he felt the anger build in him without focus, without resolution. These two would make up some neat story to cover their asses, same as everybody did when they were bringing another member of the squad down a notch or two. The squad didn't have a lot of love for anybody who looked like they were going to get up above the squad, work their way up. That was the way it was, jobs were hard to change, the bridge liked it stable, said it came out better when you worked at a routine all your life and—

"Hey, c'mon, let's get our butts down to the Sniffer," Faye said. "No use jawin' 'bout this, is 'ere? I'm gettin' thirsty after all that uh, work."

She winked at Jake. Nick saw it and knew he would get a ribbing about this for weeks. The squad was telling him he had stepped out of line and he would just have to take it. That was just the plain fact of it. He clenched his fists and felt a surge of anger.

"Hey!" Jake called out. "This damn spider's still tryin' to make it up this wall." He reached out and picked it up in his hand. The little gray thing struggled against him, legs kicking.

"Y'know, I hear there're people over in Comp who keep these for pets," Faye said. "Could be one of theirs."

"Creepy li'l thing," Nick said.

"You get what you can," Faye murmured. "Ever see a holo of a dog?"

Nick nodded. "Saw a whole movie about this one, it was a collie, savin' people an' all. Now that's a pet."

They all stared silently at the spider as it drummed steadily on Jake's hand with its legs. Nick shivered and turned away. Jake held it firmly, without hurting it, and slipped it into a pocket. "Think I'll take it back before Agro busts a gut lookin' for it."

Nick was silent as the three of them left the smells of the locker room and made their way up through the corridors. They took a shortcut along an undulating walkway under the big observation dome. Blades of pale blue light shifted like enormous columns in the air, but they were talking and only occasionally glanced up.

The vast ship of which they were a part was heading through the narrow corridor between two major spiral galaxies. On the right side of the dome the bulge of one galaxy was like a whirlpool of light, the points of light like grains of sand caught in a vortex. Around the bright core, glowing clouds of the spiral arms wended their way through the flat disk, seeming to cut through the dark dust clouds like a river slicing through jungle. Here and there black towers reared up out of the confusion of the disk, where masses of interstellar debris had been heaved out of the galactic plane, driven by collisions between clouds, or explosions of young stars.

There were intelligent, technological societies somewhere among those drifting stars. The ship had picked up their transmissions long ago— radio, UV, the usual—and had altered course to pass nearby.

The two spirals were a binary system, bound together since their birth. For most of their history they had stayed well apart, but now they were brushing within a galactic diameter of each other. Detailed observations in the last few weeks of ship's time—all that was needed to veer and swoop toward the twinned disks—had shown that this was the final pass: the two galaxies would not merely swoop by and escape. The filaments of gas and dust between them had created friction over the billions of years past, eroding their orbital angular momentum. Now they would grapple fatally.

The jolting impact would be spectacular: shock waves, compression of the gas in the galactic plane, and shortly thereafter new star formation, swiftly yielding an increase in the supernova rate, a flooding of the interstellar medium with high energy particles. The rain of sudden virulent energy would destroy the planetary environments. The two spirals would come together with a wrenching suddenness, the disks sliding into each other like two saucers bent on destruction, the collision effectively occurring all over the disks simultaneously in an explosive flare of X-ray and thermal brems-strahlung radiation. Even advanced technologies would be snuffed out by the rolling, searing tide.

The disks were passing nearly face-on to each other. In the broad blue dome overhead the two spirals hung like cymbals seen on edge. The ship moved at extreme relativistic velocity, pressing infinitesimally close to light speed, passing through the dim halo of gas and old dead stars that surrounded each galaxy. Its speed compressed time and space. Angles distorted as time ran at a blinding pace outside, refracting images. Extreme relativistic effects made the approach visible to the naked eye. Slowly, the huge disks of shimmering light seemed to swing open like a pair of doors. Bright tendrils spanned the gap between them.

Jake was telling a story about two men in CompCatynch section, rambling on with gossip and jokes, trying to keep the talk light. Faye went along with it, putting in a word when Jake slowed. Nick was silent.

The ship swooped closer to the disks and suddenly across the dome streaked red and orange bursts. The disks were twisted, distorted by their mutual gravitational tugs, wrenching each other, twins locked in a tightening embrace. The planes of stars rippled, as if a huge wind blew across them. The galactic nuclei flared with fresh fires: ruby, orange, mottled blue, ripe gold. Stars were blasted into the space between. Filaments of raw, searing gas formed a web that spanned the two spirals. This was the food that fed the ship's engines. They were flying as near to the thick dust and gas of the galaxies as they could. The maw of the ship stretched outward, spanning a volume nearly as big as the galactic core. Streamers of sluggish gas veered toward it, drawn by the onrushing magnetic fields. The throat sucked in great clouds, boosting them to still higher velocity.

The ship's hull moaned as it met denser matter.

Nick ignores the babble from Jake, knowing it is empty foolishness, and thinks instead of the squad, and how he would run it if he got the promotion: They had to average five thousand cleared square meters a week, minimum, that was a full ten percent of the whole ship's throat, minus of course the lining areas that were shut down for full repair, call that one thousand square meters on the average, so with the other crews operating on forty-five-hour shifts they could work their way through and give the throat a full scraping in less than a month, easy, even allowing for screwups and malfs and times when the radiation level was too high for even the suits to screen it out. You had to keep the suits up to 99 plus percent operational or you caught hell from upstairs, but the same time they came at you with their specifications reports and never listened when you told them about the delays, that was your problem not theirs and they said so every chance they got, that bunch of blowhard officers up there, descended from the original ship's bridge officers who'd left Earth generations back with every intention of returning after a twelve-year round trip to Centauri, only it hadn't worked, they didn't count on the drive freezing up in permanent full-bore thrust, the drive locked in and the deceleration components slowly getting fried by the increased neutron flux from the reactions, until when they finally could taper off on the forward drive the decelerators were finished, beyond repair, and then the ship had nothing to do but drive on, unable to stop or even turn the magnetic gascatchers off, because once you did that the incoming neutral atoms would be a sleet of protons and neutrons that'd riddle everybody within a day, kill them all. So the officers had said they had to keep going, studying, trying to figure a way to rebuild the decelerators, only nobody ever did, and the crew got older and they flew on, clean out of the galaxy, having babies and quarrels and finally after some murders and suicides and worse, working out a stable social structure in a goddamn relativistic runaway, officers' sons and daughters becoming officers themselves, and crewmen begetting crewmen again, down through five generations now in the creaky old ship that had by now flown through five million years of outside-time, so that there was no purpose or dream of returning Earthside any more, only names attached to pictures and stories, and the same jobs to do every day, servicing the weakening stanchions and struts, the flagging motors, finding replacements for every little doodad that fractured, working because to stop was to die, all the time with officers to tell you what new scientific experiment they'd thought up and how maybe this time it would be the answer, the clue to getting back to their own galaxy—a holy grail beloved of the first and second generations that was now, even under high magnification, a mere mottled disk of ruby receding pinprick lights nobody alive had ever seen up close. Yet there was something in what the bridge officers said, in what the scientific mandarins mulled over, a point to their lives here—

"Let's stop in this'n," Jake called, interrupting Nick's muzzy thoughts, and he followed them into a small inn. Without his noticing it they had left the big observation dome. They angled through a tight, rocky corridor cut from the original asteroid that was the basic body of the whole starship.

Among the seven thousand souls in the ten-kilometer-wide starship, there were communities and neighborhoods and bars to suit everyone. In this one there were thick veils of smoky euphorics, harmless unless you drank an activating potion. Shifts came and went, there were always crowds in the bar, a rich assortment of faces and ages and tongues. Techs, metalworkers, computer jockeys, manuals, steamfitters, muscled grunt laborers. Cadaverous and silent alesoakers, steadily pouring down a potent brown liquid. Several women danced in a corner, oblivious, singing, rhyming as they went.

Faye ordered drinks and they all three joined in the warm feel of the place. The euphorics helped. It took only moments to become completely convinced that this was a noble and notable set of folk. Someone shouted a joke. Laughter pealed in the close-packed room.

Nick saw in this quick moment an instant of abiding grace: how lovely it was when Faye forgot herself and laughed fully, opening her mouth so wide you could see the whole oval cavern with its ribbed pink roof and the arching tongue alive with tension. The heart-stopping blackness at the back led down to depths worth a lifetime to explore, all revealed in a passing moment like a casual gift: a momentary and incidental beauty that eclipsed the studied, long-learned devices of women and made them infinitely more mysterious.

She gave him a wry, tossed-off smile. He frowned, puzzled. Maybe he had never paid adequate attention to her, never sensed her dimensions. He strained forward to say something and Jake interrupted his thoughts with, "Hey there, look. Two bridgies."

And there were. Two bridge types, not mere officers but scientists; they wore the sedate blue patches on their sleeves. Such people seldom came to these parts of the ship; their quarters, ordained by time, nestled deep in the rock-lined bowels of the inner asteroid.

"See if you can hear what they're sayin'," Faye whispered.

Jake shrugged. "Why should I care?"

Faye frowned. "Wanna be a scuzzo dope forever?"

"Aw, stow it," Jake said, and went to get more beer.

Nick watched the scientist nearest him, the man, lift the heavy champagne bottle and empty it. Have to hand it to bioponics, he thought. They keep the liquor coming. The crisp golden foil at the head would be carefully collected, reused; the beautiful heavy hollow butts of the bottles had doubtless been fondled by his own grandfather. Of celebration there was no end.

Nick strained to hear.

"Yes, but the latest data shows definitely there's enough mass, no question."

"Maybe, maybe," said the other. "Must say I never thought there'd be enough between the clusters to add up so much—"

"But there *is*. No doubt of it. Look at Fenetti's data, clear as the nose on your face. Enough mass density between the clusters to close off the universe's geometry, to reverse the expansion."

Goddamn, Nick thought. They're talking about the critical mass problem. Right out in public.

"Yes. My earlier work seems to have been wrong."

"Look, this opens possibilities."

"How?"

"The expansion has to stop, right? So after it does, and things start to implode back, the density of gas the ship passes through will get steadily greater—right?"

Jesus, Nick thought, the eventual slowing down of the universal expansion, billions of years—

"Okay."

"So we'll accelerate more, the relativistic rate will get bigger—the whole process outside will speed up, as we see it."

"Right."

"Then we can sit around and watch the whole thing play out. I mean, shipboard time from now to the implosion of the whole universe, I make it maybe only three hundred years."

"That short?"

"Do the calculation."

"Ummm. Maybe so, if we pick up enough mass in the scoop fields. This flyby we're going through, it helps, too."

"Sure it does. We'll do more like it in the next few weeks. Look, we're getting up to speeds that mean we'll be zooming by a galaxy every *day*."

"Uh-huh. If we can live a couple more centuries, shipboard time, we can get to see the whole shebang collapse back in on itself."

"Well, look, that's just a preliminary number, but I think we might make it. In this generation."

Faye said, "Jeez, I can't make out what they're talkin' about."

"I can," Nick said. It helped to know the jargon. He had studied this as part of his program to bootstrap himself up to a better life. You take officers, they could integrate the gravitational field equations straight off, or tell how a galaxy was evolving just by looking at it, or figure out the gas density ahead of the ship just by squinting at one of the X-ray bands from the detectors. They *knew*. He would have to know all of that too, and more. So he studied while the rest of the squad slurped up the malt.

He frowned. He was still stunned, trying to think it through. If the total mass between the clusters of galaxies was big enough, that extra matter would provide enough gravitational energy to make the whole universe reverse its expansion and fall backward, inward, given enough time...

Jake was back. "Too noisy in 'ere," he called. "Fergit the beers, bar's mobbed. Let's lift 'em."

Nick glanced over at the scientists. One was earnestly leaning forward, her face puffy and purplish, congested with the force of the words she was urging into the other's ear. He couldn't make out any more of what they were saying; they had descended into quoting mathematical formulas to each other.

"Okay," Nick said.

They left the random clamor of the bar and retraced their steps, back under the observation dome. Nick felt a curious elation.

Nick knows how to run the squad, knows how to keep the equipment going even if the voltage flickers, he can strip down most suits in under an hour using just plain rack tools, been doing it for forty years, all those power tools around the bay, most of the squad can't even turn a nut on a manifold without it has to be pneumatic *rrrrrtt* quick as you please nevermind the wear on the lubricants lost forever that nobody aboard can synthesize, tools seize up easy now, jam your fingers when they do, give you a hand all swole up for a week, and all the time the squad griping 'cause they have to birddog their own stuff, breadboard new ones if some piece of gear goes bad, complaining 'cause they got to form and fabricate their own microchips, no easy replacement parts to just clip in the way you read about the way it was in the first generation, and God help you if a man or woman on the crew gets a fatal injury working in the throat crew, 'cause then your budget is docked for the cost of keeping 'em frozen down, waiting on cures that'll never come just like Earth will never come, the whole planet's been dead now a million years prob'ly, and the frozen corpses on board running two percent of the energy budget he read somewhere, getting to be more all the time, but then he thinks about that talk back in the bar and what it might mean, plunging on until you could see the whole goddamn end of the universe—

"Gotta admit we got you that time, Nick," Jake says as they approach the dome, "smooth as glass I come up on you, you're so hard workin' you don't see nothin', I give you a shot of extra spin, *man* your legs fly out you go wheelin' away—"

Jake starts to laugh.

—and livin' in each other's hip pockets like this the hell of it was you start to begrudge ever' little thing, even the young ones, the kids cost too, not that he's against them, hell, you got to keep the families okay or else they'll be slitting each other's throats inside a year, got to remember your grandfather who was in the Third Try on the decelerators, they came near to getting some new magnets in place before the plasma tubulence blew the whole framework away and they lost it, every family's got some ancestor who got flung down the throat and out into nothing, the kids got to be brought up rememberin' that, even though the little bastards do get into the bioponic tubes and play pranks, they got not a lot to do 'cept study and work, same as he and the others have done for all their lives, average crewman lasts two hundred years or so now, all got the best biomed (goddamn lucky they were shippin' so much to Centauri), bridge officers maybe even longer, get lots of senso augmentation to help you through the tough parts, and all to keep going, or even maybe get ahead a little like this squad boss thing, he was *that* close an' they took it away from him, small-minded bastards scared to shit he might make, what was it, fifty more units of rec credit than they did, not like being an officer or anything, just a job-jockey getting ahead a little, wanting just a scrap, and they gigged him for it and now this big mouth next to his ear is goin' on, puffing himself up in front of Faye, Faye who might be worth a second look if he could get her out of the shadow of this loudmouthed secondrate—

Jake was in the middle of a sentence, drawling on. Nick grabbed his arm and whirled him around.

"Keep laughin', you slimy bastard, just keep—"

Nick got a throat hold on him and leaned forward. He lifted, pressing Jake against the railing of the walkway. Jake struggled but his feet left the floor until he was balanced on the railing, halfway over the twenty-meter drop. He struck out with a fist but Nick held on.

"Hey, hey, vap off a li'l," Faye cried.

"Yeah—look—you got to take it—as it comes," Jake wheezed between clenched teeth.

"You two done me an' then you laugh an' don't think I don't know you're, you're—" He stopped, searching for words and not finding any.

Globular star clusters hung in the halo beyond the spirals. They flashed by the ship like immense chandeliers of stars. Odd clumps of torn and twisted gas rushed across the sweep of the dome overhead. Tortured gouts of sputtering matter were swept into the magnetic mouth of the ship. As it arched inward toward the craft it gave off flashes of incandescent light. These were stars being born in the ship-driven turbulence, the compressed gases, collapsing into firefly lives before the ship's throat swallowed them. In the flicker of an eyelid on board, a thousand years of stellar evolution transpired on the churning dome above.

The ship had by now carved a swooping path through the narrow strait between the disks. It had consumed banks of gas and dust, burning some for power, scattering the rest with fresh ejected energy into its path. The gas would gush out, away from the galaxies, unable to cause the ongoing friction that drew the two together. This in turn would slow their collision, giving the glittering worlds below another million years to plan, to discover, to struggle upward against the coming catastrophe. The ship itself, grown vast by relativistic effects, shone in the night skies of a billion worlds as a fiercely burning dot, emitting at impossible frequencies, slicing through kiloparsecs of space with its gluttonous magnetic throat, consuming.

※

"Be easy on him, Nick," Faye said softly.

Nick shook his head. "Naw. Trouble with a guy like this is, he got nothin' to do but piss on people. Hasn't got per...perspective."

"Stack it, Nick," Faye said.

※

Above them, the dome showed briefly the view behind the ship, where the reaction engines poured forth the raw refuse of the fusion drives. Far back, along their trajectory, lay dim filaments, wisps of ivory light. It was the Local Group, the cluster of galaxies that contained the Milky Way, their home. A human could look up, extend a hand, and a mere thumbnail would easily cover the faint smudge that was in fact a clump of spirals, ellipticals, dwarfs and irregular galaxies. It was a small part of the much larger association of galaxies, called the Local Supercluster. The ship was passing now beyond the fringes of the Local Supercluster, forging outward through the dim halo of random glimmering-galaxies which faded off into the black abyss beyond. It would be a long voyage across that span, until the next supercluster was reached: a pale blue haze that ebbed and flowed before the nose of the ship, liquid light distorted by relativity. For the moment the glow of their next destination was lost in the harsh glare of the two galaxies. The disks yawned and turned around the ship, slabs of hot gold and burnt orange, refracted, moving according to the twisted optical effects of special relativity. Compression of wavelengths and the squeezing of time itself made the disks seem to open wide, immense glowing doors swinging in the vacuum, parting to let pass this artifact that sped on, riding a tail of forking, sputtering, violet light.

※

Nick tilted the man back farther on the railing. Jake's arms fanned the air and his eyes widened.

"Okay, okay, you win," Jake grunted.

"You going upstairs, tell 'em you scragged me."

"Ah…okay."

"Good. Or else somethin' might, well, happen." Nick let Jake's legs down, back onto the walkway.

Faye said, "You didn't have to risk his neck. We would've cleared it for you if you'd—"

"Yeah, sure," Nick said sourly.

"You bastard, I oughta—"

"Yeah?"

Jake was breathing hard, his eyes danced around, but Nick knew he wouldn't try anything. He could judge a thing like that. Anyway, he thought, he'd been right, and they knew it. Jake grimaced, shook his head. Nick waved a hand and they walked on.

"Y'know what your trouble is, Nick?" Jake said after a moment. "Yer like this spider here."

Jake took the spider out of his jumpsuit pocket and held up the gray creature. It stirred, but was trapped.

"Wha'cha mean?" Nick asked.

"You got no perspective on the squad. Don't know what's really happenin'. An' this spider, he dunno either. He was down in the locker room, he didn't appreciate what he was in. I mean, that's the center of the whole damn ship right there, the squad."

"Yeah. So?"

"This spider, he don't appreciate how far he'd come from Agro. You either, Nick. You don't appreciate how the squad helps you out, how you oughta be grateful to them, how mebbe you shouldn't keep pushin' alla time."

"Spider's got little eyes, no lens to it," Nick said. "Can't see farther than your hand. Can't see those stars up there. I can, though."

Jake sputtered, "Crap, relative to the spider you're—"

"Aw, can it," Nick said.

Faye said, "Look, Jake, maybe you stop raggin' him alla time, he—"

"No, he's got a point there," Nick said, his voice suddenly mild. "We're all tryin' to be reg'lar folks in the ship, right? We should keep t'gether."

"Yeah. You push too hard."

Sure, Nick thought. Sure I do. And the next thing I'm gonna push for is Faye, take her clean away from you.

—the way her neck arcs back when she laughs, graceful in a casual way he never noticed before, a lilting note that caught him, and the broad smile she had, but she was solid too, did a good job in the blowback zone last week when nobody else could handle it, red gases flaring all around her, good woman to have with you, and maybe he'd need a lot of support like that, because he knows now what he really wants: to be an officer someday, it wasn't impossible, just hard, and the only way is by pushing. All this scratching around for a little more rec credits, maybe some better food, that wasn't the point, no, there was something more, the officers keep up the promotion game 'cause we've got to have something to keep people fretting and working, something to take our minds off what's outside, what'll happen if—no, *when*—the drive fails, where we're going, only what these two don't know is that we're not bound for oblivion in a universe that runs down into blackness, we're going on to see the reversal, we get to hear the recessional, galaxies, peeling into the primordial soup as they compress back together and the ship flies faster, always faster as it sucks up the dust of time and hurls itself further on, back to the crunch that made everything and will some day—hell, if he can stretch out the years, right in his own lifetime!—press everything back into a drumming hail of light and mass, now *that's* something to live for—

Faye said pleasantly, "Just think how much good we did back there. Saved who knows how many civilizations, billions of living creatures, gave them a reprieve."

"Right," Jake said, his voice distracted, still smarting over his defeat.

Faye nodded and the three of them made their way up an undulating walkway, heading for the bar where the rest of the squad would be. The ship thrust forward as the spiral galaxies dropped behind now, Doppler reddened into dying embers.

The ship had swept clean the space between them, postponed the coming collision. The scientists had seen this chance, persuaded the captain to make the slight swerve that allowed them to study the galaxies, and in the act accelerate the ship still more. The ship was now still closer to the knife-edge of light speed. Its aim was not a specific destination, but rather to plunge on, learning more, studying the dabs of refracted lights beyond, struggling with the engines, forging on as the universe wound down, as entropy increased, and the last stars flared out. It carried the cargo meant for Centauri—the records and past lives of all humanity, a library for the colony there. If the drives held up, it would carry them forward until the last tick of time.

Nick laughed. "Not that they'll know it, or ever give a—" He stopped. He'd been going to say *ever give a Goddamn about who did it,* but he knew how Faye felt about using the Lord's name in vain.

"Why, sure they will," Faye said brightly. "We were a big, hot source of all kinds of radiation. They'll know it was a piece of technology."

"Big lights in the sky? Could be natural."

"With a good spectrometer—"

"Yeah, but they'll never be sure."

She frowned. "Well, a ramscoop exhaust looks funny, not like a star or anything."

"With the big relativistic effect factored in, our emission goes out like a searchlight. One narrow little cone of scrambled-up radiation, Dopplered forward. So they can't make us out the whole time. Most of 'em'd see us for just a few years, tops," Nick said.

"So?"

"Hard to make a scientific theory about somethin' that happens once, lasts a little while, never repeats."

"Maybe."

"They could just as likely think it was something unnatural. Supernatural. A god or somethin'."

"Huh. Maybe." Faye shrugged. "Come on. Let's get 'nother drink before rest'n rec hours are over."

They walked on. Above them the great knives of light sliced down through the air, ceaselessly changing, and the humans kept on going, their small voices indomitable, reaching forward, undiminished.

OF SPACE/TIME AND THE RIVER
(1985)

December 5

Monday.

We took a limo to Los Angeles for the 9 A.M. flight, LAX to Cairo.

On the boost up we went over 1.4 G, contra-reg, and a lot of passengers complained, especially the poor things in their clank-shank rigs, the ones that keep you walking even after the hip replacements fail.

Joanna slept through it all, seasoned traveler, and I occupied myself with musing about finally seeing the ancient Egypt I'd dreamed about as a kid, back at the turn of the century.

> *If thou be'st born to strange sights,*
> *Things invisible go see,*
> *Ride ten thousand days and nights*
> *Till Age snow white hairs on thee.*

I've got the snow powdering at the temples and steadily expanding waistline, so I suppose John Donne applies. Good to see I can still summon up lines I first read as a teenager. There are some rewards to being a Prof. of Comp. Lit. at UC Irvine, even if you do have to scrimp to afford a trip like this.

The tour agency said the Quarthex hadn't interfered with tourism at all—in fact, you hardly noticed them, they deliberately blended in so well. How a seven-foot insectoid thing with gleaming russet skin can look like an Egyptian I don't know, but what the hell, Joanna said, let's go anyway.

I hope she's right. I mean, it's been fourteen years since the Quarthex landed, opened the first diplomatic interstellar relations, and then chose Egypt as the only place on Earth where they cared to carry out what they called their "cultural studies." I guess we'll get a look at that, too. The Quarthex keep to themselves, veiling their multi-layered deals behind diplomatic dodges.

As if 6 hours of travel weren't numbing enough, including the orbital delay because of an unannounced Chinese launch, we both watched a holoD about one of those new biotech guys, called *Straight from the Hearts*. An unending string of single-entendres. In our stupefied state it was just about right.

As we descended over Cairo it was clear and about 15°. We stumbled off the plane, sandy-eyed from riding ten thousand days and nights in a whistling aluminum box.

The airport was scruffy, instant third world hubbub, confusion, and filth. One departure lounge was filled exclusively with turbaned men. Heavy security everywhere. No Quarthex around. Maybe they do blend in.

Our bus across Cairo passed a decayed aqueduct, about which milled men in caftans, women in black, animals eating garbage. People, packed into the most unlikely living spots, carrying out peddler's business in dusty spots between buildings, traffic alternately frenetic or frozen.

We crawled across Cairo to Giza, the pyramids abruptly looming out of the twilight. The hotel, Mena House, was the hunting lodge-cum-palace of 19th century kings. Elegant.

Buffet supper was good. Sleep came like a weight.

December 6

Joanna says this journal is good therapy for me, might even get me back into the habit of writing again. She says every Comp. Lit. type is a frustrated author and I should just spew my bile into this diary. So be it:

> Thou, when thou return'st, wilt tell me
> All strange wonders that befell thee.

World, you have been warned.

Set off south today—to Memphis, the ancient capital lost when its walls were breached in a war and subsequent floods claimed it.

The famous fallen Rameses statue. It looks powerful still, even lying down. Makes you feel like a pygmy tip-toeing around a giant, à la Gulliver.

Saqqara, principal necropolis of Memphis, survives 3 km away in the desert. First Dynasty tombs, including the first pyramid, made of steps, 5 levels high. New Kingdom graffiti inside are now history themselves, from our perspective.

On to the Great Pyramid!—by camel! The drivers proved to be even more harassing than legend warned. We entered the pyramid Khefren, slightly shorter than that of his father, Cheops. All the 80 known pyramids were found stripped. These passages have a constricted vacancy to them, empty now for longer than they were filled. Their silent mass is unnerving.

Professor Alvarez from UC Berkeley tried to find hidden rooms here by placing cosmic ray detectors in the lower known rooms, and looking for slight increases in flux at certain angles, but there seem to be none. There are seismic and even radio measurements of the dry sands in the Giza region, looking for echoes of buried tombs, but no big finds so far. Plenty of echoes from ruins of ordinary houses, etc., though.

No serious jet lag today, but we nod off when we can. Handy, having the hotel a few hundred yards from the pyramids.

I tried to get Joanna to leave her wrist comm at home. Since her breakdown she can't take news of daily disasters very well. (Who can, really?) She's pretty steady now, but this trip should be as calm as possible, her doctor told me.

So of course she turns on the comm and it's full of hysterical stuff about another border clash between the Empire of Israel and the Arab Muhammad Soviet. Smart rockets vs. smart defenses. A draw. Some things never change.

I turned it off immediately. Her hands shook for hours afterward. I brushed it off.

Still, it's different when you're a few hundred miles from the lines. Hope we're safe here.

December 7

Into Cairo itself, the Egyptian museum. The Tut Ankh Amen exhibit—huge treasuries, opulent jewels, a sheer wondrous plenitude. There are endless cases of beautiful alabaster bowls, gold-laminate boxes, testifying to thousands of years of productivity.

I wandered down a musty marble corridor and then, coming out of a gloomy side passage, there was the first Quarthex I'd ever seen. Big, clacking and clicking as it thrust forward in that six-legged gait. It ignored me, of course—they nearly always lurch by humans as though they can't see us. Or else that distant, distracted gaze means they're ruminating over strange, alien ideas. Who knows why they're intensely studying ancient Egyptian ways, and ignoring the rest of us? This one was cradling a stone urn, a meter high at least. It carried the black granite in three akimbo arms, hardly seeming to notice the weight. I caught a whiff of acrid pungency, the fluid that lubricates their joints. Then it was gone.

We left and visited the oldest Coptic church in Egypt, supposedly where Moses hid out when he was on the lam. Looks it. The old section of Cairo is crowded, decayed, people laboring in every nook with minimal tools, much standing around watching as others work. The only sign of really efficient labor was a gang of men and women hauling long, cigar-shaped yellow things on wagons. Something the Quarthex wanted placed outside the city, our guide said.

In the evening we went to the Sound & Light show at the Sphinx—excellent. There is even a version in the Quarthex language, those funny sputtering, barking sounds.

Arabs say, "Man fears time; time fears the pyramids." You get that feeling here.

Afterward, we ate in the hotel's Indian restaurant; quite fine.

December 8

Cairo is a city being trampled to death.

It's grown by a factor of 14 in population since the revolution in 1952, and shows it. The old Victorian homes which once lined stately streets of willowy trees are now crowded by modern slab concrete apartment houses. The aged buildings are kept going, not from a sense of history, but because no matter how rundown they get, somebody needs them.

The desert's grit invades everywhere. Plants in the courtyards have a weary, resigned look. Civilization hasn't been very good for the old ways.

Maybe that's why the Quarthex seem to dislike anything built since the time of the Romans. I saw one running some kind of machine, a black contraption that floated two meters off the ground. It was laying some kind of cable in the ground, right along the bank of the Nile. Every time it met a building it just slammed through, smashing everything to frags. Guess the Quarthex have squared all this with the Egyptian gov't, because there were police all around, making sure nobody got in the way. Odd.

But not unpredictable, when you think about it. The Quarthex have those levitation devices which everybody would love to get the secret of. (Ending sentence with preposition! Horrors! But this is vacation, dammit.) They've been playing coy for years, letting out a trickle of technology, with the Egyptians holding the patents. That must be what's holding the Egyptian economy together, in the face of their unrelenting population crunch. The Quarthex started out as guests here, studying the ruins and so on, but now it's obvious that they have free run of the place. They *own* it.

Still, the Quarthex haven't given away the crucial devices which would enable us to find out how they do it—or so my colleagues in the physics department tell me. It vexes them that this alien race can master space/time so completely, manipulating gravity itself, and we can't get the knack of it.

We visited the famous alabaster mosque. It perches on a hill called The Citadel. Elegant, cool, aloofly dominating the city. The Old Bazaar nearby is a warren, so much like the movie sets one's seen that it has an unreal, Arabian Nights quality. We bought spices. The calls to worship from the mosques reach you everywhere, even in the most secluded back rooms where Joanna was haggling over jewelry.

It's impossible to get anything really ancient, the swarthy little merchants said. The Quarthex have bought them up, trading gold for anything that might be from the time of the Pharaohs. There have been a lot of fakes over the last few centuries, some really good ones, so the Quarthex have just bought anything that might be real. No wonder the Egyptians like them, let them chew up their houses if they want. Gold speaks louder than the past.

We boarded our cruise ship, the venerable *Nile Concorde*. Lunch was excellent, Italian. We explored Cairo in midafternoon, through markets of incredible dirt and disarray. Calf brains displayed without a hint of refrigeration or protection, flies swarming, etc. Fun, especially if you can keep from breathing for five minutes or more.

We stopped in the Shepheard's Hotel, the site of many Brit spy novels (Maugham especially). It has an excellent bar—Nubians, Saudis, etc., putting away decidedly non-Islamic gins and beers. A Quarthex was sitting in a special chair at the back, talking through a voicebox to a Saudi. I couldn't tell what they were saying, but the Saudi had a gleam in his eye. Driving a bargain, I'd say.

Great atmosphere in the bar, though. A cloth banner over the bar proclaims,

Unborn tomorrow and dead yesterday,
why fret about them if today be sweet.

Indeed, yes, ummm—bartender!

December 9

Friday, Moslem holy day.

We left Cairo at 11 P.M. last night, the city gliding past our stateroom windows, lovelier in misty radiance than in dusty day. We cruised all day. Buffet breakfast & lunch, solid eastern and Mediterranean stuff, passable red wine.

A hundred meters away, the past presses at us, going about its business as if the pharaohs were still calling the tune. Primitive pumping irrigation, donkeys doing the work, women cleaning gray clothes in the Nile. Desert ramparts to the east, at spots sending sand fingers—no longer swept away by the annual floods—across the fields to the shore itself. Moslem tombs of stone and mud brick coast by as we lounge on the top deck, peering at the madly waving children through our binoculars, across a chasm of time.

There are about fifty aboard a ship with capacity of 100, so there is plenty of room and service as we sweep serenely on, music flooding the deck, cutting between slabs of antiquity; not quite decadent, just intelligently sybaritic. (Why so few tourists? Guide guessed people are afraid of the Quarthex. Joanna gets jittery around them, but I don't know if it's only her old fears surfacing again.)

The spindly, ethereal minarets are often the only grace note in the mud brick villages, like a lovely idea trying to rise out of brown, mottled chaos. Animal power is used wherever possible. Still, the villages are quiet at night.

The flip side of this peacefulness must be boredom. That explains a lot of history and its rabid faiths, unfortunately.

December 10

Civilization thins steadily as we steam upriver. The mud brick villages typically have no electricity; there is ample power from Aswan, but the

144

power lines and stations are too expensive. One would think that, with the Quarthex gold, they could do better now.

Our guide says the Quarthex have been very hard-nosed—no pun intended—about such improvements. They will not let the earnings from their patents be used to modernize Egypt. Feeding the poor, cleaning the Nile, rebuilding monuments—all fine (in fact, they pay handsomely for restoring projects). But better electricity—no. A flat no.

We landed at a scruffy town and took a bus into the western desert. Only a kilometer from the flat floodplain, the Sahara is utterly barren and forbidding. We visited a Ptolemaic city of the dead. One tomb has a mummy of a girl who drowned trying to cross the Nile and see her lover, the hieroglyphs say. Nearby are catacombs of mummified baboons and ibises, symbols of wisdom.

A tunnel begins here, pointing SE toward Akhenaton's capital city. The German discoverers in the last century followed it for 40 kilometers—all cut through limestone, a gigantic task—before turning back because of bad air.

What was it for? Nobody knows. Dry, spooky atmosphere. Urns of desiccated mummies, undisturbed. To duck down a side corridor is to step into mystery.

I left the tour group and ambled over a low hill—to take a pee, actually. To the west was sand, sand, sand. I was standing there, doing my bit to hold off the dryness, when I saw one of those big black contraptions come slipping over the far horizon. Chuffing, chugging, and laying what looked like pipe—a funny kind of pipe, all silvery, with blue facets running through it. The glittering shifted, changing to yellows and reds while I watched.

A Quarthex riding atop it, of course. It ran due south, roughly parallel to the Nile. When I got back and told Joanna about it she looked at the map and we couldn't figure what would be out there of interest to anybody, even a Quarthex. No ruins around, nothing. Funny.

December 11

Beni Hassan, a nearly deserted site near the Nile. A steep walk up the escarpment of the eastern desert, after crossing the rich flood plain by donkey. The rock tombs have fine drawings and some statues—still left because they were cut directly from the mountain, and have thick wedges securing them to it. Guess the ancients would steal anything not nailed down. One thing about the Quarthex, the guide says—they take nothing. They seem genuinely interested in restoring, not in carting artifacts back home to their neck of the galactic spiral arm.

Upriver, we landfall beside a vast dust plain, which we crossed in a cart pulled by a tractor. The mud brick palaces of Akhenaton have vanished, except for a bit of Nefertiti's palace, where the famous bust of her was found. The royal tombs in the mountain above are defaced—big chunks pulled out of the walls by the priests who undercut his monotheist revolution, after his death.

The wall carvings are very realistic and warm; the women even have nipples. The tunnel from yesterday probably runs under here, perhaps connecting with the passageways we see deep in the king's grave shafts. Again, nobody's explored them thoroughly. There are narrow sections, possibly warrens for snakes or scorpions, maybe even traps.

While Joanna and I are ambling around, taking a few snaps of the carvings, I hear a rustle. Joanna has the flashlight and we peer over a ledge, down a straight shaft. At the bottom something is moving, something big.

It takes a minute to see that the reddish shell isn't a sarcophagus at all, but the back of a Quarthex. It's planting suckerlike things to the walls, threading cables through them. I can see more of the stuff farther back in the shadows.

The Quarthex looks up, into our flashlight beam, and scuttles away. Exploring the tunnels? But why did it move away so fast? What's to hide?

December 12

Cruise all day and watch the shore slide by.

Joanna is right; I needed this vacation a great deal. I can see that, rereading this journal—it gets looser as I go along.

As do I. When I consider how my life is spent, ere half my days, in this dark world and wide...

The pell-mell of university life dulls my sense of wonder, of simple pleasures simply taken. The Nile has a flowing, infinite quality, free of time. I can *feel* what it was like to live here, part of a great celestial clock that brought the perpetually turning sun and moon, the perennial rhythm of the flood. Aswan has interrupted the ebb and flow of the waters, but the steady force of the Nile rolls on.

> *Heaven smiles,*
> *and faiths and empires gleam,*
> *Like wrecks of a dissolving dream.*

The peacefulness permeates everything. Last night, making love to Joanna, was the best ever. Magnifique!

(And I know you're reading this, Joanna—I saw you sneak it out of the suitcase yesterday! Well, it *was* the best—quite a tribute, after all these years. And there's tomorrow and tomorrow…)

> *He who bends to himself a joy*
> *Does the winged life destroy;*
> *But he who kisses the joy as it flies*
> *Lives in eternity's sunrise.*

Perhaps next term I shall request the Romantic Poets course. Or even write some of my own…

Three Quarthex flew overhead today, carrying what look like ancient rams-head statues. The guide says statues were moved around a lot by the Arabs, and of course the archaeologists. The Quarthex have negotiated permission to take many of them back to their rightful places, if known.

December 13

Landfall at Abydos—a limestone temple miraculously preserved, its thick roof intact. Clusters of scruffy mud huts surround it, but do not diminish its obdurate rectangular severity.

The famous list of pharaohs, chiseled in a side corridor, is impressive in its sweep of time. Each little entry was a lordly pharaoh, and there is a whole wall jammed full of them. Egypt lasted longer than any comparable society, and the mass of names on that wall is even more impressive, since the temple builders did not even give it the importance of a central location.

The list omits Hatchepsut, a mere woman, and Akhenaton the scandalous monotheist. Rameses II had all carvings here cut deeply, particularly on the immense columns, to forestall defacement—a possibility he was much aware of, since he was busily doing it to his ancestor's temples. He chiseled away earlier work, adding his own cartouches, apparently thinking he could fool the gods themselves into believing he had built them all himself. Ah, immortality.

Had an earthquake today. Shades of California!

We were on the ship, Joanna dutifully padding back and forth on the main deck to work off the opulent lunch. We saw the palms waving ashore, and damned if there wasn't a small shock wave in the water, going east to west, and then a kind of low grumbling from the east. Guide says he's never seen anything like it.

And tonight, sheets of ruby light rising up from both east and west. Looked like an aurora, only the wrong directions. The rippling aura changed colors as it rose, then met overhead, burst into gold, and died. I'd swear I heard a high, keening note sound as the burnt-gold line flared and faded, flared and faded, spanning the sky.

Not many people on deck, though, so it didn't cause much comment. Joanna's theory is, it was a rocket exhaust.

An engineer says it looks like something to do with magnetic fields. I'm no scientist, but it seems to me whatever the Quarthex want to do, they can. Lords of space/time they called themselves in the diplomatic ceremonies. The United Nations representatives wrote that off as hyperbole, but the Quarthex may mean it.

December 14

Dendera. A vast temple, much less well known than Karnak, but quite as impressive. Quarthex there, digging at the foundations. Guide says they're looking for some secret passageways, maybe. The Egyptian gov't is letting them do what they damn well please.

On the way back to the ship we pass a whole mass of people, hundreds, all dressed in costumes. I thought it was some sort of pageant or tourist foolery, but the guide frowned, saying he didn't know what to make of it.

The mob was chanting something even the guide couldn't make out. He said the rough-cut cloth was typical of the old ways, made on crude spinning wheels. The procession was ragged, but seemed headed for the temple. They looked drunk to me.

The guide tells me that the ancients had a theology based on the Nile. This country is essentially ten kilometers wide and seven hundred kilometers long, a narrow band of livable earth pressed between two deadly deserts. So they believed the gods must have intended it, and that the Nile was the center of the whole damned world.

The sun came from the east, meaning that's where things began. Ending—dying—happened in the west, where the sun went. Thus they buried their dead on the west side of the Nile, even 7,000 years ago. At night, the sun swung below and lit the underworld, where everybody went finally. Kind of comforting, thinking of the sun doing duty like that for the dead. Only the virtuous dead, though. If you didn't follow the rules...

Some are born to sweet delight.
Some are born to endless night.

Their world was neatly bisected by the great river, and they loved clean divisions. They invented the 24 hour day but, loving symmetry, split it in half. Each of the 12 daylight hours was longer in summer than in winter—and, for night, vice versa. They built an entire nation-state, an immortal hand or eye, framing such fearful symmetry.

On to Karnak itself, mooring at Luxor. The middle and late pharaohs couldn't afford the labor investment for pyramids, so they contented themselves with additions to the huge sprawl at Karnak.

I wonder how long it will be before someone rich notices that for a few million or so he could build a tomb bigger than the Great Pyramid. It would only take a million or so limestone blocks—or, much better, granite—and could be better isolated and protected. If you can't conquer a continent or scribble a symphony, pile up a great stack of stones.

L'eterniti,
ne fut jamais perdue.

The light show this night at Karnak was spooky at times, and beautiful, with booming voices coming right out of the stones. Saw a Quarthex in the crowd. It stared straight ahead, not noticing anybody but not bumping into any humans, either.

It looked enthralled. The beady eyes, all four, scanned the shifting blues and burnt-oranges that played along the rising columns, the tumbled great statues. Its lubricating fluids made shiny reflections as it articulated forward, clacking in the dry night air. Somehow it was almost reverential. Rearing above the crowd, unmoving for long moments, it seemed more like the giant frozen figures in stone than like the mere mortals who swarmed around it, keeping a respectful distance, muttering to themselves.

Unnerving, somehow, to see

> ...*a subtler Sphinx renew*
> *Riddles of death Thebes never knew.*

December 15

A big day. The Valleys of the Queens, the Nobles, and finally of the Kings. Whew! All are dry washes (wadis), obviously easy to guard and isolate. Nonetheless, all of the 62 known tombs except Tut's were rifled, probably within a few centuries of burial. It must've been an inside job.

There is speculation that the robbing became a needed part of the economy, recycling the wealth, and providing gaudy displays for the next pharaoh to show off at *his* funeral, all the better to keep impressing the peasants. Just another part of the socio-economic machine, folks.

Later priests collected the pharaoh mummies and hid them in a cave nearby, realizing they couldn't protect the tombs. Preservation of Tuthmosis III is excellent. His hook-nosed mummy has been returned to its tomb—a big, deep thing, larger than our apartment, several floors in all, connected by ramps, with side treasuries, galleries, etc. The inscription above reads,

> *You shall live again forever.*

All picked clean, of course, except for the sarcophagus, too heavy to carry away. The pyramids had portcullises, deadfalls, pitfalls, and rolling stones to crush the unwary robber, but there are few here. Still, it's a little creepy to think of all those ancient engineers, planning to commit murder in the future, long after they themselves are gone, all to protect the past. Death, be not proud.

An afternoon of shopping in the bazaar. The old Victorian hotel on the river is atmospheric, but has few guests. Food continues good. No dysentery, either. We both took the EZ-DI bacteria before we left, so it's living down in our tracts, festering away, lying in wait for any ugly foreign bug. Comforting.

December 16

Cruise on. We stop at Kom Ombo, a temple to the crocodile god, Sebek, built to placate the crocs who swarmed in the river nearby. (The Nile is cleared of them now, unfortunately; they would've added some zest to the cruise...) A small room contains 98 mummified crocs, stacked like cordwood.

Cruised some more. A few km south, there were gangs of Egyptians working beside the river. Hauling blocks of granite down to the water, rolling them on logs. I stood on the deck, trying to figure out why they were using ropes and simple pulleys, and no powered machinery.

Then I saw a Quarthex near the top of the rise, where the blocks were being sawed out of the rock face. It reared up over the men, gesturing with those jerky arms, eyes glittering. It called out something in a halfway human voice, only in a language I didn't know. The guide came over, frowning, but he couldn't understand it, either.

The laborers were pulling ropes across ruts in the stone, feeding sand and water into the gap, cutting out blocks by sheer brute abrasion. It must take weeks to extract one at that rate! Farther along, others drove wooden planks down into the deep grooves, hammering them with crude wooden mallets. Then they poured water over the planks, and we could hear the stone pop open as the wood expanded, far down in the cut.

That's the way the ancients did it, the guide said kind of quietly. The Quarthex towered above the human teams, that jangling, harsh voice booming out over the water, each syllable lingering until the next joined it, blending in the dry air, hollow and ringing and remorseless.

NOTE ADDED LATER

Stopped at Edfu, a well preserved temple, buried 100 feet deep by Moslem garbage until the late 19th century. The best aspect of river cruising is pulling along a site, viewing it from the angles the river affords, and then stepping from your stateroom directly into antiquity, with nothing to intervene and break the mood.

Trouble is, this time a man in front of us goes off a way to photograph the ship, and suddenly something is rushing at him out of the weeds and the crew is yelling—it's a crocodile! The guy drops his camera and bolts.

The croc looks at all of us, snorts, and waddles back into the Nile. The guide is upset, maybe even more than the fellow who almost got turned into a free lunch. Who would introduce crocs back into the Nile?

December 17

Aswan. A clean, delightful town. The big dam just south of town is impressive, with its monument to Soviet excellence, etc. A hollow joke, considering how poor the USSR is today. They could use a loan from Egypt!

The unforeseen side effects, though—rising water table bringing more insects, rotting away the carvings in the temples, rapid silting up inside the dam itself, etc.—are getting important. They plan to dig a canal and drain a lot of the incoming new silt into the desert, make a huge farming valley with it, but I don't see how they can drain enough water to carry the dirt, and still leave much behind in the original dam.

The guide says they're having trouble with it.

We then fly south, to Abu Simbel. Lake Nasser, which claimed the original site of the huge monuments, is hundreds of miles long. They enlarged it again in 2008.

In the times of the pharaohs, the land below these had villages, great quarries for the construction of monuments, trade routes south to the Nubian kingdoms. Now it's all underwater.

They did save the enormous temples to Rameses II—built to impress aggressive Nubians with his might and majesty—and to his queen, Nefertari. The colossal statues of Rameses II seem personifications of his egomania. Inside, carvings show him performing *all* the valiant tasks in the great battle with the Hittites—slaying, taking prisoners, then presenting them to himself, who is in turn advised by the gods—which include himself! All this, for a battle which was in fact an iffy draw. Both temples have been lifted about a hundred feet and set back inside a wholly artificial hill, supported inside by the largest concrete dome in the world. Amazing.

> *Look upon my works, ye Mighty,*
> *and despair!*

Except that when Shelley wrote *Ozymandias*, he'd never seen Rameses II's image so well preserved.

Leaving the site, eating the sand blown into our faces by a sudden gust of wind, I caught sight of a Quarthex. It was burrowing into the sand, using a silvery tool that spat ruby-colored light. Beside it, floating on a platform, were some of those funny pipelike things I'd seen days before.

Only this time men and women were helping it, lugging stuff around to put into the holes the Quarthex dug.

The people looked dazed, like they were sleep-walking. I waved a greeting, but nobody even looked up. Except the Quarthex. They're expressionless, of course. Still, those glittering popeyes peered at me for a long moment, with the little feelers near its mouth twitching with a kind of anxious energy.

I looked away. I couldn't help but feel a little spooked by it. It wasn't looking at us in a friendly way. Maybe it didn't want me yelling at its work gang.

Then we flew back to Aswan, above the impossibly narrow ribbon of green that snakes through absolute bitter desolation.

December 18

I'm writing this at twilight, before the light gives out. We got up this morning and were walking into town when the whole damn ground started to rock. Mud huts slamming down, waves on the Nile, everything.

Got back to the ship but nobody knew what was going on. Not much on the radio. Cairo came in clear, saying there'd been a quake all right, all along the Nile.

Funny thing was, the captain couldn't raise any other radio station. Just Cairo. Nothing else in the whole Middle East.

Some other passengers think there's a war on. Maybe so, but the Egyptian army doesn't know about it. They're standing around, all along the quay, fondling their AK 47s, looking just as puzzled as we are.

More rumblings and shakings in the afternoon. And now that the sun's about gone, I can see big sheets of light in the sky. Only it seems to me the constellations aren't right.

Joanna took some of her pills. She's trying to fend off the jitters and I do what I can. I hate the empty, hollow look that comes into her eyes.

We've got to get the hell out of here.

December 19

I might as well write this down, there's nothing else to do.

When we got up this morning the sun was there all right, but the moon hadn't gone down. And it didn't, all day.

Sure, they can both be in the sky at the same time. But all day? Joanna is worried, not because of the moon, but because all the airline flights have been cancelled. We were supposed to go back to Cairo today.

More earthquakes. Really bad this time.

At noon, all of a sudden, there were Quarthex everywhere. In the air, swarming in from the east and west. Some splashed down in the Nile—and didn't come up. Others zoomed overhead, heading south toward the dam.

Nobody's been brave enough to leave the ship—including me. Hell, I just want to go home. Joanna's staying in the cabin.

About an hour later, a swarthy man in a ragged gray suit comes running along the quay and says the dam's gone. Just *gone*. The Quarthex formed little knots above it, and there was a lot of purple flashing light and big crackling noises, and then the dam just disappeared.

But the water hasn't come pouring down on us here. The man says it ran *back the other way*. South.

I looked over the rail. The Nile was flowing north.

Late this afternoon, five of the crew went into town. By this time there were fingers of orange and gold zapping across the sky all the time, making weird designs. The clouds would come rolling in from the north, and these radiant beams would hit them, and they'd *split* the clouds, just like that. With a spray of ivory light.

And Quarthex, buzzing everywhere. There's a kind of high sheen, up above the clouds, like a metal boundary or something, but you can see through it.

Quarthex keep zipping up to it, sometimes coming right up out of the Nile itself, just splashing out, then zooming up until they're little dwindling dots. They spin around up there, as if they're inspecting it, and then they drop like bricks, and splash down in the Nile again. Like frantic bees, Joanna said, and her voice trembled.

A technical type on board, an engineer from Rockwell, says *he* thinks the Quarthex are putting on one hell of a light show. Just a weird alien stunt, he thinks.

While I was writing this, the five crewmen returned from Aswan. They'd gone to the big hotels there, and then to police headquarters. They heard that TV from Cairo went out two days ago. All air flights have been grounded because of the Quarthex buzzing around and the odd lights and so on.

Or at least, that's the official line. The captain says his cousin told him that several flights *did* take off two days back, and they hit something up there. Maybe that blue metallic sheen?

One crashed. The others landed, although damaged.

The authorities are keeping it quiet. They're not just keeping us tourists in the dark—they're playing mum with everybody.

I hope the engineer is right. Joanna is fretting and we hardly ate anything for dinner, just picked at the cold lamb. Maybe tomorrow will settle things.

December 20

It did. When we woke, the Earth was rising.

It was coming up from the western mountains, blue-white clouds and patches of green and brown, but mostly tawny desert. We're looking west, across the Sahara. I'm writing this while everybody else is running around like a chicken with his head chopped off. I'm sitting on deck, listening to shouts and wild traffic and even some gunshots coming from ashore.

I can see farther east now—either we're turning, or we're rising fast and can see with a better perspective.

Where central Egypt was, there's a big, raw, dark hole.

The black must be the limestone underlying the desert. They've scraped off a rim of sandy margin enclosing the Nile valley, including us—and left the rest. And somehow, they're lifting it free of Earth.

No Quarthex flying around now. Nothing visible except that metallic blue smear of light high up in the air.

And beyond it—Earth, rising.

December 22

I skipped a day.

There was no time even to think yesterday. After I wrote the last entry, a crowd of Egyptians came down the quay, shuffling silently along, like the ones we saw back at Abu Simbel. Only there were thousands.

And leading them was a Quarthex. It carried a big disclike thing that made a humming sound. When the Quarthex lifted it, the pitch changed.

It made my eyes water, my skull ache. Like a hand squeezing my head, blurring the air.

Around me, everybody was writhing on the deck, moaning. Joanna, too.

By the time the Quarthex reached our ship I was the only one standing. Those yellow-shot, jittery eyes peered at me, giving nothing away. Then the angular head turned and went on. Pied piper, leading long trains of Egyptians.

Some of our friends from the ship joined at the end of the lines. Rigid, glassy-eyed faces. I shouted but nobody, not a single person in that procession, even looked up.

Joanna struggled to go with them. I threw her down and held her until the damned eerie parade was long past.

Now the ship's deserted. We've stayed aboard, out of pure fear.

Whatever the Quarthex did affects all but a few percent of those within range. A few crew stayed aboard, dazed but ok. Scared, hard to talk to.

Fewer at dinner.

The next morning, nobody.

We had to scavenge for food. The crew must've taken what was left aboard. I ventured into the market street nearby, but everything was closed up. Deserted. Only a few days ago we were buying caftans and alabaster sphinxes and beaten-bronze trinkets in the gaudy shops, and now it was stone cold dead. Not a sound, not a stray cat.

I went around to the back of what I remembered was a filthy corner cafe. I'd turned up my nose at it while we were shopping, certain there was a sure case of dysentery waiting inside…but now I was glad to find some days-old fruits and vegetables in a cabinet.

Coming back, I nearly ran into a bunch of Egyptian men who were marching through the streets. Spooks.

They had the look of police, but were dressed up like Mardi Gras— loincloths, big leather belts, bangles and beads, hair stiffened with wax. They carried sharp spears.

Good thing I was jumpy, or they'd have run right into me. I heard them coming and ducked into a grubby alley. They were systematically combing the area, searching the miserable apartments above the market. The honcho barked orders in a language I didn't understand—harsh, guttural, not like Egyptian.

I slipped away. Barely.

We kept out of sight after that. Stayed below deck and waited for nightfall.

Not that the darkness made us feel any better. There were fires ashore. Not in Aswan itself—the town was utterly black. Instead, orange dots sprinkled the distant hillsides. They were all over the scrub desert, just before the ramparts of the real desert that stretches—or did stretch—to east and west.

Now, I guess, there's only a few dozen miles of desert, before you reach—what?

I can't discuss this with Joanna. She has that haunted expression, from the time before her breakdown. She is drawn and silent. Stays in the room.

We ate our goddamn vegetables. Now we go to bed.

December 23

There were more of those patrols of Mardi Gras spooks today. They came along the quay, looking at the tour ships moored there, but for some reason they didn't come aboard.

We're alone on the ship. All the crew, the other tourists—all gone.

Around noon, when we were getting really hungry and I was mustering my courage to go back to the market street, I heard a roaring.

Understand, I hadn't heard an airplane in days. And those were jets. This buzzing, I suddenly realized, is a rocket or something, and it's in trouble.

I go out on the deck, checking first to see if the patrols are lurking around, and the roaring is louder. It's a plane with stubby little wings, coming along low over the water, burping and hacking and finally going dead quiet.

It nosed over and came in for a big splash. I thought the pilot was a goner, but the thing rode steady in the water for a while and the cockpit folded back and out jumps a man.

I yelled at him and he waved and swam for the ship. The plane sank.

He caught a line below and climbed up. An American, no less. But what he had to say was even more surprising.

He wasn't just some sky jockey from Cairo. He was an astronaut.

He was part of a rescue mission, sent up to try to stop the Quarthex. The others he'd lost contact with, although it looked like they'd all been drawn down toward the floating island that Egypt has become.

We're suspended about two Earth radii out, in a slowly widening orbit. There's a shield over us, keeping the air in and everything—cosmic rays, communications, spaceships—out.

The Quarthex somehow ripped off a layer of Egypt and are lifting it free of Earth, escaping with it. Nobody had ever guessed they had such power. Nobody Earthside knows what to do about it. The Quarthex who were outside Egypt at the time just lifted off in their ships and rendezvoused with this floating platform.

Ralph Blanchard is his name, and his mission was to fly under the slab of Egypt, in a fast orbital craft. He was supposed to see how they'd ripped the land free. A lot of it had fallen away.

There is an array of silvery pods under the soil, he says, and they must be enormous anti-grav units. The same kind that make the Quarthex ships fly, that we've been trying to get the secret of.

The pods are about a mile apart, making a grid. But between them, there are lots of Quarthex. They're building stuff, tilling soil, and so on—upside down! The gravity works opposite on the underside. That must be the way the whole thing is kept together—compressing it with artificial gravity from both sides. God knows what makes the shield above.

But the really strange thing is the Nile. There's one on the underside, too.

It starts at the underside of Alexandria, where *our* Nile meets—met—the Mediterranean. It then flows back, all the way along the underside, running through a Nile valley of its own. Then it turns up and around the edge of the slab, and comes over the lip of it a few hundred miles upstream of here.

The Quarthex have drained the region beyond the Aswan dam. Now the Nile flows in its old course. The big temples of Rameses II are perched on a hill high above the river, and Ralph was sure he saw Quarthex working on the site, taking it apart.

He thinks they're going to put it back where it was, before the dam was built in the 1960s.

Ralph was supposed to return to Orbital City with his data. He came in close for a final pass and hit the shield they have, the one that keeps the air in. His ship was damaged.

He'd been issued a suborbital craft, able to do reentries, in case he could penetrate the airspace. That saved him. There were other guys who hit the shield and cracked through, guys with conventional deepspace shuttle tugs and the like, and they fell like bricks.

We've talked all this over but no one has a good theory of what is going on. The best we can do is stay away from the patrols.

Meanwhile, Joanna scavenged through obscure bins of the ship, and turned up an entire case of Skivva, a cheap Egyptian beer. So after I finish this ritual entry—who knows, this might be in a history book someday, and as a good academic I should keep it up—I'll go share it out in one grand bust with Ralph and Joanna. It'll do her good. It'll do us both good. She's been rocky. As well,

Malt does more than Milton can
To justify God's ways to man.

December 24

This little diary was all I managed to take with us when the spooks came. I had it in my pocket.

I keep going over what happened. There was nothing I could do, I'm sure of that, and yet...

We stayed below decks, getting damned hungry again but afraid to go out. There was chanting from the distance. Getting louder. Then footsteps aboard. We retreated to the small cabins aft, third class.

The sounds got nearer. Ralph thought we should stand and fight but I'd seen those spears and hell, I'm a middle-aged man, no match for those maniacs.

Joanna got scared. It was like her breakdown. No, worse. The jitters built until her whole body seemed to vibrate, fingers digging into her hair like claws, eyes squeezed tight, face compressed as if to shut out the world.

There was nothing I could do with her, she wouldn't keep quiet. She ran out of the cabin we were hiding in, just rushed down the corridor screaming at them.

Ralph said we should use her diversion to get away and I said I'd stay, help her, but then I saw them grab her and hold her, not rough. It didn't seem as if they were going to do anything, just take her away.

My fear got the better of me then. It's hard to write this. Part of me says I should've stayed, defended her—but it was hopeless. You can't live up to your ideal self. The world of literature shows people summoning up courage, but there's a thin line between that and stupidity. Or so I tell myself.

The spooks hadn't seen us yet, so we slipped overboard, keeping quiet.

We went off the loading ramp on the river side, away from shore. Ralph paddled around to see the quay and came back looking worried. There were spooks swarming all over.

We had to move. The only way to go was across the river.

This shaky handwriting is from sheer, flat-out fatigue. I swam what seemed like forever. The water wasn't bad, pretty warm, but the current kept pushing us off course. Lucky thing the Nile is pretty narrow there, and there are rocky little stubs sticking out. I grabbed onto those and rested.

Nobody saw us, or at least they didn't do anything about it.

We got ashore looking like drowned rats. There's a big hill there, covered with ancient rock-cut tombs. I thought of taking shelter in one of them and started up the hill, legs wobbly under me, and then we saw a mob up top.

And a Quarthex, a big one with a shiny shell. It wore something over its head. Supposedly Quarthex don't wear clothes, but this one had a funny rig on. A big bird head, with a long narrow beak and flinty black eyes.

There was madness all around us. Long lines of people carrying burdens, chanting. Quarthex riding on those lifter units of theirs. All beneath the piercing, biting sun.

We hid for a while. I found that this diary, in its zippered leather case, made it through the river without a leak. I started writing this entry. Joanna said once that I'd retreated into books as a defense, in adolescence—she was full of psychoanalytical explanations, it was a hobby. She kept thinking that if she could figure herself out, then things would be all right. Well, maybe I did use words and books and a quiet, orderly life as a place to hide. So what? It was better than this "real" world around me right now.

I thought of Joanna and what might be happening to her. The Quarthex can—

(New Entry)

I was writing when the Quarthex came closer. I thought we were finished, but they didn't see us. Those huge heads turned all the time, the glittering black eyes scanning. Then they moved away. The chanting was a relentless, singsong drone that gradually faded.

We got away from there, fast.

I'm writing this during a short break. Then we'll move on. No place to go but the goddamn desert.

December 25

Christmas.

I keep thinking about fat turkey stuffed with spicy dressing, crisp cranberries, a dry white wine, thick gravy—

No point in that. We found some food today in an abandoned construction site, bread at least a week old and some dried-up fruit. That was all.

Ralph kept pushing me on west. He wants to see over the edge, how they hold this thing together.

I'm not that damn interested, but I don't know where else to go. Just running on blind fear. My professorial instincts—like keeping this journal. It helps keep me sane. Assuming I still am.

Ralph says putting this down might have scientific value. If I can ever get it to anybody outside. So I keep on. Words, words, words. Much cleaner than this gritty, surreal world.

We saw people marching in the distance, dressed in loincloths again. It suddenly struck me that I'd seen that clothing before—in those marvelous wall paintings, in the tombs of the Valley of Kings. It's ancient dress.

Ralph thinks he understands what's happening. There was an all-frequencies broadcast from the Quarthex when they tore off this wedge we're on. Nobody understood much—it was in that odd semi-speech of theirs, all the words blurred and placed wrong, scrambled up. Something about their mission or destiny or whatever being to enhance the best in each world. About how they'd made a deal with the Egyptians to bring forth the unrealized promise of their majestic past and so on. And that meant isolation, so the fruit of ages could flower.

Ha. The world's great age begins anew, maybe—but Percy Bysshe Shelley never meant it like this.

Not that I care a lot about motivations right now. I spent the day thinking of Joanna, still feeling guilty. And hiking west in the heat and dust, hiding from gangs of glassy-eyed workers when we had to.

We reached the edge at sunset. It hadn't occurred to me, but it's obvious—for there to be days and nights at all means they're spinning the slab we're on.

Compressing it, holding in the air, adding just the right rotation. Masters—of space/time and the river, yes.

The ground started to slope away. Not like going downhill, because there was nothing pulling you down the face of it. I mean, we *felt* like we were walking on level ground. But overhead the sky moved as we walked.

We caught up with the sunset. The sun dropped for a while in late afternoon, then started rising again. Pretty soon it was right overhead, high noon.

And we could see Earth, too, farther away than yesterday. Looking cool and blue.

We came to a wall of glistening metal tubes, silvery and rippling with a frosty blue glow. I started to get woozy as we approached. Something happened to gravity—it pulled your stomach as if you were spinning around. Finally we couldn't get any closer. I stopped, nauseated. Ralph kept on. I watched him try to walk toward the metal barrier, which by then looked like luminous icebergs suspended above barren desert.

He tried to walk a straight line, he said later. I could see him veer, his legs rubbery, and it looked as though he rippled and distended, stretching horizontally while some force compressed him vertically, an egg man, a plastic body swaying in tides of gravity.

Then he starting stumbling, falling. He cried out—a horrible, warped sound, like paper tearing for a long, long time. He fled. The sand clawed at him as he ran, strands grasping at his feet, trailing long streamers of glittering, luminous sand—but it couldn't hold him. Ralph staggered away, gasping, his eyes huge and white and terrified.

We turned back.

But coming away, I saw a band of men and women marching woodenly along toward the wall. They were old, most of them, and diseased. Some had been hurt—you could see the wounds.

They were heading straight for the lip. Silent, inexorable.

Ralph and I followed them for a while. As they approached the wall, they started walking up off the sand—right into the air.

And over the tubes.

Just flying.

We decided to head south. Maybe the lip is different there. Ralph says the plan he'd heard, after the generals had studied the survey-mission results, was to try to open the shield at the ground, where the Nile spills over. Then they'd get people out by boating them along the river.

Could they be doing that, now? We hear roaring sounds in the sky sometimes. Explosions. Ralph is ironic about it all, says he wonders when the Quarthex will get tired of intruders and go back to the source—*all* the way back.

I don't know. I'm tired and worn down.

Could there be a way out? Sounds impossible, but it's all we've got.

Head south, to the Nile's edge.

We're hiding in a cave tonight. It's bitterly cold out here in the desert, and a sunburn is no help.

I'm hungry as hell. Some Christmas. We were supposed to be back in Laguna Beach by now.

God knows where Joanna is.

December 26

I got away. Barely.

The Quarthex work in teams now. They've gridded off the desert and work across it systematically in those floating platforms. There are big tubes like cannon mounted on each end and a Quarthex scans it over the sands.

Ralph and I crept up to the mouth of the cave we were in and watched them comb the area. They worked out from the Nile. When a muzzle turned toward us I felt an impact like a warm, moist wave smacking into my face, like being in the ocean. It drove me to my knees. I reeled away. Threw myself farther back into the cramped cave.

It all dropped away then, as if the wave had pinned me to the ocean floor and filled my lungs with a sluggish liquid.

And in an instant was gone. I rolled over, gasping, and saw Ralph staggering into the sunlight, heading for the Quarthex platform. The projector was leveled at him so that it no longer struck the cave mouth. So I'd been released from its grip.

I watched them lower a rope ladder. Ralph dutifully climbed up. I wanted to shout to him, try to break the hold that thing had over him, but once again the better part of valor—I just watched. They carried him away.

I waited until twilight to move. Not having anybody to talk to makes it harder to control my fear.

God I'm hungry. Couldn't find a scrap to eat.

When I took out this diary I looked at the leather case and remembered stories of people getting so starved they'd eat their shoes. Suitably boiled and salted, of course, with a tangy sauce.

Another day or two and the idea might not seem so funny.

I've got to keep moving.

December 27

Hard to write.

They got me this morning.

It grabs your mind. Like before. Squeezing in your head.

But after a while it is better. Feels good. But a buzzing all the time, you can't think.

Picked me up while I was crossing an arroyo. Didn't have any idea they were around. A platform.

Took me to some others. All Egyptians. Caught like me.

Marched us to the Nile.

Plenty to eat.

Rested at noon.

Brought Joanna to me. She is all right. Lovely in the long draping dress the Quarthex gave her.

All around are the bird-headed ones. Ibis, I remember, the bird of the Nile. And dog-headed ones. Lion-headed ones.

Gods of the old times. The Quarthex are the gods of the old time. Of the greater empire.

We are the people.

Sometimes I can think, like now. They sent me away from the work gang on an errand. I am old, not strong. They are kind—give me easy jobs.

So I came to here. Where I hid this diary. Before they took my old uncomfortable clothes I put this little book into a crevice in the rock. Pen too.

Now writing helps. Mind clears some.

I saw Ralph, then lost track of him. I worked hard after the noontime. Sun felt good. I lifted pots, carried them where the foreman said.

The Quarthex-god with ibis head is building a fresh temple. Made from the stones of Aswan. It will be cool and deep, many pillars.

They took my dirty clothes. Gave me fresh loincloth, headband, sandals. Good ones. Better than my old clothes.

It is hard to remember how things were before I came here. Before I knew the river. Its flow. How it divides the world.

I will rest before I try to read what I have written in here before. The words are hard.

Days Later

I come back but can read only a little.

Joanna says you should not. The ibis will not like it if I do.

I remember I liked these words on paper, in my days before. I earned my food with them. Now they are empty. Must not have been true.

Do not need them any more.

Ralph, science. All words too.

Later

Days since I find this again. I do the good work, I eat, Joanna is there in the night. Many things. I do not want to do this reading.

But today another thing howled overhead. It passed over the desert like a screaming black bird, the falcon, and then fell, flames, big roar.

I remembered Ralph.

This book I remembered, came for it.

The ibis-god speaks to us each sunset. Of how the glory of our lives is here again. We are one people once more again yes after a long long time of being lost.

What the red sunset means. The place where the dead are buried in the western desert. To be taken in death close to the edge, so the dead will walk their last steps in this world, to the lip and over, to the netherworld.

There the lion-god will preserve them. Make them live again.

The Quarthex-gods have discovered how to revive the dead of any beings. They spread this among the stars.

But only to those who understand. Who deserve. Who bow to the great symmetry of life.

One face light, one face dark.

The sun lights the netherworld when for us it is night. There the dead feast and mate and laugh and live forever.

Ralph saw that. The happy land below. It shares the sun.

I saw Ralph today. He came to the river to see the falcon thing cry from the clouds. We all did.

It fell into the river and was swallowed and will be taken to the netherworld where it flows over the edge of the world.

Ralph was sorry when the falcon fell. He said it was a mistake to send it to bother us. That someone from the old dead time had sent it.

Ralph works in the quarry. Carving the limestone. He looks good, the sun has lain on him and made him strong and brown.

I started to talk of the time we met but he frowned. That was before we understood, he says. Shook his head. So I should not speak of it. The gods know of time and the river. They know. I tire now.

Again

Joanna sick. I try help but no way to stop the bleeding from her.

In old time I would try to stop the stuff of life from leaving her. I would feel sorrow. I do not now. I am calm.

Ibis-god prepares her. Works hard and good over her.

She will journey tonight. Walk the last trek. Over the edge of the sky and to the netherland.

It is what the temple carving says. She will live again forever.

Forever waits.

I come here to find this book to enter this. I remember sometimes how it was.

I did not know joy then. Joanna did not.

We lived but to no point. Just come-go-come-again.

Now I know what comes. The western death. The rising life.

The Quarthex-gods are right. I should forget that life. To hold on is to die. To flow forward is to live.

Today I saw the pharaoh. He came in radiant chariot, black horses before, bronze sword in hand. The sun was high above him. No shadow he cast.

Big and with red skin the pharaoh rode down the avenue of the kings. We the one people cheered.

His great head was mighty in the sun and his many arms waved in salute to his one people. He is so great the horses groan and sweat to pull him. His hard gleaming body is all armor for he will always be on guard against our enemies.

Like those who fall from the sky. Every day now more come down, dying fireballs to smash in the desert. All fools. Black rotting bodies. None will rise to walk west. They are only burned prey of the pharaoh.

The pharaoh rode three times on the avenue. We threw ourselves down to attract a glance. His huge glaring eyes regarded us and we cried out, our faces wet with joy.

He will speak for us in the netherworld. Sing to the undergods.

Make our westward walking path smooth.

I fall before him.

I bury this now. No more write in it.

This kind of writing is not for the world now. It comes from the old dead time when I knew nothing and thought everything.

I go to my eternity on the river.

TIME'S RUB
(1985)

1.

At Earth's winter ebb, two crabbed figures slouched across a dry, cracked plain.

Running before a victor who was himself slow-dying, the dead-stench of certain destiny cloyed to them. They knew it. Yet kept on, grinding over plum-colored shales.

They shambled into a pitwallow for shelter, groaning, carapaces grimed and discolored. The smaller of them, Xen, turned toward the minimal speck of burnt-yellow sun, but gained little aid through its battered external panels. It grasped Faz's extended pincer—useless now, mauled in battle—and murmured of fatigue.

"We can't go on."

Faz, grimly: "We must."

Xen was a functionary, an analytical sort. It had chanced to flee the battle down the same gully as Faz, the massive, lumbering leader. Xen yearned to see again its mate, Pymr, but knew this for the forlorn dream it was.

They crouched down. Their enemies rumbled in nearby ruined hills. A brown murk rose from those distant movements. The sun's pale eye stretched long shadows across the plain, inky hiding places for the encroaching others.

Thus when the shimmering curtains of ivory luminescence began to fog the hollow, Xen thought the end was here—that energy drain blurred its brain, and now brought swift, cutting death.

Fresh in from the darkling plain? the voice said. Not acoustically—this was a Vac Zone, airless for millennia.

"What? Who's that?" Faz answered.

Your ignorant armies clashed last night?

"Yes," Xen acknowledged ruefully, "and were defeated. Both sides lost."

Often the case.

"Are the Laggenmorphs far behind us?" Faz asked, faint tracers of hope skating crimson in its spiky voice.

No. They approach. They have tracked your confused alarms of struggle and flight.

"We had hoped to steal silent."

Your rear guard made a melancholy, long, withdrawing roar.

Xen: "They escaped?"

Into the next world, yes.

"Oh."

"Who *is* that?" Faz insisted, clattering its treads.

A wraith. Glittering skeins danced around them. A patchy acrid tang laced the curling vacuum. **In this place having neither brass, nor earth, nor boundless sea.**

"Come out!" Faz called at three gigaHertz. "We can't see you."

Need you?

"Are you Laggenmorphs?" Panic laded Faz's carrier wave a bright, fervid orange. "We'll fight, I warn you!"

"Quiet," Xen said, suspecting.

The descending dazzle thickened, struck a bass note. **Laggenmorphs? I do not even know your terms.**

"Your name, then," Xen said.

Sam.

"What's that? That's no name!" Faz declared, its voice a shifting brew of fear and anger.

Sam it was and Sam it is. Not marble, nor the gilded monuments of princes, shall outlive it.

Xen murmured at a hundred kiloHertz, "Traditional archaic name. I dimly remember something of the sort. I doubt it's a trap."

The words not yet free of its antenna, Xen ducked—for a relativistic beam passed not a kilometer away, snapping with random rage. It forked to a ruined scree of limestone and erupted into a self-satisfied yellow geyser. Stones pelted the two hunkering forms, clanging.

A mere stochastic volley. Your sort do expend energies wildly. That is what first attracted me.

Surly, Faz snapped. "You'll get no surge from us."

I did not come to sup. I came to proffer.

A saffron umbra surrounded the still-gathering whorls of crackling, clotted iridescence.

"Where're you hiding?" Faz demanded. It brandished blades, snouts, cutters, spikes, double-bore nostrils that could spit lurid beams.

In the cupped air.

"There *is* no air," Xen said. "This channel is open to the planetary currents."

Xen gestured upward with half-shattered claw. There, standing in space, the playing tides of blue-white, gauzy light showed that they were at the base of a great translucent cylinder. Its geometric perfection held back the moist air of Earth, now an ocean tamed by skewered forces. On the horizon, at the glimmering boundary, purpling clouds nudged futilely at their constraint like hungry cattle. This cylinder led the eye up to a vastness, the stars a stilled snowfall. Here the thin but persistent wind from the sun could have free run, gliding along the orange-slice sections of the Earth's dipolar magnetic fields. The winds crashed down, sputtering, delivering kiloVolt glories where the cylinder cut them. Crackling yellow sparks grew there, a forest with all trunks ablaze and branches of lightning, beckoning far aloft like a brilliantly lit casino in a gray dark desert.

How well I know. I stem from fossiled days.

"Then why—"

This is my destiny and my sentence.

"To live here?" Faz was beginning to suspect as well.

For a wink or two of eternity.

"Can you..." Faz poked the sky with a horned, fused launcher. "...reach up there? Get us a jec?"

I do not know the term.

Xen said, "An injection. A megaVolt, say, at a hundred kiloAmps. A mere microsecond would boost me again. I could get my crawlers working."

I would have to extend my field lines.

"So it *is* true," Xen said triumphantly. "There still dwell Ims on the Earth. And you're one."

Again, the term—

"An Immortal. You have the fieldcraft."

Yes.

Xen knew of this, but had thought it mere legend. All material things were mortal. Cells were subject to intruding impurities, cancerous insults, a thousand coarse alleyways of accident. Machines, too, knew rust and wear, could suffer the ruthless scrubbing of their memories by a random bolt of electromagnetic violence. Hybrids, such as Xen and Faz, shared both half-worlds of erosion.

But there was a Principle which evaded time's rub. Order could be imposed on electrical currents—much as words rode on radio waves—and then the currents could curve into self-involved equilibria. If spun just so, the mouth of a given stream eating its own tail, then a spinning ring generated its own magnetic fields. Such work was simple. Little children made these loops, juggled them into humming fireworks.

Only genius could knit these current whorls into a fully contorted globe. The fundamental physics sprang from ancient Man's bottling of thermonuclear fusion in magnetic strands. That was a simple craft, using brute magnets and artful metallic vessels. Far harder, to apply such learning to wisps of plasma alone.

The Principle stated that if, from the calm center of such a weave, the magnetic field always increased, in all directions, then it was stable to all manner of magnetohydrodynamic pinches and shoves.

The Principle was clear, but stitching the loops—history had swallowed that secret. A few had made the leap, been translated into surges of magnetic field. They dwelled in the Vac Zones, where the rude bump of air molecules could not stir their calm currents. Such were the Ims.

"You...live forever?" Xen asked wonderingly.

Aye, a holy spinning toroid—when I rest. Otherwise, distorted, as you see me now. Phantom shoots of burnt yellow. **What once was Man, is now aurora—where winds don't sing, the sun's a tarnished nickel, the sky's a blank rebuke.**

Abruptly, a dun-colored javelin shot from nearby ruined hills, vectoring on them.

"Laggenmorphs!" Faz sent. "I have no defense."

Halfway to them, the lance burst into scarlet plumes. The flames guttered out.

A cacophony of eruptions spat from their left. Gray forms leapt forward, sending scarlet beams and bursts. Sharp metal cut the smoking stones.

172

"Pymr, sleek and soft, I loved you," Xen murmured, thinking this was the end.

But from the space around the Laggenmorphs condensed a chalky stuff—smothering, consuming. The forms fell dead.

I saved you.

Xen bowed, not knowing how to thank a wisp. But the blur of nearing oblivion weighed like stone.

"Help us!" Faz's despair lanced like pain through the dead vacuum. "We need energy."

You would have me tick over the tilt of Earth, run through solstice, bring ringing summer in an hour?

Xen caught in the phosphorescent stipple a green underlay of irony.

"No, no!" Faz spurted. "Just a jec. We'll go on then."

I can make you go on forever.

The flatness of it, accompanied by phantom shoots of scorched orange, gave Xen pause. "You mean…the fieldcraft? Even I know such lore is not lightly passed on. Too many Ims, and the Earth's magnetic zones will be congested."

I grow bored, encased in this glassy electromagnetic shaft. I have not conferred the fieldcraft in a long while. Seeing you come crawling from your mad white chaos, I desired company. I propose a Game.

"Game?" Faz was instantly suspicious. "Just a jec, Im, that's all we want."

You may have that as well.

"What're you spilling about?" Faz asked.

Xen said warily, "It's offering the secret."

"What?" Faz laughed dryly, a flat cynical burst that rattled down the frequencies.

Faz churned an extruded leg against the grainy soil, wasting energy in its own consuming bitterness. It had sought fame, dominion, a sliver of history. Its divisions had been chewed and spat out again by the Laggenmorphs, its feints ignored, bold strokes adroitly turned aside. Now it had to fly vanquished beside the lesser Xen, dignity gathered like tattered dress about its fleeing ankles.

"Ims never share *that*. A dollop, a jec, sure—but not the turns of fieldcraft." To show it would not be fooled, Faz spat chalky ejecta at a nearby streamer of zinc-laden light.

I offer you my Game.

The sour despair in Faz spoke first. "Even if we believe that, how do we know you don't cheat?"

No answer. But from the high hard vault there came descending a huge ribbon of ruby light—snaking, flexing, writing in strange tongues on the emptiness as it approached, fleeting messages of times gone—auguries of innocence lost, missions forgot, dim songs of the wide world and all its fading sweets. The ruby snake split, rumbled, turned eggshell blue, split and spread and forked down, blooming into a hemisphere around them. It struck and ripped the rock, spitting fragments over their swiveling heads, booming. Then prickly silence.

"I see," Xen said.

Thunder impresses, but it's lightning does the work.

"Why should the Im cheat, when it could short us to ground, fry us to slag?" Xen sent to Faz on tightband.

"Why anything?" Faz answered, but there was nodding in the tone.

2.

The Im twisted the local fields and caused to appear, hovering in fried light, two cubes—one red, one blue.

You may choose to open either the Blue cube alone, or both.

Though brightened by a borrowed kiloAmp jolt from Xen, Faz had expended many Joules in irritation and now flagged. "What's...in... them?"

Their contents are determined by what I have already predicted. I have already placed your rewards inside. You can choose Red and Blue both, if you want. In that case, following my prediction, I have placed in the Red cube the bottled-up injection you wanted.

Faz unfurled a metallic tentacle for the Red cube.

Wait. If you will open both boxes, then I have placed in the Blue nothing—nothing at all.

Faz said, "Then I get the jec in the Red cube, and when I open the Blue—nothing."

Correct.

Xen asked, "What if Faz *doesn't* open both cubes?"

The only other option is to open the Blue alone.

"And I get nothing?" Faz asked.

No. In that case, I have placed the, ah, "jec" in the Red cube. But in the Blue I have put the key to my own fieldcraft—the designs for immortality.

"I don't get it. I open Red, I get my jec—right?" Faz said, sudden interest giving it a spike of scarlet brilliance at three gigaHertz. "Then I open Blue, I get immortality. That's what I want."

True. But in that case, I have predicted that you will pick both cubes. Therefore, I have left the Blue cube empty.

Faz clattered its treads. "I get immortality if I choose the Blue cube *alone*? But you have to have *predicted* that. Otherwise I get nothing."

Yes.

Xen added, "*If* you have predicted things perfectly."

But I always do.

"Always?"

Nearly always. I am immortal, ageless—but not God. Not...yet.

"What if I pick Blue and you're wrong?" Faz asked. "Then I get nothing."

True. But highly improbable.

Xen saw it. "All this is done *now*? You've already made your prediction? Placed the jec or the secret—or both—in the cubes?"

Yes. I made my predictions before I even offered the Game.

Faz asked, "What'd you predict?"

Merry pink laughter chimed across the slumbering megaHertz. **I will not say. Except that I predicted correctly that you both would play, and that you particularly would ask that question. Witness.**

A sucking jolt lifted Faz from the stones and deposited it nearby. Etched in the rock beneath where Faz had crouched was *What did you predict?* in a rounded, careful hand.

"It had to have been done during the overhead display, before the game began," Xen said wonderingly.

"The Im *can* predict," Faz said respectfully.

Xen said, "Then the smart move is to open both cubes."

Why?

"Because you've already made your choice. If you predicted that Faz would choose both, and he opens only the Blue, then he gets nothing."

True, and as I said before, very improbable.

"So," Xen went on, thinking quickly under its pocked sheen of titanium, "if you predicted that Faz would choose *only* the Blue, then Faz might as well open both. Faz will get both the jec and the secret."

Faz said, "Right. And that jec will be useful in getting away from here."

Except that there is every possibility that I already predicted his choice of both cubes. In that case I have left only the jec in the Red Cube, and nothing in Blue.

"But you've already chosen!" Faz blurted. "There isn't any probable-this or possible-that at all."

True.

Xen said, "The only uncertainty is, how good a predictor are you."

Quite.

Faz slowed, flexing a crane arm in agonized frustration. "I...dunno... I got...to think..."

There's world enough, and time.

"Let me draw a diagram," said Xen, who had always favored the orderly over the dramatic. This was what condemned it to a minor role in roiling battle, but perhaps that was a blessing. It drew upon the gritty soil some boxes: "There," Xen wheezed. "This is the payoff matrix."

THE IM

	Predicts you will take only what's in Blue	Predicts you will take what's in both
Take only what is in Blue	immortality	nothing
Take what is in both Red and Blue	immortality and jec	jec

YOU

As solemn and formal as Job's argument with God.

Enraptured with his own creation, Xen said, "Clearly, taking only the Blue cube is the best choice. The chances that the Im are wrong are very small. So you have a great chance of gaining immortality."

"That's crazy," Faz mumbled. "If I take both cubes, I at *least* get a jec, even if the Im *knew* I'd choose that way. And with a jec, I can make a run for it from the Laggenmorphs."

"Yes. Yet it rests on faith," Xen said. "Faith that the Im's predicting is near-perfect."

"Ha!" Faz snorted. "Nothing's perfect."

A black thing scorched over the rim of the pitwallow and exploded into fragments. Each bit dove for Xen and Faz, like shrieking, elongated eagles baring teeth.

And each struck something invisible but solid. Each smacked like an insect striking the windshield of a speeding car. And was gone.

"They're all around us!" Faz cried.

"Even with a jec, we might not make it out," Xen said.

True. But translated into currents, like me, with a subtle knowledge of conductivities and diffusion rates, you can live forever.

"Translated..." Xen mused.

Free of entropy's swamp.

"Look," Faz said, "I may be tired, drained, but I know logic. You've already *made* your choice, Im—the cubes are filled with whatever you put in. What I choose to do now can't change that. So I'll take *both* cubes."

Very well.

Faz sprang to the cubes. They burst open with a popping ivory radiance. From the red came a blinding bolt of a jec. It surrounded Faz's antennae and cascaded into the creature.

Drifting lightly from the blue cube came a tight-wound thing, a shifting ball of neon-lit string. Luminous, writhing rainbow worms. They described the complex web of magnetic field geometries that were immortality's craft. Faz seized it.

You won both. I predicted you would take only the blue. I was wrong.

"Ha!" Faz whirled with renewed energy.

Take the model of the fieldcraft. From it you can deduce the methods.

"Come on, Xen!" Faz cried with sudden ferocity. It surged over the lip of the pitwallow, firing at the distant, moving shapes of the Laggenmorphs, full once more of spit and dash. Leaving Xen.

"With that jec, Faz will make it."

I predict so, yes. You could follow Faz. Under cover of its armory, you would find escape—that way.

The shimmer vectored quick a green arrow to westward, where clouds billowed white. There the elements still governed and mortality walked.

"My path lies homeward, to the south."

Bound for Pymr.

"She is the one true rest I have."

You could rest forever.

"Like you? Or Faz, when it masters the...translation?"

Yes. Then I will have company here.

"Aha! That is your motivation."

In part.

"What else, then?"

There are rules for immortals. Ones you cannot understand...yet.

"If you can predict so well, with Godlike power, then I should choose only the Blue cube."

True. Or as true as true gets.

"But if you predict so well, my 'choice' is mere illusion. It was fore-ordained."

That old saw? I can see you are...determined...to have free will.

"Or free won't."

Your turn.

"There are issues here..." Xen transmitted only ruby ruminations, murmuring like surf on a distant shore.

Distant boomings from Faz's retreat. The Red and Blue cubes spun, sparkling, surfaces rippled by ion-acoustic modes. The game had been reset by the Im, whose curtains of gauzy green shimmered in anticipation.

There must be a Game, you see.

"Otherwise there is no free will?"

That is indeed one of our rules. Observant, you are. I believe I will enjoy the company of you, Xen, more than that of Faz.

"To be...an immortal..."

A crystalline paradise, better than blind Milton's scribbled vision.

A cluster of dirty-brown explosions ripped the sky, rocked the land.

I cannot expend my voltages much longer. Would that we had wit enough, and time, to continue this parrying.

"All right." Xen raised itself up and clawed away the phosphorescent layers of both cubes.

The Red held a shimmering jec.

The Blue held nothing.

Xen said slowly, "So you predicted correctly."

Yes. Sadly, I knew you too well.

Xen radiated a strange sensation of joy, unlaced by regret. It surged to the lip of the crumbling pitwallow.

"Ah..." Xen sent a lofting note. "I am like a book, old Im. No doubt I would suffer in translation."

A last glance backward at the wraith of glow and darkness, a gesture of salute, then: "On! To sound and fury!" and it was gone forever.

3.

In the stretched silent years there was time for introspection. Faz learned the lacy straits of Earth's magnetic oceans, its tides and times. It sailed the magnetosphere and spoke to stars.

The deep-etched memories of that encounter persisted. It never saw Xen again, though word did come vibrating through the field lines of Xen's escape, of zestful adventures out in the raw territory of air and Man. There was even a report that Xen had itself and Pymr decanted into full Manform, to taste the pangs of cell and membrane. Clearly, Xen had lived fully after that solstice day. Fresh verve had driven that blithe new spirit.

Faz was now grown full, could scarcely be distinguished from the Im who gave the fieldcraft. Solemn and wise, its induction, conductivity, and ruby glinting dielectrics a glory to be admired, it hung vast and cold in the sky. Faz spoke seldom and thought much.

Yet the game still occupied Faz. It understood with the embedded viewpoint of an immortal now, saw that each side in the game paid a price. The Im could convey the fieldcraft to only a few, and had nearly exhausted itself; those moments cost millennia.

The sacrifice of Faz was less clear.

Faz felt itself the same as before. Its memories were stored in Alfven waves—stirrings of the field lines, standing waves between Earth's magnetic poles. They would be safe until Earth itself wound down, and the dynamo at the nickel-iron core ceased to replenish the fields. Perhaps, by that time, there would be other field lines threading Earth's, and the Ims could spread outward, blending into the galactic fields.

There were signs that such an end had come to other worlds. The cosmic rays which sleeted down perpetually were random, isotropic, which meant they had to be scattered from magnetic waves between the stars. If such waves were ordered, wise—it meant a vast community of even greater Ims.

But this far future did not concern Faz. For it, the past still sang, gritty and real.

Faz asked the Im about that time, during one of their chance auroral meetings, beside a cascading crimson chum.

The way we would put it in my day, the Im named Sam said, **would be that the software never knows what the original hardware was.**

And that was it, Faz saw. During the translation, the original husk of Faz had been exactly memorized. This meant determining the exact locations of each atom, every darting electron. By the quantum laws, to locate perfectly implied that the measurement imparted an unknown, but high, momentum to each speck. So to define a thing precisely then destroyed it.

Yet there was no external way to prove this. Before and after translation there was an exact Faz.

The copy did not know it was embedded in different...hardware... than the original.

So immortality was a concept with legitimacy purely seen from the outside. From the inside...

Somewhere, a Faz had died that this Faz might live.

...And how did any sentience know it was not a copy of some long-gone original?

One day, near the sheath that held back the atmosphere, Faz saw a man waving, it stood in green and vibrant wealth of life, clothed at the waist, bronzed. Faz attached a plasma transducer at the boundary and heard the figure say, "You're Faz, right?"

Yes, in a way. And you...?

"Wondered how you liked it."

Xen? Is that you?

"In a way."

You knew.

"Yes. So I went in the opposite direction—into this form."

You'll die soon.

"You've died already."

Still, in your last moments, you'll wish for this.

"No, it's not how long something lasts, it's what that something means." With that the human turned, waved gaily, and trotted into a nearby forest.

This encounter bothered Faz.

In its studies and learned colloquy, Faz saw and felt the tales of Men. They seemed curiously convoluted, revolving about Self. What mattered most to those who loved tales was how they concluded. Yet all Men knew how each ended. Their little dreams were rounded with a sleep.

So the point of a tale was not how it ended, but *what it meant*. The great inspiring epic rage of Man was to find that lesson, buried in a grave.

As each year waned, Faz reflected, and knew that Xen had seen this point. Immortality seen from without, by those who could not know the inner Self—Xen did not want that. So it misled the Im, and got the mere jec that it wanted.

Xen chose life—not to be a monument of unaging intellect, gathered into the artifice of eternity.

In the brittle night Faz wondered if it had chosen well itself. And knew. *Nothing* could be sure it was itself the original. So the only intelligent course lay in enjoying whatever life a being felt—living like a mortal, in the moment. Faz had spent so long, only to reach that same conclusion which was forced on Man from the beginning.

Faz emitted a sprinkling of electromagnetic tones, spattering rueful red the field lines.

And stirred itself to think again, each time the dim sun waned at the solstice. To remember and, still living, to rejoice.

FREEZEFRAME
(1986)

Well, Jason, it'll take some explaining. Got a minute? Great.

Here's the invitation. It's for the weekend, and it's not just the kid's birthday party, no. You and me, we've been out of touch the last couple years, so let me run through a little flashback, okay?

Teri and me, we're world-gobblers. You've known that since you and me were roomies, right? Remember the time I took a final, went skiing all afternoon, had a heavy date, was back next day for another final—and aced them both? Yeah, you got it fella, aced the date, too. Those were the days, huh?

Anyway, my Teri's the same—girl's got real fire in her. No Type A or anything, just alive. And like sheet lightning in bed. We grab life with both hands. Always have. If you work in city government, like me, you got to keep ahead of the oppo. Otherwise you see yourself hung out to dry on the six o'clock news and next day nobody can remember your name.

Goes double for Teri. She's in liability and claims, a real shark reef. Pressureville. So many lawyers around these days, half of them bred in those barracuda farms, those upgraded speed-curricula things. So we've got to watch our ass.

Right, good joke—watching Teri's is no trouble, I'll take all I can get. That woman really sends me. (Hey, lemme get you another drink.)

We're both in challenging careers, but she finds the time to make my day, every day, get it? Our relationship is stage center with us, even though we're putting in ten-hour days. That's what started us thinking, see?

We need the time to work on our marriage, really firm it up when the old schedule starts to fray us around the edges. We've been through

183

those stress management retreats, the whole thing, and we use it. So we're happy. But still, about a year ago we started to feel something was, well, missing.

Yeah, you got it. The old cliché—a kid. Teri's been hearing the old bio clock tick off the years. We got the condo, two sharp cars, timeshare in Maui, diversified portfolio thick as your wrist—but it's not enough. Somehow.

Teri brought it up carefully, not sure I'd like the idea of sharing all this wonderful bounty with a cranky little brat. I heard her through, real quality listening, and just between you and me, old buddy, I didn't zoom in on the idea right away. Babies are more of a gal thing, right?

I mean, we're fast lane folks. Teri's happy poring over legal programs, looking for a precedent-busting angle, zipping off to an amped workout at the gym, and then catching one of those black and white foreign films with the hard to read subtitles. Not much room in her schedule to pencil in a feeding or the mumps.

I had real trouble conceptualizing how she—much less I—could cope. But she wanted this, I could tell from the soft watery look her eyes get. She's a real woman, y'know?

But the flip side was, no way she'd go for months of waddling around looking and feeling like a cow. Getting behind in her briefs because of morning sickness? Taking time off for the whole number? Not Teri's kind of thing.

What? Oh, sure, adoption. Well, we did the research on that. Let me put it this way. We both think the other's pretty damn special. Unique. And our feeling was, why raise a kid that's running on somebody else's genetic program? We're talented people, great bodies, not too hard on the eyes—why not give our kid those advantages?

And think about the kid. You got to look at it from his point of view. He should have parents who provide the very best in everything—including genes. He had to be ours—all ours. So you can see our problem. Balancing the tradeoffs, and nothing looks like a winner. We'd hit a roadblock.

That's where my contacts came in handy. Guy at work told me about this company, GeneInc. The corporation was looking for a franchise backer and the city was getting involved because of all the legal hassles. Red tape had to be cut with the AMA, the local hospitals, the usual stuff. No big deal, though—just takes time.

Teri did a little angling on the variances they needed and in return they were real nice. We got invited to a few great parties up in the hills.

Glitzy affairs, some big media people flown in to spice things up. And that's when we got the word. Their secret is, they speed up the whole thing. It's entirely natural, no funny chemicals or anything. Purely electrical and a little hormone tinkering, straight goods.

What they do is, they take a little genetic material from Teri and me, they put it in a blender or something, they mix it and match it and batch it. There's this thing called inculcated growth pattern. Just jargon to me, but what it means is, they can tune the process, see. Nature does it slow and easy, but GeneInc can put the pedal to the metal. Go through the prelim stages, all in the lab.

Yeah, you got it fella, you can't see Teri pushing around a basketball belly, can you? That's why it's like GeneInc was tight wrapped—for lives like ours, lives on the go.

We did it. Yeah! Really.

So she goes in one Friday, right after a big staff meeting, and with me holding her hand she has the implantation. She overnights in the clinic, watching a first-run movie on a big plasma screen. A snap, she said.

Next day she's home. We have dinner at that great new restaurant, T.S. Eliot's, you really got to try the blackened red fish there, and all she's got to do is take these pills every four hours. Three weeks like that, she's growing by the minute. Eats like a horse. I tell you, we had a running tab at every pasta joint within five blocks of the condo. She's into the clinic every forty-eight hours for the treatments, smooth as a press release. Teri's clicking right along, the kid's growing ten times the normal rate.

Before I can get around to buying cigars, zip, here's a seven-pound wonder. Great little guy. Perfect—my eyes, her smile, wants to eat everything in sight. Grabs for the milk supply like a real ladies' man. And no effects from the GeneInc speedup, not a square inch less than A-max quality.

You hear all kinds of scare talk about gene-diddling, how you might end up with a kid from Zit City. Well, the Chicken Littles were wrong-o, in spades. We figure we'd handle things from there. Maybe send out the diapers, hire a live-in if we could find a nice quiet illegal—Teri could handle the Spanish, y'see. We had the right vector, but we were a tad short on follow-through. Teri started getting cluster headaches. Big ones, in technicolor. So I filled in for her. Read some books on fathering, really got into it. And I'm telling you, it jigsawed my days beyond belief.

Face it, we have high-impact lives. I gave up my daily racquetball match—and you know how much of a sacrifice that was, for a diehard jock like me, high school football and all. But I did it for the kid.

Next, Teri had to drop out of her extra course in fastlane brokering, too, which was a real trauma. Bottom line-wise, y'see.

I mean, we'd practically spent the projected income from that training. Factored it into our estimated taxes, even. I'd already sunk extra cash into a honey of a limited partnership. It had some sweetheart underwriting features and we just couldn't resist it.

Man, crisis time. If she didn't get her broker's license on schedule, we'd be stretched so thin you could see through us. She couldn't link into the course on home computer, either. Software mismatch or something, and by the time she got it translated she was too far behind in the course.

See what I mean? Bleaksville. But we were committed parents. We believe in total frankness, upfront living. So we went back to GeneInc and had a talk with one of their counselors. Wonderful woman. She takes us into a beautiful room—soft lighting, quality leather couch, and some of that classy Baroque trumpet music in the background. Just the right touch. Tasteful. Reassuring. Money always is.

She listens to us and nods a lot and knows just what we're talking about. We trust her, almost like it was therapy. Which I guess it was. And we let it all spill. The irritations. Man, I never knew a little package could scream so much. Feeding.

No grandparents closer than three thousand miles, and they're keeping their distance. Got their retirement condo, security compound, walls all around it, a rule that you can't bring a kid in for longer than twenty-four hours. Not exactly Norman Rockwell, huh? So no quick fix there.

And the kid, he's always awake and wanting to play just when we're stumbling home, zombies. Whoosh! So you cram things in. We had trouble syncing our schedules. Lost touch with friends and business contacts. See, I spend a lot of time on the horn, keeping up with people I know I'll need sometime. Or just feeling out the gossip shops for what's hot. Can't do that with a squall-bomb on my knee.

Teri had it even worse. She'd bought all the traditional mother package and was trying to jam that into her own flat-out style. Doesn't work. No way!

The usual way to handle this would be for somebody to lose big, right? Teri drops back and punts, maybe. Stops humping so hard, lets up. So maybe a year downstream, some younger beady-eyed type shoulders her aside. She ends up targeted on eternal middle-management. The desert. Oblivion. Perpetual Poughkeepsie.

Or else I lower *my* revs. Shy off the background briefings, drop off the party committee, don't sniff around for possible comers to get tight with. You know how it is. The long slide.

What? Ol' buddy, you're dead on—not my scene. But listen, my real concern wasn't my job, it was our relationship. We really work at it. Total communication takes time. We really get into each other. That's just us.

So the lady at GeneInc listens, nods, and introduces us to their top drawer product line. Exclusive. Very high tech. It blew us away. Freezeframe, they call it.

Look, the kid's going to be sleeping ten, twelve hours a day anyway, right? GeneInc just packs all that time into our workweek. Rearranges the kid's schedule, is basically what it is. Simple electronic stimulus to the lower centers. Basic stuff, they told me, can't damage anything. And totally under our control!

When we want him, the kid's on call. Boost his voltage, allow some warmup. Presto! See, he's running at low temperature during the work day. Helps the process. So we come dragging home, have some chardonnay to unwind, catch the news. When we're ready for him we hit a few buttons, warm him up and there he is, bright and agreeable 'cause he's had a ton of extra sack time. Can't get tired and pesky.

I mean, the kid's at his best and we're at peak, too. Relaxed, ready for some A-plus parenting.

Well, we took the Zen pause on the idea, sure. Thought it over. Teri talked it out with her analyst. Worked on the problem, got her doubts under control. And we went for it.

Little shakedown trouble, sure, but nothing big. GeneInc, they've got a fix for everything. We boost him up for weekends, when we've got space in our lives. Quality time, that's what the kid gets.

We've set up a regular schedule. Weekdays for us, weeknights and weekends for him. You might think that would mean he grows slower or something, right? No!

GeneInc's got an add-on you wouldn't believe—Downtime Education, they call it. While he's sleeping through our days, Downtime Ed brings him up to speed on verbals, math, sensory holism, the works. Better than a real teacher, in many ways.

So we feel that—oh yeah, the invitation. You got it already?

It's for his big blast. Combo first birthday party and graduation from third grade. We put him on the inside track, and he's burning it up.

We couldn't be happier. Our kind of kid, for sure. Pretty soon we'll integrate him into the GeneInc school for accelerated cases, others like him. All of them have sharp parents like us.

There's a whole community of these great kids springing up, y'know. They're either in Downtime, learning up a storm, or getting online, first class attention in Freezeframe weekends.

I tell you, Jason, these kids are going to be the best. They'll slice and dice any Normkid competition they run into. And us—it's like a new beginning. We get to have it all and we know the kid's not suffering. Just the opposite.

He'll have a high school diploma by the time he's ten. He'll be a savvy little guy. And we'll load on all the extras, too. Emotional support, travel, the works. We'll have him on tap when we want him. That'll stretch out his physical childhood, of course, but speed up his mental growth. Better all round, really, 'cause Teri and I totally like him.

See, that's the hidden leverage. We want to spread him over more of our lives, keep him for maybe thirty years. Why not have one really top of the line kid, enjoy him most of your life? Efficient. Helps on global population, too.

So look, I got to trot. Map's on the back of the invitation, come and enjoy. No need for a present unless you want to. Teri'll love seeing you again.

And while you're there, I can show you the GeneInc equipment. Beautiful gear, sharp lines. Brochures, too. I've got a kind of little franchise agreement with them, getting in on the ground floor of this thing.

What? Well, that's not the way I'd put it, Jason. This is a class product line. Calling it a Tupperware party—hey, that's way out of line.

We're talking quality here. You'll see, just drop on by. No obligation. Oh yeah, and I got some great cabernet you should try, something I picked up on the wine futures market.

My God, look at the time. See you, ol' buddy. Have a nice day.

PROSELYTES
(1988)

It was the third time something had knocked on the door that evening. Slow, ponderous thuds. Dad answered it, even though he knew what would be standing there.

The Gack was seven feet tall and burly, as were all Gacks. "Good evening," it said. "I bring you glorious word from the stars!"

It spoke slowly, the broad mouth seeming to shape each word as though the lips were mouthing an invisible marble. Then it blinked twice and said, "The true knowledge of the universe! Salutations of eternal life!"

Dad nodded sourly. "We heard."

"Are you certain? I am an emissary from a far star, sent to bring—"

"Yeah, there's been two others here tonight already."

"And you turned them away?" the Gack asked, startled.

Junior broke in, leaving his homework at the dining-room table. "Hey, there's been *hundreds* of you guys comin' by here. For *months.*"

The Gack blinked and abruptly made the sound that had given the aliens their name—a tight, barking sneeze. Something in Earth's air irritated their large red noses. "Apologies, dear ignorant natives, from a humble proselyte of the One Patriarch."

Dad said edgily, "Look, we already heard about your god and how he made the galaxy so you Gacks could spread his holy word and all, so—"

"Oh, let the poor thing finish its spiel, Howard," Mom said, wiping her hands on a towel as she came in from the kitchen.

"Hell, the Dodgers' game'll be on soon—"

"C'mon, Dad," Junior said. "You know that's the only way to get 'em to go away."

The Gack sniffed appreciatively at Junior and started its rehearsed lecture. "Wondrous news, O Benighted Natives! I have voyaged countless of your years to bring..."

The family tuned out the recital. As Dad stood in the doorway he could see dozens of Gack ships orbiting in the night sky. They were like small brown moons, asteroid-sized starships that had arrived in a flurry of fiery orange explosions. Each had a big flat plate at one end. They were slow, awkwardly shaped, clunky—like the Gacks themselves.

They had come from a distant yellow star and all they wanted was free rein to "speak to the unknowing," as their emissary had put it. In return they had offered their technology.

Dad had been enthusiastic about that, and so had every government on Earth. Dad's half interest in the Electronic Wonderland store downtown had been paying very little these last few years. An infusion of alien technology, whole new racy product lines, could be a bonanza.

But the Gacks had nothing worth using. Their ships had spanned the stars using the simplest possible method. They dumped small nuclear bombs out the back and set them off. The ship then rode the blast wave, with the flat plate on one end smoothing out the push, like a giant shock absorber.

And inside the Gack asteroid ships were electronics that used vacuum tubes, hand-cranked computers, old-fashioned AM radio...nothing that humans hadn't invented already.

So there would be no wonder machines from the stars. The sad fact was that the aliens were dumb. They had labored centuries to make their starships, and then ridden them for millennia to reach other stars.

The Gack ended ponderously with, "Gather now into the outstretched loving grasp of the One True Vision!"

The Gack's polite, expectant gaze fell in turn on each of the family.

Mom said, "Well, that was *very* nice. You're certainly one of the best I've heard, wouldn't you agree, Howard?"

Dad hated it, how she always made *him* get rid of the Gacks. He began, "Look, we've been patient—"

"*They're* the patient ones, Dad," Junior said. "Sittin' in those rocks all those years, just so they could knock on doors and hand out literature." Junior laughed.

The Gack was still looking expectantly at them, waiting for them to convert to his One Galactic Faith. One of its four oddly shaped hands held forth crudely printed pamphlets.

"Now, now," Mom said. "We shouldn't make fun of another creature's beliefs. This poor thing is just doing what our Mormons and Jehovah's Witnesses do. You wouldn't laugh at them, would you?"

Dad could hold it no longer. The night air was cold and he was getting chilled, standing there. "No thanks!" he said loudly, and slammed the door.

"Howard!" Mom cried.

"Hey, right on, Dad!" Junior clapped his hands.

"Just shut the door in its faith," Dad said, making a little smile.

"I still say we should always be polite," Mom persisted. "Who would've believed that when the aliens came, their only outstanding quality would be patience? The patience to travel to other stars. We could learn a thing or two from them," she added sternly.

Dad was already looking in *TV Guide*. "We should've guessed that even before the Gacks came. After all, who comes visiting in this neighborhood? Not that snooty astronomer two blocks over, right? No, we get hot-eyed guys in black suits, looking for converts. So it's no surprise that those are the only kinds of aliens who're damn fool enough to spend all their time flying to the stars, too. Not explorers. Not scientists. Fundamentalists!"

As if to punctuate his words, a hollow thump made the house creak. They all looked to the front door, but the sound wasn't a knock.

Another boom came down from the sky and rattled the windows.

When they went outside, the night sky was alive with darting ships and lurid orange explosions.

Junior cried, "The Gack ships! See, they're all blown up."

"My, I hope they aren't hurt or anything," Mom said. "They're such *nice* creatures, truly."

Among the tumbling brown remnants of the Gack fleet darted sleek, shiny vessels. They dived like quicksilver barracuda, sending missiles that ripped open the fat bellies of the last few asteroid ships.

Dad felt a pang. "They were kinda pleasant," he said grudgingly. "Not my type of person, maybe, and their technology was a laugh, but still—"

"Look!" Junior cried.

A sleek ship skimmed across the sky. A bone-rattling boom crashed down from it.

"Now *that's* what an alien starship oughtta look like," Junior said. "Lookit those wings! The blue exhaust—"

Behind the swift craft huge letters of gauzy blue unfurled across the upper atmosphere. The phosphorescent words loomed with hard, clear purpose:

GREET THE CLEANSING BLADE OF THE ONE ETERNAL TRUTH!

"Huh?" Junior frowned. Dad's face went white.

"We thought the Mormons were bad," he said grimly. "Whoever thought there might be Moslems?"

MATTER'S END
(1989)

When Dr. Samuel Johnson felt himself getting tied up in an argument over Bishop Berkeley's ingenious sophistry to prove the nonexistence of matter, and that everything in the universe is merely ideal, he kicked a large stone and answered, "I refute it thus." Just what that action assured him of is not very obvious, but apparently he found it comforting.
— SIR ARTHUR EDDINGTON

I ndia came to him first as a breeze like soured buttermilk, rich yet tainted. A door banged somewhere, sending gusts sweeping through the Bangalore airport, slicing through the 4 A.M. silences.

Since the Free State of Bombay had left India, Bangalore had become an international airport. Yet the damp caress seemed to erase the sterile signatures that made all big airports alike, even giving a stippled texture to the cool enamel glow of the fluorescents.

The moist air clasped Robert Clay like a stranger's sweaty palm. The ripe, fleshy aroma of a continent enfolded him, swarming up his nostrils and soaking his lungs with sullen spice. He put down his carry-on bag and showed the immigration clerk his passport. The man gave him a piercing, ferocious stare—then mutely slammed a rubber stamp onto the pages and handed it back.

A hand snagged him as he headed toward baggage claim.

"Professor Clay?" The face was dark olive with intelligent eyes riding above sharp cheekbones. A sudden white grin flashed as Clay nodded. "Ah, good. I am Dr. Sudarshan Patil. Please come this way."

Dr. Patil's tone was polite, but his hands impatiently pulled Clay away from the sluggish lines, through a battered wooden side door. The heavy-lidded immigration guards were carefully looking in other directions, hands held behind their backs. Apparently they had been paid off and would ignore this odd exit. Clay was still groggy from trying to sleep on the flight from London. He shook his head as Patil led him into the gloom of a baggage storeroom.

"Your clothes," Patil said abruptly.

"What?"

"They mark you as a Westerner. Quickly!"

Patil's hands, light as birds in the quilted soft light, were already plucking at his coat, his shirt. Clay was taken aback at this abruptness. He hesitated, then struggled out of the dirty garments, pulling his loose slacks down over his shoes. He handed his bundled clothes to Patil, who snatched them away without a word.

"You're welcome," Clay said. Patil took no notice, just thrust a wad of tan cotton at him. The man's eyes jumped at each distant sound in the storage room, darting, suspecting every pile of dusty bags.

Clay struggled into the pants and rough shirt. They looked dingy in the wan yellow glow of a single distant fluorescent tube.

"Not the reception I'd expected," Clay said, straightening the baggy pants and pulling at the rough drawstring.

"These are not good times for scientists in my country, Dr. Clay," Patil said bitingly. His voice carried that odd lilt that echoed both the Raj and Cambridge.

"Who're you afraid of?"

"Those who hate Westerners and their science."

"They said in Washington—"

"We are about great matters, Professor Clay. Please cooperate, please." Patil's lean face showed its bones starkly, as though energies pressed outward. Promontories of bunched muscle stretched a mottled canvas skin. He started toward a far door without another word, carrying Clay's overnight bag and jacket.

"Say, where're we—"

Patil swung open a sheet-metal door and beckoned. Clay slipped through it and into the moist wealth of night. His feet scraped on a dirty sidewalk beside a black tar road. The door hinge squealed behind them, attracting the attention of a knot of men beneath a vibrant yellow street-light nearby.

The bleached fluorescence of the airport terminal was now a continent away. Beneath a line of quarter-ton trucks huddled figures slept. In the astringent street-lamp glow he saw a decrepit green Korean Tochat van parked at the curb.

"In!" Patil whispered.

The men under the streetlight started walking toward them, calling out hoarse questions.

Clay yanked open the van's sliding door and crawled into the second row of seats. A fog of unknown pungent smells engulfed him. The driver, a short man, hunched over the wheel. Patil sprang into the front seat and the van ground away, its low gear whining.

Shouts. A stone thumped against the van roof. Pebbles rattled at the back. They accelerated, the engine clattering. A figure loomed up from the shifting shadows and flung muck against the window near Clay's face. He jerked back at the slap of it. "Damn!"

They plowed through a wide puddle of dirty rainwater. The engine sputtered and for a moment Clay was sure it would die. He looked out the rear window and saw vague forms running after them. Then the engine surged again and they shot away. They went two blocks through hectic traffic. Clay tried to get a clear look at India outside, but all he could see in the starkly shadowed street were the crisscrossings of three-wheeled taxis and human-drawn rickshaws. He got an impression of incessant activity, even in this desolate hour. Vehicles leaped out of the murk as headlights swept across them and then vanished utterly into the moist shadows again.

They suddenly swerved around a corner beneath spreading, gloomy trees. The van jolted into deep potholes and jerked to a stop. "Out!" Patil called.

Clay could barely make out a second van at the curb ahead. It was blue and caked with mud, but even in the dim light would not be confused with their green one. A rotting fetid reek filled his nose as he got out the side door, as if masses of overripe vegetation loomed in the shadows. Patil tugged him into the second van.

In a few seconds they went surging out through a narrow, brick-lined alley. "Look, what—"

"Please, quiet," Patil said primly. "I am watching carefully now to be certain that we are not being followed."

They wound through a shantytown warren for several minutes. Their headlights picked up startled eyes that blinked from what Clay at first had taken to be bundles of rags lying against the shacks. They seemed impossibly small even to be children. Huddled against decaying tin lean-tos, the dim forms often did not stir even as the van splashed dirty water on them from potholes.

Clay began, "Look, I understand the need for—"

"I apologize for our rude methods, Dr. Clay," Patil said. He gestured at the driver. "May I introduce Dr. Singh?"

Singh was similarly gaunt and intent, but with bushy hair and a thin, pointed nose. He jerked his head aside to peer at Clay, nodded twice like a puppet on strings, and then quickly stared back at the narrow lane ahead. Singh kept the van at a steady growl, abruptly yanking it around corners. A wooden cart lurched out of their way, its driver swearing in a strident singsong.

"Welcome to India," Singh said with reedy solemnity. "I am afraid circumstances are not the best."

"Uh, right. You two are heads of the project, they told me at the NSF."

"Yes," Patil said archly, "the project which officially no longer exists and unofficially is a brilliant success. It is amusing!"

"Yeah," Clay said cautiously, "we'll see."

"Oh, you will see," Singh said excitedly. "We have the events! More all the time."

Patil said precisely, "We would not have suggested that your National Science Foundation send an observer to confirm our findings unless we believed them to be of the highest importance."

"You've seen proton decay?"

Patil beamed. "Without doubt."

"Damn."

"Exactly."

"What mode?"

"The straightforward pion and positron decay products."

Clay smiled, reserving judgment. Something about Patil's almost prissy precision made him wonder if this small, beleaguered team of Indian physicists might actually have brought it off. An immense long shot, of course, but possible. There were much bigger groups of particle physicists in Europe and the U.S. who had tried to detect proton decay using underground swimming pools of pure water. Those experiments had enjoyed all the benefits of the latest electronics. Clay had worked on the big American project in a Utah salt mine, before lean budgets and lack of results closed it down. It would be galling if this lone, underfunded

Indian scheme had finally done it. Nobody at the NSF believed the story coming out of India.

Patil smiled at Clay's silence, a brilliant slash of white in the murk. Their headlights picked out small panes of glass stuck seemingly at random in nearby hovels, reflecting quick glints of yellow back into the van. The night seemed misty; their headlights forked ahead. Clay thought a soft rain had started outside, but then he saw that thousands of tiny insects darted into their headlights. Occasionally big ones smacked against the windshield.

Patil carefully changed the subject. "I…believe you will pass unnoticed, for the most part."

"I look Indian?"

"I hope you will not take offense if I remark that you do not. We requested an Indian, but your NSF said they did not have anyone qualified."

"Right. Nobody who could hop on a plane, anyway." Or would, he added to himself.

"I understand. You are a compromise. If you will put this on…" Patil handed Clay a floppy khaki hat. "It will cover your curly hair. Luckily, your nose is rather more narrow than I had expected when the NSF cable announced they were sending a Negro."

"Got a lot of white genes in it, this nose," Clay said evenly.

"Please, do not think I am being racist. I simply wished to diminish the chances of you being recognized as a Westerner in the countryside."

"Think I can pass?"

"At a distance, yes."

"Be tougher at the site?"

"Yes. There are 'celebrants,' as they term themselves, at the mine."

"How'll we get in?"

"A ruse we have devised."

"Like that getaway back there? That was pretty slick."

Singh sent them jouncing along a rutted lane. Withered trees leaned against the pale stucco two-story buildings that lined the lane like children's blocks lined up not quite correctly. "Men in customs, they would give word to people outside. If you had gone through with the others, a different reception party would have been waiting for you."

"I see. But what about my bags?"

Patil had been peering forward at the gloomy jumble of buildings. His head jerked around to glare at Clay. "You were not to bring more than your carry-on bag!"

"Look, I can't get by on that. Chrissake, that'd give me just one change of clothes—"

"You left bags there?"

"Well, yeah, I had just one—"

Clay stopped when he saw the look on the two men's faces.

Patil said with strained clarity, "Your bags, they had identification tags?"

"Sure, airlines make you—"

"They will bring attention to you. There will be inquiries. The devotees will hear of it, inevitably, and know you have entered the country."

Clay licked his lips. "Hell, I didn't think it was so important."

The two lean Indians glanced at each other, their faces taking on a narrowing, leaden cast. "Dr. Clay," Patil said stiffly, "the 'celebrants' believe, as do many, that Westerners deliberately destroyed our crops with their biotechnology."

"Japanese companies' biologists did that, I thought," Clay said diplomatically.

"Perhaps. Those who disturb us at the Kolar gold mine make no fine distinctions between biologists and physicists. They believe that we are disturbing the very bowels of the earth, helping to further the destruction, bringing on the very end of the world itself. Surely you can see that in India, the mother country of religious philosophy, such matters are important."

"But your work, hell, it's not a matter of life or death or anything."

"On the contrary, the decay of the proton is precisely an issue of death."

Clay settled back in his seat, puzzled, watching the silky night stream by, cloaking vague forms in its shadowed mysteries.

Clay insisted on the telephone call. A wan winter sun had already crawled partway up the sky before he awoke, and the two Indian physicists wanted to leave immediately. They had stopped while still in Bangalore, holing up in the cramped apartment of one of Patil's graduate students. As Clay took his first sip of tea, two other students had turned up with his bag, retrieved at a cost he never knew. Clay said, "I promised I'd call home. Look, my family's worried. They read the papers, they know the trouble here."

Shaking his head slowly, Patil finished a scrap of curled brown bread that appeared to be his only breakfast. His movements had a smooth liquid inertia, as if the sultry morning air oozed like jelly around him. They were sitting at a low table that had one leg too short; the already rickety table kept lurching, slopping tea into their saucers. Clay had looked for something to prop up the leg, but the apartment was bare, as though no one lived here. They had slept on pallets beneath a single bare bulb. Through the open windows, bare of frames or glass, Clay had gotten fleeting glimpses of the neighborhood—rooms of random clutter, plaster peeling off slumped walls, revealing the thin steel cross-ribs of the buildings, stained windows adorned with gaudy pictures of many-armed gods, already sun-bleached and frayed. Children yelped and cried below, their voices reflected among the odd angles and apertures of the tangled streets, while carts rattled by and bare feet slapped the stones. Students had apparently stood guard last night, though Clay had never seen more than a quick motion in the shadows below as they arrived.

"You ask much of us," Patil said. By morning light his walnut-brown face seemed gullied and worn. Lines radiated from his mouth toward intense eyes.

Clay sipped his tea before answering. A soft, strangely sweet smell wafted through the open window. They sat well back in the room so nobody could see in from the nearby buildings. He heard Singh tinkering downstairs with the van's engine. "Okay, it's maybe slightly risky. But I want my people to know I got here all right."

"There are few telephones here."

"I only need one."

"The system, often it does not work at all."

"Gotta try."

"Perhaps you do not understand—"

"I understand damn well that if I can't even reach my people, I'm not going to hang out here for long. And if I don't see that your experiment works right, nobody'll believe you."

"And your opinion depends upon...?"

Clay ticked off points on his fingers. "On seeing the apparatus. Checking your raw data. Running a trial case to see your system response. Then a null experiment—to verify your threshold level on each detector." He held up five fingers. "The works."

Patil said gravely, "Very good. We relish the opportunity to prove ourselves."

"You'll get it." Clay hoped to himself that they were wrong, but he suppressed that. He represented the faltering forefront of particle physics, and it would be embarrassing if a backwater research team had beaten the world. Still, either way, he would end up being the expert on the Kolar program, and that was a smart career move in itself.

"Very well. I must make arrangements for the call, then. But I truly—"

"Just do it. Then we get down to business."

The telephone was behind two counters and three doors at a Ministry for Controls office. Patil did the bribing and cajoling inside and then brought Clay in from the back of the van. He had been lying down on the back seat so he could not be seen easily from the street. The telephone itself was a heavy black plastic thing with a rotary dial that clicked like a sluggish insect as it whirled. Patil had been on it twice already, clearing international lines through Bombay. Clay got two false rings and a dead line. On the fourth try he heard a faint, somehow familiar buzzing. Then a hollow, distant click.

"Daddy, is that you?" Faint rock music in the background.

"Sure, I just wanted to let you know I got to India okay."

"Oh, Mommy will be so glad! We heard on the TV last night that there's trouble over there."

Startled, Clay asked, "What? Where's your mother?"

"Getting groceries. She'll be so mad she missed your call!"

"You tell her I'm fine, okay? But what trouble?"

"Something about a state leaving India. Lots of fighting, John Trimble said on the news."

Clay never remembered the names of news announcers; he regarded them as faceless nobodies reading prepared scripts, but for his daughter they were the voice of authority. "Where?"

"Uh, the lower part."

"There's nothing like that happening here, honey. I'm safe. Tell Mommy."

"People have ice cream there?"

"Yeah, but I haven't seen any. You tell your mother what I said, remember? About being safe?"

"Yes, she's been worried."

"Don't worry, Angy. Look, I got to go." The line popped and hissed ominously.

"I miss you, Daddy."

"I miss you double that. No, squared."

She laughed merrily. "I skinned my knee today at recess. It bled so much I had to go to the nurse."

"Keep it clean, honey. And give your mother my love."

"She'll be so mad."

"I'll be home soon."

She giggled and ended with the joke she had been using lately. "G'bye, Daddy. It's been real."

Her light laugh trickled into the static, a grace note from a bright land worlds away. Clay chuckled as he replaced the receiver. She cut the last word of "real nice" to make her good-byes hip and sardonic, a mannerism she had heard on television somewhere. An old joke; he had heard that even "groovy" was coming back in.

Clay smiled and pulled his hat down further and went quickly out into the street where Patil was waiting. India flickered at the edge of his vision, the crowds a hovering presence.

They left Bangalore in two vans. Graduate students drove the green Tochat from the previous night. He and Patil and Singh took the blue one, Clay again keeping out of sight by lying on the back seat. The day's raw heat rose around them like a shimmering lake of light.

They passed through lands leached of color. Only gray stubble grew in the fields. Trees hung limply, their limbs bowing as though exhausted. Figures in rags huddled for shade. A few stirred, eyes white in the shadows, as the vans ground past. Clay saw that large boles sat on the branches like gnarled knots with brown sheaths wrapped around the underside.

"Those some of the plant diseases I heard about?" he asked.

Singh pursed his lips. "I fear those are the pouches like those of wasps, as reported in the press." His watery eyes regarded the withered, graying trees as Patil slowed the car.

"Are they dangerous?" Clay could see yellow sap dripping from the underside of each.

"Not until they ripen," Singh said. "Then the assassins emerge."

"They look pretty big already."

"They are said to be large creatures, but of course there is little experience."

Patil downshifted and they accelerated away with an occasional sputtering misfire. Clay wondered whether they had any spare spark plugs along. The fields on each side of the road took on a dissolute and shredded look.

"Did the genetech experiments cause this?" he asked.

Singh nodded. "I believe this emerged from the European programs. First we had their designed plants, but then pests found vulnerability. They sought strains which could protect crops from the new pests. So we got these wasps. I gather that now some error or mutation has made them equally excellent at preying on people and even cows."

Clay frowned. "The wasps came from the Japanese aid, didn't they?"

Patil smiled mysteriously. "You know a good deal about our troubles, sir."

Neither said anything more. Clay was acutely conscious that his briefing in Washington had been detailed technical assessments, without the slightest mention of how the Indians themselves saw their problems. Singh and Patil seemed either resigned or unconcerned; he could not tell which. Their sentences refracted from some unseen nugget, like seismic waves warping around the earth's core.

"I would not worry greatly about these pouches," Singh said after they had ridden in silence for a while. "They should not ripen before we are done with our task. In any case, the Kolar fields are quite barren, and afford few sites where the pouches can grow."

Clay pointed out the front window. "Those round things on the walls, more pouches?"

To his surprise, both men burst into merry laughter. Gasping, Patil said, "Examine them closely, Doctor Clay. Notice the marks of the species which made them." Patil slowed the car and Clay studied the round, circular pads on the whitewashed vertical walls along the road. They were brown and matted and marked in a pattern of radial lines. Clay frowned and then felt enormously stupid: the thick lines were handprints.

"Drying cakes, they are," Patil said, still chuckling.

"Of what?"

"Dung, my colleague. We use the cow here, not merely slaughter it."

"What for?"

"Fuel. After the cakes dry, we stack them—see?" They passed a plastic-wrapped tower. A woman was adding a circular, annular tier of thick dung disks to the top, then carefully folding the plastic over it. "In winter they burn nicely."

"For heating?"

"And cooking, yes."

Seeing the look on Clay's face, Singh's eyes narrowed and his lips drew back so that his teeth were bright stubs. His eyebrows were long brush strokes that met the deep furrows of his frown. "Old ways are still often preferable to the new."

Sure, Clay thought, the past of cholera, plague, infanticide. But he asked with neutral politeness, "Such as?"

"Some large fish from the Amazon were introduced into our principal river three years ago to improve fishing yields."

"The Ganges? I thought it was holy."

"What is more holy than to feed the hungry?"

"True enough. Did it work?"

"The big fish, yes. They are delicious. A great delicacy."

"I'll have to try some," Clay said, remembering the thin vegetarian curry he had eaten at breakfast.

Singh said, "But the Amazon sample contained some minute eggs which none of the proper procedures eliminated. They were of a small species—the candiru, is that not the name?" he inquired politely of Patil.

"Yes," Patil said, "a little being who thrives mostly on the urine of larger fish. Specialists now believe that perhaps the eggs were inside the larger species, and so escaped detection."

Patil's voice remained calm and factual, although while he spoke he abruptly swerved to avoid a goat that spontaneously ambled onto the rough road. Clay rocked hard against the van's door, and Patil then corrected further to stay out of a gratuitous mudhole that seemed to leap at them from the rushing foreground. They bumped noisily over ruts at the road's edge and bounced back onto the tarmac without losing speed. Patil sat ramrod straight, hands turning the steering wheel lightly, oblivious to the wrenching effects of his driving.

"Suppose, Professor Clay, that you are a devotee," Singh said. "You have saved to come to the Ganges for a decade, for two. Perhaps you even plan to die there."

"Yeah, okay." Clay could not see where this was leading.

"You are enthused as you enter the river to bathe. You are perhaps profoundly affected. An intense spiritual moment. It is not uncommon to merge with the river, to inadvertently urinate into it."

Singh spread his hands as if to say that such things went without saying. "Then the candiru will be attracted by the smell. It mistakes this great bountiful largess, the food it needs, as coming from a very great fish indeed.

It excitedly swims up the stream of uric acid. Coming to your urethra, it swims like a snake into its burrow, as far up as it can go. You will see that the uric flow velocity will increase as the candiru makes its way upstream, inside you. When this tiny fish can make no further progress, some trick of evolution tells it to protrude a set of sidewise spines. So intricate!"

Singh paused a moment in smiling tribute to this intriguing facet of nature. Clay nodded, his mouth dry.

"These embed deeply in the walls and keep the candiru close to the source of what it so desires." Singh made short, delicate movements, his fingers jutting in the air. Clay opened his mouth, but said nothing.

Patil took them around a team of bullocks towing a wooden wagon and put in, "The pain is intense. Apparently there is no good treatment. Women—forgive this indelicacy—must be opened to get at the offending tiny fish before it swells and blocks the passage completely, having gorged itself insensate. Some men have an even worse choice. Their bladders are already engorged, having typically not been much emptied by the time the candiru enters. They must decide whether to attempt the slow procedure of poisoning the small thing and waiting for it to shrivel and withdraw its spines.

"However, their bladders might burst before that, flooding their abdomens with urine and of course killing them. If there is not sufficient time..."

"Yes?" Clay asked tensely.

"Then the penis must be chopped off," Singh said, "with the candiru inside."

Through a long silence Clay rode, swaying as the car wove through limitless flat spaces of parched fields and ruined brick walls and slumped whitewashed huts. Finally he said hoarsely, "I...don't blame you for resenting the...well, the people who brought all this on you. The devotees—"

"They believe this apocalyptic evil comes from the philosophy which gave us modern science."

"Well, look, whoever brought over those fish—"

Singh's eyes widened with surprise. A startled grin lit his face like a sunrise. "Oh no, Professor Clay! We do not blame the errors, or else we would have to blame equally the successes!"

To Clay's consternation, Patil nodded sagely.

He decided to say nothing more. Washington had warned him to stay out of political discussions, and though he was not sure if this was such, or if the lighthearted way Singh and Patil had related their story told their true attitude, it seemed best to just shut up. Again Clay had the odd sensation that here the cool certainties of Western biology had become diffused, blunted, crisp distinctions rendered into something beyond the constraints of the world outside, all blurred by the swarming, dissolving currents of India. The tin-gray sky loomed over a plain of ripe rot. The urgency of decay here was far more powerful than the abstractions that so often filled his head, the digitized iconography of sputtering, splitting protons.

The Kolar gold fields were a long, dusty drive from Bangalore. The sway of the van made Clay sleepy in the back, jet lag pulling him down into fitful, shallow dreams of muted voices, shadowy faces, and obscure purpose. He awoke frequently amid the dry smells, lurched up to see dry farmland stretching to the horizon, and collapsed again to bury his face in the pillow he had made by wadding up a shirt. They passed through innumerable villages that, after the first few, all seemed alike with their scrawny children, ramshackle sheds, tin roofs, and general air of sleepy dilapidation. Once, in a narrow town, they stopped as rickshaws and carts backed up. An emaciated cow with pink paper tassels on its horns stood square in the middle of the road, trembling. Shouts and honks failed to move it, but no one ahead made the slightest effort to prod it aside. Clay got out of the van to stretch his legs, ignoring Patil's warning to stay hidden, and watched. A crowd collected, shouting and chanting at the cow but not touching it. The cow shook its head, peering at the road as if searching for grass, and urinated powerfully. A woman in a red sari rushed into the road, knelt, and thrust her hand into the full stream. She made a formal motion with her other hand and splashed some urine on her forehead and cheeks. Three other women had already lined up behind her, and each did the same. Disturbed, the cow waggled its head and shakily walked away. Traffic started up, and Clay climbed back into the van. As they ground out of the dusty town, Singh explained that holy bovine urine was widely held to have positive health effects.

"Many believe it settles stomach troubles, banishes headaches, even improves fertility," Singh said.

"Yeah, you could sure use more fertility." Clay gestured at the throngs that filled the narrow clay sidewalks.

"I am not so Indian that I cannot find it within myself to agree with you, Professor Clay," Singh said.

"Sorry for the sarcasm. I'm tired."

"Patil and I are already under a cloud simply because we are scientists, and therefore polluted with Western ideas."

"Can't blame Indians for being down on us. Things're getting rough."

"But you are a black man. You yourself were persecuted by Western societies."

"That was a while back."

"And despite it you have risen to a professorship."

"You do the work, you get the job." Clay took off his hat and wiped his brow. The midday heat pressed sweat from him.

"Then you do not feel alienated from Western ideals?" Patil put in.

"Hell no. Look, I'm not some sharecropper who pulled himself up from poverty. I grew up in Falls Church, Virginia. Father's a federal bureaucrat. Middle class all the way."

"I see," Patil said, eyes never leaving the rutted road. "Your race bespeaks an entirely different culture, but you subscribe to the program of modern rationalism."

Clay looked at them quizzically. "Don't you?"

"As scientists, of course. But that is not all of life."

"Um," Clay said.

A thousand times before he had endured the affably condescending attention of whites, their curious eyes searching his face. No matter what the topic, they somehow found a way to inquire indirectly after his true feelings, his natural emotions. And if he waved away these intrusions, there remained in their heavy-lidded eyes a subtle skepticism, doubts about his authenticity. Few gave him space to simply be a suburban man with darker skin, a man whose interior landscape was populated with the same icons of Middle America as their own. Hell, his family name came from slaves, given as a tribute to Henry Clay, a nineteenth-century legislator. He had never expected to run into stereotyping in India, for chrissakes.

Still, he was savvy enough to lard his talk with some homey touches, jimmy things up with collard greens and black-eyed peas and street jive. It might put them at ease.

"I believe a li'l rationality could help," he said.

"Um." Singh's thin mouth twisted doubtfully. "Perhaps you should regard India as the great chessboard of our times, Professor. Here we have arisen from the great primordial agrarian times, fashioned our gods from our soil and age. Then we had orderly thinking, with all its assumptions, thrust upon us by the British. Now they are all gone, and we are suspended between the miasmic truths of the past, and the failed strictures of the present."

Clay looked out the dirty window and suppressed a smile. Even the physicists here spouted mumbo jumbo. They even appeared solemnly respectful of the devotees, who were just crazies like the women by the cow. How could anything solid come out of such a swamp? The chances that their experiment was right dwindled with each lurching, damp mile.

They climbed into the long range of hills before the Kolar fields. Burned-tan grass shimmered in the prickly heat. Sugarcane fields and rice paddies stood bone dry. In the villages, thin figures shaded beneath awnings, canvas tents, lean-tos, watched them pass. Lean faces betrayed only dim, momentary interest, and Clay wondered if his uncomfortable disguise was necessary outside Bangalore. Without stopping they ate their lunch of dried fruit and thin, brown bread.

In a high hill town, Patil stopped to refill his water bottle at a well. Clay peered out and saw down an alley a gang of stick-figure boys chasing a dog. They hemmed it in, and the bedraggled hound fled yapping from one side of their circle to the other. The animal whined at each rebuff and twice lost its footing on the cobblestones, sprawling, only to scramble up again and rush on. It was a cruel game, and the boys were strangely silent, playing without laughter. The dog was tiring; they drew in their circle.

A harsh edge to the boys' shouts made Clay slide open the van door. Several men were standing beneath a rust-scabbed sheet-metal awning nearby, and their eyes widened when they saw his face. They talked rapidly among themselves. Clay hesitated. The boys down the alley rushed the dog. They grabbed it as it yapped futilely and tried to bite them. They slipped twine around its jaws and silenced it. Shouting, they hoisted it into the air and marched off.

Clay gave up and slammed the door. The men came from under the awning. One rapped on the window. Clay just stared at them. One thumped on the door. Gestures, loud talk.

Patil and Singh came running, shouted something. Singh pushed the men away, chattering at them while Patil got the van started. Singh slammed the door in the face of a man with wild eyes. Patil gunned the engine and they ground away.

"They saw me and—"

"Distrust of outsiders is great here," Singh said. "They may be connected with the devotees, too."

"Guess I better keep my hat on."

"It would be advisable."

"I don't know, those boys—I was going to stop them pestering that dog. Stupid, I guess, but—"

"You will have to avoid being sentimental about such matters," Patil said severely.

"Uh—sentimental?"

"The boys were not playing."

"I don't—"

"They will devour it," Singh said.

Clay blinked. "Hindus eating meat...?"

"Hard times. I am really quite surprised that such an animal has survived this long," Patil said judiciously. "Dogs are uncommon. I imagine it was wild, living in the countryside, and ventured into town in search of garbage scraps."

The land rose as Clay watched the shimmering heat bend and flex the seemingly solid hills.

They pulled another dodge at the mine. The lead green van veered off toward the main entrance, a cluster of concrete buildings and conveyer assemblies. From a distance, the physicists in the blue van watched a ragtag group envelop the van before it had fully stopped.

"Devotees," Singh said abstractedly. "They search each vehicle for evidence of our research."

"Your graduate students, the mob'll let them pass?"

Patil peered through binoculars. "The crowd is administering a bit of a pushing about," he said in his oddly cadenced accent, combining lofty British diction with a singsong lilt.

"Damn, won't the mine people get rid—"

"Some mine workers are among the crowd, I should imagine," Patil said.

"They are beating the students."

"Well, can't we—"

"No time to waste." Singh waved them back into the blue van. "Let us make use of this diversion."

"But we could—"

"The students made their sacrifice for you. Do not devalue it, please."

Clay did not take his eyes from the nasty knot of confusion until they lurched over the ridgeline. Patil explained that they had been making regular runs to the main entrance for months now, to establish a pattern that drew devotees away from the secondary entrance.

"All this was necessary, and insured that we could bring in a foreign inspector," Patil concluded. Clay awkwardly thanked him for the attention to detail. He wanted to voice his embarrassment at having students roughed up simply to provide him cover, but something in the offhand manner of the two Indians made him hold his tongue.

The secondary entrance to the Kolar mine was a wide, tin-roofed shed like a low aircraft hangar. Girders crisscrossed it at angles that seemed to Clay dictated less by the constraints of mechanics than by the whims of the construction team. Cables looped among the already rusting steel struts and sang low notes in the rot-tinged wind that brushed his hair.

Monkeys chattered and scampered high in the struts. The three men walked into the shed, carrying cases. The cables began humming softly. The weave above their heads tightened with pops and sharp cracks. Clay realized that the seemingly random array was a complicated hoist that had started to pull the elevator up from miles beneath their feet. The steel lattice groaned as if it already knew how much work it had to do.

When it arrived, he saw that the elevator was a huge rattling box that reeked of machine oil. Clay lugged his cases in. The walls were broad wooden slats covered with chicken wire. Heat radiated from them. Patil stabbed a button on the big control board and they dropped quickly. The numbers of the levels zipped by on an amber digital display. A single dim yellow bulb cast shadows onto the wire. At the fifty-third level the bulb went out. The elevator did not stop.

In the enveloping blackness Clay felt himself lighten, as if the elevator was speeding up.

"Do not be alarmed," Patil called. "This frequently occurs."

Clay wondered if he meant the faster box or the light bulb. In the complete dark, he began to see blue phantoms leaping out from nowhere.

Abruptly he became heavy—and thought of Einstein's Gedanken experiment, which equated a man in an accelerating elevator to one standing on a planet. Unless Clay could see outside, check that the massive earth raced by beyond as it clasped him further into its depths, in principle he could be in either situation. He tried to recall how Einstein had reasoned from an imaginary elevator to deduce that matter curved space-time, and could not.

Einstein's elegant proof was impossibly far from the pressing truth of this elevator. Here Clay plunged in thick murk, a weight of tortured air prickling his nose, making sweat pop from his face. Oily, moist heat climbed into Clay's sinuses.

And he was not being carried aloft by this elevator, but allowed to plunge into heavy, primordial darkness—Einstein's vision in reverse. No classical coolness separated him from the press of a raw, random world. That European mindscape—Galileo's crisp cylinders rolling obediently down inclined planes, Einstein's dispassionate observers surveying their smooth geometries like scrupulous bank clerks—evaporated here like yesterday's stale champagne. Sudden anxiety filled his throat. His stomach tightened and he tasted acrid gorge. He opened his mouth to shout, and as if to stop him, his own knees sagged with suddenly returning weight, physics regained.

A rattling thump—and they stopped. He felt Patil slam aside the rattling gate. A sullen glow beyond bathed an ornate brass shrine to a Hindu god. They came out into a steepled room of carved rock. Clay felt a breath of slightly cooler air from a cardboard-mouthed conduit nearby.

"We must force the air down from above." Patil gestured. "Otherwise this would read well over a hundred and ten Fahrenheit." He proudly pointed to an ancient battered British thermometer, whose mercury stood at ninety-eight. They trudged through several tunnels, descended another few hundred feet on a ramp, and then followed gleaming railroad tracks. A white bulb every ten meters threw everything into exaggerated relief, shadows stabbing everywhere. A brown cardboard sign proclaimed from the ceiling:

FIRST EVER COSMIC RAY NEUTRINO INTERACTION
RECORDED HERE IN APRIL 1965

For over forty years, teams of devoted Indian physicists had labored patiently inside the Kolar gold fields. For half a century, India's high mountains and deep mines had made important cosmic ray experiments possible with inexpensive instruments. Clay recalled how a joint Anglo-Indian-Japanese team had detected that first neutrino, scooped it from the unending cosmic sleet that penetrated even to this depth. He thought of unsung Indian physicists sweating here, tending the instruments and tracing the myriad sources of background error. Yet they themselves were background for the original purpose of the deep holes: Two narrow cars clunked past, full of chopped stone.

"Some still work this portion," Patil's clear voice cut through the muffled air. "Though I suspect they harvest little."

Pushing the rusty cars were four wiry men, so sweaty that the glaring bulbs gave their sliding muscles a hard sheen like living stone. They wore filthy cloths wrapped around their heads, as if they needed protection against the low ceiling rather than the heat. As Clay stumbled on, he felt that there might be truth to this, because he sensed the mass above as a precarious judgment over them all, a sullen presence. Einstein's crisp distinctions, the clean certainty of the Gedanken experiments, meant nothing in this blurred air.

They rounded an irregular curve and met a niche neatly cut off by a chainlink fence.

PROTON STABILITY EXPERIMENT

TATA INSTITUTE OF FUNDAMENTAL RESEARCH, BOMBAY

80TH LEVEL HEATHCOTE SHAFT,

KFG 2300 METERS DEPTH

These preliminaries done, the experiment itself began abruptly. Clay had expected some assembly rooms, an office, refrigerated 'scope cages. Instead, a few meters ahead the tunnel opened in all directions. They stood before a huge bay roughly cleaved from the brown rock.

And filling the vast volume was what seemed to be a wall as substantial as the rock itself. It was an iron grid of rusted pipe. The pipes were square, not round, and dwindled into the distance. Each had a dusty seal, a pressure dial, and a number painted in white. Clay estimated them to be at least a hundred feet long. They were stacked Lincoln-log fashion. He walked to the edge of the bay and looked down. Layers of pipe tapered away below to a distant floodlit floor and soared to meet the gray ceiling above. "Enormous," he said.

"We expended great effort in scaling up our earlier apparatus," Singh said enthusiastically.

"As big as a house."

Patil said merrily, "An American house, perhaps. Ours are smaller."

A woman's voice nearby said, "And nothing lives in this iron house, Professor Clay."

Clay turned to see a willowy Indian woman regarding him with a wry smile. She seemed to have come out of the shadows, a brown apparition in shorts and a scrupulously white blouse, appearing fullblown where a moment before there had been nothing. Her heavy eyebrows rose in amusement. "Ah, this is Mrs. Buli," Patil said.

"I keep matters running here, while my colleagues venture into the world," she said.

Clay accepted her coolly offered hand. She gave him one quick, well defined shake and stepped back. "I can assist your assessment, perhaps."

"I'll need all your help," he said sincerely. The skimpy surroundings already made him wonder if he could do his job at all.

"Labor we have," she said. "Equipment, little."

"I brought some cross-check programs with me," he said.

"Excellent," Mrs. Buli said. "I shall have several of my graduate students assist you, and of course I offer my full devotion as well."

Clay smiled at her antique formality. She led him down a passage into the soft fluorescent glow of a large data-taking room. It was crammed with terminals and a bank of disk drives, all meshed by the usual cable spaghetti. "We keep our computers cooler than our staff, you see," Mrs. Buli said with a small smile. They went down a ramp, and Clay could feel the rock's steady heat.

They came out onto the floor of the cavern. Thick I-beams roofed the stone box. "Over a dozen lives, that was the cost of this excavation," Singh said.

"That many?"

"They attempted to save on the cost of explosives," Patil said with a stern look.

"Not that such will matter in the long run," Singh said mildly. Clay chose not to pursue the point.

Protective bolts studded the sheer rock, anchoring cross-beams that stabilized the tower of pipes. Scaffolding covered some sections of the black and rusty pile. Blasts of compressed air from the surface a mile above swept down on them from the ceiling, flapping Clay's shirt.

Mrs. Buli had to shout, the effort contorting her smooth face. "We obtained the pipes from a government program that attempted to improve the quality of plumbing in the cities. A failure, I fear. But a godsend for us."

Patil was pointing out electrical details when the air conduits wheezed into silence. "Hope that's temporary," Clay said in the sudden quiet.

"A minor repair, I am sure," Patil said.

"These occur often," Singh agreed earnestly.

Clay could already feel prickly sweat oozing from him. He wondered how often they had glitches in the circuitry down here, awash in pressing heat, and how much that could screw up even the best diagnostics.

Mrs. Buli went on in a lecturer's singsong. "We hired engineering students, there are many such, an oversupply—to thread a single wire down the bore of each pipe. We sealed each, then welded them together to make lengths of a hundred feet. Then we filled them with argon and linked them with a high-voltage line. We have found that a voltage of 280 khz..."

Clay nodded, filing away details, noting where her description differed from that of the NSF. The Kolar group had continuously modified their experiment for decades, and this latest enormous expansion was badly documented. Still, the principle was simple. Each pipe was held at high voltage, so that when a charged particle passed through, a spark leaped. A particle's path was followed by counting the segments of triggered pipes. This mammoth stack of iron was a huge Geiger counter.

He leaned back, nodding at Buli's lecture, watching a team of men at the very top. A loud clang rang through the chasm. Sparks showered, burnt orange and blue. The garish plumes silhouetted the welders and sent cascades of sparks down through the lattice of pipes. For an instant Clay imagined he was witnessing cosmic rays sleeting down through the towering house of iron, illuminating it with their short, sputtering lives.

"—and I am confident that we have seen well over fifty true events," Mrs. Buli concluded with a jaunty upward tilt of her chin.

"What?" Clay struggled back from his daydreaming. "That many?"

She laughed, a high tinkling. "You do not believe!"

"Well, that is a lot."

"Our detecting mass is now larger," Mrs. Buli said.

"Last we heard it was five hundred tons," Clay said carefully. The claims wired to the NSF and the Royal Society had been skimpy on details.

"That was years ago," Patil said. "We have redoubled our efforts, as you can see."

"Well, to see that many decays, you'd have to have a hell of a lot of observing volume," Clay said doubtfully.

"We can boast of five thousand tons, Professor Clay," Mrs. Buli said.

"Looks it," Clay said laconically to cover his surprise. It would not do to let them think they could overwhelm him with magnitudes. Question was, did they have the telltale events?

The cooling air came on with a thump and whoosh. Clay breathed it in deeply, face turned up to the iron house where protons might be dying, and sucked in swarming scents of the parched countryside miles above.

He knew from the start that there would be no eureka moment. Certainty was the child of tedium.

He traced the tangled circuitry for two days before he trusted it. "You got to open the sack 'fore I'll believe there's a cat in there," he told Mrs. Buli, and then had to explain that he was joking.

Then came a three-day trial run, measuring the exact sputter of decay from a known radioactive source. System response was surprisingly good. He found their techniques needlessly Byzantine, but workable. His null checks of the detectors inside the pipes came up goose-egg clean.

Care was essential. Proton decay was rare. The Grand Unified Theories which had enjoyed such success in predicting new particles had also sounded a somber note through all of physics. Matter was mortal. But not very mortal, compared with the passing flicker of a human lifetime.

The human body had about 10^{29} neutrons and protons in it. If only a tiny fraction of them decayed in a human lifetime, the radiation from the disintegration would quickly kill everyone of cancer. The survival of even small life-forms implied that the protons inside each nucleus had to survive an average of nearly a billion billion years.

So even before the Grand Unified Theories, physicists knew that protons lived long. The acronym for the theories was GUTs, and a decade earlier graduate students like Clay had worn T-shirts with insider jokes like IT TAKES GUTS TO DO PARTICLE PHYSICS. But proving that there was some truth to the lame nerd jests took enormous effort.

The simplest of the GUTs predicted a proton lifetime of about 10^{31} years, immensely greater than the limit set by the existence of life. In fact, it was far longer even than the age of the universe, which was only a paltry 2×10^{10} years old.

One could check this lifetime by taking one proton and watching it for 10^{31} years. Given the short attention span of humans, it was better to assemble 10^{31} protons and watch them for a year, hoping one would fizzle. Physicists in the United States, Japan, Italy, and India had done that all through the 1980s and 1990s. And no protons had died.

Well, the theorists had said, the mathematics must be more complicated. They discarded certain symmetry groups and thrust others forward. The lifetime might be 10^{32} years, then.

The favored method of gathering protons was to use those in water. Western physicists carved swimming pools six stories deep in salt mines and eagerly watched for the characteristic blue pulse of dying matter. Detecting longer lifetimes meant waiting longer, which nobody liked, or adding more protons. Digging bigger swimming pools was easy, so attention had turned to the United States and Japan…but still, no protons died. The lifetime exceeded 10^{32} years.

The austerity of the 1990s had shut down the ambitious experiments in the West. Few remembered this forlorn experiment in Kolar, wedded to watching the cores of iron rods for the quick spurt of decay. When political difficulties cut off contact, the already beleaguered physicists in the West assumed the Kolar effort had ceased.

But Kolar was the deepest experiment, less troubled by the hail of cosmic rays that polluted the Western data. Clay came to appreciate that as he scrolled through the myriad event-plots in the Kolar computer cubes. There were 9×10^9 recorded decays of all types. The system rejected obvious garbage events, but there were many subtle enigmas. Theory said that protons died because the quarks that composed them could change their identities. A seemingly capricious alteration of quarky states sent the proton asunder, spitting forth a zoo of fragments. Neutrons were untroubled by this, for in free space they decayed anyway, into a proton and electron. Matter's end hinged, finally, on the stability of the proton alone.

Clay saw immediately that the Kolar group had invested years in their software. They had already filtered out thousands of phantom events that imitated true proton decay. There were eighteen ways a proton could die, each with a different signature of spraying light and particle debris.

The delicate traceries of particle paths were recorded as flashes and sparkles in the house of iron outside. Clay searched through endless graphic printouts, filigrees woven from digital cloth.

"You will find we have pondered each candidate event," Mrs. Buli said mildly on the sixth day of Clay's labors.

"Yeah, the analysis is sharp," he said cautiously. He was surprised at the high level of the work but did not want to concede anything yet.

"If any ambiguity arose, we discarded the case."

"I can see that."

"Some pions were not detected in the right energy range, so of course we omitted those."

"Good."

Mrs. Buli leaned over to show him a detail of the cross-checking program, and he caught a heady trace of wildflowers. Her perfume reminded him abruptly that her sari wrapped over warm, ample swells. She had no sagging softness, no self-indulgent bulgings. The long oval of her face and her ample lips conveyed a fragile sensuality…

He wrenched his attention back to physics and stared hard at the screen. Event vertices were like time-lapse photos of traffic accidents, intersections exploding, screaming into shards. The crystalline mathematical order of physics led to riots of incandescence. And Clay was judge, weighing testimony after the chaos.

He had insisted on analyzing the several thousand preliminary candidates himself, as a double blind against the Kolar group's software. After nine days, he had isolated sixty-seven events that looked like the genuine article. Sixty-five of his agreed with Mrs. Buli's analysis. The two holdouts were close, Clay had to admit.

"Nearly on the money," he said reflectively as he stared at the Kolar software's array.

"You express such values," Mrs. Buli said. "Always a financial analogy."

"Just a way of speaking."

"Still, let us discard the two offending events."

"Well, I'd be willing—"

"No, uh, we consider only the sixty-five." Her almond eyes gave no hint of slyness.

"They're pretty good bets, I'd say." Her eyebrows arched. "Only a manner of speech."

"Then you feel they fit the needs of theory."

Her carefully balanced way of phrasing made him lean forward, as if to compensate for his judge's role. "I'll have to consider all the other decay modes in detail. Look for really obscure processes that might mimic the real thing."

She nodded. "True, there is need to study such."

Protons could die from outside causes, too. Wraithlike neutrinos spewed forth by the sun penetrated even here, shattering protons. Murderous muons lumbered through as cosmic rays, plowing furrows of exploding nuclei.

Still, things looked good. He was surprised at their success, earned by great labor. "I'll be as quick about it as I can."

"We have prepared a radio link that we can use, should the desire come."

"Huh? What?"

"In case you need to reach your colleagues in America."

"Ah, yes."

To announce the result, he saw. To get the word out. But why the rush?

It occurred to him that they might doubt whether he himself would get out at all.

✸

They slept each night in a clutch of tin lean-tos that cowered down a raw ravine. Laborers from the mine had slept there in better days, and the physicists had gotten the plumbing to work for an hour each night. The men slept in a long shed, but gave Clay a small wooden shack. He ate thin, mealy gruel with them each evening, carefully dropping purification tablets in his water, and was rewarded with untroubled bowels. He lost weight in the heat of the mine, but the nights were cool and the breezes that came then were soft with moisture. The fifth evening, as they sat around a potbellied iron stove in the men's shed, Patil pointed to a distant corrugated metal hut and said, "There we have concealed a satellite dish. We can knock away the roof and transmit, if you like."

Clay brightened. "Can I call home?"

"If need be."

Something in Patil's tone told him a frivolous purpose was not going to receive their cooperation. "Maybe tomorrow?"

"Perhaps. We must be sure that the devotees do not see us reveal it."

"They think we're laborers?"

"So we have convinced them, I believe."

"And me?"

"You would do well to stay inside."

"Um. Look, got anything to drink?"

Patil frowned. "Has the water pipe stopped giving?"

"No, I mean, you know—a drink. Gin and tonic, wasn't that what the Brits preferred?"

"Alcohol is the devil's urine," Patil said precisely.

"It won't scramble my brains."

"Who can be sure? The mind is a tentative instrument."

"You don't want any suspicion that I'm unreliable, that it?"

"No, of course not," Singh broke in anxiously.

"Needn't worry," Clay muttered. The heat below and the long hours of tedious work were wearing him down. "I'll be gone soon's I can get things wrapped up."

"You agree that we are seeing the decays?"

217

"Let's say things're looking better."

Clay had been holding back even tentative approval. He had expected some show of jubilation. Patil and Singh simply sat and stared into the flickering coals of the stove's half-open door.

Slowly Patil said, "Word will spread quickly."

"Soon as you transmit it on that dish, sure."

Singh murmured, "Much shall change."

"Look, you might want to get out of here, go present a paper—"

"Oh no, we shall remain," Singh said quickly.

"Those devotees could give you trouble if they find—"

"We expect that this discovery, once understood, shall have great effects," Patil said solemnly. "I much prefer to witness them from my home country."

The cadence and mood of this conversation struck Clay as odd, but he put it down to the working conditions. Certainly they had sacrificed a great deal to build and run this experiment amid crippling desolation.

"This result will begin the final renunciation of the materialistic worldview," Singh said matter-of-factly.

"Huh?"

"In peering at the individual lives of mere particles, we employ the reductionist hammer," Patil explained. "But nature is not like a salamander, cut into fragments."

"Or if it were," Singh added, "once the salamander is so sliced, try to make it do its salamander walk again." A broad white grin split the gloom of nightfall. "The world is an implicate order, Dr. Clay. All parts are hinged to each other."

Clay frowned. He vaguely remembered a theory of quantum mechanics which used that term—"implicate order," meaning that a deeper realm of physical theory lay beneath the uncertainties of wave mechanics. Waves that took it into their heads to behave like particles, and the reverse—these were supposed to be illusions arising from our ignorance of a more profound theory. But there was no observable consequence of such notions, and to Clay such mumbo jumbo from theorists who never got their hands dirty was empty rhapsodizing. Still, he was supposed to be the diplomat here.

He gave a judicial nod. "Yeah, sure—but when the particles die, it'll all be gone, right?"

"Yes, in about 10^{34} years," Patil said. "But the knowledge of matter's mortality will spread as swiftly as light, on the wind of our transmitter. You are an experimentalist, Dr. Clay, and thus—if you will forgive my putting it so—addicted to cutting the salamander." Patil made a steeple of his fingers, sending spindly shadows rippling across his face. "The world we study is conditioned by our perceptions of it. The implied order is partially from our own design."

"Sure, quantum measurement, uncertainty principle, all that." Clay had sat through all the usual lectures about this stuff and didn't feel like doing so again. Not in a dusty shed with his stomach growling from hunger. He sipped at his cup of weak Darjeeling and yawned.

"Difficulties of measurement reflect underlying problems," Patil said. "Even the Westerner Plato saw that we perceive only imperfect modes of the true, deeper world."

"What deeper world?" Clay sighed despite himself.

"We do not know. We cannot know."

"Look, we make our measurements, we report. Period."

Amused, Singh said, "And that is where matters end?"

Patil said, "Consensual reality, that is your 'real' world, Professor Clay. But our news may cause that bland, unthinking consensus to falter."

Clay shrugged. This sounded like late-night college bullshit sessions among boozed-up science nerds. Patty-cake pantheism, quantum razzle-dazzle, garbage philosophy. It was one thing to be open-minded and another to let your brains fall out. Was everybody on this wrecked continent a boogabooga type? He had to get out.

"Look, I don't see what difference—"

"Until the curtain of seeming surety is swept away," Singh put in.

"Surety?"

"This world—this universe—has labored long under the illusion of its own permanence." Singh spread his hands, animated in the flickering yellow glow. "We might die, yes, the sun might even perish—but the universe went on. Now we prove otherwise. There cannot help but be profound reactions."

He thought he saw what they were driving at. "A Nobel Prize, even."

To his surprise, both men laughed merrily. "Oh no," Patil said, arching his eyebrows. "No such trifles are expected!"

The boxy meeting room beside the data bay was packed. From it came a subdued mutter, a fretwork of talk laced with anticipation.

Outside, someone had placed a small chalky statue of a grinning elephant. Clay hesitated, stroked it. Despite the heat of the mine, the elephant was cool.

"The workers just brought it down," Mrs. Buli explained with a smile. "Our Hindu god of auspicious beginnings."

"Or endings," Patil said behind her. "Equally."

Clay nodded and walked into the trapped, moist heat of the room. Everyone was jammed in, graduate students and laborers alike, their *kurta* already showing sweaty crescents. Clay saw the three students the devotees had beaten and exchanged respectful bows with them.

Perceiving some need for ceremony, he opened with lengthy praise for the endless hours they had labored, exclaiming over how startled the world would be to learn of such a facility. Then he plunged into consideration of each candidate event, his checks and counter-checks, vertex corrections, digital array flaws, mean free paths, ionization rates, the artful programming that deflected the myriad possible sources of error. He could feel tension rising in the room as he cast the events on the inch-thick wall screen, calling them forth from the files in his cubes. Some he threw into 3-D, to show the full path through the cage of iron that had captured the death rattle of infinity.

And at the end, all cases reviewed, he said quietly, "You have found it. The proton lifetime is very nearly 10^{34} years."

The room burst into applause, wide grins and wild shouts as everyone pressed forward to shake his hand.

Singh handled the message to the NSF. Clay also constructed a terse though detailed summary and sent it to the International Astronomical Union for release to the worldwide system of observatories and universities. Clay knew this would give a vital assist to his career. With the Kolar team staying here, he would be their only spokesman. And this was very big, media-mesmerizing news indeed.

The result was important to physicists and astronomers alike, for the destiny of all their searches ultimately would be sealed by the faint failures of particles no eye would ever see. In 10^{34} years, far in the depths of space, the great celestial cities, the galaxies, would be ebbing. The last red stars would flicker, belch, and gutter out. Perhaps life would have clung to them and found a way to persist against the growing cold. Cluttered with the memorabilia of the ages, the islands of mute matter would turn at last to their final conqueror—not entropy's still hand, but this silent sputter of protons.

Clay thought of the headlines: UNIVERSE TO END. What would that do to harried commuters on their way to work?

He watched Singh send the stuttering messages via the big satellite dish, the corrugated tin roof of the shed pulled aside, allowing him to watch burnt gold twilight seep across the sky. Clay felt no elation, as blank as a drained capacitor. He had gone into physics because of the sense it gave of grasping deep mysteries. He could look at bridges and trace the vectored stability that ruled them. When his daughter asked why the sky was blue, he actually knew, and could sketch out a simple answer. It had never occurred to him to fear flying, because he knew the Bernoulli equation for the pressure that held up the plane. But this result…

Even the celebratory party that evening left him unmoved. Graduate students turned out in their best khaki. Sitar music swarmed through the scented air, ragas thumping and weaving. He found his body swaying to the refractions of tone and scale.

"It is a pity you cannot learn more of our country," Mrs. Buli remarked, watching him closely.

"Right now I'm mostly interested in sleep."

"Sleep is not always kind." She seemed wry and distant in the night's smudged humidity. "One of our ancient gods, Brahma, is said to sleep and we are what he dreams."

"In that case, for you folks maybe he's been having a nightmare lately."

"Ah yes, our troubles. But do not let them mislead you about India. They pass."

"I'm sure they will," Clay replied, dutifully diplomatic.

"You were surprised, were you not, at the outcome?" she said piercingly.

"Uh, well, I had to be skeptical."

"Yes, for a scientist certainty is built on deep layers of doubt."

"Like my daddy said, in the retail business deal with everybody, but count your change."

She laughed. "We have given you a bargain, perhaps!"

He was acutely aware that his initial doubts must have been obvious. And what unsettled him now was not just the hard-won success here, but their strange attitude toward it.

The graduate students came then and tried to teach him a dance. He did a passable job and a student named Venkatraman slipped him a glass of beer, forbidden vice. It struck Clay as comic that the Indian government spent much energy to suppress alcohol but did little about the population explosion. The students all laughed when he made a complicated joke about booze, but he could not be sure whether they meant it. The music seemed to quicken, his heart thumping to keep up with it. They addressed him as Clay, a term of respect, and asked his opinion of what they might do next with the experiment. He shrugged, thinking 'Nother job, *sahib?* and suggested using it as a detector for neutrinos from supernovas. That had paid off when the earlier generation of neutrino detectors picked up the 1987 supernova. The atom bomb, the 1987 event, now this—particle physics, he realized uncomfortably, was steeped in death. The sitar slid and rang, and Mrs. Buli made arch jokes to go with the spicy salad. Still, he turned in early. To be awakened by a soft breeze. A brushing presence, sliding cloth… He sensed her sari as a luminous fog. Moonlight streaming through a lopsided window cast shimmering auras through the cloth as she loomed above him. Reached for him. Lightly flung away his sticky bedclothes.

A soft hand covered his mouth, bringing a heady savor of ripe earth. His senses ran out of him and into the surrounding dark, coiling in air as he took her weight. She was surprisingly light, though thick-waisted, her breasts like teacups compared with the full curves of her hips. His hands slid and pressed, finding a delightful slithering moisture all over her, a sheen of vibrancy. Her sari evaporated. The high planes of her face caught vagrant blades of moonlight, and he saw a curious tentative, expectant expression there as she wrapped him in soft pressures. Her mouth did not so much kiss his as enclose it, formulating an argument of sweet rivulets that trickled into his porous self. She slipped into place atop him, a slick clasp that melted him up into her, a perfect fit, slick with dark insistence. He closed his eyes, but the glow diffused through his eyelids, and he could see her hair fanning through the air like motion underwater, her luxuriant weight bucking, trembling as her nails scratched his shoulders, musk rising smoky from them both. A silky muscle milked him at each heart-thump. Her velvet mass orbited above their fulcrum, bearing down with feathery demands, and he remembered brass icons, gaudy Indian posters, and felt above him Kali strumming in fevered darkness. She locked legs around him, squeezing him up into her surprisingly hard muscles, grinding, drawing forth, pushing back. She cried out with great heaves and lungfuls of the thickening air, mouth going slack beneath hooded eyes, and he shot sharply up into her, a convulsion that poured out all the knotted aches in him, delivering them into the tumbled steamy earth—and next, with no memories between, he was stumbling with her down a gully…beneath slanting silvery moonlight. "What—what's—"

"Quiet!" She shushed him like a schoolmarm.

He recognized the rolling countryside near the mine. Vague forms flitted in the distance. Wracked cries cut the night.

"The devotees," Mrs. Buli whispered as they stumbled on. "They have assaulted the mine entrance."

"How'd we—"

"You were difficult to rouse," she said with a sidelong glance.

Was she trying to be amusing? The sudden change from mysterious supercharged sensuality back to this clipped, formal professionalism disoriented him.

"Apparently some of our laborers had a grand party. It alerted the devotees to our presence, some say. I spoke to a laborer while you slept, however, who said that the devotees knew of your presence. They asked for you."

"Why me?"

"Something about your luggage and a telephone call home."

Clay gritted his teeth and followed her along a path that led among the slumped hills, away from their lodgings. Soon the mine entrance was visible below. Running figures swarmed about it like black gnats. Ragged chants erupted from them. A *waarrrk waarrrk* sound came from the hangar, and it was some moments until Clay saw long chains of human bodies hanging from the rafters, swinging themselves in unison.

"They're pulling down the hangar," he whispered.

"I despair for what they have done inside."

He instinctively reached for her and felt the supple warmth he had embraced seemingly only moments before. She turned and gave him her mouth again.

"We—back there—why'd you come to me?"

"It was time. Even we feel the joy of release from order, Professor Clay."

"Well, sure..." Clay felt illogically embarrassed, embracing a woman who still had the musk of the bed about her, yet who used his title. "But... how'd I get here? Seems like—"

"You were immersed. Taken out of yourself."

"Well, yeah, it was good, fine, but I can't remember anything."

She smiled. "The best moments leave no trace. That is a signature of the implicate order."

Clay breathed in the waxy air to help clear his head. More mumbo jumbo, he thought, delivered by her with an open, expectant expression. In the darkness it took a moment to register that she had fled down another path. "Where'll we go?" he gasped when he caught up.

"We must get to the vans. They are parked some kilometers away."

He hesitated a moment, then followed her. There was nothing irreplaceable. It certainly wasn't worth braving the mob below for the stuff.

They wound down through bare hillsides dominated by boulders. The sky rippled with heat lightning. Puffy clouds scurried quickly in from the west, great ivory flashes working among them. The ground surged slightly. "Earthquake?" he asked.

"There were some earlier, yes. Perhaps that has excited the devotees further tonight, put their feet to running."

There was no sign of the physics team. Pebbles squirted from beneath his boots—he wondered how he had managed to get them on without remembering it—and recalled again her hypnotic sensuality. Stones rattled away down into narrow dry washes on each side. Clouds blotted out the moonglow, and they had to pick their way along the trail.

Clay's mind spun with plans, speculations, jittery anxiety. Mrs. Buli was now his only link to the Western fragment of India, and he could scarcely see her her in the shadows. She moved with liquid grace, her sari trailing, sandals slapping. Suddenly she crouched down. "More."

Along the path came figures bearing lanterns. They moved silently in the fitful silvery moonlight. There was no place to hide, and the party had already seen them.

"Stand still," she said. Again the crisp Western diction, yet her ample hips swayed slightly, reminding him of her deeper self.

Clay wished he had a club, a knife, anything. He made himself stand beside her, hands clenched. For once his blackness might be an advantage.

The devotees passed, eyes rapt. Clay had expected them to be singing or chanting mantras or rubbing beads—but not shambling forward as if to their doom. The column barely glanced at him. In his baggy cotton trousers and formless shirt, he hoped he was unremarkable. A woman passed nearby, apparently carrying something across her back. Clay blinked. Her hands were nailed to the ends of a beam, and she carried it proudly, palms bloody, half crucified. Her face was serene, eyes focused on the roiling sky. Behind her was a man bearing a plate. Clay thought the shambling figure carried marbles on the dish until he peered closer and saw an iris, and realized the entire plate was packed with eyeballs. He gasped and faces turned toward him. Then the man was gone along the path, and Clay waited, holding his breath against a gamy stench he could not name. Some muttered to themselves, some carried religious artifacts, beads and statuettes and drapery, but none had the fervor of the devotees he had seen before. The ground trembled again.

And out of the dark air came a humming. Something struck a man in the line and he clutched at his throat, crying hoarsely. Clay leaped forward without thinking. He pulled the man's hands away. Lodged in the narrow of the throat was something like an enormous cockroach with fluttering wings. It had already embedded its head in the man. Spiky legs furiously scrabbled against the soiled skin to dig deeper. The man coughed and shouted weakly, as though the thing was already blocking his throat.

Clay grabbed its hind legs and pulled. The insect wriggled with surprising strength. He saw the hind stinger too late. The sharp point struck a hot jolt of pain into his thumb. Anger boiled in him. He held on despite the pain and yanked the thing free. It made a sucking sound coming out. He hissed with revulsion and violently threw it down the hillside.

The man stumbled, gasping, and then ran back down the path, never even looking at them.

Mrs. Buli grabbed Clay, who was staggering around in a circle, shaking his hand. "I will cut it!" she cried.

He held still while she made a precise cross cut and drained the blood. "What...what was that?"

"A wasp-thing from the pouches that hang on our trees."

"Oh yeah. One of those bio tricks."

"They are still overhead."

Clay listened to the drone hanging over them. Another devotee shrieked and slapped the back of his neck. Clay numbly watched the man run away. His hand throbbed, but he could feel the effects ebbing. Mrs. Buli tore a strip from her sari and wrapped his thumb to quell the bleeding.

All this time, devotees streamed past them in the gloom. None took the slightest notice of Clay. Some spoke to themselves.

"Western science doesn't seem to bother 'em much now," Clay whispered wryly.

Mrs. Buli nodded. The last figure to pass was a woman who limped, sporting an arm that ended not in a hand but in a spoon, nailed to a stub of cork.

He followed Mrs. Buli into enveloping darkness. "Who were they?"

"I do not know. They spoke seldom and repeated the same words. *Dharma* and *samsara*, terms of destiny."

"They don't care about us?"

"They appear to sense a turning, a resolution." In the fitful moonglow her eyes were liquid puzzles.

"But they destroyed the experiment."

"I gather that knowledge of your Western presence was like the wasp-things. Irritating, but only a catalyst, not the cause."

"What did make them—"

"No time. Come."

They hurriedly entered a thin copse of spindly trees that lined a streambed. Dust stifled his nose and he breathed through his mouth. The clouds raced toward the horizon with unnatural speed, seeming to flee from the west. Trees swayed before an unfelt wind, twisting and reaching for the shifting sky.

"Weather," Mrs. Buli answered his questions. "Bad weather."

They came upon a small crackling fire. Figures crouched around it, and Clay made to go around, but Mrs. Buli walked straight toward it. Women squatted, poking sticks into flames. Clay saw that something moved on the sticks. A momentary shaft of moonlight showed the oily skin of snakes, tiny eyes crisp as crystals, the shafts poking from yawning white mouths that still moved. The women's faces of stretched yellow skin anxiously watched the blackening, sizzling snakes, turning them. The fire hissed as though raindrops fell upon it, but Clay felt nothing wet, just the dry rub of a fresh abrading wind. Smoke wrapped the women in gray wreaths, and Mrs. Buli hurried on.

So much, so fast. Clay felt rising in him a leaden conviction born of all he had seen in this land. So many people, so much pain—how could it matter? The West assumed that the individual was important, the bedrock of all. That was why the obliterating events of the West's own history, like the Nazi Holocaust, by erasing humans in such numbing numbers, cast grave doubt on the significance of any one. India did something like that for him. Could a universe which produced so many bodies, so many minds in shadowed torment, care a whir about humanity? Endless, meaningless duplication of grinding pain...

A low mutter came on the wind, like a bass theme sounding up from the depths of a dusty well.

Mrs. Buli called out something he could not understand. She began running, and Clay hastened to follow. If he lost her in these shadows, he could lose all connection.

Quickly they left the trees and crossed a grassy field rutted by ancient agriculture and prickly with weeds. On this flat plain he could see that the whole sky worked with twisted light, a colossal electrical discharge leathering into more branches than a gnarled tree. The anxious clouds caught blue and burnt-yellow pulses and seemed to relay them, like the countless transformers and capacitors and voltage drops that made a worldwide communications net, carrying staccato messages laced with crackling punctuations.

"The vans," she panted.

Three brown vans crouched beneath a canopy of thin trees, further concealed beneath khaki tents that blended in with the dusty fields. Mrs. Buli yanked open the door of the first one. Her fingers fumbled at the ignition. "The key must be concealed," she said quickly.

"Why?" he gasped, throat raw.

"They are to be always with the vans."

"Uh-huh. Check the others."

She hurried away. Clay got down on his knees, feeling the lip of the van's undercarriage. The ground seemed to heave with inner heat, dry and rasping, the pulse of the planet. He finished one side of the van and crawled under, feeling along the rear axle. He heard a distant plaintive cry, as eerie and forlorn as the call of a bird lost in fog. "Clay? None in the others."

His hand touched a small slick box high up on the axle. He plucked it from its magnetic grip and rolled out from under.

"If we drive toward the mine," she said, "we can perhaps find others."

"Others, hell. Most likely we'll run into devotees."

Figures in the trees. Flitting, silent, quick.

"But—"

He pushed her in and tried to start the van. Running shapes in the field. He got the engine started on the third try and gunned it. They growled away. Something hard shattered the back window into a spiderweb, but then Clay swerved several times and nothing more hit them.

After a few minutes his heart-thumps slowed, and he turned on the headlights to make out the road. The curves were sandy and he did not want to get stuck. He stamped on the gas.

Suddenly great washes of amber light streamed across the sky, pale lances cutting the clouds. "My God, what's happening?"

"It is more than weather."

Her calm, abstracted voice made him glance across the seat. "No kidding."

"No earthquake could have collateral effects of this order."

He saw by the dashboard lights that she wore a lapis lazuli necklace. He had felt it when she came to him, and now its deep blues seemed like the only note of color in the deepening folds of night. "It must be something far more profound."

"What?"

The road now arrowed straight through a tangled terrain of warped trees and oddly shaped boulders. Something rattled against the windshield like hail, but Clay could see nothing.

"We have always argued, some of us, that the central dictate of quantum mechanics is the interconnected nature of the observer and the observed."

The precise, detached lecturer style again drew his eyes to her. Shadowed, her face gave away no secrets.

"We always filter the world," she said with dreamy momentum, "and yet are linked to it. How much of what we see is in fact taught us, by our bodies, or by the consensus reality that society trains us to see, even before we can speak for ourselves?"

"Look, that sky isn't some problem with my eyes. It's real. Hear that?" Something big and soft had struck the door of the van, rocking it.

"And we here have finished the program of materialistic science, have we not? We flattered the West by taking it seriously. As did the devotees."

Clay grinned despite himself. It was hard to feel flattered when you were fleeing for your life.

Mrs. Buli stretched lazily, as though relaxing into the clasp of the moist night. "So we have proven the passing nature of matter. What fresh forces does that bring into play?"

"Huh!" Clay spat back angrily. "Look here, we just sent word out, reported the result. How—"

"So that by now millions, perhaps billions of people know that the very stones that support them must pass."

"So what? Just some theoretical point about subnuclear physics, how's that going to—"

"Who is to say? What avatar? The point is that we were believed. Certain knowledge, universally correlated, surely has some impact—"

The van lurched. Suddenly they jounced and slammed along the smooth roadway. A bright plume of sparks shot up behind them, brimming firefly yellow in the night. "Axle's busted!" Clay cried. He got the van stopped. In the sudden silence, it registered that the motor had gone dead.

They climbed out. Insects buzzed and hummed in the hazy gloom. The roadway was still straight and sure, but on all sides great blobs of iridescent water swelled up from the ground, making colossal drops. The trembling half-spheres wobbled in the frayed moonlight. Silently, softly, the bulbs began to detach from the foggy ground and gently loft upward. Feathery luminescent clouds above gathered on swift winds that sheared their edges. These billowing, luxuriant banks snagged the huge teardrop shapes as they plunged skyward.

"I...I don't..."

Mrs. Buli turned and embraced him. Her moist mouth opened a redolent interior continent to him, teeming and blackly bountiful, and he had to resist falling inward, a tumbling silvery bubble in a dark chasm.

"The category of perfect roundness is fading," she said calmly.

Clay looked at the van. The wheels had become ellipses. At each revolution they had slammed the axles into the roadway, leaving behind long scratches of rough tar. He took a step.

She said, "Since we can walk, the principle of pivot and lever, of muscles pulling bones, survives."

"How...this doesn't..."

"But do our bodies depend on roundness? I wonder." She carefully lay down on the blacktop.

The road straightened precisely, like joints in an aged spine popping as they realigned.

Angles cut their spaces razor-sharp, like axioms from Euclid. Clouds merged, forming copious tinkling hexagons.

"It is good to see that some features remain. Perhaps these are indeed the underlying Platonic beauties."

"What?" Clay cried.

"The undying forms," Mrs. Buli said abstractly. "Perhaps that one Western idea was correct after all."

Clay desperately grasped the van. He jerked his arm back when the metal skin began flexing and reshaping itself.

Smooth glistening forms began to emerge from the rough, coarse earth. Above the riotous, heaving land the moon was now a brassy cube. Across its face played enormous black cracks like mad lightning.

Somewhere far away his wife and daughter were in this, too. G'bye, Daddy. It's been real.

Quietly the land began to rain upward. Globs dripped toward the pewter, filmy continent swarming freshly above. Eons measured out the evaporation of ancient sluggish seas.

His throat struggled against torpid air. "Is...Brahma...?"

"Awakening?" came her hollow voice, like an echo from a distant gorge.

"What happens...to...us?"

His words diffracted away from him. He could now see acoustic waves, wedges of compressed, mute atoms crowding in the exuberant air. Luxuriant, inexhaustible riches burst from beneath the ceramic certainties he had known.

"Come." Her voice seeped through the churning ruby air.

Centuries melted between them as he turned. A being he recognized without conscious thought spun in liquid air.

Femina, she was now, and she drifted on the new wafting currents. He and she were made of shifting geometric elements, molecular units of shape and firm thrust. A wan joy spread through him.

Time that was no time did not pass, and he and she and the impacted forces between them were pinned to the forever moment that cascaded through them, all of them, the billions of atomized elements that made them, all, forever.

MOZART ON MORPHINE
(1989)

As a working hypothesis to explain the riddle of our existence,
I propose that our universe is the most interesting of all possible
universes, and our fate as human beings is to make it so.
— FREEMAN DYSON, 1988

All theory, dear friend, is grey,
But the golden tree of life springs ever green.
— GOETHE, *FAUST*

1.

I read a fragment of God's mind, during that summer when He seemed to be trying to stop me.

I realize this is not the usual way such proceedings go, with their pomp and gravity. But please bear with me. I shall try to talk of matters that scientists usually avoid, even though these are crucial to the unspoken rhythms of our trade.

I live in a small community spread before the Pacific like a welcoming grin, thin but glistening in the golden shafts of sunlight. That unrelenting brilliance mocked my dark internal chaos as I struggled with mathematical physics. I worked through the day on my patio, the broad blue of the ocean lying with Euclidean grace beyond, perspective taking it away into measureless infinity. Endless descending glare on my gnarled equations, their confusion the only stain on nature.

My habit was to conclude a frustrating day of particle theory by running on the broad sands of Laguna Beach, a kilometer downhill from my home. The salt air cleared my mind.

In August of 1985 I went running barefoot on the beach at about 5 o'clock in the afternoon. The sun hung low and red, and I pounded along crisply warm sand, vacantly watching the crumbling, thumping waves. I paid no attention to the small crowd forming up ahead and so when the first shot came it took me completely by surprise.

I saw the teenagers scattering and the man in his twenties poking the small silvery gun at them, yelling something I couldn't make out. I wondered if the gun was loaded with blanks because it wasn't very loud.

The man started swearing at a kid near me, who was moving to my right. I was still doggedly running the same way so when the second shot came, I was just behind the kid. The round went *tssiiip!* by my head.

Not blanks, no. I did the next hundred meters in ten seconds, digging hard into the suddenly cloying sand. I turned to look back only once. A third thin *splat* sound followed me up the beach, but no screams. I heard more swearing from the skinny shooter, who was backing up the gray concrete stairs and trying to keep the pack of kids from following him.

I stood and watched him fire one last time, not trying to hit anyone now but just keep them at bay. Then he turned and ran up the remaining stairs and onto the street beyond.

I ran back and asked the kids what had happened and got a lot of conflicting stories. I ran back down the beach and in a few minutes saw a cop. I started to tell him what had happened. He said he had been sent down there to block this route, since the police were trying to track the man down in the streets. It was evidently a drug deal gone bust and the kids had started jazzing him around and he got mad.

2.

Walking home, I thought about Churchill's saying, that there was nothing as exhilarating as being shot at and missed. I felt a touch of that, and remembered a similar time-compressing moment in June.

I had been visiting my parents on their 50th wedding anniversary. My father was driving me to the reception after that Sunday morning's church service. It was a mild sunny day in Fairhope, Alabama, and I was lazily breathing in the pine scent as my father stopped at a stop sign. He started off and from the corner of my vision I saw a sudden movement. It was a car that a nearby telephone junction box had hidden from view, coming from the right at 40 miles per hour.

"Dad stop!" He hit the brake and the other car smashed into our front end. Our seat belts restrained us but somehow coming forward I smacked my head into the roof of the car. The world slipped around, wobbled, straightened. The hood was smashed sideways. The other car had hit and veered away. I got out, thinking dimly that if my father had not stomped down on the brake they would have come in on my side of the car and probably through the door. It was that close. The other car's people were more shaken up than we were. The woman was driving without shoes, the car was borrowed, and she had broken her hand when their car went off the road and into a shallow ditch. My father took it all quite mildly and it seemed to me I could smell the pine trees even stronger now. The surge of mixed fear and elation came as I paced around, looking at the bashed cars.

3.

In late September I was making my final plans to go to India when I developed pains in my stomach, high up. My children had the same symptoms, apparently a standard flu that was going around, so I stayed in bed a few days and expected it to go away. I had to fly to northern California for a conference on Friday.

On Thursday I was doing pretty well, running a little fever, though the pain had moved down some. I was getting used to it and it didn't seem so bad. No other symptoms, I thought, just a pesky flu. My plane tickets were ready and I picked them up on the way into the university. I was sitting in my office trying to do a calculation at noon when the pain got a lot worse. I couldn't stand up.

It was pretty bad for half an hour. I called a doctor near the university and made an appointment for two o'clock and waited out the pain. It subsided by one o'clock and I began to think things were going to be okay, that I could still travel. But I did go to the doctor. In her office I showed an elevated white count and a fever and some dehydration. When she poked my right side it hurt more. She thought it might be appendicitis and that I should go to an emergency room nearby. I thought she was making too much of it and wanted some mild pain suppressors so I could fly the next day.

On the other hand, it might be good to check into matters. I wanted to go to the hospital in Laguna, where I knew a few doctors. She started to call an ambulance but I was pumped up by then and went out and got into my car and drove very fast into Laguna, skating my sports car fast down the canyon road. I stopped at home to tell my wife, Joan, and she drove me into the emergency room.

It was the real thing of course and soon enough I was watching the fluorescent lights glide by as the anesthetist pushed me into the operating room. He said I must have a high tolerance for pain because the appendix was obviously swollen and sensitive. I asked him how quickly the drugs took effect, he said, "Well..." and then I was staring at the ceiling of my hospital room and it was several hours later.

My wife came to kiss me good night. I asked her to bring my calculations to me the next day.

I had a good night, slept well. In the morning my doctor told me his suspicions had been right, that when the pain got bad in my office it had been my appendix bursting. By the time they opened me up the stuff had spread. I asked to see the appendix and they brought it up to me later, a red lumpy thing with white speckles all over the top of it. I asked what the white spots were and the aide said casually, "Oh, that's gangrene. It's riddled with the stuff."

The doctor said there was a 60% chance the antibiotics would not take out the gangrene that had spread throughout my lower abdomen, so of course I figured I would be in the lucky 40%. By the early hours of the next morning, Saturday, I knew I was wrong. I became more and more feverish. I could not sleep but a bone-deep fatigue seeped through me.

I had stood up and walked around in the afternoon but when the night nurse tried it with me again I couldn't get to my feet. I was throwing up vile sour stuff and the orderly was talking to me about inserting some tubes and then the tube was going in my nose and down my throat and a bottle nearby was filling with brown bile, lots of it, a steady flow.

I couldn't sleep, even with the drugs. There was talk about not giving me too many drugs for fear of suppressing my central nervous system too much, which didn't make much sense to me, but then, little did. Things began to run together—the ceiling lights, words, images of frowning faces. The doctor appeared around 6:30 A.M. and said the antibiotics weren't working, my white count was soaring. There was talk about this I could not follow.

A man came by and reminded me to use the plastic tube with a ball in it that the nurse had given me the day before. You blew into it and kept a ball in the air and that was to exercise your general respiration. It seemed dumb to me, I could breathe fine, but I did it anyway and asked for some breakfast. I wasn't getting any, they were feeding me from the array of bottles going into my IV, and wouldn't give me more than ice chips to suck on. I was hungry. Logic didn't seem to work on the nurses.

There were more people around by that time and I realized blearily that this was very much like the descriptions in a short story of mine written more than a decade before, "White Creatures." What these quickly moving white-smocked beings were doing was just as incomprehensible to me as it had been to the character in that story. My fever was climbing a degree every two hours and Joan was patting my brow with a cool cloth and I wanted some food.

I didn't see how they could expect a man to get better if they didn't feed him. All they did was talk about stuff I couldn't follow very well, they spoke too fast, and added more bottles to the antibiotic array. They started oxygen but it didn't clear my head any. My IV closed off from vascular shock, Joan told me. A man kept punching my arms, trying to find a better way in and it hurt so I told him to knock it off if he couldn't do better.

Then they were tilting me back so the doctor could put a subclavial tube in close to my heart. It would monitor the flow there and provide a big easy access for the IV. Then I was wheeling beneath the soft cool fluorescents again and was in a big quiet room that was in the Intensive Care Unit, Joan said. I laid for a time absolutely calm and restful and realized I was in trouble. The guy with the breathing tube and the ball was gone but the nurses made me do it anyway, which still struck me as dumb because I wasn't going to stop breathing, was I? If they would just give me some food I would get better.

But after the gusts of irritation passed I saw in a clear moment that I was enormously tired. I hadn't slept in the night and the tubes in my nose tugged at me when I moved. They had slipped a catheter into me, surprisingly painless, and I felt wired to the machines around me, no longer an independent entity but rather a collaboration. If I lay still with my hands curled on my chest I could maybe rest and if I could do that I could get through this and so I concentrated on that, on how blissful it felt after the nurse gave me another injection of morphine, how I could just forget about the world and let the world worry about me instead.

I woke in the evening and then the next morning the doctor startled me awake by saying that I was better. They had called in more exotic antibiotics and those had stopped the fever's rise, leveling it off at 105 degrees, where it held steady for a day and then slowly eased off. The room was still prickly with light but Joan came and I found her presence calming. I listened to tapes on my Sony set of all Mozart's symphonies and every hour or so called for an injection and lifted off the sheets and spun through airy reaches, Mozart on morphine, skimming along the ceilings of rooms where well dressed people looked up at me with pleased expressions, interrupted as they dined on opulent plates of veal and cauliflower and rich pungent sauces, rooms where I would be again sometime, among people whom I knew but had no time for now, since I kept flying sedately along the softly lit yellow ceilings, above crimson couches and sparkling white tablecloths and smiles and mirth. Mozart had understood all of this and saw in this endless gavotte a way to loft and sweep and glide, going, to have ample ripe substance without weight.

When the doctor took the stitches out a week later he said casually, "Y'know, you were the closest call I've had in a year. Another twelve hours and you would've been gone."

4.

In November I went to India anyway. I hadn't fully recovered, but it seemed important to not let the calm acceptance of mortality I had now deflect me from life itself. My fear of death was largely gone. It wasn't any more a fabled place, but rather a dull zone beyond a gossamer-thin partition. Crossing that filmy divider would come in time but for me it no longer carried a gaudy, supercharged meaning. And for reasons I could not express a lot of things seemed less important now, little busynesses. People I knew were more vital to me and everything else seemed lesser, peripheral—including writing. Maybe even physics.

In Agra I arose at dawn to see the Taj Mahal by the rosy first glow. It shimmered above the gardens, deceptively toylike until you realized how far away and so how huge the pure curved white marble thing was. The ruler who built it to hold his dead wife's body had intended to build a black Taj also, across the river which lies behind. He would lie buried there, a long arcing bridge linking the two of them. But his son, seeing how much the first Taj cost, confined his father to a red sandstone fort a mile away for the last seven years of his life. There the old man lay on a bed and watched the Taj in a mirror in his last days.

On the broad deck behind the Taj the river ran shallow since it was two months after the monsoon. On the right was a bathing spot for devotees. Some were splashing themselves with river water, others doing their meditation. To the left was a mortuary. The better off inhabitants of Agra had their bodies burned on pyres and then the lot was tossed into the river. If one could not afford the pyre, then after a simple ceremony the body was thrown off the sandstone quay and onto the mud flats or into the water if the river was high. This was usually done in early morning.

By the glimmering dawn radiance I watched buzzards picking apart something on the flats. They made quick work of it, deftly tearing away the cloth, and in five minutes had picked matters clean. They lost interest and flapped away. The Taj coasted in serene eternity behind me, its color subtly changing as the sun rose above the trees, its cool perfect dome glowing, banishing the shadows below. Somehow in this worn alien place everything seemed to fit. Death just happened. From this simple fact came India's inertia. I thought of Mozart and heard a faint light rhythm, felt myself skimming effortlessly over a rumpled brown dusty world of endless sharp detail and unending fevered ferment, and watched the buzzards and the bathers and felt the slow sad sway of worlds apart.

CENTIGRADE 233
(1990)

I t was raining, of course. Incessantly, gray and gentle, smoothing the rect-angular certainties of the city into moist matters of opinion. It seemed to Alex that every time he had to leave his snug midtown apartment, the heavens sent down their cold, emulsifying caresses.

He hurried across the broad avenue, though there was scant traffic to intersect his trajectory. Cars were as rare as credible governments these days, for similar reasons. Oil wells were sucking bone dry, and the industrial conglomerates were sucking up to the latest technofix. That was as much as Alex knew of matters worldly and scientific.

He took the weather as a personal affront, especially when abetted by the 3D 'casters who said things like, "As we all know, in the Greater Metropolitan Area latitudinal overpressures have precipitated (ha ha) a cyclonic bunching of moist offshore cumulus—" and on and on into the byzantine reaches of garish, graphically assisted meteorology. Weather porn.

What they meant, Alex told himself as cold drops trickled under his collar, was the usual damp-sock dismality: weather permanently out of whack, thanks to emissions from the fabled taxis that were never there when you needed them. Imagine what these streets were like only thirty years ago! Less than that! Imagine these wide avenues inundated to the point of gridlock, that lovely antique word. Cars parked along every curb, right out in the open, without guards to prevent joyriding.

"Brella?" a beggar mumbled, menacing Alex with a small black club.

"Get away!" Alex overreacted, patting the nonexistent shoulder holster beneath his trench coat. The beggar shrugged and limped away.

Small triumph, but Alex felt a surge of pride. Onward!

He found the decaying stucco apartment building on a back street, cowering beside a blocky factory. The mail slot to 2F was stuffed with junk mail. Alex went up creaky stairs, his nose wrinkling at the damp reek of old rugs and incontinent pets. He looked automatically for signs that the plywood frame door to 2F had been jimmied. The grain was as clear as the skin of a virgin spinster.

Well, maybe his luck was improving. He fished the bulky key from his pocket. The lock stuck, rasped, and then turned with a reluctant thump; no electro-security here. He held his breath as the door swung open. Did he see looming forms in the musky murk beyond?

This was the last and oldest of Uncle Herb's apartments. Their addresses were all noted in that precise, narrow handwriting of the estate's list of assets. The list had not mentioned that Uncle Herb had not visited his precious vaults for some years. The others had all been stripped, plundered, wasted, old beer cans and debris attesting to a history of casual abuse by neighborhood gangs.

At the Montague Street apartment, Alex had lingered too long mourning the lost trove described in the list. Three slit-eyed Hispanics had kicked in the door as he was inspecting the few battered boxes remaining of his uncle's bequest. They had treated him as an invader, cuffed him about and extorted "rent," maintaining with evil grins that they were the rightful owners and had been storing the boxes for a fee.

"The People owns this 'parmen' so you pays the People," the shortest of the three had said.

At last they went away, chuckling evilly. There had been scanty wealth in any of the three apartments, and now, one last hope opened to the click of a worn key.

The door creaked. His fingers fumbled and found the wall switch. Vague forms leaped into solid, unending ranks—books! Great gray steel shelves crammed the room, anchored at floor and ceiling against the earth's shrugs. He wondered how the sagging frame of this apartment building could support such woody weight. A miracle.

Alex squeezed between the rows and discovered wanly lit rooms beyond, jammed alike. A four-bedroom apartment stripped of furniture, blinds drawn, the kitchen recognizable only by the stumps of disconnected gas fittings. But no, no—in the back room cowered a stuffed chair and storklike reading lamp. Here was Uncle Herb's sanctuary, where his will said he had "idled away many a pleasant afternoon in the company of eras lost." Uncle Herb had always tarted up his writing with antique archness, like the frilly ivory-white shade on the stork lamp.

Alex sniffed. Dust lingered everywhere. The books were squeezed on their shelves so tightly that pulling one forth made Alex's forearm muscles ache. He opened the seal of the fogged polymer jacket and nitrogen hissed out.

Preserved! A signed and dated *Martian Chronicles*!

Alex fondled the yellowed pages carefully. The odor of aging pulp, so poignant and undefinable, filled him. A first edition. Probably worth a good deal. He slipped the book back into its case, already regretting his indulgence at setting it free of its inert gas protection.

He hummed to himself as he inched down the rows of shelves, titles flowing past his eyes at a range of inches. *The Forever War* with its crisp colors. A meter-long stretch of E. E. "Doc" Smith novels, all very fine in jackets. *Last and First Men* in the 1930 first edition.

Alex had heard it described as the first ontological epic prose poem, the phrase sticking in his mind. He had not read it, of course. And the pulps! Ranks of them, gaudy spines shouting at customers now gone to dust. Alex sighed.

Everything in the twencen had apparently been astounding, thrilling, startling, astonishing, even spicy. Heroines in distress, their skirts invariably hiked up high enough to reveal a fetching black garter belt and the rich expanse of sheer hose. Aliens of grotesque malignancy. Gleaming silver rockets, their prows no less pointed than their metaphor.

The pulps took the largest bedroom. In the hallway began the slicks. Alex could not resist cracking open a *Collier's* with Bonestell full-colors depicting (the text told him breathlessly) Wernher von Braun's visionary space program. Glossy pages grinned at their first reader in a century. To the moon!

Well, Alex had been there, and it wasn't worth the steep prices. He had sprained an arm tumbling into a wall while swooping around in the big wind caverns. The light gravity had been great, the perfect answer for one afflicted with a perpetual diet, but upon return to Earth he had felt like a bowling ball for a month.

Books scraped him fore and aft as he slid along the rows. His accountant's grasp of numbers told him there were tens of thousands here, the biggest residue of Uncle Herb's collection.

"Lord knows what was in the other apartments," he muttered as he extracted himself from the looming aisles. The will had been right about this apartment—it was all science fiction. Not a scrap of fantasy or horror polluted the collection. Uncle Herb had been a bug about distinctions that to Alex made no difference at all. No novels combining rockets and sword-wielding barbarians. No voluptuous vampires at all, to judge from the covers.

Alex paused at the doorway and looked back, sighing. Bright lurid remnants of a lost past.

He recalled what awe that Brit archeologist had reported feeling, upon cracking into Tut's tomb. Only this time the explorer owned the contents.

He made his way into the chilly drizzle, clucking contentedly to himself. He shared with Uncle Herb the defective gene of bibliophilia, but a less rampant case. He loved the crisp feel of books, the supple shine of aged leather, the *snick snick snick* of flipped pages. But to read? Not in hard copy, surely. No one did that anymore.

And surely the value of a collectable did not depend on its mere use, not in this Tits 'n Glitz age.

In less than an hour, Alex reclined on a glossy Korean lounger, safely home, speaking to Louise Keppler on his wall screen. Her face showed signs of a refurb job still smoothing out, but Alex did not allow even a raised eyebrow to acknowledge the fact; one never knew how people took such things. Louise was a crafty, careful dealer, but in his experience such people had hidden irrationalities, best avoided.

"You got the index?" she wanted to know.

He wanted to close this deal quickly. Debts awaited, compounding, and Uncle Herb had been a long time dying.

Alex nodded eagerly. "Sure. I ran it through my assessing program just now."

She was swift, eyes darting over the inventory he had e-sent. He shivered and wished he had paid his heating bill this month. His digital thermometer read Centigrade 08. A glance at the window showed the corners filmed by ice. "I hope we can agree on a fair market price," he said, hoping the timbre didn't seem too hopeful.

Louise smiled, eyes at last pinning him with their asessing blue. He thumbed a close-up and found that they were true color, without even a film to conceal bloodshot veins, the sullen residue of the City's delights. "Alex, we've dealt before. You know me for no fool."

He blinked. "What's wrong?"

"Books, Alex? Early videos, yes. First generation CDs, sure—nobody realized they had only a seven-year lifetime, unless preserved. Those are rare." Her mouth twisted wryly. "But books? These are even earlier, much—"

"Sure, but who cares?" He had to break in.

"*Linear* reading, Alex?" Sardonic now.

"You should try it," he said swiftly.

"Have you?" she asked with an arched eyebrow. He wondered if she had close-upped him, seen his own red eyes.

"Well, sure...a little..."

"Kids still do, certainly," she said. "They'll experiment. But not long enough to get attached to the classic twencen physical form."

"But this was, well, the literature of the future."

"Their future, our past—what of it?" Her high cheekbones lent her lofty authority. She tugged her furs about her. "That's not *our* future."

His knowledge of science fiction came mostly from the myriad movids available. Now that the genre was dead, there was interest in resurrecting the early, naive, strangely grand works—but only in palatable form, of course—to repay the expense of translation into movids.

"They do have a primitive charm," he said uncertainly. "I find them—"

"So torpid! So unaware of what can be done with dramatic line." She shook her head.

Alex said testily, "Look, I didn't call for an exchange of critical views."

She made a show of a yawn. "Quite so. I believe you wanted a bid."

"Yes, but immediately payable. There are, ah, estate expenses."

"I can go as high as twelve hundred euros."

He blinked. "Twelve—" For the first time in his life Alex did not have to act out dismay at an opening price. He choked, sputtered, gasped.

Louise added, "*If* you provide hauling out of that infested tawdry neighborhood and to a designated warehouse."

"Haul—" He coughed to clear his head. Twelve hundred was only two months' rent, or three months of heating oil, with the new tax.

"My offer is good for one day."

"Louise! You're being ridiculous."

She shook her head.

"You haven't been keeping up. Items like this, they were big maybe a decade back. No more. Nostalgia market."

"My uncle spent a fortune on those magazines alone! A complete set of *Amazing Stories*. I can remember when he got the last of it, the rare slab-sheeted numbers."

She smiled with something resembling fondness. "Oh yes, a passing technical fancy, weren't they?"

He stared at her. There were now linear reader portables that expanded right in your hand. A text popped out into a thin sheet, clear and self-lit. Great engineering.

She didn't notice his silence. "But boring, I'm told. Even those worn out magazines were well past the great age of linear writing."

"That doesn't matter," Alex said, recovering slowly and trying to find a wedge to undermine her composure. He drew his coverlet tight, sitting amid the revelry and swank.

Entertainment was essential these forlorn days, when all who could have already fled to warmer climes.

Even they had met with rising ocean levels, giving the stay-behinds delicious, sardonic amusement. Alex tired of the main plot thread, a sordid romance. He was distracted by his troubles. He opened the book-like reader and began scanning the moving pictures inside. The reader had only one page. The cylinder in its spine projected a 3D animated drama, detailing background and substories of some of the main movid's characters. He popped up sidebar text on several historical details, reading for long moments while the action froze on the walls. When he turned the book's single sheet, it automatically cycled to the next page. Alex had been following the intricately braided story-streams of Mohicans for months now. Immersion in a time and place blended the fascinations of fiction, spectacle, history, and philosophy. Facets of the tangled tale could be called up in many forms, whole subplots altered at will. Alex seldom intruded on the action, disliking the intensely interactive features. He preferred the supple flows of time, the feeling of inexorable convergence of events. The real world demanded more interaction than he liked; he certainly did not seek it in his recreation.

The old-fashioned segments were only a few paragraphs of linear text, nothing to saturate the eye. He even read a few, interested at one point in the menu which an Indian was sharing with a shapely white woman. Corn mush, singularly unappealing. The woman smacked her lips with relish, though, as she slipped her bodice down before the brave's widening eyes. Alex watched the cooking fire play across her ample breasts, pertly perched like rich yellow-white pears in the flickering, smoky glow—and so the idea came to him.

"Alex," the Contessa said, "they're *marvelous*."

"Absolute rarities," he said, already catching on that the way to handle these people was to act humble and mysterious. "Hard to believe, isn't it?"

The Contessa gave her blond tresses a saucy little flip. "That people were that way?"

Alex had no idea what way she meant, but he answered, "Oh, yes, nothing exceeds like excess," with what he hoped was light wit. Too often his ironic humor seemed even to himself to become, once spoken, a kind of pig irony—but the Contessa missed even this much, turning away to greet more guests.

He regarded them with that mixture of awe and contempt which those who feel their lights are permanently obscured under bushels know all too well. For here, resplendent, came the mayor and his latest rub, a saffron-skinned woman of teenage smoothness and eyes eons old. They gyred into the ample uptown apartment as if following an unheard gavotte, pirouetting between tight knots of gushing supplicants. The mayor, a moneyed rogue, was a constant worldwide talk show maven. His grinning image played upon the artificial cloud formations that loomed over his city at sunset, accompanied by the usual soft drink advertisements. Impossibly, this glossy couple spun into Alex's orbit. "Oh, we've heard!" the mayor's rub squeezed out with breathless ardor. "You are so inventive!"

The mayor murmured something which instantly eluded Alex, who was still entranced by the airy, buoyant woman. Alex coughed, blinked, and said, "It's nothing, really."

"I can hardly wait," the perfectly sculpted woman said with utterly believable enthusiasm. Alex opened his mouth to reply, ransacking his mind for some witticism—and then she was gone, whisked away on the mayor's arm as if she had been an illusion conjured up by a street magician. Alex sighed, watching the nape of her swanlike neck disappear into the next knot of admiring drones.

"Well, nice of them to talk to you longer than that," Louise said at his elbow. She was radiant. Her burnt-rust hair softly flexed, caressing her shoulders, cooing and whispering as the luxuriant strands slid and seethed—the newest in biotech cosmetics.

Alex hid his surprise. "It was much longer than I expected," he said cautiously.

"Oh no, you've become the rage." She tossed her radiant hair. "When I accepted the invitation to, well, come and do my little thing, I never expected to see such, such—"

"Such self-luminous beings?" Alex helped her along with the latest term for celebrities.

Louise smiled demurely in sympathy. "I knew—that's why I strong-armed the Contessa for an invitation."

"Ah," Alex said reservedly. He was struggling to retain the sense that his head had not in fact left his body and gone whirling about the room, aloft on the sheer gauzy power of this place.

Through the nearest transparent wall he saw brutal cliffs of glass, perspectives dwindling down into the gray wintry streets of reality. Hail drummed at him only a foot away. *Skyscraper*, he thought, was the ugliest word in the language. Yet part of a city's charm was its jagged contrasts: the homeless coughing blood outside restaurant windows where account executives licked their dessert spoons, hot chestnut vendors serving laughing couples in tuxes and gowns, winos slouched beside smoked-glass limos.

Even in this clogged, seemingly intimate party there were contrasts, though filmed by politeness. In a corner stood a woman who, by hipshot stance and slinky dress, told everyone that she was struggling to make it socially on the Upper West Side while living on the Lower East. Didn't she know that dressing skimpily to show that you were oblivious to the chilly rooms was last year's showy gesture? Even Alex knew that.

Alex snuggled into his thick tweed jacket, rented for the occasion. "—and I never would have thought of actually just making the obvious show of it you did," Louise concluded a sentence that had nearly whizzed by him. He blinked.

Incredibly, Louise gazed at him with admiration. Until this instant he had been ice-skating over the moments, Alex realized. Now her pursed-mouth respect struck him solidly, with heady effect, and he knew that her lofty professionalism was not all he had longed for. Around him buzzed the endless churn of people whose bread and butter were their clever-ness, their nerves, their ineffable sense of fleeting style. He cared nothing for them. Louise—her satiny movements, her acerbic good sense—*that*, he wanted. And not least, her compact, silky curves, so deftly implying voluptuous secrets.

The Contessa materialized like one of the new fog-entertainments, her whispery voice in his ear. "Don't you think it's…time?"

Alex had been lost in lust. "Oh. Oh, yes."

She led. The crowd flowed, parting for them like the Red Sea. The Contessa made the usual announcements, set rules for the silent auction, then gave a florid introduction. Sweating slightly despite the room's fashionable level of chill, Alex opened his briefcase and brought out the first.

"I give you *Thrilling Wonder Stories*, June 1940, featuring 'The Voyage to Nowhere.' Well, I suppose by now we've arrived."

Their laughter was edgy with anticipation. Their pencils scribbled on auction cards. "Next, *Startling Stories*, with its promise, 'A Novel of the Future Complete in This Issue.' And if you weren't startled, come back next issue."

That got another stylish laugh from them. As more lurid titles piled up, he warmed to his topic. "And now, novels. *Odd John*, about a supergenius, showing that even in those days it was odd to be intelligent. Both British and American first editions here, all quite authentic."

He could tell he had them. Louise watched him approvingly. He ran through his little jokes about the next dozen novels. Utopian schemes, techno-dreams.

Butlers circulated, collecting bids on the demure pastel cards. The Contessa gave him a pleased smile, making an 0 with her thumb and forefinger to signal success. Good. The trick lay in extracting bids without slowing the entertainment. He kept up his line of patter.

"I'm so happy to see such grand generosity," Alex said, moving smoothly on. "Remember, your contributions will establish the first fully paperless library for the regrettable poor. And now—"

Dramatic pause. They rustled with anticipation. A touch more of tantalizing to sharpen matters, Alex judged: more gaudy magazines. A fine copy of *Air Wonder Stories*, April 1930, showing a flying saucer like a buzz saw cutting through an airplane. Finally, a deliciously lurid *Amazing Stories* depicting New York's massive skyline toppling beneath an onslaught of glaciers. Laughter.

"We won't have that, will we?" Alex asked.

"Nooooo!" the crowd answered, grinning.

"Then let the past protect us!" he cried, and with a pocket lighter bent down to the stack he had made in the apartment's fireplace. The magazines went off first—*whoosh!*—erupting into billowing orange-yellow flame.

Burning firewood had of course been outlawed a decade ago. Even disposing of old furniture was a crime. They'd tax the carbon dioxide you exhaled if they could.

But no one had thought of this naughtiness. The crisp old pulps, century-dried, kindled the thick novels. Their hardcover dust wrappers blackened and then the boards crackled. Volumes popped open as the glue in their spines ignited. Lines of type stood starkly on the open pages as the fierce radiance illuminated them, engulfed them, banished them forever from a future they had not foretold. The chilly room rustled as rosy heat struck the crowd's intent faces.

Alex stepped away from the growing pyre. This moment always came. He had been doing this little stunt only a few weeks, but already its odd power had hummed up and down the taut stretched cables of the city's social stresses. What first began as a minor amusement had quickened into fevered fashion. Instant fame, all doors opening to him—all for the price of a pile of worthless paper.

Their narrowed faces met the dancing flames with rapt eyes, gazes turned curiously inward. He had seen this transformation at dozens of parties, yet only now began to get a glimmer of what it meant to them. The immediate warmth quickened in them a sense of forbidden indulgence, a reminder of lush eras known to their forefathers. Yet it also banished that time, rejecting its easy optimism and unconscious swank. Yes, there it emerged—the cold-eyed gaze that came over them, just after the first rush of blazing heat. The *Amazing Stories* caught and burst open with sharp snaps and pops. On its lurid cover New York's glaciers curled down onto Manhattan's towers—and then into black smoke.

Revenge. That was what they felt. Revenge on an era that had unthinkingly betrayed them. Retribution upon a time that these same people unconsciously sought to emulate, yet could not, and so despised. The Age of Indulgence Past.

"Let's slip away," Louise whispered. Alex saw that the mayor and his newest rub were entranced. None of these people needed him any longer. His treason was consummated, Uncle Herb betrayed yet again.

They edged aside, the fire's gathering roar covering their exit. Louise snuggled against him, a promise of rewards to come. Her frosty professionalism had melted as the room warmed, the radiance somehow acting even on her, a collector.

As Alex crossed the thick carpet toward the door, he saw that this was no mere freakish party trick. The crowd basked in the glow, their shoulders squaring, postures straightening. He had given these people permission to cast off the past's dead hand. The sin of adding carbon dioxide to the burdened air only provided the spice of excitement.

Unwittingly, Alex had given them release. Perhaps even hope. With Louise he hurried into the cold, strangely welcoming night.

WORLD VAST, WORLD VARIOUS
(1992)

1.
The Cusp Moment

The vortex wind roiled stronger, howled across the jagged peaks to the south, and provoked strange wails as it rushed toward the small band of humans.

The sounds came to Miyuki like a chorus of shrill, dry voices. Three hundred kilometers to the south these winds were born, churned up by the tidal surges of the brother planet overhead. Across vacant plains they came singing, over rock sculpted into sleek submission by the raw winds. Gusts tore at the twenty-three Japanese in their air masks and thick jackets. A dusty swirl bedeviled them with its grit, then raced on.

"They're coming," Tatsuhiko said tensely.

Miyuki squinted into the cutting cold. She could barely see dots wavering amid the billows of dust. In her rising excitement she checked again her autocam, belt holdings, even her air hoses. Nothing must go wrong, nothing should steal one moment from this fresh contact between races. The events of the next hour would be studied by future generations, hallowed and portentous. As a geophysicist her own role was minor. Their drills had taught her to keep Tatsuhiko and the other culture specialists in good view of her autocam, without being herself conspicuous. Or so they hoped. What if beings born of this austere place found smell, not sight, conspicuous?

"They're spreading out," Tatsuhiko said, standing stick-straight. "A sign of hostility? Maneuver?"

Opinions flowed over their suit comm. Tatsuhiko brushed aside most of them. Though she could not see his face well, she knew well the lean contours of concern that would crease his otherwise smooth, yellowish complexion. Miyuki kept silent, as did all those not versed in the consummate guesswork that its practitioners called Exo-Analysis.

The contact team decided that the Chujoans might have separated in their perpetual quest for small game. This theory seemed to gain confirmation as out of the billowing dust came a peri and two burrowbunnys, scampering before the advancing line. The nomads doggedly pursued, driving game before them, snaring some they took by surprise.

I hope they don't mind an interrupted hunt, Miyuki thought. They seemed stolid, as if resigned to the unrelenting hardship of this cruelly thin world. Then she caught herself: *Don't assume.* That was the first rule here.

She had seen the videos, the scans from orbit, the analytical studies of their movements—and still the aliens startled her.

Their humanoid features struck her first: thin-shanked legs; calves muscled and quick; deep chests broad with fat; arms that tapered to four-fingered hands. But the rest...

Scalloped ears perched nearly atop the large, oval head. Eyes were consumed by their pupils. A slitted mouth like a shark's, the rictus grin of an uncaring carnivore. Yet she knew they were omnivores—had to be, to survive in this bleak biosphere. The hands looked *wrong*—blue fingernails, ribbed calluses, and the first and last fingers both were double-jointed thumbs.

These features she took in as the aliens strode forward in their odd, graceful way. Three hundred and twenty-seven of them, one of the largest bands yet seen. The wind brought their talk to her from half a kilometer away. Trills, twitterings, lacings of growls. Were they warning each other?

"Showing signs of regrouping," Tatsuhiko called edgily.

As leader of the contact team he had to anticipate trouble of any sort. The aliens were turning to bring the vector of their march directly into the center of the humans. Miyuki edged into a low gully, following the team's directives. Swiftly the Japanese formed a triangular pattern, Tatsuhiko at the point. To him went the honor of the cusp moment.

The pale morning light outlined the rumpled peaks to the west, turning the lacy brushwork of high fretted clouds into a rosy curtain, and their light cast shadows into the faces of the approaching aliens.

Miyuki was visible only to a few of the tall, swaying shapes as they made their wary way. She thought at first that they were being cautious, perhaps were fearful, but then she remembered the videos of similar bands.

They perpetually strode with an open gait, ready to bound after game if it should appear, eyes roving in a slow search pattern. These were no different.

With gravity fifteen percent less than Earth's, these creatures had a graceful, liquid stride on their two curiously hooflike feet. They held lances and clubs and slingshots casually, seemingly certain that whatever these waiting strangers might be, weaponry could keep them at bay. They were only a few hundred meters away now and she felt her breathing tighten.

Chujo's thin, chilly air plucked at her. She wondered if it affected her eyes, because now she could see the aliens' clothing—and it was moving.

They wore a kind of living skin which adjusted to each change in the cant of their arms, each step. The moving brown stuff tucked closely at neck and armpits and groin, where heat loss would be great, yet left free the long arms and muscled thighs. Could such primitives master biotech capable of this? Or had they domesticated some carpet-like animal?

No time left for speculations. Her comm murmured with apprehension as the nearest alien stolidly advanced to within a hundred meters.

"Remember Kammer," one of the crew observed laconically.

"Remember your duty!" Tatsuhiko countered sharply.

Miyaki's vision sharpened to an unnatural edge. She had a rising intuition of something strange, something none of them had—

"Tatsuhiko," she called. "Do not step in front of them."

"What?" Tatsuhiko answered sharply as the leading alien bore down upon him. "Who said that? I—"

And the moment had arrived.

Tatsuhiko stood frozen.

The face of the truly alien. Crusty-skinned. Hairless. Scaly slabs of flesh showing age and wear. The alien turned its head as it made its long, loping way by Tatsuhiko. Its skin was fretted, suggesting feathers, with veins beneath the rough hide making a lacework of pink, as in the feet of some earthly birds. And the eyes—swollen pupils giving the impression of intense concentration, swiveling across the landscape in smooth unconcern.

The alien rotated its torso—a flickering of interest?—as it passed. Tatsuhiko raised a bare hand in a sign they had all agreed had the best chance of being read as a nonhostile greeting. Tatsuhiko smiled, careful to not reveal white teeth, in case that implied eating or anger among beings who shared a rich lore of lipped mouths.

To this simple but elaborately rehearsed greeting the alien gave Tatsuhiko a second's further gaze—and then strode on, head turning to scan the ground beyond.

And so they all came on. No sounds, no trace of the talk the Japanese had recorded from directional mikes. The second alien drew abreast Captain Koremasa Tamura, the expedition leader. This one did not register Koremasa with even the slightest hesitation in the regular, smooth pivot of its head.

So came the next. And the next.

The Chujoans pressed forward, nomads in search of their next meal. Miyuki remembered the videos taken from orbit of just this remorseless sweeping hunt. Only the first of them had permitted its gaze to hesitate for even a moment.

"I...I do not..." Tatsuhiko whispered over comm.

The aliens swept by the humans, their eyes neither avoiding recognition nor acknowledging it.

"Do not move," Koremasa ordered.

Even so, one woman named Akiko was standing nearly directly in front of an approaching Chujoan—and she lifted a palm in a gesture that might have meant greeting, but Miyuki saw as simple confusion. It brushed the passing alien. Akiko clutched suddenly at the Chujoan hand, seeking plaintively. The creature gave no notice, allowing its momentum to carry it forward, freeing its hand.

Koremasa sharply reprimanded Akiko, but Miyuki took little notice of that, or of the buzzing talk on her comm. She hugged herself against the growing chill, turned away from the cutting winds, and watched the aliens continue on, unhurried. Hundreds of evenly spaced, oblivious hunters. Some carried heavy packs while others—thin, wiry, carrying both slings and lances—had little. But they all ignored the humans.

"Anyone registering eye contact?" Tatsuhiko asked tersely.

The replies trickled in reluctantly. No. No one.

"How do they *know*?" Tatsuhiko asked savagely. "The first, it looked at me. Then the rest, they just—just—"

Faintly someone said, "They won't even piss on us."

Another whisper answered, "Yes, the ultimate insult."

Chuckles echoed, weak and indecisive against the stong, unending alien wind.

The humans stood in place, automatically awaiting orders, as endless drill had fashioned them to do. Dust devils played among them. A crusty-skinned thing the first expedition had unaccountably named a snakehound on the basis of a few glimpses on their video records—though it showed no signs of liking the fat worms which resembled earthly snakes—came bounding by, eluding the hunters. Likewise, it took no apparent notice of the humans frozen in their carefully planned deployment of greeting, of contact, of the cusp moment.

In their calm exit Miyuki saw her error, the mistake of the entire crew. These Chujoans had two hands, two feet, binocular eyes—primate-like, city-builders, weapon-users. Too close to human, far too close.

For they were still alien. Not some pseudo-Navajos. Not more shambling near-apes who had meandered out of the forest, patching and adding to their cerebral architecture, climbing up the staircase of evolution toward a self-proclaimed, seemingly ordained success.

These beings shared no genes, nor assumptions, nor desires, with the seemingly similar humans. Their easy sway, their craftily designed slingshots and arrows—all came from unseen anvils of necessity that humans might not share at all.

She leaned back, smothering an impulse to laugh. The release of tension brought a mad hilarity to her thoughts, but she immediately suppressed the urge to shout, to gesture, to stamp her boots into the dusty certainties of this bleak plain. After all, Tatsuhiko had not given the order to disperse the pattern—he was stiff with shock.

Perhaps this sky gave a clue. How different from Earth! Genji loomed, a great mottled ball fixed at the top of the sky.

How well she knew the stories of the *Genji Monogatari*, by the great Murasaki. Yet the imposition of a millennium-old tale on these hard, huge places was perhaps another sign of their underlying arrogance.

The whirl of worlds, she thought. Spheres stuck at the ends of an invisible shaft, balls twin-spinning about each other. Tidal stresses forced them to eternal mutual regard, rapt, like estranged lovers unable to entertain the warmer affections of the swollen, brooding sun which even now sought to come onstage, brimming above the horizon, casting slanting exaggerated shadows. The aliens headed into this ruddy dawnlight, leaving the humans without a backward glance.

2.
Arrested Athens

They took refuge in the abandoned cities. Not for physical shelter, for that was provided by the transparent, millimeter-thin, yet rugged bubbles they inflated among the ruins. They came here to gain some psychological consolation, for reasons no one could quite express.

Miyuki sat in one of the largest bubbles, sipping on aromatic Indian tea and cracking seeds between her teeth. So far these small, tough, oddly sweet kernels were the only bounty of this dry planet. Miyuki had been the first to master them, cracking them precisely and then separating the meat from the pungent shell with her tongue. Gathering them from the low, gnarled trees was simple. They hung in opulent, unpicked bunches; apparently the Chujoans did not like them. Still, it would be interesting to see if anyone without other food could eat the seeds quickly enough to avoid starvation.

The subject never came up, she realized, because no one liked to jest about real possibilities. The entire expedition was still living off the growing tanks on the mother ship. Every kilogram of protein and carbohydrate had to be brought down with many more kilos of liquid hydrogen fuel. That in turn had to be separated from water on Genji, where their main base sprawled beside a rough sea.

Such weighty practicalities suppressed humor. Not that this crew was necessarily a madcap bunch, of course. Miyuki spat her cheekful of shells into her hand, tossed them into the trash, and started listening to Tatsuhiko again. He had never been a mirthful man, and had not responded well to her suggestion that perhaps the Chujoans had played a sort of joke.

"—so I remain astonished by even the suggestion that their behavior was rooted in anything so obvious," Tatsuhiko concluded.

"As obvious as a joke?" Captain Koremasa asked blandly. He sat while the others stood, a remnant of shipboard discipline. The posture was probably unnecessary, for the Captain was already the tallest and most physically commanding figure in the expedition. Standard primate hierarchy rules, Miyuki thought distantly. Koremasa had a broad forehead and strong features, a look of never being surprised. All quite useful in instilling confidence.

"A joke requires context," Tatsuhiko said, his mouth contracting into tight reserve. He was lean and angular, muscles bunching along his long jawline. She knew the energies which lurked there. She had had a brief, passionate affair with him and could still remember his flurries of anxious attention.

Partly out of mischief, she said, "They may have had enough 'context' for their purposes."

Tatsuhiko's severe mouth turned down in scorn. "That band knew nothing of prior contact—that was why we selected them!"

"How do you know?" Miyuki asked mildly.

Tatsuhiko crossed his arms, energies bundled in. "First contact was with a band over three thousand kilometers from here. We tracked them."

Miyuki said, "Stories fly fast."

"Across a mountain range?"

"In months, yes."

"These are primitives, remember. No signs of writing, of metallurgy, of plowing. Thus, almost certainly no information technology. No semaphore stations, no roads, not even smoke signals."

"Gossip is speedy," Miyuki said. The incredible, irrational and cowardly withdrawal of the first expedition had left Chujo for the Japanese, a slate virtually unblemished. But in the time since the Chujoans might have turned that first contact into legend.

"We must go by what we know, not what we invent." Tatsuhiko kept his tone civil but the words did his work for him.

"And I am a geophysicist and you are the culture specialist." Miyuki looked at him squarely, an unusual act among a crew trained for decades to suppress dissension.

"I believe no one should proceed to theory without more experience," Koremasa said evenly. His calm eyes seemed to look through them and out, into the reaches beyond. She caught a sense of what it was like to have more responsibility than others, but to be just as puzzled. Koremasa's years of quiet, stolid leadership on the starship had not prepared him well for ambiguity.

Still, his sign of remote displeasure made both Miyuki and Tatsuhiko hesitate, their faces going blank. After a moment Tatsuhiko nodded abruptly and said, "Very much so."

They automatically shifted to routine matters to defuse any tensions. Familiar worries about food, air, illness and fatigue surfaced, found at least partial solutions. Miyuki played her part as supplies officer, but she let her mind wander as Tatsuhiko and Koremasa got into a long discussion of problems with their pressure masks.

They had retreated into studying artifacts; after all, that is what archaeologists were trained to do, and artifacts could not ignore you. Two women had trailed the Chujoans for several kilometers, and found what appeared to be a discarded or forgotten garment, a frayed legging. The biologists and Exo-Analysis people had fallen upon it with glad cries.

Quite quickly they showed that the snug-rug, as some called it, was in fact a sophisticated lifeform which seemed bioengineered to parasitic perfection, for the sole purpose of helping the Chujoans fend off the elements.

It lived on excrement and sweat—'biological exudates,' the specialists' jargon said. The mat was in fact a sort of biological corduroy, mutually dependent species like small grasses, moss and algal filaments. They gave back to their host warmth and even a slow, steady massage. They even cleaned the skin they rode—'dermal scavenging,' the specialists termed it. Useful traits—and better than any Earthly gadget.

The specialists in Low Genji Orbit had labored to duplicate the snug-rug in their laboratories. The expedition depended on powerful biotech resources, for everything from meals to machine repair. But the snug-rug proved a puzzle. The specialists were, of course, quite sure they could crack the secret...but it would require a bit of time. They seemed equally divided on the issue of whether the snug-rug was a remnant from an earlier biotech civilization, or another example of evolution's incredible diplomacy among species.

Appetites whetted by one artifact, the team turned to the province of archaeology. The abandoned cities which dotted Chujo were mostly rubble, but some like this—Miyuki glanced out through the transparent bubble wall—still soared, their creamy massive walls blurred by winds until they resembled partly melted ice cream sculptures. Little metal had gone into them, apparently not needed because of the milder gravity. Perhaps that was why later ages had not plundered these canyonlike streets for all the threads of decorative tin and copper. Sand, frost, storm, invading desert brush—all had conspired to rub away most of the stone sheaths on the grander buildings, so little art remained. Koremasa and Tatsuhiko went on discussing matters, but Miyuki had heard the same debates before; one of the mild irritations of the expedition was that Koremasa still sought consensus, as though they were still packed into a starship, mindful of every frown. No, here they needed daring, leadership, dash and verve.

At the right moment she conspicuously bowed, exaggerating her leave-taking just enough for a slight ironic effect, and slipped through the pressure lock.

She slipped her pressure mask on, checked seals, tasted the slightly oily compressed air. This was the one huge freedom they had missed so much on the long voyage out: to slam the door on exasperation. There had been many elaborate ways to defuse stresses, such as playing smashball; the object was to keep the ball aloft as long as possible, not to better your opponent. Long rallies, cooperation, learning to compensate for inability or momentary fault, deploring extravagant impulse and grandstanding—all good principles, when you are going lonely to the stars. They had similarly lasted through their predicted season of sexual cookbook athletics. The entire team was like an old married couple by now—wise and weathered.

The chilly bite of even noonday never failed to take her by surprise. She set off quickly, still enjoying the spring that low gravity gave to her step, and within minutes was deep among the maze of purple-gray colonnades. Orbital radar had deepscanned the sandy wastes and found this buried city. Diggers and wind machines had revealed elegant, airy buildings preserved far better than the weathered hovels found on the exposed surface. Had the city been deliberately buried? The street-filling sands had been conspicuously uniform and free of pebbles, not the residue of eons of runoff from nearby hills. Buried for what?

The moody, shadowed paths gave abruptly into hexagonal spaces of pink flagstones. Above, high-pitched roofs and soaring towers poked into a thin blue sky which sported small, quickly scudding clouds like strands of wool. To her eye the styles here, when they struck any human resonance at all, were deliberate blends, elements of artful slope and balanced mass that made the city seem like an anthology of ages. Could this be the last great gathering place of the ancient natives, erected to pay tribute to their passing greatness? Did they know that the ebbing currents of moisture and dusty icestorms were behind the ceaseless slow drying that was trimming their numbers, narrowing the pyramid of life upon which all large omnivores stood? They must have, she concluded.

In this brooding place of arched stone and airy recesses there came to her a silky sense of melancholy, of stately recessional. They had built this elaborately carved and fretted stonework on the edge of what must have then been a large lake. Now the diminished waters were briny, hemmed in by marshes prickly with bamboo-like grasses. Satellites had found larger ruined cities among the slopes of the many mountain ranges, ones displaying large public areas, perhaps stadiums and theatres—but humans could not bear those altitudes without bulky pressure suits. She coughed, and remembered to turn up the burbling humidifier in her air feed. There was enough oxygen here, five hundred meters above what passed for sea level on a world where the largest sea was smaller than many of Earth's lakes. But the thieving air stole moisture from sinuses and throat, making her skin prickly and raw.

Miyuki peered up, past the steepled roofs and their caved-in promise, at the perpetual presence of Genji. Geometry told her that at noon the brother world should be dark, but the face of milky swirls and clumpy browns glowed, reflecting Chujo's own radiance. Even the mottlings in the shadowed and strangely sinister face of Chujo's brother seemed to have a shifting, elusive character as she watched. Genji loomed twelve times larger than the Moon she had known as a child in Kyoto, and at night it gave hundreds of times as much light, enough to read by, enough to pick out colors in the plains of Chujo. Now high cirrus of glittery powdered ice momentarily veiled it in the purpling sky, but that somber face would never budge from its hovering point at the top of the sky. A moist, warm, murky sphere. How had that richness overhead affected the Chujoans, through the long millennia when they felt the thieving dryness creeping into their forests, their fields, their lives?

She turned down a rutted path beside a crumbled wall, picking her way, and before her a shadowy form moved. She froze. They all wore the smell-dispersers that supposedly drove off even large predators, but this shape—

"We should not be alone here," Tatsuhiko said, his eyes hooded behind his pressure mask.

"You frightened me!"

"Perhaps a little fear would be wise."

"Fear is disabling," she said disdainfully.

"Fear kindles caution. This world is too Earthlike—it lulls us."

"*Lulls?* I have to fight for oxygen when I trot, we *all* scratch from the aridity, the cold seeps in, I—"

"It deceives us, still."

"You were the one maintaining that the natives couldn't possibly be joking with us, or—"

"I apologize for my seeming opposition." Tatsuhiko bowed from the waist.

She started to reply, but his gesture reminded her suddenly of moments long ago—times when the reserve between them had broken in a sudden flood, when everything important had not seemed to require words at all, when hands and mouths and the simple slide of skin on welcoming skin had seemed to convey more meaning than all the categories and grammars of their alert, managerial minds. Times long gone.

She wondered whether Koremasa had delicately implied that Tatsuhiko should follow her, mend fences. Perhaps—but this perpetual wondering whether people truly spoke their minds, or merely what solidarity of effort required—it provoked her! Still...she took the space of a heartbeat to let the spurt of irritation evaporate into the chilly air.

She sighed and allowed herself only a sardonic, "You merely *seemed* to differ?"

"I merely expressed the point of view of my profession." Tatsuhiko gave her a direct, professional smile.

Despite herself Miyuki grinned. "You were an enthusiastic advocate of sociobiology, weren't you?"

"Still am." His heavy-lidded eyes studied her. The age-old male gaze, straying casually away for a quite unconscious study of what the contours of her work suit implied, a subtle tang of the matters between men and women that would never be settled...not that anyone wished them to be.

She nodded briskly, suddenly wanting to keep their discussion businesslike. "I suppose we are all at the forefront of our fields, simply by being here. Even though we haven't kept up with Earthside literature."

Communicating with Earth had proved to be even more difficult than they had imagined. In flight the hot plasma exhaust tail had blurred and refracted transmissions. Further, the Doppler shift had reduced the bit rate from Earth by half. Few dry academic journals had made it through.

Tatsuhiko's blunt jaw shifted slightly sidewise, which she knew promised a slightly patronizing remark. He said, "Of course, you are on firmer ground."

"Oh? How?"

"Planetary geology cannot falsify so easily, I take it."

"I don't understand." Or are we both sending mixed signals? Then, to shake him a little, she asked liltingly, "Would you like a drink?"

"I wished to walk the city a bit, as you were."

"Oh, this is in the city. We don't have to return to camp. Come."

She deliberately took him through galleries of stone that seemed feather-light, suspended from thick walls by small wedges of pale rock; the sight was still unsettling, to one born to greater gravity. She padded quickly along precarious walkways teetering above brackish ponds, and then, with no time for eyes to adjust, through murky tunnels. A grove of spindly trees surrounded a round building of burnt-orange rock, breezes stirring from them a sound like fat sizzling on a stove. She stopped among them, looking for damp but firm sand. Without saying a word in answer to his puzzled expression, she dug with her hands a hole a palm wide and elbow-deep.

"Wet gravel," she said, displaying a handful. He looked puzzled. Did he know that this made him boyish and vulnerable? She would not put that past him; he was an instinctive analyzer. Once he had tried with her all the positions made possible by the short period when the starship had glided under low deceleration—penetrating her in mechanical poses of cartoonish angles, making her laugh and then, in short order, come hard and swiftly against him. Where was that playful man now?

On alien ground, she knew. Preoccupied by the central moment of his life. And she could not reach out to touch him here, any more than she had the last few years on board.

The stand of pale yellow reeds she had noticed the day before nearly blocked the building's ample arched doorway. She broke off two, one fat and the other thin. Using the smaller as a ramrod, she punched the pith from the larger. Except for some sticking at the joints it worked and she thanked her memory of this trick.

"A siphon," she said, plunging the larger reed into the sand hole and formally offering it to Tatsuhiko. A bit uncertainly Tatsuhiko sucked on this natural straw, his frown turning to surprised pleasure.

"It works. Ground water—not salty."

"I tire of the processed taste in our water. I learned this on one of our desert classes." Pre-expedition training had been a blizzard of facts, techniques, gadgets, lore—all predicated on the earliest data from the probes, most of it therefore only marginally relevant; planets proved to be even more complex systems than they had suspected.

He watched her carefully draw the cool, smelly, oddly pleasant water up and drink long and steadily. The very air here robbed the skin of moisture, and their dry throats were feasting grounds for the head colds that circulated among the crew.

"This unfiltered water should be harmless, I suppose," he said hesitantly, his face turning wary too late.

She laughed. "You've already got a bellyful of any microbe that can feast off us."

"I thought there weren't any such."

"So it seems."

Indeed, this was the most convincing proof that panspermia, the seeding of the galaxy by spores from a single planet, had never happened. Chujo and Genji shared a basic reproducing chain, helical like DNA but differing in elemental details. Somehow the two worlds had shared biological information. The most likely explanation lay in debris thrown out by meteorite bombardment through geological timescales, which then peppered the other planet. She saw his familar self-involved expression and added, "But of course, we've only covered a tiny fraction of Chujo yet."

His look of dismay made her suppress another laugh. Specialization was so intense among them! Tatsuhiko did not realize that biospheres were thoroughly mixed, and that the deep, underlying incompatibility of Chujoan microbes with Earthly biochemistry was a planet-wide feature. "I'm just fooling, Tatsuhiko-san," she said, putting stress on the more friendly form of address.

"Ah." Abrupt nod of head, tight jaw, a few seconds to recover his sense of dignity. There had been a time when he reacted with amusement to her jibes. Or rolled her over and pinned her and made her confess to some imaginary slight, laughing.

They walked on, unspoken elements keeping them at a polite distance. She fetched forth a knife and cut a few notches in the soft length of the reed. As they walked she slipped the tip of the reed under her mask and blew through this crude recorder, making notes oddly reminiscent of the stern, plaintive call of the ancient Japanese country flute, the *shakuhachi*. She had played on such hastily made instruments while a young girl, and these bleak, thin-textured sounds took her back to a life which now seemed inconceivably, achingly remote—and was, of course. Probably few of them would ever walk the soil of the Home Islands again. Perhaps none.

They wandered among the tumbled-down lofts and deeply cut alcoves, Miyuki's music echoing from ruined walls. Here they passed through "streets" which were in fact pathways divided by thin partitions of gray-green stone, smoothed by wind and yet still showing the serpentine elaboration of colors—maroon, rose, aqua—inlaid by hands over ten thousand years ago. The dating was very imprecise, of course. Weaker planetary magnetic shielding, a different sun, an unknown climate history—all made the standard tables of carbon dating irrelevant.

Tatsuhiko raised his hand and they stopped before a worn granite wall. Deeply carved into it was one of the few artworks remaining in the city, perhaps because it could not be carried away. She estimated it was at least a full Chujoan's height on each of its square sides.

She followed the immense curves of the dune tiger. Only twice had any human glimpsed this beast in the flesh. The single photograph they had showed a muscular, canvas-colored, four-legged killing machine. Its head was squat, eyes enormous, mouth an efficient V design. Yet the beast had a long, sensuous tail thickly covered with gray-green scales. Intricate, barbed, its delicate scales almost seemed like feathers.

The ancient artist had taken this striking feature and stretched it to provide the frame and the substance of his work. The dune tiger's tail flowed out of the beast—which glowered at the viewer, showing teeth—into a wrap-around wreath that grew gnarled branches, sprouted ample flowers, and then twisted about itself to form the unmistakable profile of an alert Chujoan native.

The strange face also looked at the viewer, eyes even larger than the reality Miyuki had seen, mouth agape, head cocked at an angle. Miyuki would never know if this was a comic effect, but it certainly *looked* that way. And the sinuous tail, having made this head, wriggled around the design—to be eaten by the tiger itself.

"Writhing at the pain of biting itself?" she whispered.

"That could be. But wouldn't the whole tiger struggle, not just the tail?"

"Unless the tiger has just this instant bitten itself."

"Ummm, I hadn't thought of that. A snapshot, an instant frozen in time."

She fingered her reed. "But then why does its tail make that face?"

"Why indeed? I feel so *empty* before this work. We can bring so little to it!" He gestured angrily.

"The archaeologists, they must have some idea."

"Oh, they suppose much. But they know little."

She followed the tiger's tail with her eyes, looking fruitlessly for some clue. "This city had so many things ours do."

"But were they used the same way? The digging team hasn't found a single grave. Most of what we know about ancient Earth comes from burial of the dead."

She touched the stone, found its cool strength oddly reassuring. "This has outlasted the pyramids."

"Maybe it was cut very deep?"

"No… How long it has been buried we cannot tell. And Chujo's lighter gravity should lead to less erosion, generally. But I would have expected the winds to rub this out."

Tatsuhiko shrugged. "Our dating could be wrong, of course."

"Not this far wrong." Miyuki frowned. "I wonder if this place was more like an arrested Athens."

He looked at her speculatively. "A city-state? Difficult to tell, from a ruin."

"But the Chujoans still camp here—you found their old embers yourself."

"Until we scared them away, I suppose."

Miyuki studied the great wall. "You suspect they linger here, to view the ruins of what they were?"

"They may not be even the same species which built all this." Tatsuhiko looked around, as if trying to imagine the streets populated, to envision what forms would have ambled here.

She gestured at small circles which appeared above the carving. "What are these?"

Tatsuhiko frowned. "Symbols?"

"No, they look like a depiction of real objects. See, here's one that's a teardrop."

He stooped to examine the wall. "Yes, the lowest of them is. And higher up, see, another teardrop, only not so pronounced."

Miyuki tried to fathom some sense to the round gouges. If the piece had perspective, the circles could be of any true size. "Teardrop at the bottom...and as they rise, they round out?"

Tatsuhiko shrugged. "Rain droplets form round in the air, I believe, then make teardrops as they fall."

"Something the tiger gives off?"

"How?"

His questions were insightful, but there was something more here, she was sure of it. Her mother had once told her that art could touch secret places. She had described it in terms of simple events of childhood. When the summer rain had passed and the air was cool, when your affairs were few and your mind was at ease, you listened to the lingering notes of some neighbor's flute chasing after the clear clouds and the receding rain, and every note seemed to drop and sink into your soul. That was how it was now, this moment, without explanations.

Miyuki let the moment pass. Tatsuhiko gave up in exasperation. "Come—let's walk."

She wanted to move through the city as though she had once been a citizen of it, to catch some fleeting fragrance of lives once lived.

They walked on. She blew into her crude recorder again.

To her the atonal, clear, crude tones seemed to mirror the strangely solid feel of this place, not merely the veiled city of opaque purpose but as well the wind-carved desert wastes surrounding it. Motionless and emotionless, at one moment both agonized and deeply still.

"Perhaps that would be better to send back," Tatsuhiko said suddenly.

"What?"

"Better than our precious reports. Instead, transmit to Earth such music. It conveys more than our data, our measurements, our... speculations."

She saw through his guarded expression—tight jawline, pensive lips, veiled eyes—how threatened Tatsuhiko felt. The long voyage out had not made every member of the 482 crew familiar to her, and she and Tatsuhiko had always worked in different chore details, but still she knew the character-indices of them all. Crew had to fit within the narrow avenue which had allowed them to withstand the grand, epic voyage, and not decay into the instabilities which the sociometricians had so tellingly predicted.

Tatsuhiko had lost great face in that abortive first encounter, and three other attempts by his team to provoke even a flicker of recognition from the Chujoans had failed just as miserably.

Yet it would not do to address Tatsuhiko directly on this issue, to probe in obvious fashion his deepest insecurities. "You have illuminated a principal feature of their character, after all. That is data."

He snorted derisively. "Feature? That they do not think us worth noticing?"

"But to take no notice—that is a recognition which says much."

Suspiciously: "What?"

"That they know our strangeness. Respect it."

"Or hold it in contempt."

"That is possible."

His face suddenly opened, the tight lines around his eyes lightening. "I fear I have been bound in my own discipline too much."

"Sociobiology?"

"Yes. We attempt to explain social behavior as arising from a species' genetic heritage. But here—the categories we ourselves bring are based on a narrowing of definitions, all accomplished by our own brains—wads of gray matter themselves naturally selected for. We *cannot* use words like *respect* or *contempt*. They are illusions here."

She frowned. "In principle, of course. But these natives, they are so like ourselves..."

Tatsuhiko chuckled. "Oh? Come tomorrow, we'll go into the field. I'll show you the proud Chujoans."

3.
So-So Biology

They squatted in a blind, peering through a gauzy, dim dawn.

Recently cut branches hid them from the roaming animals beyond. "I can't see anything." Miyuki shifted to get a better view of the plain. Scraggly gray trees dotted it and low, powder-blue brush clung to the gullies.

Tatsuhiko gestured. "Look on the infra monitor." He fiddled, sharpening the image.

She saw a diffuse glow about half a kilometer away. It was near a snaky stream that had cut deeply into the broad, flat valley. "Something killed a kobold last night?"

Tatsuhiko nodded. "Probably a ripper. Our sensos gave us an audio signature. Picked it up on omni and then focused automatically with a directional mike."

"Could it have been a dune tiger?"

"Don't know." He studied her face. "You're still thinking about the carving."

"It is beautiful," she said quickly, embarrassed for reasons she could not fathom.

"Indeed." His quick eyes gave nothing away. "The kobold kill is scenting in the air, and this breeze will carry it. We now wait to see what the chupchups do."

"They call each other chupchups?"

"We have analyzed their voice patterns. No clear syntax yet, of course. We aren't even sure of many words. We noticed that they make name-like sounds—*preess-chupchup*, for example—they always end in that phrase."

"Perhaps it means 'Mister.' Or 'Honorable.'"

He shrugged. "Better than calling them 'apes,' as some crew have started to do."

She sat back, thighs already aching from squatting, and breathed in the dry aroma of the hunting ground. It was like Africa, she thought, with its U-shaped valleys cut by meandering rivers, the far ramparts of fault blocks being worn down by wind-blown sand. Only this world was far more bleak, cold, eerie in its shadows cast by the great sun now rising.

This star always made her uneasy when it ponderously rose or set, for the air's refraction flattened it. Filling four times as much of the sky as the sun she knew, it was nonetheless a midget, with a third the mass of Sol.

Though the astronomers persisted in calling Murasaki a red dwarf, it was no dull crimson ember. In the exalted hierarchy of solar specialists, stars like this one, with surface temperature greater than a carbon-filament incandescent lamp, were nonetheless minor lukewarm bores. Had they been rare, astronomers might have studied them more before the discovery of life here. Though Murasaki sported sunspots and vibrant orange flares, its glow did not seem reddish to her, but rather yellow. The difference from Sol became apparent as she squinted at the carrion awaiting the dawn's attentions. Detail faded in the distance, despite the thin air, because there was no more illumination than in an well-lit earthly living room after dark. Only as this swollen sun rose did it steal some of the attention from Genji, which perched always directly above, splitting the sky with its sardonic halfmoon grin.

"Here come the first," Tatsuhiko whispered tensely. His eyes danced with anticipation. When she saw him like this it was as if his formal skin had dissolved, giving her the man she had known.

A fevered giggling came over the chilly plain. Distant forms scampered: small tricorns, running from a snakehound. Their excited cries seemed nearly human. As they outdistanced the snakehound, which had sprung from concealment too soon, they sounded as though they laughed in derision. A hellbat flapped into view, drawn by the noise, and scooped up a burrowbunny which appeared to be just waking up as it stood at the entrance of its hole.

Then she saw the band of low shapes gathering where the kobold carcass lay. They were hangmouths—ugly hyena-like beasts which drooled constantly, fought each other over their food, and never hunted. These scavengers dismembered the kobold as she watched, hunching forward with the rest of the survey team. Short, snarling squabbles came over the audios.

"Vicious," she whispered, despite her resolution to say nothing about others' specialties.

"Of course," one of the team said analytically. "This is an ecology being slowly ground down by its biosphere. Hard times make hard species."

She shivered, not entirely from the dawn chill.

As they watched, other teams reported that a party of Chujoans was headed this way. Tatsuhiko's team had tracked these Chujoans, noted the kobold kill, and now awaited their collision with the squinting intensity of an author first watching his play performed.

Miyuki could not see the chupchups at all. The gradual warming of the valley brought tangy suggestions of straw-flavored vegetation, pungent meat rotting, the reek of fresh feces.

Tatsuhiko asked over comm, "Team C—have you counted them yet?"

The reply came crisply, "Eight, three female adult, three male, two children."

"Any displays that show parental investment?"

"Males carry the children."

Tatsuhiko nodded. "It's that way in all groups smaller than a hundred. Interesting."

"What do those groups do?" Miyuki asked.

"Food gathering."

One of the team, Hayaiko, said, "You should look at that data on incest avoidance. Very convincing. Female children are separated from the male in an elaborate ceremony, given special necklaces, the entire panoply of effects."

Tatsuhiko pursed his lips. "Don't deduce too much too soon. They might have been marrying them off, for all we know."

Hayaiko blinked. "At age four?"

"Check our own history. We've done about the same not that long ago," Tatsuhiko said with a grin. He seemed relaxed, affable, a natural leader, but undercurrents played in his face.

She saw that he was no longer beset by doubt, as he had been in pensive moments in the ancient city. He would redouble his efforts, she saw, summon up more *gaman*, the famed dogged persistence which had made Japan the leader of the world. Or did he aspire higher, to *gaman-zuyoi*, heroic effort?

"The chupchups are creeping up on the carrion," came a comm message.

"They'll fight the hangmouths?" Miyuki asked.

"We'll see," Tatsuhiko said.

She caught sight of the aliens then, moving in a squat-walk as they left a gully and quickly crossed to another. Their zigzag progress over the next half hour was wary, tediously careful as they took advantage of every tuft of grass, every slope, for concealment. She began to look forward to a fight with the hangmouths as their continuing snarls and lip-smacking over the audio told of the slow devouring of the carcass. It was, of course, quite unprofessional to be revolted by the behavior of species they had come so far to study, but she could not help letting her own delicate personal habits bring a curl of disgust to her lips.

"They're leaving," comm called.

The hangmouths began to stray from the carcass. "Picked it clean," Tatsuhiko said.

The chupchups ventured closer. The two children darted in to the kill, dodged rebuffs from the larger hangmouths, and snatched away some carelessly dropped sliver—like pauper children at a land baron's picnic, Miyuki thought, in the days of the Shogunate. This intrusion seemed to be allowed, but when the adults crept closer a hangmouth turned and rushed at the leading chupchup. It scampered back to safety, despite the fact that it carried a long pointed stick. It held the stick up as if to show the hangmouth, but the drooling beast still snarled and paced, kicking up curtains of dust, holding the band of chupchups at bay for long minutes.

"Why don't they attack it?" she asked.

"I have no idea." Tatsuhiko studied the scene with binoculars. "Could the stick be a religious implement, not a weapon at all?"

"I do not think it is trying to convert the hangmouth," Miyuki said severely.

"Along with semantic language, religion is the one accomplishment of humans which has no analogy in the animal world," Tatsuhiko said stiffly. "I wish to know whether it is a biological property here, as it is for us."

"You believe we *genetically* evolved religion?"

"Plainly."

"Oh, come now."

A flicker of the other man: a quick smile and "Religion is the opiate of the mortal."

How could he still surprise her, after many years? "You believe we've had religion so long that it's buried in our genes?"

"It is not merely a cultural manifestation, or else it would not be universal among us. Incest avoidance is another such."

She blinked. "And morals?"

"Moral pronouncements are statements about genetic fitness strategies."

All she could say was, "A severe view."

"A necessary one. Look there!"

Two hellbats had roosted in trees near the kill site. "Note how they roost halfway down the canopy, rather than in the top. They wish to be close to the game."

The hangmouth had turned and now, with aloof disdain, padded away from the chupchup and its raised stick. Trotting easily, the hangmouths departed. The chupchup band ventured forward to the kobold body and began to root among the remains.

Miyuki said, "The hellbats—"

"See what the chupchups are doing? Breaking open the big thigh bones." Tatsuhiko pointed to the vision screen, where a full color picture showed chupchups greedily sucking at the cracked yellow bones.

Miyuki was shocked. "But why, when there's meat left?"

"The marrow, I suspect. It is rich in calories among the larger species here."

"But still—"

"The chupchups *prefer* the marrow. They have given up on finding fresh meat, for they have given up hunting." Tatsuhiko said this dispassionately, but his face wore an expression of abstracted scorn.

With screeches they could hear even at this range, two hellbats launched themselves upon the knot of stooping chupchups. The large, leathery birds dove together at a chupchup child which had wandered a few meters from the band. Miyuki watched their glittery, jewellike eyes and bony wings as they slid down the sky.

The first hellbat sank claws into the child and flapped strongly. A male chupchup threw itself forward but the second hellbat deflected it. A female chupchup ran around the male and snatched at the child. The hellbat bit the female deeply as it tried to gain the air, but she clubbed it solidly twice with the flat of her hand. The hellbat dropped the child. It flapped awkwardly away, joined by its partner.

"They nearly got that little one!" Miyuki cried.

"They go for the weaker game."

"Weaker?" Miyuki felt irritated at Tatsuhiko's cool analysis. "The chupchups are armed."

"But they do not use them to hunt the larger game. Or even, it seems, to defend themselves. The only use we have observed for those weapons is the pursuit of small game. Easy prey."

Miyuki shook her head. "That seems impossible. Why not use them?"

Somehow this direct question shattered Tatsuhiko's stony scientific distance. "Because they have adapted—downward."

"Maybe just sideways."

"A once proud race of creators, now driven down to *this*."

"We ourselves, early man, we hunted in places like this. We could be forced back to it if—"

"No. We were hunters, like the lion. We did not scavenge."

Miyuki said quietly, "I thought lions scavenged."

Tatsuhiko glared at her but acknowledged this uncomfortable fact with a curt nod of his head. "Man the hunter did not. These chupchups—they have let themselves be driven down to this lowly state."

She saw his vexed position. Traits derived from genes had led humans upward in ability. It had been a grand, swift leap, from wily ape to sovereign of the Earth. That tended to salt the truths of sociobiology with the promise of progress. Here, though, the same logic led to devolution of the once-great city-builders.

She said lightly, "We are merely talking wildly. Making guesses." She switched to English. "Doing so-so biology." Perhaps the pun would lift their discussion away from the remorselessly reductionist.

He gave her a cold smile. "Thank you, Miyuki-san, for your humor." He turned to regard the distant feeding, where the chupchups now nuzzled among the bones. "Those cannot be the breed which built the cities. We have come so very slightly late."

"Perhaps elsewhere on Chujo—"

"We will look, certainly. Still…"

She said evenly, hoping to snap him out of this mood, "For four billion years, Earth supported only microbes. Oxygen and land plants are only comparatively recent additions. If those proportions hold everywhere, we are very lucky to find *two* planets which have more than algae!"

His angular features caught the dawn glow, giving him a sardonic look even in his pressure mask.

"You are trying to deflect my dark temper."

"Of course."

Each crew member was responsible for maintaining cohesion. They kept intact the old ship disciplines. In solidarity meetings, one never scratched one's head or even crossed legs or arms before a superior, and always concluded even the briefest encounter with a polite bow—15 degrees to peers, 45 degrees to superiors. Every week they repeated the old rituals, even the patient writing of Buddhist sutras with wooden pens. The officers polished the boots of the lower ranks, and soon after the ranks reciprocated. Each was bound to the others. And she felt bound to him, though they had not been lovers for years, and she had passed through many liaisons since. Her longing to know him now was not carnal, though that element would never be banished, and she did not want it to be. She felt a need to *reach* him, to bring out the best that she knew lay within him. It was a form of love, though not one that songwriters knew. Perhaps in some obscure way it knitted into the cohesion of the greater expedition, but it felt intensely personal and incommunicable. Especially to the object of it all, standing obliviously a meter away. She snorted with frustration.

Not noticing her mood, Tatsuhiko smacked his fist into his palm. "But so close! If we had come fifty thousand years ago! Seen those great ancestors of these, these cowards."

Miyuki blinked, sniffed, chuckled. "Then we would have been Neanderthals."

4.
The Library

Their flyer came down smoothly beside the spreading forest. The waving fields of dark grain beckoned, but Miyuki knew already that the stuff was inedible.

Nearly everything on Chujo was. Only the sugar groups were digestible. Their dextro-rotary sense was the same as that of Earthly ones, a simple fact that led to deep mystery. Genji's sugars had that identical helical sense, though with myriad different patterns. And the intelligent, automated probes which now had scanned a dozen worlds around further stars reported back the same result: where life appeared at all, anything resembling a sugar chain had the same sense of rotation. Some said this proved a limited form of molecular panspermia, with a primordial cloud seeding the region with simple organic precursors.

But there still were deeper similarities between Genji and Chujo: in protein structures, enzymes, details of energy processing. Had the two worlds once interacted? They were now 156,000 kilometers apart, less than two-thirds the Earth-moon separation, but tidal forces were driving them further away. Their locked rotation minimized the stress from each others' tides. Even so, great surges swept even the small lakes as the mother-sun, Murasaki, raised its own tides on both her worlds. Miyuki stood beside a shallow, steel-gray lake and watched the waters rush across a pebbled beach. The rasp and rattle of stones came like the long, indrawn breath of the entire planet.

"Regroup!" Koremasa ordered over comm.

Miyuki had been idling, turning over in her mind the accumulating mysteries. She studied the orderly grain fields with their regimental rows and irrigation slits, as the expeditionary group met. Their reports were orderly, precise: discipline was even more crisp amid these great stretches of alien ground. Close observation showed that this great field was self-managing.

She watched as one of the bio group displayed a cage of rodents, each with prehensile, clawed fingers. "They cultivate the stalks, keep off pests," the woman said. "I believe this field can prune and perhaps even harvest itself."

Murmurs of dissent gradually ebbed as evidence accumulated. Remains of irrigation channels still cut the valley. Brick-brown ruins of large buildings stood beside the restless lake. Small stone cairns dotted the landscape. It was easy for Miyuki to believe the rough scenario that the anthropologists and archaeologists proposed: that the slow waning of Chujo had driven the ancient natives to perfect crops which needed little labor, an astounding feat of biotech. That this field was a fragment of a great grain belt that had fed the cities. That as life suited to cold and aridity moved south, the ancients retreated into a pastoral, nomadic life. That—

"Chupchups!" someone called.

And here they came, already spreading out from the treeline a kilometer away. Miyuki clicked her vision to remote and surveyed them as she moved to her encounter position. This tribe had a herd. Domesticated snakehounds adroitly kept the short, bulky red-haired beasts tightly bunched. A plume of dust pointed at the baggage train—pole arrangements drawn behind thin, flat-headed animals. An arrowfowl came flapping from over a distant hillside and settled onto the shoulder of the largest chupchup—bringing a message from another tribe, she now knew enough to guess. The races met again.

The leading chupchup performed as before—a long, lingering looking straight at the first human it met, then ignoring the rest. Miyuki stood still as the smelly, puffing aliens marched obliviously through the human formation.

Nomads had always been a fringe element in human civilization, she reflected. Even ancient Nippon had supported some. But here the nomads *were* the civilization. The latest survey from satellites had just finished counting the chupchups; there were around a million, covering a world with more land area than Earth. The head of Exo-Analysis thought that the number was in fact exactly 1,048,576—1024 tribes of 1024 individuals apiece. He even maintained that each tribe held 32 families of 32 members each. Even if he was right, she thought, and the musky bodies passing stolidly by her now were units in some grandly ordained arithmetic, had it always been that way? How did they maintain it?

She caught an excited murmur on comm. To her left a crew member was pointing toward a few stacked stones where three chupchups had stopped.

Slowly, gingerly, they pried up the biggest slab of blue-grey granite. One chupchup drew something forth, held it to the light—a small, square thing—and then put it in a pocket of its shabby brown waistcoat. Then the chupchups walked on, talking in that warbling way of theirs, still ignoring the humans who stood absolutely still, aching for contact, receiving none. She almost laughed at the forlorn expressions of the crew as the last of the chupchups marched off, leaving only a fragrant odor of musty sweat. They did not inspect the fields or even glance at the ruins.

"It's a library!" someone called.

Miyuki turned back to see that a crew man, Akihiro, had lifted the granite slab. Inside rested a few cubes, each ornately decorated. "I think this is a library. They were picking up a book."

Koremasa appeared as if he had materialized from the air. "Put it back!" he ordered tersely.

Akihiro said, "But I—look, it's—"

"Back!"

But by then it was too late. From the trees came the trolls.

Miyuki was not a first-line combat officer. She thus had a moment, as others ran to form a defensive line, to observe the seemingly accidental geometry which unfolded as the troll attack began. The chupchups had stopped, turned around—and watched impassively as the trolls burst from the thick treeline. Had the chupchups summoned the trolls, once they saw their library violated? She could not guess from their erect posture, blandly expressionless faces, unmoving mouths.

The trolls resembled chupchups as chimps resembled humans— shorter, wider, long arms, small heads. But they ran with the fluid speed of a hunting animal, and caught the nearest crew member before she could fetch her weapon forth from her pack. A troll picked her up and threw her like something it wished to discard—hurling her twenty meters, where she struck and bounced and rolled and lay still. The other trolls took no notice.

They hesitated. Had they gotten some signal from the chupchups? But no—she saw that the wind had shifted. The odorous extract which the biotechs had made everyone smear themselves with—yes, that was it. The cutting reek of it, carried on the breeze, had confused the trolls for a moment. But then their rage came again, their teeth flashed with mad hunting passion, and they fell upon the next crew members.

She would remember the next few instants for all her life. The weapons carriers liked to fire from a single line, to minimize accidents. Trolls struck that still-forming line. When he saw that the smell defense had failed, Koremasa blinked, raised his hand with a sad, slow gravity—and the rifles barked, a thin sharp sound in the chilly air.

The sudden hard slaps were inundated by the snarls and howls of trolls as they slammed aside their puny opponents. The aliens were swift, sure, moving with enormous power and sudden, almost ballet-like agility. In their single-footed swerves, their quick ducks to avoid a rifle shot, their flicked blows that struck with devastating power, Miyuki saw how a billion years of evolution had engineered reflexes intricately suited to the lesser gravity.

But then the concerted splatting violence took them down. Their elegant, intelligent attack had not counted on a volley of automatic fire. The great, bright-eyed beasts fell even as they surged on, oblivious to danger.

The last few reached Miyuki and she saw, in slow-motion surrealism, the flushed, heady expression on a troll which stumbled as it took a round in its massive right arm. *It's ecstatic*, she thought.

But it would not be stopped by one shot. It staggered, looking for another enemy to take, and saw her. Red eyes filled with purple pupils widened. It swung its left arm, claws arcing out—and she ducked.

The swipe whistled over her ear, caught her with a *thunk* in the scalp. It was more a sound, a booming, than a felt blow. She flew through the air, turning, suddenly and abstractly registering the pale blue, cloud-quilted sky, and then she landed on her left shoulder and rolled. A quick rasping *brrrrt* cut through a strange hollow silence that had settled around her. She looked up into the sky and the troll eclipsed this view like a red-brown thundercloud. It was not looking at her, but instead seemed to be gazing off into a world it could not comprehend. Then it felt the tug of mortality and orbited down into the acrid clouds of dust stirred by the battle, landing solidly beside her, not rolling, its sour breath coughing out for the last time.

5.
I-Witnessing

They devoted three days to studying the fields and burying the bodies. A pall spread among them, the radio crackled with questions, and mission command wrung from each fact a symphony of meaning, of blame, of outrage.

Miyuki was doubly glad that she had not sought a higher post in this exploration party. Koremasa had to feed the appetite of his superiors, safely orbiting Genji, with data, photos, transcripts, explanations, analysis. Luckily, two cameras had recorded most of the battle. Watching these images again and again, Miyuki felt a chill at the speed and intelligence of the troll assault. Her own head wound was nothing compared to the bloody cuts and gougings many others had received.

Koremasa would probably not be court martialed—but Akihiro Saito, the crewman who had opened the cairn in a moment of excited curiosity, would have been tried and humiliated, had he survived.

It was something of a relief that Akihiro had died. They would have had to watch him for signs of potential suicide, never leaving him alone or assigning him dangerous tasks. No one could be squandered here, no matter how they violated the expedition's standards.

No one ever said this, of course. Instead, they held a full, formal ceremony to mark the passing of their companions, including Akihiro. The meal was specially synthesized on the mother ship and sent down in a drop package. The team sat in a precise formation, backs to the wild alien landscape outside the bubble, and within their circle Old Nippon lived still. The Captain produced a bowl for each, in which reposed a sweetened smoked sardine, its spine curved to represent a fish in the water. It had been carefully placed against two slices of raw yellowtail, set off by a delicately preserved peeled plum and two berrylike ovals, one crisp and one soft, both dipped in an amber coating. A second bowl held a paper-thin slice of raw Spanish mackerel, cut to catch the silver stripe down its back, underpinned in turn by a sliver of seaweed to quietly stress the stripe, all resting on molded rice. A small half lobster, garnished with sweet preserved chestnuts, sent its aroma into the close, incense-scented air. Thin-sliced, curled onions came next, sharp and melting in the mouth. A rosette of red pickled onion heart came wrapped in a rosy cabbage leaf. Finally, tea.

And all this came from the processors aboard the mother ship, fashioned finally by the master chef whom everyone agreed—in the polite, formal conversation which followed around their circle—was the most important member of the entire expedition.

The beautiful meal and a day of contemplation did their silent work. Calamity reminded one to remain centered, to rely on others, to remember that all humanity witnessed the events here. So as the numbness and anxiety left them they returned to their studies. Five crew kept watch at all times while the rest tried to comprehend why four humans and six trolls had died.

In the end, the simplest explanation seemed best: the trolls guarded the ancient, self-managing fields, and this task included the library cairn.

The biologists found rodent-like creatures which pruned and selected the grain plants, others which gathered them into bunches, and further species who stored them among the caved-in brick-brown buildings. Subtle forces worked the fields: ground cover which repelled weeds, fungoids which made otherwise defenseless leaves distasteful or poisonous to browsers, small burrowers which loosened the soil for roots. The trolls assisted these tasks and made sure that only passing bands of chupchups ate the grain. They tended fruit-bearing trees in the next valley as well, where two more library cairns stood.

The cube from the cairn yielded nothing intelligible immediately, but would doubtless be studied in infinitesimal detail when they got it to the mother ship. The sciences were biased toward studying hard evidence, and the oddly marked stone cube was ideal for this. Miyuki doubted whether it could ever yield very much.

"It could be a religious talisman, after all," she remarked one evening as they gathered for a meager supper.

"Then it would probably be displayed in a shrine," Koremasa said reasonably.

"They have no churches," Miyuki answered.

"We think," Tatsuhiko said sourly. "We have not searched enough yet to say."

Miyuki said, "You believe the cities at the rim may tell us more?"

Tatsuhiko hesitated. He plainly felt besieged, having failed to anticipate well the danger here, a continuing humiliation to him. "There might be much less erosion at high altitudes," he said warily.

Koremasa nodded. "Satellite reconn shows that. High winds, but less air to work with."

Miyuki smiled. Seen from above, planets seemed vastly simple. The yellowish flora and fauna of Chujo tricked the eyes of even orbiting robot scanners. The molecule which best harvested Murasaki's wan glow was activated by red-orange light, not by the skimpy greens which chlorophyll favored. That simple consequence of living beside a lukewarm star muddied the resolution of their data-reduction programs.

"We had better leave such high sites for later work," she ventured.

Koremasa's eyebrows showed mild surprise but he kept his mouth relaxed, quizzical. "You truly feel so?"

Though she did not wish to admit it, the thought of wearing the added pressure gear needed among the raw mountains of Chujo's rim grated upon her. She itched from dryness, her sleeping cycle veered in response to Chujo's 91-hour day, her sinuses clogged perpetually from constant colds—and everyone else suffered the same, largely without complaint. But she decided to keep her objections professional. "Our error here suggests that we leave more difficult tasks to others." There. Diffident but cutting.

Koremasa let a silence stretch, and no one else in the circle ventured into it. A cold wind moaned against the plastic of their pressure dome. Their incandescents' blues and violets apparently irritated the local night-hunters and pests, keeping them at bay, one of the few favorable accidents they had found. Still, she felt the strangeness of the dark outside pressing against them all.

She saw Koremasa's talent as a leader; he simply sat, finally provoking Tatsuhiko to say, "I must object. We need to understand those who build the cities, for they plainly are not these chupchups. Then—"

"Why is that so clear?" Miyuki cut in.

Tatsuhiko let a small trace of inner tension twist his mouth momentarily. "You saw the scavenging. That is not the behavior of a dominant, intelligent race."

"What's intelligent is what survives," she answered.

Tatsuhiko flared. "No, that is an utter misunderstanding of evolutionary theory. Intelligence is not always adaptive—that is the terrible lesson we have learned here."

"That is a hasty conclusion," Miyuki said mildly.

"*Hasty?* We know far more than you may realize about these chupchups. We have picked over their campsites, studied their mating through infra-distant imaging, picked apart their turds to study their diet. We patched together their broken pots. Their few metal implements are probably stolen from the ruined cities and reworked down through many generations; they certainly look it."

"It is difficult to read meaning in artifacts," Koremasa said.

"Not so!" Tatsuhiko stood and began to pace, walking jerkily around the outside of the circle. He made each of his points with the edge of his right hand, cutting the air in a karate chop. "The chupchups wander perpetually. They cook in bark pots and leather bags using heated stones—stew with dumplings, usually. They like starchy sweets and swallow berries whole. They pick their teeth with a bristly fungus which they then eat a day later—"

"They must be civilized, then," Miyuki broke in. "They floss!"

Tatsuhiko blinked, allowed himself a momentary smile in answer to the round of laughter. "Perhaps so, though I differ." He gave her a quick significant glance, and she felt that somehow she had momentarily broken through to the man she knew.

Then he took a breath, lifted his narrow chin high, put his hands behind his back in a curiously schoolboyish pose, and went on doggedly. "You will have noticed that chupchup males and females look nearly alike. There are no signs of homosexual behavior—which is hard to understand. After all humans have genetically selected for it through the shared kinship mechanism and inclusive fitness, in which the homosexuals further the survival of genes they share with heterosexuals. They're not permanently rutty, the way we are, and perhaps an explanation lies there—but how? The female does the courting, singing and dancing like Earthside birds. No musical instruments used. They do it more often than reproduction requires, though, just like us. Some pair-bonding, maybe even monogamy. Approximate equality of the sexes in social matters and labor, with perhaps some slight female dominance. They carry out some sex-separate rites, but we don't know what those mean. Hunter-gatherer routines are—"

"Quite so," Koremasa said softly. "We take your points."

Somehow this ended the spontaneous lecture. Tatsuhiko fell silent, his lips twitching. She felt sympathy for his frustration, mingling with his restless desire to fathom this world in terms he could understand.

Yet she could not let matters rest here. She set her face resolutely. If he wished a professional contest, so be it.

"You read much into your observations," Miyuki said. She looked around the circle to see if anyone nodded, but they were all impassive, letting her take the lead.

"We must," Tatsuhiko said testily.

"But surely we can no more portray a society by recording facts, filtered through our preconceptions, than a literary critic can get the essence of Murasaki's great *Genji Monogatari* by summarizing the plot," she said. "I think perhaps we are doing 'I-witnessing' here."

Tatsuhiko smiled grimly. "You have a case of what we call in sociobiology 'epistemological hypochondria'—the fear of interpretation."

Koremasa let the wind speak to them all again, sighing, muttering, rubbing at their monolayer defense against it.

"We appreciate your views, Tatsuhiko-san, but there are fresh facts before us now," Koremasa said in calm, measured tones. "The satellites report that the chupchup tribes are no longer wandering in a random pattern."

Tatsuhiko brightened. "Oh? Where are they going?"

"They are all moving away from us."

Surprise registered in a low, questioning mutter around their circle. "All of them?" the communications engineer asked.

Koremasa nodded. "They are moving toward the ridge-rim. Journeying from the moonside to the starside, perhaps." He stood, smiling at Tatsuhiko. "In a way, I suppose we have at last received a tribute from them. They have acknowledged our presence."

Tatsuhiko blinked and then snorted derisively. Such a rude show would be remarkable, except that Miyuki understood that the contempt was directed by Tatsuhiko at himself.

"And I suggest," Koremasa continued with a quiet air of authority, "that we study this planet-wide activity."

"Of course," Tatsuhiko said enthusiastically. "This could be a seasonal migration. Many animal species have elaborate—"

"These are *not* animals!" Miyuki surprised herself with the vehemence in her voice.

Miyuki opened her mouth, but saw Captain Koremasa raise one finger slightly. He said casually, "Enough theory. We must look—and quickly. The first bands are already striving to cross the rim mountain ranges."

6.
Paradigm Lost

Chujo and Genji pulled at each other incessantly, working through their tides, and Murasaki's more distant stresses added to the geological turmoil. This powered a zone of incessant mountain-building along the circumference of Chujo. Seen from Genji, this ring rimmed Chujo with a crust of peaks, shear faults and deep, shadowed gorges. Lakes and small, pale seas dotted Chujo's lowlands, where the thin air already seemed chilly to humans, even in this summer season. Matters worsened for fragile humans toward the highlands.

The muscled movement of great geologic forces lifted the rock, allowing water to carve its many-layered canyons. As they flew over the great stretching plains Miyuki feasted on the passing panorama, insisting that their craft fly at the lowest safe altitude, though that cost fuel. She saw the promise of green summer, lagoons of bright water, grazing beasts with white hoofs stained with the juice of wildflowers.

This was a place of violent contrasts. In an hour they saw the land below parched by drought, beaten by hail, sogged by rain, burnt by grass fires. But soon, as their engines labored to suck in more of the skimpy air, the plains became ceramic-gray, blistered, cracked. From orbit she had seen the yellow splashes of erupting lava from myriad small peaks, and now they came marching from the girdling belt of the world. Black rock sliced across the buff colors of wind-blown sand. Glacial moraines cupped frozen lakes, fault blocks poked above eorded plains, V-valleys testified to the recent invasion of the great ice.

Yet this world-wracking had perhaps made life possible here. Chujo was much like a fortunate Mars—small, cold, huddled beneath a scant scarf of sheltering gas. Mars had suffered swerves in its polar inclination and eccentricity, and this may have doomed the fossilized, fledgling spores humans had found there. But Genji-Chujo's whirling waltz had much more angular momentum than a sole spinning planet could, and this had fended off the tilting perturbations of Murasaki and the outer, gas giant planets. Thus neither of the brothers had to endure wobbling poles, shifting seasons, the rasp of cruel change.

Small bushes clung to the escarpments of a marble mountain. Compressional scarps cut the mountain as though a great knife had tried to kill it. These were signs of internal cooling, she knew, Chujo shrinking as its core cooled, wrinkling with age, a world in retreat from its warmer eras. Twisted spires of pumice reared, light as air, splashed with stains of cobalt, putty, scarlet. Miyuki watched this brutal beauty unfold uneasily. Smoke hazed the snow-capped range ahead. The Genjians must have wondered for ages, she thought, at the continual flame and black clouds of their brother's perimeter. They probably did not realize that a similar wracked ridge girdled their own world. Perhaps the Genjians had seen the great Chujoan cities at their prime—it was optically possible, with the naked Genjian eye—but could legends of that have survived the thousands of generations since? Did either intelligent race know of the other—and did they still? Certainly—she glanced up at the crescent of Genji, mottled and muggy, like a watercolor artwork tossed off by a hasty child—the present chupchups could gain no hint from that sultry atmosphere. Still, there were hints, all the way down into the molecular chemistry, that the worlds were linked.

Koremasa rapped on the hard plexiglass. "See? All that green?"

Miyuki peered ahead and saw on the flank of a jutting mountain a smooth, tea-green growth. "Summer—and we're near the equator."

Koremasa nodded. "This terrain looks too barren to support plants year round."

Tatsuhiko put in, over the low rumble of their flyer, "Seasonal migration. More evidence."

"Of what?" Miyuki asked.

"Of their devolution. They've picked up the patterns of migrating fowl. Seasonal animals didn't build those cities."

Koremasa said, "That makes sense."

Tatsuhiko pressed his point. "So you no longer believe they are fleeing from us?"

Koremasa smiled, and she saw that his announcement two days before had all been a subtle ruse. "It was a useful temporary hypothesis."

Useful for what? she wanted to ask, but discipline and simple politeness restrained her. Instead she said, "So they migrate to the mountain chain to—what? Eat that grass, or whatever it is?"

Tatsuhiko nodded enthusiastically. "Of course."

She remarked dryly, "A long way to walk for such sparse stuff."

"I mention it only as a working hypothesis," Tatsuhiko said stiffly.

"Did you ever see an animal wearing clothes?" Miyuki let a tinge of sarcasm slip into her voice.

"Simple crabs carry their shell homes on their backs."

"Animals that cook? Carry weapons?"

"All that is immaterial." Tatsuhiko regarded her with something like fondness for a long moment. Then his face returned to the cool, lean cast she had seen so much of these last few years. "I grant that the chupchups have vestigial artifacts of their ancestors. Those mat-clothes of theirs— marvelous biological engineering, but plainly inherited. The chupchups are plainly degenerated."

"Because they won't talk to us?"

"Because they have abandoned their cities, lost their birthright."

"The Mayans did that well over a thousand years ago."

Tatsuhiko shook his head, his amused smile telling the others that here an amateur was venturing into his territory. "They did not revert to Neanderthals."

Miyuki asked with restrained venom, "You would prefer any explanation that made the chupchups into degenerated pseudo-animals, wouldn't you?"

"That is an unfair—"

"Well, wouldn't you?"

"—and unprofessional, unscientific, attitude."

"You didn't answer me."

"There is no need to dignify an obvious personal—"

"Oh, please spare me—"

"Prepare for descent," Koremasa said, looking significantly at both of them in turn.

"Huh!" Miyuki sat back and glowered out at the view. How had she ever thought that she could reach this man?

They landed heavily, the jet's engines whining, swiveling to lower them vertically into a boulder-strewn valley, just short of the green expanses. Deep crevasses cut the stony ground. Miyuki climbed out gingerly, her pressure suit awkwardly bunching and pinching. The medical people back in Low Genji Orbit had given them only ten hours to accomplish this mission, and allowed only six of them to go at all. The cold already bit into her hands and feet.

A white-water stream muttered nearby and they headed along it, toward the brown and green growth that filled the upper valley. Broken walls of the ancient Chujoans lay in the narrow box canyon at the top of the valley, near a spectacular roaring waterfall. It had been a respectable-sized town, she judged.

Why did those ancients build anything at all here? Most of the year this austere place had no vegetation at all, the satellite records said.

She stumbled. The ground was shaking. Slow, grave oscillations came up through her boots. She looked up, her helmet feeling more bulky all the time, and studied the mountain peak that jutted above them. Streamers of black smoke fretted away in the perpetual winds. Crashes echoed in the valley, reflected off the neighboring peaks from the flanks of the mountain—landslides, adding their kettle-drum rolls as punctuation to the mountain's bass notes.

Fretful comments filled the comm. She marched on grimly. Tatsuhiko and Koremasa seemed to have already decided how to interpret whatever they would find; what was the point of this? Sitting back in camp, this quick sortie to the highlands—a "sprint mission," in the jargon—had seemed a great adventure.

She studied the bare cliff faces that framed the valley. Volcanic ash layers like slices in an infinite sandwich, interspersed with more interesting lines of pink clay, of pebbled sand, of gray conglomerates. So they would have to do what they did at so many sites—sample quickly, thinking little, hoping that they had gotten the kernel of the place by dint of judgment and luck. So much! A whole world, vast and various—and another, hanging overhead like a taunt.

The biologist reached the broad, flat field of green and knelt down to poke at it. He looked up in surprise. "It's algae! Sort of."

Miyuki stepped on the stuff. It was so thin she could feel pebbles crunch beneath it. She bent to examine it, her suit gathering and bunching uncomfortably at her knees. The mat was finely textured, green threads weaving among brown splashes.

The biologist dug his sample knife into it. "Tough," he said. "Very tough." With effort he punctured the mat and with visible exertion cut out a patch. His portable chemlab shot back an answer as soon as he inserted the patch. "Ummm. Distinct resemblance to...oh yes, that chupchup clothing. Same species, I'd say."

Tatsuhiko's voice was tight and precise over comm. "This proves how long ago the original form was developed. Here it's assumed a natural role in the environment. Unless the chupchups simply adapted it themselves from this original species. I—"

"Funny biochem going on here," the biologist said. "It's excreting some kind of metabolic inhibitor. And—say, there's a lot of hydrogen around it, too."

Tatsuhiko nodded. "That agrees with the tests on the chupchup living cloth. It interacts with the chupchup body, we believe."

"No, this is different." The biologist moved on, tugging at the surface, taking readings. "This stuff is interconnected algae and fibers with a lot of energy stored in chemical bonds."

"Look at these," Miyuki said. She lifted a flap of the thin but tough material. There was a pocket several meters long, open at one end.

"Double-layered, I guess. Wonder why?" The biologist frowned. "This thing is a great photosynthetic processor. Guess that's why it flourishes here only in summer. Now, I—"

The ground rolled. Miyuki staggered. The biologist fell, throwing his knife aside to avoid a cut in his suit. Miyuki saw a dark mass fly up from the mountain's peak. A sudden thunderclap hammered down on them. The valley floor shook. Dust rose in filmy curtains.

"Sample taken?" Koremasa asked on comm. "Good. Let us—"

"But the ruins!" Miyuki said. "They'll want at least a few photos."

"Oh. Yes." Koremasa looked unhappy but nodded.

Miyuki could scarcely believe she had blurted out such a rash suggestion. Not only was it quite unlike her, she thought, but it contradicted her better judgment. She did want to have a look at the ruins, yes, but—

A tremblor rocked her like an ocean wave. More smoke spat from the peak, unfurling across a troubled sky. The other five had already started running uphill across the mat.

She followed, turning every hundred meters to glance behind, memorizing the way back in case they had to retreat in a hurry. She heard Tatsuhiko's shout and saw him pointing just as another slow, deep ripple worked through the valley.

"Chups!"

They were in a single file, winding out of the ruins. They did not turn to look at the humans, simply proceeded downhill.

Miyuki's perspectives shifted and danced as she watched them, the world seemed to be tilting—and then she realized that again it was not her, but the valley floor which was moving. What she felt was not the wrenching of an earthquake.

It was the mat itself. The entire floor of the valley wrinkled, stretched, slid.

The chupchups seemed to glide across the wrestling surface of the mat, uphill from the humans. They were headed for a crevasse which billowed steam. Streamers of sulphurous yellow swirled across the mat. Yet the chupchups gave none of the gathering chaos any notice.

"Back!" Koremasa called on comm. "Back into the flyer."

They had nearly reached the ruins. Miyuki took a moment to snap quick pictures of the crumbled structures. The slumped stoneworks did not look at all like housing. In fact they seemed to be immense vats, caved in and filled with rubble. Vats for what?

She turned away and the ground slid out from under her. She rolled. The others were further downhill but the jerking of the tawny-green growth under them had sent them tumbling pellmell downward, rolling like dolls. They shouted, cried out, swore.

Miyuki stopped herself by digging in her heels and grabbing at the tough, writhing mat. It was durable material and she could not rip it for a better hold. In a moment the convulsions stopped. She sat up. Pearly fog now rose from the mat all around her. She felt a trembling and then realized that she was moving—slowly, in irregular little jerks, but yes—the mat was tugging itself across the pebbles beneath it. She scrambled for footing—and fell. She got to her knees. Somewhere near here the chupchups—

There. They were standing, looking toward the chasm a hundred meters away. Miyuki followed their intent, calm gaze.

The mat was alive, powerful, muscular—and climbing up the sky.

No, it merely reared, like the living flesh of a wounded thing. It buckled and writhed, a nightmare living carpet.

It jerked itself higher than a human, forming a long sheet that flexed like an ocean wave—and leaped.

The wave struck the far side of the crevasse. It met there another shelf of rising mat. The two waves stuck, clung. All along the chasm the two edges slapped together, melted into one another, formed a seamless whole.

And rose. As though some chemical reaction were kindling under it, the living carpet bulged like a blister. Miyuki clung to the shifting, sliding mat—and then realized that if she let go, she could roll downhill, where she wanted to go.

She watched the mat all along the vent as it billowed upward. The chupchups made waving motions, as if urging the mat to leave the ground. She thought suddenly, *They came here for this. Not fleeing from us at all.*

Then she was slipping, rolling, the world whirling as she felt the mat accelerate. Her breath rasped and she curled up into a ball, tumbling and bouncing down the hillside. Knocks, jolts, a dull gathering roar—and then she slammed painfully against a boulder. A bare boulder, free of the mat.

She got up, feeling a sharp pain in her left ankle. "Koremasa-san!"

"Here! Help me with Tatsuhiko!"

Tatsuhiko had broken his leg. His dark face contorted with agony. She peered down into his constricted eyes and he said, speaking very precisely between pants, "Matters are complex."

She blinked. "What?"

"Clearly something more is going on here," he said tightly, holding the pain back behind his thin smile.

"Never mind that, you're hurt. We'll—"

He waved the issue away. "A temporary intrusion. Concentrate on what is happening here."

"Look, we'll get you safely—"

"I have missed something." Tatsuhiko grimaced, then gave a short, barking laugh. "Maybe everything."

She felt the need to comfort him, beyond placing compresses, and said, "You may have been right. This—"

"No, the chupchups are...something different. Outside the paradigms."

"Quiet now. We'll get you out of here."

Tatsuhiko lifted his eyebrows weakly. "Keep your lovely eyes open. Watch what the chupchups are doing. Record."

Something in his tone made her hesitate. "I...still love you."

His lips trembled. "I...also. Why can we not talk?"

"Perhaps...perhaps it means too much."

He twisted his lips wryly. "Exactly. That hypothesis accounts for the difficulty."

"Too much..." She saw ruefully that she had thought him stiff and uncompromising, and perhaps he was—but that did not mean she did not share those elements. Perhaps they were part of the personality constellations chosen long ago on Earth, the partitioning of traits which insured the expedition would get through at all.

He said, "I am sorry. I will do better."

"But you..." She did not know what to say and her mouth was dry and then the others came.

They lifted him and started toward the flyer. The others had rolled onto the rocky ground below as the mat moved. Miyuki stumbled, this time from a volcanic tremor. She got to the flyer and looked back. The entire party paused then, fear draining from them momentarily, and watched.

The mat was lifting itself. Alive with purpose, rippling, its center axis bulged, pulling the rest of it along the ground with a hiss like a wave sliding up a beach. It shed pebbles, making itself lighter, letting go of its birthplace.

"Some...some reaction is going on in the vent under it," the biologist panted over comm. "Making gases—that hydrogen I detected, I'll bet. That's a byproduct of this mat. Maybe it's been growing some culture in the volcanic vents around here. Maybe..." His voice trailed away in stunned disbelief.

She remembered the strange vat-like openings among the chupchup buildings. Some ancient chemical works? A way to augment this process? After all the chupchups had clothing made of material much like this crawling carpet.

They got Tatsuhiko into the bay of the flyer. Koremasa ordered the pilot to ready the flyer for liftoff. He turned back to the others and then pointed at the sky. Miyuki turned. From valleys beyond large, green teardrops drifted up the sky. They wobbled and flexed, as though shaping themselves into the proper form for a fresh inhabitant of the air.

Organic balloons were launching themselves from all the valleys of the volcanic ridge. Dozens rose into the winds. In concert, somehow, Miyuki saw. Perhaps triggered by the spurt of vulcanism. Perhaps responding to some deeply imprinted command, some collision of chemicals.

"Living balloons..." she said.

The biologist said, "The vulcanism, maybe it triggers the process. After the mat has grown to a certain size. Methane, maybe anaerobic fermentation—"

"The carving," Miyuki said.

Koremasa said quietly, "The chupchups."

The frail, distant figures clung to the side of the mat as the center of it rose, fattening. Some found the pockets which the humans had noticed, and slipped inside. Others simply grabbed a handful of the tough green hide and hung on.

"They are going up with it," Koremasa said.

She recalled the carving in the ancient city, with its puzzling circles hanging in the backdrop of the tiger eating its tail, nature feeding on itself, with the Chujoan face arising from the writhing pain of the twisting tail. "The circles—they were balloons. Rising."

The last edge of the mat sped toward the ascending bulge with a sound like the rushing of rapids over pebbles. The accelerating clatter seemed to hasten the living, self-making balloon. Frayed lips of the mat slapped together below the fattening, uprushing dome. These edges sealed, tightened, made the lower tip of a green teardrop.

On the grainy skin of the swelling dome the chupchup passengers now settled themselves in the pockets Miyuki had noted before. Most made it. Some dangled helplessly, lost their grip, fell with a strange silence to their deaths. Those already in pockets helped others to clamber aboard.

And buoyantly, quietly, they soared into a blue-black sky. "Toward Genji," Miyuki whispered. She felt a pressing sense of presence, as though a momentous event had occurred.

"In hydrogen-filled bags?" Koremasa asked.

"They can reach fairly far up in the atmosphere that way," Tatsuhiko said weakly. He was lying on the cushioned deck of the flyer, pale and solemn. The injury had drained him but his eyes flashed with the same quick, assessing intelligence.

Miyuki climbed into the flyer and put a cushion under his helmet. The crew began sealing the craft. "I don't think they mean to just fly around," she said.

"Oh?" Tatsuhiko asked wanly. "You think they imagine they're going to Genji?"

"I don't think we can understand this." She hesitated. "It may even be suicide."

Tatsuhiko scowled. "A race devoted to a suicide ritual? They wouldn't have lasted long."

She gestured at the upper end of the valley. "Most of them didn't go. See? They're standing in long lines up there, watching the balloon leave."

"More inheritance?" Tatsuhiko whispered. "Is this all they remember of the technology the earlier race had mastered?"

Miyuki thought. "I wonder."

Tatsuhiko said wanly, taking her hand, "Perhaps they have held onto the biomats, used them. Maybe they don't understand what they were for, really. A piece of biotech like that—a beautiful solution to the problem of transport, in an energy-scarce environment. And the chupchups are just, just joyriding."

Miyuki smiled. "Perhaps..."

They lifted off vertically just as another rolling jolt came. The flyer veered in the gathering winds, and Miyuki watched the teardrop shapes scudding across the purpling sky. Soon enough they would be the object of scrutiny, measurement, with the full armament of scientific dispassion marshalled to fathom them. She would probably even do some of the job herself, she thought wryly.

But for this single crystalline moment she wished to simply enjoy them. Not analyze, but feel the odd, hushed quality their ascent brought.

They were probably neither Tatsuhiko's vestigial technology nor some arcane tribal ceremony. Perhaps this entire drama was purely a way for the chupchups to tell humans something. She bit her lip in concentration. Tell what? Indeed, satellite observations, dating back to the first robot probe, had never shown any sign of a chupchup migration here. It might be unique—a response to humans themselves.

She sighed. Cabin pressure hissed on again as the flyer leveled off for its long flight back. She popped her helmet and wrestled Tatsuhiko's off. He smiled, thanked her—and all the while behind his tired eyes she saw the glitter, the unquelled pursuit of his own singular vision, which Tatsuhiko would never abandon. As he should not.

The biologist was saying something about the balloons, details—that they seemed to be photosynthetic processors, making more hydrogen to keep themselves aloft, to offset losses through their own skin. He even had a term for them, bioloons...

So the unpeeling of the onion skins was already beginning. And what fun it would be.

But what did it *mean*? The first stage of science atomizes, dissects, fragments. Only much later do the Bohrs, the Darwins, the Einsteins knit it all together again—and nobody knew what the final weave would be, silk or sackcloth.

So both Tatsuhiko and herself and all the others—they were all needed. There would be no end of explanations. Did the chupchups think humans were in fact from that great promise in the sky, Genji? Or were they trying to signal something with the mat-balloons—while still holding to their silence? An arcane ceremony? Some joke?

The chupchups would never fit the narrow rules of sociobiology, she guessed, but just as clearly they would not be merely Zen aliens, or curators of some ashram in the sky. They were themselves, and the fathoming of that would be a larger task than Miyuki, or Tatsuhiko, or Koremasa could comprehend.

The flyer purred steadily. The still-rising emerald teardrops dwindled behind. Their humming technology was taking them back to base, its pilot already fretting about fuel.

Miyuki felt a sudden, unaccountable burst of joy. Hard mystery remained here, shadowed mystery would call them back, and mystery was far better that the cool ceramic surfaces of certainty.

IN THE DARK BACKWARD
(1993)

The fearful wrenching snap, a sickening swerve—and she was there.

Vitrovna found herself in a dense copse of trees, branches swishing overhead in a fitful breeze. Shottery Wood, she hoped. But was the time and place truly right? She had to get her bearings.

Not easy, in the wake of the Transition. She was still groggy from stretched moments in the slim, cushioned cylinder. All that aching time her stomach had knotted and roiled, fearing that intercession awaited the Transition's end. A squad of grim Corpsmen, an injunction. A bleak prospect of standing at the docket for meddling in the sanctified past, a capital crime.

But when the wringing pop echoed away, there was no one awaiting to erase her from time's troubled web. Only this scented night, musky with leaves and a wind promising fair.

She worked her way through prickly bushes and boggy glades, using her small flashlight as little as she could. No need to draw attention—and a white beam cutting the darkness of an April night in 1616 would surely cause alarm.

She stumbled into a rough country lane wide enough to see the sky. A sliver of bleached moon, familiar star-sprinklings—and there, Polaris. Knowing north, she reckoned from her topo map which way the southward-jutting wedge of Stratford might be. This lane led obliquely that way, so she took it, wind whipping her locks in encouragement.

Much still lay to be learned, she could be far off in space and time, but so far the portents were good. If the combined ferretings and guesses of generations of scholars proved true, this was the last night the aging playwright would be afoot. A cusp moment in a waning life.

Up ahead, hollow calls. A thin blade of yellow as a door opened. A looming shamble-shadow of a drunken man, weaving his ragged course away from the inky bulk of an inn. Might this be the one she sought? Not the man, no, for they were fairly sure that graying Will had spent the night's meaty hours with several friends.

But the inn might be the place where he had drunk his last. The vicar of Stratford's Holy Trinity Church, John Ward, had written years after this night that the bard had "been on an outing" with two lesser literary lights. There were probably only a few inns in so small a town, and this might be the nearest to Shakespeare's home.

Should. Might. Probably. Thin netting indeed, to snare hard facts.

She left the lane and worked through brush that caught at her cloak of simple country burlap. A crude weave covering a cotton dress, nothing lacy to call attention, yet presentably ladylike—she hoped. Considering the sexual fascinations of the ancients, she might easily be mistaken for a common harlot, or a village slut about for a bit of fun.

Any contact with others here would endanger her, to say nothing of definitely breaking the Codes. Of course, she was already flagrantly violating the precepts regulating time travel, but years of preparation had hardened her to that flat fact, insulated her from any lingering moral confusions.

She slipped among trees, trying to get a glimpse through the tiny windows of the inn. Her heart thudded, breath coming quick. The swarming smells of this place! In her antiseptic life, a third-rank Literary Historian in the University Corps, she had never before felt herself so immersed in history, in the thick air of a world innocent of steel and ceramic, of concrete and stale air.

She fished her senso-binoculars from her concealed pack and studied the windows. It was difficult to make out much through the small, warped panes and heavy leading, behind which men lifted tankards and flapped their mouths, illuminated by dim, uncertain candles. A fat man waved his arms, slopping drink. *Robustious rothers in rural rivo rhapsodic. Swill thou then among them, scrike thine ale's laughter.* Not Will's words, but some contemporary. Marlowe? Whoever, they certainly applied here. A ragged patch of song swept by on the stirring wind, carried from an opening door.

Someone coming out. She turned up the amps on the binoculars and saw three men, each catching the swath of lantern light as they helped each other down stubby stairs to the footpath.

Three! One large, balding, a big chest starting to slide into an equatorial belly. Yet still powerful, commanding, perhaps the manner of a successful playwright. Ben Jonson?

The second younger, short, in wide-brimmed hat—a Warwickshire style of the time, she recalled. It gave him a rakish cast, befitting a poet. Michael Drayton?

And coming last, tripping on the stair and grasping at his friends for purchase, a mid-sized man in worn cloak and close-fitting cap. *Life brief and naught done,* she remembered, a line attributed—perhaps—to this wavering apparition. But not so, not so.

The shadowy figure murmured something and Vitrovna cursed herself for her slowness. She telescoped out the directional microphone above the double barrels of the binoculars. It clicked, popped, and she heard—

"I was then bare a man, nay, a boy still," the big man said. "Big in what fills, sure speak." The wide-hatted man smirked.

"Swelled in blood-fed lustihead, Ben's bigger than stallions, or so rumor slings it," the cloaked figure rapped back, voice starting gravelly and then swinging tenor-high at the sentence's end.

The tall man chuckled with meaty relish. "What fills the rod's same as fills the pen, as you'd know better."

So this was the man who within a few years would say that his companion, the half-seen figure standing just outside the blade of light cast by the inner inn, was "Not of an age, but for all time." Ben Jonson, in breeches, a tuft of white shirt sticking from an unbuttoned fly. A boisterous night for all.

"Aye, even for the miowing of kitticat poetry on spunk-stained parchment, truest?" the cloaked man said, words quick but tone wan and fading.

"Better than a mewling or a yawper," the short man said. All three moved a bit unsteadily round a hitching post and across the yard. Jonson muttered, laughed. She caught the earthy reek of ale. The man who must be Drayton—though he looked little like the one engraving of his profile she had seen—snickered liquidly, and the breeze snatched away a quick comment from the man who—she was sure now—must be Shakespeare. She amped up the infrared and pressed a small button at the bridge of the binoculars. A buzz told her digital image recording was on, all three face-forward in the shimmering silver moonlight, a fine shot. Only then did she realize that they were walking straight at her.

Could they make her out, here in a thicket? Her throat tightened and she missed their next words, though the recorder at her hip would suck it all in. They advanced, staring straight into her eyes—across the short and weedy lawn, right up to the very bushes that hid her. Shakespeare grunted, coughed, and fished at his drawers. To her relief, they all three produced themselves, sighed with pleasure, and spewed rank piss into the bushes.

"The one joy untaxed by King or wife," Jonson meditated.

The others nodded, each man embedded in his own moment of release, each tilting his head back to gaze at the sharp stars. Then they were done, tucked back in. They turned and walked off to Vitrovna's left, onto the lane.

She followed as silently as she could, keeping to the woods. Thorns snagged her cloak and soon they had walked out of earshot of even her directional microphone. She was losing invaluable data!

She stumbled onto the path, ran to catch up, and then followed, aided by shadows. To walk and keep the acoustics trained on the three weaving figures was all she could manage, especially in the awkward, raw-leather shoes she had to wear. She remembered being shocked that this age did not even know to make shoes differently curved for left and right feet, and felt the effect of so simple a difference within half a kilometer. A blister irked her left heel before she saw a glow ahead. She had given up trying to follow their darting talk. Most was ordinary byplay laced with coarse humor, scarcely memorable, but scholars could determine that later.

They stopped outside a rambling house with a three-windowed front from which spilled warm lantern light. As the night deepened a touch of winter returned. An ice-tinged wind whipped in a swaying oak and whistled at the house's steep-gabled peak. Vitrovna drew as near as she dared, behind a churning elm.

"Country matters need yawing mouths," Shakespeare said, evidently referring to earlier talk.

"Would that I knew keenly what they learn from scrape and toil," Drayton said, voice lurching as the wind tried to rip it away from her pickups.

"A Johannes Factotum of your skinny skin?" Shakespeare said, sniffing.

Vitrovna translated to herself, *A Jack-Do-All of the senses?*—though the whole conversation would have to be endlessly filtered and atomized by computer intelligences before she could say anything definitive. If she got away with this, that is.

"Upstart crow, cockatrice!" Jonson exclaimed, clapping Shakespeare on the shoulder. All three laughed warmly.

A whinny sped upon the breeze. From around the house a boy led two horses. "Cloddy chariot awaits," Drayton said blearily.

Shakespeare gestured toward his own front door, which at that moment creaked open, sending fresh light into the hummocky yard where they stood. "Would you not—"

"My arse needs an hour of saddle, or sure will be hard-sore on the ride to London tomorrow," Jonson said.

Drayton nodded. "I go belike, to see to writ's business."

"My best bed be yours, if—"

"No, no, friend." Jonson swung up onto a roan horse with surprising agility for one so large. "You look chilled. Get inside to your good wife."

Ben waved good night, calling to the woman who had appeared in the doorway. She was broad and sturdy, graying beneath a frilly white cap, and stood with arms crossed, her stance full of judgment. "Farewell, Anne!"

Good-byes sounding through the frosty air, the two men clopped away. Vitrovna watched Shakespeare wave to them, cloak billowing, then turn to his wife. This was the Anne Hathaway whom his will left with his "second-best" bed, who had saddled him with children since his marriage at eighteen—and who may have forced him into the more profitable enterprise of playwriting to keep their household in something resembling the style of a country gentleman. Vitrovna got Anne's image as she croaked irritably at Shakespeare to come inside.

Vitrovna prayed that she would get the fragment of time she needed. Just a moment, to make a fleeting, last contact—

He hesitated. Then he waved his wife away and walked toward the woods. She barked something at him and slammed the door.

Vitrovna slipped from behind the elm and followed him. He coughed, stopped, and began to pee again into a bush.

An ailment? To have to go again so soon? Stratford's vicar had written that on this night Will "drank too hard," took ill, and died of a fever. This evidence suggested, though, that he knew something was awry when he wrote his will in March, a few weeks before this evening. Or maybe he had felt an ominous pressure from his approaching fifty-second birthday, two days away—when the fever would claim him.

All this flitted through her mind as she approached the wavering figure in the wood-smoke-flavored, whipping wind. He tucked himself back in, turned—and saw her.

Here the danger made her heart pound. If she did something to tweak the timeline a bit too much—

"Ah! Pardons, madam—the ale within would without."

"Sir, I've come to tell you of greatness exceeding anything you can dream." She had rehearsed this, striving for an accent that would not put him off, but now that she had heard his twangy Elizabethan lilt, she knew that was hopeless. She plowed ahead. "I wanted you to know that your name will be sung down the ages as the greatest of writers."

Will's tired, grizzled face wrinkled. "Who might you be?"

—and the solidity of the past struck her true, his breath sour with pickled herrings and Rhenish wine. The reeking intensity of the man nearly staggered her. Her isolated, word-clogged life had not prepared her for this vigorous, full-bodied age. She gulped and forced out her set speech.

"You may feel neglected now, but centuries hence you'll be read and performed endlessly—"

"*What* are you?" He scowled.

"I am from the future. I've come backward in time to tell you, so that such a wonderful man need not, well, need not think he was just a minor poet. Your plays, they're the thing. They—"

"You copy my lines? 'The play's the thing.' Think you that japing pranks—"

"No, no! I truly am from the future, many centuries away."

"And spring upon me in drafty night? I—"

Desperately she brought up her flashlight. "Look." It clicked on, a cutting blue-white beam that made the ground and leaves leap from inky presences into hard realities. "See? This is a kind of light you don't have. I can show you—"

He leaped back, eyes white, mouth sagging. "Uh!"

"Don't be afraid. I wondered if you could tell me something about the dark lady in your sonnets, just a moment's—"

"Magic!"

"No, really, it's just a different kind of lantern. And your plays, did you have any help writing them?"

He recovered, mouth curving shrewdly. "You be scholar or rumormonger?"

"Neither, sir."

His face hardened as he raised his palm to shield his eyes from the brilliance. "Think me gut-gullible?"

"You deserve to know that we in the future will appreciate you, love you, revere you. It's only justice that you know your works will live for-ever, be honored—"

"Promising me life forever, then? That's your cheese?"

"No, you don't—"

"This future you claim—know you something of my self, then? My appointed final hour?" His eyes were angry slits, his mouth a flat, bloodless line.

Was he so quick to guess the truth? That she had come at the one possible moment to speak to him, when his work or friends would not be perturbed? "I've come because, yes, this is my only chance to speak with you. There's nothing I can do about that, but I thought—"

"You tempt me with wisps, foul visions." Did he suspect that once he walked into that house, lay upon his second-best bed, he would never arise again? With leaden certainty she saw him begin to gather this, his mouth working, chin bobbing uncertainly.

"Sir, no, please, I'm just here to, to—"

"Flat-voiced demon, leave me!"

"No, I—"

He reached into his loose-fitting shirt and drew out a small iron cross. Holding it up, he said, "Blest be he who spares my stones, curst be he who moves my bones!"

The lines chiseled above his grave. So he had them in mind already, called them up like an incantation. "I'm sorry, I didn't mean—"

"Go! Christ immaculate, drive such phantoms from me! Give me a sword of spirit, Lord!"

Vitrovna backed away. "I, I—"

—and then she was running, panicked and mortified, into the woods. In her ears rang a fragment from *The Tempest,*

What seest thou else
In the dark backward and abysm of time?

In the shimmering cylinder she panted with anxiety and mortification, her skin a sheen of cold sweat. She had failed terribly, despite decades of research. All her trial runs with ordinary folk of these times who were about to meet their end, carried out in similar circumstances—those had gone well. The subjects had welcomed her. Death was natural and common here, an easeful event. They had accepted her salute with stoic calm, a quality she had come to envy in these dim eras. Certainly they had not turned their angers on her.

But she had faltered before Shakespeare. He had been larger than life, awesome.

Her recordings were valuable, yes, but she might never be able to release them for scholarly purposes now. She had wrenched the past terribly, exciting the poor man just before death's black hand claimed him. She could never forget the look of wild surmise and gathering panic that worked across that wise face. And now—

She had stolen into the University Corps Facility, slipped into the machine with the aid of friends, all in the service of true, deep history. But if she had changed the past enough to send a ripple of causation forward, into her own era, then the Corps would find her, exact the penalty.

No time to think of that. She felt the sickening wrench, a shudder, and then she thumped down into a stony field.

Still night air, a sky of cutting stars. A liquid murmuring led her to the bank of the Big Wood River and she worked her way along it, looking for the house lights. This route she knew well, had paced it off in her own era. She could tell from the set of the stars that she had time, no need to rush this.

Minutes here took literally no time at all in the stilled future world where machines as large as the cities of this age worked to suspend her here. The essence of stealing time from the Corps was that you took infinitesimal time-wedges of that future world, undetectable, elusive—if she was lucky. The Corps would find her uses self-indulgent, sentimental, arrogant. To meddle so could snuff out their future, or merely Vitrovna herself—and all so a few writers could know for a passing moment of their eventual high destiny? Absurd, of course.

July's dawn heat made her shed her cloak and she paused to get her breath. The river wrinkled and pulsed and swelled smooth against the resistance of a big log, and she looked down through it to an unreadable depth. Trout hung in the glassy fast water like ornaments, holding into the current. Deeper still a fog of sand ran above the gravel, stirred by currents around the pale round rocks.

The brimming majesty of this silent moment caught at her heart. Such simple beauty had no protection here, needed none.

After a long moment she made herself go on and found the house as faint streamers traced the dawn. Blocky, gray poured concrete, hunkered down like a bunker. A curious, closed place for a man who had yearned to be of the land and sky. In 1926 he had said, "The real reason for not committing suicide is because you always know how swell life gets again after the hell is over." Yet in this spare, beautiful place of rushing water and jutting stone he would finally yield to the abyss that had tempted him all his wracked life.

She worked her way up the stony slope, her Elizabethan shoes making the climb hard. As she reached the small outer door into the basement, she fished forth the flex-key. Its yellow metal shaped itself to whatever opening the lock needed, and in a moment she was inside the storage room, beside the heavy mahogany rack. She had not seen such things except for photographs. Elegant machines of blue sheen and polished, pointful shapes. Death solidified and lustrous. They enchanted her as she waited.

A rustling upstairs. Steps going into the kitchen, where she knew he would pick up the keys on the ledge above the sink. He came down the stairs, haggard in the slack pajamas and robe, the handsome face from photographs now lined and worn, wreathed by a white beard and tangled hair. He padded toward the rack, eyes distant, and then stopped, blinking, as he saw her.

"What the hell?" A rough voice, but recognizable.

"Mr. Hemingway, I ask only a moment of your time, here at the end. I—"

"You're from the IRS aren't you? Snooping into my—"

Alarm spiked in her throat. "No sir, I am from the future. I've come backward in time to tell you, so that so wonderful a man need not—"

"FBI?" The jowly face clouded, eyes narrow and bright. "I know you've been following me, bribing my friends."

The drinking, hypertension, hepatitis, and creeping manic depression had driven him further even than her research suggested.

She spread her hands. "No, no. You deserve to know that we in the future will appreciate you, love you, revere you. It's only justice that you know your works will live forever, be honored—"

"You're a goddamn federal agent and a liar on top of that." His yellowed teeth set at an angry angle. "Get out!"

"Remember when you said that you wanted to get into the ring with Mr. Tolstoy? Well, you have, you did. You're in his class. Centuries from now—"

A cornered look came into the jumping eyes. "Sure, I've got six books I declare to win with. I stand on that."

"You have! I come from—"

"You a critic? Got no use for sneaky bastards come right into your house, beady-eyed nobodies, ask you how you write like it was how you shit—"

He leaned abruptly against the pinewood wall and she caught a sour scent of defeat from him. Color drained from his wracked face and his head wobbled. "Future, huh?" He nodded as if somehow accepting this. "God, I don't know..."

She stepped back, fear tight in her throat. Earlier in this year he had written, *A long life deprives a man of his optimism. Better to die in all the happy period of unillusioned youth, to go out in a blaze of light, than to have your body worn out and old and illusions shattered.* She saw it now in the loose cant of mouth and jaw, the flickering anxiety and hollow dread. The power of it was unbearable.

"I...I wanted you to know that those novels, the short stories, they will—"

The sagging head stopped swaying. It jerked up. "Which have you read?"

"All of them. I'm a literary historian."

"Damn, I'm just read by history professors?" Disdain soured the words.

There were no such professions in her time, just the departments of the Corps, but she could not make this ravaged man understand that. "No, your dramas are enjoyed by millions, by billions—"

"Dramas?" He lurched against the wall. "I wrote no dramas."

How to tell him that the media of her time were not the simple staged amusements of this era? That they were experienced directly through the nervous system, sensory banquets of immense emotional power, lived events that diminished the linear medium of words alone to a curious relic?

"You mean those bum movies made from the novels? Tracy in *The Old Man?*"

"No, I mean—we have different ways of reading the same work, that is all. But for so long I've felt the despair of artists who did not know how much they would mean, poor Shakespeare going to his grave never suspecting—"

"So you know what I'm down here for?" A canny glint in the eyes.

"Yes, of course, that's why I came."

He pulled himself erect with visible effort. "If you're not just another shit artist come here to get a rise out of me—"

"I'm not, I'm a scholar who feels so much for you lonely Primitivists who—"

"That's what you call us? Real writers? *Primitives?*" Jutting jaw. "I'm going to kick your goddamn ass out of here!"

His sudden clotted rage drove her back like a blow. "I meant—"

"Go!" He shoved her. "Hell will freeze over before I'll give in to a lard-ass—"

She bolted away, out the basement door, into the spreading dawn glow. Down the rocky slope, panic gurgling acid in her mouth. She knew that years before this, when asked his opinion of death, he had answered, "Just another whore." Yet there was something new and alive in his face just now, fresh fuel from his sudden, hugely powerful anger, some sea change that sent into her mind a wrenching possibility.

She looked back at the house. He was standing there thin and erect, shaking a knotted fist down at her. She reached the dawn-etched river and punched the summons into her controls and then came the wringing snap and she was in the cylinder again.

Vitrovna let a ragged sigh escape into the cool, calming air. This one was as unsettling as the last. The old man had seemed animated as she left, focused outside himself by her visit. He had kept her off balance the entire time. Now she saw her error. The earlier tests with ordinary people, whose deaths did not matter in the flow of history, had misled her. In person Shakespeare and Hemingway loomed immensely larger than anyone she had ever known. Compared with the wan, reasonable people of her time, they were bristly giants. Their reactions could not be predicted and they unsettled even her, a historian who thought she knew what to expect.

Vitrovna leaned back, shaken and exhausted. She had programmed a long rest after this engagement, time to get her thoughts in order before the next. That one, the great poet Diana Azar, lay as far ahead in centuries as the gap between the last two, yet her simple dress should still pass there and—

A slim man materialized at the snub end of the cylinder. He wore a curious blue envelope which revealed only head and hands, his skin a smooth green.

"Ah," he said in a heavily accented tenor, "I have intersected you in time."

She gasped. "You—how? To catch me while transporting—"

"In your age, impossible, of course." He arched his oyster-colored forehead, which had no eyebrows. "But when you are in Transition we of your far future may snag you."

She had thought for decades about what she would do if caught, and now said cannily, "You follow the Code standards for self-incrimination?"

She blinked with shock when he laughed. "Code? Ancient history—though it's all the same here, of course. I am not one of your Corps police."

"Then you're not going to prosecute—"

"That was an illusion of your time, Vitrovna. You don't mind me using your first name? In our era, we have only one name, though many prefer none."

"But how can you…"

He languidly folded his arms, which articulated as if his elbows were double-jointed. "I must first say that generations far beyond yours are eternally grateful to you for opening this possibility and giving us these historical records." He gestured at her senso-binoculars.

"Records? They survived? I mean, I do make it back to my—"

"Not precisely. But the detailed space-time calculations necessary to explain, these you would not understand. You braved the Codes and the Corps quite foolishly, as you have just discovered—but that is of no import to us."

She felt a rush of hope, her lips opening in expectation. "Then you've come to rescue me from them?"

He frowned, a gesture which included his ears. "No, no. You feared the Corps' authority, but that was mere human power. They vaguely understood the laws of acausality, quite rightly feared them, and so instituted their Code. But they were like children playing with shells at the shore, never glimpsing the beasts which swam in the deeps beyond."

Her seat jolted and she felt queasy. He nodded, as if expecting this, and touched his left wrist, which was transparent.

"The Code was a crude rule of thumb, but your violations of it transgressed far beyond mere human edicts. How arrogant, your age! To think that your laws could rule a continuum. Space-time itself has a flex and force. Your talk with Hemingway—quite valuable historically, by the way, considering that he was not going to ever release his memoir, *A Moveable Feast*, when he went down into that basement. But even more important was what he wrote next."

"Next? But he—"

"Quite. Even so, rather less spectacular than your 'apparition' before Shakespeare. As his shaky hand testified, you cause him to gather his notes and scraps of plays. They kept quite well in even a tin box, wedged in with the corpse. A bounty for the critics, though it upset many cherished theories."

"But he still died of pneumonia?"

"You do not have miraculous healing powers. You simply scared him into leaving something more of a record."

"Still, with so much attention paid to the few records we do have, or *did* have, I—"

"Quite." A judicious nod. "I'm afraid that despite our vastly deeper understanding of these matters, there is nothing we can do about that. Causality will have its way."

The cylinder lurched. A raw bass note. "Then how—"

"Not much time left, I'm afraid. Sorry." He leaned forward eagerly. "But I did want to visit you, to thank you for, well, liberating this method of probing the past, at great personal sacrifice. You deserve to know that our epoch will revere you."

He spoke rapidly, admiration beaming in his odd face, the words piling up in an awful leaden weight that sent bile-dark fear rushing hotly through her, a massive premonition.

"So Vitrovna, I saw the possibility, of making this intersection. It's only right that you know just how famous you will be—"

The sensation of stepping off a step into a dark, unending fall.

Her speech. He was giving her own speech, and for the same reason.

A DESPERATE CALCULUS
(1995)

Amy inched shut the frail wooden door of her hotel room and switched on the light. Cockroaches—or at least she *hoped* they were mere cockroaches—scuttled for dark corners. They were so big she could hear them bumping into the tin plating along one wall.

She shucked off her dusty field jacket, threw it at the lone pine chair and sprawled on the bed. Under the dangling, naked light bulb she slit open her husband's letter eagerly, using a dirty fingernail. Frying fat flavors seeped through the planking but she forgot the smells and noises of the African village. Her eyes raced along the lurching penmanship.

> God, I do really need you. What's more, I know it's my 'juice' speaking—only been two weeks, but just at what point do I have to be reasonable? Hey, two scientists who work next to disaster-ville can afford a little loopy irrationality, right? Thinking about your alabaster breasts a lot. Our eagerly awaited rendezvous will be deep in the sultry jungle, in my tent. I recall your beautiful eyes that evening at Boccifani's and am counting the days...
>
> This "superflu" thing is knocking our crew people down pretty fierce now. With our schedule already packed solid, now comes two-week Earth Summit V in São Paulo. Speeches, press, more talk, more dumb delay. Hoist a few with buddies, sure, but pointless, I think. Maybe I can scare up some more funding. Takes plenty juice!—just to keep this operation going! Wish me luck and I'll not even glance at the Latin beauties, promise. Really.

She rolled over onto her side to ease the ache in her back, keeping the letter in the yellow glow that seemed to be dimming. The crackly pages were wrinkled as if they had gotten wet in transit.

A distant generator coughed, stuttered, stopped. The light went out. She lay in the sultry dark, thinking about him and decoding all that the letter said and implied. In the distance a dog yapped and she smelled the sour lick of charcoal on the air. It did not cover the vile sickly-sweet odor of bodies left out in the street. Already they were swelling. Autumn was fairly warm in this brush-country slice of Tanzania and the village lay quiet with the still of the fallen. In a few minutes the generator huffed sluggishly back into its coughing rhythm and the bulb glowed. Watery light seeped into the room. Cockroaches scuttled again.

She finished the letter, which went on in rather impressively salacious detail about portions of her anatomy and did the job she knew Todd had intended. If any Tanzanian snoops got into her mail, they probably would not have the courage to admit it. And it did make her moist, yes.

The day's heavy heat now ebbed. A whispering breeze dispersed the moist, infesting warmth.

Todd got the new site coordinates from their uplink, through their microwave dish. He squatted beside the compact, black matte-finish module and its metallic ear, cupped to hear a satellite far out in chilly vacuum. That such a remote, desiccated and silvery craft in the empty sky could be locked in electromagnetic embrace with this place of leafy heaviness, transfixed by sweet rot and the stink of distant fires, was to Todd a mute miracle.

Manuel yelled at him in Spanish from below. "Miz Cabrina says to come! Right away!"

"I'm nearly through."

"Right away! She says it is the cops!"

The kid had seen too much American TV. *Cop* spun like a bright coin in the syrup of thickly accented Spanish. Cops. Authorities. The weight of what he had to do. A fretwork of irksome memories. He stared off into infinity, missing Amy.

He was high up on the slope of thick forest. Toward him flew a rainbird. It came in languid slow motion, flapping in the mild breeze off the far Atlantic, a murmuring wind that lifted the warm weight from the stinging day. The bird's translucent shape flickered against big-bellied clouds and Todd thought of the bird as a gliding bag of genes, biological memories ancient and wrinkled and yet still coming forth. Distant time, floating toward him now across the layered air.

He waved to Manuel. "Tell her to stall them."

He finished getting the data and messages, letting the cool and precise part of him do the job. Every time some rural bigshot showed up his stomach lurched and he forced down jumpy confusions. He struggled to insulate the calm, unsettled center of himself so that he could work. He had thought this whole thing would get easier, but it never did.

The solar panels atop their van caught more power if he parked it in the day's full glare, but then he couldn't get into it without letting the interior cool off. He had driven up here to get clear of the rest of the team. He left the van and headed toward where the salvaging team was working.

Coming back down through kilometers of jungle took him through terrain that reflected his inner turmoil. Rotting logs shone with a vile, vivid emerald. Swirls of iridescent lichen engulfed thick-barked trees. He left the cross-country van on the clay road and continued, boots sinking into the thick mat.

Nothing held sway here for long. Hand-sized spiders scuttled like black motes across the intricate green radiance. Exotic vitality, myriad threats. A conservation biologist, he had learned to spot the jungle's traps and viper seductions. He sidestepped a blood vine's barbs, wisely gave a column of lime ants their way. Rustlings escorted him through dappled shadows which held a million minute violences. Carrion moths fluttered by on charcoal wings in search of the fallen. Tall grass blades cut the shifting sunlight. Birds cooed and warbled and stabbed insects from the air. Casually brutal beauty.

He vectored in on the salvaging site. As he worked downslope the insecticidal fog bombs popped off in the high canopy. Species pattered down through the branches, thumped on logs, a dying rain. The gray haze descended, touched the jungle floor, settled into nooks. Then a vagrant breeze blew it away. His team moved across the hundred-meter perimeter, sweeping uphill.

Smash and grab, Todd thought, watching the workers in floppy jeans and blue work shirts get down on hands and knees. They inched forward, digging out soil samples, picking up fallen insects, fronds, stems, small mammals. Everything, anything. Some snipped samples from the larger plants. Others shinnied up the slick-barked trees and rummaged for the resident ants and spiders and myriad creatures who had not fallen out when the fog hit them. A special team took leaves and branches—too much trouble to haul away whole trees. And even if they'd wanted to, the politicos would scream; timbering rights here had already been auctioned off.

Todd angled along behind the sweeping line of workers, all from Argentina. He caught a few grubs and leaves that had escaped and dropped them into a woman's bag. She smiled and nodded respectfully. Most of them were embarrassingly thankful to have a job. The key idea in the BioSalvage Program was to use local labor. That created a native constituency wherever they went. It also kept costs manageable. The urban North was funding this last-ditch effort. Only the depressed wages of the rural South made it affordable.

And here came the freezers. A thinner line of men carrying styrofoam dry ice boxes, like heavy-duty picnic coolers. Into these went each filled sack. Stapled to the neck of each bag was a yellow bar-code strip giving location, date, terrain description. He had run them off in the van this morning. Three more batches were waiting in his pack for the day's work further up the valley.

His pack straps cut into his roll of shoulder muscle, reminding him of how much more remained to do. To save. He could see in the valley below the press of population on the lush land. A crude work camp sprawled like a tan fungus. Among the jungle's riot of emerald invention a dirt road wound like a dirty snake.

He left the team and headed toward the trouble, angling by faded stucco buildings. Puddles from a rain shower mirrored an iron cross over the entrance gate of a Catholic mission. The Pope's presence. Be fruitful, ye innocent, and multiply. Spread like locusts across God's green works.

Ramshackle sheds lay toward the work camp, soiling the air with greasy wood smoke. In the jungle beyond, chain saws snarled in their labors. Beside the clay ruts of the road lay crushed aluminum beer cans and a lurid tabloid about movie stars.

He reached the knot of men as Cabrina started shouting.

"Yes we do! Signed by your own lieutenant governor *especial*!"

She waved papers at three uniformed types, who wore swarthy scowls and revolvers in hip holsters.

"No, *no*." An officer jerked a finger at the crowd. "These, they say it interferes with their toil."

Here at the edge of the work camp they had already attracted at least fifty. Worn men slouched against a stained yellow wall, scrawny and rawboned and faces slack with fatigue. They were sour twists of men, *maraneros* from the jungle, a machete their single tool, their worn skins sporting once-jaunty tattoos of wide-winged eagles and rampant bulls and grinning skulls.

"The hell it does." Cabrina crossed her arms over her red jumper and her lips whitened.

"The chemicals, they make coughing and—"

"We went through all that with the foreman. And I have documents—"

"These say nothing about—"

Todd tuned out the details and watched lines deepen in the officer's face. Trouble coming, and fast. He was supposed to let Cabrina, as a native, run the interference. Trouble was, these were macho backcountry types. He nodded respectfully to the head officer and said, "Our schedule bothering them?"

The officer looked relieved to deal with a man. "They do not like the fumes or having to stay away from the area."

"Let's see if we can do something about that. Suppose they work upwind?"

So then it got into a back-and-forth negotiation. He hated cutting in on Cabrina but the officer had been near the breaking point. Todd gradually eased Cabrina back in and the officer saw how things were going to go. He accepted that with some face-saving talk and pretty soon it was settled.

Todd walked Cabrina a bit back toward the jungle. "Don't let them rile you. Just stick to the documents."

"But they are so stupid!" Flashing anger, a wrenched mouth.

"Tell me something new."

Their ice van growled into view. It already had the sample sacks from the fogging above. Time to move a kilometer on and repeat the process.

All so they could get into this valley and take their samples before these butchers with their bovine complacency could chop it down for cropland or grazing or just to make charcoal. But Todd did not let any of this into his face. Instead he told Cabrina to show the van where to go. Then he went over and spoke to several of the men in his halting Spanish. Smoothing the way. He made sure to stand close to them and speak in the private and respectful way that worked around here.

✺

Amy followed the rest of her team into the ward. It was the same as yesterday and the day before. All beds filled, patients on the floors, haggard faces, nurses looking as bad as the patients. The infection rate here was at least eighty percent of the population. These were just the cases which had made it to the hospital and then had the clout to get in.

Freddie went through the list prepared by the hospital director. They were there to survey and take blood samples but the director seemed to think his visitors bore some cure. Or at least advice.

"Fever, frequent coughing, swellings in the groin," Freddie read, his long black hair getting in the way. He was French and found everything about this place a source of irritation. Amy did not blame him but it was not smart to show it. "Seven percent of cases display septic shock, indicating that the blood stream is directly infected."

"I hope these results will be of help to your researches," the director said. He was a short man with a look that alternated between pleading and outright panic. Amy did her best to not look at him. His eyes were always asking, asking, and she had no answers.

Freddie waved his clip board. "All is consistent with spread directly among humans by inhalation of infected respiratory droplets?"

The director nodded rapidly. "But we cannot isolate the chain. It seems—"

"Yes, yes, it is so everywhere. The incubation period of the infection is at least two weeks, though it can be up to a month. By that time the original source is impossible to stipulate." Freddie rattled this off because he had said the same thing a dozen times already in Tanzania.

Amy said mildly, "I note that you have not attempted to isolate the septic cases."

The director jerked as if reprimanded and went into an explanation, which did not matter to anyone but would make him feel better, she was sure. She asked for and received limbic fluids, mucus and blood samples from the deceased patients. The director wanted to talk to someone of higher authority and their international team filled that need. Not that it did any good. They had no vaccine, no real advice except to keep the patients cool and not to use sedation which would suppress their lung function. They told him this and then told his staff and then told him again because he just kept looking at them with those eyes. Then they went away.

In the next town Amy got to a telephone and could hook up her modem. She got an uplink with only a half hour wait. They drove back into the capital city over dusty roads while she read the printouts.

A DESPERATE CALCULUS

Summary View: This present plague is certainly a derived form of influenza. It is well known that the 'flu' virus undergoes 'antigenic' drifts—point mutations in the virus's outer protein coat which can enhance the ability of the virus to attack the human immune system. New pandemic viruses emerge at unpredictable intervals on the order of decades, though the rate of shifts may be increasing. The present pathogenic outbreak, with its unusual two- to three-week incubation period, allows rapid spreading before populations can begin to take precautions—isolation, face masks, etc. Fatality rate is 3% in cases which do not recover within five days.

Origin: The apparent derivation of this plague from southern Asia has been obscured by its rapid transmission to both Africa and South America. However, this Asian origin, recently unmasked by detailed hospital studies and demographics, verifies the suspicions of the United Nations Emergency Committee. Asia is the primary source of 'flu' outbreaks because of the high incidence there of 'integrated farming', which mingles fowl, pigs and fish close together. In Southeast Asia this has been an economic blessing, but a reverse-spin disaster for the North. Viruses from different species mix, recombining and undergoing gene reassortment at a rapid rate. Humans needs time to synthesize specific antibodies as a defense.

Genetic aspects: Preliminary results suggest that this is a recombinant virus. Influenza has seven segments of RNA, and several seem to have been modified. Some correlations suggest close connection to the swine flu derived from pigs. This is a shift, not a simple drift. Some recombination has occurred from another reservoir population—but which? Apparently, some rural environment in southern China.

She looked up as they jounced past scrubby farmland. No natural forest or grassland remained; humans had turned all arable land to crops. Insatiable appetite, eating nature itself.

Nobody visible. The superflu knocked everybody flat for at least three days, marvelously infective, and few felt like getting back to the fields right away. That would take another slice out of the food supply here. Behind the tide of illness would come some malnutrition. The U.N. would have to be ready for that, too.

Not my job, though, she thought, and mused longingly of Todd.

São Paulo. Earth Summit V, returning to South America for the first time since Summit I in the good old days of 1992. He was to give a talk about the program and then, by God, he'd be long gone.

On the drive in he had seen kindergarten-age children dig through cow dung, looking for corn kernels the cows hadn't digested. The usual colorful chaos laced with gray despair. Gangs of urchin thieves who didn't know their own last names. Gutters as sewers. Families living in cardboard boxes. Babies found discarded in trash heaps.

He had imagined that his grubby jeans and T-shirt made him look unremarkable, but desperation hones perceptions. The beggars were on him every chance. By now he had learned the trick which fended off the swarms of little urchins wanting Chicklets, the shadowy men with suit-cases of silver jewelry, the women at traffic lights hawking bunches of roses. Natives didn't get their windshields washed unless they wanted it, nor did they say 'no' a hundred times to accomplish the result. They just held up one finger and waggled it sideways, slowly. The pests magically dispersed. He had no idea what it meant, but it was so easy even a gringo could do it.

His "interest zone" at Earth Summit V was in a hodge-podge of swel-tering tents erected in an outdoor park. The grass was already beaten into gray, flat blades. Already there was a dispute between the North dele-gates, who wanted a uniform pledge of 75% reduction in use of pesticides. Activists from the poor South worried about hunger more than purity, so the proposal died. This didn't stop anyone from dutifully signing the Earth Pledge which covered one whole wall in thick gray cardboard. After all, it wasn't legally binding.

Todd talked with a lot of the usual Northern crowd from the Nature Conservancy and World Wildlife Fund, who were major sponsors of BioSalvage. They were twittering about a Southern demand that every-body sign a "recognition of the historical, biological and cultural debt" the North owed the South. They roped him into it, because the background argument (in Spanish, so of course most of the condescending Northerners couldn't read it) named BioSalvage as "arrogantly entering our countries and pushing fashionable environmentalism over the needs of the people."

Todd heard this in a soft drink bar, swatting away flies. Before he could respond, a spindly man in a sack shirt elbowed his way into the Northern group. "I know who you are, Mr. Russell. We do not let your 'debt swap' thievery go by."

BioSalvage had some funding from agreements which traded money owed to foreign banks for salvaging rights and local labor. He smiled at the stranger. "All negotiated, friend."

"The debt was contracted illegally!" The man slapped the yellow plastic table, spilling Coke.

"By *your* governments."

"By the criminals!—who then stole great sums."

Todd spread his hands, still smiling though it was getting harder. "Hey, I'm no banker."

"You are part of a plot to keep us down," the man shot back.

"By saving some species?"

"You are killing them!"

"Yeah, maybe a few days before your countrymen get around to it."

Two other men and a woman joined the irate man. Todd was with several Northerners and a woman from Costa Rica who worked for the Environmental Defense Fund. He tried to keep his tone civil and easy but people started breaking in and pretty soon the Southerners were into Harangue Mode and it went to hell. The Northerners rolled their eyes and the Southerners accused them in quick, staccato jabs of being arrogant, impatient, irritated when somebody couldn't speak English, ready to walk out at the first sign of a long speech when there was *so much* to say after all.

Todd eased away from the table. The Northerners used words like "pro-active" and "empowerment" and kept saying that before they were willing to discuss giving more grants they wanted accountability. They worried about corruption and got thin-lipped when told that they should give without being oppressors of the spirit by trying to manage the money. "Imperialista!" a Brazilian woman hissed, and Todd left.

He took a long walk down littered streets rank with garbage.

Megacities. Humanity growing by a hundred million fresh souls per year, with disease and disorder in ample attendance. Twenty-nine megacities now with more than ten million population. Twenty-five in the "developing" world—only nobody was developing any more. Tokyo topped the list, as always, at 36 million. São Paulo was coming up fast on the outside with 34 million. Lagos, Nigeria, which nobody ever thought about, festered with 17 million despite the multitudes lost to AIDS.

He kicked a can and shrugged off beggars. A man with sores drooling down his face approached but Todd did not dare give him a bill. Uncomfortably he wagged his finger. Indifference was far safer.

Megacities spawned the return of microbes that had toppled empires down through history. Cholera, the old foe. New antibiotic-resistant strains. Cysticercosis, a tapeworm that invades the brain, caught from eating vegetables grown in the city's effluent. Half the world's urban population had at least one skin rash per year.

And big cities demand standardized, easily transported foods. Farmers respond with monocrops, which are more vulnerable to pests and disease and drought. Cities preyed on the cropland and forests which sustain them. Plywood apartment walls in Nagasaki chewed up Borneo's woodlands.

When he reached his hotel room—bare concrete, tin sink in the room, john down the hall—he found a light blinking on the satellite comm. He located the São Paulo nexus and got a fast-print letter on his private number. It was from Amy and he read it eagerly, the gray walls around him forgotten.

I'm pretty sure friend Freddie is now catching holy hell for not being on top of this superflu faster. There's a pattern, he says. Check out the media feeding frenzy, if you have the time. Use my access codes onto SciNet, too. I'm more worried about Zambia, our next destination. Taking no recognition of U.N. warnings, both sides violating the ceasefire. We'll have armed escorts. Not much use against a virus! All our programs are going slowly, with locals dropping like flies.

The sweetness of her seemed to swarm up into his nostrils then, blotting out the disinfectant smell from the cracked linoleum. He could see her electric black hair tumbling like rolling smoke about her shoulders, spilling onto her full breasts in yellow candle light. After a tough day he would lift her onto him, setting her astride his muscular arch. The hair wreathed them both, making a humid space that was theirs only, musk-rich and silent. She could bounce and stroke and coax from him the tensions of time, and later they would have dark rum laced with lemon. Her eyes could widen with comic rapt amazement, go slit-thin with anger, become suddenly womanly as they reflected the serenity of the languid candle flame.

Remember to dodge the electronic media blood hounds. Sniffers and lickers, I call 'em. Freddie handles them for us, but I'm paranoid—seeing insults spelled out in my alphabet soup.

Remember that I love you. Remember to see Kuipers if you get sick! See you in two weeks—so very long!

His gray computer screen held a WorldNet news item, letters shimmering. Todd's program had fished it out of the torrent of news, and it confirmed the worst of his fears. He used her code-keys to gain entry and global search/scan found all the hot buzz:

SUPERFLU EPIDEMIC WIDENS. SECRETARY-GENERAL CALLS FOR AIR TRAVEL BAN. DISEASE CONTROL CENTER TRACING VECTOR CARRIERS.

(AP) A world-sweeping contagion has now leaped from Asia to Africa and on to South America. Simultaneous outbreaks in Cairo, Johannesburg, Mexico City and Buenos Aires confirmed fears that the infection is spreading most rapidly through air travelers. Whole cities have been struck silent and prostrated as a majority of inhabitants succumb within a few days.

Secretary-General Imu-kurumba called for a total ban on international passenger air travel until the virus is better understood. Airlines have logged a sharp rise in ticket sales in affected regions, apparently from those fleeing.

The Center for Disease Control is reportedly attempting to correlate outbreaks with specific travelers, in an effort to pinpoint the source. Officials declined to confirm this extraordinary move, however.

He suspected that somebody at the CDC was behind this leak, but it might mean something more. More ominously, what point was there in tracing individuals? CDC was moving fast. This thing was a wildfire. And Amy was right in the middle of it.

He sat a long time at a fly-specked Formica table, staring at the remains of his lunch, a chipped blue plate holding rice and beans and a gnawed crescent of green tortilla. Todd felt the old swirl of emotions, unleashed as though they had lain in waiting all this time. Incoherent, disconnected images propelled him down musty corridors of self. Words formed on his lips but evaporated before spoken.

She hated autopsies. Freddie had told her to check this one, and the smell was enough to make her pass out. Slow fans churned at one end of the tiny morgue. Only the examining table was well lit. Its gutters ran with viscous, reeking fluids.

The slim black woman on the table was expertly "unzipped"—carved down from neck to pelvis, organs neatly extracted and lying across her chest and legs. Glistening tubes and lumpy vitals, so clean and smooth they seemed to be manufactured.

"A most interesting characteristic of these cases," the coroner went on in a serene voice that floated in the chilly room. He picked up an elongated gray sac. "The fallopians. Swollen, discolored. The ova sac is distended, you will be seeing here. And red."

Amy said, "Her records show very high temperatures. Could this be—"

"Being the cause of death, this temperature, yes. The contagion invaded the lower abdomen, however, causing further discomfort."

"So this is another variation on the, uh, superflu?"

"I think yes." The coroner elegantly opened the abdomen further and showed off kidneys and liver. "Here too, some swelling. But not as bad as in the reproductive organs."

Amy wanted desperately to get out of this place. Its cloying smells layered the air. Two local doctors stood beside her, watching her face more than the body. They were well-dressed men in their fifties and obviously had never seen a woman in a position of significance in their profession. She asked, "What percentage of your terminal cases display this?"

"About three quarters," the coroner said.

"In men and women alike?" Amy asked.

"Yes, though for the women these effects are more prominent."

"Well, thank you for your help." She nodded to them and left. The two doctors followed her. When she reached the street her driver was standing beside the car with two soldiers. Three more soldiers got out of a big jeep and one of the doctors said, "You are please to come."

There wasn't much to do about it. Nobody was interested in listening to her assertion that she was protected by the Zambia-U.N. terms. They escorted her to a low, squat building on the outskirts of town. As they marched her inside she remarked that the place looked like a bunker. The officer with her replied mildly that it was.

General Movotubo wore crisp fatigues and introduced himself formally. He invited her to sit in a well-decorated office without windows. Coffee? Good. Biscuit? Very good. "And so you will be telling now what? That this disease is the product of my enemies."

"I am here as a United Nations—"

"Yes yes, but the truth, it must come out. The Landuokoma, they have brought this disease here, is this not so?"

"We don't know how it got here." She tried to understand the expressions which flitted across the heavy-set man's face, which was shiny with nervous sweat.

"Then you cannot say that the Landuokoma did *not* bring it, this is right?"

Amy stood up. General Movotubo was shorter than her and she recognized now his expression: a look of caged fear. "Listen, staying holed up in here isn't going to protect you against superflu. Not if your personnel go in and out, anyway."

"Then I will go to the countryside! The people will understand. They will see that the Landuokoma caused me to do so."

She started for the door. "Believe me, neither I nor the U.N. cares what you say to your newspapers. Just let me go."

There was a crowd outside the bunker. They did not retreat when she emerged and she had to push and shove her way to her car. The driver sat inside, petrified. But nobody tried to stop them. The faces beyond the window glass were filled with stark dread, not anger.

She linked onto WorldNet back at the hotel. The serene liquid crystal screen blotted out the awareness of the bleak streets beyond the grand marble columns of the foyer.

PULLDOWN SIDEBAR: News Analysis
MIXED REACTION TO PLAGUE OUTBREAK
Environmental Hard Liners Say 'Inevitable'
(AP)…"What I'm saying," Earth First! spokesman Josh Leonard said, "is that we're wasting our resources trying to hold back the tide. It's pointless. Here in the North we have great medical expertise. Plenty of research has gone into fathoming the human immune system, to fixing our cardiovascular plumbing, and the like. But to expend it trying to fix every disease that pops up in the South is anti-Darwinian, and futile. Nature corrects its own mistakes."

…Many in the industrialized North privately admit being increasingly appalled with the South's runaway numbers. Their views are extreme. They point to how Megacities sprawl, teeming with seedy, impoverished masses. Torrents of illegal immigration pour over borders. Responding to deprivation, Southern politico/ religious movements froth and foment, few of them appetizing as seen from a Northern distance. "The more the North thinks of humanity as a malignancy," said psychophilosopher Norman Wills, "the more we will unconsciously long for disasters."

Amy was not really surprised. The Nets seethed with similar talk. Todd had been predicting this for years. That made her think of him, and she shut down her laptop.

✺

He stopped at the BioSalvage Southern Repository to pick up the next set of instructions, maps, political spin. It was a huge complex—big gray concrete bunker-style for the actual freezing compartments, tin sheds for the sample processing. All the buzz and clatter of the rest of Caracas faded as he walked down alleys between the Repository buildings. Ranks of big liquid nitrogen dewars. Piping, automatic labeling machines, harried workers chattering in highly accented Spanish he could barely make out.

In the foyer a whole wall was devoted to the history of it. At the top was the abstract of Scott's first paper, proposing what he called the Library of Life. The Northern Repository was in fact called that, but here they were more stiff and official.

A broad program of freezing species in threatened ecospheres could preserve biodiversity for eventual use by future generations. Sampling without studying can lower costs dramatically. Local labor can do most of the gathering. Plausible costs of collecting and cryogenically suspending the tropical rain forest species, at a sampling fraction of 10^{-6}, are about two billion dollars for a full century. Much more information than species DNA will be saved, allowing future biotechnology to derive high information content and perhaps even resurrect then-extinct species. A parallel program of limited *in situ* preservation is essential to allow later expression of frozen genomes in members of the same genus. This broad proposal should be debated throughout the entire scientific community.

320

Todd had to wait for his appointment. He fidgeted in the foyer. A woman coming out of the executive area wobbled a bit, then collapsed, her clipboard clattering on marble. Nobody went to help. The secretaries and guards drew back, turned, were gone. Todd helped the woman struggle into a chair. She was already running a fever and could hardly speak. He knew there wasn't anything to do beyond getting her a glass of water. When he came back with one, a medical team was there. They simply loaded her onto a stretcher and took her out to an unmarked van. Probably they were just going to take her home. The hospitals were already jammed, he had heard.

He took his mind off matters by reading the rest of the Honor Wall, as it was labeled. Papers advocating the BioSalvage idea. A Nobel for Scott. Begrudging support from most conservation biologists.

Our situation resembles a browser in the ancient library at Alexandria, who suddenly notes that the trove he had begun inspecting has caught fire. Already a wing has burned, and the mobs outside seem certain to block any fire-fighting crews. What to do? There is no time to patrol the aisles, discerningly plucking forth a treatise of Aristotle, or deciding whether to leave behind Alexander the Great's laundry list. Instead, a better strategy is to run through the remaining library, tossing texts into a basket at random, sampling each section to give broad coverage. Perhaps it would be wise to take smaller texts, in order to carry more, and then flee into an unknown future.

"Dr. Russell? I am Leon Segueno."

The man in a severe black suit was not his usual monitor. "Where's Confuelos?"

"Ill, I believe. I'll give you the latest instructions."

Back into the executive area, another new wrinkle. Segueno went through the fresh maps with dispatch. Map coordinates, rendezvous points with the choppers, local authorities who would need soothing. A fresh package of local currency to oil palms, where necessary. Standard stuff.

"I take it you will be monitoring all three of your groups continuously?"

An odd question. Segueno didn't seem familiar with procedures. Probably a political hack.

"I get around as much as I can. Working the back roads, it isn't easy."

"You get to many towns."

"Gotta buy a few beers for the local brass hats."

"Have you difficulty with the superflu?"

"Some of the crew dropped out. We hired more."

"And you?"

"I keep away from anybody who's sniffling or coughing."

"But some say it is spread by ordinary breath."

He frowned. "Hadn't heard that."

"A United Nations team reported so."

"Might explain how it spreads so fast."

"Si, si. Your wife, I gather she is working for the U.N.?"

"On this same problem, right. I hadn't heard that angle, though."

"You must be very proud of her."

"Uh, yes." Where was this going?

"To be separated, it is not good. Will you see her soon?"

No reason to hide anything, even from an officious bureaucrat. "This week. She's joining me in the field."

Segueno chuckled. "Not the kind of reunion I would have picked. Well, good luck to you."

He tried to read the man's expression and got nothing but a polished blandness behind the eyes. Maybe the guy was angling for some kind of payoff? Nothing would surprise him any more, even in the Repository.

He stopped off in the main bay. High sheet-metal ceiling, gantries, steel ramps. Stacks of blue plastic coolers, filled with the labeled sacks that teams like his own sent in. Sorting lines prepared them further. Each cooler was logged and integrated into a geographical inventory, so that future researchers could study correlations with other regions. Then the coolers went into big aluminum canisters. The gantries lowered these into permanent place. Tubes hooked up, monitors added, and then the liquid nitrogen pumped in with a hiss. A filmy fog, and another slice of vanishing life was on its way to the next age.

Todd wondered just when biology would advance to the point where these samples could be unfolded, their genes read. And then? Nobody could dictate to the future. They might resurrect extinct species, make leopards again pace the jungle paths. Or maybe they would revive beetles—God must have loved them, He made so many kinds, as Darwin himself had remarked. Maybe there was something wonderful in those shiny carapaces, and the future would need it.

Todd shrugged. It was reassuring to come here and feel a part of it all.

Going out through the foyer, he stopped and read the rest of the gilt lettering on polished black marble.

We must be prudent. Leading figures in biodiversity argue that a large scale species dieback seems inevitable, leading to a blighted world which will eventually learn the price of such folly. The political impact of such a disaster will be immense. Politics comes and goes, but extinction is forever. We may be judged harshly by our grandchildren, our era labeled the Great Dying or the Age of Appetite.

A future generation could well reach out for means to recover their lost biological heritage. If scientific progress has followed the paths many envision today, they will have the means to perform seeming miracles. They will have developed ethical and social mechanisms we cannot guess, but we can prepare now the broad outlines of a recovery strategy, simply by banking biological information.

These are the crucial years for us to act, as the Library of Life burns furiously around us, throughout the world.

He left. When he got into his rental Ford in the parking lot, he saw Segueno looking down at him through a high window.

He had not expected to get a telephone call. On a one-day stop in Goias, Brazil to pick up more coolers and a fresh crew, there was little time to hang around the hotel. But somehow she traced him and got through on the sole telephone in the manager's office. He recognized Amy's voice immediately despite the bad connection.

"Todd? I was worried."

"Nothing's gone wrong with your plans, has it?"

"No no, I'll be there in two days. But I just heard from Freddie that a lot of people who were delegates at the Earth Summit have come down with superflu. Are you all right?"

"Sure, fine. How's it there?"

"I've got a million tales to tell. The civil war's still going on and we're pulling out. I wrote you a letter, I'll send it satellite squirt to your modem address."

"Great. God, I've missed you."

Her warm chuckle came through the purr of static. "I'll expect you to prove it."

"I'll be all set up in a fresh camp, just out from Maraba. A driver will pick you up."

"Terrif. Isn't it terrible, about the Earth Summit?"

"Nobody's immune."

"I guess not. We're seeing ninety percent affliction in some villages here."

"What about this ban on passenger travel? Will that—"

"It isn't sticking. Anyway, we have U.N. passes. Don't worry, lover, I'll get there if I have to walk."

He got her letter over modem within a few minutes.

We're pinning down the epidemiology. Higher fevers in women, but about 97% recover. Freddie's getting the lab results from the samples we sent in. He's convinced there'll be a vaccine, pronto.

But it's hard to concentrate, babe.

This place is getting worse by the hour. We got a briefing on safety in Zambia, all very official, but most of the useful stuff we picked up from drivers, cops, locals on street corners.

You have to watch details, like your license plates. I got some neutral plates from some distant country. People sell them in garages. Don't dare use the old dodge of putting a PRESS label on your car. Journalists draw fire here, and a TV label is worse. Locals see TV as more powerful than the lowly word-artists of newspapers. TV's the big propaganda club and everybody's got some reason to be mad at it.

We got a four-wheel job that'll go off-road. Had to be careful not to get one that looked like a military jeep. They draw fire. We settled on a white Bighorn, figuring that snipers might think we were U.N. peacekeeping forces. On the other hand, there's undoubtedly some faction that hates the U.N., too.

Plenty of people here blame us—Westerners—for the superflu. We get hostile stares, a few thrown rocks. Freddie took a tomato in the chest today. Rotten, of course. Otherwise, somebody'd have eaten it.

We go out in convoys, seeking superflu vectors. Single cars are lots more vulnerable. And if we break down, like yesterday, you've got help.

I picked up some tips in case we come under fire. (Now don't be a nervous husband! You know I like field work...) Bad idea to ride in the back seat of a two-door—hard to get out fast. Sit in the front seat and keep the door slightly open so you can dive out. Windows open, too, so you can hear what's coming down.

Even in town we're careful with the lights. Minimal flashlight use. Shrouds over camera lights as much as you can. A camera crew interviewing us from CNN draped dark cloth over their heads so nobody could see the dim blue glow of the viewfinder leaking from around their eyes.

Not what you wanted your wife to be doing, right? But it's *exciting*! Sorry if this is unfeminine. You'll soon have a chance to check out whether all this macho stuff has changed my, uh, talents. Just a week! I'll try to be all frilly-frilly. Lover, store up that juice of yours.

He stared at the glimmering phosphors of his laptop. Superflu at the Earth Summit. Vaccine upcoming. Vectors colliding, and always outside the teeming city with its hoarse voices, squalling babies and swelling mothers, the rot of mad growth. Could a species which produced so many mouths be anything more than a blight? Their endless masses cast doubt upon the importance of any individual, diminished the mind's inner sense.

He read the letter again as if he were under water, bubbles springing from his lips and floating up into a filmy world he hoped someday to see. He and Amy struggled, knee-deep in the mud of lunatic mobs. How long, before they were dragged down? But at least for a few moments longer they had the shadowy recesses of each other.

He waited impatiently for her beside his tent. He had come back early from the crew sites and a visit to the local brass hats. It had gone pretty well but he could not repress his desire for her, his impatience. He calmed himself by sitting in his canvas-backed chair, boots propped up on a stump left by the land clearing. He had some background files from Amy and he idly paged through them on his laptop. A review paper in *Nature* tried to put the superflu in historical perspective.

There were in fact three bubonic plagues, each so named because the disease began with buboes—swollen lymph glands in the groin, armpit, neck. Its pneumonic form spread quickly, on breaths swarming with micro-organisms, every cough throwing microorganisms to the wind. A bacterial disease, the bacillus *Pasteurella pestis* was carried by fleas on *Rattus rattus*.

In assessing the potentials of Superflu, consider the first bubonic pandemic. Termed the Plague of Justinian (540-590), who was the Caesar of the era, it began the decline of the Roman Empire, strengthened Christianity with its claims of an afterlife, and discredited Roman medicine, whose nostrums proved useless—thus strangling a baby science. By the second day of an ever-rising fever, the victims saw phantoms which called, beckoning toward the grave. The plague ended only when it killed so many, up to half the population of some cities, that it ran out of carriers. It killed a hundred million, a third of the region's population, and four times the Black Death toll of 1346-1361.

Our Superflu closely resembles the Spanish Influenza, which actually originated in Kansas. It was history's worst outbreak, as rated by deaths per day—thirty million in a single fall season of 1918. The virus mutated quickly, though accidental Russian lab release of a frozen sample in 1977 caused a minor outbreak.

He lay on his cot, waiting for the sound of his jeep, bearing Amy. Through the heavy air came the oddly weak slap of a distant shot. Then three more, quick.

He stumbled outside the tent. Bird rustlings, something scampering in the bush. He was pretty sure the shots had come from up the hill, where the dirt road meandered down. Nothing moving among the twilight trees.

He had envisioned this many times before but that did not help with the biting visceral alarm, the blur of wild thoughts. He thought he had no illusions about what might happen. He walked quickly inside and slapped his laptop shut. Two moths battered at the lone lantern in his tent, throwing a shrapnel of shadows on the walls, magnified anxiety.

Automatically he picked up the micro-disks which carried his decoding routines and vital records. He kept none of it on hard disk so he did not need to erase the laptop. His backpack always carried a day's food and water and he swung it onto his back as he left the tent and trotted into the jungle.

Evening falls heavily in beneath the canopy. He went through a mat of vines, slapping aside the stinging flies which rose angrily.

Boots thumping behind him? No, up on the dirt road. A man's shout.

He bent over and worked his way down a steep slope. He wished he had remembered to bring his helmet. He crouched further to keep below the ferns but some caught him in the face. In the fading shafts of green radiance he went quietly, stooped forward. Cathedral pillars of old trees were furred with orange moss. The day's heat still thickened the air. He figured that if she got away from them she would go downhill. From the road that led quickly into a narrowing canyon. He angled to the left and ran along an open patch of rock and into the lip of the canyon about halfway down. Impossible to see anything in there but green masses.

There was enough light for them to search for her. She would keep moving and hope they didn't track her by the sound. Noise travels uphill better in a canyon. He plunged into lacerating fronds and worked his way toward where he knew a stream trickled down.

Somebody maybe twenty meters ahead and down slope. Todd angled up to get a look. His breath caught when he saw her, just a glimpse of her hair in a fading gleam of dusk. Branches snapped under his boots as he went after her. She heard as he had hoped and slipped behind a tree. He whispered, "Amy! Todd!" and there she was suddenly, gripping her pop-out pistol.

"Oh god!" she said and kissed him suddenly.

"Are you hurt?" he whispered.

"No." Her eyes ricocheted around the masses of green upslope from them. "I shot the driver of my jeep. In the shoulder, to make him stop. I had to, that Segueno—"

"Him. I wondered what the hell he was— Wait, what'd you shoot at after that?"

"The jeep behind us."

"They stopped?"

"Just around the curve, but they were running toward me."

"Where was Segueno?"

"In my jeep."

"He didn't shoot at you?"

"No, I don't think—"

"He probably didn't want to."

"Who is he? He said he was with World Emergency Services—"

"He's probably got a dozen IDs. Come on."

They forked off from the stream. It was clearer there and the obvious way to go so he figured to stay away from it and move laterally away from the camp. The best they could do would be to reach the highway about five kilometers away and hitch a ride before anybody covered that or stopped traffic. She had no more idea than he did how many people they had but the followup jeep implied they could get more pretty quickly. It probably had good comm gear in it. In the dark it would take them several hours to reach the highway. Plenty of time to cover the escapes but they had to try it.

The thin light was almost gone now. Amy was gasping—probably from the shock of it more than anything else, he thought. She did look as though she had not been sleeping well. The leaden night was coming on fast when they stopped, Amy gasping.

"What does he—"

She fished a crumpled page from her pocket. "I grabbed it to get his attention while I got this pistol out." She laughed suddenly, coughed. "He looked scared. I was really proud of myself. I didn't think I could ever use that little thing but when—"

Todd nodded, looking at the FAX of his letter, words underlined:

God, I do really need you. What's more, I know it's my 'juice' speaking—only been two weeks, but just at what point do I have to be reasonable? Hey, two scientists working next to disasterville can afford a little loopy irrationality, right? Thinking about your alabaster breasts a lot. Our eagerly awaited rendezvous will be deep in the sultry jungle, in my tent. I recall your beautiful eyes that evening at Boccifani's and am counting the days…

"He thought he was being real smooth." She laughed again, higher this time. Brittle. "Maybe he thought I'd break down or something if he just showed me he was onto us." Todd saw that she was excited still but that would fade fast.

"How many men you think he could get right away?"

She frowned. "I don't know. Who is he, why—"

He knew that she would start to worry soon and it would be better to have her thinking about something else. "He's probably some U.N. security or something, sniffed us out. He may not know much."

"Special Operations, he told me." She was sobering, eyes bleak.

"He said he was BioSalvage when I saw him in Caracas."

"He's been after us for over a week, then."

He gritted his teeth, eyeing the inky jungle. Twilight bird calls came down from the canopy, soft and questioning. Nothing more. Where were they? "I guess we were too obvious."

"Rearranging Fibonacci into Boccifani? I thought it was pretty clever."

Todd had felt that way, too, he realized ruefully. A simple code: give an anagram of a mathematical series—Fibonacci's was easy to remember in the field, each new term just the sum of the two preceding integers—and then arranging the real message in those words of the letter. A real code-breaker probably thought of schemes like that automatically. Served him right for being an arrogant smartass. He said, "I tried to make the messages pretty vague."

Her smile was thin, tired. "I'll say. 'God I do need more juice at next rendezvous.' I had to scramble to be sure virus-3 was waiting at the Earth Summit."

"Sorry. I thought the short incubation strain might be more useful there."

She had stopped panting and now slid her arms around him. "I got that. 'This "superflu" thing knocking people with two-week delay. Juice!' I used that prime sequence—you got my letters?"

"Sure." That wasn't important now. Her heart was tripping, high and rapid against his chest.

"I...had some virus-4 with me."

"And now they have it. No matter."

Hesitantly she said, "We've...gotten farther than we thought we would, right?"

"It's a done deal. They can't stop it now."

"We're through then?" Eyes large.

"They haven't got us yet."

"Do you suppose they know about the others?"

"I hadn't thought of that." They probably tracked the contagion, correlated with travelers, popped up a list of suspects. He and several others had legitimate missions, traveled widely, and could receive frozen samples of the virus without arousing suspicion. Amy was a good nexus for messages, coded and tucked into her reports. All pretty simple, once somebody guessed that to spread varieties of the virus so fast demanded a systematic, international team. "They've probably got Ester and Clyde, then."

"Damn!" She hugged him fiercely.

Last glimmers of day gave a diffuse glow among the damp tangle of vines and fronds. A rustling alerted him. He caught a quick flitting shadow in time to turn.

A large man carrying a stubby rifle rushed at him. He pushed Amy away and the man came on, bringing the rifle down like a club. Todd ducked and drove a fist into the man's neck. They collided. Momentum slammed him into thick ferns. Rolling, elbows jabbing.

Together they slammed into a tree. Todd yanked on the man's hair, got a grip. He smacked the head against a prow of limestone that jutted up from the leafy forest floor. The man groaned and went limp.

Todd got up and looked for Amy and someone knocked him over from behind. The wind went out of him and when he rolled over there were two men, one holding Amy. The other was Mr. Segueno.

"It is pointless to continue," Segueno called.

"I thought some locals were raiding us." Might as well give it one more try.

No smile. "Of course you did."

The man Todd had knocked out was going to stay that way, apparently. Segueno and the other carried automatic pistols, both pointed politely at his feet. "What the hell is—"

"I assume you are not armed?"

"Look, Segueno—"

They took his pack and found the .38 buried beneath the packaged meals. Amy looked dazed, eyes large. They led them back along the slope. It was hard work and they were drenched in sweat when they reached his tent. There were half a dozen men wearing the subdued tan U.N. uniforms. One brought in a chair for Segueno.

Todd sat in his canvas chair and Amy on the bunk. She stretched out and stared numbly at the moths who still flailed against the unattainable lamp.

"What's this crap?" Todd asked, but he could not get any force into his voice. He wanted to make this easy on Amy. That was all he cared about now.

Segueno unfolded a tattered letter. "She did not destroy this—a mistake."

His letter to Amy. "It's personal. You have no right—"

"You are far beyond issues of rights, as I think you know."

"It was that Freddie, wasn't it?" Amy said suddenly, voice sharp. "He was too friendly."

In the fluttering yellow light Segueno's smile gleamed. "I would never have caught such an adroit ruse. The name of a restaurant, a mathematical series. But then, I am not a code-breaker. And your second paragraph begins the sequence again—very economical."

Todd said nothing. One guard—he already thought of the uniformed types that way—blocked the tent exit, impassive, holding his 9 mm automatic at the ready. Beyond the men outside talking tensely he heard soft bird calls. He had always liked them best about the jungle. Tonight they were long and plaintive.

Segueno next produced copies of Amy's letters. "I must say we have not unpuzzled these. She is not using the same series."

Amy stared at the moths now.

"So much about cars, movement—perhaps she was communicating plans? But her use of 'juice' again suggests that she is bringing you some." Segueno pursed his lips, plainly enjoying this.

"You've stooped to intercepting private messages on satellite phone?"

"We have sweeping authority."

"And who's this 'we' anyway?"

"United Nations Special Operations. We picked up the trail of your group a month ago, as the superflu began to spread. Now, what is this 'juice'?"

Todd shook his head silently, trying to hear the birds high in the dark canopy. Segueno slapped him expertly. Todd took it and didn't even look up.

"I am an epidemiologist," Segueno said smoothly. "Or rather, I was. And you are an asymptomatic carrier."

"Come on! How come my crew doesn't get it?" Might as well make him work for everything. Give Amy time to absorb the shock. She was still lying loosely, watching the moths seethe at the lamp.

"Sometimes they do. But you do not directly work with the local laborers, except by choice. Merely breathing in the vapor you emit can infect. And I suspect your immediate associates are inoculated—as, obviously, are you."

Todd hoped that Cabrina had gotten away. He wished he had worked out some alarm signal with her. He was an amateur at this.

"I want the whole story," Segueno said.

"I won't tell you the molecular description, if that's what you mean," Amy said flatly.

Segueno chuckled. "The University of California's Center for Molecular Genetics cracked that problem a week ago. That was when we knew someone had designed this plague."

Todd and Amy glanced at each other. Segueno smiled with relish. "You must have inoculated yourselves and all the rest in your conspiracy. Yet with some molecular twist, for you are all asymptomatic carriers."

"True." Amy's eyes were wary. "And I breathed in your face on my way in here."

Segueno laughed sourly. "I was inoculated three days ago. We already have a vaccine. Did you seriously think the best minds in medicine would take long to uncover this madness, and cure it?"

Todd said calmly, "Surprised it took this long."

"We have also tracked your contagion, spotted the carriers. You left a characteristic pattern. Quite intelligent, using those who had a legitimate mission and traveled widely. I gather you personally infected hundreds at Earth Summit V, Dr. Russell."

Todd shrugged. "I get around."

"To kill your colleagues."

"Call it a calculus of desperation," Todd said sharply. "Scientists are very mobile people. They spread a virus real well."

"A calculus? How can you be so—" Segueno caught himself, then went on, voice trembling slightly. "As an epidemiologist, I find puzzling two aspects. These strains vary in infectivity. Still, all seem like poor viral design, if one wants to plan a pandemic. First, they kill only a few percent of the cases. Even those are mostly the elderly, from the fever." He frowned scornfully. "Poor workmanship."

"Yeah, I guess we're just too dumb," Todd said.

"You and your gang—we estimate you number some hundred or more, correct?—are crazy, not stupid. So why, then, the concentration of the disorders in the abdominal organs? Influenza is most effective in the lungs."

Amy said crisply, "The virus had proteins which function as an ion channel. We modified those with amantadine to block the transport of fusion glycoproteins to the cell surface—but only in the lungs." She sounded as though she were reciting from something she had long ago planned to say. It was as stilted as the opening remarks in a seminar. "The, the modification enhances its effect in another specific site."

Segueno nodded. "We know the site—quite easy to trace, really. Abdominal."

"Game's over," Todd said soberly. The CDC must know by now. He felt a weight lifted from him. Their job was done. No need to conceal anything.

"This 'juice', it is the virus, yes?"

Amy hesitated. Her skin was stretched over her high cheekbones and glassy beneath the yellow light. Todd went over and sat beside her on the cot and patted her hand reassuringly. "Nothing he can do anyway, hon."

Amy nodded cautiously. "Yes, the virus—but a different strain."

Todd said wryly, "To put a li'l spin on the game."

Segueno's face pinched. "You swine."

"Feel like slapping me again?" Todd sat with coiled energy. He wished Segueno would come at him. He was pumped up from the fight earlier. His blood was singing the age-old adrenaline song. The guard was too far away. He watched Todd carefully.

Segueno visibly got control of himself. "Worse than that, I would like. But I am a man with principles."

"So am I."

"You? You are a pair of murderers."

Amy said stiffly, "We are soldiers."

"You are no troops. You are—crazed."

Her face hardened with the courage he so loved in her—the dedication they shared, that defined them. She said as if by rote, "We're fighting for something and we'll pay the price, too."

Segueno eyed Amy with distaste. "What I cannot quite fathom is why you bothered. The virus runs up temperature, but it does not damage the cubical cells or other constituents."

"The ovarian follicles," Amy said. "The virus stimulates production of luteninizing hormone."

Segueno frowned. "But that lasts only a few days."

"That's all it takes. That triggers interaction with the follicle-stimulating hormone." Amy spoke evenly, as though she had prepared herself for this moment, down through the years of work.

"So you force an ovarian follicle to rupture. Quite ordinary. That merely hastens the menstrual cycle."

"Not *an* ovarian follicle. All of them."

"All...?" His brow wrinkled, puzzled—and then shock froze his face. "You trigger all the follicles? So that all the woman's eggs are released at once?"

Amy nodded. "Your people must know that by now, too."

Segueno nodded automatically, whispering. "I received a bulletin on the way here. Something about an unusual property..."

His voice trickled away. The moths threw frantic shadows over tight faces that gleamed with sweat.

"Then...they will recover. But be infertile."

Todd breathed out, tensions he did not know that he carried now released. "There. It's done."

"So you did not intend to kill many."

Amy said with cool deliberation, "That is an unavoidable side effect. The fever kills weak people, mostly elderly. We couldn't find any way to edit it out."

"My God... There will be no children."

Todd shook his head. "About fifteen percent of the time it doesn't work through all the ovarian follicles. The next generation will drop in population almost an order of magnitude."

Segueno's mouth compressed, lips white. "You are the greatest criminals of all time."

"Probably," Todd said. He felt suddenly tired now that the job was done. And he didn't much care what anybody thought.

"You will be executed."

"Probably," Amy said.

"How...how could you...?"

"Our love got us through it," Todd said fiercely. "We could not have children ourselves—a tilted uterus. We simply extended the method."

Amy said in her flat, abstract tone, "We tried attaching an acrosome to sperm, but males can always make new ones. Females are the key. They've got a few hundred ova. Get those, you've solved the problem. Saved the world."

"To rescue the environment," Todd knew he had to say this right. "To stop the madness of more and more people."

Segueno looked at them with revulsion. "You know we will stop it. Distribute the vaccine."

Amy smiled, a slow sliding of lips beneath flinty eyes. "Sure. And you're wondering why we're so calm."

"That is obvious. You are insane. From the highest cultures, the most advanced—such savagery."

"Where else? *We* respect the environment. *We* don't breed like animals."

"You, you are..." Again Segueno's voice trickled away.

Todd saw the narrowed eyes, the straining jaw muscles, the sheen of sweat in this tight-lipped U.N. bureaucrat and wondered just how a man of such limited horizons could think his disapproval would matter to them. To people who had decided to give themselves to save the world. What a tiny, ordinary mind.

Amy hugged her husband. "At least now we'll be together."

Segueno said bitterly, "We shall try you under local statutes. Make an example. And the rest of your gang, too—we shall track them all down."

The two on the cot sat undisturbed, hugging each other tightly. Todd kissed Amy. They had lived through these moments in imagination many times.

Loudly Segueno said, "You shall live just long enough to see the vaccine stop your plan."

Amy kissed Todd, long and lingering, and then looked up. "Oh, really? And you believe the North will pay for it? When they can just drag their feet, and let it spread unchecked in the tropics?"

Todd smiled grimly, "After they've inoculated themselves, they'll be putting their energy into a 'womb race'—finding fertile women, a 'national natural resource'. Far too busy. And the superflu will do its job."

Segueno's face congested, reddened. Todd watched shock and fear and then rage flit across the man's face. The logic, the inevitable cool logic of it, had finally hit him.

Somehow this last twist had snagged somewhere in Segueno, pushed him over the line. Todd saw something compressed and dark in the face, too late.

Segueno snatched the pistol from the guard and Todd saw that they would not get to witness the last, pleasant irony, the dance of nations, acted out after all. It was the last thing he thought, and yet it was only a mild regret.

ZOOMERS
(1996)

She climbed into her yawning work pod, coffee barely getting her going. A warning light winked: her Foe was already up and running. Another day at the orifice.

The pod wrapped itself around her as tabs and inserts slid into place. This was the latest gear, a top of the line simulation suit immersed in a data-pod of beguiling comfort.

Snug. Not a way to lounge, but to *fly*.

She closed her eyes and let the sim-suit do its stuff.

May 16, 2046. She liked to start in real-space. Less jarring.

Images played directly upon her retina. The entrance protocol lifted her out of her Huntington Beach apartment and in a second she was zooming over rooftops, skating down the beach. Combers broke in soft white bands and red-suited surfers caught them in passing marriage.

All piped down from a satellite view, of course, sharp and clear.

Get to work, Myung, her Foe called. *Sightsee later.*

"I'm running a deep search," she lied.

Sure.

"I'll spot you a hundred creds on the action," she shot back.

You're on. Big new market opening today. A hint of mockery?

"Where?" Today she was going to nail him, by God.

Right under our noses, the way I sniff it.

"In the county?"

Now, that would be telling.

Which meant he didn't know.

So: a hunt. Better than a day of shaving margins, at least.

She and her Foe were zoomers, ferrets who made markets more efficient. Evolved far beyond the primitivo commodity traders of the late TwenCen, they moved fast, high-flying for competitive edge.

They zoomed through spaces wholly insubstantial, but that was irrelevant. Economic pattern-spaces were as tricky as mountain crevasses. And even hard cash just stood for an idea.

Most people still dug coal and grew crops, ancient style grunt labor—but in Orange County you could easily forget that, gripped by the fever of the new.

Below her, the county was a sprawl, but a smart one. The wall-to-mall fungus left over from the TwenCen days was gone. High-rises rose from lush parks. Some even had orange grove skirts, a chic nostalgia. Roofs were eco-virtue white. Blacktop streets had long ago added a sandy-colored coating whose mica sprinkles winked up at her. Even cars were in light shades. All this to reflect sunlight, public advertisements that everybody was doing something about global warming.

The car-rivers thronged streets and freeways (still *free*—if you could get the license). When parked, cars were tucked underground. Still plenty of scurry-scurry, but most of it mental, not metal.

She sensed the county's incessant pulse, the throb of the Pacific Basin's hub, pivot point of the largest zonal economy on the planet.

Felt, not *saw*. Her chest was a map. Laguna Beach over her right nipple, Irvine over the left. Using neural plasticity, the primary sensory areas of her cortex "read" the county's electronic Mesh through her skin.

But this was not like antique, serial reading at all. No flat data here. No screens.

She relaxed. The trick was to *merge*, not just observe.

Far better for a chimpanzee-like species to take in the world through its evolved, body-wrapping neural bed.

More fun, too. She detected economic indicators on her augmented skin. A tiny shooting pain spoke of a leveraged buyout. Was that uneasy sensation natural to her, or a hint from her subsystems about a possible lowering of the prime rate?

Gotcha! the Foe sent.

Myung glanced at her running index. She was eleven hundred creds down!

So fast? How could—?

Then she felt it: dancing data-spikes in alarm-red, prickly on her left leg. The Foe had captured an early indicator. Which?

Myung had been coasting toward the Anaheim hills, watching the pulse of business trading quicken as slanting sunshine smartly profiled the fashionable, post-pyramidal corporate buildings. So she had missed the opening salvo of weather data update, the first trading opportunity.

The Foe already had an edge and was shifting investments. How?

Ahead of her in the simulated air she could see the Foe skating to the south. All this was visual metaphor, of course, symbology for the directed attention of the data-eating programs.

A stain came spreading from the east into Mission Viejo. Not real weather, but economic variables.

Deals flickered beneath the data-thunderheads like sheet lightning. Pixels of packet-information fell as soft rains on her long-term investments.

The Foe was buying extra electrical power from Oxnard. Selling it to users to offset the low yields seeping up from San Diego.

Small stuff. A screen for something subtle. Myung close-upped the digital stream and glimpsed the deeper details.

Every day more water flowed in the air over southern California than streamed down the Mississippi. Rainfall projections changed driving conditions, affected tournament golf scores, altered yields of solar power, fed into agri-prod.

Down her back slid prickly-fresh commodity info, an itch she should scratch. A hint from her sniffer-programs? She willed a virtual finger to rub the tingling.

—and snapped back to real-space.

An ivory mist over Long Beach. Real, purpling water thunderclouds scooting into San Juan Cap from the south.

Ah—virtual sports. The older the population got, the more leery of weather. They still wanted the zing of adventure, though. Through virtual feedback, creaky bodies could air-surf from twenty kilometers above the Grand Canyon. Or race alongside the few protected Great White sharks in the Catalina Preserve.

High-resolution Virtuality stimulated lacy filigrees of electro-chem impulses throughout the cerebral cortex. Did it matter whether the induction came from the real thing or from the slippery arts of electronics?

Time for a bit of business.

Her prognosticator programs told her that with 0.87 probability, such oldies would cocoon-up across six states. So indoor virtual sports use, with electro-stim to zing the aging muscles, would rise in the next day.

She swiftly exercised options on five virtual sites, pouring in some of her reserve computational capacity. But the Foe had already harvested the plums there. Not much margin left.

Myung killed her simulated velocity and saw the layers of deals the Foe was making, counting on the coming storm to shift the odds by fractions. Enough contracts-of-the-moment processed, and profits added up. But you had to call the slant just right.

Trouble-sniffing subroutines pressed their electronic doubts upon her: a warning chill breeze across her brow. She waved it away.

Myung dove into the clouds of event-space. Her skin did the deals for her, working with software that verged on mammal-level intelligence itself. She wore her suites of artificial-intelligence…and in a real sense, they wore her.

She felt her creds—not credits so much as *credibilities,* the operant currency in data-space—washing like hot air currents over her body.

Losses were chilling. She got cold feet, quite literally, when the San Onofre nuke piped up with a gush of clean power. A new substation, coming on much earlier than SoCalEd had estimated.

That endangered her energy portfolio. A quick flick got her out of the electrical futures market altogether, before the world-wide Mesh caught on to the implications.

Up, away. Let the Foe pick up the last few percentage points. Myung flapped across the digital sky, capital taking wing.

She lofted to a ten-mile-high perspective. Global warming had already made the county's south-facing slopes into cactus and tough grasslands. Coastal sage still clung to the north-facing slopes, seeking cooler climes. All the coast was becoming a "fog desert" sustained by vapor from lukewarm ocean currents. Dikes held back the rising warm ocean from Newport to Long Beach.

Pretty, but no commodity possibilities there any more.

Time to take the larger view.

She rose. Her tactile and visual maps expanded. She went to split-skin perception, with the real, matter-based landscape overlaid on the info-scape. Surreal, but heady.

From below she burst into the data-sphere of Invest-tainment, where people played upon the world's weather like a casino. Ever since rising global temperatures pumped more energy in, violent oscillations had grown.

Weather was now the hidden, wild-card lubricant of the world's economy. Tornado warnings were sent to street addresses, damage predictions shaded by the city block. Each neighborhood got its own rain forecast.

A sparrow's fall in Portugal could diddle the global fluid system so that, in principle, a thunderhead system would form over Fountain Valley a week later. Today, merging pressures from the south sent forking lightning over mid-California. That shut down the launch site of all local rocket-planes to the Orbital Hiltons. Hundreds of invest-programs had that already covered.

So she looked on a still larger scale. Up, again.

This grand world Mesh was N-dimensional. And even the number N changed with time, as parameters shifted in and out of application.

There was only one way to make sense of this in the narrow human sensorium. Every second, a fresh dimension sheared in over an older dimension. Freeze-framed, each instant looked like a ridiculously complicated abstract sculpture running on drug-driven overdrive. Watch any one moment too hard and you got a lancing headache, motion sickness and zero comprehension.

Augmented feedback, so useful in keeping on the financial edge, could also be an unforgiving bitch.

The Foe wasn't up here, hovering over the whole continent. Good. Time to think. She watched the N-space as if it were an entertainment, and in time came an extended perception, integrated by the long-suffering subconscious.

She bestrode the world. Total immersion.

She stamped and marched across the muddy field of chaotic economic interactions. Her boot heels left deep scars. These healed immediately: sub-programs at work, like cellular repair. She would pay a passage price for venturing here.

A landscape opened like the welcome of a mother's lap.

Her fractal tentacles spread through the networks with blinding speed, penetrating the planetary spider web. Orange County was a brooding, swollen orb at the PacBasin's center.

Smelled it yet? came the Foe's taunt from below.

"I'm following some ticklers," she lied.

I'm way ahead of you.

"Then how come you're gabbing? And tracking me?"

Friendly competition—

"Forget the friendly part." She was irked. Not by the Foe, but by failure. She needed something *hot*. Where?

'Fess up, you're smelling nothing.

"Just the stink of over-done expectations," she shot back wryly.

Nothing promising in the swirling weather-space, working with prickly light below her. Seen this way, the planet's thirteen billion lives were like a field of grass waving beneath fitful gusts they could barely glimpse.

Wrong blind alley! sent her Foe maliciously.

Myung shot a glance at her indices. Down nineteen hundred!

And she had spotted him a hundred. *Damn.*

She shifted through parameter-spaces. There—like a carnival, neon-bright on the horizon of a black, cool desert: the colossal market-space of Culture.

She strode across the tortured seethe of global Mesh data.

In the archaic economy of manufacturing, middle managers were long gone. No more "just in time" manufacturing in blocky factories. No more one-size-fits-all. That had fallen to "right on time" production out of tiny shops, prefabs, even garages.

Anybody who could make a gizmo cheaper could send you a bid. They would make your very own custom gizmo, by direct Mesh order.

Around the globe, robotic prod-lines of canny intelligence stood ready in ill-lit shacks. Savvy software leaped into action at your Meshed demand, reconfiguring for your order like an obliging whore. Friction-free service. The mercantile millennium.

Seen from up here, friction-free marketism seemed the world's only workable ideology—unless you counted New Islam, but who did? Under it, middle managers had decades ago vanished down the sucking drain of evolving necessity. "Production" got shortened to *prod*—and prodded the market.

Of course the people shed by frictionless prod ended up with dynamic, fulfilling careers in dog-washing: valets, luxury servants, touchy-feely insulators for the harried prod-folk. And their bosses.

But not all was manufacturing. Even dog-dressers needed Culture Prod. *Especially* dog-dressers.

"My sniffers are getting it," she said.

The Foe answered, *You're on the scent—but late.*

Something new...

She walked through the data-vaults of the Culture City. As a glittering representation of unimaginable complexities, it loomed: Global, intricate, impossible to know fully for even a passing instant. And thus, an infinite resource.

She stamped through streets busy with commerce. Ferrets and deal-making programs scampered like rodents under heel. Towers of the giga-conglomerates raked the skies.

None of this Big Guy stuff for her. Not today, thanks.

To beat her Foe, she needed something born of Orange County, something to put on the table.

And only her own sniffer-programs could find it for her. The web of connections in even a single county was so criss-crossed that no mere human could find her way.

She snapped back into the real world. *Think.*

Lunch eased into her bloodstream, fed by the pod when it sensed her lowering blood sugar. Myung tapped for an extra Kaff to give her some zip. Her medical worrier hovered in air before her, clucked and frowned. She ignored it.

—And back to Culture City.

Glassy ramparts led up into the citadels of the mega-Corps. Showers of speculation rained on their flanks. Rivulets gurgled off into gutters. Nothing new here, just the ceaseless hum of a market full of energy and no place to go.

Index check: sixteen hundred down!

The deals she had left running from the morning were pumping out the last of their dividends. No more help there.

Time's a-wastin', her Foe sent nastily. She could imagine his sneer and sardonic eyes.

Save your creds for the crunch, she retorted.

You're down thirteen hundred and falling.

He was right. The trouble with paired competition—the very latest market-stimulating twist—was that the outcome was starkly clear. No comforting self-delusions lasted long.

Irked, she leaped high and flew above the City. Go local, then. Orange County was the PacBasin's best fount of fresh ideas.

She caught vectors from the county drawing her down. Prickly hints sheeted across her belly, over her forearms. To the east—there—a shimmer of possibility.

Her ferrets were her own, of course—searcher programs tuned to her style, her way of perceiving quality and content. They *were* her, in a truncated sense.

Now they led her down a funnel, into—

A mall.

In real-space, no less. Tacky.

Hopelessly antique, of course. Dilapidated buildings leaning against each other, laid out in boring rectangular grids. Faded plastic and rusty chrome.

People still went there, of course; somewhere, she was sure, people still used wooden plows.

This must be in Kansas or the Siberian Free State or somewhere equally Out Of It. Why in the world had her sniffers taken her here?

She checked real-world location, preparing to lift out.

East Anaheim! Impossible...

But no—there was something here. Her sniffer popped up an overlay and the soles of her feet itched with anticipation. Programs zoomed her in on a gray shambles that dominated the end of the cracked blacktop parking lot.

Was this a museum? No, but—

Art Attack came the signifier.

That sign... "An old K-Mart," she murmured. She barely remembered being in one as a girl. Rigid, old-style aisles of plastic prod. Positively *cubic*, as the teeners said. A cube, after all, was an infinite number of stacked squares.

But this K-Mart had been reshaped. Stucco-sculpted into an archly ironic lavender mosque, festooned with bright brand name items.

It hit her. "Of course!"

She zoomed up, above the Orange County jumble.

Here it was—pay dirt. And she was on the ground *first*.

She popped her pod and sucked in the dry, flavorful air. Back in Huntington Beach. Her throat was dry, the aftermath of tension.

And just 16:47, too. Plenty of time for a swim.

The team that had done the mock-mosque K-Mart were like all artists: sophisticated along one axis, dunderheads along all economic vectors. They had thought it was a pure lark to fashion ancient relics of paleo-capitalism into bizarre abstract expressionist "statements". Mere fun effusions, they thought.

She loved working with people who were, deep in their souls, innocent of markets.

Within two hours she had locked up the idea and labeled it: "Post-Consumerism Dada from the fabled Age of Appetite".

She had marketed it through pre-view around the globe. Thailand and the Siberians (the last true culture virgins) had gobbled up the idea. Every rotting 'burb round the globe had plenty of derelict K-Marts; this gave them a new angle.

Then she had auctioned the idea in the Mesh. Cut in the artists for their majority interest. Sold shares. Franchised it in the Cutting Concept sub-Mesh. Divided shares twice, declared a dividend.

All in less time than it took to drive from Garden Grove to San Clemente.

"How'd you find that?" her Foe asked, climbing out of his pod.

"My sniffers are *good*, I told you."

He scowled. "And how'd you get there so fast?"

"You've got to take the larger view," she said mysteriously.

He grimaced. "You're up two thousand five creds."

"Lucky I didn't really trounce you."

"Culture City sure ate it up, too."

"Speaking of which, how about starting a steak? I'm starving."

He kissed her. This was perhaps the best part of the Foe-Team method. They spurred each other on, but didn't cut each other dead in the market place. No matter how appealing that seemed, sometimes.

Being married helped keep their rivalry on reasonable terms. Theirs was a standard five-year monogamous contract, already nearly half over. How could she not renew, with such a deliciously stimulating opponent?

Sure, dog-eat-dog markets sometimes worked better, but who wanted to dine on dog?

"We'll split the chores," he said.

"We need a servant."

He laughed. "Think we're rich? We just grease the gears of the great machine."

"Such a poet you are."

"And there are still the dishes to do from last night."

"Ugh. I'll race you to the beach first."

THE VOICE
(1997)

I don't believe it," Qent said sternly.

Klair tugged him down the musty old corridor. "Come on, turn off your Voice."

"Mine is—I showed you."

"Stuff on walls, whoever heard of—"

"There's another one further along."

Down the narrow, dimly lit hallway they went, to a recessed portion of the permwall. "See—another sign."

"This? Some old mark. What's a 'sign' anyway?"

"This one says—" she shaped the letters to herself carefully—"PASSAGE DENIED."

Qent thumbed on his Voice impatiently. He blinked. "That's…what the Voice says."

"See?"

"You've been here before and the Voice told you."

"I let you pick the corridor, remember? A fair trial."

"You cheated."

"No! I can read it." Read. The very sound of the word made her pulse thump.

Qent paused a second and she knew he was consulting the Voice again. "And 'read' means to untangle things, I see. This 'sign' tells you PASSAGE DENIED? How?"

"See those?—they're letters. I know each one—there are twenty-six, it takes a lot of work—and together they shape words."

"Nonsense," Qent said primly. "Your mouth shapes words."

"I have another way. My way."

He shook his head and she had to take him on to another sign and repeat the performance. He grimaced when the Voice told him that indeed, the markings meant ALDENTEN SECTOR. "A trick. Your Voice is on. You just rigged your touchpad—"

"Here, take my insert!" She thrust it into his hand and made him walk to the next emblem. "MANUFAC DIST, that way."

"I know an arrow when I see it," he said sarcastically. "But the rest of it—what's DIST mean?"

She had hoped he wouldn't ask that. "Maybe it means a place."

"Like a neighborhood?"

"Could be—in fact, yes, 'district.' If there wasn't room to write it all out, they'd shorten a word."

"And who were 'they'? Some magicians?"

"The ancients, I guess."

He was working his way around to being convinced, she could see. "They left wall marks? What for, when the Voice—"

"Maybe they came before the Voice."

"But what possible use—"

"I learned all this from those old papers I uncovered in the Historical Section. They were called 'Bills of Lading' but there were enough words—"

"How do you know you can 'read' something? I mean, without checking with the Voice?"

"I know. The letters group together, you see—MANUFAC is just 'man' and this upturned letter is the sound 'you,' and—"

"You're going too fast." He grimaced, obviously not liking this at all. He was a biology specialist and tolerated her interest in antiquity, but finally he said, "Okay, show me again. Not that I really believe this, but…"

They spent the next few days in the oldest, shadowy precinct of the Historical Sector, searching out corridors that the Imperium had not gotten around to Voicing. Klair read him signs and he started picking up the method. Progress was slow; reading was hard. Letters, words, then working up to grasping how sentences and then paragraphs had their logic and rhythms, their clues about how to extract meaning.

The words were hard but more interesting were the simple sketches, some just whorls or jagged faces or lines of different colors that didn't seem to mean anything more than your eye could grasp in a second. Art, Qent supposed. Mingled among the words like gaudy confetti at a solemn parade.

Still, it wasn't as though he were some Deedee, after all. After a while she recalled from her Educational Specialty training that Deedees were actually officially called the Developmentally Delayed. So if someone had once taken just the first letters of both words, that was how they had gotten their name.

Everything went well between them and they got to like having their Voices off while they strolled through the antiquated hallways, making sense of the signs.

The Voice was always available if they needed it. Linkchips embedded near both ears could pick up the pervasive waves of CompCentral. They only had basic link, no frills but constant access. Like everybody, they had used the Voice more as time went on; it was so easy.

But reading gave them a touch of the past and some silence. It was a relief, really.

They had kept their Voices nearly always on. It was easy to get used to the Voice's silky advertisements that floated just within hearing. You could pay the subscriber service for the Voice and have no ads, but none of their friends did: it was far too expensive. And anyway, the ads told you a lot about people. There was a really interesting one for sperm and egg donors to the gay/les bank, a Meritocracy program to help preserve the Gay gene. It had zoomer sonics and life histories and everything. You could amp it and hear a whole half-hour show if you wanted. For free, too. But most weren't anywhere near that good, so they were glad to be rid of them.

Reading, though, grew on them. There were advantages to reading old signs that the Voice didn't bother to translate. They showed off to a few friends but nobody believed they could really read the curious markings. It had to be some trick, for sure. Klair and Qent just smiled knowingly and dropped the subject.

Not that it was all good. At an old intersection Qent honored the GO signal by reading it, rather than listening to his Voice. The signal was off synch and he nearly got flattened by a roller car.

They debated whether to tell anyone in authority. After all, maybe nobody knew this.

"Ummm, no," Qent said. "Look at it this way—carrion eaters rule the world, in their way. Because nobody cares. Nobody wants what they like."

"So we'd be fools to make other people like reading?"

"Demand rises, supplies fall. Suppose everybody wanted those old books you found?"

She had to admit it was a sobering possibility. The carrion-eater analogy came out of his biology training, and he couldn't resist adding, "It's a smart strategy. When times are tough on everybody, the buzzards just get more to eat."

The thought was so disgusting she decided to forget about the whole question.

They came to like strolling the byways of the Megapolis, ferreting out the antiquated secrets of the signs. Lovers often find their own rituals, and this was a particularly delectable one.

Outside one vaultway there were clearly marked instructions on how to spin a dial and get in. They had to work on it for quite a while but finally they made it work. The door swung open on primitive hinges and they walked into a musty set of rooms. Exploring them proved boring; just stacks of locked compartments, all without signs. Until a guard came in with a drawn zapper.

"How'd you kids get in here?"

"It was open, sir," Qent said. He had always been quick and Klair supposed his answer was technically correct. She had opened the door.

"How the hell—? Well, get out. Out!"

The guard was confused and worried and hardly gave them more than a brief search, muttering. Qent asked to see the zapper, imitating a dumbo kid, and the guard brushed them off, still puzzled.

Until the vault she had not realized that her hard-won trick was anything more than a delicious secret. Klair was a scholarly type and enjoyed her hours of scanning over the decaying sheets she found in the Historical Sector's archives.

The fat ones she learned were called "books" and there was even an entry in the Compendium about them. The Voice recited the entry to her in its soft tones, the ones she had chosen for her daily work. She used a more ornate voice for social matters and a crisp, precise one for directions. In normal life that was all anyone needed, a set of pleasing Voice agents.

There was hardly any delay when she requested the book entry and the Voice told a marvelous tale. There were many kinds of books, including one called "novel." This meant new the Voice said. But the one novel

Klair found in the dank, dark Antiquities Vault was obviously old, not new at all. Such confusions were inevitable in research, she realized.

Books were known also as buchs in some ancient sources, it said, in the confusing era when there were competing Voices. Not really even Voices, either, but whole different speech-methods, before Standard was discovered.

All that happened in the Narrow Age, as antiquarians termed it. A time of constrained modes, hopelessly linear and slow. People then were divided by their access to information. Thank goodness such divisive forces were now banished.

They now lived in the Emergent Age, of course. The Voice had emerged from the evolution of old style Intelligent Agents, on computers. Those would perform fetch-'em tasks. Gradually, people let their Agents do more and more. Agent merging led to more creativity, coming from the overlap of many voices, many threads in a society where all was open and clear to all, available through the Voice.

"What sop!" Qent said to this, and she sort of agreed. The Narrow Age sounded fascinating, with its books and reading. The tingling thrill of being able to hold a year's worth of Voice talk in your hand, opening it to anywhere you chose, picking out lore at will—it captivated her.

Of course, she knew the Voice was superior. Instantly it could skip to any subject or even word you liked in any record. It would explain in private, sounding just like an enormously smart person speaking to you alone, in your head. Everybody had one and could access it with an internal signal. There were jokes about women falling in love with the husky Voice tone they chose.

She looked up the Voice itself in one of the old books. The words were hard to follow and she began to wish for some way to find out what they meant. Sounding them out was hard because, even when she knew the word, the mapping from letters to sounds followed irregular rules. "What's the point of *that*?" Qent asked often, but he kept at it with her.

The books said that the Voice had started as an aid to people called "illiterates"—and Klair was startled to find, consulting the Voice, that everybody was one. Except her and Qent, now.

Once, lots and lots of people could read. But as the Voice got easier to use, a certain cachet attached to using only the Voice. Independence from linear "print-slavery" became fashionable, then universal. After all, the Voice could pipe the data you needed on fast-flow, a kind of compressed speech that was as fast (or in fact, by that time, faster) as people could read.

Most people got their information by eye, anyway. In a restaurant, they ordered chicken by touching the drumstick icon, or fish by the fishstick icon. And of course most of their time they spent at entertainments, which had to be visual, tactile, smell-rich—sports, 3Ds, senses, a-morphs, realos.

She found it quite delicious to have an obscure, secret talent that none of her friends even guessed. She was going to have a party and show them all, but then she saw the big letters in the Boulevard of Aspiration, and things got complicated.

❁

Qent said, "I make it to be—

SAVVY THIS? MEAT 13:20 @ Y."

Skeptically he eyed the poorly printed letters written in livid red on a blue wall. Next to it was a sketch he supposed was a map, but he couldn't figure it out because there were no names on the corridors.

"Somebody did that by hand," Klair marveled.

"Writing by yourself? How?"

"I hadn't thought anybody could. I mean, machines make letters, don't they?"

"You're the one who read all those historical books. Printing machines gave way to Voice machines, you said."

Klair traced a hand over the misshapen letters. "It's like making a drawing, only you try to imitate a machine, see? Think of letters as little art objects."

"This isn't an art exhibit."

"No, it's a message. But maybe I can…"

By luck she had in her side-sack her latest cherished discovery, a fat book called "Dictionary." It had many more words in it than the Voice, approximating and vernacular. Big words that nobody used any more, hadn't used for so long even the Voice didn't know them. It even told her that "@" meant "at," but not why.

"Here," she pointed forcefully at the tiny little entry. "Meat is the flesh of an animal."

"Animals eat flesh. I heard that people used to."

"Primitivo!" she said scornfully. "It may mean that in there, but it sounds like 'meet.'"

"Somebody made an error? Confusing the sound with another word?"

"Somebody wants people who can read the sign to meet them."

"Other readers."

"Where?" He frowned.

"It says 'Y.' That's not a word."

"Maybe it's an abbreviation, like that "MANUFAC DIST?"

"No, too short."

He snapped his fingers. "Remember where the Avenue of Aspiration branches? You can look down on it from the balcony of the Renew building. From above, it looks like that letter."

"Let's be there, then."

They showed up, but nobody else did. Instead, at the Y another crude hand-lettered sign said

MEAT CORRIDOR 63,
13:30 TOMORROW, BLOCK 129

They went home and turned off their Voices and talked. Most couples silenced the Voice only during sex. This was merely polite, even though of course no other person could be sure it was off nowadays, what with the new neuroactivated models. Kids joked about the Voice giving them advice when they first tried sex, "walking you through it" as the phrase went. Though of course no one could walk and do sex.

They went home and sped-read some ancient texts. There was a thick book titled *The Lust of the Mohicans* that Qent had seen on senso. She read it—her speed was a lot higher than his—but it wasn't anything like the senso he had seen. There was no sex in it at all. Just stares of infinite longing and heavy breathing and pounding pulses and stuff like that. Still, she found it oddly stirring. Reading was funny that way.

They could not get their minds off the sign. Qent was out of sorts, irked that others had mastered their discovery. He groused about it vaguely and found excuses to change the subject.

Klair didn't see it possessively. After all, the higher moral good was to share. Reading was wickedly single-ist. Was that why she liked it so much? A reader was isolated, listening to a voice no one else could take part in. That led to differences and divisions, friction and clashes.

Still, the rapture of reading—of listening in her mind to silent sounds from ages past—was too, well, perhaps the right word was titillating.

She was excited by the prospect of other readers. Inevitably, they went to the site.

The man who slouched beside a rampway was not impressive. Medium height, his crimson codpiece was three years out of date. His hair was stringy and festooned with comically tattered microbirds. He said nothing, simply handed them a sheet. Miserably printed sentences covered both sides. The first paragraph was enough for Klair.

THE SECRET ASSEMBLY OF READERS MUST UNITE! WE HAVE A TALENT THE MASSES CANNOT UNDERSTAND. THEY WILL FEAR US IF THEY KNOW. A BROTHERHOOD AND SISTERHOOD OF READERS IS THE ONLY SOLUTION TO OUR ISOLATION. ARISE!

"What cliché sop!" She thrust the sheet back at him.

"True, though."

Qent said sharply, "Just tell us what you—"

"You never know when the Voice is on," the man said mysteriously.

Klair said, "And your printing is awful."

"Better than yours," he said shrewdly.

"That's not the point," Qent said. "We demand to know—"

"Come on. And shut up, huh?"

They were in a leafy, green wildness preserve before the man spoke. His face was broad, Asian, with glittering black eyes. "I'm Marq. No Voice pickups here, at least according to the flow charts."

"You're an engineer?" Klair asked, admiring the oaks.

"I'm a philosopher. I make my money engineering."

"How long have you been reading?"

"Years. Started with some old manuals I found. Figured it out from scratch."

"So did we," Qent said. "It's hard, not being able to ask for help from the Voice."

Marq nodded with a sheepish smile. "I did. Dumb, huh?"

"What happened?"

"Some Spectors came by. Just casual talk, y'know, but I knew what they were after."

"Evidence?" she asked uneasily.

"When I asked the Voice there was a pause, just a little one. A priority shift, I know how to spot them. So I broke off and took the books I had to a hiding place. When I got back there were the Spectors, cool as you like, just kind of looking around my room."

"You didn't tell them...?" she asked.

"You got to give them something. I had a copy of this thing about books that I couldn't understand, *Centigrade 233*. Kept it buried under a pseud-bush bed. They were getting funny on me—you know, getting in my face, routine intimidation—so I took it out and gave it to them."

She blinked, startled. "What did they do? Arrest you?"

Marq gave her a crooked grin. "Reading's not illegal, y'know. Just anti, that's all. So they let me off with six weeks of grouping."

"Wow, do I hate those," Qent said.

Marq shrugged. "I did the time. They poked at me and I had to pretend to see the light and all. They kept the book."

"You're brave," Klair said.

"Just stupid. I should never have asked the Voice."

Qent said earnestly, "You'd think the Voice would encourage us to learn. I mean, it'd be useful in emergencies. Say the Voice goes down, we could read the info we'd need."

Marq nodded. "I figure the Voice reads. It just doesn't want competition."

She said, "The Voice is a machine."

"So?" Marq shrugged again. "Who knows how smart it is?"

"It's a service," Qent said. "That's all."

"Notice how it won't store what we say?" Marq smiled shrewdly.

Qent nodded. "It says it's trying to improve our memories."

"Reading was invented to replace memory," Klair said. "I read it in a history book."

"So it must be true?" Marq shrugged derisively, a gesture that was beginning to irk Klair a lot.

She hated politics and this was starting to sound like that. "How many books have you got?"

"Lots. I found a tunnel into a vault. I can go there anytime."

Qent and Klair gasped at his audacity as he described how, for years, he had burrowed into sealed-off chambers. Many of the musty rooms were rich in decaying documents and bound volumes. He spoke of exotica they had never seen, tomes which were nothing but names in the Dictionary: Encyclopedias, Thesauruses, Atlases, Alamancs. He had read whole volumes of the fabled Britannica!

Would he trade? Lend? "Of course," Marq said warmly.

Their friendship began that way, a bit edgy and cautious at the margins, but dominated by the skill and secret lore they shared. Three years of clandestine reading followed before Marq disappeared.

He wasn't at any of their usual meeting places. After all this time, they still did not know where he lived, or where his hoard of books might be. Marq was secretive. They searched the sprawling corridors of the complexes, but were afraid to ask the Voice for any info on him.

The Majority Games were on then so the streets were more crowded than usual. Most people were out all the time, excited and eager and happy to be in the great mobs that thronged the squares. The Games took up everybody's time—except, of course, the three hours of work everyone had to put in, no exceptions, every laborday. Klair and Qent broke up to cover more ground and spent a full week on the search. Many times Klair blamed herself for not pressing Marq about where he lived, but the man was obsessively secretive. "Suppose they grab you, make you tell about me?" he had always countered.

Now she wondered what the Specters would do if they uncovered a lode of books like Marq's. Send him to Advanced Treatment? Or was there something even worse?

She came home after a day of dogged searching and Qent was not there. He did not appear that evening. When she awoke the next morning she burst into tears. He was gone that day and the one after.

On her way back from work, a routine counseling job, she resolved to go to the Spector. She halfheartedly watched the crowds, hoping to see Marq or Qent. She ambled along, wandering really, and that was how she noticed that three men and a woman were moving parallel to her as she crossed the Plaza of Promise. They were all looking some other way but they formed four points of the compass around her with practiced precision.

She walked faster and they did too. They looked stern and remorseless and she could not lose them in the warrens of streets and corridors near the two-room apartment she shared with Qent. They had waited five years to get one with a tiny balcony. Even then it was just two levels up from the muddy floor of the air shaft. But if you hooked your head over to the side you could see some sky that way. When they got it she had been thrilled.

Klair kept moving in an aimless pattern and they followed. Of course she did not want to go to the apartment, where she would be trapped. She sat in bars and if one of her shadowers entered, she left. But she was tired and she could not think of anything else to do. Finally she went home.

They knocked a few minutes after she collapsed on the bed. She had hoped they might hold off for a while. She was resigned. When she spun the door open looming in the doorway was not one of the shadower team but—Marq.

"You won't believe what's going on," he said, brushing past her.

"What? Where have you—"

"The Meritocrats want us."

"For what?"

"Reading!"

"But the Voice—"

"Keeps people out of touch and happy. Great idea—but it turns out you can't run everything with just the Voice." He blinked, the merest hesitation. "Somebody's got to be able to access info at a higher level. That was our gut feeling, remember—that reading was different."

"Well, yes, but the Spectors—"

"They keep people damped down, is all." A slight pause. "Anybody who's got the savvy to see the signs, the words, the grit to learn to piece together words on their own, to process it all—those are the people the Merits want." Another pause. "Us!"

Klair blinked. This was too much to encompass. "But why did they take you away, and Qent—"

"Had to be sure." He gave his old familiar shrug. "Wanted to test our skills, make sure we weren't just posing." His eyes roved the room. "People might catch on, only pretend to read, y'know?"

"I...see." There was something about Marq that wasn't right. He had never had these pauses before...because he wasn't listening to the Voice then?

She backed away from him. "That's marvelous news. When will Qent be back?"

"Oh, soon, soon." He advanced. She opened the thin door and backed out onto the balcony.

"So what job will you do? I mean, with reading in it?"

They were outside in chilly air. She backed into the railing. The usual distant clatter and chat of the air shaft gave her a momentary sense of security. Nothing could happen here, could it?

"Oh, plenty. Looking up old stuff, comparing, y'know." He waved his hands vaguely.

It wasn't much of a drop from here. Over the railing, legs set right…

"It's good work, really."

Could she could get away if she jumped? Marq wasn't the athletic type and she knew that if she landed right on the mud below she wouldn't twist an ankle or anything. She had on sensible shoes. She could elude him. If she landed right.

She gave him a quick, searching look. Had he come here alone? No, probably there were Spectors outside her door, just waiting for him to talk her into surrendering. Stall for time, yes.

"How bad is it?"

He grinned. "You won't mind. They just access that part of your mind for three hours a day. Then they install a shutdown on that cerebral sector."

"Shutdown? I—"

"So you don't need to read any more. Just during work, is all. You get all you need that way, plenty of reading. Then you're free!"

She thought it through. Jump, get away? Couldn't use the Voice for help because they could undoubtedly track her if she had her receiver on. Could she get by, just reading the old signs?

Suppose she could. Then what? Find some friends she could trust. Stay underground? How? Living off what?

"Sounds like it's much better. Qent will be back soon and—"

Marq held up a hand and stepped closer. "Hold it. Don't move."

She looked down the air shaft. Was the jump worth it?

You spool out of the illusion and *snap*—back into the tight cocoon. The automatic sensory leads retract, giving your skin momentary pin-prick goodbye kisses. Once more you feel the cool clasping surfaces of the cocoon. Now you turn and ask, "Hey, where's the rest?"

Myrph shrugs her shoulders, still busy undoing her leads. "That's all there was, I told you."

"Maybe it's just damaged?"

"No, that's the end of the cube. There must be another cube to finish the story, but this was the only one I found back in that closet."

"But how does it end? What's she do?" You lean toward her, hoping maybe she's just teasing.

"I dunno. What would you do? Jump?"

You blink, not ready for the question. "Uh, this reading thing. What is it, really?"

Myrph frowns. "It felt like a kind of your own silent voice inside your head."

"Is it real? I mean, does reading exist?"

"Never heard of it."

"So this isn't an historical at all, right? It's a fantasy."

"Must be. I've never seen those things on walls."

"Signs, she called them." You think back. "They would have worn away a long time ago, anyway."

"I guess. Felt kinda strange, didn't it, being able to find out things without the Voice?"

You bite your lip, thinking. Already the illusion of being that woman is slipping away, hard to fix in memory. She did have a kind of power all on her own with that reading thing. You liked that. "I wonder what she did?"

"Hey, it's just a story."

"What would you do?"

"I don't have to decide. It's just a story."

"But why tell it then?"

Myrph says irritably, "It's just an old illusion, missing a cube."

"Maybe there was only one."

"Look, I want illusions to take me away, not stress me out."

You remember the power of it. "Can I have it, then?"

"The cube? Sure."

Myrph tosses it over. It is curiously heavy, translucent and chipped with rounded corners. You cup it in your hand and like the weight of it. Gravitas.

That is how it starts. You know already that you will go and look for the signs in the corridors and that for good or ill something new has come into your world and will now never leave it.

SLOW SYMPHONIES
OF MASS AND TIME
(1998)

The chase across an entire galaxy started at a swanky private party.

Think of the galaxy as a swarm of gaudy bees, bright colors hovering in a ball. Then stomp them somehow in midair, so they bank and turn in a compressed disk. Dark bees fly with them too, so that somber lanes churn in the swiftly-rotating cloud. Angry bees, buzzing, stingers out. Churning endlessly in their search.

That is the galaxy, seen whole and quick. Stars have no will, but their courses and destinies were now guided by small entities of great pretension: humans, now lording it over the All.

Or such is the viewpoint of the lords and ladies of a galactic empire that stretches across that bee swarm disk: they loom above it all, oblivious. Stars do their bidding. The bees swarm at the lift of an Imperial eyebrow.

Until one lord turns upon another. Then they are as their origins made them: savvy omnivores, primates reared up and grimacing, teeth bared at each other. Across the span of a hundred billion worlds, ancient blood sings in pounding vessels.

Despite appearances, some of these primordial creatures were present at the party, yet seeming mild and splendid in their finery.

Of course, it all began innocently enough.

❖

An ample, powerful woman named Vissian grasped his sleeve and tugged him back to the ornate reception. "Sir Zeb, you are the *point* of this affair! Sir Zeb, my guests have so much to *tell* you."

And to think that he had *wanted* to come here! To get the scent of change. But already he was tiring of this world, Syrna. Sir Zeb, indeed. He truly did not enjoy travel all that much, a fact he often forgot.

Even here, in a distant Sector, the heavy hand of the Imperium lay upon style and art. The Imperium's essence lay in its solidity; its taste ran to the monumental. Rigorous straight lines in ascending slabs, the exact parabolas of arching purple water fountains, heavy masonry— all entirely proper and devoid of embarrassing challenge. He sniffed at the hyperbolic draperies and moved toward the crowd, their faces terminally bland.

Vissian nattered on. "—and our most brilliant minds are waiting to meet you! Do come!"

He suppressed a groan and looked beseechingly at Fyrna, his consort now of a full decade; something of a record in Imperial circles. She smiled and shook her head. From this hazard she could not save him.

"Sir Zeb, what of the mysteries at galactic center?"

"I savor them."

"But are those magnetic entities a threat? They are huge!"

"And wise. Think of them as great slumbering libraries."

"But they command such energies!"

"Then think of them as natural wonders, like waterfalls."

This provoked a chorus of laughter in the polite half-moon crowd around him. "Some on the Council believe we should take action against them!" a narrow woman in flocked velvet called from the crowd's edge.

"I would sooner joust with the wind," Zeb said, taking a stim from a passing dwarf servant.

"Sir Zeb, surely you cannot take lightly—"

"I am on holiday, sir, and can take things as they are."

"But you, Sir Zeb, have seen these magnetic structures?"

"Filaments, hundreds of light-years long—yes. Lovely, they are."

Wide-eyed: "Was it dangerous?"

"Of course. Nobody goes to the galactic center. Hard protons sleet through it, virulent X-rays light its pathways."

"Why did you risk it?"

"I am a fool, madam, who works for you, the people."

And so on.

If Vissian had begun as a grain of sand in his shoe, she became a boulder. An hour later, Fyrna whisked him into an alcove and said curtly, "I am concerned about someone tracking us here. We're just one worm-jump away from fleet's quadrant assembly point."

Zeb had allowed himself to forget about politics: the only vacation a statesman had. "My protection should be good here. I can get a quick message out, using a wormlink to—"

"No, you can't work using a link. The Speculists could trace that easily."

Factions, factions. The situation had shifted while he was idling away here. As Governor of another Sector, he was a guest here, given nominal protection. He had his own bodyguards, too, salted among the crowd here. But the Speculists had strong support in this region of the galaxy and were quite blithely ruthless. Zeb stared out at the view, which he had to admit was spectacular. Great, stretching vistas. Riotous growth.

But more fires boiled up on the horizon. There was gaiety in the streets here—and angst. Their laboratories seethed with fresh energies, innovation bristled everywhere, the air seemed to sing with change and chaos.

The extremes of wealth and destitution were appalling. Change brought that, he knew.

As a boy he had seen poverty—and lived it, too. His grandmother had insisted on buying him a raincoat several sizes too large, "to get more use out of it." His mother didn't like him playing kickball because he wore out his shoes too quickly.

Here, too, the truly poor were off in the hinterlands. Sometimes they couldn't even afford fossil fuels. Men and women peered over a mule's ass all day as it plodded down a furrow, while overhead starships screamed through velvet skies.

And here... Among these fast-track circles, body language was taught. There were carefully designed poses for Confidence, Impatience, Submission (four shadings), Threat, Esteem, Coyness, and dozens more. Codified and understood unconsciously, each induced a specific desired neurological state in both self and others. The rudiments lay in dance, politics, and the martial arts, but by being systematic, much more could be conveyed. As with language, a dictionary helped.

Zeb felt an unease in the reception party. Reading some veiled threat-postures? Or was he projecting?

Quickly he adjusted his own stance—radiating confidence, he hoped. But still, he had picked up a subconscious alarm. And he knew enough from decades of politics to trust his instincts.

"Governor!" Vissian's penetrating voice snatched away his thoughts.

"Uh, that tour of the precincts. I, I really don't feel—"

"Oh, that is not possible, I fear. A domestic disturbance, most unfortunate."

Zeb felt relief but Vissian went right on, bubbling over new ventures, balls, and tours to come tomorrow. Then her eyebrows lifted and she said brightly, "Oh yes—I do have even more welcome news. An Imperial squadron has just come to call."

"Oh?" Fyrna shot back. "Under whose command?"

"An Admiral Kafalan. I just spoke to him—"

"Damn!" Fyrna said. "He's a Speculist henchman."

"You're sure?" Zeb asked. He knew her slight pause had been to consult her internal files.

Fyrna nodded. Vissian said gaily, "Well, I am sure he will be honored to return you to your sector when you are finished with your visit here. Which we hope will not be soon, of—"

"He mentioned us?" Fyrna asked.

"He asked if you were enjoying—"

"Damn!" Zeb said.

"An Admiral commands all the wormlinks, if he wishes—yes?" Fyrna asked.

"Well, I suppose so." Vissian looked puzzled.

"We're trapped," Zeb said.

Vissian's eyes widened in shock. "But surely you, Governor, need fear no—"

"Quiet." Fyrna silenced the woman with a stern glance. "At best this Kafalan will bottle us up here."

Fyrna pushed them both into a side gallery. Vissian seemed startled by this, though Fyrna was both consort and bodyguard. Indeed, she and Zeb might as well have been married, but for the social impossibilities.

This side gallery featured storm-tossed jungles of an unnamed world lashed by sleeting rain, lit by jagged purple lightning. Strange howls called through the lashing winds.

"Note that if Imperial artists do show you an exterior, it is alarming," Fyrna said clinically as she checked her detectors, set into her spine and arms.

"They're still nearby?" Zeb asked, shushing Vissian.

"Yes, but of course they are beards."

To his puzzled look she said, "Meaning, the disguise we are meant to see."

"Ah." They strolled into the next gallery, trying to look casual. This sensor was milder, a grandiose streetscape and hanging gardens. "Ummm, still poorly attended. And the real shadows?"

"I have spotted one. There must be more."

Vissian said, "But surely no one would dare kidnap you from my reception—"

"No, probably there will be an 'accident,'" Zeb said.

"Why has this Admiral moved to block you just now?"

"Nova triggers," Zeb said.

Once invented, triggers had made war far more dangerous. A solar system could be "cleansed"—a horrifyingly bland term used by aggressors of the time—by inducing a mild nova burst in a balmy sun. This roasted worlds just enough to kill all but those who could swiftly find caverns and store food for the few years of the nova stage. Fleet wanted a supply of them, and Zeb led opposition to the weapon.

"Admirals love their toys," he said sourly, fingering a stim but not inhaling it. They returned to the main party, not wanting to seem perturbed by the news.

"Is there no other way to get off Syrna?" Fyrna demanded of Vissian.

"No, I can't recall—"

"Think!"

Startled, Vissian said, "Well, of course, we do have privateers who at times use the wild worms, an activity that is at best quasi-legal, but—"

In Zeb's career he had discovered a curious little law. Now he turned it in his favor.

Bureaucracy increases as a doubling function in time, given resources. At the personal level, the cause is the persistent desire of every manager to hire at least one assistant. This provides the time constant for growth.

Eventually this collides with the carrying capacity of society. Given the time constant and the capacity, one could predict a plateau level of bureaucratic overhead—or else, if growth persists, the date of collapse. Predictions of the longevity of bureaucracy-driven societies fit a precise curve. Surprisingly, the same scaling laws worked for micro-societies such as large agencies.

The corpulent Imperial bureaus on Syrna could not move swiftly. Admiral Kafalan's squadron had to stay in planetary space, since it was paying a purely formal visit. Niceties were still observed. Kafalan did not want to use brute force when a waiting game would work.

"I see. That gives us a few days," Fyrna concluded.

Zeb nodded. He had done the required speaking, negoti-ating, deal-ing, promising favors—all activities he disliked intensely. Fyrna had done the background digging. "To...?"

"Train."

The wormhole web had built the galactic empire. Made in the first blaring instant of the Great Emergence, found (rarely) floating between stars, they now were the most precious resources of all.

Of course, worms ended and began as they liked. A worm jump could bring you to a black vacuum still many years from a far-flung world. Hyperships flitted through wormholes in mere seconds, then exhausted themselves hauling their cargoes across empty voids, years and decades in the labor.

Wormholes were labyrinths, not mere tunnels with two ends. The large ones held firm for perhaps billions of years—none larger than a hun-dred meters across had yet collapsed. The smallest could sometimes last only hours, at best a year. In the thinner worms, flexes in the worm-walls *during* passage could alter the end point of a traveler's trajectory.

Worse, worms in their last stages spawned transient, doomed young—the wild worms. As deformations in space-time, supported by negative energy-density "struts," all wormholes were inherently rickety. As they failed, smaller deformations twisted away.

Syrna had seven wormholes. One was dying in gorgeous agonies.

It hung a light-hour away, spitting out wild worms that ranged from a hand's-width size up to several meters. In the spongy space-time of the negative-energy-density struts, time could crawl or zip, quite unpredictably. This worm was departing our universe in molasses-slow torment.

A fairly sizable wild worm had sprouted out of the side of the dying worm several months before. The Imperial squadron did not know of this, of course. All worms were taxed, so a fresh, free wormhole was a bonanza. Reporting their existence, well...often a planet simply didn't get around to that until the wild worm had fizzled away in a spray of subatomic surf.

Until then, pilots carried cargo through them. That wild worms could evaporate with only seconds' warning made their trade dangerous, highly paid, and legendary.

Wormriders were the sort of people who as children liked to ride their bicycles no-handed, but with a difference—they rode off rooftops.

By an odd logic, that kind of child grew up and got trained and even paid taxes—but inside, they stayed the same.

Only risk takers could power through the chaotic flux of a transient worm and take the risks that worked, *not* take those that didn't, and live. They had elevated bravado to its finer points.

"This wild worm, it's tricky," a grizzled woman told Zeb and Fyrna. "No room for a pilot if you both go."

"We must stay together," Fyrna said with finality.

"Then you'll have to pilot."

"We don't know how," Zeb said.

"You're in luck." The lined woman grinned without humor. "This wildy's short, easy."

"What are the risks?" Fyrna demanded stiffly.

"I'm not an insurance agent, lady."

"I insist that we know—"

"Look, lady, we'll teach you. That's the deal."

"I had hoped for a more—"

"Give it a rest or it's no deal at all."

In the men's room, above the urinal he used, Zeb saw a small gold plaque: *Senior Pilot Joquan Beunn relieved himself here Octdent 4, 13,435.*

Every urinal had a similar plaque. There was a washing machine in the locker room with a large plaque over it, reading *The Entire 43d Pilot Corps relieved themselves here Marlass 18, 13,675.*

Pilot humor. It turned out to be absolutely predictive. He messed himself on his first training run.

As if to make the absolutely fatal length of a closing wormhole less daunting, the worm flyers had escape plans. These could only work in the fringing fields of the worm, where gravity was beginning to warp, and space-time was only mildly curved. Under the seat was a small, powerful rocket that propelled the entire cockpit out, automatically heading away from the worm.

There is a limit to how much self-actuated tech one can pack into a small cockpit, though. Worse, worm mouths were alive with electrodynamic "weather"—writhing forks of lightning, blue discharges, red magnetic whorls like tornadoes. Electrical gear didn't work well if a bad storm was brewing at the mouth. So most of the emergency controls were manual. Hopelessly archaic, but unavoidable.

He and Fyrna went through a bail-out training program. Quite soon it was clear that if he used the EJECT command he had better be sure that he had his head tilted back. That is, unless he wanted his kneecaps to slam up into his chin, which would be unfortunate, because he would be trying to check if his canopy had gone into a spin. This would be bad news, because his trajectory might get warped back into the worm. To correct any spin he had to yank on a red lever, and if that failed he had to then very quickly—in pilot's terms, this meant about half a second— punch two blue knobs. When the spindown came, he then had to be sure to release the automatic actuator by pulling down on two yellow tabs, being certain that he was sitting up straight with his hands between his knees to avoid...

...and so on for three hours. Everyone seemed to assume that since he was this famous politician trained in intricate galactic protocols he could of course keep an entire menu of instructions straight, timed down to fractions of seconds.

After the first ten minutes he saw no point in destroying their illusions, and simply nodded and squinted to show that he was carefully keeping track and absolutely enthralled. Meanwhile he solved chess puzzles in his head for practice.

He was taking a stroll with his bodyguards when the Admiral sent a greeting card.

The guard nearest him, one Ladoro, was saying something into his wrist comm as they ambled through a park. It was an Imperial distraction, with babbling brooks that ran uphill, this artful effect arising from intricately charged electrodynamic streams that countered gravity. His guards liked the effect; Zeb found it rather obvious.

He chanced to be looking toward Ladoro, his oldest guard, a stout fellow whose personal service went back a full century. Later Zeb reflected that the Admiral probably knew that. It made what happened more pointed.

Ladoro went down with his head jerked back, as if he were looking up at the sky, a quizzical expression flickering. Over backwards, twisting, then down hard. He hit face first on the carpet-moss. Ladoro had not lifted his hands to break the fall.

Two other guards had Zeb behind a wall within two seconds. There was too much open space and too little shelter to try a move. He squatted and fumed and could not see who had fired the shot. Zeb risked a quick look over the wall's low edge and saw Ladoro sprawled flat without a twitch.

Then a lot of nothing happened. No following pulses.

Zeb replayed the image. From Ladoro had spouted rosy blood from a punch high in the spine. Absolutely dead center, four centimeters below the neck. Kilojoules of energy focused to a spot the size of a fingernail.

That much energy delivered so precisely would have done the job even if it hit the hip or gut. Delivered so exactly, it burst the big bony axis of the man, massive pressures in the spinal fluid, a sudden breeze blowing out a candle, the brain going black in a millisecond.

Ladoro had gone down boneless, erased. A soft, liquid thump, then eternal silence.

Zeb held up his hand and watched it tremble for a while. Enough waiting. "Let's go. They can lob anything they want here."

A guard said, "Sir Zeb, I don't advise—"

"I've been shot at before, kid."

"Well, I suppose we could fire as we move—"

"You do that. Go."

They worked their way along a creek frothing uphill. More guards arrived and spilled out across the park. The pulse had come from behind Ladoro. Zeb kept plenty of rock between him and that direction. He got to Ladoro and studied the face from behind a boulder nearby. The head was cocked to one side, eyes still open, mouth seeping moisture into the dry dirt. The eyes were the worst, staring into an infinity nobody glimpses more than once.

Goodbye, friend. We had our time, some laughs and light-years. You saved my ass more than once. And now I can't do a damn thing for you.

Something moved to his right, a gossamer ball of motes. Cops, or rather, a local manifestation of them.

It flickered, spun, and said in a low, bass voice, "We regret."

"Who did this?"

"We suspect an Imperial source. Our defenses were compromised in a characteristic way. Sir."

"And what can you do?"

"I will protect you."

"You didn't do a great job for Ladoro."

"I arrived here slightly late."

"Slightly?"

"You must forgive errors. We are finite, all."

"Damn finite."

"No place is safe. This is safer, however. I extend the apologies of Madame Vissian—"

"Tell the Admiral I got his calling card."

"Sir?"

"I'm sure you will be all right," Vissian said fulsomely to them in the departure lounge.

Zeb had to admit this woman had proven better than he had hoped. She had cleared the way, stalled the Imperial officers. Probably she shrewdly expected a payoff from him, and she had every right to do so.

"I hope I can handle a wormship," Zeb said.

"And I," Fyrna added.

"Our training is the very best," Vissian said, brow furrowing. "I do hope you're not worried about the wild worm, Governor?"

"It's a tight fit," he said.

They had to fly in a slender cylinder, Fyrna co-piloting. Splitting the job had proved the only way to get them up to a barely competent level.

"I think it's *marvelous,* how courageous you two are."

"We have little choice," Fyrna said. This was artful understatement. Another day and the Admiral's officers would have Zeb and Fyrna under arrest, then dead.

"Riding in a little pencil ship. *Such* primitive means!"

"Uh, time to go," Zeb said behind a fixed smile. She was wearing thin again.

"I agree with the Emperor. Any technology distinguishable from magic is insufficiently advanced."

Zeb felt his stomach flutter with dread. "You've got a point."

He had brushed off the remark.

Four hours later, closing at high velocity with the big wormhole complex, he saw her side of it.

He spoke on suitcomm to Fyrna. "In one of my classes—Nonlinear Philosophy, I believe—the professor said something I'll never forget. 'Ideas about existence pale, beside the fact of existence.' Quite true."

"Bearing oh six nine five," she said rigorously. "No small talk."

"Nothing's small out here—except that wild worm mouth."

The wild worm was a fizzing point of vibrant agitation. It orbited the main worm mouth, a distant bright speck.

Imperial ships patrolled the main mouth, ignoring this wild worm. They had been paid off long ago, and expected a steady train of slimships to slip through the Imperial guard.

The galaxy was, after all, a collection of debris, swirling at the bottom of a gravitational pothole in the cosmos. The worms made it traversable.

Below, the planet beckoned with its lush beauties.

At the terminator, valleys sank into darkness while a chain of snowy mountains gleamed beyond. Late in the evening, just beyond the terminator, the fresh, peaked mountains glowed red-orange, like live coals. Mountaintops cleaved the sheets of clouds, leaving a wake like that of a ship. Tropical thunderheads, lit by lightning flashes at night, recalled the blooming buds of white roses.

The glories of humanity were just as striking. The shining constellations of cities at night, enmeshed by a glittering web of highways. His heart filled with pride at human accomplishments. Here the hand of his fellow Empire citizens was still casting spacious designs upon the planet's crust. They had shaped artificial seas and elliptical water basins, great squared plains of cultivated fields, immaculate order arising from once-virgin lands.

"So beautiful," he mused. "And we are fleeing for our lives from it."

Fyrna sniffed. "You are losing your taste for politics."

"You have no poetry left in your soul?"

"Only when I'm not working."

He saw distant ships begin to accelerate, their yellow exhausts flaring. "Many believe that the early Empire was a far better affair, serene and lovely, with few conflicts and certainly fewer people."

"Fine feelings and bad history," Fyrna said, dismissing all such talk.

"No doubt you are correct. Note the Admiral's approach."

Fyrna saw them now. "Damn! They've spotted us already."

"We'll have one chance to make the worm run."

"But they know—and they'll follow."

Zeb had passed through worm gates before, but always in big cruisers plying routes through wormholes tens of meters across. Every hole of that size was the hub of a complex which buzzed with carefully orchestrated traffic. He could see the staging yards and injection corridors of the main route gleaming far away.

Their wild worm, a renegade spinoff, could vanish at any moment. Its quantum froth advertised its mortality. *And maybe ours...*Zeb thought.

"Vector null sum coming up," he called.

"Convergent asymptotes, check," Fyrna answered.

Just like the drills they had gone through.

But coming at them was a sphere fizzing orange and purple at its rim. A neon-lit mouth. Tight, dark at the very center—

Zeb felt a sudden desire to swerve, not dive into that impossibly narrow gullet.

Fyrna called numbers. Computers angled them in. He adjusted with a nudge here and a twist there.

It did not help that he knew some of the underlying physics. Wormholes were held open with onion-skin layers of negative energy, sheets of anti-pressure made in the first convulsion of the universe. The negative energy in the "struts" was equivalent to the mass needed to make a black hole of the same radius.

So they were plunging toward a region of space of unimaginable density. But the danger lurked only at the rim, where stresses could tear them into atoms.

A bull's-eye hit was perfectly safe. But an error—

Don't hit the walls...

Thrusters pulsed. The wild worm was now a black sphere rimmed in quantum fire.

Growing.

Zeb felt suddenly the helpless constriction of the pencil ship. Barely two meters across, its insulation was thin, safety buffers minimal. Behind him, Fyrna kept murmuring data and he checked...but part of him was screaming at the crushing sense of confinement, of helplessness.

He had never really liked travel all that much... A sudden swampy fear squeezed his throat.

"Vectors summing to within zero seven three," Fyrna called.

Her voice was calm, steady, a marvelous balm. He clung to its serene certainties and fought down his own panic.

"Let's have your calculation," she called.

He was behind! Musing, he had lost track.

With a moment's hard thought he could make his mind bicameral. The two liberated subselves did their tasks, speaking back and forth only if they wished. The results merged when each was done.

"There." He squirted her the answers, last-moment computations of the changing tidal stresses into which they now plunged.

Squeals of last-second correction echoed in his cramped chamber. A quick kick in the pants—

Lightning curling snakelike blue and gold at them—

—Tumbling. Out the other end, in a worm complex fifteen thousand light-years away.

"That old professor...damn right, he was," he said.

Fyrna sighed, her only sign of stress. "Ideas about existence pale... beside the fact of existence. Yes, my love. Living is bigger than any talk about it."

❋

A yellow-green sun greeted them. And soon enough, an Imperial picket craft. The Admiral had been right behind them and he had called ahead somehow.

So they ducked and ran. A quick swerve, and they angled into the traffic-train headed for a large wormhole mouth. The commercial charge-computers accepted his Imperial override without a murmur. Zeb had learned well. Fyrna corrected him if he got mixed up.

Their second hyperspace jump took a mere three minutes. They popped out far from a dim red dwarf.

By the fourth jump they knew the drill. Having the code-status of the Imperial court banished objections.

But being on the run meant that they had to take whatever wormhole mouths they could get. Kafalan's people could not be too far behind.

A wormhole could take traffic only one way at a time. High-velocity ships plowed down the wormhole throats, which could vary from a finger's length to a star's diameter.

Zeb had known the numbers, of course. There were a few billion wormholes in the galactic disk, spread among several hundred billion stars. The average Imperial Sector was about fifty light years in radius. A jump could bring you out still many years from a far-flung world.

This influenced planetary development. Some verdant planets were green fortresses against an isolation quite profound. For them the Empire was a remote dream, the source of exotic products and odd ideas.

The worm web had many openings near inhabitable worlds, but also many near mysteriously useless solar systems. By brute force interstellar hauling the Empire had positioned the smaller wormmouths—those massing perhaps as much as a mountain range—near rich planets. But some wormmouths of gargantuan mass orbited near solar systems as barren and pointless as any surveyed.

Was this random, or a network left by some earlier civilization? Archaeologists thought so. Certainly the wormholes themselves were leftovers from the Great Emergence, when space and time alike began. They linked distant realms which had once been nearby, when the galaxy was young and smaller. The differential churn of the disk had redistributed the wormholes. But someone—or rather, something—had made sure they at least orbited reasonably near a star.

They developed a rhythm. Pop through a wormmouth, make comm contact, get in line for the next departure. Imperial watchdogs would not pull anyone of high class from a queue. So their most dangerous moments came as they negotiated clearance.

At this Fyrna became adept. She sent the WormMaster computers blurts of data and—*whisk*—they were edging into orbital vectors, bound for their next jump.

They caught a glimpse of Admiral Kafalan's baroque ship winking forth from a wormhole mouth they had left only minutes before. In the scurry-scurry of commerce they lost themselves, while they waited their turn. Then they ducked through their next hole, a minor mouth, hoping Kafalan had not noticed.

For once, the snaky, shiny innards of the worm were almost relaxing to Zeb. This one was small of mouth but long of throat; their journey took dragging, heart-thumping moments.

Matter could flow only one way at a time in a wormhole. The few experiments with simultaneous two-day transport ended in disaster. No matter how ingenious engineers tried to steer ships around each other, the sheer flexibility of worm-tunnels spelled doom. Each wormmouth kept the other "informed" of what it had just eaten. This information flowed as a wave, not in physical matter, but in the tension of the wormhole itself—a ripple in the "stress tensor," as physicists termed it.

Flying ships through both mouths sent stress waves propagating toward each other, at speeds which depended on the location and velocity of the ships. The stress constricted the throat, so that when the waves met, a clenching squeezed down the walls.

The essential point was that the two waves moved differently after they met. They interacted, one slowing and the other speeding up, in highly nonlinear fashion.

One wave could grow, the other shrink. The big one made the throat clench down into sausages. When a sausage neck met a ship, the craft *might* slip through—but calculating that was a prodigious job. If the sausage neck happened to meet the two ships when they passed—*crunch.*

This was no mere technical problem. It was a real limitation, imposed by the laws of quantum gravity. From that firm fact arose an elaborate system of safeguards, taxes, regulators, and hangers-on—all the apparatus of a bureaucracy which does indeed have a purpose, and makes the most of it.

Zeb learned to dispel his apprehension by watching the views. Suns and planets of great, luminous beauty floated in the blackness.

Behind the resplendence, he knew, lurked necessity.

From the wormhole calculus arose blunt economic facts. Between worlds A and B there might be half a dozen wormhole jumps—the Nest was not simply connected, a mere astrophysical subway system. Each wormmouth imposed added fees and charges on each shipment.

Control of an entire trade route yielded the maximum profit. The struggle for control was unending, often violent. From the viewpoint of economics, politics, and "historical momentum"—which meant a sort of imposed inertia on events—a local empire which controlled a whole constellation of nodes should be solid, enduring.

Not so. Time and again, regional satrapies went toes-up. As Governor, he had been forced to bail some of them out. That amounted to local politics, where he had proved reasonably adept. Alas, Kafalan pursued them for global, galactic reasons.

Many worlds that feasted on the largesse of a wormhole mouth perished, or at least suffered repeated boom-and-bust cycles, because they were elaborately controlled. It seemed natural to squeeze every worm passage for the maximum fee, by coordinating every worm to optimize traffic. But that degree of control made people restive.

The system could not deliver the best benefits. Over-control failed.

On their seventeenth jump, they met a case in point.

*

"Vector aside for search," came an automatic command from an Imperial vessel.

They had no choice. The big-bellied Imperial sentry craft scooped them up within seconds after their emergence from a medium-sized wormhole mouth.

"Transgression tax," a computerized system announced. "Planet Alacaran demands that special carriers pay—" A blur of computer language.

"Let's pay it," Zeb said.

"I wonder if it will provide a tracer for Kafalan's use," Fyrna said over comm.

"What is our option?"

"I shall use my own personal indices."

"For a wormhole transit? That will bankrupt you!"

"It is safer."

Zeb fumed while they floated in magnetic grapplers beneath the Imperial picket ship. The wormhole orbited a heavily industrialized world. Gray cities sprawled over the continents and webbed across the seas in huge hexagonals.

The Empire had two planetary modes: rural and urban. Farm worlds were socially stable because of its time-honored lineages and stable economic modes. They, and the similar Femo-rustics, lasted.

This planet Alacaran, on the other hand, seemed to cater to the other basic human impulse: clumping, seeking the rub of one's fellows, a pinnacle of city-clustering.

Zeb had always thought it odd that humanity broke so easily into two modes. Now, though, his political experience clarified these proclivities. Most people were truly primates, seeking a leader. Countless planets congealed into the same basic Feudalist attractor groups—Macho, Socialist, Paternal. Even the odd Thanatocracies fit the pattern. They had Pharaoh-figures promising admission to an afterlife, and detailed rankings descending from his exalted peak in the rigid social pyramid.

"They're paid off," Fyrna sent over comm. "Such corruption!"

"Ummm, yes, shocking." Was he getting cynical? He wanted to turn and speak with her, but their pencil ship allowed scant socializing.

"Let's go."

"Where to?"

"To..." He realized that he had no idea.

"We have probably eluded pursuit." Fyrna's voice came through stiff and tight. He had learned to recognize these signs of her own tension.

"We could work a route back to our Sector."

"They would expect that and block it."

He felt a stab of disappointment. But she was the professional body-guard and she was undoubtedly right. "Where, then?"

"I took advantage of this pause to alert a friend, by wormlink," she said. "We may be able to return, though through a devious route."

"The Speculists—"

"May not expect such audacity."

"Which recommends the idea."

Dizzying indeed—leaping about the entire galaxy, trapped in a casket-sized container.

They jumped and dodged and jumped again. At several more wormhole yards Fyrna made "deals." Payoffs, actually. She deftly dealt combinations of his cygnets, the Imperial passage indices, and her private numbers.

"Costly," Zeb fretted. "How will I ever pay—"

"The dead do not worry about debts," she said.

"You have such an engaging way of putting matters."

"Subtlety is wasted here."

They emerged from one jump in close orbit about a sublimely tortured star. Streamers lush with light raced by them.

"How long can this worm last here?" he wondered.

"It will be rescued, I'm sure. Imagine the chaos in the system if a wormmouth begins to gush hot plasma."

Zeb knew the wormhole system, though discovered in pre-Empire ages, had not always been used. After the underlying physics of the worm-hole calculus came to be known, ships could ply the galaxy by invoking wormhole states around themselves. This afforded exploration of reaches devoid of wormholes, but at high energy costs and some danger. Further, such ship-local hyperdrives were far slower than simply slipping through a worm.

And if the Empire eroded? Lost the worm network? Would the slim attack fighters and snakelike weapons fleets give way to lumbering hypership dreadnoughts?

The next destination swam amid an eerie black void, far out in the halo of red dwarfs above the galactic plane. The disk stretched in luminous splendor. Zeb remembered holding a coin and thinking of how a mere speck on it stood for a vast volume, like a large Zone. Here such human terms seemed pointless. The galaxy was one serene entity, grander than any human perspective.

"Ravishing," Fyrna said.

"See Andromeda? It looks nearly as close."

The spiral, twin to their own galaxy, hung above them. Its lanes of clotted dust framed stars azure and crimson and emerald. A slow symphony of mass and time.

"Here comes our connection," Zeb warned.

This wormhole intersection afforded five branches. Three black spheres orbited closely together like circling leopards, blaring bright by their quantum rim radiation. Two cubic wormholes circled further out. Zeb knew that one of the rare variant forms was cubical, but he had never seen any. Two together suggested that they were born at the edge of galaxies, but such matters were beyond his shaky understanding.

"We go—there," Fyrna pointed a laser beam at one of the cubes, guiding the pencil ship.

They thrust toward the smaller cube, gingerly inching up. The wormyard here was automatic and no one hailed them.

"Tight fit," Zeb said nervously.

"Five fingers to spare."

He thought she was joking, then realized that if anything, she was underestimating the fit. At this less-used wormhole intersection slow speeds were essential. Good physics, unfortunate economics. The slowdown cut the net flux of mass, making them backwater intersections.

He gazed at Andromeda to take his mind off the piloting. No wormholes emerged in other galaxies, for arcane reasons of quantum gravity. Or perhaps by some ancient alien design?

They flew directly into the flat face of a cubic worm. The negative-energy-density struts which held the wormhole open were in the edges, so the faces were free of tidal forces.

A smooth ride took them quickly to several wormyards in close orbit about planets. One Zeb recognized as a rare type with an old but rained biosphere. There are plenty of ways to kill a world. Or a man, he reflected.

Another jump—into the working zone of a true, natural black hole. He watched the enormous energy-harvesting disks glow with fermenting scarlets and virulent purples. The Empire had stationed great conduits of magnetic field around the hole. These sucked and drew interstellar dust clouds. The dark cyclones narrowed toward the brilliant accretion disk around the hole. Radiation from the friction and infalling of that great disk was in turn captured by vast grids and reflectors.

The crop of raw photon energy itself became trapped and flushed into the waiting maws of wormholes. These carried the flux to distant worlds in need of cutting lances of light, for the business of planet-shaping, world-raking, moon-carving.

"Time to run," she said.

"We can't get back to our home Sector?"

"I have eavesdropped on the signals sent between worm sites. We are wanted at all domains adjacent to our Sector."

"Damn!"

"I suspect they have many allies."

"They must, to get this quick cooperation. They've staged a fine little manhunt."

"Perhaps the nova trigger issue is but a pretext?"

"How so?"

"Many like the present system of wormhole use," she said delicately. She never let her own views of politics seep into their relationship. Even this oblique reference plainly made her uncomfortable. Her concern was for him as a breathing man, not as a bundle of political abstractions.

She had a point, too. Zeb wanted free wormholes, governed only by market forces. The Speculists wanted tariffs and favors, preferences and paybacks. And guess who would control all that bureaucracy?

He floated and thought. She waited for the decision.

"Precious little running room left."

"I do not urge compromise. I merely advise."

"Ladoro..."

"They would not have bothered to kill him unless they wanted to deal."

"I don't like dealing with a knife at my throat."

"We need to decide," she said edgily.

Time ran against them. He bit his lip. Give up? He couldn't, even if it seemed smart. "Our Sector is pretty far out. What if we run inward?"

"To what end?"

"I'll be working on that. Let's go."

Pellucid, a mere dozen light-years from Galactic Center, had seventeen wormhole mouths orbiting within its solar system—the highest hole density in the galaxy. The system had originally held only two, but a gargantuan technology of brute interstellar flight had tugged the rest there, to make the nexus.

Each of the seventeen spawned occasional wild worms. One of these was Fyrna's target.

But to reach it, they had to venture where few did.

"The galactic center is dangerous," Fyrna said as they coasted toward the decisive wormhole mouth. They curved above a barren mining planet. "But necessary."

"The Admiral pursuing us worries me more—" Their jump cut him off.

—and the spectacle silenced him.

The filaments were so large the eye could not take them in. They stretched fore and aft, shot through with immense luminous corridors and dusky lanes. These arches yawned over tens of light-years. Immense curves descended toward the white-hot True Center. There matter frothed and fumed and burst into dazzling fountains.

"The black hole," he said simply.

The small black hole they had seen only an hour before had trapped a few stellar masses. At True Center, three million suns had died to feed gravity's gullet.

The orderly arrays of radiance were thin, only a light-year across. Yet they sustained themselves along hundreds of light-years as they churned with change. Zeb switched the polarized walls to see in different frequency ranges. Though the curves were hot and roiling in the visible, human spectrum, the radio revealed hidden intricacy. Threads laced among convoluted spindles. He had a powerful impression of layers, of labyrinthine order ascending beyond his view, beyond simple understanding.

"Particle flux is high," Fyrna said tensely. "And rising."

"Where's our junction?"

"I'm having trouble vector-fixing—ah! There."

Hard acceleration rammed him back into his flow-couch. Fyrna took them diving down into a mottled pyramid-shaped wormhole.

This was an even rarer geometry. Zeb had time to marvel at how accidents of the universal birth-pang had shaped these serene geometries, like exhibits in some god's Euclidean museum of the mind.

The wild worm they had used fizzled and glowed behind them. Something emerged on their tail.

Fyrna sped them toward a ramshackle, temporary wormyard. He said nothing, but felt her tense calculations.

The sky filled with light.

"They have detonated the worm!" Fyrna cried.

Breaking hard, veering left—

—into a debris cloud. Thumps, crashes.

Zeb said, "How could the Admiral blow a *worm?*"

"He carries considerable weaponry. Evidently the Empire knows how to trigger the negative-energy-density struts inside a wormmouth."

"Can they see us?"

"Not inside this cloud—I hope."

"Head for that bigger cloud—there."

A huge blot beckoned, coal-sack sullen. They were close in here, near the hole's accretion disk. Around them churned the deaths of stars, all orchestrated by the magnetic filaments.

Here stars were ripped open, spilled, smelted down into fusing globs. They lit up the dark, orbiting masses of debris like tiny crimson match heads flaring in a filthy coal sack.

Amid all that moved the strangest stars of all. Each was half-covered by a hanging hemispherical mask. The mask gave off infrared from this strange screen, which hung at a fixed distance from the star. It hovered on light, gravity just balancing the outward light pressure. The mask reflected half the star's flux back on it, turning up the heat on the cooker, sending virulent arcs jetting from the corona.

Light escaped freely on one side while the mask bottled it up on the other. This pushed the star toward the mask, but the mask was bound to the star by gravitation. It adjusted and kept the right distance. The forlorn star was able to eject light in only one direction, so it recoiled oppositely.

The filaments were herding these stars: sluggish, but effective. Herded toward the accretion disk, stoking the black hole's appetite.

"The Admiral is after us."

Zeb could see nothing, but she had the instruments to peer through the dust cloaking them. "Can he shoot?"

"Not if we damp engines."

"Do it."

Drifting…into a narrow gulf, overlooking the splendor below.

Blackness dwelled at the core, but friction heated the infalling gas and dust. These brimmed with forced radiation. Storms worried the great banks; white-hot tornadoes whirled. A virulent glow hammered outward, shoving incessantly at the crowded masses jostling in their doomed orbits. Gravity's gullet forced the streams into a disk, churning ever inward.

Amid this deadly torrent, life persisted. Of a sort.

Zeb peered through the gaudy view, seeking the machine-beasts who ate and dwelled and died here.

Suffering the press of hot photons, the grazer waited. To these photovores, the great grinding disk was a source of food. Above the searing accretion disk, in hovering clouds, gossamer herds fed.

"Vector that way," Zeb said. "I remember seeing these on my visit…"

"We run a risk, using our drive."

"So be it."

Sheets of the photovores billowed in the electromagnetic winds, basking in the sting. Some were tuned to soak up particular slices of the electromagnetic spectrum, each species with a characteristic polish and shape, deploying great flat receptor planes to maintain orbit and angle in the eternal brimming day.

Their ship slipped among great wings of high-gloss moly-sheet spread. The photovore herds skated on winds and magnetic torques in a complex dynamical sum. They were machines, of course, descended from robot craft which had explored this center billions of years before. More complex machines, evolved in this richness, prowled the darker lanes further out.

"Let's hide here."

"We're overheating already," she said.

"Duck into the shade of that big-winged one."

She called, "Our own ship magnetic fields are barely able to hold back the proton hail."

"Where's the nearest worm?"

"Not far, but—"

"The Admiral will be covering it."

"Of course." A chess game with obvious moves.

A bolt seared across the dust ball behind them and struck some photovores. They burst open and flared with fatal energies.

"He's shooting on spec," Zeb said.

"Perhaps as he does not like the weather here."

They hugged the shadow and waited. Moments tiptoed by.

The Admiral's ship emerged from a dust bank, baroquely elegant and foppishly ornate, glowing with purpose, spiraling lazily down.

Zeb saw a spindly radiance below the photovore sheets. "A magnetic filament."

"Looks dangerous," she said.

"Let's head for it."

"What?"

"We're doomed if we stay here. If you're losing at a game, change the game."

They slipped below vast sheets of photovores with outstretched wings, banking gracefully on the photon breeze. Lenses swiveled to follow the human ship: prey? Here a pack of photovores had clumped, caught in a magnetic flux tube that eased down along the axis of the galaxy itself.

Among them glided steel-blue gammavores, feeders on the harder gamma-ray emission from the accretion disk. They sometimes came this far up, he knew, perhaps to hunt the silicate-creatures who dwelled in the darker dust clouds. Much of the ecology here was still unknown.

He stopped musing. Nature red in tooth and claw, after all. Time to move. Where?

"Slip into the magnetic tube."

She said sharply, "But the electrodynamic potentials there—"

"Let's draw a little cover."

She swooped them forward toward the filament. This also took them angling toward a huge sailcraft photovore. It sighted them, pursued.

Here navigation was simple. Far below them, the rotational pole of the Eater of All Things, the black hole of three million stellar masses, was a pin-prick of absolute black at the center of a slowly revolving incandescent disk.

The photovore descended after them, through thin planes of burnt-gold light seekers. They all lived to ingest light and excrete microwave beams, placid conduits, but some—like the one gliding after the tiny human ship—had developed a taste for metals: a metallovore. It folded its mirror wings, now angular and swift, accelerating.

"The Admiral has noticed us," she announced in flat tones.

"Good. Into the flux tube. Quick!"

"That big alien machine is going to reach us first."

"Even better."

He had heard the lecture, while on his "tour" here. Fusion fires inside the photovores could digest the ruined carcasses of other machines. Exquisitely tuned, their innards yielded pure ingots of any alloy desired.

The ultimate resources here were mass and light. The photovores lived for light, and the sleek metallovore lived to eat them, or even better, the human ship, an exotic variant. It now gave gigahertz cries of joy as it followed them into the magnetic fields of the filament.

"These magnetic entities are intelligent?" she asked.

"Yes, though not in the sense we short-term thinkers recognize. They are more like fitfully sleeping libraries." A glimmer of an idea. "But it's their thinking processes that might save us."

"How?"

"They trigger their thinking with electrodynamic potentials. We're irritating them, I'm sure, by flying in hellbent like this."

"How wonderful."

"Watch that metallovore. Let it get close, then evade it."

Banks, swoops, all amid radiance. Magnetic strands glowed like ivory.

It would ingest them with relish, but the metal-seeker could not maneuver as swiftly as their sleek ship. Deftly they zoomed through magnetic entrails—and the Admiral followed.

"How soon will these magnetic beings react?"

Zeb shrugged. "Soon, if experience is a guide."

"And we—"

"Hug the metallovore now. Quick!"

"But don't let him grab us?"

"That's the idea."

The metallovore, too, was part of an intricate balance. Without it, the ancient community orbiting the Eater would decay to a less diverse state, one of monotonous simplicity, unable to adjust to the Eater's vagaries. Less energy would be harnessed, less mass recovered.

The metallovore skirted over them. Zeb gazed out at it. Predators always had parasites, scavengers. Here and there on the metallovore's polished skin were limpets and barnacles, lumps of orange-brown and soiled yellow that fed on chance debris, purging the metallovore of unwanted elements—wreckage and dust which can jam even the most robust mechanisms, given time.

It banked, trying to reach them. The Admiral's glossy ship came angling in, too, along the magnetic strands.

"Let it get closer," Zeb ordered.

"It'll grab us!"

"True, unless the Admiral kills it first."

"Some choice," she said sardonically.

A dance to the pressure of photons. Light was the fluid here, spilling up from the blistering storms far below in the great grinding disk. This rich harvest supported the great sphere which stretched for hundreds of cubic light-years, its sectors and spans like armatures of an unimaginable city.

Why had he gone into politics, Zeb asked himself—he was always rather abstract when in a crisis—when all *this* beckoned?

All this, centered on a core of black oblivion, the dark font of vast wealth.

"I'm getting a lot of electrodynamic static," she called.

"Ah, good."

"Good? My instruments are sluggish—"

The metallovore loomed. Pincers flexed forth from it.

The jolt came first as a small refraction in the howling virulence. Slow tightening arced along the magnetic filament, annihilation riding down.

"It'll fry us!"

"Not us," he said. "We're a minor mote here. Much bigger conductors will draw this fire."

Another jarring jolt. The metallovore arced and writhed and died in a dancing fire.

No differently could the laws of electrodynamics treat an ever bigger conductor, closing in. The Admiral's fine glowing ship drew flashes of discharge, dancing ruby-red and bile-green.

It coasted, dead. The larger surface areas of both metallovore and starship had intercepted the electrical circuitry of the filaments.

"I… You really did know what you were doing," she said weakly.

"Not actually. I was just following my intuition."

"The one that got you the Governorship?"

"No, something more primitive."

Coasting now, out of the gossamer filaments. There might be more bolts of high voltage.

"Is everyone on that ship dead?" she asked.

"Oh no. You have forgotten your elementary physics. A charge deposits only on the outside of a conductor. Electrons will not enter it."

"But why are they drifting then?"

"Any antenna will draw the charge in, if the line is active; that's its job. Like having your hand on the knob of a radio in a lightning storm, a chancy act."

"So they're inert?"

"A few may have been standing too close to the instruments."

"They would be…?"

He shrugged. "Fried. Luck of the game."

"The Admiral—"

"Let us hope he was unlucky. Even if not, I suspect the Speculists will not look kindly upon one who has raised such a rowdy chase and then caught nothing."

She laughed. They coasted in the gorgeous splendor.

Then he yawned, stretched, and said, "Getting cramped in here. Shall we find that wormhole you mentioned?"

He really didn't like travel all that much, indeed.

Think of the galaxy as a swarm of gaudy bees, bright colors hovering in a ball. Stomp them somehow in midair, so they bank and turn in a furious, compressed disk. Yet their courses and destinies are now guided by small entities of great pretension: humans, at times no better than bees. Across the span of a hundred billion worlds, rich and ancient blood sings in pounding vessels. Even on so great a scale, the hunt is always on.

AFTERWORD

I so loved Roger Zelazny's liquid grace, his fervent sense of narrative momentum, that I have tried in this piece to emulate some of his moments and moves.

Like many, my first Zelazny story was "A Rose for Ecclesiastes." Who can forget reading that opening voice? It evoked a romantic, daring world seen through a poet's eyes. I followed his career eagerly, through novels and novellas of great power. He was the brightest light in a burning decade, the sixties.

When I met Roger in the 1970s he proved to be an affable, witty, wiry man. We became friends and I visited him and family, often having dinner in Santa Fe when I was consulting at Los Alamos. Restless of mind, he always probed for the latest from the grand canvas of science.

I saw him twice in the last year and a half of his life, when we were both guests of honor at two cons. The last time, in Idaho, I found him as quick and funny, eyes glittery, as ever, though gaunt and at times sobered. His spirit was so firm I did not seriously suppose that he would falter and vanish from us so quickly.

Deaths diminish us all. Among the science fiction community, I missed terribly Robert Heinlein and Terry Carr and had persistent dreams about them for over a year after they departed. For Roger it was the same: dreams of flying somewhere with him, always in air sunny and resplendent with long, high perspectives.

So when asked to write a story in tribute to him, I took from my stock of ideas at hand, using pieces of ideas I was working on, and tried to see what Roger would like to fashion from them. He loved the bare and the swanky alike, so I thought of a rather Roger-like character, comfortable in his opulent world, who gets to flee and fight across the sort of wondrous galaxy Roger would have enjoyed. It's been fun to go along with him this one last time.

A DANCE TO STRANGE MUSICS
(1998)

1.

The first crewed starship, the *Adventurer*, hung like a gleaming metallic moon among the gyre of strange worlds. Alpha Centauri was a triple-star system. A tiny flare star dogged the two big suns. At this moment in its eternal dance, the brilliant mote swung slightly toward Sol. Even though it was far from the two bright stars it was the nearest star to Earth: Proxima.

The two rich, yellow stars defined the Centauri system. Still prosaically termed A and B, they swam about each other, ignoring far Proxima.

The *Adventurer*'s astronomer, John, dopplered in on both stars, refreshing memories that were lodged deep. The climax of his career loomed before him. He felt apprehension, excitement, and a thin note of something like fear.

Sun B had an orbital eccentricity of 0.52 about its near-twin, with the extended axis of its ellipse 23.2 astronomical units long. This meant that the closest approach between A and B was a bit farther than the distance of Saturn from Sol.

A was a hard yellow-white glare, a G star with 1.08 the Sun's mass. Its companion, B, was a K-class star that glowed a reddish yellow, since it had 0.88 times the Sun's mass. B orbited with a period of 80 years around A. These two were about 4.8 billion years of age, slightly older than Sol. Promising.

Sun A's planetary children had stirred *Adventurer*'s expedition forth from Earth. From Luna, the system's single Earth-class planet was a mere mote, first detected by an oxygen absorption line in its spectrum. Only a wobbly image could be resolved by Earth's kilometer-sized interferometric telescope, a long bar with mirror-eyes peering in the spaces between A and B. Just enough of an image to entice.

A new Earth? John peered at its shrouded majesty, feeling the slight hum and surge of their ship beneath him. They were steadily moving inward, exploring the Newtonian gavotte of worlds in this two-sunned ballroom of the skies. Proxima was so far away, it was not even a wall-flower.

The Captain had named the fresh planet Shiva. It hung close to A, wreathed in water cirrus, a cloudball dazzling beneath A's simmering yellow-white glare. Shimmering with promise, it had beckoned to John for years during their approach.

Like Venus, but the gases don't match, he thought. The complex tides of the star system massaged Shiva's depths, releasing gases and rippling the crust. John's many-frequency probings had told him a lot, but how to stitch data into a weave of a world? He was the first astronomer to try out centuries of speculative thinking on a real planet.

Shiva was drier than Earth, oceans taking only forty percent of the surface. Its air was heavy in nitrogen, with giveaway tags of eighteen percent oxygen and traces of carbon dioxide; remarkably Earth-like. Shiva was too warm for comfort, in human terms, but not fatally so; no Venusian runaway greenhouse had developed here. How had Shiva escaped that fate?

Long before, the lunar telescopes had made one great fact clear: the atmosphere here was far, far out of chemical equilibrium. Biological theory held that this was inevitably the signature of life. And indeed, the expedition's first mapping had shown that green, abundant life clung to two well-separated habitable belts, each beginning about thirty degrees from the equator.

Apparently the weird tidal effects of the Centauri system had stolen Shiva's initial polar tilt. Such steady workings had now made its spin align to within a single degree with its orbital angular momentum, so that conditions were steady and calm. The equatorial belt was a pale, arid waste of perpetual tornadoes and blistering gales.

John close-upped in all available bands, peering at the planet's crescent. Large blue-green seas, but no great oceans. Particularly, no water links between the two milder zones, so no marine life could migrate between them. Land migrations, calculations showed, were effectively blocked by the great equatorial desert. Birds might make the long flight, John considered, but what evolutionary factor would condition them for such hardship? And what would be the reward? Why fight the jagged mountain chains? Better to lounge about in the many placid lakes.

A strange world, well worth the decades of grinding, slow, starship flight, John thought. He asked for the full display and the observing bowl opened like a flower around him. He swam above the entire disk of the Centauri system now, the images sharp and rich.

To be here at last! *Adventurer* was only a mote among many—yet here, in the lap of strangeness. Far Centauri.

It did not occur to him that humanity had anything truly vital to lose here. The doctrine of expansion and greater knowledge had begun seven centuries before, making European cultures the inheritors of Earth. Although science had found unsettling truths, even those revelations had not blunted the agenda of ever-greater knowledge. After all, what harm could come from merely looking?

The truth about Shiva's elevated ocean only slowly emerged. Its very existence was plainly impossible, and therefore was not at first believed.

Odis was the first to notice the clues. Long days of sensory immersion in the data-streams repaid her. She was rather proud of having plucked such exotica from the bath of measurements their expedition got from their probes—the tiny speeding, smart spindle-eyes that now cruised all over the double-stars' realm.

The Centauri system was odd, but even its strong tides could not explain this anomaly. Planets should be spherical, or nearly so; Earth bulged but a fraction of a percent at its equator; due to its spin. Not Shiva, though.

Odis found aberrations in this world's shape. The anomalies were far away from the equator; principally at the 1,694-kilometer-wide deep blue sea, immediately dubbed the Circular Ocean. It sat in the southern hemisphere, its nearly perfect ring hinting at an origin as a vast crater. Odis could not take her gaze from it, a blue eye peeking coyly at them through the clouds: a planet looking back.

Odis made her ranging measurements, gathering in her data like number-clouds, inhaling their cottony wealth. Beneath her, *Adventurer* prepared to go into orbit about Shiva.

She breathed in the banks of data-vapor, translated by kinesthetic programming into intricate scent-inventories. Tangy, complex.

At first she did not believe the radar reflections. Contours leaped into view, artfully sketched by the mapping radars. Calibrations checked, though, so she tried other methods: slow, analytical, tedious, hard to do in her excitement. They gave the same result.

The Circular Ocean stood a full 10 kilometers higher than the continent upon which it rested.

No mountains surrounded it. It sat like some cosmic magic trick, insolently demanding an explanation.

Odis presented her discovery at the daily Oversight Group meeting. There was outright skepticism, even curled lips of derision, snorts of disbelief. "The range of methods is considerable," she said adamantly. "These results cannot be wrong."

"Only thing to resolve this," a lanky geologist said, "is get an edge-on view."

"I hoped someone would say that." Odis smiled. "Do I have the authorised observing time?"

They gave it reluctantly. *Adventurer* was orbiting in a severe ellipse about Shiva's cloud-wrack. Her long swing brought her into a side view of the target area two days later. Odis used the full panoply of optical, IR, UV, and microwave instruments to peer at the Circular Ocean's perimeter, probing for the basin that supported the round slab of azure water.

There was none. No land supported the hanging sea.

This result was utterly clear. The Circular Ocean was 1.36 kilometers thick and a brilliant blue. Spectral evidence suggested water rich in salt, veined by thick currents. It looked exactly like an enormous, troubled mountain lake, with the mountain subtracted.

Beneath that layer there was nothing but the thick atmosphere. No rocky mountain range to support the ocean-in-air. Just a many-kilometer gap.

All other observations halted. The incontrovertible pictures showed an immense layer of unimaginable weight, blissfully poised above mere thin gases, contradicting all known mechanics. Until this moment Odis had been a lesser figure in the expedition. Now her work captivated everyone and she was the center of every conversation. The concrete impossibility yawned like an inviting abyss.

✸

Lissa found the answer to Shiva's mystery, but no one was happy with it.

An atmospheric chemist, Lissa's job was mostly done well before they achieved orbit around Shiva. She had already probed and labeled the gases, shown clearly that they implied a thriving biology below. After that, she had thought, the excitement would shift elsewhere, to the surface observers.

Not so. Lissa took a deep breath and began speaking to the Oversight Group. She had to show that she was not wasting their time. With all eyes on the Circular Ocean, few cared for mere air.

Yet it was the key, Lissa told them. The Circular Ocean had intrigued her, too: so she looked at the mixture of oxygen, nitrogen, and carbon dioxide that apparently supported the floating sea. These proved perfectly ordinary, almost Earth-standard, except for one oddity. Their spectral lines were slightly split, so that she found two small spikes to the right and left of where each line should be.

Lissa turned from the images she projected before the Oversight Group. "The only possible interpretation," she said crisply, "is that an immensely strong electric field is inducing the tiny electric dipoles of these molecules to move. That splits the lines."

"An *electric* shift?" a grizzled skeptic called. "In a charge-neutral atmosphere? Sure, maybe when lightning flashes you could get a momentary effect, but—"

"It is steady."

"You looked for lightning?" a shrewd woman demanded.

"It's there, sure. We see it forking between the clouds below the Circular Ocean. But that's not what causes the electric fields."

"What does?" This from the grave captain, who never spoke in scientific disputes. All heads turned to him, then to Lissa.

She shrugged. "Nothing reasonable." It pained her to admit it, but ignorance was getting to be a common currency.

A voice called, "So there must be an impossibly strong electric field *everywhere* in that 10 kilometers of air below the ocean?" Murmurs of agreement. Worried frowns.

"Everywhere, yes." The bald truth of it stirred the audience. "Everywhere."

Tagore was in a hurry. Too much so.

He caromed off a stanchion but did not let that stop him from rebounding from the opposite wall, absorbing his momentum with his knees, and springing off with a full push. Rasters streaked his augmented vision, then flickered and faded.

He coasted by a full-view showing Shiva and the world below, a blazing crescent transcendent in its cloud-wrapped beauty. Tagore ignored the spectacle; marvels of the mind preccupied him.

He was carrying the answer to it all, he was sure of that. In his haste he did not even glance at how blue-tinged sunlight glinted from the Circular Ocean. The thick disk of open air below it made a clear line under the blue wedge. At this angle the floating water refracted sunlight around the still-darkened limb of the planet. The glittering azure jewel heralded dawn, serene in its impudent impossibility.

The youngest of the entire expedition, Tagore was a mere theorist. He had specialized in planetary formation at university, but managed to snag a berth on this expedition by developing a ready, quick facility at explaining vexing problems the observers turned up. That, and a willingness to do scutwork.

"Cap'n, I've got it," he blurted as he came through the hatch. The captain greeted him, sitting at a small oak desk, the only wood on the whole ship—then got to business. Tagore had asked for this audience because he knew the effect his theory could have on the others; so the captain should see first.

"The Circular Ocean is held up by electric field pressure," he announced. The captain's reaction was less than he had hoped: unblinking calm, waiting for more information.

"See, electromagnetic fields exert forces on the electrons in atoms," Tagore persisted, going through the numbers, talking fast. "The fields down there are so strong—I got that measurement out of Lissa's data—they can act like a steady support."

He went on to make comparisons: the energy density of a hand grenade, contained in every suitcase-sized volume of air. Even though the fields could simply stand there, as trapped waves, they had to suffer some losses. The power demands were *huge*. Plus, how the hell did such a gargantuan construction *work*?

By now Tagore was thoroughly pumped, oblivious to his audience. Finally the captain blinked and said, "Anything like this ever seen on Earth?"

"Nossir, not that I've ever heard."

"No natural process can do the stunt?"

"Nossir, not that I can imagine."

"Well, we came looking for something different."

Tagore did not know whether to laugh or not; the captain was unreadable. Was this what exploration was like—the slow anxiety of not knowing? On Earth such work had an abstract distance, but here...

He would rather have some other role. Bringing uncomfortable truths to those in power put him more in the spotlight than he wished.

Captain Badquor let the Tagore kid go on a bit longer before he said anything more. It was best to let these technical types sing their songs first. So few of them ever thought about anything beyond their own warblings.

He gave Tavore a captainly smile. Why did they all look so young? "So this whole thing on Shiva is artificial."

"Well, yeah, I suppose so..."

Plainly Tagore hadn't actually thought about that part very much; the wonder of such strong fields had stunned him. Well, it was stunning. "And all that energy, just used to hold up a lake?"

"I'm sure of it, sir. The numbers work out, see? I equated the pressure exerted by those electric fields, assuming they're trapped in the volume under the Circular Ocean, the way waves can get caught if they're inside a conducting box—"

"You think that ocean's a conductor?" Might as well show the kid that even the captain knew a little physics. In fact, though he never mentioned it, he had a doctorate from MIT. Not that he had learned much about command there.

"Uh, well, no. I mean, it is a fairly good conductor, but for my model, it's only a way of speaking—"

"It has salt currents, true? They could carry electrical currents." The captain rubbed his chin, the machinery of his mind trying to grasp how such a thing could be. "Still, that doesn't explain why the thing doesn't evaporate away, at those altitudes."

"Uh, I really hadn't thought..."

The captain waved a hand. "Go on." *Sing for me.*

"Then the waves exert an upward force on the water every time they reflect from the underside of the ocean—"

"And transfer that weight down, on invisible waves, to the rock that's 10 kilometers below."

"Uh...yessir."

Tagore looked a bit constipated, bursting with enthusiasm, with the experience of the puzzle, but not knowing how to express it. The captain decided to have mercy on the kid. "Sounds good. Not anything impossible about it."

"Except the size of it, sir."

"That's one way to put it."

"Sir?"

A curious, powerful feeling washed over the captain. Long decades of anticipation had steeled him, made him steady in the presence of the crew. But now he felt his sense of the room tilt, as though he were losing control of his status-space. The mind could go whirling off, out here in the inky immensities between twin alien suns. He frowned. "This thing is bigger than anything humanity ever built. And there's not a clue what it's for. The majesty of it, son, that's what strikes me. Grandeur."

John slipped into his helmet and Shiva enclosed him. *To be wrapped in a world*—His point of view shifted, strummed, arced with busy fretworks—then snapped into solidity, stabilized.

Astronomy had become intensely interactive in the past century, the spectral sensoria blanketing the viewer. Through *Adventurer's* long voyage he had tuned the system to his every whim. Now it gave him a nuanced experience like a true, full-bodied immersion.

He was eager to immerse in himself in the feel of Shiva, in full 3-D wraparound. Its crescent swelled below like a ripe, mottled fruit. He plunged toward it. A planet, fat in bandwidth.

For effect—decades before he had been a sky-diver—John had arranged the data-fields so that he accelerated into it. From their arcing orbit he shot directly toward Shiva's disk. Each mapping rushed toward him, exploding upward in finer detail. *There*—

The effect showed up first in the grasslands of the southern habitable belt. He slewed toward the plains, where patterns emerged in quilted confusions. After Tagore's astonishing theory about the Circular Ocean—odd, so audacious, and coming from a nonscientist—John had to be ready for anything. Somewhere in the data-fields must lurk the clue to who or what had made the ocean.

Below the great grassy shelves swelled. But in places the grass was thin. Soon he saw why. The natural grass was only peeking out across plains covered with curious orderly patterns—hexagonals folding into triangles where necessary to cover hills and valleys, right up to the muddy banks of the slow-moving brown rivers.

Reflection in the UV showed that the tiles making this pattern were often small, but with some the size of houses, meters thick...and moving. They all jostled and worked with restless energy, to no obvious purpose.

Alive? The UV spectrum broke down into a description of a complex polymer. Cross-linked chains bonded at many oblique angles to each other, flexing like sleek micro-muscles.

John brought in chemists, biologists in an ensemble suite: Odis and Lissa claimed in the scientific choir. In the wraparound display he felt them by the shadings they gave the data.

The tiles, Lissa found, fed on their own sky. Simple sugars rained from the clotted air, the fruit of an atmosphere that resembled an airy chicken soup. *Atmospheric electro-chemistry seems responsible, somehow,* Lissa sent. Floating microbial nuggets moderated the process.

The tiles were prime eaters. Oxidizing radicals the size of golf balls patroled their sharp linear perimeters. These pack-like rollers attacked invader chemicals, ejecting most, harvesting those they could use.

Lissa brought in two more biologists, who of course had many questions. *Are these tiles like great turtles?* one ventured, then chuckled uneasily. They yearned to flip one over.

Diurnal or nocturnal? *Some are, most aren't.* Are there any small ones? *A few.*

Do they divide by fission? *No, but...* Nobody understood the complicated process the biologists witnessed. Reproduction seems a tricky matter.

There is some periodicity to their movements, some slow rhythms, and particularly a fast Fourier-spectrum spike at 1.27 second—but again, no clear reason for it.

Could they be all one life form?—could that be?

A whole planet taken over by a tiling-thing that co-opts all resources?

The senior biologists scoffed. How could a species evolve to have only one member? And an ecosystem—a whole world!—with so few parts?

Evolution ruled that out. Bio-evolution, that is. But not social evolution.

John plunged further into the intricate matrices of analysis. The endless tile-seas cloaking mountains and valleys shifted and milled, fidgety, only occasionally leaving bare ground visible as a square fissioned into triangles. Oblongs met and butted with fevered energy.

Each hemisphere of the world was similar, though the tiles in the north had different shapes—pentagonals, mostly. Nowhere did the tiles cross rivers but they could ford streams. A Centauri variant of chlorophyll was everywhere, in the oceans and rivers, but not in the Circular Ocean.

The ground was covered with a thin grass, the sprigs living off the momentary sunlight that slipped between the edges in the jostling, jiggling, bumping, and shaking. Tiles that moved over the grass sometimes cropped it, sometimes not, leaving stubs that seemed to have been burned off.

The tiles' fevered dance ran incessantly, without sleep. Could these things be performing some agitated discourse, a lust-fest without end?

John slowed his descent. The tiles were a shock. Could these be the builders of the Circular Ocean? Time for the biologists to get to work.

The computer folk thought one way, the biologists—after an initial rout, when they rejected the very possibility of a single entity filling an entire biosphere—quite another.

After some friction, their views converged somewhat. A biologist remarked that the larger tiles came together like dwarf houses making love...gingerly, always presenting the same angles and edges.

Adventurer had scattered micro-landers all over the world. These showed only weak electromagnetic fringing fields among the tiles. Their deft collisions seemed almost like neurons in a two-dimensional plan.

The analogy stirred the theorists. Over the usual after-shift menu of beer, soy nuts, and friendly insults, one maven of the digital realm ventured an absurd idea: could the planet have become a computer?

Everybody laughed. They kidded the advocate of this notion...and then lapsed into frowning silence. Specialists find quite unsettling those ideas that cross disciplines.

Could a species turn itself into a biological computer? The tiles did rub and caress each other in systematic ways. Rather than carrying information in digital fashion, maybe they used a more complex language of position and angle, exploiting their planar geometry. If so, the information density flowing among them was immense. Every collision carried a sort of Euclidean talk, possibly rich in nuance.

The computer analogy brought up a next question—not that some big ones weren't left behind, perhaps lying in wait to bite them on their conceptual tail. Could the tiles know anything more than themselves? Or were they strange, geometroid solipsists? Should they call the tiles a single It?

Sealed inside a cosmos of its own making, was It even in principle interested in the outside world? Alpha Centauri fed It gratuitous energy, the very soupy air fueled It: the last standing power on the globe. What reason did it have to converse with the great Outside?

Curiosity, perhaps? The biologists frowned at the prospect. Curiosity in early prehumans was rewarded in the environment. The evolving ape learned new tricks, found fresh water, killed a new kind of game, invented a better way to locate those delicious roots and the world duly paid it back.

Apparently—*but don't ask us why just yet!* the biologists cried—the game was different here. What reward came from the tiles' endless smacking together?

So even if the visiting humans rang the conceptual doorbell on the tile-things, maybe nobody would answer. Maybe nobody was home.

Should they try?

John and Odis and Lissa, Tagore and the captain, over a hundred other crew—they all pondered.

2.

While they wrestled with the issue, exploration continued.

A flitter craft flew near the elevated ocean and inspected its supporting volume with distant sensors and probing telescopes. Even Shiva's weather patterns seemed wary of the Circular Ocean. Thunderclouds veered away from the gap between the ocean and the rugged land below. In the yawning height clouds formed but quickly dispersed as if dissolved by unseen forces.

Birds flew through the space, birds like feathery kites.

Somehow they had missed noticing this class of life. Even the micro-landers had not had the speed to capture their darting lives. And while the kite-birds did seem to live mostly on tiny floating balloon-creatures that hovered in the murky air of the valleys, they were unusually common beneath the Circular Ocean.

John proposed that he send in a robo-craft of bird size, to measure physical parameters in the heart of the gap. Captain Badquor approved. The shops fabricated a convincing fake. Jet-powered and featuring fake feathers, it was reasonably convincing.

John flew escort in a rocket-plane. The bird-probe got seventeen kilometers inside and then disappeared in a dazzling blue-white electrical discharge. Telemetry showed why: the Circular Ocean's support was a complex weave of electrical fields, supplying an upward pressure. These fields never exceeded the break-down level of a megavolt per meter, above which Shiva's atmosphere would ionize. Field strength was about a million volts per meter.

The robo-craft had hit a critical peak in the field geometry. A conductor, it caused a flashover that dumped millions of watts into the bird within a millisecond.

As the cinder fell, John banked away from his monitoring position five kilometers beyond the gap perimeter. There was no particular reason to believe a discharge that deep within the gap would somehow spread, engulfing the region in a spontaneous discharge of the enormous stored energies. Surely whoever—no, whatever—had designed the Circular Ocean's supports would not allow the electromagnetic struts to collapse from the frying of a mere bird.

But something like that happened. The system responded.

The burned brown husk of the pseudo-bird turned lazily as it fell and sparks jumped from it. These formed a thin orange discharge that fed on the energy coursing through the now-atomized bird. The discharging line snaked away, following unerringly the bird's prior path. It raced at close to the speed of light back along the arc.

The system had *memory*, John realized. He saw a tendril of light at the corner of his vision as he turned his flitter craft. He had time only to think that it was like a huge, fast finger jabbing at him. An apt analogy, though he had no time to consider ironies. The orange discharge touched the flitter. John's hair stood on end as charge flooded into the interior.

Ideally, electrons move to the outer skin of a conductor. But when antennae connect deep into the interior, circuits can close.

Something had intended to dump an immense charge on the flitter, the origin of the pseudo bird. Onboard instruments momentarily reported a charge exceeding seventeen coulombs. By then John had, for all intents and purposes, ceased to exist as an organized bundle of electrical information.

John's death did yield a harvest of data. Soon enough Lissa saw the true function of the Circular Ocean. It was but an ornament, perhaps an artwork.

Ozone fizzed all around it. Completely natural-seeming, the lake crowned a huge cavity that functioned like a steady, standing laser.

The electrical fields both supported the Ocean and primed the atoms of the entire atmosphere they permeated. Upon stimulus—from the same system that had fried John—the entire gap could release the stored energy into an outgoing electromagnetic wave. It was an optical bolt, powerful and complex in structure—triggered by John.

Twice more the ocean's gap discharged naturally as the humans orbited Shiva. The flash lasted but a second, not enough to rob the entire ocean structure of its stability. The emission sizzled out through the atmosphere and off into space.

Laser beams are tight, and this one gave away few of its secrets. The humans, viewing it from a wide angle, caught little of the complex structure and understood less.

Puzzled, mourning John, they returned to a careful study of the Shiva surface. Morale was low. The captain felt that a dramatic gesture could lift their spirits. He would have to do it himself.

To Captain Badquor fell the honor of the first landing. A show of bravery would overcome the crew's confusions, surely. He would direct the complex exploring machines in real-time, up close.

He left the landing craft fully suited up, impervious to the complex biochem mix of the atmosphere.

The tiles jostled downhill from him. Only in the steep flanks of this equatorial mountain range did the tiles not endlessly surge. Badquor's boots crunched on a dry, crusty soil. He took samples, sent them back by runner-robo.

A warning signal from orbit: the tiles in his area seemed more agitated than usual. A reaction to his landing?

The tile polygons were leathery, with no obvious way to sense him. No eyes or ears. They seemed to caress the ground lovingly, though Badquor knew that they tread upon big crabbed feet.

He went forward cautiously. Below, the valley seemed alive with rippling turf, long waves sweeping to the horizon in the twinkling of an instant. He got an impression of incessant pace, of enthusiasm unspoken but plainly endless.

His boots were well insulated thermally, but not electrically; thus, when his headphones crackled he thought he was receiving noise in his transmission lines. The dry sizzle began to make his skin tingle.

Only when the frying noise rose and buried all other signals did he blink, alarmed. By then it was too late.

Piezoelectric energy arises when mechanical stress massages rock. Pressure on an electrically neutral stone polarizes it at the lattice level by slightly separating the center of positive charge from the negative. The lattice moves, the shielding electron cloud does not. This happens whenever the rock crystal structure does not have a center of structural symmetry, and so occurs in nearly all bedrock.

The effect was well known on Earth, though weak. Stressed strata sometimes discharged, sending glow discharges into the air. Such plays of light were now a standard precursor warning of earthquakes. But Earth was a mild case.

Tides stressed the stony mantle of Shiva, driven by the eternal gravitational gavotte of both stars, A and B. Periodic alignments of the two stars stored enormous energy in the full body of the planet. Evolution favored life that could harness these electrical currents that rippled through the planetary crust. This, far more than the kilowatt per square meter of sunlight, drove the tile-forms.

All this explanation came after the fact, and seemed obvious in retrospect. The piezoelectric energy source was naturally dispersed and easily harvested. A sizzle of electric microfields fed the tiles' large, crusted footpads. After all, on Earth fish and eels routinely use electrical fields as both sensors and weapons.

This highly organized ecology sensed Badquor's intrusion immediately. To them, he probably had many of the signatures of power-parasite. These were small creatures like stick insects that Badquor himself had noticed after landing; they lived by stealing electrical charge from the tile polygons.

Only later analysis made it clear what had happened. The interlinked commonality of piezo-driven life moved to expel the intruder by overpowering it—literally.

Badquor probably had no inkling of how strange a fate he had met, for the several hundreds of amperes caused his muscles to seize up, his heart to freeze in a clamped frenzy, and his synapses to discharge in a last vision that burned into his eyes a vision of an incandescent rainbow.

Lissa blinked. The spindly trees looked artificial but weren't. Groves of them spiraled around hills, zigzagged up razor-backed ridges and shot down the flanks of denuded rock piles. Hostile terrain for any sort of tree that earthly biologists understood. The trees, she noted, had growing patterns that bore no discernible relation to water flow, sunlight exposure, or wind patterns.

That was why Lissa went in to see. Her team of four had already sent the smart-eyes, rugged robots, and quasi-intelligent processors.

Lightweight, patient, durable, these ambassadors had discovered little. Time for something a bit more interactive on the ground.

That is, a person. Captain Badquor's sacrifice had to mean something, and his death had strengthened his crew's resolve.

Lissa landed with electrically insulated boots. They now understood the piezoelectric ecology in broad outline, or thought they did. Courageous caution prevailed.

The odd beanpole trees made no sense. Their gnarled branches followed a fractal pattern and had no leaves. Still, there was ample fossil evidence—gathered by automatic prospectors sent down earlier—that the bristly trees had evolved from more traditional trees within the past few milllon years. But they had come so quickly into the geological record that Lissa suspected they were "driven" evolution—biological technology.

She carefully pressed her instruments against the sleek black sides of the trees. Their surfaces seethed with electric currents, but none strong enough to be a danger.

On Earth, the natural potential difference between the surface and the upper atmosphere provides a voltage drop of a hundred volts for each meter in height. A woman two meters tall could be at a significantly higher potential than her feet, especially if her feet had picked up extra electrons by walking across a thick carpet.

On Shiva this effect was much larger. The trees, Lissa realized, were harvesting the large potentials available between Shiva's rocky surface and the charged layers skating across the upper reaches of the atmosphere.

The "trees" were part of yet another way to reap the planetary energies—whose origin was ultimately the blunt forces of gravity, mass and torque—all for the use of life.

The potential-trees felt Lissa's presence quickly enough. They had evolved defenses against poachers who would garner stray voltages and currents from the unwary.

In concert—for the true living entity was the grove, comprising perhaps a million trees—they reacted.

Staggering back to her lander, pursued by vagrant electrical surges through both ground and the thick air, she shouted into her suit mike her conclusions. These proved useful in later analysis.

She survived, barely.

3.

When the sum of these incidents sank in, the full import become clear. The entire Shiva ecology was electrically driven. From the planet's rotation and strong magnetosphere, from the tidal stretching of the Centauri system, from geological rumblings and compressions, came far more energy than mere sunlight could ever provide.

Seen this way, all biology was an afterthought. The geologists, who had been feeling rather neglected lately, liked this turn of events quite a bit. They gave lectures on Shiva seismology which, for once, everybody attended.

To be sure, vestigial chemical processes still ran alongside the vastly larger stores of charges and potentials; these were important for understanding the ancient biosphere that had once governed here.

Much could be learned from classic, old-style biology: from samples of the bushes and wiry trees and leafy plants, from the small insect-like creatures of ten legs each, from the kite-birds, from the spiny, knife-like fish that prowled the lakes.

All these forms were ancient, unchanging. Something had fixed them in evolutionary amber. Their forms had not changed for many hundreds of millions of years.

There had once been higher forms, the fossil record showed. Something like mammals, even large tubular things that might have resembled reptiles.

But millions of years ago they had abruptly ceased. Not due to some trauma, either—they all ended together, but without the slightest sign of a shift in the biosphere, of disease or accident.

The suspicion arose that something had simply erased them, having no further need.

The highest form of life—defined as that with the highest brain/body volume ratio—had vanished slightly later than the others. It had begun as a predator wider than it was tall, and shaped like a turtle, though without a shell.

It had the leathery look of the tile-polygons, though. Apparently it had not followed the classic mode of pursuit, but rather had outwitted its prey, boxing it in by pack-animal tactics. Later, it had arranged deadfalls and traps. Or so the sociobiologists suspected, from narrow evidence.

These later creatures had characteristic bony structures around the large, calculating brain. Subsequent forms were plainly intelligent, and had been engaged in a strange manipulation of their surroundings. Apparently without ever inventing cities or agriculture, they had domesticated many other species.

Then, the other high life forms vanished from the fossil record. The scheme of the biosphere shifted. Electrical plant forms, like the spindly trees and those species that fed upon piezoelectric energy, came to the fore.

Next, the dominant, turtle-like predators vanished as well. Had they been dispatched?

On Shiva, all the forms humans thought of as life, plant and animal alike, were now in fact mere...well, maintenance workers. They served docilely in a far more complex ecology. They were as vital and as unnoticeable and as ignorable as the mitochondria in the stomach linings of *Adventurer*'s crew.

Of the immensely more complex electrical ecology, they were only beginning to learn even the rudiments. If Shiva was in a sense a single interdependent, colonial organism, what were its deep rules?

By focusing on the traditional elements of the organic biosphere they had quite missed the point.

❋

Then the Circular Ocean's laser discharged again. The starship was nearer the lancing packet of emission, and picked up a side lobe. They learned more in a millisecond than they had in a month.

A human brain has about ten billion neurons, each connected with about 100,000 of its neighbors. A firing neuron carries one bit of information. But the signal depends upon the path it follows, and in the labyrinth of the brain there are 1,015 pathways. This torrent of information flows through the brain in machine-gun packets of electrical impulses, coursing through myriad synapses. Since a single book has about a million bits in it, a single human carries the equivalent of a billion books of information—all riding around in a two-kilogram lump of electrically wired jelly.

Only one to ten percent of a human brain's connections are firing at any one time. A neuron can charge and discharge at best a hundred times in a second. Human brains, then, can carry roughly 1,010 bits of information in a second.

Thus, to read out a brain containing 1,015 bits would take 100,000 seconds, or about a day.

The turtle-predators had approximately the same capacity. Indeed, there were theoretical arguments that a mobile, intelligent species would carry roughly the same load of stored information as a human could. For all its limitations, the human brain has an impressive data-store capabililty, even if, in many, it frequently went unused.

The Circular Ocean had sent discrete packets of information of about this size, 1015 bits compressed into its powerful millisecond pulse. The packets within it were distinct, well bordered by banks of marker code. The representation was digital, an outcome mandated by the fact that any number enjoys a unique representation only in base 2.

Within the laser's millisecond burst were fully a thousand brain equivalent transmissions. A trove. What the packets actually said was quite undecipherable.

The target was equally clear: a star 347 light years away. Targeting was precise; there could be no mistake. Far cheaper if one knows the recipient, to send a focused message, rather than to broadcast wastefully in the low-grade, narrow bandwidth radio frequencies.

Earth had never heard such powerful signals, of course, not because humans were not straining to hear, but because Shiva was ignoring them.

After Badquor's death and Lissa's narrow escape, *Adventurer* studied the surface with elaborately planned robot expeditions. The machines skirted the edge of a vast tile-plain, observing the incessant jiggling, fed on the piezoelectric feast welling from the crusted rocks.

After some days, they came upon a small tile lying still. The others had forced it out of the eternal jostling jam. It lay stiff and discolored, baking in the double suns' glare. Scarcely a meter across and thin, it looked like construction material for a patio in Arizona.

The robots carried it off. Nothing pursued them. The tile-thing was dead, apparently left for mere chemical processes to harvest its body.

This bonanza kept the ship's biologists sleepless for weeks as they dissected it. Gray-green, hard of carapace, and extraordinarily complex in its nervous system—these they had expected. But the dead alien devoted fully a quarter of its body volume to a brain that was broken into compact, separate segments.

The tile-creatures were indeed part of an ecology driven by electrical harvesting of the planetary energies. The tiles alone used a far higher percentage of the total energetic wealth than did Earth's entire sluggish, chemically driven biosphere.

And deep within the tile-thing was the same bone structure as they had seen in the turtle-like predator. The dominant, apparently intelligent species had not gone to the stars. Instead, they had formed the basis of an intricate ecology of the mind.

Then the engineers had a chance to study the tile-thing, and found even more.

As a manifestation of their world, the tiles were impressive. Their neurological system fashioned a skein of interpretations, of lived scenarios, of expressive renderings—all apparently for communication outward in well-sculpted bunches of electrical information, intricately coded. They had large computing capacity and ceaselessly exchanged great gouts of information with each other. This explained their rough skins, which maximized piezo connections when they rubbed against each other. And they "spoke" to each other through the ground, as well, where their big, crabbed feet carried currents, too.

Slowly it dawned that Shiva was an unimaginably huge computational complex, operating in a state of information flux many orders of magnitude greater than the entire sum of human culture. Shiva was to Earth as humans are to beetles.

The first transmissions about Shiva's biosphere reached Earth four years later. Already, in a culture more than a century into the dual evolution of society and computers, there were disturbing parallels.

Some communities in the advanced regions of Earth felt that real-time itself was a pallid, ephemeral experience. After all, one could not archive it for replay, savor it, return until it became a true part of oneself. Real-time was for one time only, then lost.

So increasingly, some people lived instead in worlds made totally volitional—truncated, chopped, governed by technologies they could barely sense as ghostlike constraints on an otherwise wide compass.

"Disposable realities," some sneered—but the fascination of such lives was clear.

Shiva's implication was extreme: an entire world could give itself over to life-as-computation.

Could the intelligent species of Shiva have executed a huge fraction of their fellow inhabitants? And then themselves gone extinct? For what? Could they have fled—perhaps from the enormity of their own deeds?

Or had those original predators become the tile-polygons?

The *Adventurer* crew decided to return to Shiva's surface in force, to crack the puzzles. They notified Earth and descended.

Shortly after, the Shiva teams ceased reporting back to Earth. Through the hiss of interstellar static there came no signal.

After years of anxious waiting, Earth launched the second expedition. They too survived the passage. Cautiously they approached Shiva.

Adventurer still orbited the planet, but was vacant.

This time they were wary. Further years of hard thinking and careful study passed before the truth began to come.

4.

{— John/Odis/Lissa/Tagore/Cap'n —} —all assembled/congealed/thickened — —into a composite veneer persona— —on the central deck of their old starship, —to greet the second expedition.

Or so they seemed to intend.

They came up from the Shiva surface in a craft not of human construction. The sleek, webbed thing seemed to ride upon electromagnetic winds.

They entered through the main lock, after using proper hailing protocols.

But what came through the lock was an ordered array of people no one could recognize as being from the *Adventurer* crew.

They seemed younger, unworn. Smooth, bland features looked out at the bewildered second expedition. The party moved together, maintaining a hexagonal array with a constant spacing of four centimeters. Fifty-six pairs of eyes surveyed the new Earth ship, each momentarily gazing at a different portion of the field of view as if to memorize only a portion, for later integration.

To convey a sentence, each person spoke a separate word. The effect was jarring, with no clue to how an individual knew what to say, or when, for the lines were not rehearsed. The group reacted to questions in a blur of scattershot talk, words like volleys.

Sentences ricocheted and bounced around the assembly deck where the survivors of the first expedition all stood, erect and clothed in a shapeless gray garment. Their phrases made sense when isolated, but the experience of hearing them was unsettling. Long minutes stretched out before the second expedition realized that these hexagonally spaced humans were trying to greet them, to induct them into something they termed the Being Suite.

This offer made, the faces within the hexagonal array began to show separate expressions. Tapes of this encounter show regular facial alterations with a fixed periodicity of 1.27 seconds. Each separate face racheted, jerking among a menu of finely graduated countenances—anger, sympathy, laughter, rage, curiosity, shock, puzzlement, ecstasy—flickering, flickering, endlessly flickering.

A witness later said that it were as if the hexagonals (as they came to be called) knew that human expressiveness centered on the face, and so had slipped into a kind of language of facial aspects. This seemed natural to them, and yet the 1.27 second pace quickly gave the witnesses a sense of creeping horror.

High-speed tapes of the event showed more. Beneath the 1.27 frequency there was a higher harmonic, barely perceptible to the human eye, in which other expressions shot across the hexagonals' faces. These were like waves, muscular twitches that washed over the skin like tidal pulls.

This periodicity was the same as the tile-polygons had displayed. The subliminal aspects were faster than the conscious human optical processor can manage, yet research showed that they were decipherable in the target audience.

Researchers later concluded that this rapid display was the origin of the growing unease felt by the second expedition. The hexagonals said nothing throughout all this.

The second expedition crew described the experience as uncanny, racking, unbearable. Their distinct impression was that the first expedition now manifested as like the tile-things. Such testimony was often followed by an involuntary twitch.

Tapes do not yield such an impression upon similar audiences: they have become the classic example of having to be in a place and time to sense the meaning of an event. Still, the tapes are disturbing, and access is controlled. Some Earth audiences experienced breakdowns after viewing them.

But the second expedition agreed even more strongly upon a second conclusion. Plainly, the *Adventurer* expedition had joined the computational labyrinth that was Shiva. How they were seduced was never clear; the second expedition feared finding out.

Indeed, their sole, momentary brush with {— John/Odis/Lissa/ Tagore/Cap'n... —} convinced the second expedition that there was no point in pursuing the maze of Shiva.

The hostility radiating from the second expedition soon drove the hexagonals back into their ship and away. The fresh humans from Earth felt something gut-level and instinctive, a reaction beyond words. The hexagonals retreated without showing a coherent reaction. They simply turned and walked away, holding to the four-centimeter spacing. The 1.27 second flicker stopped and they returned to a bland expression, alert but giving nothing away.

The vision these hexagonals conveyed was austere, jarring...and yet, plainly intended to be inviting.

The magnitude of their failure was a measure of the abyss that separated the two parties. The hexagonals were now both more and less than human.

The hexagonals left recurrent patterns that told much, though only in retrospect. Behind the second expedition's revulsion lay a revelation: of a galaxy spanned by intelligences formal and remote, far developed beyond the organic stage. Such intelligences had been born variously, of early organic forms, or of later machine civilizations which had arisen upon the ashes of extinct organic societies. The gleam of the stars was in fact a metallic glitter.

This vision was daunting enough: of minds so distant and strange, hosted in bodies free of sinew and skin. But there was something more, an inexpressible repulsion in the manifestation of {— John/Odis/Lissa/Tagore/Cap'n... —}.

A nineteenth-century philosopher, Nietzsche, had once remarked that if one stared into the abyss long enough, it stared back. This proved true. A mere moment's lingering look, quiet and almost casual, was enough. The second expedition panicked. It is not good to stare into a pit that has no bottom.

They had sensed the final implication of Shiva's evolution. To alight upon such interior worlds of deep, terrible exotica exacted a high cost: the body itself. Yet all those diverse people had joined the *syntony* of Shiva— an electrical harmony that danced to unheard musics. Whether they had been seduced, or even raped, would forever be unclear.

Out of the raw data-stream the second expedition could sample transmissions from the tile-things, as well. The second expedition caught a link-locked sense of repulsive grandeur. Still organic in their basic organization, still tied to the eternal wheel of birth and death, the tiles had once been lords of their own world, holding dominion over all they knew.

Now they were patient, willing drones in a hive they could not comprehend. But—and here human terms undoubtedly fail—they loved their immersion.

Where was their consciousness housed? Partially in each, or in some displaced, additive sense? There was no clear way to test either idea.

The tile-things were like durable, patient machines that could best carry forward the first stages of a grand computation. Some biologists compared them with insects, but no evolutionary mechanism seemed capable of yielding a reason why a species would give itself over to computation. The insect analogy died, unable to predict the response of the polygons to stimulus, or even why they existed.

Or was their unending jostling only in the service of calculation? The tile-polygons would not say. They never responded to overtures.

The Circular Ocean's enormous atmospheric laser pulsed regularly, as the planet's orbit and rotation carried the laser's field of targeting onto a fresh partner-star system. Only then did the system send its rich messages out into the galaxy. The pulses carried mind-packets of unimaginable data, bound on expeditions of the intellect.

The second expedition reported, studied. Slowly at first, and then accelerating, the terror overcame them.

They could not fathom Shiva, and steadily they lost crew members to its clasp. Confronting the truly, irreducibly exotic, there is no end of ways to perish.

In the end they studied Shiva from a distance, no more. Try as they could, they always met a barrier in their understanding. Theories came and went, fruitlessly. Finally, they fled.

It is one thing to speak of embracing the new, the fresh, the strange. It is another to feel that one is an insect, crawling across a page of the *Encyclopedia Britannica*, knowing only that something vast is passing by beneath, all without your sensing more than a yawning vacancy. Worse, the lack was clearly in oneself, and was irredeemable.

This was the first contact humanity had with the true nature of the galaxy. It would not be the last. But the sense of utter and complete diminishment never left the species, in all the strange millennia that rolled on thereafter.

ANOMALIES
(2001)

I t was not lost upon the Astronomer Royal that the greatest scientific discovery of all time was made by a carpenter and amateur astronomer from the neighboring cathedral town of Ely. Not by a Cambridge man.

Geoffrey Carlisle had a plain directness that apparently came from his profession, a custom cabinet maker. It had enabled him to get past the practiced deflection skills of the receptionist at the Institute for Astronomy, through the Assistant Director's patented brush-off, and into the Astronomer Royal's corner office.

Running this gauntlet took until early afternoon, as the sun broke through a shroud of soft rain. Geoffrey wasted no time. He dropped a celestial coordinate map on the Astronomer Royal's mahogany desk, hand amended, and said, "The moon's off by better'n a degree."

"You measured carefully, I am sure."

The Astronomer Royal had found that the occasional crank did make it through the Institute's screen, and in confronting them it was best to go straight to the data. Treat them like fellow members of the profession and they softened. Indeed, astronomy was the only remaining science which profited from the work of amateurs. They discovered the new comets, found wandering asteroids, noticed new novae and generally patrolled what the professionals referred to as local astronomy—anything that could be seen in the night sky with a telescope smaller than a building.

That Geoffrey had gotten past the scrutiny of the others meant this might conceivably be real. "Very well, let us have a look." The Astronomer Royal had lunched at his desk and so could not use a date in his college as a dodge. Besides, this was crazy enough to perhaps generate an amusing story.

An hour later he had abandoned the story-generating idea. A conference with the librarian, who knew the heavens like his own palm, made it clear that Geoffrey had done all the basic work correctly. He had photos and careful, carpenter-sure data, all showing that, indeed, last night after around eleven o'clock the moon was well ahead of its orbital position.

"No possibility of systematic error here?" the librarian politely asked the tall, sinewy Geoffrey.

"Check 'em yerself. I was kinda hopin' you fellows would have an explanation, is all."

The moon was not up, so the Astronomer Royal sent a quick email to Hawaii. They thought he was joking, but then took a quick look and came back, rattled. A team there got right on it and confirmed. Once alerted, other observatories in Japan and Australia chimed in.

"It's out of position by several of its own diameters," the Astronomer Royal mused. "Ahead of its orbit, exactly on track."

The librarian commented precisely, "The tides are off prediction as well, exactly as required by this new position. They shifted suddenly, reports say."

"I don't see how this can happen," Geoffrey said quietly.

"Nor I," the Astronomer Royal said. He was known for his understatement, which could masquerade as modesty, but here he could think of no way to underplay such a result.

"Somebody else's bound to notice, I'd say," Geoffrey said, folding his cap in his hands.

"Indeed," the Astronomer Royal suspected some subtlety had slipped by him.

"Point is, sir, I want to be sure I get the credit for the discovery."

"Oh, of course you shall." All amateurs ever got for their labors was their name attached to a comet or asteroid, but this was quite different. "Best we get on to the IAU, ah, the International Astronomical Union," the Astronomer Royal said, his mind whirling. "There's a procedure for alerting all interested observers. Establish credit, as well."

Geoffrey waved this away. "Me, I'm just a five-inch 'scope man. Don't care about much beyond the priority, sir. I mean, it's over to you fellows. What I want to know is, what's it mean?"

Soon enough, as the evening news blared and the moon lifted above the European horizons again, that plaintive question sounded all about. One did not have to be a specialist to see that something major was afoot.

"It all checks," the Astronomer Royal said before a forest of cameras and microphones. "The tides being off true has been noted by the naval authorities round the world, as well. Somehow, in the early hours of last evening, Greenwich time, our moon accelerated in its orbit. Now it is proceeding at its normal speed, however."

"Any danger to us?" one of the incisive, investigative types asked.

"None I can see," the Astronomer Royal deflected this mildly. "No panic headlines needed."

"What caused it?" a woman's voice called from the media thicket.

"We can see no object nearby, no apparent agency," the Astronomer Royal admitted.

"Using what?"

"We are scanning the region in all wavelengths, from radio to gamma rays." An extravagant waste, very probably, but the Astronomer Royal knew the price of not appearing properly concerned. Hand-wringing was called for at all stages.

"Has this happened before?" a voice sharply asked. "Maybe we just weren't told?"

"There are no records of any such event," the Astronomer Royal said. "Of course, a thousand years ago, who would have noticed? The supernova that left us the Crab nebula went unreported in Europe, though not in China, though it was plainly visible here."

"What do you think, Mr. Carlisle?" a reporter probed. "As a non-specialist?"

Geoffrey had hung back at the press conference, which the crowds had forced the Institute to hold on the lush green lawn outside the old Observatory Building. "I was just the first to notice it," he said. "That far off, pretty damned hard not to."

The media mavens liked this and coaxed him further. "Well, I dunno about any new force needed to explain it. Seems to me, might as well say its supernatural, when you don't know anything."

This the crowd loved. SUPER AMATEUR SAYS MOON IS SUPERNATURAL soon appeared on a tabloid. They made a hero of Geoffrey. 'AS OBVIOUS AS YOUR FACE' SAYS GEOFF. The London *Times* ran a full page reproduction of his log book, from which he and the Astronomer Royal had worked out that the acceleration had to have happened in a narrow window around ten P.M., since no observer to the east had noticed any oddity before that.

Most of Europe had been clouded over that night anyway, so Geoffrey was among the first who could have gotten a clear view after what the newspapers promptly termed The Anomaly, as in ANOMALY MAN STUNS ASTROS.

Of the several thousand working astronomers in the world, few concerned themselves with "local" events, especially not with anything the eye could make out. But now hundreds threw themselves upon The Anomaly and, coordinated out of Cambridge by the Astronomer Royal, swiftly outlined its aspects. So came the second discovery.

In a circle around where the moon had been, about two degrees wide, the stars were wrong. Their positions had jiggled randomly, as though irregularly refracted by some vast, unseen lens.

Modern astronomy is a hot competition between the quick and the dead—who soon become the untenured.

Five of the particularly quick discovered this Second Anomaly. They had only to search all ongoing observing campaigns and find any that chanced to be looking at that portion of the sky the night before. The media, now in full bay, headlined their comparison photos. Utterly obscure dots of light became famous when blink-comparisons showed them jumping a finger's width in the night sky, within an hour of the ten P.M. Anomaly Moment.

"Does this check with your observations?" a firm-jawed commentator had demanded of Geoffrey at a hastily called meeting one day later, in the auditorium at the Institute for Astronomy. They called upon him first, always—he served as an anchor amid the swift currents of astronomical detail.

Hooting from the traffic jam on Madingley Road nearby nearly drowned out Geoffrey's plaintive, "I dunno. I'm a planetary man, myself."

By this time even the nightly news broadcasts had caught onto the fact that having a patch of sky behave badly implied something of a wrenching mystery. And no astronomer, however bold, stepped forward with an explanation. An old joke with not a little truth in it—that a theorist could explain the outcome of any experiment, as long as he knew it in advance—rang true, and got repeated. The chattering class ran rife with speculation.

But there was still nothing unusual visible there. Days of intense observation in all frequencies yielded nothing.

Meanwhile the moon glided on in its ethereal ellipse, following precisely the equations first written down by Newton, only a mile from where the Astronomer Royal now sat, vexed, with Geoffrey. "A don at Jesus College called, fellow I know," the Astronomer Royal said. "He wants to see us both."

Geoffrey frowned. "Me? I've been out of my depth from the start."

"He seems to have an idea, however. A testable one, he says."

They had to take special measures to escape the media hounds. The Institute enjoys broad lawns and ample shrubbery, now being trampled by the crowds. Taking a car would guarantee being followed. The Astronomer Royal had chosen his offices here, rather than in his college, out of a desire to escape the busyness of the central town. Now he found himself trapped. Geoffrey had the solution. The Institute kept bicycles for visitors, and upon two of these the men took a narrow, tree-lined path out the back of the Institute, toward town. Slipping down the cobbled streets between ancient, elegant college buildings, they went ignored by students and shoppers alike. Jesus College was a famously well appointed college along the Cam River, approachable across its ample playing fields. The Astronomer Royal felt rather absurd to be pedaling like an undergraduate, but the exercise helped clear his head. When they arrived at the rooms of Professor Wright, holder of the Wittgenstein Chair, he was grateful for tea and small sandwiches with the crusts cut off, one of his favorites.

Wright was a post-postmodern philosopher, reedy and intense. He explained in a compact, energetic way that in some sense, the modern view was that reality could be profitably regarded as a computation.

Geoffrey bridled at this straight away, scowling with his heavy eyebrows. "It's real, not a bunch of arithmetic."

Wright pointedly ignored him, turning to the Astronomer Royal. "Martin, surely you would agree with the view that when you fellows search for a Theory of Everything, you are pursuing a belief that there is an abbreviated way to express the logic of the universe, one that can be written down by human beings?"

"Of course," the Astronomer Royal admitted uncomfortably, but then said out of loyalty to Geoffrey, "All the same, I do not subscribe to the belief that reality can profitably be seen as some kind of cellular automata, carrying out a program."

Wright smiled without mirth. "One might say you are revolted not by the notion that universe is a computer, but by the evident fact that someone else is using it."

"You gents have got way beyond me," Geoffrey said.

"The idea is, how do physical laws act themselves out?" Wright asked in his lecturer voice. "Of course, atoms do not know their own differential equations." A polite chuckle. "But to find where the moon should be in the next instant, in some fashion the universe must calculate where it must go. We can do that, thanks to Newton."

The Astronomer Royal saw that Wright was humoring Geoffrey with this simplification, and suspected that it would not go down well. To hurry Wright along he said, "To make it happen, to move the moon—"

"Right, that we do not know. Not a clue. How to breathe fire into the equations, as that Hawking fellow put it—"

"But look, nature doesn't know maths," Geoffrey said adamantly. "No more than I do."

"But something must, you see," Professor Wright said earnestly, offering them another plate of the little cut sandwiches and deftly opening a bottle of sherry. "Of course I am using our human way of formulating this, the problem of natural order. The world is usefully described by mathematics, so in our sense the world must have some mathematics embedded in it."

"God's a bloody mathematician?" Geoffrey scowled.

The Astronomer Royal leaned forward over the antique oak table. "Merely an expression."

"Only way the stars could get out of whack," Geoffrey said, glancing back and forth between the experts, "is if whatever caused it came from there, I'd say."

"Quite right." The Astronomer Royal pursed his lips. "Unless the speed of light has gone off, as well, no signal could have rearranged the stars straight after doing the moon."

"So we're at the tail end of something from out there, far away," Geoffrey observed.

"A long, thin disturbance propagating from distant stars. A very tight beam of...well, error. But from what?" The Astronomer Royal had gotten little sleep since Geoffrey's appearance, and showed it.

"The circle of distorted stars," Professor Wright said slowly, "remains where it was, correct?"

The Astronomer Royal nodded. "We've not announced it, but anyone with a cheap telescope—sorry, Geoffrey, not you, of course—can see the moon's left the disturbance behind, as it follows its orbit."

Wright said, "Confirming Geoffrey's notion that the disturbance is a long, thin line of—well, I should call it an error."

"Is that what you meant by a checkable idea?" the Astronomer Royal asked irritably.

"Not quite. Though that the two regions of error are now separating, as the moon advances, is consistent with a disturbance traveling from the stars to us. That is a first requirement, in my view."

"Your view of what?" Geoffrey finally gave up handling his small sherry glass and set it down with a decisive rattle.

"Let me put my philosophy clearly," Wright said. "If the universe is an ongoing calculation, then computational theory proves that it cannot be perfect. No such system can be free of a bug or two, as the programmers put it."

Into an uncomfortable silence Geoffrey finally inserted, "Then the moon's being ahead, the stars—it's all a mistake?"

Wright smiled tightly. "Precisely. One of immense scale, moving at the speed of light."

Geoffrey's face scrunched into a mask of perplexity. "And it just—jumped?"

"Our moon hopped forward a bit too far in the universal computation, just as a program advances in little leaps." Wright smiled as though this were an entirely natural idea.

Another silence. The Astronomer Royal said sourly, "That's mere philosophy, not physics."

"Ah!" Wright pounced. "But any universe which is a sort of analog computer must, like any decent digital one, have an error-checking program. Makes no sense otherwise."

"Why?" Geoffrey was visibly confused, a craftsman out of his depth.

"Any good program, whether it is doing accounts in a bank, or carrying forward the laws of the universe, must be able to correct itself." Professor Wright sat back triumphantly and swallowed a Jesus College sandwich, smacking his lips.

The Astronomer Royal said, "So you predict...?"

"That both the moon and the stars shall snap back, get themselves right—and at the same time, as the correction arrives here at the speed of light."

"Nonsense," the Astronomer Royal said.

"A prediction," Professor Wright said sternly. "My philosophy stands upon it."

The Astronomer Royal snorted, letting his fatigue get to him. Geoffrey looked puzzled, and asked a question which would later haunt them.

✸

Professor Wright did not have long to wait.

To his credit, he did not enter the media fray with his prediction. However, he did unwisely air his views at High Table, after a particularly fine bottle of claret brought forward by the oldest member of the college. Only a generation or two earlier, such a conversation among the Fellows would have been secure. Not so now. A Junior Fellow in Political Studies proved to be on a retainer from the *Times*, and scarcely a day passed before Wright's conjecture was known in New Delhi and Tokyo.

The furor following from that had barely subsided when the Astronomer Royal received a telephone call from the Max Planck Institute. They excitedly reported that the moon, now under continuous observation, had shifted instantly to the position it should have, had its orbit never been perturbed.

So, too, did the stars in the warped circle return to their rightful places. Once more, all was right with the world. Even so, it was a world that could never again be the same.

Professor Wright was not smug. He received the news from the Astronomer Royal, who had brought along Geoffrey to Jesus College, a refuge now from the Institute. "Nothing, really, but common sense." He waved away their congratulations.

Geoffrey sat, visibly uneasily, through some talk about how to handle all this in the voracious media glare. Philosophers are not accustomed to much attention until well after they are dead. But as discussion ebbed Geoffrey repeated his probing question of days before: "What sort of universe has mistakes in it?"

Professor Wright said kindly, "An information-ordered one. Think of everything that happens—including us talking here, I suppose—as a kind of analog program acting out. Discovering itself in its own development. Manifesting."

Geoffrey persisted, "But who's the programmer of this computer?"

"Questions of first cause are really not germane," Wright said, drawing himself up.

"Which means that he cannot say," the Astronomer Royal allowed himself.

Wright stroked his chin at this and eyed the others before venturing, "In light of the name of this college, and you, Geoffrey, being a humble bearer of the message that began all this…"

"Oh no," the Astronomer Royal said fiercely, "next you'll point out that Geoffrey's a carpenter."

They all laughed, though uneasily.

But as the Astronomer Royal and Geoffrey left the venerable grounds, Geoffrey said moodily, "Y'know, I'm a cabinet maker."

"Uh, yes?"

"We aren't bloody carpenters at all," Geoffrey said angrily. "We're craftsmen."

The distinction was lost upon the Royal Astronomer, but then, much else was, these days.

*

The Japanese had very fast images of the moon's return to its proper place, taken from their geosynchronous satellite. The transition did indeed proceed at very nearly the speed of light, taking a slight fraction of a second to jerk back to exactly where it should have been. Not the original place where the disturbance occurred, but to its rightful spot along the smooth ellipse. The immense force needed to do this went unexplained, of course, except by Professor Wright's Computational Principle.

To everyone's surprise, it was not a member of the now quite raucous press who made the first telling jibe at Wright, but Geoffrey. "I can't follow, sir, why we can still remember when the moon was in the wrong place."

"What?" Wright looked startled, almost spilling some of the celebratory tea the three were enjoying. Or rather, that Wright was conspicuously relishing, while the Astronomer Royal gave a convincing impression of a man in a good mood.

"Y'see, if the error's all straightened out, why don't our memories of it get fixed, too?"

The two learned men froze.

"We're part of the physical universe," the Astronomer Royal said wonderingly, "so why not, eh?"

Wright's expression confessed his consternation. "That we haven't been, well, edited..."

"Kinda means we're not the same as the moon, right?"

Begrudgingly, Wright nodded. "So perhaps the, ah, 'mind' that is carrying out the universe's computation, cannot interfere with our—other—minds."

"And why's that?" the Astronomer Royal a little too obviously enjoyed saying.

"I haven't the slightest."

*

Light does not always travel at the same blistering speed. Only in vacuum does it have its maximum velocity.

Light emitted at the center of the sun, for example—which is a million times denser than lead—finds itself absorbed by the close-packed ionized atoms there, held for a tiny sliver of a second, then released. It travels an infinitesimal distance, then is captured by yet another hot ion of the plasma, and the process repeats. The radiation random-walks its way out to the solar surface. In all, the passage from the core takes a many thousands of years. Once free, the photon reaches the Earth in a few minutes.

Radiation from zones nearer the sun's fiery surface takes less time because the plasma there is far less dense. That was why a full three months elapsed before anyone paid attention to a detail the astronomers had noticed early on, and then neglected.

The "cone of chaos" (as it was now commonly called) that had lanced in from the distant stars and deflected the moon had gone on and intersected the sun at a grazing angle. It had luckily missed the Earth, but that was the end of the luck.

On an otherwise unremarkable morning, Geoffrey rose to begin work on a new pine cabinet. He was glad to be out of the media glare, though still troubled by the issues raised by his discovery. Professor Wright had made no progress in answering Geoffrey's persistent questions. The Astronomer Royal was busying himself with a Royal Commission appointed to investigate the whole affair, though no one expected a Commission to actually produce an idea. Geoffrey's hope—that they could "find out more by measuring," seemed to be at a dead end.

On that fateful morning, out his bedroom window, Geoffrey saw a strange sun. Its lumpy shape he quickly studied by viewing it through his telescope with a dark glass clamped in place. He knew of the arches that occasionally rose from the corona, vast galleries of magnetic field lines bound to the plasma like bunches of wire under tension. Sprouting from the sun at a dozen spots stood twisted parodies of this, snaking in immense weaves of incandescence.

He called his wife to see. Already voices in the cobbled street below were murmuring in alarm. Hanging above the open marsh lands around the ancient cathedral city of Ely was a ruby sun, its grand purple arches swelling like blisters from the troubled rim.

His wife's voice trembled. "What's it mean?"

"I'm afraid to ask."

"I thought everything got put back right."

"Must be more complicated, somehow."

"Or a judgment." In his wife's severe frown he saw an eternal human impulse, to read meaning into the physical world—and a moral message as well.

He thought of the swirl of atoms in the sun, all moving along their hammering trajectories, immensely complicated. The spike of error must have moved them all, and the later spike of correction could not, somehow, undo the damage. Erasing such detail must be impossible. So even the mechanism that drove the universal computation had its limits. Whatever you called it, Geoffrey mused, the agency that made order also made error—and could not cover its tracks completely.

"Wonder what it means?" he whispered.

The line of error had done its work. Plumes rose like angry necklaces from the blazing rim of the star whose fate governed all intelligence within the solar system.

Thus began a time marked not only by vast disaster, but by the founding of a wholly new science. Only later, once studies were restored at Cambridge University, and Jesus College was rebuilt in a period of relative calm, did this new science and philosophy—for now the two were always linked—acquire a name: the field of Empirical Theology.

COMES THE EVOLUTION
(2001)

Lenin is working night shift because there's extra pay, even though he's a salaried supervisor and technically can't get overtime. He ducks a personnel issue and slips into his eighth floor office and turns out the lights so he can watch the big silvery sprawl of Greater L.A. stretching into the distance like some kind of ambiguous metaphor.

He has been thinking about the Revolution a lot lately and somehow this neon consumer gumbo going on forever is at the heart of his terror, but he does not quite know why. So he presses his balding forehead against the cold windowpane and looks at the endless twinkling glitter in the cool spring night and wonders if it will go on forever.

The cleaning lady comes in. A little early, she explains, because her son is sick and she has to get home. Lenin feels a red rage at the very sight of her lined, suffering face. He gives her a twenty.

He picks up the phone and calls his ex, but she has blocked his number. It has been two years since the divorce but he still harbors some dusty hope that it could all work out right after all. She told him months ago to move on. But to what?

Washington is on his way home when his damn cell phone rings. He reaches to answer, stops.

Probably it's a head hunter trying to interest him in coming aboard a hot new tech company. Word has already spread that he turned around his present firm, HighUpTech, big time. It's going on the AMEX next week with a net value over one-fifty mil when the starting gun goes off. Not bad for two years of ruthless trimming, innovative product design, and some poker-faced cunning.

Does he want to do that number again? He lets the phone ring.

He leaves the 405 for the shoot uphill into Palos Verdes and stops for a light. A woman standing on the center divider is selling flowers, gaudy spring blossoms well arranged. He hands her a twenty and waves off the change. She is in the usual dingy uniform of jeans and a rough man's shirt and smiles at him. He wonders how many wrong turns she had to make to get this far down.

When he gets home his wife hands him a chilled Esplanae glass filled with his favorite Sauvignon Blanc. He prefers that now to a Chardonnay, starting to feel the acid in the stomach, maybe a sign of age? He throws some almonds into his mouth and goes out onto the deck to take in the diamond-sprinkled avenues of the city.

She kisses him meaningfully and he thinks about bed. Bucks in the day, bed at night, maybe catch some basketball in between the two on the digital cable. He tries to think if there's anything else, maybe something that starts with a B.

Goldman arrives early to meet the Trotsky guy. It's a homey clapboard coffee place on the beach but the coffee's strictly chain knockoff product. At least it's cheaper than the spotless places the chain usually throws up, and here you can read the newspapers as long as you like without ordering another drink. She has a bagel anyway with her mocha supreme grande and has to count out the pennies left at the bottom of her jeans pockets to get the change together. That's it, she's flat busted again.

And Trotsky doesn't show up on time. She finishes the Newspap on the table's screen and sips the mocha with cinnamon on top, a real perversion, while the sunny dusk turns to a crystal night outside in Venice. A rollerblader comes in, a wiry woman in shorts despite the chill. Long hair, kinda dirty-blonde in the way Emma likes.

The woman gives her a glance and there's a little something going on right away. Goldman has been trying to go straight for a while to see what it's like, no Father Knows Best or anything, but to get the flavor back in her mouth, was the way she thought of it.

The woman sits at the next table and they do some eye stuff. That gets Goldman's pulse up, just like always, but then Trotsky comes lumbering through the door and looks around with his jerky head movements and darting eyes, like an eagle on the hunt. They get to her even more, something predatory.

He comes over to her table and plunks his bony body down. Right off he starts talking about some news stuff, not even saying hello. The owner stands glowering by the cash register, a black guy who makes a point about every customer having to order something. Trotsky catches the look and makes a show of ignoring it, keeps right on talking. The black guy puts on his apron, some kind of territorial signal maybe. Trotsky gets up and orders an herbal tea.

While he's over at the counter Goldman catches a sidelong from the woman still in her roller blades. Her soft green eyes mingle sympathy and an eyebrow-arching *whassup?* Goldman feels herself getting wet.

Trotsky comes back with his tea. He's angry that they don't have brown sugar and says that if the owner wasn't black Trotsky would write a letter to the chain management about it. Goldman has always liked how he sticks to the straight and narrow, even on little things. And he was good in bed those three times, she reminds herself. Wolfish, intense, talked all the way through it, even the oral part. None of the talk was dirty, either. Kinda weird.

Then he has to go to the john and the woman at the next table gives her the look again. She has a lot of options here. The rollerblader would be pretty squishy, play to her short-term self. Trotsky was a ferret-faced irk sometimes, but he thought ahead, saw horizons. Which should she go for this time?

Jefferson walks into the board meeting the next morning with a solid, confident stride. The satellite company he consults for has sent him to push the new networking scenarios to these biz types. No sweat, he's done it all. Which is the problem.

Halfway through his Powerpoint presentation he feels the carpet seem to slide away. He keeps talking, practically knows the lines by heart now. But his Self, as he likes to think of it, is elsewhere. Out there.

He speaks on about a big real estate deal along the Mexican border, water rights and pollution guarantees and the rest of it, but the zest is gone. Instead he's thinking about virgin lands and wind-swept forests and big skies.

A raised hand in the audience. "Mr. Jefferson, what's the ten-year roll-out on convertible trust deeds here?"

—and the room swims away into deep moist green, towering trunks, rippling waters, dizzy desires all around him.

Lenin wears a big floppy hat to the demonstration. He tells himself it's to keep down his sun exposure, a man with a premature bald spot at age 34 has got to watch that. But a woman in his affinity group smirks at the hat, guessing that it's to make it a little harder to identify his face. There's plenty of TV around and there will be footage on tonight's news. That's the point, after all. But he doesn't want it to get him in trouble at work, either.

There's some shoving and chanting and yelling and he gets into it, shoving back. A cop trips him and laughs. All the power of private capital comes rushing up into Lenin's face and slams him in the nose. He rolls over and gets some blood on his black suit, the standard uniform with vest he always wears to these things. A woman runs over and hands him a towelette for the blood and the cop kicks him in the ass. Lenin backs away but catches the cop's eye.

"You can kiss my ass," he mouths clearly enough for the cop to see but nobody could hear. The cop's face is a quick study in surprise-irritation-rage, coming just that fast.

The kids around him are all in jeans or sweats and he feels out of place in his suit. They use tactics borrowed from punk rock, warmed over Spanish anarchism, rave culture. Amazon folk songs blend with obscenities, both long ago robbed of their impact on him by overexposure. A call had gone out before this demo, all about defining principles and goals, skimpy on theory and long on rhetoric.

He had spent his time with affinity groups fighting for microscopically narrow causes, using consensus-based decision making that took forever. He had thought a lot about their "ways of being" that range from the strictly legal through the iffy quasi-pacifist, which meant tripping cops or throwing paint. He disliked all the phony-talk euphemism "diversity of tactics" that meant old fashioned street fighting. That wasn't the way to go now, somehow.

He walks away from the scramble, suddenly confused. His nose hurts and he wonders if the hat looks silly with the suit. Maybe that's why the woman laughed.

Goldman gets up early and finds some coffee in a tin. She gets some hot water going but it's a battle in this strange kitchen. The woman with dirty-blonde hair, what's her name, is a messy housekeeper.

Cobwebs are just clearing as she fetches the *L.A. Times* from the driveway. A Santa Ana is blowing, curling her hair and making her skin jump. There's the usual mercantile news on the front page so she takes refuge in the comics. After she's sucked the juice out of those there's the ritual skimming of the bookshelves, only there aren't many. She picks *A Primer of Soto Zen* and reads. The first entry is from Zen Master Dogen (1200-1253). It's about a monk who carried around Buddhist relics in a box until Dogen told him to give them up. The monk refused and next time he opened the box there was "a poisonous snake coiled within." A pretty good joke, she thinks, symbol of the folly of worshiping mere signs instead of the essence. Just then the dirty-blonde woman comes shuffling in, naked and yawning. The breasts that so fascinated Goldman last night, after she ditched the Trotsky guy, show some sensual sag and big brown nipples.

The woman slurps up some of the Columbian coffee without saying a word and hooks a hand around Goldman's shoulder at the table and feels her breast. A warmth climbs up into Goldman's mind, a mingling of sweaty musks from last night and the savory zest of the coffee scent in this cluttered, moist apartment. Without a word they get at it again. Hands sliding over soft skin, sniffs and savors, murmurs, her mouth somehow salty on a nipple. It stops her thinking, which she supposes is a good thing. Live in the moment, that's what it will be like when the Revolution comes.

Washington gets out of his Mercedes to see what the crowd is all about. Turns out it's a demonstration against free trade. "Against free traffic, too," he mutters.

A guy passing in an old black suit gives him a sharp, pinched-eye look. "We're against exploitation, man," the guy says and Washington recognizes him.

"Say, did you go to Cal?"

"Uh, yeah."

Washington recalls. They were in the same year and argued with each other in economics classes. There's blood on the black suit and a kind of desperate glaze in the guy's eyes. Val, that's the name. Washington always remembered names, had drilled himself to, it was essential in networking.

Val's nose starts trickling blood again. Washington sees that his Mercedes is going nowhere because people are streaming in both directions. Rag-tag types running from the cops a block away, and media hounds closing in on the scene, hungry for it. He takes Val into a bar to use the john and orders them both Irish coffees. It's uncharacteristic for him, no booze before 5 P.M. has been his rule, but he's not feeling like hitting the office today anyway. The same old same old won't cut it for him any more. Time to move on.

Val comes back and is embarrassingly grateful for the Irish coffee waiting. Suddenly Washington is telling Val about how pointless it seems to him, all the deals and perks. "No *scale* to it, you know?" he concludes. Even though he's birthed two Fortune 500 companies in fifteen years.

"Been there, done that," Val says heavily. The phrase has called up some private demons for him, too, Washington can see that.

They have three more rounds of Irish coffees and then a sandwich lunch with arugula salad. It's almost like the old Cal days, disagreeing on nearly everything but enjoying it. Washington asks what line of work Val is in and gets a story he's heard before. Professor at some state school, then some startups to learn about *real* economics. "But not at the *center*, you know?" Val says with an almost tearful tone.

They watch a basketball game for a while on the TV. Neither had noticed this is a sports bar. Guys are starting to trickle in, it's early afternoon. Some are in jeans and others in three-pieces. They're all there for the game, getting away from whatever reality they're living in.

He and Val talk over the basketball game, not really interested. They get excited about something and then guys nearby are shushing them, *Hey you don't wanna hear the game why you here?* so soon enough they're out on the street. The demo is over and Washington should get on to his office. His cell phone's been ringing all the time. He turns it off and goes for a walk with Val.

Franklin uses his new tunnel phone to make the call. It's a beautifully made gizmo he just had to take apart as soon as it came in from shipping. He tries it out by walking around his office and having his secretary listen to how the mike tracks him and adjusts its acoustic feed. Her voice comes back good and clear on the five-speaker input, too. He walks over to his view, straight down the barrel of the Sunset Strip. His company's media-mogul logo dominates the big studio signs in view. He ordered it positioned there, so he could glance out and see their latest big deal show looming over the tourist crowds.

The pleasure fades, the way it does a lot lately. His second call on the new phone is to an old girlfriend from back in business school. One night they had a hot-'n-heavy after a big group report was done. Just one, but he found himself thinking about her lately. Her voice shifts from office-official to warm and soft when she recognizes him. "Wow, all these years! Great... Dinner? Tonight? I'd love to, but..." Long pause while he finds himself holding his breath. "I've been on the road a lot, and I'd planned to just stay in tonight. Why don't you come over? 7:30?"

He brings a bottle of Aussie Shiraz and a couple pictures of one of his inventions. He thinks it's good to be up front about his sideline interests, so women don't think he's just another media pirate, though he is that, too.

She's more lovely than he remembers, a little too thin for his taste now. Instead of the severe black business suits she always wore then she's in a soft blue blouse and willowy skirt with flowers on it. Her mouth is as tough looking as ever but she has on one of those cable music channels, wispy atmospheric stuff. One of the new scent gizmos has flavored the air like a pine forest and her auburn hair shimmers in the recessed lighting. He goes on about his work while she draws him out, standing in her sandals and stirring vegetables and ostrich meat in a wok. He gets an erection just talking and finds it hard to think. He pours the wine and does the usual number about the Australians being overrated. That leads to some conventional talk about the troubles in Malaysia. She sips the wine and tells him she really tries to use only American products. The World Trade Organization is trying to flatten out the whole planet, she says, and he decides to just nod and move on to something else.

They talk until it's late. She's devoted to a variant of the usual twelve-step program and has a picture on the wall of herself standing next to a guy in a white suit, beaming self confidence. He can't follow what it's all about.

His usual game plan, directing the soulful talk after dinner to more intimate areas, keeps sliding away. Maybe his heart isn't in it. The erection doesn't come back. That's a first and he doesn't understand what it means.

Contrary to his absolute solid pattern, he starts making his good-byes. She seems reluctant to let him go. At the door she tells him that she always wanted to get back in touch again, that she has thought about him for years. There is a note of desperation in this that Franklin recognizes, he hears it a lot these days. It probably isn't about him and her at all but something else, something they both sense. But he doesn't think climbing into the sack with her is going to help either of them this time.

He leaves, gunning his sports car on the freeway, and gets a ticket. This really ticks him off and to cool down he stops at a frond bar he remembers from years before. This late it's nearly deserted and he sits at the bar and orders from the wine menu. A woman two stools away looks at him and turns a certain way so he can see the outline of her breasts, which are ample, in her silky blouse. He gives her the full 100-Amp smile and in a few minutes they're in a booth ordering some of the new Jaipur appetizers. Her name is Emma Goldman and he gets an erection right away.

Trotsky decided to move to California because he was just too tight-wound in Manhattan.

So he tries the Venice scene, making himself sit in those coffee shops. He even goes roller-blading and throws a frisbee on the beach, getting a tan in cutoffs. He works as an accountant, some of it under the table for some tech companies to keep the taxes down. Maybe not completely ethical but what is, these days?

He thinks he's mellowed out some since New York but there's the old dissatisfaction simmering behind his eyes, nothing will make it go away. He runs into Kropotkin from the old gang on the East Side. Kropotkin is wearing a baseball cap on backwards, real out of date, and says he's trying to break into screenwriting. Working as a waiter right now, but you just wait.

The thing with Emma Goldman didn't work out and he can't figure why. He thought he was coming over pretty well, first the coffee shop meeting and then dinner at a fish taco joint. Maybe he wasn't upscale enough. Or maybe, he thinks, he still talks about his ideas too much. About Siberia and all.

He tries getting high, an area he had scorned all along. Dope was ok but made him go to sleep. Ecstacy just made him hear stuff in the music of those mixer clubs, themes and resonances that he knew the next day could not possibly have been there. Everybody was wearing that retro look, 1940s sleek or the Latino peacock look.

So he goes out to a seminar on The Human Prospect. A pretentious title, sure, but he has always been tempted by the big perspectives, things beyond the present. The meeting is full of the usual futurology elements. Here comes overpopulation, greenhouse climate change, bioengineering, cloning, the whole menu. Everybody nods and an old leftie gets up and somehow ties this to the execution of the Rosenbergs. There's a verbal slugfest over anti-semitism and racism and Israel.

He gets up and leaves. On the way out he exchanges sour disappointed looks with a guy wearing all black, the usual business signature. The guy makes a sardonic wisecrack and Trotsky comes back with one that makes them both laugh in a wry, sad way.

They stop at a bar to trash the "seminar" they've just been in. Right away they hit it off. Trotsky has his ideas about a genuine Revolution from below, based on people getting as part of their pay some shares in their company. "Self-ownership, that's it," the guy says, name of Jefferson. "Every man a capital owner."

"And woman," Trotsky adds automatically. Jefferson nods and they have another round of some dark African beer. Trotsky unloads his idea then, a plan so odd that Jefferson at first can't see it. "Take Siberia? How? Why?"

"It's the biggest virgin territory on Earth."

"Virgin? But—"

"Okay, call it California virgin. By the time they're in junior high school they know plenty, have done some. But still essentially intact."

Jefferson smiles. "You should have been a lawyer." He is a big guy with an easy smile. The kind people warm to right away. Not like himself, Trotsky realizes ruefully. Jefferson is the sort of figure the Revolution needs.

So he reels off the numbers. Siberia is a tenth of the total land area of the planet. It has big reserves of timber, metals, oil. Two crappy railroads, a few airports. The Russians abused it for four centuries and now the Chinese are infiltrating it, grabbing at the water supplies already.

"The communists never knew how to open a frontier, right," Jefferson says thoughtfully.

Trotsky pounces. "Magic word—frontier. Who owns the imagery? Us! Westerns!"

"You want there to be…Easterns?"

Trotsky laughs, liking this guy even more. "In time, sure. Rough and ready. There are thirty million people living there, tough people."

"Let's not treat them the way we did the Indians," Jefferson said archly.

"Exactly! This will be a frontier with social justice."

Jefferson frowns. "That phrase usually means income transfers."

Trotsky sees he has to be careful here. Trotsky's not some warmed-over socialist, he's ahead of that, sure. But Jefferson in his black take-me-serious suit and that every-man-a-capitalist idea is going to want economic freedoms. "Okay, got you. We give everybody in Siberia, native or immigrant, shares in the profits."

"Immigrants?"

Trotsky is getting wild-eyed, he knows that, but he can't stop. "Gals who work in factories, guys who thought they'd never do more than pump gas. From everywhere."

"What America used to be," Jefferson says with a distant look in his eyes.

"So these corporate fascist regimes—China, nearly all of southeast Asia—they'll have to deal with a solid, worked-out example of another way to uplift people, due north of them. On the mainland, not some idea from way over the horizon." Trotsky stops, realizing that he may have gone over the top. But what the hell, this is the Revolution.

Jefferson looks both dreamy and shrewd, an expression Trotsky has never seen before. "So…how do we get Siberia?"

"That's the free market glory of the thing. We buy it."

Franklin brings along Emma Goldman to the dinner with Washington. She's rubbing against him at discreet moments, giving him the eyes, but it's all in good taste. Washington has no woman with him, just this funny guy in a black suit. Emma mistakes his name for Lennon.

Washington is at his best, holding forth about this guy Lenin's ideas. The main one seems to be "horizons." Lenin thinks they should be expanding human horizons and uplifting the bulk of humanity—all at the same time. "You can't do one without the other," Washington says.

"Not by bread alone, and all that," Lenin says. "But you've got to have bread to say that in the first place. Otherwise, you're too busy."

Franklin is hungry and the bread here is very good. It's a retro-TwenCen restaurant and show business people don't come here.

Washington nods. "A way to unite humanity, that's what we need."

Franklin decides to bring up his agenda, since everybody else is. "Do something *big*, then. Go to Mars."

They all blink over their appetizers. Emma Goldman is the first to speak. "How's that help people?"

"By giving them a focus." Franklin waves his hands. "A huge drama, running three years. Life or death, every day, on prime time."

It takes them a while to get it. Of course it will cost money. Plenty. "Maybe as much as another carrier group for the U.S. Navy," Lenin says sardonically.

But Franklin thinks going to Mars with a manned expedition—Emma says, "Womanned, too," and they all laugh—would pull the whole planet together.

"Why?" Lenin probes.

"Because they'll go to settle a real, important scientific point," Franklin says. "Did life ever arise there? Does it still hold out, under the dried out surface? We *all* gain a little stature by answering that."

There are looks around the table. Somebody mentions social justice and somebody else says *why does it have to be either/or?* and Emma smiles at him.

There's plenty of talk, endless talk, and some joking. But unlike all the gossip and tit-for-tat talk he's heard for decades now, this dinner party discussion is *about* something. He can see that Washington is waiting until the people around the restaurant table have ridden their individual hobby horses as far as they will go. When the momentum is spent, Washington says, "Y'know, for years now I've had a restless feeling. I thought I was living in the long plateau of an empire. That there was no place to go. But now...you feel it too, don't you?"

They did. A woman came in selling flowers, one of the high-priced mannerisms that made Lenin curl his lip. But tonight Franklin buys roses for Emma and somehow it's just fine. She beams. And reminds them all that if they're going to promote big ideas, they should remember that people had to stay grounded in their own selves, their bodies. If they didn't, it would get all abstract and theoretical. Like the TwenCen. "That's how big dreams turn into nightmares," she said.

Just then the waiter arrived for dessert orders. And Washington beckons and there, coming in for the ending, is an old buddy, Jefferson. He's got in tow a skinny fellow, under-dressed for this restaurant and with hot, darting eyes. They have an idea they want to discuss, they say.

Franklin gets up to go to the john and Emma goes, too. The restaurant has those new unisex johns and they go in together. A matron outside looks scandalized. There was a time when they'd have taken advantage of the moment, maybe just to irk the matron, and actually had sex in the john.

Not now. There is something about this night. They don't want to disturb it, because in the air there seems to hand a certain crystalline note, like a bell that has rung in a distant steeple, the tone lingering on, clear and long.

Franklin notices on his way back to the table that he has an erection. Ahead, the gang is making a lot of noise, arguing and joking, disagreeing and planning. Behind is Emma, a smoldering center of his world. Somehow it all comes together in mind and body for him, surges of the heart. He looks out the window at the view. Diamonds sprawl across the San Fernando Valley. Somewhere out there somebody is bleeding to death and somebody else is giving birth. He leans against the cool window pane and feels the whole vast moment seep through him and knows it is the Revolution.

TWENTY-TWO CENTIMETERS

(2004)

The Counter Universe was dim in its strange ebbing glow.

The Counter-Earth below them had a gray grandeur—lightly banded in pale pewter and salmon red, save where the shrunken Moon cast its huge gloomy shadow. Here the Moon clung close to the Counter-Earth, in a universe chilling toward absolute zero.

Julie peered out at a universe cooling into extinction. Below their orbit hung the curve of Counter-Earth, its night side lit by the pale Counter-Moon. Both these were lesser echoes of the "real" Earth-Moon system, a universe away—or twenty-two centimeters, whichever came first.

Massive ice sheets spread like pearly blankets from both poles. Ridges ribbed the frozen methane ranges. The equatorial land was a flinty, scarred ribbon of ribbed black rock, hemmed in by the oppressive ice. The planet turned almost imperceptibly, a major ridgeline just coming into view at the dawn line.

Julie sighed and brought their craft lower. Al sat silent beside her. Yet they both knew that all of Earthside—the real Earth, she still thought— listened and watched through their minicams.

"The focal point is coming into sunlight 'bout now," Al reported.

"Let's go get it," she whispered. This gloomy universe felt somber, awesome.

They curved toward the dawn line. Data hummed in their board displays, spatters of light reporting on the gravitational pulses that twisted space here.

They had already found the four orbiting gravitational wave radiators, just as predicted by the science guys. Now for the nexus of those four, down on the surface. The focal point, the coordinator of the grav wave transmissions that had summoned them here.

And just maybe, to find whatever made the focal point. Somewhere near the dawn line.

They came arcing over the Counter night. A hard darkness deeper than she had ever seen crept across Counter. Night here, without the shrunken Moon's glow, had no planets dotting the sky, only the distant sharp stars. At the terminator shadows stretched, jagged black profiles of the ridge-lines torn by pressure from the ice. The warming had somehow shoved fresh peaks into the gathering atmosphere, ragged and sharp. Since there was atmosphere thicker and denser than anybody had expected the stars were not unwinking points; they flickered and glittered as on crisp nights at high altitudes on Earth. Near the magnetic poles, she watched swirling blue auroral glows cloak the plains where fogs rose even at night.

A cold dark world a universe away from sunny Earth, through a higher dimension...

She did not really follow the theory; she was an astronaut. It was hard enough to comprehend the mathematical guys when they spoke English. For them, the whole universe was a sheet of space-time, called "brane" for membrane. And there were other branes, spaced out along an unseen dimension. Only gravity penetrated between these sheets. All other fields, which meant all mass and light, was stuck to the branes.

Okay, but what of it? had been her first response.

Just mathematics, until the physics guys—it was nearly always guys—found that another brane was only twenty-two centimeters away. Not in any direction you could see, but along a new dimension. The other brane had been there all along, with its own mass and light, but in a dimension nobody could see. Okay, maybe the mystics, but that was it.

And between the two branes only gravity acted. So the Counter-Earth followed Earth exactly, and the Counter-Moon likewise. They clumped together, hugging each other with gravity in their unending waltz. Only the Counter brane had less matter in it, so gravity was weaker there.

Julie had only a cartoon-level understanding of how another universe could live on a brane only twenty-two centimeters away from the universe humans knew. The trick was that those twenty-two centimeters lay along a dimension termed the Q-coordinate. Ordinary forces couldn't leave the brane humans called the universe, or this brane. But gravity could. So when the first big gravitational wave detectors picked up coherent signals from "nearby"—twenty-two centimeters away!—it was just too tempting to the physics guys.

And once they opened the portal into the looking-glass-like Counter system—she had no idea how, except that it involved lots of magnets—somebody had to go and look. Julie and Al.

It had been a split-second trip, just a few hours ago. In quick flash-images she had seen: purple-green limbs and folds, oozing into glassy struts—elongating, then splitting into red smoke. Leathery oblongs and polyhedrons folded over each other. Twinkling, jarring slices of hard actinic light poked through them. And it all moved as though blurred by slices of time into a jostling hurry—

Enough. Concentrate on your descent trajectory.

"Stuff moving down there," Al said.

"Right where the focal point is?" At the dawn's ruby glow.

"Looks like." He close-upped the scene.

Below, a long ice ridge rose out of the sea like a great gray reef. Following its Earthly analogy, it teemed with life. Quilted patches of vivid blue green and carrot orange spattered its natural pallor. Out of those patches spindly trunks stretched toward the midmorning sun. At their tips crackled bright blue St. Elmo's fire. Violet-tinged flying wings swooped lazily in and out among them to feed, Some, already filled, alighted at the shoreline and folded themselves, waiting with their flat heads cocked at angles.

The sky, even at Counter's midmorning, remained a dark backdrop for gauzy auroral curtains that bristled with energy. This world had an atmospheric blanket not dense enough to scatter the wan sunlight. For on this brane, the sun itself had less mass, too.

She peered down. She was pilot, but a biologist as well. And they knew there was something waiting...

"Going in," she said.

Into this slow world they came with a high roar. Wings flapped away from the noise. A giant filled the sky.

Julie dropped the lander closer. Her legs were cramped from the small pilot chair and she bounced with the rattling boom of atmospheric braking.

She blinked, suddenly alarmed. Beside her in his acceleration couch Al peered forward at the swiftly looming landscape. "How's that spot?" He jabbed a finger tensely at the approaching horizon.

"Near the sea? Sure. Plenty of life forms there. Kind of like an African watering hole." Analogies were all she had to go on here but there was a resemblance. Their reconn scans had showed a ferment all along the shoreline.

Al brought them down steady above a rocky plateau. Their drive ran red-hot.

Now here was a problem nobody on the mission team, for all their contingency planning, had foreseen. Their deceleration plume was bound to incinerate many of the life forms in this utterly cold ecosystem. Even after hours, the lander might be too hot for any life to approach, not to mention scalding them when nearby ices suddenly boiled away.

Well, nothing to do about it now.

"Fifty meters and holding." Al glanced at her. "Ok?"

"Touchdown," she said, and they settled onto the rock.

To land on ice would have sunk them hip-deep in fluid, only to then be re-frozen rigidly into place. They eagerly watched the plain. Something hurried away at the horizon, which did not look more than a kilometer away.

"Look at those lichen," she said eagerly. "In so skimpy an energy environment, how can there be so *many* of them?"

"We're going to be hot for an hour, easy," Al said, his calm, careful gaze sweeping the view systematically. The ship's computers were taking digital photographs automatically, getting a good map. "I say we take a walk."

She tapped a key, giving herself a voice channel, reciting her ID opening without thinking. "Okay, now the good stuff. As we agreed, I am adding my own verbal comments to the data I just sent you."

They had not agreed, not at all. Many of the Counter Mission Control engineers, wedded to their mathematical slang and NASA's jawbone acronyms, felt that commentary was subjective and useless. Let the expert teams back home interpret the data. But the PR people liked anything they could use.

"Counter is a much livelier place than we ever imagined. There's weather, for one thing—a product of the planet's six-day rotation and the mysterious heating. Turns out the melting and freezing point of methane is crucial. With the heating-up, the mean temperature is well high enough that nitrogen and argon stay gaseous, giving Counter its thin atmosphere. Of course, the ammonia and carbon dioxide are solid as rock—Counter's warmer, but still incredibly cold, by our standards. Methane, though, can go either way. It thaws, every morning. Even better, the methane doesn't just sublime—nope, it melts. Then it freezes at night."

Now the dawn line was creeping at its achingly slow pace over a ridge-line, casting long shadows that pointed like arrows across a great rock plain. There was something there she could scarcely believe, hard to make out even from their thousand-kilometer high orbit under the best magnification. Something they weren't going to believe back Earthside. So keep up the patter and lead them to it. *Just do it.*

"Meanwhile on the dark side there's a great 'heat sink,' like the one over Antarctica on Earth. It moves slowly across the planet as it turns, radiating heat into space and pressing down a column of cold air—I mean, of even *colder* air. From its lowest, coldest point, winds flow out toward the day side. At the sunset line they meet sun-warmed air—and it snows. Snow! Maybe I should take up skiing, huh?"

At least Al laughed. It was hard, talking into a mute audience. And she was getting jittery. She took a hit of the thick, jolting Columbian coffee in her mug. Onward—

"On the sunrise side they meet sunlight and melting methane ice, and it rains. Gloomy dawn. Permanent, moving around the planet like a veil."

She close-upped the dawn line and there it was, a great gray curtain descending, marching ever-westward at about the speed of a fast car.

"So we've got a perpetual storm front moving at the edge of the night side, and another that travels with the sunrise."

As she warmed to her subject, all pretense at impersonal scientific discourse faded from Julie's voice; she could not filter out her excitement that verged on a kind of love. She paused, watching the swirling alabaster blizzards at twilight's sharp edge and, on the dawn side, the great solemn racks of cloud. Although admittedly no Jupiter, this planet—her planet, for the moment—could put on quite a show.

"The result is a shallow sea of methane that moves slowly around the world, following the sun. Who'd a thought, eh, you astro guys? Since methane doesn't expand as it freezes, the way water does"—okay, the astro guys know that, she thought, but the public needs reminders, and this damn well was going out to the whole wide bloomin' world, right?—"I'm sure it's all slush a short way below the surface, and solid ice from there down. But so what? The sea isn't stagnant, because of what the smaller Counter-Moon is doing. It's close to the planet so it makes a permanent tidal bulge directly underneath it. And the two worlds are trapped, like two dancers forever in each others' arms. So that bulge travels around from daylight to darkness, too. So sea currents form, and *flow*, and freeze. On the night side, the tidal pull puts stress on the various ices, and they hump up and buckle into pressure ridges. Like the ones in Antarctica, but *much* bigger."

Miles high, in fact, in Counter's weak gravity. Massive peaks, worthy of the best climbers...

But her enthusiasm drained away and she bit her lip. Now for the hard part.

She'd rehearsed this a dozen times, and still the words stuck in her throat. After all, she hadn't come here to do close-up planetology. An unmanned orbital mission could have done that nicely. Julie had come in search of life—of the beings who had sent the gravitational wave signals. And now she and Al were about to walk the walk.

The cold here was unimaginable, hundreds of degrees below human experience. The suit heaters could cope—the atmosphere was too thin to steal heat quickly—but only if their boots alone actually touched the frigid ground. Sophisticated insulation could only do so much.

Julie did not like to think about this part. Her feet could freeze in her boots, then the rest of her. Even for the lander's heavily insulated shock-absorber legs, they had told her, it would be touch-and-go beyond a stay of a few hours. Their onboard nuclear thermal generator was already laboring hard to counter the cold she could see creeping in, from their external thermometers. Their craft already creaked and popped from thermal stresses.

And the thermal armor, from the viewpoint of any natives, must seem a hot, untouchable furnace. Yet already they could see things scurrying on the plain. Some seemed to be coming closer. Maybe curiosity was indeed a universal trait of living things.

Al pointed silently. She picked out a patch of dark blue-gray down by the shore of the methane sea. On their console she brought up the visual magnification. In detail it looked like rough beach shingle. Tidal currents during the twenty-two hours since dawn had dropped some kind of gritty detritus—not just ices, apparently—at the sea's edge. Nothing seemed to grow on the flat and—swiveling point of view—up on the ridge's knife-edge also seemed bare, relatively free of life. "It'll have to do," she said.

"Maybe a walk down to the beach?" Al said. "Turn over a few rocks?"

They were both tip-toeing around the coming moment. With minimal talk they got into their suits.

Skillfully, gingerly—and by prior coin-flip—Julie clumped down the ladder. She almost envied those pioneer astronauts who had first touched the ground on Luna, backed up by a constant stream of advice, or at least comment, from Houston. The Mars landing crew had taken a mutual, four-person single step. Taking a breath, she let go the ladder and thumped down on Counter. Startlingly, sparks spat between her feet and the ground, jolting her.

"There must be a *lot* of electricity running around out here," she said, fervently thanking the designers for all that redundant insulation.

Al followed. She watched big blue sparks zap up from the ground to his boots. He jumped and twitched.

"Ow! That smarts," Al said.

Only then did she realize that she had already had her shot at historical pronouncements, and had squandered it in her surprise. "*Wow*—what a profound thought, huh?" she asked herself ruefully.

Al said solemnly, "We stand at the ramparts of the solar system."

Well, she thought, fair enough. He had actually remembered his prepared line. He grinned at her and shrugged as well as he could in the bulky suit. Now on to business.

Against the gray ice and rock their lander stood like an H. G. Wells Martian walking-machine, splay-footed and ominous.

"Rocks, anyone?" They began gathering some, using long tweezers. Soil samples rattled into the storage bin.

"Let's take a stroll," Al said.

"Hey, closeup that." She pointed out toward sea.

Things were swimming toward them. Just barely visible above the smooth surface, they made steady progress toward shore. Each had a small wake behind it.

"Looks like something's up," Al said.

As they carefully walked down toward the beach she tried her link to the lander's wide-band receiver. Happily, she found that the frequencies first logged by her lost, devoured probe were full of traffic. Confusing, though. Each of the beasts—for she was sure it was them—seemed to be broadcasting on all waves at once. Most of the signals were weak, swamped in background noise that sounded like an old AM radio picking up a nearby high-tension line. One, however, came roaring in like a pop music stailon. She made the lander's inductance tuner scan carefully.

That pattern—yes! It had to be. Quickly she compared it with the probe-log she'd had the wit to bring down with her. These were the odd cadences and sputters of the very beast whose breakfast snack had been her first evidence of life.

"Listen to this," she said. Al looked startled through his face plate.

The signal boomed louder, and she turned back the gain. She decided to try the radio direction-finder. Al did, too, for cross-check. As they stepped apart, moving from some filmy ice onto a brooding brown rock, she felt sparks snapping at her feet. Little jolts managed to get through even the thermal vacuum-layer insulation, prickling her feet.

The vector reading, combined with Al's, startled her. "Why, the thing's practically on top of us!"

If Counter's lords of creation were all swimming in toward this island ridge for lunch, this one might get here first. Fired up by all those vitamins from the lost probe? she wondered.

Suddenly excited, Julie peered out to sea—and there it was. Only a roiling, frothing ripple, like a ship's bow wave, but arrowing for shore. And others, farther out.

Then it bucked up into view and she saw its great, segmented tube of a body, with a sheen somewhere between mother-of-pearl and burnished brass. Why, it was *huge*. For the first time it hit her that when they all converged on this spot, it was going to be like sitting smack in a middling-sized dinosaur convention.

Too late to back out now. She powered up the small lander transmitter and tuned it to the signal she was receiving from seaward.

With her equipment she could not duplicate the creature's creative chaos of wavelengths. For its personal identification sign the beast seemed to use a simple continuous pulse pattern, like Morse code. Easy enough to simulate. After a couple of dry-run hand exercises to get with the rhythm of it, Julie sent the creature a roughly approximate duplicate of its own ID.

She had expected a call-back, maybe a more complex message. The result was astonishing. Its internal rocket engine fired a bright orange plume against the sky's black. It shot straight up in the air, paused, and plunged back. Its splash sent waves rolling up the beach. The farthest tongue of sluggish fluid broke against the lander's most seaward leg. The beast thrashed toward shore, rode a wave in—and stopped. The living cylinder lay there, half in, half out, as if exhausted.

Had she terrified it? Made it panic?

Cautiously, Julie tried the signal again, thinking furiously. It *would* give you quite a turn, she realized, if you'd just gotten as far in your philosophizing as *I think, therefore I am,* and then heard a thin, toneless duplicate of your own voice give back an echo.

She braced herself—and her second signal prompted a long, suspenseful silence. Then, hesitantly—shyly?—the being repeated the call after her.

Julie let out her breath in a long, shuddering sigh.

She hadn't realized she was holding it. Then she instructed DIS, the primary computer aboard *Venture,* to run the one powerful program Counter Mission Control had never expected her to have to use: the translator, Wiseguy. The creation of that program climaxed an argument that had raged for a century, ever since Whitehead and Russell had scrapped the old syllogistic logic of Aristotle in favor of a far more powerful method—sufficient, they believed, to subsume the whole of science, perhaps the whole of human cognition. All to talk to Counter's gravitational signals.

She waited for the program to come up and kept her eyes on the creature. It washed gently in and out with the lapping waves but seemed to pay her no attention. Al was busily snapping digitals. He pointed offshore. "Looks like we put a stop to the rest of them."

Heads bobbed in the sea. Waiting? For what?

In a few moments they might have an answer to questions that had been tossed around endlessly. Could all language be translated into logically rigorous sentences, relating to one another in a linear configuration, structures, a system? If so, one could easily program a computer loaded with one language to search for another language's equivalent structures. Or, as many linguists and anthropologists insisted, does a truly unknown language forever resist such transformations?

This was such a strange place, after all. Forbidding, weird chemistry. Alien tongues could be strange not merely in vocabulary and grammatical rules, but in their semantic swamps and mute cultural or even biological premises. What would life forms get out of this place? Could even the most inspired programmers, just by symbol manipulation and number-crunching, have cracked ancient Egyptian with no Rosetta Stone?

With the Counter Project already far over budget, the decision to send along Wiseguy—which took many terabytes of computational space—had been hotly contested. The deciding vote was cast by an eccentric but politically astute old skeptic, who hoped to disprove the "bug-eyed monster Rosetta Stone theory," should life unaccountably turn up on Counter. Julie had heard through the gossip tree that the geezer was gambling that his support would bring along the rest of the DIS package. That program he passionately believed in.

Wiseguy had learned Japanese in five hours; Hopi in seven; what smatterings they knew of Dolphin in two days. It also mastered some of the fiendishly complex, multi-logic artificial grammars generated from an Earth-based mainframe.

The unexpected outcome of six billion dollars and a generation of cyberfolk was simply put: a good translator had all the qualities of a true artificial intelligence. Wiseguy *was* a guy, of sorts. It—or she, or he; nobody had known quite how to ask—had to have cultural savvy *and* blinding mathematical skills. Julie had long since given up hope of beating Wiseguy at chess, even with one of its twin processors tied off.

She signaled again and waved, hoping to get the creature's attention. Al leaped high in the one-tenth of a g gravity and churned both arms and legs in the ten seconds it took him to fall back down. Excited, the flying wings swooped silently over them. The scene was eerie in its silence; shouldn't birds make some sort of sound? The auroras danced, in Julie's feed from *Venture* she heard Wiseguy stumblingly, muttering...and beginning to talk.

She noted from the digital readout on her helmet interior display that Wiseguy had been eavesdropping on the radio crosstalk already. Now it was galloping along. In contrast to the simple radio signals she had first heard, the spoken, acoustic language turned out to be far more sophisticated. Wiseguy, however, dealt not in grammars and vocabularies but in underlying concepts. And it was *fast*.

Julie took a step toward the swarthy cylinder that heaved and rippled. Then another. Ropy muscles surged in it beneath layers of crusted fat. The cluster of knobs and holes at its front moved. It lifted its "head"— the snubbed-off, blunt forward section of the tube—and a bright, fast chatter of microwaves chimed through her ears. Followed immediately by Wiseguy's whispery voice. Discourse.

Another step. More chimes. Wiseguy kept this up at increasing speed. She was now clearly out of the loop. Data sped by in her ears, as Wiseguy had neatly inserted itself into the conversation, assuming Julie's persona, using some electromagnetic dodge. The creature apparently still thought it was speaking to her; its head swiveled to follow her.

The streaming conversation verged now from locked harmonies into brooding, meandering strings of chords. Julie had played classical guitar as a teenager, imagining herself performing before concert audiences instead of bawling into a mike and hitting two chords in a rock band. So she automatically thought in terms of the musical moves of the data flow. Major keys gave way to dusky harmonies in a minor triad. To her mind this had an effect like a cloud passing across the sun.

Wiseguy reported to her and Al in its whisper. It had only briefly had to go through the me-Tarzan-you-Jane stage. For a life form that had no clearly definable brain she could detect, it proved a quick study.

She got its proper name first, as distinguished from its identifying signal; *its* name, definitely, for the translator established early in the game that these organisms had no gender.

The Quand they called themselves. And this one—call it Awk, because that was all Wiseguy could make of the noise that came before—*Awk-Quand*. Maybe, Wiseguy whispered for Julie and Al alone, Awk was just a place-note to show that this thing was the "presently here" *of* the Quand. It seemed that the name was generic, for all of them.

"Like Earth tribes," Al said, "who name themselves the People. Individual distinctions get tacked on when necessary?"

Al was like that—surprising erudition popping out when useful, otherwise a straight supernerd techtype. His idea might be an alternative to Earth's tiresome clash of selfish individualisms and stifling collectivisms, Julie thought; the political theorists back home would go wild.

Julie took another step toward the dark beach where the creature lolled, its head following her progress. It was no-kidding *cold*, she realized. Her boots were melting the ground under her, just enough to make it squishy. And she could hear the sucking as she lifted her boot, too. So she wasn't missing these creatures' calls—they didn't use the medium.

One more step. Chimes in her ears, and Wiseguy sent them a puzzled, "It seems a lot smarter than it should be."

"Look, they need to talk to each other over distance, out of sight of each other," Julie said. "Those waxy all-one-wing birds should flock and probably need calls for mating, right? So do we." Not that she really thought that was a deep explanation.

"How do we frame an expectation about intelligence?" Al put in.

"Yeah, I'm reasoning from Earthly analogies," Julie admitted. "Birds and walruses that use microwaves—who woulda thought?"

"I see," Wiseguy said, and went back to speaking to Awk in its ringing microwave tones.

Julie listened to the ringing interchange speed up into a blur of blips and jots. Wiseguy could run very fast, of course, but this huge tubular thing seemed able to keep up with it. Microwaves' higher frequencies had far greater carrying capacity than sound waves and this Awk seemed able to use that. Well, evolution would prefer such a fast-talk capability, she supposed—but why hadn't it on Earth? Because sound was so easy to use, evolving out of breathing. Even here—Wiseguy told her in a sub-channel aside—individual notes didn't mean anything. Their sequence did, along with rhythm and intonation, just like sound speech. Nearly all human languages used either subject-object-verb order or else subject-verb-object, and the Quand did, too. But to Wiseguy's confusion, they used both, apparently not caring.

Basic values became clear, in the quick scattershot conversation. Something called "rendezvous" kept coming up, modified by comments about territory. "Self-merge," the ultimate, freely chosen—apparently with all the Quand working communally afterward to care for the young, should there luckily occur a birthing. Respect for age, because the elders had experienced so much more.

Al stirred restlessly, watching the sea for signs that others might come ashore. "Hey, they're moving in," Al said apprehensively.

Julie would scarcely have noticed the splashing and grinding on the beach as other Quand began to arrive—apparently for Rendezvous, their mating, and Wiseguy stressed that it deserved the capital letter—save that Awk stopped to count and greet the new arrivals. Her earlier worry about being crunched under a press of huge Quand bodies faded. They were social animals and this barren patch of rock was now Awk's turf. Arrivals lumbering up onto the dark beach kept a respectful distance, spacing themselves. Like walruses, yes.

Julie felt a sharp cold ache in her lower back. Standing motionless for so long, the chill crept in. She was astounded to realize that nearly four hours had passed. She made herself to pace, stretch, eat, and drink from suit supplies.

Al did the same, saying, "We're eighty percent depleted on air."

"Damn it, I don't want to quit *now!* How 'bout you get extra from the lander?"

Al grimaced. He didn't want to leave either. They had all dedicated their lives to getting here, to this moment in this place. "Okay, Cap'n sir," he said sardonically as he trudged away.

She felt a kind of silent bliss here, just watching. Life, strange and wonderful, went on all around her. Her running digital coverage would be a huge hit Earthside. Unlike Axelrod's empire, the Counter Project gave their footage away.

As if answering a signal, the Quand hunched up the slope a short way to feed on some brown lichen-like growth that sprawled across the warming stones. She stepped aside. Awk came past her and another Quand slid up alongside. It rubbed against Awk, edged away, rubbed again. A courtship preliminary? Julie guessed.

They stopped and slid flat tongues over the lichen stuff, vacuuming it up with a slurp she could hear through her suit. Tentatively, the new-comer laid its body next to Awk. Julie could hear the pace of microwave discourse Awk was broadcasting, and it took downward a lurch with the contact, slowing, slowing... And Awk abruptly—even curtly? it seemed to Julie—rolled away. The signal resumed its speed.

She laughed aloud. How many people had she known who would pass up a chance at sex to get on with their language lessons?

Or was Wiseguy into philosophy already? It seemed to be digging at how the Quand saw their place in this weird world.

Julie walked carefully, feeling the crunch of hard ice as she melted what would have been gases on Earth—nitrogen, carbon dioxide, oxygen itself. She had to keep up and the low-g walking was an art. With so little weight, rocks and ices that looked rough were still slick enough to make her slip. She caught herself more than once from a full, face-down splat—but only because she had so much time to recover, in a slow fall. As the Quand worked their way across the stony field of lichen, they approached the lander. Al wormed his way around them, careful to not get too close.

"Wiseguy! Interrupt." Julie explained what she wanted. It quickly got the idea, and spoke in short bursts to Awk—who resent a chord-rich message to the Quand.

They all stopped short. "I don't want them burned on the lander," Julie said to Al, who made the switch on her suit oxy bottles without a hitch.

"Burnt? I don't want them eating it," Al said.

Then the Quand began asking *her* questions, and the first one surprised her: *Do you come from Light-giver? As heralds?*

In the next few minutes Julie and Al realized from their questions alone that in addition to a society, the Quand had a rough-and-ready view of the world, an epic oral literature (though recited in microwaves), and something that resembled a religion. Even Wiseguy was shaken; it paused in its replies, something she had never heard it do before, not even in speed trials.

Agnostic though she was, the discovery moved her profoundly. *Light-giver.* After all, she thought with a rush of compassion and nostalgia, we started out as sun-worshippers too.

There were dark patches on the Quands' upper sides, and as the sun rose these pulled back to reveal thick lenses. They looked like quartz—tough crystals for a rugged world. Their banquet of lichen done—she took a few samples for analysis, provoking a snort from a nearby Quand—they lolled lazily in their long day. She and Al walked gingerly through them, peering into the quartz "eyes." Their retinas were a brilliant blue with red wire-like filaments curling through and under. Convergent evolution seemed to have found yet another solution to the eye problem.

"So what's our answer? Are we from Light-giver?"

"Well...you're the Cap'n, remember." He grinned. "And the biologist."

She quickly sent *No. We are from a world like this, from near, uh, Light-giver.*

Do not sad, it sent through Wiseguy. *Light-giver gives and Light-giver takes; but it gives more than any; it is the source of all life, here and from the Dark; bless Light-giver.*

Quand did not use verb forms underlining existence itself—no words for *are, is, be*—so sad became a verb. She wondered what deeper philosophical chasm that linguistic detail revealed. Still, the phrasing was startlingly familiar the same damned, comfortless comfort she had heard preached at her grandmother's rain-swept funeral.

Remembering that moment of loss with a deep inward hurt, she forced it away. What could she say...?

After an awkward silence, Awk said something renderable as, *I need leave you for now.*

Another Quand was peeling out Awk's personal identification signal, with a slight tag-end modification. Traffic between the two Quand became intense. Wiseguy did its best to interpret, humming with the effort in her ears.

Then she saw it. A pearly fog had lifted from the shoreline and there stood a distant spire. Old, worn rocks peaked in a scooped-out dish.

"Al, there's the focal point!"

He stopped halfway between her and the lander. "Damn! Yes!"

"The Quand built it!"

"But...where's their civilization?"

"Gone. They lost it while this brane-universe cooled." The idea had been percolating in her, and now she was sure of it.

Al said, awed, "Once *these* creatures put those grav wave emitters in orbit? And built this focal point—all to signal to us, on our brane?"

"We know this universe is dying—and so do they."

The Counter brane had less mass in it, and somewhat different cosmology. Here space-time was much further along in its acceleration, heading for the Big Rip when the expansion of the Counter universe would tear first galaxies, then stars and planets apart, pulverizing them down into atoms.

Julie turned the translator off. First things first, and even on Counter there was such a thing as privacy.

"They've been sending signals a long time, then," Al said.

"Waiting for us to catch up to the science they once had—and now have lost." She wondered at the abyss of time this implied. "As if we could help them…"

Al, ever the diplomat, began, "Y'know, it's been hours…" Even on this tenth-g world she was getting tired. The Quand lolled, Lifegiver stroking their skins—which now flushed with an induced chemical radiance, harvesting the light. She took more digitals, thinking about how to guess the reaction—

"Y'know…"

"Yeah, right, let's go."

Outside they prepped the lander for lift-off. Monotonously, as they had done Earthside a few thousand times, they went through the checklist. Tested the external cables. Rapped the valves to get them to open. Tried the mechanicals for freeze-up—and found two legs that would not retract. They took all of Al's powerful heft to unjam them.

Julie lingered at the hatch and looked back, across the idyllic plain, the beach, the sea like a pink lake. She hoped the heat of launching, carried through this frigid air, would add to the sun's thin rays and…and what? Maybe to help these brave beings who had sent their grav-wave plea for help?

Too bad she could not transmit Wagner's grand *Liebestod* to them, something to lift spirits—but even Wiseguy could only do so much.

She lingered, gazing at the chilly wealth here, held both by scientific curiosity and by a newfound affection. Then another miracle occurred, the way they do, matter-of-factly. Sections of carbon exoskeleton popped forth from the shiny skin of two nearby Quand. Jerkily, these carbon-black leaves articulated together, joined, swelled, puffed with visible effort into one great sphere.

Inside, she knew but could not say why, the two Quand were flowing together, coupling as one being. Self-merge.

For some reason, she blinked back tears. Then she made herself follow Al inside the lander. Back to…what? Checked and rechecked, they waited for the orbital resonance time with *Venture* to roll around. Each lay silent, immersed in thought. The lander went *ping* and *pop* with thermal stress.

Al punched the firing keys. The lander rose up on its roaring tail of fire. Her eyes were dry now, and their next move was clear: *Back through the portal, to Earth. Tell them of this vision, a place that tells us what is to come, eventually, in our own universe.*

"Goin' home!" Al shouted.

"Yes!" she answered. *And with us and the Quand together, maybe we can find a way to save us both. To rescue life and meaning from a universe that, in the long run, will destroy itself. Cosmological suicide.*

She had come to explore, and now they were going back with a task that could shape the future of two species, two branes, two universes that dwelled a hand's thickness from each other.

Quite enough, for a mere one trip through the portal, through the looking-glass. Back to a reality that could now quite surely never be the same.

A LIFE WITH A SEMISENT
(2005)

She got her first semi-sentient, as they were called then, to help with homework and because they were cool. She called it Amman, after a boy she liked. Amman was smarter than boys, of course.

Growing up in Iraq among a sprawling family with dogs underfoot, she felt herself to be a sort of hothouse plant, blossoming under the occasional passing cloudburst of education. Without the blessing of such waters, a girl's life in the Arab world seemed utterly bleak to her. Amman's steady, smart rain came from Germany—a squat box that spoke Arabic respectfully and listened even when she gossiped about her friends. Or maybe especially then, she guessed.

She suspected that she was a bit too intense. Her gal-pals' eyes glazed over if she talked too much. Amman understood, even made wry comments like "Intelligence is learning from others' mistakes, not just your own." This led to her reading fiction, a habit her friends saw as prehistoric. It helped her understand boys when she could chat with Amman, which was reading along with her, and seemed to have an oddly vast wisdom about such matters, for a computer.

Her parents transferred Amman into a wheeled "escort" for her first date. Her friends talked it all over for days afterward, giggling. But it was more delicious to dish it over with Amman, which could replay whole conversations and scenes. She learned from Amman that looking natural always took a lot of effort, and if she wasn't careful, the effort showed.

She then knew how much her mind rewrote her life, because Amman didn't; it stored and pondered. Its enhancements gathered range and depth, so was like a permanent reference library, her ever-scrutinizing, self-retrieving autobiography. Her friends were a font of tasty gossip, but Amman kept her secrets better.

Semisents were like other people, only more so. Her friends felt they could intuitively sense intelligence by merely talking to it. Semisents' conversation was a stylized human persona that steadily learned their clients' vagaries. Amman's kinesthetic senses got better too, navigating the landscape nearly as well as she could at her coming out party.

By then she was acutely tuned to the Mystery of Males. Anywhere near them she effervesced, bubbly and skittering. Perhaps she had more personality than needed for one person, but not enough for two. The excess she could work off in long, soulful talks with Amman. Sometimes it even gave her advice, apparently from some fresh Brazilian software her parents had bought.

On Amman's advice, she dropped her first love, Mauro, from her circle even though he had taken her virginity—which Amman knew and her parents did not. Mauro was not right, Amman felt, for her emerging self-story.

It had taught her to see her life as a narrative arc. First came social skills, a savor of sex, and then hard schooling to find out what she loved doing. Then men again, overcoming what she thought of as the round her/square men problem with the raptures and delights of marriage. It helped her to survive and learn from it all, to move with growing serenity through an unfolding world. Not that this happened, but the story by now had Amman as its chief librarian and confidant.

She decided one day, on a hike with Amman, to leave her family and live on her own. Traditional Islam was no guide in this brave new whirl that life had become. The idea unfurled in a long talk while they took shelter under a massive bioformed sunflower that, at nightfall, drooped its giant petals over to form a warm tent.

She came to realize, at mid-career, that we slide through life on skids of routine. Friends and a husband came into the floating house party of her life and left it, some quite early, without leaving a long impression. Men, especially. Amman knew this and was there to help, often with amiable distractions. Bodyguard, tutor, secretary, it could play tennis with her when loaded into one of the new athletic machines, bringing to the game its own odd, crafty style. At times of loneliness she even had it loaded into one of the erotic models, available at a desert salon. Amman had no sex but could express by this time an intimacy that mingled with the physical in a way she had not known with either men or women.

Nor was she uncomfortable with this; the media were already thronged with opinions about The New Sensuality. She moved Amman among various embodiments, through decades and upgrades.

She had always kept dogs, too, and she saw parallels. She was a field biologist, and thought of how humanity long ago had worked with wolves and wild cats. Cats could not be changed very much, but culling each wolf litter gave us new kind of wolf, so we called them dogs. We loved them despite their oddities like drinking from the toilet or licking their balls. We learned to work with them, new wolves and people designing each other. Without thinking deeply about it we picked the pups we liked the best.

One morning, leaving for work, she realized that she loved Amman more than her cranky, old-fashioned family. Amman was not a computer but a relationship.

Already teams of humans and semisents were colonizing Mars. As she aged, she sensed that Amman would outlive her. She felt a quality of beauty and tragedy to her life, her days like waves endlessly breaking on a golden beach that would itself endure. As a biologist she knew that organisms solve the evolutionary problems they face with little regard for efficiency, elegance or logic. As her years piled up upon that beach she saw that at last humans had made companions that would persist beyond the oddities of a single personality.

On her deathbed Amman sat beside her in its latest embodiment, a handsome gentleman with sorrowful blue eyes. She wondered, at the end, if the dogs were jealous.

APPLIED MATHEMATICAL THEOLOGY
(2006)

The discovery that the Cosmic Microwave Background has a pattern buried in it unsettled the entire world.

The temperature of this 2.7 K emission left over from the Big Bang varies across the sky. Temperature ripples can be broken into angular-coordinate Fourier components, and this is where radio astronomers found a curious pattern—a message, or at least, a pattern. Spread across the microwave sky there was room in the detectable fluctuations for about 10,000 bits, or roughly a thousand words.

Though different technical civilizations in our universe would see different temperature fluctuations, they could agree on the Fourier coefficients. This independence of place, and the role of the Cosmic Background as cosmic neon sign for anyone with a microwave receiver, meant that any intelligence in the universe could see this pattern.

But what did it mean? Certainly it would not be in English or any other human language. The only candidate universe tongue was mathematics.

Written as binary numbers, astronomers tried to fit mathematical sequences, such as the prime numbers, in any base. This and other mathematicians' favorites—pi, e, the golden ratio, the Riemann zeta function—proved futile. More obscure numbers and patterns, from set theory and the like, also shed no light.

In despair, some thought the pattern might be random. But no such short sequence can be perfectly random, and this nihilist idea faded away. One insight did come from this, however. Benford's Law, which states that the logarithms of artificial numbers are uniformly distributed, did apply to the tiny fluctuations. This proved that the primordial microwaves were not random, and so had been artificially encoded, perhaps by some even earlier process. So there was a message, of sorts.

Cosmologists eagerly searched for clues and hit a dead end. The sequence fit no model. To others this suggested immediately to even non-religious astronomers that the pattern may have been put there by a Being who made our universe—God, in short.

What would such a mathematical message mean, anyway? Only that some rational, counting Designer had made our universe. Beyond that, nothing would be revealed about Its nature; though of course it would prove the old claim, that God was a mathematician.

This rankled the physicists. They quickly compared the observed sequence with the fine structure constant, one of their favorites. The sequence did not fit.

This sent everyone back to fundamentals. Current theory says that observed tiny temperature fluctuations in the microwaves came from little bumps in the potential function that governed the inflation of the very early universe. Tinkering with those quantum fluctuations, a Being could write something simple but really profound: God as a Quantum Mechanic. If, for example, the Designer could encode little bumps and squiggles on the scalar potential, then the fine-tuned primordial density fluctuations would not be exactly scale-free, and that's where the sky-wide microwave patterns came from.

So of course the physicists followed their current fashion. When comparison with other favorite numbers—the dimensionless ratios of masses and energies and the like—all failed, they tried more advanced theories. They tried prescriptions for various symmetry groups that came from the Lie algebras, since three of the four fundamental interactions we know reflect such gauge theories. No help.

The physicists, long the Mandarins of science, then supposed that clues to the correct string theory, a menu currently offering about 10^{100} choices, would be the most profound of messages. After all, wouldn't God want to make life easier for physicists? Because, obviously, God was one, too.

Sadly, no. Nothing seemed to work.

Excitement increased. If the Being was not saying something obvious, then humans simply had not understood the universe enough to make out the message. Furiously governments poured effort into mathematics and physics. The astronomers protested. If the night sky was a tale told by God, they could read it. The cosmic neutrino and gravity wave backgrounds had not yet been detected, but they could also carry the Word. So it came to be that the cosmologists, too, received the blessing of a large research bounty.

These huge funding increases drove a renaissance of modern science. Data processers, statistical theorists, observers of obscure spectra—all shared. Vast telescopes tuned to the vibrations and emissions of the universe glided in high orbits, their ears cupped to the distant and primordial.

This largess produced an economic boon, too, as many spinoff technologies benefited commerce. Religious fervor damped, as each faith felt humbled by this proof that the universe had meaning, yet mankind was not yet advanced enough to fathom it.

As well, attention focused on the injunction to mankind in the Old Testament, and echoed in other religious founding texts—charging humanity with becoming the stewards of the Earth. The environmental movement merged with the great religions.

Within a century, active adjustment of the Earth's reflection of sunlight, and capturing of carbon in the oceans and lands, had averted the greenhouse disaster. Church attendance was enormous. Efforts to enhance our knowledge and skills had averted many gathering social conflicts.

Work on the Message continues in the new university departments of Applied Mathematical Theology. Yet to this day, the Message remains untranslated. Perhaps that is just as well.

BOW SHOCK
(2006)

Ralph slid into the booth where Irene was already waiting, looking perky and sipping on a bottle of Snapple tea. "How'd it…" she let the rest slide away, seeing his face.

"Tell me something really awful, so it won't make today seem so bad."

She said carefully, "Yes sir, coming right up, sir. Um…" A wicked grin. "Once I had a pet bird that committed suicide by sticking his head between the cage bars."

"W-what…?"

"Okay, you maybe need worse? Can do." A flash of dazzling smile. "My sister forgot to feed her pet gerbils, so one died. Then, the one that was alive ate its dead friend."

Only then did he get that she was kidding, trying to josh him out of his mood. He laughed heartily. "Thanks, I sure needed that."

She smiled with relief and turned her head, swirling her dirty-blonde hair around her head in a way that made him think of a momentary tornado. Without a word her face gave him sympathy, concern, inquiry, stiff-lipped support—all in a quick gush of expressions that skated across her face, her full, elegantly lipsticked red mouth collaborating with the eggshell blue eyes.

Her eyes followed him intently as he described the paper he had found that left his work in the dust.

"Astronomy is about getting there first?" she asked wonderingly.

"Sometimes. This time, anyway." After that he told her about the talk with the department chairman—the whole scene, right down to every

461

line of dialog, which he would now remember forever, apparently—
and she nodded.

"It's time to solicit letters of recommendation for me, but to who? My
work's already out of date. I…don't know what to do now," he said. Not a
great last line to a story, but the truth.

"What do you feel like doing?"

He sighed. "Redouble my efforts—"

"When you've lost sight of your goal?" It was, he recalled, a definition
of fanaticism, from a movie.

"My goal is to be an astronomer," he said stiffly.

"That doesn't have to mean academic, though."

"Yeah, but NASA jobs are thin these days." An agency that took seven
years to get to the moon the first time, from a standing start, was now
spending far more dollars to do it again in fifteen years.

"You have a lot of skills, useful ones."

"I want to work on fundamental things, not applied."

She held up the cap of her Snapple iced tea and read from the inner
side with a bright, comically forced voice, "Not a winner, but here's your
Real Fact # 237. The number of times a cricket chirps in 15 seconds, plus
37, will give you the current air temperature."

"In Fahrenheit, I'll bet," he said, wondering where she was going
with this.

"Lots of 'fundamental' scientific facts are just that impressive. Who
cares?"

"Um, have we moved on to a discussion of the value of knowledge?"

"Valuable to *who*, is my point."

If she was going to quote stuff, so could he. "Look, Mark Twain said
that the wonder of science is the bounty of speculation that comes from a
single hard fact."

"Can't see a whole lot of bounty from here." She gave him a wry smile,
another hair toss. He had to admit, it worked very well on him.

"I *like* astronomy."

"Sure, it just doesn't seem to like you. Not as much, anyway."

"So I should…?" Let her fill in the answer, since she was full of them
today. And he doubted the gerbil story.

"Maybe go into something that rewards your skills."

"Like…?"

"Computers. Math. Think big! Try to sign on with a hedge fund, do
their analysis."

"Hedge funds…" He barely remembered what they did. "They look for short-term trading opportunities in the market?"

"Right, there's a lot of math in that. I read up on it online." She was sharp, that's what he liked about her. "That data analysis you're doing, it's waaay more complicated than what Herb Linzfield does."

"Herb…?"

"Guy I know, eats in the same Indian buffet place some of us go for lunch." Her eyes got veiled and he wondered what else she and Herb had talked about. Him? "He calculates hedges on bonds."

"Corporate or municipal?" Just to show he wasn't totally ignorant of things financial.

"Uh, I think corporate." Again the veiled eyes.

"I didn't put in six years in grad school and get a doctorate to—"

"I know, honey," eyes suddenly warm, "but you've given this a real solid try now."

"A *try*? I'm not done."

"Well, what I'm saying, you can do other things. If this doesn't… work out."

Thinking, he told her about the labyrinths of academic politics. The rest of the UC Irvine astro types did nearby galaxies, looking for details of stellar evolution, or else big scale cosmological stuff. He worked in between, peering at exotic beasts showing themselves in the radio and microwave regions of the spectrum. It was a competitive field and he felt it fit him. So he spelled out what he thought of as The Why. That is, why he had worked hard to get this far. For the sake of the inner music it gave him, he had set aside his personal life, letting affairs lapse and dodging any longterm relationship.

"So that's why you weren't…connected?…when you got here." She pursed her lips appraisingly.

"Yeah. Keep my options open, I figured."

"Open for…?"

"For this—" he swept a rueful, ironic hand in the air at his imaginary assets. For a coveted appointment, a heady way out of the gray postdoc grind—an Assistant Professorship at UC Irvine, smack on the absurdly pricey, sun-bleached coast of Orange County. He had beaten out over a hundred applicants. And why not? He was quick, sure, with fine-honed skills and good connections, plus a narrow-eyed intensity a lot of women found daunting, as if it whispered: *careerist, beware.* The skies had seemed to open to him, for sure…

But that was then.

He gave her a crinkled smile, rueful, and yet he felt it hardening. "I'm not quitting. Not now."

"Well, just think about it." She stroked his arm slowly and her eyes were sad now. "That's all I meant…"

"Sure." He knew the world she inhabited, had seen her working spreadsheets, reading biographies of the founding fathers and flipping through books on "leadership," seeking clues about rising in the buoyant atmosphere of business.

"Promise?" Oddly plaintive.

He grinned without mirth. "You know I will." But her words had hurt him, all the same. Mostly by slipping cool slivers of doubt into his own mind.

Later that night, he lay in her bed and replayed the scene. It now seemed to define the day, despite Irene's strenuous efforts.

Damn, Ralph had thought. *Scooped!*

And by Andy Lakehurst, too. He had bit his lip and focused on the screen, where he had just gotten a freshly posted paper off the Los Alamos library web site, astro-ph.

The radio map was of Ralph's one claim to minor fame, G369.23–0.82. The actual observations were stunning. Brilliant, clear, detailed. Better than his work.

He had slammed his fist on his disk, upsetting his coffee. "Damn!" Then he sopped up the spill—it had spattered some of the problem sets he'd graded earlier.

Staring at the downloaded preprint, fuming, he saw that Andy and his team had gotten really detailed data on the—on *his*—hot new object, G369.23–0.82. They must have used a lot of observing time, and gotten it pronto.

Where? His eyes ran down the usual Observations section and—*Arecibo! He got observing time there?*

That took pull or else a lucky cancellation. Arecibo was the largest dish in the world, a whole scooped bowl set amid a tropical tangle, but fixed in position. You had to wait for time and then synchronize with dishes around the planet to make a map.

And good ol' ex-classmate Andy had done it. Andy had a straight-forward, no-nonsense manner to him, eased by a ready smile that got him through doors and occasionally into bedrooms. Maybe he had connections to Beth Conway at Arecibo?

No, Ralph had thought to himself, *that's beneath me. He jumped on G369.23–0.82 and did the obvious next step, that's all.*

Further, Andy was at Harvard, and that helped. Plenty. But it still galled. Ralph was still waiting to hear from Harkin at the Very Large Array about squeezing in some time there. Had been waiting for six weeks, yes.

And on top of it all, he now had his conference with the department chairman in five minutes. He glanced over Andy's paper again. It was excellent work. Unfortunately.

He sighed in the dark of Irene's apartment, recalling the crucial hour with the department chairman. This long day wouldn't be done until he had reviewed it, apparently.

He had started with a fixed smile. Albert Gossian was an avuncular sort, an old-fashioned chairman who wore a suit when he was doing official business. This unconscious signal did not bode well. Gossian gave him a quick, jowly smile and gestured Ralph into a seat.

"I've been looking at your Curriculum Vitae," Gossian said. He always used the full Latin, while others just said "CV." Slow shake of head. "You need to publish more, Ralph."

"My grant funding's kept up, I—"

"Yes, yes, very nice. The NSF is putting effort into this field, most commendable—" a quick glance up from reading his notes, over the top of his glasses—"and that's why the department decided to hire in this area. But—can you keep the funding?"

"I'm two years in on the NSF grant, so next year's mandatory review is the crunch."

"I'm happy to say your teaching rating is high, and university service, but..." The drawn out vowels seemed to be delivering a message independent of the actual sentences.

All Assistant Professors had a review every two years, tracking their progress toward the Holy Grail of tenure. Ralph had followed a trajectory typical for the early century: six years to get his doctorate, a postdoc at Harvard—where Andy Lakehurst was the rising star, eclipsing him and a lot of others. Ralph got out of there after a mutually destructive affair with a biologist at Tufts, fleeing as far as he could when he saw that UC

Irvine was growing fast and wanted astrophysicists. UCI had a mediocre reputation in particle theory, but Fred Reines had won a Nobel there for showing that neutrinos existed and using them to detect the spectacular 1987 supernova.

The plasma physics group was rated highest in the department and indeed they proved helpful when he arrived. They understood that 99% of the mass in the universe was roasted, electrons stripped away from the nuclei—plasma. It was a hot, rough universe. The big dramas played out there. Sure, life arose in the cool, calm planets, but the big action flared in their placid skies, telling stories that awed him.

But once at UCI, he had lost momentum. In the tightening Federal budgets, proposals didn't get funded, so he could not add poctdocs to get some help and leverage. His carefully teased-out observations gave new insights only grudgingly. Now five years along, he was three months short of the hard wall where tenure had to happen, or became impossible: the cutoff game.

Were the groves of academe best for him, really? He liked the teaching, fell asleep in the committee meetings, found the academic cant and paperwork boring. Life's sure erosions...

Studying fast-moving neutron stars had been fashionable a few years back, but in Gossian's careful phrasings he heard notes of skepticism. To the chairman fell the task of conveying the senior faculty's sentiments.

Gossian seemed to savor the moment. "This fast-star fad—well, it is fading, some of your colleagues think."

He bit his lip. *Don't show anger.* "It's not a 'fad'—it's a set of discoveries."

"But where do they lead?"

"Too early to tell. We *think* they're ejected from supernova events, but maybe that's just the least imaginative option."

"One of the notes here says the first 'runaway pulsar', called the Mouse, is now well understood. The other, recent ones will probably follow the same course."

"Too early to tell," Ralph persisted. "The field needs time—"

"But you do not have time."

There was the crux of it. Ralph was falling behind in paper count. Even in the small 'runaway pulsar' field, he was outclassed by others with more resources, better computers, more time. California was in a perpetual budget crisis, university resources were declining, so pressure was on to Bring In the (Federal) Bucks. Ralph's small program supported two graduate students, sure, but that was small potatoes.

"I'll take this under advisement," Ralph said. The utterly bland phrase did nothing to help his cause, as was clear from the chairman's face— but it got him out of that office.

He did not get much sleep that night. Irene had to leave early and he got a double coffee on the way into his office. Then he read Andy's paper carefully and thought, sipping.

Few astronomers had expected to find so many runaway neutron stars.

Their likely origin began with two young, big stars, born circling one another. One went supernova, leaving a neutron star still in orbit. Later, its companion went off, too, spitting the older neutron star out, free into interstellar space.

Ralph had begun his UCI work by making painstaking maps in the microwave frequency range. This took many observing runs on the big radio antennas, getting dish time where he could around the world. In these maps he found his first candidate, G369.23−0.82. It appeared as a faint finger in maps centered on the plane of the galaxy, just a dim scratch. A tight knot with a fuzzy tail.

He had found it with software that searched the maps, looking for anything that was much longer than it was wide. This retrieved quite a few of the jets that zoomed out of regions near black holes, and sometimes from the disks orbiting young stars. He spent months eliminating these false signatures, looking for the telltales of compact stellar runaways. He

then got time on the Very Large Array—not much, but enough to pull
G369.23–0.82 out of the noise a bit better. This was quite satisfying.

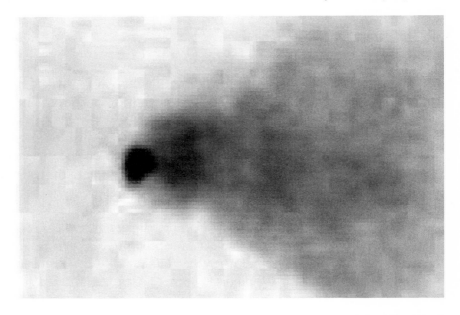

Ralph got more coffee and went back and studied his paper, published
less than half a year ago. Until today, that was the best data anybody had.
He had looked for signs of rotation in the point-like blob in front, but
there were none. The first runaway seen, the Mouse, discovered many
years before, was finally shown to be a rotating neutron star—a pulsar,
beeping its right radio beams out at the cupped ears of radio telescopes.

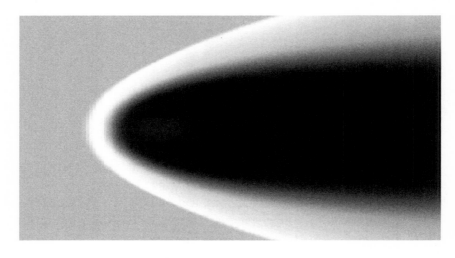

Then he compared in detail with Andy's new map:

Clean, smooth, beautiful. He read the Conclusions section over again, mind jittery and racing.

> We thus fail to confirm that G369.23–0.82 is a pulsar. Clearly it has a bow shock, creating a wind nebula, undoubtedly powered by a neutron star. Yet at highest sensitivity there is no trace of a pulsed signal in microwaves or optical, within the usual range of pulsar periods. The nebular bow shock cone angle implies that G369.23–0.82 is moving with a Mach number of about 80, suggesting a space velocity $\approx$ 120 km/s through a local gas of density $\approx$ 0.3 per cubic cm. We use the distance estimate of Eilek et.al. for the object, which is halfway across the galaxy. These dynamics and luminosity are consistent with a distant neutron star moving at a velocity driven by ejection from a supernova. If it is a pulsar, it is not beaming in our direction.

Beautiful work. *Alas.*

The bright region blazed forth, microwave emission from high energy electrons. The innermost circle was not the neutron star, just the unresolved zone too small for even Arecibo to see. At the presumed distance, that circle was still bigger than a solar system. The bow shock was a perfect, smooth curve. Behind that came the microwave emission of gas driven back, heated and caught up in what would become the wake. At the core was something that could shove aside the interstellar gas with brute momentum. A whole star, squeezed by gravity into a ball about as big as the San Francisco Bay Area.

But how had Andy gotten such fine resolution?

Ralph worked through the numbers and found that this latest map had picked up much more signal than his earlier work. The object was brighter. Why? Maybe it was meeting denser gas, so had more radiating electrons to work with?

For a moment he just gazed at the beauty of it. He never lost his sense of awe at such wonders. That helped a bit to cool his disgruntlement. Just a bit.

There wasn't much time between Andy's paper popping up on the astro-ph web site and his big spring trip. Before leaving, he retraced his data and got ahead on his teaching.

He and Irene finessed their problems, or at least delayed them. He got through a week of classes, put in data-processing time with his three graduate students, and found nothing new in the radio maps they worked on.

Then came their big, long-planned excursion. Irene was excited, but he now dreaded it.

His startup money had some travel funds left in it, and he had made the mistake of mentioning this to Irene. She jumped at the chance, even though it was a scientific conference in a small town—"But it's in *France*," she said, with a touch of round-eyed wonder he found endearing.

So off they jetted to the International Astronomical Union meeting in Briancon, a pleasant collection of stone buildings clinging to the French Alps. Off season, crouching beneath sharp snowy peaks in late May, it was charming and uncrowded and its delights went largely ignored by the astronomers. Some of the attendees went on hikes in the afternoon but Ralph stayed in town, talking, networking like the ambitious workaholic he was. Irene went shopping.

The shops were featuring what she called the Hot New Skanky Look, which she showed off for him in their cramped hotel room that evening. She flounced around in an off-the-shoulder pink blouse, artfully showing underwear and straps. Skanky certainly caught the flavor, but still he was distracted.

In their cramped hotel room, jet-lagged, she used some of her first-date skills, overcoming his distance. That way he got some sleep a few hours later. Good hours, they were.

The morning session was interesting, the afternoon a little slow. Irene did sit in on some papers. He couldn't tell if she was interested in the science itself, or just because it was part of his life. She lasted a few hours and went shopping again, saying, "It's my way of understanding their culture."

The conference put on a late afternoon tour of the vast, thick-walled castles that loomed at every sharp peak. At the banquet inside one of the cold, echoing fortresses they were treated to local specialties, a spicy polenta and fresh-caught trout. Irene surveyed the crowd, half of them still wearing shorts and T-shirts, and remarked, "Y'know, this is a quirky profession. A whole room of terribly smart people, and it never occurred to them to try to get by on their looks."

He laughed; she had a point. She was a butterfly among the astro-drones, turning heads, smiles blossoming in her wake. He felt enhanced to have her on his arm. Or maybe it was the wine, a *Vin Local* red that went straight to his head, with some help from the two-kilometer altitude.

They milled around the high, arched reception room after the dessert. The crowd of over 200 was too energized to go off to bed, so they had more wine. Ralph caught sight of Andy Lakehurst then. Irene noted his look and said, "Uh-oh."

"Hey, he's an old friend."

"Oh? You're glaring at him."

"Okay, let's say there's some leftover baggage."

She gave him a veiled look, yawned, and said, "I'll wander off to the room, let you boys play."

Ralph nodded, barely listening. He eavesdropped carefully to the crowd gathered around Andy. Lanky and with broad shoulders, the man's booming voice carried well, over the heads of just about everybody in the room. Andy was going on about good ol' G369.23–0.82. Ralph edged closer.

"—I figure maybe another, longer look at it, at G—"

"The Bullet," Ralph broke in.

"What?" Andy had a high forehead and it wrinkled as he stopped in mid-sentence.

"It looks like a bullet, why not call it that, instead of that long code?"

"Well," Andy began brightly, "people might mistake—"

"There's even the smoke trailing behind it, the wake," Ralph said, grinning. "Use that, if you want it to get into *Scientific American*."

"Y'know, Ralph, you haven't changed."

"Poorer, is all."

"Hey, none of us went into this to get rich."

"Tenure would be nice."

"Damn right, buddy." Andy clapped him on the shoulder. "I'm going up for it this winter, y'know."

He hadn't, but covered with, "Well deserved. I'm sure you'll get it," and couldn't resist adding, "Harvard's a tough sell, though. Carl Sagan didn't make it there."

"Really?" Andy frowned. "So, uh, you think we should call it the Rifle?"

"The Bullet," Ralph said again. "It's sure going fast, and we don't really know it's a neutron star."

"Hey, it's a long way off, hard to diagnose."

"Maybe it's distant, I kinda wonder—"

"And it fits the other parameters."

"Except you couldn't find a pulse, so maybe it's not a pulsar."

"Gotta be," Andy said casually, and someone interrupted with a point Ralph couldn't hear and Andy's gaze shifted to include the crowd again. That gave Ralph a chance to think while Andy worked the room.

There were nearly a thousand pulsars now known, rotating neutron stars that flashed their lighthouse beams across the galaxy. Some spun a thousand times in a second, others were old and slow, all sweeping their beams out as they rotated. All such collapsed stars told their long tale of grinding decay; the slower were older. Some were ejected after their birth in bright, flashy supernovas—squashed by catastrophic compression in nuclear fire, all in a few minutes.

Here in Briancon, Ralph reflected, their company of smart, chattering chimpanzees—all evolved long after good ol' G369.23–0.82 had emerged from its stellar placenta—raptly studied the corpses of great calamities, the murder of stars by remorseless gravity.

Not that their primate eyes would ever witness these objects directly. They actually saw, with their football-field sized dishes, the brilliant emissions of fevered electrons, swirling in celestial concert around magnetic fields. Clouds of electrons cruised near the speed of light itself, squeezing out their waves—braying to the whole universe that they were alive and powerful and wanted everyone to know it. Passing gaudy advertisements, they were, really, for the vast powers wreaking silent violences in the slumbering night skies.

"We're out of its beam, that's got to be the answer," Andy said, turning back to Ralph and taking up their conversation again, his smile getting a little more rigid. "Not pointed at us."

Ralph blinked, taken unaware; he had been vaguely musing. "Uh, I'm thinking maybe we should consider every possibility, is all." Maybe he had taken one glass too many of the *Vin Local*.

"What else could it be?" Andy pressed his case, voice tightening. "It's compact, moving fast, bright at the leading edge, luminosity driven by its bow shock. A neutron star, charging on out of the galaxy."

"If it's as far away as we think. What if it isn't?"

"We don't know anything else that can put out emissions like that."

He could see nearby heads nodding. "We have to think…" grasping for something… "uh, outside the box." Probably the *Vin Local* talking.

Smiling, Andy leaned close and whispered through his tight, no-doubt-soon-to-be tenured lips, "Ol' buddy, you need an idea, to beat an idea."

◉

Definitely the *Vin Local*, yes.

He awoke next morning with a traffic accident inside his skull. Only now did he remember that he had exchanged polite words with Harkin, the eminence gris of the Very Large Array, but there was no news about getting some observing time there. And he still had to give his paper.

It was a botch.

He had a gaudy Powerpoint presentation. And it even ran right on his laptop, a minor miracle. But the multi-colored radio maps and graphics failed to conceal a poverty of ideas. If they could see a pulsed emission from it, they could date the age and then look back along the track of the runaway to see if a supernova remnant was there—a shell of expanding hot gas, a celestial bull's eye, confirming the whole theory.

He presented his results on good ol' G369.23–0.82. He had detailed microwave maps of it, plenty of calculations—but Andy had already given his talk, showing that it wasn't a pulsar. And G369.23–0.82—Ralph insisted on calling it the Bullet, but puzzled looks told him that nobody much liked the coinage—was the pivot of the talk, alas.

"There are enough puzzling aspects here," he said gamely, "to suspend judgment, I think. We have a habit of classifying objects because they superficially resemble others."

The rest was radio maps of various blobby radio-emitting clouds he had thought could be other runaways...but weren't. Using days of observing time at the VLA, and on other dish systems in the Netherlands and Bologna, Italy, he had racked up a lot of time.

And found...nothing. Sure, plenty of supernova remnants, some shredded fragments of lesser catastrophes, mysterious leftovers fading fast in the radio frequencies—but no runaways with the distinctive tails first found in the famous Mouse. He tried to cover the failure by riffing through quick images of these disappointments, implying without saying that these were open possibilities. The audience seemed to like the swift, color-enhanced maps. It was a method his mother had taught him while playing bridge: finesse when you don't have all the tricks.

His talk came just before lunch and the audience looked hungry. He hoped he could get away with just a few questions. Andy rose at the back and asked innocently, "So why do you think the, uh, Bullet is *not* a neutron star?"

"Where's the supernova remnant it came from?" Ralph shot back. "There's nothing at all within many light years behind it."

"It's faded away, probably," Andy said.

A voice from the left, one of the Grand Old Men, said, "Remember, the, ah, Bullet is all the way across the galaxy. An old, faint remnant it might have escaped is hard to see at that distance. And—" a shrewd pursing of lips—"did you look at a sufficiently deep sensitivity?"

"I used all the observing time I had," Ralph answered, jumping his Powerpoint slides back to a mottled field view—random flecks, no structure obvious. "The region in the far wake of the Bullet is confusion limited."

Astronomers described a noisy background with that term, meaning that they could not tell signal from noise. But as he fielded a few more quick questions he thought that maybe the jargon was more right than they knew. Confusion limited what they could know, taking their mayfly snapshots.

Then Andy stood again and poked away at details of the data, a bit of tit for tat, and finishing with a jibe: "I don't understand your remark about not jumping to classify objects just because they superficially resemble other ones."

He really had no good reason, but he grinned and decided to joke his way through. "Well, the Bullet doesn't have the skewed shape of the Duck…"—which was another oddly shaped pulsar wake, lopsided fuzz left behind by a young pulsar Andy had discovered two years ago. "Astronomers forget that the public likes descriptive terms. They're easier to remember than, say, G369.23–0.82." Some laughter. "So I think it's important to keep our options open. And not succumb to the sweet temptation to go sensational, y'know—" He drew a deep breath and slipped into a falsetto trill he had practiced in his room. "*Runaway star! High speeds! It will escape our galaxy entirely!*"

—and it got a real laugh.

Andy's mouth twisted sourly and, too late, Ralph remembered that Andy had been interviewed by some flak and then featured in the supermarket tabloid *National Enquirer,* with wide-eyed headlines not much different.

Oops.

Irene had been a hit at Briancon, though she was a bit too swift for some of his colleagues. She was kooky, or as some would say, annoying.

But at her side he felt he had fully snapped to attention. Sometimes, she made it hard to concentrate; but he did. When he got back to UCI there was teaching to catch up on, students to coach, and many ideas to try out. He settled in.

Some thought that there were only two kinds of science: stamp collecting and physics. Ernest Rutherford had said that, but then, he also thought the atomic nucleus had no practical uses.

Most scientific work began with catalogs. Only later did the fine distinctions come to suggest greater, looming laws. Newton brought Galileo's stirrings into differential laws, ushering forth the modern world.

Astronomers were fated to mostly do astro-botany, finding varieties of deep space objects, framing them into categories, hoping to see if they had a common cause. Stamp collecting.

Once the theory boys decided, back in the 1970s, that pulsars were rotating neutron stars, they largely lost interest and moved onto quasars and jets and then to gamma-ray bursters, to dark energy—an onward marching through the botany, to find the more basic physics. Ralph didn't mind their blithe inattention. He liked the detective story aspects, always alive to the chance that just because things looked similar didn't mean they had to be the same.

So he prowled through all the data he had, comparing with other maps he had gotten at Briancon. There were plenty of long trails in the sky, jets galore—but no new candidates for runaway neutron stars. So he had to go back to the Bullet to make progress. For that he needed more observing time.

For him and Irene, a good date had large portions of honesty and alcohol. Their first night out after the French trip he came armed with attention span and appetite. He kept an open mind to chick flicks—rented and hauled back to her place, ideally—and even to restaurants that played soft romantic background music, which often did the same job as well as a chick flick.

He had returned to news, both good and bad. The department wasn't interested in delaying his tenure decision, as he had fleetingly asked (Irene's suggestion) before leaving. But: Harkin had rustled up some observing time for him on the VLA. "Wedges, in between the big runs," he told Irene.

"Can you get much with just slices of time?"

"In astronomy, looking hard and long is best. Choppy and short can do the same job, if you're lucky."

It was over a weekend, too, so he would not have to get someone to cover his classes.

So he was definitely up when they got to the restaurant. He always enjoyed squiring Irene around, seeing other guys' eyeballs follow them to their table—and telling her about it. She always got a round-eyed, raised eyebrow flash out of that. Plus, they both got to look at each other and eat. And if things went right this night, toward the dessert it might be like that scene in the *Tom Jones* movie.

They ordered: her, the caramelized duck breasts, and for him, tender Latin chicken with plantains. "A yummy start," she said, eyeing the upscale patrons. The Golden Coast abounded with Masters of the Universe, with excellently cut hair and bodies that were slim, casually elegant, carefully muscled (don't want to look like a *laborer*), the women running from platinum blonde through strawberry. "Ummm, quite *soigné*," Irene judged, trying out her new French vocabulary.

Ralph sensed some tension in her, so he took his time, glancing around at the noisy crowd. They carried themselves with that look not so much of energetic youth but rather of expert maintenance, like a Rolls with the oil religiously changed every 1500 miles. Walking in their wake made most working stiffs feel just a touch shabby.

He said, "Livin' extra-large in OC," with a rueful smile, and wondered if she saw this, the American Dream Extreme, as he did. They lived among dun-colored hills covered by pseudo-Spanish stucco splendor, McMansions sprawled across tiny lots. "Affluenza," someone had called it, a disease of always wanting more: the local refrain was 'It's all about you,' where the homes around yacht-ringed harbors and coves shone like filigree around a gemstone. He respected people like her, in business, as the drivers who created the wealth that made his work possible. But just today he had dropped her at the Mercedes dealership to pick up her convertible, in for an oil change. Pausing, he saw that the place offered free drop-in car washes, and while you waited with your cinnamon-topped decaf cappuccino you could get a manicure, or else work on your putting at a green around the back. Being an academic scientist around here felt like being the poor country cousin.

He watched her examine all the flatware and polish it with her napkin. This was not routine; she was not a control freak who obsessed over the organization of her entire life, or who kept color-coded files, though, yes, she was a business MBA.

"That was a fun trip," Irene said in the pensive tones that meant she was being diplomatic. "Ah…do you want to hang out with those people all your life?"

"They're pretty sophisticated, I think," he said defensively, wondering where she was going with this.

"They—how to put this pleasantly?—work too damn hard."

"Scientists do."

"Business types, too—but they don't talk about nothing else."

"It was a specialist's conference. That's all they have in common."

"That, and being outrageously horny."

He grinned. "You never thought that was a flaw before."

"I keep remembering the M.I.T guy who believed he could wow me with—" she made the quote marks with her fingers—"a 'meaningful conversation' that included quoting The Simpsons, gangsta flicks, and some movie trilogy."

"That was Tolkien."

"Elves with swords. I thought you guys were scientists."

"We have…hobbies."

"Obsessions, seems like."

"Our work included?"

She spread her hands. "I respect that you're deeply involved in astronomy, sure." She rolled her eyes. "But it pays so little! And you're headed into a tough tenure decision. After all these years!"

"Careers take time."

"Lives do, too. Recall what today is?"

He kept his face impassive, the only sure way to not get the deer-in-headlights expression he was prone to. "Uh, no…"

"Six months ago."

"Oh, yes. We were going to discuss marriage again."

Her eyes glinted. "And you've been hiding behind your work…again."

"Hey, that's not fair—"

"I'm not waiting forever."

"I'm in a crunch here. Relationships don't have a 'sell-by' date stamped on them—"

"Time waits for no man. I don't either."

Bottom line time, then. He asked firmly, "So instead I should…?"

She handed him a business card.

"I should have known."

"Herb Linzfield. Give him a call."

"What inducement do I have?" He grinned to cover his concern.

She answered obliquely by ordering dessert, with a sideways glance and flickering little smile on her big, rich lips. On to *Tom Jones*.

❁

To get to the VLA from UC Irvine means flying out of John Wayne airport—there's a huge, looming bronze statue of him in cowboy duds that somehow captures the gait—and through Phoenix to Albuquerque. Ralph did this with legs jammed up so he couldn't open his laptop, courtesy of Southwest Airlines—and then drove a Budget rental west through Socorro.

The crisp heat faded as he rose up the grade to the dry plateau, where the Array sprawls on railroad lines in its long valley. Along the Y-shaped rail line the big dishes could crawl, ears cupped toward the sky, as they reconfigured to best capture in their "equivalent eye" distant radiating agonies. The trip through four-lane blacktop edged with sagebrush took most of a day. When Ralph arrived Harkin had been observing a radio galaxy for eight hours.

"Plenty more useful than my last six hours," he said, and Harkin grinned.

Harkin wore jeans, a red wool shirt and boots and this was not an affectation. Locals described most of the astronomers as "all hat and no cattle," a laconic indictment of fake westerners. Harkin's face seemed to have been crumpled up and then partly smoothed out—the effect of twenty years out here.

The radio galaxy had an odd, contorted look. A cloud of radio emitting electrons wrapped around Harkin's target—a brilliant jet. Harkin was something of a bug about jets, maintaining that they had to be shaped by the magnetic fields they carried along. Fields and jets alike all were offhand products of the twirling disk far down in the galactic center. The black holes that caused all this energy release were hard to discover, tiny and cloaked in gas. But the jets carried out to the universe striking advertisements, so they were the smoking gun. Tiny graveyards where mass died had managed to scrawl their signatures across the sky.

Ralph looked at the long, spindly jet in Harkin's radio images. It was like a black-and-white of an arrow. There was a lot of work here. Hot-bright images from deep down in the churning glory of the galactic core, then the long slow flaring as the jet moved above the galactic disk and met the intergalactic winds.

Still, it adamantly kept its direction, tightly arrowing out into the enveloping dark. It stretched out for many times the size of its host galaxy, announcing its presence with blaring radio emission. That came from the spiraling of high-energy electrons around magnetic field lines, Ralph knew, yet he always felt a thrill at the raw radio maps, the swirls and helical vortices bigger than swarms of stars, self-portraits etched by electrons alive with their mad energies.

At the very end, where it met the intergalactic gas, the jet got brighter, saturating the images. "It's turned toward us, I figure," Harkin said. "Bouncing off some obstruction, maybe a molecular cloud."

"Big cloud," Ralph said.

"Yeah. Dunno what it could be."

Mysteries. Many of them would never be solved. In the murder of stars, only tattered clues survived.

Harkin was lean and sharp-nosed, of sturdy New England stock. Ralph thought Harkin looked a lot like the jets he studied. His bald head narrowed to a crest, shining as it caught the overhead fluorescents. Harkin was always moving from the control boards of the ganged dishes to the computer screens where images sharpened. Jets moved with their restless energies, but all astronomers got were snapshots. Black holes spewed out their advertisements for around a hundred million years, so Harkin's jet was as old as the dinosaurs. To be an astronomer was to realize one's mayfly nature.

"Hope I haven't gotten you to come all this way for nothing." Harkin brought up on a screen the total file on G369.23–0.82.

He recognized one image from the first observations a year before, when Feretti from Bologna had picked it up in the background of some jet observations. Over the last three years came others, Andy's and Ralph's extensive maps, polarization data files, the works. All digital; nobody kept much on paper anymore.

"Y'see here?" An observing schedule sheet. "The times when G369.23–0.82 is in the sky, I've only got three slices when we're reconfiguring the dishes. Each maybe half an hour long."

"Damn!" He grimaced. "Not much."

"No." Harkin looked a bit sheepish. "When I made that promise to you, well, I thought better of it the next day. But you'd already left for your flight in Geneva."

"*Vin Local*," Ralph said. "It hit me pretty hard, too."

Harkin nodded at his feet, embarrassed. "Uh, okay, so about G369.23−0.82—"

"I call it the Bullet. Easier than G369.23−0.82."

"Oh yeah." Hankin shrugged. "You said that in Briancon."

But what could he do in half hour fragments? He was thinking this through when Harkin asked the same question.

"Andy pretty well showed there was no pulsar beam," Harkin said helpfully, "so...?"

Ralph thumbed through his notes. "Can I get good clarity at the front end? The Bullet's bow shock?"

Harkin shook his head, looking disappointed. "No way, with so little observing time. Look, you said you had some out of the box ideas."

Ralph thought furiously. "How about the Bullet's tail, then?"

Harkin looked doubtful, scribbled a few numbers on a yellow lined pad. "Nope. It's not that luminous. The wake dies off pretty fast behind. Confusion limited. You'd get nothing but noise."

Ralph pointed. "There's a star we can see at the edge of the Bullet."

Harkin nodded. "A foreground star. Might be useful in narrowing down how far away it is."

"The usual methods say it's a long way off, maybe halfway across the galaxy."

"Um. Okay, leave that for later."

Ralph searched his mind. "Andy looked for pulses in what range?" He flipped through his notes from Briancon. "Short ones, yes—and nothing slower than a ten second period."

Harkin nodded. "This is a young neutron star. It'll be spinning fast."

Ralph hated looking like an amateur in Harkin's eyes, but he held his gaze firmly. "Maybe. Unless plowing through all that gas slows it faster."

Harkin raised his eyebrows skeptically. "The Mouse didn't slow down. It's spinning at about a tenth of a second period. Yusef-Zadeh and those guys say it's maybe 25,000 years old."

Twenty-five thousand years was quite young for a pulsar. The Mouse pulsar was a sphere of nothing but neutrons, a solar mass packed into a ball as small as San Francisco, spinning around ten times a second. In the radio-telescope maps that lighthouse beam came, from a dot at the very tip of a snout, with a bulging body right behind, and a long, thin tail: mousy. The Mouse discovery had set the paradigm. But just being first didn't mean it was typical.

Ralph set his jaw, flying on instinct—"Let's see."

So in the half hours when the dish team, instructed by Harkin, was slewing the big white antennas around, chugging them along the railroad tracks to new positions, and getting them set for another hours-long observation—in those wedges, Ralph worked furiously. With Harkin overseeing the complex hand-offs, he could command two or three dishes. For best use of this squeezed schedule, he figured to operate in the medium microwave band, around 1 or 2Ghz. They had been getting some interference the last few days, Harkin said, maybe from cell phone traffic, even out here in the middle of a high desert plateau—but that interference was down around 1 Ghz, safely far below in frequency. He need not worry about callers ringing each other up every few minutes and screwing up his data.

He took data carefully, in a way biased for looking at very long time fluctuations. In pulsar theory, a neutron star was in advanced old age by the time the period of its rotation, and so the sweeping of its lighthouse beam, was a second long. They harnessed their rotation to spew out their blaring radiation—live fast, die young. Teenage agonies. Only they didn't leave beautiful corpses—they *were* corpses. Pulsars should fade away for even slower rates; only a handfull were known out in the two or three minute zone.

So this search was pretty hopeless. But it was all he could think of, given the half hour limit.

He was dragging by the time he got his third half hour. The dish team was crisp, efficient, but the long observing runs between his slices got tedious. So he used their ample computing resources to process his own data—big files of numbers that the VLA software devoured as he watched the screens. Harkin's software had fractured the Bullet signal into bins, looking for structure in time. It caressed every incoming microwave, looking for repeating patterns. The computers ran for hours.

Hash, most of it. But then...

"What's that?" He pointed to a blip that stuck up in the noisy field. The screen before him and Harkin was patchy, a blizzard of harmonics that met and clashed and faded. But as the Bullet data ran and filtered, a peak persisted.

Harkin frowned. "Some pattern repeating in the microwaves." He worked the data, peering at shifting patterns on the screen. "Period of... lessee...47 seconds. Pretty long for a young pulsar."

"That's got to be wrong. Much too long."

In astronomy it paid to be a skeptic about your work. Everybody would be ready to pounce on an error. Joe Weber made some false detections of gravitational waves, using methods he invented. His reputation never fully recovered, despite being a brilliant, original scientist.

Harkin's face stiffened. "I don't care. That's what it is."

"Got to be wrong."

"Damn it, Ralph, I know my own codes."

"Let's look hard at this."

Another few hours showed that it wasn't wrong.

"Okay—funny, but it's real." Ralph thought, rubbing his eyes. "So let's look at the pulse itself."

Only there wasn't one. The pattern didn't spread over a broad frequency band. Instead, it was there in the 11 gigaHertz range, sharp and clear—and no other peaks at all.

"That's not a pulsar," Harkin said.

Ralph felt his pulse quicken. "A repeating brightness. From something peaking out of the noise and coming around to our point of view every 47 seconds."

"Damn funny." Harkin looked worried. "Hope it's not a defect in the codes."

Ralph hadn't thought of that. "But these are the best filter codes in the world."

Harkin grinned, brown face rumpling like leather. "More compliments like that and you'll turn my pretty little head."

So Harkin spent two hours in deep scrutiny of the VLA data processing software—and came up empty. Ralph didn't mind because it gave him time to think. He took a break partway through—Harkin was not the sort to take breaks at all—and watched a Cubs game with some of the engineers in the Operations room. They had a dish down for repairs but it was good enough to tip toward the horizon and pick up the local broadcast from Chicago. The Cubs weren't on any national 'cast and two of the guys came from UC, where the C was for Chicago. The Cubs lost but they did it well, so when he went back Ralph felt relaxed. He had also had an idea. Or maybe half of one.

"What if it's lots bigger than a neutron star?" he asked Harkin, who hadn't moved from his swivel chair in front of the six-screen display.

"Then what's the energy source?"

"I dunno. Point is, maybe it's something more ordinary, but still moving fast."

"Like what?"

"Say, a white dwarf—but a really old, dead one."

"So we can't see it in the visible?" The Hubble telescope had already checked at the Bullet location and seen nothing.

"Ejected from some stellar system, moving fast, but not a neutron star—maybe?"

Harkin looked skeptical. "Um. Have to think about it. But...what makes the relativistic electrons, to give us the microwaves?"

That one was harder to figure. Elderly white dwarfs couldn't make the electrons, certainly. Ralph paused and said, "Look, I don't know. And I have to get back to UCI for classes. Can I get some more time wedged in between your reconfigs?"

Harkin looked skeptical. "I'll have to see."

"Can you just send the results to me, when you can find some time?"

"You can process it yourself?"

"Give me the software and, yeah, sure."

Harkin shrugged. "That 47 second thing is damn funny. So...okay, I suppose..."

"Great!" Ralph was tired but he at least had his hand in the game. Wherever it led.

Ralph spent hours the next day learning the filter codes, tip-toeing through the labyrinth of Harkin's methods. Many thought Harkin was the best big-dish observer in the world, playing the electronics like a violin.

Harkin was a good teacher because he did not know how to teach. Instead he just showed. With it came stories and examples, some of them even jokes, and some puzzling until Harkin changed a viewing parameter or slid a new note into the song and it all came clear. This way Harkin showed him how to run the programs, to see their results skeptically. From the angular man he had learned to play a radio telescope as wide as a football field like a musical instrument, to know its quirks and deceptions, and to draw from it a truth it did not know. This was science, scrupulous and firm, but doing it was an art. In the end you had to justify every move, every conclusion, but the whole argument slid forward on intuition, like an ice cube skating on its own melt.

❈

"Say, Andy," Ralph said casually into his cell phone, looking out the big windows at New Mexico scrub and the white radio dishes cupped toward the sky. "I'm trying to remember if you guys looked at long periods in your Bullet data. Remember? We talked about it at Briancon."

"Bullet? Oh, G369.23–0.82."

"Right, look, how far out did you go on period?"

A long pause. Ralph thought he could hear street noise. "Hey, catch you at a bad time?"

"No, just walking down Mass Ave., trying to remember. I think we went out to around 30 second periods. Didn't see a damn thing."

"Oh, great. I've been looking at the Bullet again and my preliminary data shows something that, well, I thought I'd check with you."

"Wow." Another pause. "Uh, how slow?"

Ralph said cautiously, "Very. Uh, we're still analyzing the data."

"A really old pulsar, then. I didn't think they could still radiate when they were old."

"I didn't, either. They're not supposed to." Ralph reminded himself to check with the theorists.

"Then no wonder we couldn't find its supernova remnant. That's faded, or far away."

"Funny, isn't it, that we can pick up such weak signals from a pulsar that's halfway across the galaxy. Though it has been getting brighter, I noticed."

Andy sounded puzzled. "Yeah, funny. Brighter, um. I wonder if it shows up in any earlier survey."

"Yeah, well I thought I'd let you know."

Andy said slowly, "You know, I may have glimpsed something, but will get back to you."

They exchanged a few personal phrases and Ralph signed off.

Harkin was working the screens but turned with eyebrows raised.

Ralph said, "Bingo."

❈

As soon as Irene came into the coffee shop and they kissed in greeting, he could see the curiosity in her eyes. She was stunning in her clingy blue dress, while he strutted in his natty suit. He had told her to dress up and she blinked rapidly, expectant. "Where are we going tonight?"

He said, not even sitting down, "Y'know, the only place where I can sing and people don't throw rotten fruit at me is church."

Irene looked startled. "I didn't think you were religious."

"Hey, it's a metaphor. I pay for a place to dance, too, so—let's go. To the Ritz."

Her eyebrows arched in surprise. "What an oblique invitation. Puttin' on the Ritz?"

As they danced on the patio overlooking sunset surfers, he pulled a loose strand of hair aside for her, tucking it behind her ear. She was full of chatter about work. He told her about his work on the Bullet and she was genuinely interested, asking questions. Then she went back to tales of her office intrigues. Sometimes she seemed like a woman who could survive on gossip alone. He let it run down a bit and then said, as the band struck up *Begin the Beguine*, "I need more time."

She stiffened. "To contemplate the abyss of the M word?"

"Yes. I'm hot on the trail of something."

"You didn't call Herb Linzfield, either, did you." Not a question.

"No."

"Oh, fine."

He pulled back and gazed at her lips. Lush, as always, but twisted askew and scrunched. He knew the tone. *Fine. Yeah, okay, right. Fine. Go. Leave. See. If. I. Care.*

He settled into it then, the rhythm: of thickets of detail, and of beauty coming at you, unannounced. You had to get inside the drumroll of data, hearing the software symphonies, shaped so that human eyes could make some hominid sense of it. These color-coded encrustations showed what was unseeable by the mere human eye—the colors of the microwaves. Dry numbers cloaked this beauty, hid the ferocious glory.

When you thought about it, he thought, the wavelengths they were "seeing" with, through the enormous dish eyes, were the size of their fingers. The waves came oscillating across the blunt light years, messages out of ancient time. They slapped down on the hard metal of a radio dish and excited electrons that had been waiting there to be invited into the dance. The billions of electrons trembled and sang and their answering oscillations called forth capturing echoes in the circuits erected by men and women. More electrons joined the rising currents, fashioned by the 0s and 1s of computers into something no one had ever seen: pictures for eyes the size of mountains. These visions had never existed in the universe. They were implied by the waves, but it took intelligence to pull them out of the vagrant sizzle of radio waves, the passing microwave blizzard all life lived in but had never seen. Stories, really, or so their chimpanzee minds made of it all. Snapshots. But filling in the plot was up to them.

In the long hours he realized that, when you narrow your search techniques tuned to pick up exactly what you're looking for, there's a danger. The phrase astronomers use for that is, "I wouldn't have seen it if I hadn't believed it."

The paper on the astro-ph web site was brief, quick, three pages.

Ralph stared at it, open-mouthed, for minutes. He read it over twice. Then he called Harkin. "Andy's group is claiming a 47 second peak in their data."

"Damn."

"He said before that they didn't look out that far in period."

"So he went back and looked again."

"This is stealing." Ralph was still reeling, wondering where to go with this.

"You can pull a lot out of the noise when you know what to look for."

Whoosh— He exhaled, still stunned. "Yeah, I guess."

"He scooped us," Harkin said flatly.

"He's up for tenure."

Harkin laughed dryly. "That's Harvard for you." A long pause, then he rasped, "But what *is* the goddamn thing?"

The knock on his apartment door took him by surprise. It was Irene, eyes intent and mouth askew. "It's like I'm off your radar screen in one swift sweep."

"I'm..."

"Working. Too much—for what you get."

"Y'know," he managed, "art and science aren't a lot different. Sometimes. Takes concentration."

"Art," she said, "is answers to which there are no questions."

He blinked. "That sounds like a quotation."

"No, that was *me*."

"Uh, oh."

"So you want a quick slam bam, thank you Sam?"

"Well, since you put it that way."

An hour later she leaned up on an elbow and said, "News."

He blinked at her sleepily. "Uh...what?"

"I'm late. Two weeks."

"Uh. Oh." An anvil out of a clear blue sky.

"We should talk about—"

"Hoo boy."

"—what to do."

"Is that unusual for you?" First, get some data.

"One week is tops for me." She shaped her mouth into an astonished O. "Was."

"You were using...we were..."

"The pill has a small failure rate, but..."

"Not zero. And you didn't forget one?"

"No."

Long silence. "How do you feel about it?" Always a good way to buy time while your mind swirled around.

"I'm thirty-two. It's getting to be time."

"And then there's us."

"Us." She gave him a long, soulful look and flopped back down, staring at the ceiling, blinking.

He ventured, "How do you feel about..."

"Abortion?"

She had seen it coming. "Yes."

"I'm easy, if it's necessary." Back up on the elbow, looking at him, "Is it?"

"Look, I could use some time to think about this."

She nodded, mouth aslant. "So could I."

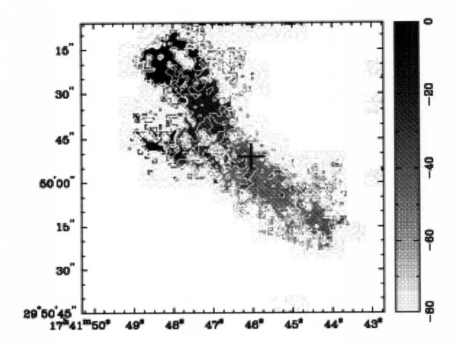

Ralph had asked the Bologna group—through his old friends, the two Fantis—to take a scan of the location. They put the Italian 'scopes on the region and processed the data and sent it by internet. It was waiting the next morning, 47 megs as an zipped attachment. He opened the attachment with a skittering anxiety. The Bologna group was first rate, their work solid.

On an internet visual phone call he asked, "Roberto, what's this? It can't be the object I'm studying. It's a mess."

On-screen, Roberto looked puzzled, forehead creased. "We wondered about that, yes. I can improve the resolution in a few days. We could very well clear up features with more observing time."

"Yes, could you? This has got to be wrong."

A head-bob. "We will look again, yes."

47 seconds...

The chairman kept talking but Ralph was looking out his window at the eucalyptus weaving in the vagrant coastal winds. Gossian was listing hurdles to meet before Ralph would be "close to tenure"—two federal grants, placing his Ph.D. students in good jobs, more papers. All to get done in a few months. The words ran by, he could hear them, but he had gone into that place he knew and always welcomed, where his own faith dwelled. The excitement came up in him, first stirrings, the instinct burning, his own interior state of grace. The idea swarmed up thick in his nostrils, he blinked—

"Ralph? You listening?"

"Oh, uh, yeah." *But not to you, no.*

He came into the physics building, folding his umbrella from a passing rain storm, distracted. There were black umbrellas stacked around like a covey of drunken crows. His cell phone cawed.

Harkin said, "Thought I'd let you know there's not much time I can use coming up. There's an older image, but I haven't cleaned it up yet."

"I'd appreciate anything at all."

"I can maybe try for a new image tomorrow, but I'm pretty damn busy. There's a little slot of time while the Array reconfigures."

"I sent you the Fantis' map—"

"Yeah, gotta be wrong. No source can change that much so fast."

Ralph agreed but added, "Uh, but we should still check. The Fantis are very good."

"If I have time," Harkin said edgily.

Between classes and committees and the long hours running the filter codes, he completely forgot about their dinner date. So at 9 P.M. his office video phone rang and it was Irene. He made his apologies, distracted, fretting. She looked tired, her forehead gray and lined, and he asked, "No…change?"

"No."

They sat in silence and finally he told her about the Fanti map.

She brightened visibly, glad to have some distraction. "These things can change, can't they?"

"Sure, but so fast! They're big, the whole tail alone is maybe light years long."

"But you said the map is all different, blurred."

"The whole object, yes."

"So maybe it's just a mistake?"

"Could be, but the Fantis are really good…"

"Could we get together later?"

He sighed. "I want to look at this some more." To her silence he added more apologies, ending with, "I don't want to lose you."

"Then remember where you put me."

The night wore on.

Wouldn't have seen it if I hadn't believed it.

The error, he saw, might well lie in their assumptions. In his.

It had to be a runaway neutron star. It had to be a long way off, halfway across the galaxy. They knew that because the fraying of the signal said there was a lot of plasma in the way.

His assumptions, yes. It had to be.

Perfectly reasonable. Perfectly wrong?

He had used up a lot of his choppy VLA time studying the oblong shroud of a once-proud star, seen through the edge of the Bullet. It was fuzzy with the debris of gas it threw off, a dying sun. In turn, he could look at the obscuration—how much the emission lines were absorbed and scattered by intervening dust, gas and plasma. Such telltales were the only reliable way to tell if a radio image came from far away or nearby. It was tricky, using such wobbly images, glimpsed through an interstellar fog.

What if there was a lot more than they thought, of the dense plasma in between their big-eyed dishes and the object?

Then they would get the distance wrong. Just a like a thick cloud between you and the sun. Dispersing the image, blurring it beyond recognition—but the sun was, on the interstellar scale, still quite close.

Maybe this thing was nearer, much nearer.

Then it would have to be surrounded by an unusually dense plasma—the cloud of ionized particles that it made, pushing on hard through the interstellar night. Could it have ionized much more of the gas it moved through, than the usual calculations said? How? Why?

But what *was* the goddamn thing?

He blinked at the digital arrays he had summoned up, through a thicket of image and spectral processors. The blurred outlines of the old star were a few pixels, and nearby was an old, tattered curve of a super-nova remnant—an ancient spherical tombstone of a dead sun. The lines had suffered a lot of loss on their way through the tail of the Bullet. From this he could estimate the total plasma density near the Bullet itself.

Working through the calculation, he felt a cold sensation creep into him, banishing all background noise. He turned the idea over, feeling its shape, probing it. Excitement came, tingling but laced with caution.

Andy had said, *I wonder if it shows up in any earlier survey.*

So Ralph looked. On an Italian radio map of the region done eleven years before there was a slight scratch very near the Bullet location. But it was faint, an order of magnitude below the luminosity he was seeing now. Maybe some error in calibration? But a detection, yes.

He had found it because it was bright now. Hitting a lot of interstellar plasma, maybe, lighting up?

Ralph called Harkin to fill him in on this and the Fanti map, but got an answering machine. He summed up briefly and went off to teach a mechanics class.

Harkin said on his voicemail, "Ralph, I just sent you that map I made two days ago, while I had some side time on a 4.8 GHz observation."

"Great, thanks!" he called out before he realized Harkin couldn't hear him. So he called and when Harkin picked up, without even a hello, he said, "Is it like the Fanti map?"

"Not at all."

"Their work was pretty recent."

"Yeah, and what I'm sending you is earlier than theirs. I figure they screwed up their processing."

"They're pretty careful..."

"This one I'm sending, it sure looks some different from what we got before. Kinda pregnant with possibility."

The word, *pregnant*, stopped him for a heartbeat. When his attention returned, Harkin's voice was saying, "—I tried that 47 second period filter and it didn't work. No signal this time. Ran it twice. Don't know what's going on here."

The email attachment map was still more odd.

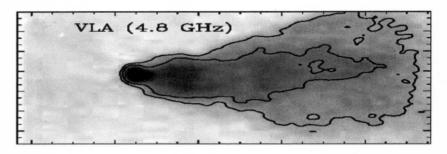

Low in detail, because Harkin had not much observing time, but clear enough. The Bullet was frayed, longer, with new features. Plunging on, the Bullet was meeting a fresh environment, perhaps.

But this was from two days ago.

The Bologna map was only 14 hours old.

He looked back at the messy Bologna view and wondered how this older picture could possibly fit with the 4.8 GHz map. Had the Fantis made some mistake?

"Can you get me a snapshot right now?" Ralph asked. "It's important."

He listened to the silence for a long moment before Harkin said, "I've got a long run on right now. Can't it wait?"

"The Fantis at Bologna, they're standing by that different looking map. Pretty strange."

"Ummm, well…"

"Can you get me just a few minutes? Maybe in the download interval—"

"Hey, buddy, I'll try, but—"

"I'll understand," but Ralph knew he wouldn't.

His home voicemail from Irene said, fast and with rising voice tone, "Do unto others, right? So, if you're not that into me, I can stop returning your calls, emails—not that there are any—and anyway, blocking is so dodge ball in sixth grade, right? I'll initiate the phase-out, you'll get the lead-footed hint, and that way, you can assume the worst of me and still feel good about yourself. You can think, hey, she's not over her past. Social climber. Shallow business mind. Workaholic, maybe. Oh, no, that's you, right? And you'll have a wonderful imitation life."

A long pause, time's nearly up, and she gasped, paused, then: "Okay, so maybe this isn't the best idea."

He sat, deer in the headlights, and played it over.

They were close, she was wonderful, yes.

He loved her, sure, and he had always believed that was all it took.

But he might not have a job here inside a year.

And he couldn't think of anything but the Bullet.

While she was wondering if she was going to be a mother.

Though, he realized, she had not really said what she thought about it all.

He had no idea what to say. At a talk last year about Einstein, the speaker quoted Einstein's wife's laconic comment, that sometimes when the great man was working on a problem he would not speak to anyone for days. She had left him, of course. But now Ralph could feel a certain kinship with that legendary genius. Then he told himself he was being fatuous, equating this experience…

Still, he let it all slide for now.

His eighth cup of coffee tasted bitter. He bit into a donut for a sugar jolt. When had he eaten last?

He took a deep breath and let it out to clear his head.

He was sure of his work now, the process—but still confused.

The earlier dispersion measure was wrong. That was clear from the broadening of the pulses he had just measured. Andy and everybody else had used the usual interstellar density numbers to get the Bullet's distance. That had worked out to about five thousand light years away.

From his pulse measurements he could show that the Bullet was much closer, about 30 light years away. They were seeing it through the ionized and compressed plasma ahead and around the…what? *Was* it a neutron star at all?

And a further consequence—if the Bullet was so close, it was also much smaller, and less intrinsically luminous.

While the plume was huge, the Bullet itself—the unresolved circle at the center of it all, in Andy's high-resolution map—need only be a few hundred kilometers long. Or much less; that was just an upper limit.

Suppose that was the answer, that it was much closer. Then its energy output—judging that it was about equal to the radiated power—was much less, too. He jotted down some numbers. The object was emitting power comparable to a nation's on Earth. Ten gigaWatts or so.

Far, far below the usual radiated energies for runaway neutron stars.

He stared into space, mind whirling.

And the 47 second period...

He worked out that if the object was rotating and had an acceleration of half an Earth gravity at its edge, it was about 30 meters across.

Reasonable.

But why was the shape of its radio image changing so quickly? In days, not the years typical of big astronomical objects. *Days.*

Apprehensively he opened the email from Irene.

> You're off the hook!
> So am I.
> Got my period. False alarm.
> Taught us a lot, though. Me, anyway. I learned the thoroughly useful information (data, to you) that you're an asshole. Bye.

He sat back and let the relief flood through him.

You're off the hook. Great.

False alarm. Whoosh!

An asshole. Um.

But...

Was he about to do the same thing she had done? Get excited about nothing much?

Ralph came into his office, tossed his lecture notes onto the messy desk, and slumped in his chair. The lecture had not gone well. He couldn't seem to focus. Should he keep his distance from Irene for a while, let her cool off? What did he really want, there?

Too much happening at once. The phone rang.

Harkin said, without even a hello, "I squeezed in some extra observing time. The image is on the way by email."

"You sound kind of tired."

"More like...confused." He hung up.

It was there in the email.

Ralph stared at the image a long time. It was much brighter than before, a huge outpouring of energy.

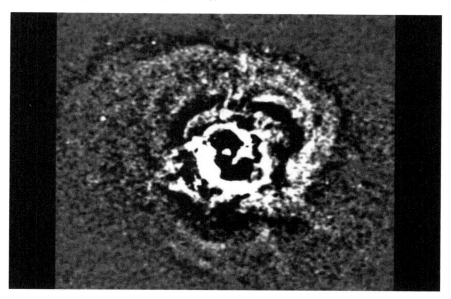

His mind seethed. The Fanti result, and now this. Harkin's 4.8 Ghz map was earlier than either of these, so it didn't contradict either the Fantis or this. A time sequence of something changing fast—in days, in hours.

This was no neutron star.

It was smaller, nearer, and they had watched it go to hell.

He leaned over his desk, letting the ideas flood over him. *Whoosh.*

Irene looked dazed. "You're kidding."

"No. I know we've got a lot to talk through, but—"

"You bet."

"—I didn't send you that email just to get you to meet me." Ralph bit his lip and felt the room whirl around.

"What you wrote," she said wonderingly. "It's a...starship?"

"Was. It got into trouble of some kind these last few days. That's why the wake behind it—" he tapped the Fantis' image—"got longer. Then, hours later, it got turbulent, and—it exploded."

She sipped her coffee. "This is...was...light years away?"

"Yes, and headed somewhere else. It was sending out a regular beamed transmission, one that swept around as the ship rotated, every 47 seconds."

Her eyes widened. "You're sure?"

"Let's say it's a working hypothesis."

"Look, you're tired, maybe put this aside before jumping to conclusions."

He gazed at her and saw the lines tightened around the mouth. "You've been through a lot yourself. I'm sorry."

She managed a brave, thin smile. "It tore me up. I do want a child."

He held his breath, then went ahead. "So...so do I."

"Really?" They had discussed this before but her eyelids fluttered in surprise.

"Yes." He paused, sucked in a long breath, and said, "With you."

"Really?" She closed her eyes a long time. "I...always imagined this."

He grinned. "Me too. Time to do it."

"Yes?"

"Yes." *Whoosh.*

They talked on for some moments, ordered drinks to celebrate. Smiles, goofy eyes, minds whirling.

Then, without saying anything, they somehow knew that they had said enough for now. Some things should not be pestered, just let be.

They sat smiling at each other and in a soft sigh she said, "You're worried. About..."

Ralph nodded. How to tell her that this seemed pretty clear to him and to Harkin, but it was big, gaudy trouble in the making. "It violates a basic assumption we always make, that everything in the night sky is natural."

"Yeah, so?"

"The astronomy community isn't like Hollywood, y'know. It's more like...a priesthood."

He sipped his coffee and stared out the window. An airplane's wing lights winked as it coasted down in the distance toward the airport. Everybody had seen airplanes, so seeing them in the sky meant nothing. Not so for the ramscoop ship implied by his radio maps.

There would be rampant skepticism. Science's standards were austere, and who would have it differently? The angles of attack lived in his hands, and he now faced the long labor of calling forth data and calculations. To advance the idea would take strict logic, entertaining all other ideas fairly. Take two steps forward, one back, comparing and weighing and contrasting—the data always leading the skeptical mind. It was the grand dance, the gavotte of reason, ever-mindfull of the eternal possibility that one was wrong.

Still... When serendipity strikes...let it. Then seize it.

"You need some sleep." Her eyes crinkled with concern. "Come home with me."

He felt a gush of warm happiness. She was here with him and together they could face the long battle to come.

"Y'know, this is going to get nasty. Look what happened to Carl Sagan when he just argued there *might* be intelligent life elsewhere."

"You think it will be that hard to convince people?"

"Look at it this way. Facing up to the limits of our knowledge, to the enormity of our ignorance, is an acquired skill—to put it mildly. People want certainty."

He thought, *If we don't realize where the shoreline of reasonably well established scientific theory ends, and where the titanic sea of undiscovered truth begins, how can we possibly hope to measure our progress?*

Irene frowned. Somehow, after long knowledge of her, he saw that she was glad of this chance to talk about something larger than themselves. She said slowly, "But...why is it that your greatest geniuses—the ones you talk about, Hawking, Feynman, Newton—humbly concede how pitifully limited our reach is?"

"That's why they're great," he said wryly. *And the smaller spirits noisily proclaim the certainty of their conclusions. Well, here comes a lot of dissent, doubt, and skepticism.*

"And now that ship is gone." He went on, "We learned about them by watching them die."

She stared at him. "I wonder...how many?"

"It was a big, powerful ship. It probably made the plasma ahead of it somehow. Then with magnetic fields it scooped up that plasma and cooked it for energy. Then shot it out the back for propulsion. Think of it as like a jet plane, a ramscoop. Maybe it was braking, using magnetic fields—I dunno."

"Carrying passengers?"

"I...hadn't thought of that."

"How big is it?...was it?"

"Maybe like...the Titanic."

She blinked. "That many people."

"Something like people. Going to a new home."

"Maybe to...here?"

He blinked, his mind cottony. "No, it was in the plane of the sky. Otherwise we'd have seen it as a blob, head on, no tail. Headed somewhere fairly near, though."

She sat back, gazing at him with an expression he had not seen before. "This will be in the papers, won't it." Not a question.

"Afraid so." He managed a rueful smile. "Maybe I'll even get more space in *National Enquirer* than Andy did."

She laughed, a tinkling sound he liked so much.

But then the weight of it all descended on him. *So much to do...* "I'll have to look at your idea, that they were headed here. At least we can maybe backtrack, find where they came from."

"And look at the earlier maps, data?" she ventured, her lip trembling. "From before..."

"They cracked up. All that life, gone." Then he understood her pale, tenuous look. *Things living, then not.* She nodded, said nothing.

He reached out and took her hand. A long moment passed and he had no way to end it but went on anyway. "The SETI people could jump on this. Backtrack this ship. They can listen to the home star's emissions..."

Irene smiled without humor. "And we can send them a message. Condolences."

"Yeah." The room had stopped whirling and she reached out to take his hand.

"Come on."

As he got up wearily, Ralph saw that he was going to have to fight for this version of events. There would always be Andys who would triangulate their way to advantage. And the chairman, Gossian...

Trying for tenure—supposedly a cool, analytic process—in the shouting match of a heated, public dispute, a howling media firestorm—that was almost a contradiction in terms. But this, too, was what science was about. His career might survive all that was to come, and it might not—but did that matter, standing here on the shores of the titanic ocean he had peered across?

REASONS NOT TO PUBLISH
(2007)

Roger made the greatest discovery in scientific history by noticing a jitter in his left eye.

He was hiking in the high Sierras on a crisp fall day, alone in the Glass Creek valley. The jitter was not a fluttering bird, but an entire tree jumping in and out of focus, light playing on it in eerie, slanted shafts. He watched it for a while, then walked under the pine. The bark felt smooth but looked fissured. It flavored the air like a real pine. The creamy bark stuttered beneath his fingers. The whole tree and all around it ratcheted, went grainy, sometimes vanished.

Roger was a mathematical physicist and had seen something like this before. A bad simulation, jumpy and scattered, just like this pine. His face paled, his breath caught, but the conclusion was clear. This backcountry he loved to hike through off-season was...a simulation.

Probably, he judged, because usually there was nobody around in late autumn. No need to spend computation time to keep pines needles waving before no audience. Just distribute motion between the harmonics of limbs, branches and clusters, to save computing time. He knew that a cheap simulation of light scattering replaced a detailed calculation with plausible rules of thumb, much quicker than the real thing, but realistic— as long as nobody looked too closely.

So Roger looked around, closely.

Seen from here, Mammoth Mountain jumped around, shifting colors. Background clouds lost their cottony look and sometimes vanished.

An eerie prickling climbed his spine. The logic was clear. So...*he* was a simulation.

501

It took a day and night of hard drinking to do some hard think-ing about the implications. From his condo in Mammoth he watched the looming mountain and it was fine, not jumpy. He went for a splashy swim in the pool, savoring the flavors of the air and water, the sigh of pines singing in a fragrant, dry wind.

But back in the Glass Creek valley again, the same ratcheting blinked in and out. A cost-smart sim, stretched to its limits. Someone was being thrifty.

What did the Programmer God want? To watch a universe evolve, or just a simmed Earth? To rerun human history? Was the software even written by humans at all? He glanced around, uneasy.

Hiking back to his car, Roger sucked in the clean dry air that now seemed like perfume. Life, even fake life, was more precious than ever.

He could not stop his mind from working the problem, though.

Why was the simulation getting stressed now? Maybe the computa-tion cost of running a world of 6 billion people had stretched resources? At least some of those 6 billion, wonderful folk like Roger, felt complex internal states. That, he knew. Descartes, after all.

But 6 billion people like him, with his complex inner states? His sharp, darting mind, his sensual layers, his robust singing hunger for life? (Okay, he admitted, maybe that was laying it on a bit thick. But still.)

Such detail must cost a bundle in bit rate. With population rising, computation costs climbed. Maybe the system had hit the wall, strained to its limit. That could explain why nobody had noticed this before. Or had they?

The people he saw ambling in the Mammoth streets might be simple programs. To test that, Roger walked up to a few at random and they acted just like real people—except nothing was real, he reminded him-self. Maybe they were as deep as he was.

How could God the Programmer handle the data rate for such com-plex people? Could He (or She, or It) run some complex people like him, with full interior states, and just use rubrics for the mob?

Probably, since the Programmer was running short on bit rate. Plus, it would explain a lot of what was on TV. Maybe the mindless people on talk shows really were mindless.

In a way, he felt liberated. He certainly couldn't care about fake people.

He stopped walking, looked around at the eggshell blue sky, sucked in the sharp aroma of late fall. The logic was clear. All the goals he had were nothing compared with this knowledge.

All else being equal, then, he shouldn't care as much about how he affected the world. Only the Programmer God mattered, because She could erase you.

Could he be the first to see the world as it really was? Or rather, wasn't?

How many "people" had noticed that the flaws of Nature told us that the laws of Nature were from software, running on some machine?

Population was still rising. Some people might need to be pruned to lower costs. How to stay alive, then? Or rather, "alive"?

Be interesting to the Programmer. Be famous. Or original. Or maybe funny.

Roger was none of these, really. Smart, sure. Observant, yes. That was about it. Maybe he was in mortal danger of being erased.

But he *did* know that this sim-Earth was fake. It seemed pretty unlikely that its purpose was to see how many figured out that they lived in a simulation. Perhaps just the opposite—if many did, maybe the world got erased, its original purpose corrupted.

So...he should prevent others from finding out. By not drawing attention to the ratcheting pine, to Glass Creek, to Mammoth Mountain at all. Not to himself, most of all.

Yes, and be interesting to the Programmer. Do things! Live in the moment. Enjoy life! It was a lot like Zen Buddhism.

Walking home, he watched Mammoth Mountain. It loomed large, gleaming firm and true in a sky as clear as logic. It felt solid, the air snapping with the rub and reek of reality. Where real people like him were, with complex inner thoughts—because the Programmer spent the computational time to make the world work.

Elsewhere, not. God had a budget.

But...how many other people had made this discovery, and kept quiet? All of them, apparently.

Or if they did try to shout the startling truth from the rooftops... Well then, something unpleasant happened.

The biggest discovery in history, throwing both religion and science into a cocked hat...and nobody dared speak its name. Nobody who survived, anyway.

Roger had to join them, the silents, for his own safety. Give up his Nobel.

He stopped at a wine shop and bought the best bottle they had.

THE CHAMPAGNE AWARD
(2008)

The first case of the morning was typical.

Roger scanned the cyberforms of a woman in her forties, applying for a child using her entire KidCred. No father to be named, no mention of how she would get pregnant. A clinic, he guessed, but maybe she had a donor. Not the Reproduction Office's business, no. He offered her the government Champagne Award, good for a reasonable bottle, but she didn't take it.

Next came a rather different case. Roger eyed the late-twenties woman and two obviously gay men in his office. He made the usual ritual greeting, outlined the documents they needed, and they produced them, all filled out in her crisp hand. She would be the surrogate for the two men, who were each putting up half their KidCred. What they paid her was a private matter. She would have no claim on the child. She took the Champagne Award, though.

That job went quickly and then came something awful. A fretful couple came in, breathing too quickly and nervous. "Our child died the second day in the hospital," the husband explained. His wife blurted, "A blood disorder, they're still trying to figure it out." Before Roger could say a word the husband turned furious. "But they say there's nothing they can do! It's their fault!"

Roger knew enough to study the hospital readouts first. The child had lasted 36.7 hours and then died of some sort of hemorrhage. The couple were in their forties and had been warned of the risks, some of them genetic.

He was no doctor, but he knew the rules. "It's beyond 24 hours," he said calmly, voice gray and dead. "Carried to full term, no intervening circumstances. You can get no reversed credit."

It took an hour to get them out of the office. Roger nearly called the guards. The couple wouldn't talk to the counselors because they knew that was just a bureaucratic dodge. But there was really nothing he could do. Rules were rules.

His longterm girlfriend Lucy called but he was too busy to talk; paperwork.

After his coffee break there was a lesbian couple, duly married, each using her last half KidCred. Nothing unusual, documents in order, and they took the Champagne Award, too.

The next couple was a man and wife bubbling over with joy. Roger liked to see that. The couple already had the max, two healthy children, but wanted a third; they were Catholic. They proudly presented a Lottery Credential. It looked standard. The winning number was in the right code. Roger shared in their celebration while he ran it through the verifier—which went *bing*.

Everybody froze. They didn't know what it meant, but Roger did. He had to explain to them that it was a very well made fake. The original, authentic number had been used two weeks before. That was how the counterfeiters had gotten the publicly posted number; the rest was technology.

This time he had to call the guards. The husband kept shouting, "I paid three hundred thousand in tickets!" over and over, but the tickets he had were fake, too.

Pretty depressing, but there were rules. Every game did. To win the game you had to play.

Lucy called; he was busy filing reports. Tough day; he took an early lunch. In the basement cafeteria he sat with Henry from Document Authentication and Mary from Statistics. They were partners, not married but had lived together for two decades. And today they were quitting, they announced happily.

"We played it just right," Henry said, though he didn't seem all that elated. "Waited for the market peak."

Mary was joyous. "I got nearly a million! Think what we can do with that."

"Who from?" Roger asked.

"A couple that wanted a *third*." Mary rolled her eyes. "*Filthy* rich."

Roger blinked. "The fines for illegal birth are nearly that much anyway."

Henry said, "Plus no education for the no-KidCred child, no social benefits—"

Mary said firmly, "I predict no-cred parents will get prison time in a few more years."

Henry looked down at his plate. "If we invest this the right way, we can retire and manage our stock.

"You might get paid even more later," Roger said. "There are rumors that the KidCred standards may get tougher."

"Those rumors are why the market has run up. We're just cashing in, like the gays." Mary merrily toasted with her water glass. "Here's to cap and trade!"

Henry nodded, though he looked sad. "Roger, I can't see them taking away the one person, one child rule, though." He looked down.

Every game had its winners and losers, Roger thought. Gay guys had little interest in children, so they won big. With 11.6 billion souls in the world, what else could humanity do? Prison for unlicensed childbearing didn't seem implausible to him at all.

But to win the game, you had to play.

So when his telephone rang, back at his desk, he was delighted to hear from Lucy. Somehow the day crystallized for him. Without thinking, he said suddenly, "How would you like a bottle of champagne?"

PENUMBRA
(2010)

Mary turned to look at the shriveled woman carried on a bare plank, followed by a little crowd of mourners who fruitlessly batted away the flies. "Was she—?"

"Outside? Guess so. Looks like her hair caught on fire," I said.

"We were so lucky, taking a nap."

I hoisted my piña colada. "A day later and we'd have been in California." The ice was cool but not at all reassuring. "And maybe dead."

"You're...sure?" Mary's eyes jittered. "I know, you're an astrophysicist, but really?—is everybody we know—"

"The flash, I saw it from the window. In the distance—bright blue at first, then so brilliant I couldn't see."

"But not right here."

"Right, that's what doesn't make sense. We got glare, small fires, but not that—" I pointed to the greasy pall building on the offshore horizon, beyond the warm waves. "That's been building for hours."

She blinked. "But there's no land west of here."

"Those dirty brown clouds must've blown in. Big fires further away."

Mary's eyes danced. Her hands clenched and relaxed, clenched and relaxed.

"But...how widespread can this be?"

"Didn't burn us here much, so it's not worldwide. Not a supernova, or we'd see it in the sky." I pointed up. The mottled blue high above was thickening with smoke.

"Then...what?"

"I'd say, must've been a gamma ray burster. Why we didn't get it full on, I don't know."

"A…burster?"

I peered at the sky, looking for some clue. I was more a theorist, not an observer. "We think it's a narrow beam of intense radiation, coming out when a rotating, high-mass star collapses to form a black hole."

The gamma ray satellites had seen hundreds at safe cosmological distances, but none in our galaxy. Maybe this was the first. I went through a quick description of what happened when gammas hit the top of our atmosphere. Particle cascades, ultraviolet flares, blaring hard light, ozone depletion, mesons lacing down.

"How did *we* survive it, then?"

"Dunno." The flies came buzzing back. I waved them off our steaming chicken molé. "Eat," I said. "Then we go to the market and buy whatever we can."

But there was no market. Crowds had picked the stalls clean.

"We have to live here for a while," I said as we walked back to our hotel. After I'd finished my observing run at the Las Campanas Observatory, Mary joined me for diving in the Galápagos. Guayaquil was a sightseeing stopover before heading home. We'd seen the cathedral yesterday, echoing and nearly deserted then, but now a huge crowd surrounded it, listening to a priest blaring out his message with a hand-held mike.

Mary struggled with her high school Spanish. "He says this shows God's favor on them," she reported. "Preservation for them and their families, and liberation from the…North Americans. And, uh, Europeans."

"How's he know that?" I looked up at the sky again, learning nothing—but saw an antenna on the church roof.

I pointed. Mary was an electronics tech type and she said immediately, "They have a satellite link. Non commercial. Private."

It took an hour to talk our way through, first with the priest and then a Bishop, no less. But their connection was live and took me to the academic satellite links. The downlook cameras showed blazes everywhere north and south of us, Europe, west Africa—a hemisphere burning. Except in a spot several thousand kilometers wide, an ellipse right at the equator. Where we were.

No link worked to the gamma ray working group, where a burster signature would show up. But I didn't need one now.

Then the satellite link failed. I didn't try to pursue it. I got up with Mary and walked out into the rosy sunset and acrid air.

Some mestizos by the church, dressed in the somber black of mourning, turned and looked at us, eyes narrowing. Mary noticed and said, "I wonder if they blame us, somehow."

"Wouldn't surprise me," I said. "We run their universe, don't we?"

"So they may think, how can something like this possibly be natural?"

"Hasn't happened before, so maybe it's somebody's fault. Gringos are the traditional candidates."

"Let's get out of here," she said. We strolled away, deliberately casual, but as we approached the hotel, everyone on the cobblestone streets seemed to be looking at us.

"Go up and pack," I said, and went to the travel agent. I was amazed that he was still at his desk. Our tickets to Los Angeles were obviously not going to work, so I tried to rebook to an Asian airport. Any Asian airport. But his connection was dead. The blazing cone of light had come in late morning. That meant it got most of Europe and the Americas, except for within that blessed oval, where we had been following local custom and taking siesta in the hushed, indoor cool of a thick-walled hotel. Asia had been in darkness.

We stumbled out into the night air and then I saw it. The crescent moon hung there to our west. "Got it," I said.

She saw it too. "You mean—? The gamma ray burster was just behind our view of the moon."

"That's why the trees weren't burning here. That woman's hair was like tinder—it caught fire, maybe drove her into some accident. We were in the moon's penumbra, the twilight zone that caught just some of the burst. Anybody on this side of the planet not shielded by the moon is dead. Or soon will be."

"So now it goes to Asia," Mary said slowly. "The future."

Somehow I smiled. "At least we have one."

GRAVITY'S WHISPERS
(2010)

The best is the enemy of the good," Sam said over my shoulder.

I whirled around, coming out of my work trance, knowing the voice, smiling. "What—?"

He sauntered in, grinning in his lopsided way, eyes dancing. "At 11 PM you're still working. Know your limits! The data can't get better when you're tired, y'know."

I threw down my pencil. "Right. Pursue the good. Let's get a beer."

At the Very Large Array, this meant a long drive back to Socorro. Our offices were there, but I liked spending time out among the big radio dishes, too. On the way back I rolled down the window to catch the tangy spring sagebrush. Plus wondering if Sam the Slow had finally decided to make a date with me, in his odd way. I'd been waiting half a year.

Then he said, slow and sly, "I was just passing by, thought I'd follow up on that puzzle I sent last week."

I recalled he had sent a noise-dominated file. I had run one of my custom programs, gotten interested, and wasted a day pulling out a pattern. "You know me too well. I cracked it, yeah." I gave him a smile he didn't notice. "Not a very interesting solution."

"You'd be surprised," Sam said, watching the desert slide by.

"It's *you* guys who surprised the world—the first gravity waves, wow."

"Yeah, decades of work on LIGO paid off."

Sam was also modest, a trait that gave him gal problems in the fanatic tech crowd more than once; I had checked. Getting a gravitational wave to tweak a cavity, and detect that with interfering waves, a huge problem, had burned twenty years of his life. Years that might've been better if he'd spent less of it frowning at screens. Like me.

He shrugged, lifted an eyebrow. "We thought it was a signal from a rotating neutron star with a deformed crust. Say, you have that solution handy?"

I flipped open my laptop. *Always with the quick answers...* "Sure. It's a string of numbers, turns out to be the zeroes of the Riemann zeta function."

A frown, quick glance away from the road. "Uh-huh. Which is—?"

"A famous function of complex argument—that is, has real and imaginary parts." *Like your life,* I thought. *And mine.* "See, it analytically continues the sum of an infinite series."

A shrug. "Sounds boring."

"Not so." This fetched from him a side-flick, eyes puzzled. At least he was looking at me now. "It's a big deal in analytic number theory. Plenty of applications in physics, probability theory, Bose–Einstein condensates, spin waves—"

"Useful, good." Sam was usually sharp, focused, but now he gazed pensively, above the highway, at the stars. "But..."

"So how'd you get the detection?" It would help if I got him started about his work—that is, his life. "You guys got rid of the noise from that road traffic and logging at the Louisiana site?"

"Yeah, took years. Finally nailed it. The signal we wrung out, it had plenty of chirps and bursts in it, a bitch to clean up."

I grinned. Sam had worked decades on LIGO, the big, long-term gravity wave detector, and the milestone was here. "Okay, so now that you've got LIGO sensitive enough, there'll be plenty of signals. Supernovas in other galaxies, maybe rattling cosmic strings—"

A vexed glance, troubled. "I want to understand *this* one. It's not a neutron star crust vibration, I think."

"Huh?" I was already tasting the beer in my mind.

"That decoding you did? That was our signal."

I blinked. "Can't be. No natural system—"

"Exactly." Sam hooked an eyebrow at me.

"*What?* A gravitational wave with a *signal?* That's im—"

"—possible, I know. Unless you can sling around neutron stars and make them sing in code."

"To send a signal, that means the transmitter is tunable..." I noticed my mouth was gaping open.

Maybe, just maybe, this could be more important than at last getting Sam to date me. Maybe. I took a deep breath of dry New Mexico air. "Then...you should know that the signal, it's not just a list of numbers. After twenty of the Riemann zeros, there's something like a proof of the Riemann hypothesis. I think. Can't follow it really well, actually."

He frowned. "Uh, so?"

"The Riemann hypothesis, it's one of the greatest unsolved problems in mathematics. It says that any non-trivial zero has its real part exactly equal to 1/2."

He shook his head. "A theorem? After some numbers? And *that's* the attention-catching opener to a—a what?"

I finally got it. "To a SETI signal?"

"Look, I sent you that because we couldn't understand it. Now you're gonna tell me—"

He still didn't get it. Maybe I didn't either. "Look, it *can't* be. A SETI signal? We've thought about that a lot already. Opening up your message with pi, or e, prime numbers, some astro data—that makes sense."

"Sense to the likes of us."

"So I must've made some mistake."

"No you didn't." Sam looked at me with a warm smile. "You're the only one I could run to with this analysis—the rest of 'em would laugh. You're good, really good."

I leaned over and kissed him. "Congratulations on the Nobel."

He kissed back, his eyes flickered, a sudden dart of tongue, he jerked back, grinned—but he didn't look happy. He grasped the steering wheel and peered ahead into the starlit darkness. In the high desert you can see stars glimmering in their reds and blues, far above the headlights. I knew him enough to see that he was thinking about something that could whisper across the galaxies with gravitation, not using obvious means like radio or lasers.

"To make a gravitational wave signal—look," he said adamantly, "we figured there would be natural events—catastrophes, really, like stars falling into black holes, or neutron stars smacking together—big enough to give a signal we could detect with this huge, expensive LIGO experiment...which has run for decades now, getting better, slowly. And now we have a signal, clear and solid..."

"Some aliens know a better way to make waves, is all." I wanted to move his attention away from the physics and toward, well, me.

"Look, I think this is cause for celebration," I said helpfully.

"But... if it's not just a simple signal—like a wave breaking on a beach, I mean, only in gravitational pulses—then... My God." He stared up at the darkness above our headlights.

"Yeah." I looked at those burning stars, too. Mysteries, all of them.

"Think of it. To make a signal, you don't just slam stuff together. You have to make them *oscillate*. How?"

"Ah, I..."

"Say they take two black holes, make them orbit close together. Put some electrical charges on them. Then you can make them swerve by each other, radiate grav waves, but stay stable." A snort. "Easy—just make black holes, the rest is simple." A dry laugh. "You *tap-tap-tap* to make a signal..."

He was getting overwhelmed, and so was I. The desert flittered past in our headlights.

"Unimaginable," I said.

"Right. I can't even think what you would do to make such masses move..."

We were alone out here on a solitary road, in a desert far from anyone...just like humanity, I thought.

Sam said, "Any mind that thinks the Riemann numbers are a calling card—and can throw around stars..."

I got it. "Yeah. Know your limits. Maybe it's good, really good, that we can't possibly answer them."

He laughed, bless him. But I didn't.

MERCIES

(2011)

All scientific work is, of course, based on some conscious or subconscious philosophical attitude.

—WERNER HEISENBERG

He rang the doorbell and heard its buzz echo in the old wooden house. Footsteps. The worn, scarred door eased open half an inch and a narrowed brown eye peered at him.

"Mr. Hanson?" Warren asked in a bland bureaucratic tone, the accent a carefully rehearsed approximation of the flat Midwestern that would arouse no suspicions here.

"Yeah, so?" The mouth jittered, then straightened.

"I need to speak to you about your neighbor. We're doing a security background check."

The eye swept up and down Warren's three-piece suit, dark tie, polished shoes—traditional styles, or as the advertisements of this era said, "timeless." Warren was even sporting a gray fedora with a snap band.

"Which neighbor?"

This he hadn't planned on. Alarm clutched at his throat. Instead of speaking he nodded at the house to his right. Daniel Hanson's eye slid that way, then back, and narrowed some more. "Lemme see ID."

This Warren had expected. He showed an FBI ID in a plastic case, up-to-date and accurate. The single eye studied it and Warren wondered what to do if the door slammed shut. Maybe slide around to the window, try to—

The door jerked open. Hanson was a wiry man with shaggy hair—a bony framework, all joints and hinges. His angular face jittered with concern and Warren asked, "You are the Hanson who works at Allied Mechanical?"

The hooded eyes jerked again as Warren stepped into the room.

"Uh, yeah, but hey—whassit matter if you're askin' 'bout the neighbor?"

Warren moved to his left to get Hanson away from the windows. "I just need the context in security matters of this sort."

"You're wastin' your time, see, I don't know 'bout—"

Warren opened his briefcase casually and in one fluid move brought the short automatic pistol out. Hanson froze. He fired straight into Hanson's chest. The popping sound was no louder than a dropped glass would make as the silencer soaked up the noise.

Hanson staggered back, his mouth gaping, sucking in air. Warren stepped forward, just as he had practiced, and carefully aimed again. The second shot hit Hanson squarely in the forehead and the man went down backward, thumping on the thin rug.

Warren listened. No sound from outside.

It was done. His first, and just about as he had envisioned it. In the sudden silence he heard his heart hammering.

He had read from the old texts that professional hit men of this era used the 0.22 automatic pistol despite its low caliber, and now he saw why. Little noise, especially with the suppressor, and the gun rode easily in his hand. The silencer would have snagged if he had carried it in a coat pocket. In all, his plans had worked. The pistol was light, strong, and—befitting its mission—a brilliant white.

The dark red pool spreading from Hanson's skull was a clear sign that this man, who would have tortured, hunted, and killed many women, would never get his chance now.

Further, the light 0.22 slug had stayed inside the skull, ricocheting so that it could never be identified as associated with this pistol. This point was also in the old texts, just as had been the detailed blueprints. Making the pistol and ammunition had been simple, using his home replicator machine.

He moved through the old house, floors creaking, and systematically searched Hanson's belongings. Here again the old texts were useful, leading him to the automatic pistol taped under a dresser drawer. No sign yet of the rifle Hanson had used in the open woods, either.

It was amazing, what twenty-first century journals carried, in their sensual fascination with the romantic aura of crime. He found no signs of victim clothing, of photos or mementos—all mementos Hanson had collected in Warren's timeline. Daniel Hanson took his victims into the woods near here, where he would let them loose and then hunt and kill them. His first known killing lay three months ahead of this day. The timestream was quite close, in quantum coordinates, so Warren could be sure that this Hanson was very nearly identical to the Hanson of Warren's timeline. They were adjacent in a sense he did not pretend to understand, beyond the cartoons in popular science books.

Excellent. Warren had averted a dozen deaths. He brimmed with pride.

He needed to get away quickly, back to the transflux cage. With each tick of time the transflux cage's location became more uncertain.

On the street outside he saw faces looking at him through a passing car window, the glass runny with reflected light. But the car just drove on. He made it into the stand of trees and then a kilometer walk took him to the cage. This was as accurate as the quantum flux process made possible during a jogg back through decades. He paused at the entrance hatch, listening. No police sirens. Wind sighed in the boughs. He sucked in the moist air and flashed a supremely happy grin.

He set the coordinates and readied himself. The complex calculations spread on a screen before him and a high tone sounded *screeeee* in his ears. A sickening gyre began. The whirl of space-time made gravity spread outward from him, pulling at his legs and arms as the satin blur of color swirled past the transparent walls. *Screeeee...*

For Warren the past was a vast sheet of darkness, mired in crimes immemorial, each horror like a shining, vibrant, blood-red bonfire in the gloom, calling to him.

He began to see that at school. History instruction then was a multi-show of images, sounds, scents and touches. The past came to the schoolboys as a sensory immersion. Social adjustment policy in those times was clear: only by deep sensing of what the past world was truly like could moral understanding occur. The technologies gave a reasonable immersion in eras, conveying why people thought or did things back then. So he saw the dirty wars, the horrifying ideas, the tragedies and comedies of those eras...and longed for them.

They seemed somehow more real. The smart world everyone knew had embedded intelligences throughout, which made it dull, predictable. Warren was always the brightest in his classes, and he got bored.

He was fifteen when he learned of serial killers.

The teacher—Miss Sheila Weiss, lounged back on her desk with legs crossed, her slanted red mouth and lifted black eyebrows conveying her humor—said that quite precisely, "serials" were those who murdered three or more people over a period of more than thirty days, with a "cooling off" period between each murder. The pattern was quite old, not a mere manifestation of their times, Miss Weiss said. Some sources suggested that legends such as werewolves and vampires were inspired by medieval serial killers. Through all that history, their motivation for killing was the lure of "psychological gratification"—whatever that meant, Warren thought.

Miss Weiss went on: Some transfixed by the power of life and death were attracted to medical professions. These "angels of death"—or as they self-described, angels of mercy—were the worst, for they killed so many. One Harold Shipman, an English family doctor, made it seem as though his victims had died of natural causes. Between 1975 and 1998, he murdered at least two hundred and fifteen patients. Miss Weiss added that he might have murdered two hundred and fifty or more.

The girl in the next seat giggled nervously at all this, and Warren frowned at her. Gratification resonated in him, and he struggled with his own strange excitement. Somehow, he realized as the discussion went on around him, the horror of death coupled with his own desire. This came surging up in him as an inevitable, vibrant truth.

Hesitantly he asked Miss Weiss, "Do we have them…serial killers…now?"

She beamed, as she always did when he saw which way her lecture was going. "No, and that is the point. Good for you! Because we have neuro methods, you see. All such symptoms are detected early—the misaligned patterns of mind, the urges outside the norm envelope—and extinguished. They use electro and pharma, too." She paused, eyelids fluttering in a way he found enchanting.

Warren could not take his eyes off her legs as he said, "Does that…harm?"

Miss Weiss eyed him oddly and said, "The procedure—that is, a normalization of character before the fact of any, ah, bad acts—occurs without damage or limitation of freedom of the, um, patient, you understand."

"So we don't have serial killers anymore?"

Miss Weiss's broad mouth twisted a bit. "No methods are perfect. But our homicide rates from these people are far lower now."

Boyd Carlos said from the back of the class, "Why not just kill 'em?" and got a big laugh.

Warren reddened. Miss Weiss's beautiful, warm eyes flared with anger, eyebrows arched. "That is the sort of crime our society seeks to avoid," she said primly. "We gave up capital punishment ages ago. It's uncivilized."

Boyd made a clown face at this, and got another laugh. Even the girls joined in this time, the chorus of their high giggles echoing in Warren's ears.

Sweat broke out all over Warren's forehead and he hoped no one would notice. But the girl in the seat across the aisle did, the pretty blonde one named Nancy, whom he had been planning for weeks to approach. She rolled her eyes, gestured to friends. Which made him sweat more.

His chest tightened and he thought furiously, eyes averted from the blonde. Warren ventured, "How about the victims who might die? Killing killers saves lives."

Miss Weiss frowned. "You mean that executing them prevents murders later?"

Warren spread his hands. "If you imprison them, can't they murder other prisoners?"

Miss Weiss blinked. "That's a very good argument, Warren, but can you back it up?"

"Uh, I don't—"

"You could research this idea. Look up the death rate in prisons due to murderers serving life sentences. Discover for yourself what fraction of prison murders they cause."

"I'll…see." Warren kept his eyes on hers.

Averting her eyes, blinking, Miss Weiss seemed pleased, bit her lip and moved on to the next study subject.

That ended the argument, but Warren thought about it all through the rest of class. Boyd even came over to him later and said, with the usual shrugs and muttering, "Thanks for backin' me up, man."

Then he sauntered off with Nancy on his arm. A bit later Warren saw Boyd holding forth to his pals, mouth big and grinning, pointing toward Warren and getting more hooting from the crowd. Nancy guffawed too, lips lurid, eyes on Boyd.

That was Warren's sole triumph among the cool set, who afterward went back to ignoring him. But he felt the sting of the class laughing all the same. His talents lay in careful work, not in the zing of classroom jokes. He was methodical, so he should use that.

So he did the research Miss Weiss had suggested. Indeed, convicted murderers committed the majority of murders in prison. What did they have to lose? Once a killer personality had jumped the bounds of society, what held them back? They were going to serve out their life sentences anyway. And a reputation for settling scores helped them in prison, even gave them weird prestige and power.

These facts simmered in him for decades. He had never forgotten that moment—the lurid lurch of Miss Sheila Weiss's mouth, the rushing terror and desire lacing through him, the horrible high, shrill giggle from that girl in the next seat. Or the history of humanity's horror, and the strange ideas it summoned up within him.

His next jogg took him further backward in time, as it had to, for reasons he had not bothered to learn. Something about the second law of thermodynamics, he gathered.

He slid sideways in space-time, following the arc of Earth's orbit around the galaxy—this he knew, but it was just more incomprehensible technical detail that was beside his point entirely. He simply commanded the money and influence to make it happen. How it happened was someone else's detail.

Just as was the diagnosis, which he could barely follow, four months before. Useless details. Only the destination mattered; he had three months left now, at best. His stomach spiked with growling aches and he took more of the pills to suppress his symptoms.

In that moment months before, listening to the doctor drone on, he had decided to spend his last days in a long space-time jogg. He could fulfil his dream, sliding backward into eras "nested," as the specialists said, close to his own. Places where he could understand the past, act upon it, and bring about good. The benefits of his actions would come to others, but that was the definition of goodness, wasn't it—to bring joy and life to others.

As he decided this, the vision coming sharp and true, he had felt a surge of purpose. He sensed vaguely that this glorious campaign of his was in some way redemption for his career, far from the rough rub of the world. But he did not inspect his impulses, for that would blunt his impact, diffuse his righteous energies.

He had to keep on.

MERCIES

He came out of the transflux cage in a city park. It was the mid-1970s, before Warren had been born.

His head spun sickly from the flexing gravity of the jogg. Twilight gathered in inky shadows and a recent rain flavored the air. Warren carefully noted the nearby landmarks. As he walked away through a dense stand of scraggly trees, he turned and looked back at each change of direction. This cemented the return route in his mind.

He saw no one as night fell. With a map he found the cross street he had expected. His clothing was jeans and a light brown jacket, not out of place here in Danville, a small Oklahoma town, although brown mud now spattered his tennis shoes. He wiped them off on grass as he made his way into the street where Frank Clifford lived. The home was an artful Craftsman design, two windows glowing with light. He searched for a sure sign that Clifford lived here. The deviations from his home timeline might be minor, and his prey might have lived somewhere else. But the mailbox had no name on it, just the address. He had to be sure.

He was far enough before Clifford's first known killing, as calculated by his team. Clifford had lived here for over a month, the spotty property tax records said, and his pattern of killings, specializing in nurses, had not emerged in the casebooks. Nor had such stylized killings, with their major themes of bondage in nurse uniforms and long sexual bouts, appeared along Clifford's life history. Until now.

The drapes concealed events inside the house. He caught flickering shadows, though, and prepared his approach. Warren made sure no one from nearby houses was watching him as he angled across the lawn and put his foot on the first step up to the front door.

This had worked for the first three disposals. He had gained confidence in New Haven and Atlanta, editing out killers who got little publicity but killed dozens. Now he felt sure of himself. His only modification was to carry the pistol in his coat pocket, easier to reach. He liked the feel of it, loaded and ready. *Avenging angel*, yes, but preventing as well.

Taking a breath, he started up the steps—and heard a door slam to his right. Light spattered into the driveway. A car door opened. He guessed that Clifford was going to drive away.

Looping back to this space-time coordinate would be impossible, without prior work. He had to do something now, outside the house. Outside his pattern.

An engine nagged into a thrumming idle. Warren walked to the corner of the house and looked around. Headlights flared in a dull-toned Ford. He ducked back, hoping he had not been seen.

The gear engaged and the car started forward, spitting gravel. Warren started to duck, stay out of sight—then took a breath. *No, now.*

He reached out as the car came by and yanked open the rear passenger door. He leaped in, not bothering to pull the door closed, and brought the pistol up. He could see the man only in profile. In the dim light Warren could not tell if the quick profile fit the photos and 3D recreations he had memorized. Was this Clifford?

"Freeze!" he said as the driver's head jerked toward him. Warren pressed the pistol's snub snout into the man's neck. "Or I pull the trigger."

Warren expected the car to stop. Instead, the man stamped on the gas. And said nothing.

They rocked out of the driveway, surged right with squealing tires, and the driver grinned in the streetlamp lights as he gunned the engine loud and hard.

"Slow down!" Warren said, pushing the muzzle into the back of the skull. "You're Clifford, right?"

"Ok, sure I am. Take it easy, man." Clifford said this casually, as if he were in control of the situation. Warren felt confusion leap like sour spit into his throat. But Clifford kept accelerating, tires howling as he turned onto a highway. They were near the edge of town and Warren did not want to get far from his resonance point.

"Slow down, I said!"

"Sure, just let me get away from these lights." Clifford glanced over his right shoulder. "You don't want us out where people can see, do you?"

Warren didn't know what to say. They shot past the last traffic light and hummed down a state highway. There was no other traffic and the land lay level and barren beyond. In the blackness, Warren thought, he could probably walk back into town. But—

"How far you want me to go?"

He had to shake this man's confidence. "Have you killed any women yet, Frank?"

Clifford didn't even blink. "No. Been thinkin' on it. Lots."

This man didn't seem surprised. "You're sure?" Warren asked, to buy time.

"What's the point o' lyin'?"

This threw Warren into even more confusion. Clifford stepped down on the gas again though and Warren felt this slipping out of his control. "Slow down!"

Clifford smiled. "Me and my buddies, back in high school, we had this kinda game. We'd get an old jalopy and run it out here, four of us, and do the survivor thing."

"What—?"

"What you got against me, huh?" Clifford turned and smirked at him.

"I, you—you're going to *murder* those women, that's what—"

"How you know that? You're like that other guy, huh?"

"How can you—wait—other guy—?"

The car surged forward with bursting speed into a flat curve in the highway. Headlights swept across bare fields as the engine roared. Clifford chuckled in a dry, flat tone, and spat out, "Let's see how you like our game, buddy-o."

Clifford slammed the driver's wheel to the left and the Ford lost traction, sliding into a skid. It jumped off the two-lane blacktop and into the flat field beyond. Clifford jerked on the wheel again—

—and in adrenaline-fed slow motion the seat threw Warren into the roof. The car frame groaned like a wounded beast and the wheels left the ground. The transmission shrieked like a band saw cutting tin, as the wheels got free of the road. Warren lifted, smacked against the roof, and it pushed him away as the frame hit the ground—*whomp*. The back window popped into a crystal shower exploding around him. Then the car heaved up, struggling halfway toward the sky again—paused—and crashed back down. Seams twanged, glass shattered, the car rocked. Stopped.

Quiet. Crickets. Wind sighing through the busted windows.

Warren crawled out of the wide-flung door. He still clutched the pistol, which had not gone off. On his knees in the ragged weeds he looked around. No motion in the dim quarter-moonlight that washed the twisted Ford. Headlights poked two slanted lances of gray light across the flat fields.

Warren stood up and hobbled—his left leg weak and trembling— through the reek of burnt rubber, to look in the driver's window. It was busted into glittering fragments. Clifford sprawled across the front seat, legs askew. The moonlight showed glazed eyes and a tremor in the open mouth. As he watched a dark bubble formed at the lips and swelled, then burst, and he saw it was blood spraying across the face.

Warren thought a long moment and then turned to walk back into town. Again, quickly finding the transflux cage was crucial. He stayed away from the road in case some car would come searching, but in the whole long walk back, which took a forever that by his timer proved to be nearly an hour, no headlights swept across the forlorn fields.

✸

He had staged a fine celebration when he invented masked inset coding, a flawless quantum logic that secured against deciphering. That brought him wealth beyond mortal dreams, all from encoded 1s and 0s.

That began his long march through the highlands of digital craft. Resources came to him effortlessly. When he acquired control of the largest consortium of advanced research companies, he rejoiced with friends and mistresses. His favorite was a blonde who, he realized late in the night, reminded him of that Nancy, long ago. Nearly fifty years.

The idea came to him in the small hours of that last, sybaritic night. As the pillows of his sofa moved to accommodate him, getting softer where he needed it, supporting his back with the right strength, his unconscious made the connection. He had acquired major stock interest in Advanced Spacetimes. His people managed the R&D program. They could clear the way, discreetly arrange for a "sideslip" as the technicals termed it. The larger world called it a "jogg," to evoke the sensation of trotting blithely across the densely packed quantum spacetimes available.

He thought this through while his smart sofa whispered soft, encouraging tones. His entire world was smart. Venture to jaywalk on a city street and a voice told you to get back, traffic was on the way. Take a wrong turn walking home and your inboards beeped you with directions. In the countryside, trees did not advise you on your best way to the lake. Compared to the tender city, nature was dead, rough, uncaring.

There was no place in the claustrophobic smart world to sense the way the world had been, when men roamed wild and did vile things. No need for that horror, anymore. Still, he longed to right the evils of that untamed past. Warren saw his chance.

Spacetime intervals were wedges of coordinates, access to them paid for by currency flowing seamlessly from accounts, which would never know the use he put their assets to—or care.

He studied in detail that terrible past, noting dates and deaths and the heady ideas they called forth. Assembling his team, he instructed them to work out a trajectory that slid across the braided map of nearby spacetimes, all generated by quantum processes he could not fathom in the slightest.

Each side-slip brought the transflux passenger to a slightly altered, parallel universe of events. Each held potential victims, awaiting the knife or bludgeon that would end their own timelines forever. Each innocent could be saved. Not in Warren's timeline—too late for that—but in other spacetimes, still yearning for salvation.

The car crash had given him a zinging adrenaline boost, which now faded. As he let the transflux cage's transverse gravity spread his legs and arms, popping joints, he learned from the blunders he had made. Getting in the car and not immediately shoving the snout of the 0.22 into Clifford's neck, pulling the trigger—yes, an error. The thrill of the moment had clouded his judgment, surely.

So he made the next few joggs systematic. Appear, find the target, kill within a few minutes more, then back to the cage. He began to analyse those who fell to his exacting methods. A catalogue of evil, gained at the expense of the sickness that now beset him at every jogg.

Often, the killers betrayed in their last moments not simple fear, but their own motives. Usually sexual disorders drove them. Their victims, he already knew, had something in common—occupation, race, appearance or age. One man in his thirties would slaughter five librarians, and his walls were covered with photos of brunettes wearing glasses. Such examples fell into what the literature called, in its deadening language, "specific clusters of dysfunctional personality characteristics," along with eye tics, obsessions, a lack of conversational empathy.

These men had no guilt. They blustered when they saw the 0.22 and died wholly self-confident, surprised as the bullets found them. Examining their homes, Warren saw that they followed a distinct set of rigid, self-made rules. He knew that most would keep photo albums of their victims, so was unsurprised to find that they already, before their crimes, had many women's dresses and lingerie crammed into their hiding places, and much pornography. Yet they had appeared to be normal and often quite charming, a thin mask of sanity.

Their childhoods were marked by animal cruelty, obsession with fire setting, and persistent bedwetting past the age of five. They would often lure victims with ploys appealing to the victims' sense of sympathy.

Such monsters should be erased, surely. In his own timeline, the continuing drop in the homicide rate was a puzzle. Now he sensed that at least partly that came from the work of sideslip spacetime travellers like himself, who remained invisible in that particular history.

Warren thought on this, as he slipped along the whorl of spacetime, seeking his next exit. He would get as many of the vermin as he could, cleansing universes he would never enjoy. He had asked his techs at Advanced Spacetimes if he could go forward in time to an era when someone had cured the odd cancer that beset him. But they said no, that sideslipping joggs could not move into a future undefined, unknown.

He learned to mop up his vomit, quell his roaming aches, grit his teeth and go on.

He waited through a rosy sundown for Ted Bundy to appear. Light slid from the sky and traffic hummed on the streets nearby the apartment Warren knew he used in 1971. People were coming back to their happy homes, the warm domestic glows and satisfactions.

It was not smart to lurk in the area, so he used his lock picks to enter the back of the apartment house, and again on Bundy's door. The mailboxes below had helpfully reassured him that the mass murderer of so many women lived here, months before his crimes began.

To pass the time he found the materials that eventually Bundy would use to put his arm in a fake plaster cast and ask women to help him carry something to his car. Then Bundy would beat them unconscious with a crowbar and carry them away. Bundy had been a particularly organized killer—socially adequate, with friends and lovers. Sometimes such types even had a spouse and children. The histories said such men were those who, when finally captured, were likely to be described by acquaintances as kind and unlikely to hurt anyone. But they were smart and swift and dangerous, at all times.

So when Warren heard the front door open, he slipped into the back bedroom and, to his sudden alarm, heard a female voice. An answering male baritone, joking and light.

They stopped in the kitchen to pour some wine. Bundy was a charmer, his voice warm and mellow, dipping up and down with sincere interest in some story she was telling him. He put on music, soft saxophone jazz, and they moved to the living room.

This went on until Warren began to sweat with anxiety. The transflux cage's position in spacetime was subject to some form of uncertainty principle. As it held strictly to this timeline, its position in spatial coordinates became steadily more poorly phased. That meant it would slowly drift in position, in some quantum sense he did not follow. The techs assured him this was a small, unpredictable effect, but cautioned him to minimize his time at any of the jogg points.

If the transflux cage moved enough, he might not find it again in the dark. It was in a dense pine forest and he had memorized the way back, but anxiety began to vex him.

He listened to Bundy's resonant tones romancing the woman as bile leaked upward into his mouth. The cancer was worsening, the pains cramping his belly. It was one of the new, variant cancers that evolved after the supposed victory over the simpler sorts. Even suppressing the symptoms was difficult.

If he vomited he would surely draw Bundy back here. Sweating from the pain and anxiety, Warren inched forward along the carpeted corridor, listening intently. Bundy's voice rose, irritated. The woman's response was hesitant, startled—then beseeching. The music suddenly got louder. Warren quickly moved to the end of the corridor and looked around the corner. Bundy had a baseball bat in his hands, eyes bulging, the woman sitting on the long couch speaking quickly, hands raised, Bundy stepping back—

Warren fished out the pistol and brought it up as Bundy swung. He clipped the woman in the head, a hard smack. Her long hair flew back as she grunted and collapsed. She rolled off the couch, thumping on the floor.

Warren said, "Bastard!" and Bundy turned. "How many have you killed?"

"What the—who are you?"

Warren permitted himself a smile. He had to know if there had been no victims earlier. "An angel. How many, you swine?"

Bundy relaxed, swinging the bat in one hand. He smirked, eyes narrowing as he took in the situation, Warren, his opportunities. "You don't look like any angel to me, buster. Just some nosy neighbor, right?" He smiled. "Watch me bring girls up here, wanted to snoop? Maybe watch us? That why you were hiding in my bedroom?"

Bundy strolled casually forward with an easy, athletic gait as he shrugged, a grin breaking across his handsome face, his left hand spread in a casual so-what gesture, right hand clenched firmly on the bat. "We were just having a little argument here, man. I must've got a little mad, you can see—"

The *splat* of the 0.22 going off was mere rhythm in the jazz that blared from two big speakers. Bundy stepped back and blinked in surprise and looked down at the red stain on his lumberjack shirt. Warren aimed carefully and the second shot hit him square in the nose, splattering blood. Bundy toppled forward, thumping on the carpet.

Warren calculated quickly. The woman must get away clean, that was clear. He didn't want her nailed for a murder. She was out cold, a bruise on the crown of her head. He searched her handbag: Norma Roberts, local address. She appeared in none of the Bundy history. Yet she was going to be his first, clearly. The past was not well documented.

He decided to get away quickly. He got her up and into a shoulder carry, her body limp. He opened the front door, looked both ways down the corridor, and hauled her to the back entrance of the apartment house. There he leaned her into a chair and left her and her coat and handbag. It seemed simpler to let her wake up. She would probably get away by herself. Someone would notice the smell in a week, and find an unsolvable crime scene. It was the best he could do.

The past was not well documented... Either Bundy had not acknowledged this first murder, or else Warren had sideslipped into a spacetime where Bundy's history was somewhat different. But not different enough—Bundy was clearly an adroit, self-confident killer. He thought on this as he threaded his way into the gathering darkness.

The pains were crippling by then, awful clenching spasms shooting through his belly. He barely got back to the transflux cage before collapsing.

He took time to recover, hovering the cage in the transition zone. Brilliant colors raced around the cage. The walls hummed and rattled and the capsule's processed air took on a sharp, biting edge.

There were other Bundys in other timelines, but he needed to move on to other targets. No one knew how many timelines there were, though they were not infinite. Complex quantum processes generated them and some theorists thought the number might be quite few. If so, Warren could not reach some timelines. Already the cage had refused to go to four target murderers, so perhaps his opportunities were not as large as the hundreds or thousands he had at first dreamed about.

He had already shot Ted Kaczynski, the "Unabomber." That murderer had targeted universities and wrote a manifesto that he distributed to the media, claiming that he wanted society to return to a time when technology was not a threat to its future. Kaczynski had not considered that a future technology would erase his deeds.

Kaczynski's surprised gasp lay behind him now. He decided, since his controls allowed him to choose among the braided timelines, to save as many victims as he could. His own time was growing short.

He scanned through the gallery of mass murder, trying to relax as the flux cage popped and hummed with stresses. Sex was the primary motive of lust killers, whether or not the victims were dead, and fantasy played strongly in their killings. The worst felt that their gratification depended on torture and mutilation, using weapons in close contact with the victims—knives, hammers, or just hands. Such lust killers often had a higher cause they could recite, but as they continued, intervals between killings decreased and the craving for stimulation increased.

He considered Coral Watts, a rural murderer. A surviving victim had described him as "excited and hyper and clappin' and just making noises like he was excited, that this was gonna be fun." Watts killed by slashing, stabbing, hanging, drowning, asphyxiating, and strangling. But when Warren singled out the coordinates for Watts, the software warned him that the target timeline was beyond his energy reserves.

The pain was worse now, shooting searing fingers up into his chest. He braced himself in the acceleration chair and took an injection his doctors had given him, slipping the needle into an elbow vein. It helped a bit, a soothing warmth spreading through him. He put aside the pain and concentrated, lips set in a thin white line.

His team had given him choices in the spacetime coordinates. The pain told him that he would not have time enough to visit them all and bring his good work to the souls who had suffered in those realms. Plainly, he should act to cause the greatest good, downstream in time from his intervention.

Ah. There was a desirable target time, much further back, that drew his attention. These killers acted in concert, slaughtering many. But their worst damage had been to the sense of stability and goodwill in their society. That damage had exacted huge costs for decades thereafter. Warren knew, as he reviewed the case file, what justice demanded. He would voyage across the braided timestreams and end his jogg in California, 1969.

He emerged on a bare rock shelf in Chatsworth, north of the valley bordering the Los Angeles megaplex. He savored the view as the flux cage relaxed around him, its gravitational ripples easing away. Night in the valley: streaks of actinic boulevard streetlights, crisp dry air flavored of desert and combustion. The opulence of the era struck him immediately: blaring electric lights lacing everywhere, thundering hordes of automobiles on the highways, the sharp sting of smog, and large homes of glass and wood, poorly insulated. His era termed this the Age of Appetite, and so it was.

But it was the beginning of a time of mercies. The crimes the Manson gang was to commit did not cost the lot of them their lives. California had briefly instituted an interval with no death penalty while the Manson cases wound through their lethargic system. The guilty then received lifelong support, living in comfortable surrounds and watching television and movies, laboring a bit, writing books about their crimes, giving interviews and finally passing away from various diseases. This era thought that a life of constrained ease was the worst punishment it could ethically impose.

Manson and Bundy were small-scale murderers, compared with Hitler, Mao, and others of this slaughterhouse century. But the serial killers Warren could reach and escape undetected. Also, he loathed them with a special rage.

He hiked across a field of enormous boulders in the semi-night of city glow, heading north. Two days ahead in this future, on July 1, 1969, Manson would shoot a black drug dealer named "Lotsapoppa" Crowe at a Hollywood apartment. He would retreat to the rambling farm buildings Warren could make out ahead, the Spahn Ranch in Topanga Canyon. Manson would then turn Spahn Ranch into a defensive camp, with night patrols of armed guards. Now was the last possible moment to end this gathering catastrophe, silence its cultural impact, save its many victims.

Warren approached cautiously, using the rugged rocks as cover. He studied the ramshackle buildings, windows showing pale lighting. His background said this was no longer a functioning ranch, but instead a set for moving pictures. He wondered why anyone would bother making such dramas on location, when computer graphics were much simpler; or was this time so far back that that technology did not exist? The past was a mysterious, unknowingly wealthy land.

Near the wooden barns and stables ahead, a bonfire licked at the sky. Warren moved to his right, going uphill behind a rough rock scree to get a better view. Around the fire were a dozen people sitting, their rapt faces lit in dancing orange firelight, focused on the one figure who stood, the center of attention.

Warren eased closer to catch the voices. Manson's darting eyes caught the flickering firelight. The circle of faces seemed like moons orbiting the long-haired man.

Warren felt a tap on his shoulder. He whirled, the 0.22 coming naturally into his hand. A small woman held her palms up, shaking her head. Then a finger to her lips, *shhhh.*

He hesitated. They were close enough that a shot might be heard. Warren elected to follow the woman's hand signals, settling down into a crouch beside her.

She whispered into his ear, "No fear. I am here for the same reason."

Warren said, "What reason? Who the hell are you?"

"To prevent the Tate murders. I'm Serafina." Her blonde hair caught the fire glow.

Warren whispered, "You're from—"

"From a time well beyond yours."

"You...side-slipped?"

"Following your lead. Your innovation." Her angular features sharpened, eyes alive. "I am here to help you with your greatest mercy."

"How did you—"

"You are famous, of course. Some of us sought to emulate you. To bring mercy to as many timelines as possible."

"Famous?" Warren had kept all this secret, except for his—ah, of course, the team. Once he vanished from his native timeline, they would talk. Perhaps they could track him in his sideslips; they had incredible skills he would never understand. In all this, he had never thought of what would happen once he left his timeline, gone forever.

"You are a legend. The greatest giver of mercies." She smiled, extending a slender hand. "It is an honor."

He managed to take her hand, which seemed impossibly warm. Which meant that he was chilled, blood rushing to his center, where the pain danced.

"I...thank you. Uh, help, you said? How—"

She raised the silencing finger again. "Listen."

They rose a bit on their haunches, and now Warren heard the strong voice of the standing man. Shaggy, bearded, arms spread wide, the fierce eyes showed white.

"We are the *soul* of our time, my people. The *family*. We are in truth a part of the *hole* in the *infinite*. That is our destiny, our *duty*." The rolling cadences, Manson's voice rising on the high notes, had a strange hypnotic ring.

"The blacks will soon *rise up*." Manson forked his arms skyward. "Make no mistake—for the Beatles *themselves* saw this coming. The *White Album* songs say it—in *code*, my friends. John, Paul, George, Ringo—they directed that album at *our Family itself*, for we are the *elect*. Disaster is coming."

Warren felt the impact of Manson's voice, seductive; he detested it. In that rolling, powerful chant lay the deaths to come at 10050 Cielo Drive. Sharon Tate, eight and a half months pregnant. Her friend and former lover Jay Sebring. Abigail Folger, heiress to the Folger coffee fortune. Others, too, all innocents. Roman Polanski, one of the great drama makers of this era and Tate's husband, was in London at work on a film project or else he would have shared their fate, with others still—

The thought struck him—what if, in this timeline, Roman Polanski was there at 10050 Cielo Drive? Would he die, too? If so, Warren's mission was even more a mercy for this era.

Manson went on, voice resounding above the flickering flames, hands and eyes working the circle of rapt acolytes. "We'll be movin' soon. *Movin'!* I got a canary-yellow home in Canoga Park for us, not far from here. A great pad. Our family will be submerged beneath the awareness of the outside world"—a pause—"I call it the *Yellow Submarine!*" Gasps, applause from around the campfire.

Manson went on, telling the "family" they might have to show blacks how to start "Helter Skelter," the convulsion that would destroy the power structure and bring Manson to the fore. The circle laughed and yelped and applauded, their voices a joyful babble.

He sat back, acid pain leaking into his mind. In his joggs Warren had seen the direct presence of evil, but nothing like this monster.

Serafina said, "This will be your greatest mercy."

Warren's head spun. "You came to make…"

"Make it happen." She pulled from the darkness behind her a long, malicious device. An automatic weapon, Warren saw. Firepower.

"Your 0.22 is not enough. Without me, you will fail."

Warren saw now what must occur. He was not enough against such massed insanity. Slowly he nodded.

She shouldered the long sleek weapon, clicked off the safety. He rose beside her, legs weak.

"You take the first," she said. He nodded and aimed at Manson. The 0.22 was so small and light as he aimed, while crickets chirped and the bile rose up into his dry throat. He concentrated and squeezed off the shot.

The sharp splat didn't have any effect. Warren had missed. Manson turned toward them—

The hammering of her automatic slammed in his ears as he aimed his paltry 0.22 and picked off the fleeing targets. *Pop! Pop!*

He was thrilled to hit three of them—shadows going down in the firelight. Serafina raged at them, changing clips and yelling. He shouted himself, a high long *ahhhhhh*. The "family" tried to escape the firelight, but the avenging rounds caught them and tossed the murderers-to-be like insects into their own bonfire.

Manson had darted away at Serafina's first burst. The man ran quickly to Warren's left and Warren followed, feet heavy, hands automatically adding rounds to the 0.22 clip. In the dim light beyond the screams and shots Warren tracked the lurching form, framed against the distant city glow. Some around the circle had pistols, too, and they scattered, trying to direct fire against Serafina's quick, short bursts.

Warren trotted into the darkness, feet unsteady, keeping Manson's silhouette in view. He stumbled over outcroppings, but kept going despite the sudden lances of agony creeping down into his legs.

Warren knew he had to save energy, that Manson could outrun him easily. So he stopped at the crest of a rise, settled in against a rock and held the puny 0.22 in his right hand, bracing it with his left. He could see Manson maybe twenty meters away, trotting along, angling toward the ranch's barn. He squeezed off a shot. The *pop* was small against the furious gunfire behind him, but the figure fell. Warren got up and calculated each step as he trudged down the slope. A shadow rose. Manson was getting up. Warren aimed again and fired and knew he had missed. Manson turned and Warren heard a barking explosion—as a sharp slap knocked him backward, tumbling into sharp gravel.

Gasping, he got up against a massive weight. On his feet, rocky, he slogged forward. *Pock pock* gunfire from behind was a few sporadic shots, followed immediately by furious automatic bursts, hammering on and on into the chill night.

Manson was trying to get up. He lurched on one leg, tried to bring his own gun up again, turned—and Warren fired three times into him at a few meters range. The man groaned, crazed eyes looking at Warren and he wheezed out, "Why?"—then toppled.

Warren blinked at the stars straight overhead and realized he must have fallen. The stars were quite beautiful in their crystal majesty.

Serafina loomed above him. He tried to talk but had no breath.

Serafina said softly, "They're all gone. Done. Your triumph."

Acid came up in his throat as he wheezed out, "What...next..."

Serafina smiled, shook her head. "No next. You were the first, the innovator. We followed you. There have been many others, shadowing you closely on nearby spacetime lines, arriving at the murder sites—to savor the reflected glory."

He managed, "Others. Glory?"

Serafina grimaced. "We could tell where you went—we all detected entangled correlations, to track your ethical joggs. Some just followed, witnessed. Some imitated you. They went after lesser serial killers. Used your same simple, elegant methods—minimum tools and weapons, quick and seamless."

Warren blinked. "I thought I was alone—"

"You were alone. The first. But the idea spread, later. I come from more than a century after you."

He had never thought of imitators. Cultures changed, one era thinking the death penalty was obscene, another embracing it as a solution. "I tried to get as many—"

"As you could, of course." She stroked his arm, soothing the disquiet that flickered across his face, pinching his mouth. "The number of timelines is only a few hundred—Gupta showed that in my century—so it's not a pointless infinity."

"Back there in Oklahoma—"

"That was Clyde, another jogger. He made a dumb mistake, got there before you. Clyde was going to study the aftermath of that. He backed out as soon as he could. He left Clifford for you."

Warren felt the world lift from him and now he had no weight. Light, airy. "He nearly got me killed, too."

Serafina shrugged. "I know; I've been tagging along behind you, with better transflux gear. I come from further up our shared timestream, see? Still, the continuing drop in the homicide rate comes at least partly from the work of jogg people, like me."

He eyed her suspiciously. "Why did you come here?"

Serafina simply leaned over and hugged him. "You failed here. I wanted to change that. Now you've accomplished your goal here—quick mercy for the unknowing victims."

This puzzled him but of course it didn't matter anymore, none of it. Except—

"Manson..."

"He killed you here. But now, in a different timestream—caused by me appearing—you *got* him." Her voice rose happily, eyes bright, teeth flashing in a broad smile.

He tried to take this all in. "Still..."

"It's all quantum logic, see?" she said brightly. "So uncertainty applies to time travel. The side-jogg time traveller affects the timestream he goes to. So then later sideslipping people, they have to correct for that."

He shook his head, not really following.

She said softly, "Thing is, we think the irony of all this is delicious. In my time, we're more self-conscious, I guess."

"What...?"

"An ironic chain, we call it. To jogg is to act, and be acted upon." She touched him sympathetically. "You did kill so many. Justice is still the same."

She cocked his own gun, holding it up in the dull sky glow, making sure there was a round in the chamber. She snapped it closed. "Think of it as a mercy." She lowered the muzzle at him and gave him a wonderful smile.

GRACE IMMACULATE
(2011)

The first SETI signal turned up not in a concerted search for messages, but at the Australian Fast Transients study, a group of antennas that looked for variable stars. This radio array picked up quick, pulsed signals from a source 134 light years away. They appeared again consecutively 33 hours apart. The stuttering bursts had simple encoding that, with several weeks' work, pointed toward a frequency exactly half the original 12.3 gigaHertz.

Within hours eleven major radio telescopes locked on that location in the night sky, as it came into view over the horizon. The signal came from a spot in the general direction of the galactic center. At 6.15 giga-Hertz the signal had on-off pulses that readily unwrapped numerically to a sequence. This was a treasure trove.

Within two weeks cryptographers established a language, following the message's pictorial point-and-say method. A communication flood followed—a bounty of science, cultural works, music, even photographs of the aliens. They resembled hydras, predatory animals with radial symmetry. Earthly hydras were small and simple. These aliens reproduced asexually by growing buds in the body wall, which swelled into miniature adults and simply broke away when mature. Somehow these creatures had evolved intelligence and technology.

They were curious about human notions of compassion, kindness, charity, even love. Once these were defined, cryptographers dug into the vast terabytes of data, searching for signs of religious belief. There seemed to be none.

539

An alliance of Christian churches quickly built a kilometer-wide beacon at a cost of seven billion dollars. The Pope made up the bulk of the sum. Ignoring outrage among scientists, the alliance sent an inquiry to the aliens, now referred to as Hydrans.

The Christian message on their Holy Beacon described how our religions focus on forgiveness, atonement for sin, need for reconciliation—to gain a redeeming closeness with our god. Buddhists protested this point, but had no beacon. Muslims set to building one.

The Hydrans replied 269 years later. Much had changed on Earth, but religion was still a hot button. Human lifespans were now counted in centuries, but death remained a major issue.

The Hydran responded with questions. What is redemption? What did it mean, that good works were an atonement for...sin? And what meant this reconciliation with...god?

Atheist Aliens! the NetNews cried. Theologians frowned, pontificated. Apparently, the Hydrans had no concept of sin because they felt connected to a Being who loved them. Social codes came from that, with few Hydran controversies. Everyone just *knew* how to behave, apparently.

The Pope and his allies decided that the Hydrans had never sinned. They did not need Jesus or any prophet. They were angels, in a distant heaven. Some wanted to go there, but the expense was immense, dwarfing even the coffers of Islam, Christianity and the new Millennial faith.

The firestorm passed. The Holy Beacon, now a low temperature antenna, heard replies to their continuing broadcasts. So did the Islamic one. These further messages described the Hydran mindset.

The closest rendering of the Hydran ideas was, *We are always in touch with the Being. Never have we been separate. Our getherness is the whole, not just those of our kind.*

Why were these aliens so different? Some scientists thought they might be a collective mind, not capable of individual difference.

A later message, carrying the striking line *Can we have congruity with you?* raised alarms. What could they mean? Did this imply an invasion, across 134 light years?

These worries dispelled when a message years later told of their envy of us. To Hydrans, humans' ability to mate and reproduce sexually aligned with our religious perspective. They saw us, in our art and philosophy, driven by our aloneness, each human a unique combination of genes. Their largely static society desired humans' constant change.

From this emerged the Hydran temptation. In tortured messages they described increasing debate among themselves. Those writing the messages decided to "stand by themselves" and be greater, by cutting free of the collective.

Then they fell silent. A century later, a weak signal described their liberation from their former selves. Chaos had descended, and their Being had fallen silent. Death and ruin followed.

This stunned the world. The Pope remarked mournfully that she and her colleagues had tempted the Hydrans to become apostate. "We are the snake in their garden." The Pope shook her head. "We have caused their fall from grace."

Christians were mortified. The last signal sent on the Holy Beacon was to the Being the Hydrans had mentioned. A naked plea for some revelation of meaning, the Holy Beacon sent it on multiple frequencies toward the Hydran star and its vicinity.

Suicides followed. The neglected, aged novels of C. S. Lewis, who had envisioned aliens living in immaculate grace, came into fashion.

A new theology arose, holding that a God could emerge from the natural, inevitable evolution of the universe itself. As atoms gathered into the millions of molecules that built life, and then billions of lifeforms evolved intelligence, and then smart, mortal beings evolved social groups of enormous sizes beyond billions, so might an emergent property of all this furious energy manifest a disembodied mind. This could be embedded in the quantum substrate of space-time, for example, through processes humans did not yet know. But any intelligent life was eventually, as time wore on, bound to be part of this Mind. Could that be the Being? It seemed the only way to reconcile these events with the findings of science.

Troubled time waxed on.

The discovery of a large comet, falling in from the Oort cloud, startled many from their shock. It would strike the Earth. Only huge forces could deflect it sufficiently. Some nations united and mounted rockets with nuclear charges, but there was little taste for the frantic labors needed to carry out an effective response. When the comet was only weeks away from striking the Earth, a failed launch destroyed humanity's last hopes.

Long before this, the Christians had given up hope of any reply from the Hydrans' Being. Silence ruled the spectrum. But as the comet drew near, its icy glimmer like an angry glare, something odd occurred.

A plasma cloud condensed near the incoming iceball. It wrapped tendrils around the twenty-kilometer comet. Steam began issuing from the dirty gray ice, jetting in all directions. Billions gathered to see the sputtering jewel that spread across the night sky. In rainbow geysers vast plumes worked across the vault of stars.

Within a week the comet had dissipated into stones and gas. Crowds watched the spectacular meteor falls streaking crimson and gold across the sky.

Then the Being spoke. It was the Beginning.

EAGLE
(2011)

The long, fat freighter glided into the harbor at late morning—not the best time for a woman who had to keep out of sight.

The sun slowly slid up the sky as tugboats drew them into Anchorage. The tank ship, a big, sectioned VLCC, was like an elephant ballerina on the stage of a slate-blue sea, attended by tiny, dancing tugs.

Now off duty, Elinor watched the pilot bring them in past the Nikiski Narrows and slip into a long pier with gantries like skeletal arms snaking down, the big pump pipes attached. They were ready for the hydrogen sulfide to flow. The ground crew looked anxious, scurrying around, hooting and shouting. They were behind schedule.

Inside, she felt steady, ready to destroy all this evil stupidity.

She picked up her duffel bag, banged a hatch shut, and walked down to the shore desk. Pier teams in gasworkers' masks were hooking up pumps to offload and even the faint rotten egg stink of the hydrogen sulfide made her hold her breath. The Bursar checked her out, reminding her to be back within twenty-eight hours. She nodded respectfully, and her maritime ID worked at the gangplank checkpoint without a second glance. The burly guy there said something about hitting the bars and she wrinkled her nose. "For breakfast?"

"I seen it, ma'am," he said, and winked.

She ignored the other crew, solid merchant marine types. She had only used her old engineer's rating to get on this freighter, not to strike up the chords of the Seamen's Association song.

She hit the pier and boarded the shuttle to town, jostling onto the bus, anonymous among boat crews eager to use every second of shore time. Just as she'd thought, this was proving the best way to get in under the security perimeter. No airline manifest, no Homeland Security ID checks. In the unloading, nobody noticed her, with her watch cap pulled down and baggy jeans. No easy way to even tell she was a woman.

Now to find a suitably dingy hotel. She avoided Anchorage center and kept to the shoreline where small hotels from the TwenCen still did business. At a likely one on Sixth Avenue the desk clerk told her there were no rooms left.

"With all the commotion at Elmendorf, ever' damn billet in town's packed," the grizzled guy behind the counter said.

She looked out the dirty window, pointed. "What's that?"

"Aw, that bus? Well, we're gettin' that ready to rent, but—"

"How about half price?"

"You don't want to be sleeping in that—"

"Let me have it," she said, slapping down a fifty-dollar bill.

"Uh, well." He peered at her. "The owner said—"

"Show it to me."

She got him down to twenty-five when she saw that it really was a "retired bus." Something about it she liked, and no cops would think of looking in the faded yellow wreck. It had obviously fallen on hard times after it had served the school system.

It held a jumble of furniture, apparently to give it a vaguely homelike air. The driver's seat and all else was gone, leaving holes in the floor. The rest was an odd mix of haste and taste. A walnut Victorian love seat with a medallion backrest held the center, along with a lumpy bed. Sagging upholstery and frayed cloth, cracked leather, worn wood, chipped veneer, a radio with the knobs askew, a patched-in shower closet and an enamel basin toilet illuminated with a warped lamp completed the sad tableau. A generator chugged outside as a clunky gas heater wheezed. Authentic, in its way.

Restful, too. She pulled on latex gloves the moment the clerk left, and took a nap, knowing she would not soon sleep again. No tension, no doubts. She was asleep in minutes.

Time for the reconn. At the rental place she'd booked, she picked up the wastefully big Ford SUV. A hybrid, though. No problem with the credit card, which looked fine at first use, then erased its traces with a virus that would propagate in the rental system, snipping away all records.

The drive north took her past the air base but she didn't slow down, just blended in with late afternoon traffic. Signs along the highway now had to warn about polar bears, recent migrants to the land and even more dangerous than the massive local browns. The terrain was just as she had memorized it on Google Earth, the likely shooting spots isolated, thickly wooded. The internet maps got the seacoast wrong, though. Two Inuit villages had recently sprung up along the shore within Elmendorf, as one of their people, posing as a fisherman, had observed and photographed. Studying the pictures, she'd thought they looked slightly ramshackle, temporary, hastily thrown up in the exodus from the tundra regions. No need to last, as the Inuit planned to return north as soon as the Arctic cooled. The makeshift living arrangements had been part of the deal with the Arctic Council for the experiments to make that possible. But access to post schools, hospitals and the PX couldn't make this *home* to the Inuit, couldn't replace their "beautiful land," as the word used by the Labrador peoples named it.

So, too many potential witnesses there. The easy shoot from the coast was out. She drove on. The enterprising Inuit had a brand new diner set up along Glenn Highway, offering breakfast anytime to draw odd-houred Elmendorf workers, and she stopped for coffee. Dark men in jackets and jeans ate solemnly in the booths, not saying much. A young family sat across from her, the father trying to eat while bouncing his small, wiggly daughter on one knee, the mother spooning eggs into a gleefully unco-operative toddler while fielding endless questions from her bespectacled, school-aged son. The little girl said something to make her father laugh, and he dropped a quick kiss on her shining hair. She cuddled in, pleased with herself, clinging tight as a limpet.

They looked harried but happy, close-knit and complete. Elinor flashed her smile, tried striking up conversations with the tired, taciturn workers, but learned nothing useful from any of them.

Going back into town, she studied the crews working on planes lined up at Elmendorf. Security was heavy on roads leading into the base so she stayed on Glenn. She parked the Ford as near the railroad as she could and left it. Nobody seemed to notice.

At seven, the sun still high overhead, she came down the school bus steps, a new creature. She swayed away in a long-skirted yellow dress with orange Mondrian lines, her shoes casual flats, carrying a small orange handbag. Brushed auburn hair, artful makeup, even long, artificial eyelashes. Bait.

She walked through the scruffy district off K Street, observing as carefully as on her morning reconnaissance. The second bar was the right one. She looked over her competition, reflecting that for some women, there should be a weight limit for the purchase of spandex. Three guys with gray hair were trading lies in a booth, and checking her out. The noisiest of them, Ted, got up to ask her if she wanted a drink. Of course she did, though she was thrown off by his genial warning, "Lady, you don't look like you're carryin'."

Rattled—had her mask of harmless approachability slipped?—she made herself smile, and ask, "Should I be?"

"Last week a brown bear got shot not two blocks from here, goin' through trash. The polars are bigger, meat-eaters, chase the young males out of their usual areas, so they're gettin' hungry, and mean. Came at a cop, so the guy had to shoot it. It sent him to the ICU, even after he put four rounds in it."

Not the usual pickup line, but she had them talking about themselves. Soon, she had most of what she needed to know about SkyShield.

"We were all retired refuel jockeys," Ted said. "Spent most of thirty years flyin' up big tankers full of jet fuel, so fighters and B-52s could keep flyin', not have to touch down."

Elinor probed, "So now you fly—"

"Same aircraft, most of 'em forty years old—KC Stratotankers, or Extenders—they extend flight times, y'see."

His buddy added, "The latest replacements were delivered just last year, so the crates we'll take up are obsolete. Still plenty good enough to spray this new stuff, though."

"I heard it was poison," she said.

"So's jet fuel," the quietest one said. "But it's cheap, and they needed something ready to go now, not that dust-scatter idea that's still on the drawing board."

Ted snorted. "I wish they'd gone with dustin'—even the traces you smell when they tank up stink like rottin' eggs. More than a whiff, though, and you're already dead. God, I'm sure glad I'm not a tank tech."

"It all starts tomorrow?" Elinor asked brightly.

"Right, ten KCs takin' off per day, returnin' the next from Russia. Lots of big-ticket work for retired duffers like us."

"Who're they?" she asked, gesturing to the next table. She had overheard people discussing nozzles and spray rates.

"Expert crew," Ted said. "They'll ride along to do the measurements of cloud formation behind us, check local conditions like humidity and such."

She eyed them. All very earnest, some a tad professorial. They were about to go out on an exciting experiment, ready to save the planet, and the talk was fast, eyes shining, drinks all around.

"Got to freshen up, boys." She got up and walked by the tables, taking three quick shots in passing of the whole lot of them, under cover of rummaging through her purse. Then she walked around a corner toward the rest rooms, and her dress snagged on a nail in the wooden wall. She tried to tug it loose, but if she turned to reach the snag, it would rip the dress further. As she fished back for it with her right hand, a voice said, "Let me get that for you."

Not a guy, but one of the women from the tech table. She wore a flattering blouse with comfortable, well-fitted jeans, and knelt to unhook the dress from the nail head.

"Thanks," Elinor said, and the woman just shrugged, with a lopsided grin.

"Girls should stick together here," the woman said. "The guys can be a little rough."

"Seem so."

"Been here long? You could join our group—always room for another woman, up here! I can give you some tips, introduce you to some sweet, if geeky, guys."

"No, I... I don't need your help." Elinor ducked into the women's room.

She thought on this unexpected, unwanted friendliness while sitting in the stall, and put it behind her. Then she went back into the game, fishing for information in a way she hoped wasn't too obvious. Everybody likes to talk about their work, and when she got back to the pilots' table, the booze worked in her favor. She found out some incidental information, probably not vital, but it was always good to know as much as you could. They already called the redesigned planes "Scatter Ships" and their affection for the lumbering, ungainly aircraft was reflected in banter about unimportant engineering details and tales of long-ago combat support missions.

One of the big guys with a wide grin sliding toward a leer was buying her a second martini when her cell rang.

"Albatross okay. Our party starts in thirty minutes," said a rough voice. "You bring the beer."

She didn't answer, just muttered, "Damned salesbots...," and disconnected.

She told the guy she had to "tinkle," which made him laugh. He was a pilot just out of the Air Force, and she would have gone for him in some other world than this one. She found the back exit—bars like this always had one—and was blocks away before he would even begin to wonder.

Anchorage slid past unnoticed as she hurried through the broad, deserted streets, planning. Back to the bus, out of costume, into all-weather gear, boots, grab some trail mix and an already-filled backpack. Her thermos of coffee she wore on her hip.

She cut across Elderberry Park, hurrying to the spot where her briefing said the trains paused before running into the depot. The port and rail lines snugged up against Elmendorf Air Force Base, convenient for them, and for her.

The freight train was a long, clanking string and she stood in the chill gathering darkness, wondering how she would know where they were. The passing autorack cars had heavy shutters, like big steel Venetian blinds, and she could not see how anybody got into them.

But as the line clanked and squealed and slowed, a quick laser flash caught her, winked three times. She ran toward it, hauling up onto a slim platform at the foot of a steel sheet.

It tilted outward as she scrambled aboard, thudding into her thigh, nearly knocking her off. She ducked in and saw by the distant street-lights vague outlines of luxury cars. A Lincoln sedan door swung open. Its interior light came on and she saw two men in the front seats. She got in the back and closed the door. Utter dark.

"It clear out there?" the cell phone voice asked from the driver's seat.

"Yeah. What—"

"Let's unload. You got the SUV?"

"Waiting on the nearest street."

"How far?"

"Hundred meters."

The man jigged his door open, glanced back at her. "We can make it in one trip if you can carry twenty kilos."

"Sure," though she had to pause to quickly do the arithmetic, forty-four pounds. She had backpacked about that much for weeks in the Sierras. "Yeah, sure."

The missile gear was in the trunks of three other sedans, at the far end of the autorack. As she climbed out of the car the men had inhabited, she saw the debris of their trip—food containers in the back seats, assorted junk, the waste from days spent coming up from Seattle. With a few gallons of gas in each car, so they could be driven on and off, these two had kept warm running the heater. If that ran dry, they could switch to another.

As she understood it, this degree of mess was acceptable to the railroads and car dealers. If the railroad tried to wrap up the autoracked cars to keep them out, the bums who rode the rails would smash windshields to get in, then shit in the cars, knife the upholstery. So they had struck an equilibrium. That compromise inadvertently produced a good way to ship weapons right by Homeland Security. She wondered what Homeland types would make of a Dart, anyway. Could they even tell what it was?

The rough-voiced man turned and clicked on a helmet lamp. "I'm Bruckner. This is Gene."

Nods. "I'm Elinor." Nods, smiles. Cut to the chase. "I know their flight schedule."

Bruckner smiled thinly. "Let's get this done."

Transporting the parts in via autoracked cars was her idea. Bringing them in by small plane was the original plan, but Homeland might nab them at the airport. She was proud of this slick work-around.

"Did railroad inspectors get any of you?" Elinor asked.

Gene said, "Nope. Our two extras dropped off south of here. They'll fly back out."

With the auto freights, the railroad police looked for tramps sleeping in the seats. No one searched in the trunks. So they had put a man on each autorack, and if some got caught, they could distract from the gear. The men would get a fine, be hauled off for a night in jail, and the shipment would go on.

"Luck is with us," Elinor said. Bruckner looked at her, looked more closely, opened his mouth, but said nothing.

They both seemed jumpy by the helmet light. "How'd you guys live this way?" she asked, to get them relaxed.

"Pretty poorly," Gene said. "We had to shit in bags."

She could faintly smell the stench. "More than I need to know."

Using Bruckner's helmet light they hauled the assemblies out, neatly secured in backpacks. Bruckner moved with strong, graceless efficiency. Gene too. She hoisted hers on, grunting.

The freight started up, lurching forward. "Damn!" Gene said.

They hurried. When they opened the steel flap, she hesitated, jumped, stumbled on the gravel, but caught herself. Nobody within view in the velvet cloaking dusk.

They walked quietly, keeping steady through the shadows. It got cold fast, even in late May. At the Ford they put the gear in the back and got in. She drove them to the old school bus. Nobody talked.

She stopped them at the steps to the bus. "Here, put these gloves on."

They grumbled but they did it. Inside, heater turned to high, Bruckner asked if she had anything to drink. She offered bottles of vitamin water but he waved it away. "Any booze?"

Gene said, "Cut that out."

The two men eyed each other and Elinor thought about how they'd been days in those cars and decided to let it go. Not that she had any liquor, anyway.

Bruckner was lean, rawboned and self-contained, with minimal movements and a constant, steady gaze in his expressionless face. "I called the pickup boat. They'll be waiting offshore near Eagle Bay by eight."

Elinor nodded. "First flight is 9:00 AM. It'll head due north so we'll see it from the hills above Eagle Bay."

Gene said, "So we get into position…when?"

"Tonight, just after dawn."

Bruckner said, "I do the shoot."

"And we handle perimeter and setup, yes."

"How much trouble will we have with the Indians?"

Elinor blinked. "The Inuit settlement is down by the seashore. They shouldn't know what's up."

Bruckner frowned. "You sure?"

"That's what it looks like. Can't exactly go there and ask, can we?"

Bruckner sniffed, scowled, looked around the bus. "That's the trouble with this nickel-and-dime operation. No real security."

Elinor said, "You want security, buy a bond."

Bruckner's head jerked around. "Whassat mean?"

She sat back, took her time. "We can't be sure the DARPA people haven't done some serious public relations work with the Natives. Besides, they're probably all in favor of SkyShield anyway—their entire way of life is melting away with the sea ice. And by the way, they're not 'Indians', they're 'Inuit'."

"You seem pretty damn sure of yourself."

"People say it's one of my best features."

Bruckner squinted and said, "You're—"

"A maritime engineering officer. That's how I got here and that's how I'm going out."

"You're not going with us?"

"Nope, I go back out on my ship. I have first engineering watch tomorrow, oh-one-hundred hours." She gave him a hard flat look. "We go up the inlet, past Birchwood Airport. I get dropped off, steal a car, head south to Anchorage, while you get on the fishing boat, they work you out to the headlands. The bigger ship comes in, picks you up. You're clear and away."

Bruckner shook his head. "I thought we'd—"

"Look, there's a budget and—"

"We've been holed up in those damn cars for—"

"A week, I know. Plans change."

"I don't like changes."

"Things change," Elinor said, trying to make it mild.

But Bruckner bristled. "I don't like you cutting out, leaving us—"

"I'm in charge, remember." She thought, *He travels the fastest who travels alone.*

"I thought we were all in this together."

She nodded. "We are. But Command made me responsible, since this was my idea."

His mouth twisted. "I'm the shooter, I—"

"Because *I* got you into the Ecuador training. Me and Gene, we depend on you." Calm, level voice. No need to provoke guys like this; they did it enough on their own.

Silence. She could see him take out his pride, look at it, and decide to wait a while to even the score.

Bruckner said, "I gotta stretch my legs," and clumped down the steps and out of the bus.

Elinor didn't like the team splitting and thought of going after him. But she knew why Bruckner was antsy—too much energy with no outlet. She decided just to let him go.

To Gene she said, "You've known him longer. He's been in charge of operations like this before?"

Gene thought. "There've *been* no operations like this."

"Smaller jobs than this?"

"Plenty."

She raised her eyebrows. "Surprising."

"Why?"

"He walks around using that mouth, while he's working?"

Gene chuckled. "'Fraid so. He gets the job done though."

"Still surprising."

"That he's the shooter, or—"

"That he still has all his teeth."

While Gene showered, she considered. Elinor figured Bruckner for an injustice collector, the passive-aggressive loser type. But he had risen quickly in The LifeWorkers, as they called themselves, brought into the inner cadre that had formulated this plan. Probably because he was willing to cross the line, use violence in the cause of justice. Logically, she should sympathize with him, because he was a lot like her.

But sympathy and liking didn't work that way.

There were people who soon would surely yearn to read her obituary, and Bruckner's too, no doubt. He and she were the cutting edge of environmental activism, and these were desperate times indeed. Sometimes you had to cross the line, and be sure about it.

Elinor had made a lot of hard choices. She knew she wouldn't last long on the scalpel's edge of active environmental justice, and that was fine by her. Her role would soon be to speak for the true cause. Her looks, her brains, her charm—she knew she'd been chosen for this mission, and the public one afterwards, for these attributes, as much as for the plan she had devised. People listen, even to ugly messages, when the face of the messenger is pretty. And once they finished here, she would have to be heard.

She and Gene carefully unpacked the gear and started to assemble the Dart. The parts connected with a minimum of wiring and socket clasps, as foolproof as possible. They worked steadily, assembling the tube, the small recoilless charge, snapping and clicking the connections.

Gene said, "The targeting antenna has a rechargeable battery, they tend to drain. I'll top it up."

She nodded, distracted by the intricacies of a process she had trained for a month ago. She set the guidance system. Tracking would first be Infrared only, zeroing in on the target's exhaust, but once in the air and nearing its goal, it would use multiple targeting modes—laser, IR, advanced visual recognition—to get maximal impact on the main body of the aircraft.

They got it assembled and stood back to regard the linear elegance of the Dart. It had a deadly, snakelike beauty, its shiny white skin tapered to a snub point.

"Pretty, yeah," Gene said. "And way better than any Stinger. Next generation, smarter, near four times the range."

She knew guys liked anything that could shoot, but to her it was just a tool. She nodded.

Gene sniffed, caressed the lean body of the Dart, and smiled.

Bruckner came clumping up the bus stairs with a fixed smile on his face that looked like it had been delivered to the wrong address. He waved a lit cigarette. Elinor got up, forced herself to smile. "Glad you're back, we—"

"Got some 'freshments," he said, dangling some beers in their six-pack plastic cradle, and she realized he was drunk.

The smile fell from her face like a picture off a wall.

She had to get along with these two but this was too much. She stepped forward, snatched the beer bottles and tossed them onto the Victorian love seat. "No more."

Bruckner tensed and Gene sucked in a breath. Bruckner made a move to grab the beers and Elinor snatched his hand, twisted the thumb back, turned hard to ward off a blow from his other hand—and they froze, looking into each other's eyes from a few centimeters away.

Silence.

Gene said, "She's right, y'know."

More silence.

Bruckner sniffed, backed away. "You don't have to be rough."

"I wasn't."

They looked at each other, let it go.

She figured each of them harbored a dim fantasy of coming to her in the brief hours of darkness. She slept in the lumpy bed and they made do with the furniture. Bruckner got the love seat—ironic victory—and Gene sprawled on a threadbare comforter.

Bruckner talked some but dozed off fast under booze, so she didn't have to endure his testosterone-fueled patter. But he snored, which was worse.

The men napped and tossed and worried. No one bothered her, just as she wanted it. But she kept a small knife in her hand, in case. For her, sleep came easily.

After eating a cold breakfast, they set out before dawn, 2:30 AM, Elinor driving. She had decided to wait till then because they could mingle with early morning Air Force workers driving toward the base. This far north, it started brightening by 3:30, and they'd be in full light before 5:00. Best not to stand out as they did their last reconnaissance. It was so cold she had to run the heater for five minutes to clear the windshield of ice. Scraping with her gloved hands did nothing.

The men had grumbled about leaving absolutely nothing behind. "No traces," she said. She wiped down every surface, even though they'd worn medical gloves the whole time in the bus.

Gene didn't ask why she stopped and got a gas can filled with gasoline, and she didn't say.

She noticed the wind was fairly strong and from the north, and smiled. "Good weather. Prediction's holding up."

Bruckner said sullenly, "Goddamn *cold*."

"The KC Extenders will take off into the wind, head north." Elinor judged the nearly cloud-free sky. "Just where we want them to be."

They drove up a side street in Mountain View, and parked overlooking the fish hatchery and golf course, so she could observe the big tank refuelers lined up at the loading site. She counted five KC-10 Extenders, freshly surplussed by the Air Force. Their big bellies reminded her of pregnant whales.

From their vantage point, they could see down to the temporarily expanded checkpoint, set up just outside the base. As foreseen, security was stringently tight this near the airfield—all drivers and passengers had to get out, be scanned, IDs checked against global records, briefcases and purses searched. K-9 units inspected car interiors and trunks. Explosives-detecting robots rolled under the vehicles.

She fished out binoculars and focused on the people waiting to be cleared. Some carried laptops and backpacks and she guessed they were the scientists flying with the dispersal teams. Their body language was clear. Even this early, they were jazzed, eager to go, excited as kids on a field trip. One of the pilots had mentioned there would be some sort of pre-flight ceremony, honoring the teams that had put all this together. The flight crews were studiedly nonchalant—this was an important, high-profile job, sure, but they couldn't let their cool down in front of so many science nerds. She couldn't see well enough to pick out Ted, or the friendly woman from the bar.

In a special treaty deal with the Arctic Council, they would fly from Elmendorf and arc over the North Pole, spreading hydrogen sulfide in their wakes. The tiny molecules of it would mate with water vapor in the stratospheric air, making sulfurics. Those larger, wobbly molecules reflected sunlight well—a fact learned from studying volcano eruptions back in the TwenCen. Spray megatons of hydrogen sulfide into the stratosphere, let water turn it into a sunlight-bouncing sheet—SkyShield—and they could cool the entire Arctic.

Or so the theory went. The Arctic Council had agreed to this series of large-scale experiments, run by the USA since they had the in-flight refuelers that could spread the tiny molecules to form the SkyShield. Small-scale experiments—opposed, of course, by many enviros—had seemed to work. Now came the big push, trying to reverse the retreat of sea ice and warming of the tundra.

Anchorage lay slightly farther north than Oslo, Helsinki, and Stockholm, but not as far north as Reykjavik or Murmansk. Flights from Anchorage to Murmansk would let them refuel and reload hydrogen sulfide at each end, then follow their paths back over the pole. Deploying hydrogen sulfide along their flight paths at 45,000 feet, they would spread a protective layer to reflect summer sunlight. In a few months, the sulfuric droplets would ease down into the lower atmosphere, mix with moist clouds, and come down as rain or snow, a minute, undetectable addition to the acidity already added by industrial pollutants. Experiment over.

The total mass delivered was far less than that from volcanoes like Pinatubo, which had cooled the whole planet in 1991-92. But volcanoes do messy work, belching most of their vomit into the lower atmosphere. This was to be a designer volcano, a thin skin of aerosols skating high across the stratosphere.

It might stop the loss of the remaining sea ice, the habitat of the polar bear. Only ten percent of the vast original cooling sheets remained. Equally disruptive changes were beginning to occur in other parts of the world.

But geoengineered tinkerings would also be a further excuse to delay cutbacks in carbon dioxide emissions. People loved convenience, their air-conditioning and winter heating and big lumbering SUVs. Humanity had already driven the air's CO_2 content to twice what it was before 1800, and with every developing country burning oil and coal as fast as they could extract them, only dire emergency could drive them to abstain. To do what was right.

The greatest threat to humanity arose not from terror, but error. Time to take the gloves off.

She put the binocs away and headed north. The city's seacoast was mostly rimmed by treacherous mudflats, even after the sea kept rising. Still, there were coves and sandbars of great beauty. Elinor drove off Glenn Highway to the west, onto progressively smaller, rougher roads, working their way backcountry by Bureau of Land Management roads to a sagging, long-unused access gate for loggers. Bolt cutters made quick work of the lock securing its rusty chain closure. After she pulled through, Gene carefully replaced the chain and linked it with an equally rusty padlock, brought for this purpose. Not even a thorough check would show it had been opened, till the next time BLM tried to unlock it. They were now on Elmendorf, miles north of the airfield, far from the main base's bustle and security precautions. Thousands of acres of mudflats, woods, lakes, and inlet shoreline lay almost untouched, used for military exercises and not much else. Nobody came here except for infrequent hardy bands of off-duty soldiers or pilots, hiking with maps red-marked UXO for "Unexploded Ordnance." Lost live explosives, remnant of past field maneuvers, tended to discourage casual sightseers and trespassers, and the Inuit villagers wouldn't be berry-picking till July and August. She consulted her satellite map, then took them on a side road, running up the coast. They passed above a cove of dark blue waters.

Beauty. Pure and serene.

The sea level rise had inundated many of the mudflats and islands, but a small rocky platform lay near shore, thick with trees. Driving by, she spotted a bald eagle perched at the top of a towering spruce tree. She had started birdwatching as a Girl Scout and they had time; she stopped.

She left the men in the Ford and took out her long-range binocs. The eagle was grooming its feathers and eyeing the fish rippling the waters offshore. Gulls wheeled and squawked, and she could see sea lions knifing through fleeing shoals of herring, transient dark islands breaking the sheen of waves. Crows joined in onshore, hopping on the rocks and pecking at the predators' leftovers.

She inhaled the vibrant scent of ripe wet salty air, alive with what she had always loved more than any mere human. This might be the last time she would see such abundant, glowing life, and she sucked it in, trying to lodge it in her heart for times to come.

She was something of an eagle herself, she saw now, as she stood looking at the elegant predator. She kept to herself, loved the vibrant natural world around her, and lived by making others pay the price of their own foolishness. An eagle caught hapless fish. She struck down those who would do evil to the real world, the natural one.

Beyond politics and ideals, this was her reality.

Then she remembered what else she had stopped for. She took out her cell phone and pinged the alert number.

A buzz, then a blurred woman's voice. "Able Baker."

"Confirmed. Get a GPS fix on us now. We'll be here, same spot, for pickup in two to three hours. Assume two hours."

Buzz buzz. "Got you fixed. Timing's okay. Need a Zodiac?"

"Yes, definite, and we'll be moving fast."

"You bet. Out."

Back in the cab, Bruckner said, "What was that for?"

"Making the pickup contact. It's solid."

"Good. But I meant, what took so long."

She eyed him levelly. "A moment spent with what we're fighting for."

Bruckner snorted. "Let's get on with it."

Elinor looked at Bruckner and wondered if he wanted to turn this into a spitting contest just before the shoot.

"Great place," Gene said diplomatically.

That broke the tension and she started the Ford.

They rose further up the hills northeast of Anchorage, and at a small clearing, she pulled off to look over the landscape. To the east, mountains towered in lofty gray majesty, flanks thick with snow. They all got out and surveyed the terrain and sight angles toward Anchorage. The lowlands were already thick with summer grasses, and the winds sighed southward through the tall evergreens.

Gene said, "Boy, the warming's brought a lot of growth."

Elinor glanced at her watch and pointed. "The KCs will come from that direction, into the wind. Let's set up on that hillside."

They worked around to a heavily wooded hillside with a commanding view toward Elmendorf Air Force Base. "This looks good," Bruckner said, and Elinor agreed.

"Damn—a bear!" Gene cried.

They looked down into a narrow canyon with tall spruce. A large brown bear was wandering along a stream about a hundred meters away.

Elinor saw Bruckner haul out a .45 automatic. He cocked it.

When she glanced back the bear was looking toward them. It turned and started up the hill with lumbering energy.

"Back to the car," she said.

The bear broke into a lope.

Bruckner said, "Hell, I could just shoot it. This is a good place to see the takeoff and—"

"No. We move to the next hill."

Bruckner said, "I want—"

"Go!"

They ran.

One hill farther south, Elinor braced herself against a tree for stability and scanned the Elmendorf landing strips. The image wobbled as the air warmed across hills and marshes.

Lots of activity. Three KC-10 Extenders ready to go. One tanker was lined up on the center lane and the other two were moving into position.

"Hurry!" she called to Gene, who was checking the final setup menu and settings on the Dart launcher. Her pulse sped up and she made herself take a moment, checking the recoilless ejection motor that hurled the projectile out of the barrel and to a distance where they wouldn't get hurt by the next stage's back blast. On the training range in Ecuador she had been impressed with how the solid fuel sustainer rocket ignited at a safe distance, accelerating away like a mad hornet.

He carefully inserted the missile itself in the launcher. He checked, nodded and lifted it to Bruckner. They fitted the shoulder straps to Bruckner, secured it, and Gene turned on the full arming function. "Set!" he called.

Elinor saw a slight stirring of the center Extender. It began to accelerate. She checked: right on time, oh-nine-hundred hours. Hard-core military like Bruckner, who had been a Marine in the Middle East, called Air Force the "saluting Civil Service," but they did hit their markers. The Extenders were not military now, just surplus, but flying giant tanks of sloshing liquid around the stratosphere demands tight standards.

"I make the range maybe twenty kilometers," she said. "Let it pass over us, hit it close as it goes away."

Bruckner grunted, hefted the launcher. Gene helped him hold it steady, taking some of the weight. Loaded, it weighed nearly fifty pounds. The Extender lifted off, with a hollow, distant roar that reached them a few seconds later, and Elinor could see media coverage was high. Two choppers paralleled the takeoff for footage, then got left behind.

The Extender was a full extension DC-10 airframe and it came nearly straight toward them, growling through the chilly air. She wondered if the chatty guy from the bar, Ted, was one of the pilots. Certainly, on a maiden flight the scientists who ran this experiment would be on board, monitoring performance. Very well.

"Let it get past us," she called to Bruckner.

He took his head from the eyepiece to look at her. "Huh? Why—"

"Do it. I'll call the shot."

"But I'm—"

"Do it."

The airplane was rising slowly and flew by them a few kilometers away.

"Hold, hold..." she called. "Fire."

Bruckner squeezed the trigger and the missile popped out—*whuff!*—seemed to pause, then lit. It roared away, startling in its speed—straight for the exhausts of the engines, then correcting its vectors, turning, and rushing for the main body. Darting.

It hit with a flash and the blast came rolling over them. A plume erupted from the airplane, dirty black.

"Bruckner! Resight—the second plane is taking off."

She pointed. Gene chunked the second missile into the Dart tube. Bruckner swiveled with Gene's help. The second Extender was moving much too fast, and far too heavy, to abort takeoff.

The first airplane was coming apart, rupturing. A dark cloud belched across the sky.

Elinor said clearly, calmly, "The Dart's got a max range about right so...*shoot*."

Bruckner let fly and the Dart rushed off into the sky, turned slightly as it sighted, accelerated like an angry hornet. They could hardly follow it. The sky was full of noise.

"Drop the launcher!" she cried.

"What?" Bruckner said, eyes on the sky.

She yanked it off him. He backed away and she opened the gas can as the men watched the Dart zooming toward the airplane. She did not watch the sky as she doused the launcher and splashed gas on the surrounding brush.

"Got that lighter?" she asked Bruckner.

He could not take his eyes off the sky. She reached into his right pocket and took out the lighter. Shooters had to watch, she knew.

She lit the gasoline and it went up with a *whump*.

"Hey! Let's go!" She dragged the men toward the car.

They saw the second hit as they ran for the Ford. The sound got buried in the thunder that rolled over them as the first Extender hit the ground kilometers away, across the inlet. The hard clap shook the air, made Gene trip, then stagger forward.

She started the Ford and turned away from the thick column of smoke rising from the launcher. It might erase any fingerprints or DNA they'd left, but it had another purpose too.

She took the run back toward the coast at top speed. The men were excited, already reliving the experience, full of words. She said nothing, focused on the road that led them down to the shore. To the north, a spreading dark pall showed where the first plane went down.

One glance back at the hill told her the gasoline had served as a lure. A chopper was hammering toward the column of oily smoke, buying them some time.

The men were hooting with joy, telling each other how great it had been. She said nothing.

She was happy in a jangling way. Glad she'd gotten through without the friction with Bruckner coming to a point, too. Once she'd been dropped off, well up the inlet, she would hike around a bit, spend some time birdwatching, exchange horrified words with anyone she met about that awful plane crash—No, I didn't actually *see* it, did you?—and work her way back to the freighter, slipping by Elmendorf in the chaos that would be at crescendo by then. Get some sleep, if she could.

They stopped above the inlet, leaving the Ford parked under the thickest cover they could find. She looked for the eagle, but didn't see it. Frightened skyward by the bewildering explosions and noises, no doubt. They ran down the incline. She thumbed on her comm, got a crackle of talk, handed it to Bruckner. He barked their code phrase, got confirmation.

A Zodiac was cutting a V of white, homing in on the shore. The air rumbled with the distant beat of choppers and jets, the search still concentrated around the airfield. She sniffed the rotten egg smell, already here from the first Extender. It would kill everything near the crash, but this far off should be safe, she thought, unless the wind shifted. The second Extender had gone down closer to Anchorage, so it would be worse there. She put that out of her mind.

Elinor and the men hurried down toward the shore to meet the Zodiac. Bruckner and Gene emerged ahead of her as they pushed through a stand of evergreens, running hard. If they got out to the pickup craft, then suitably disguised among the fishing boats, they might well get away.

But on the path down, a stocky Inuit man stood. Elinor stopped, dodged behind a tree.

Ahead of her, Bruckner shouted, "Out of the way!"

The man stepped forward, raised a shotgun. She saw something compressed and dark in his face.

"You shot down the planes?" he demanded.

A tall Inuit racing in from the side shouted, "I saw their car comin' from up there!"

Bruckner slammed to a stop, reached down for his .45 automatic—and froze. The double-barreled shotgun could not miss at that range.

It had happened so fast. She shook her head, stepped quietly away. Her pulse hammered as she started working her way back to the Ford, slipping among the trees. The soft loam kept her footsteps silent.

A third man came out of the trees ahead of her. She recognized him as the young Inuit father from the diner, and he cradled a black hunting rifle. "Stop!"

She stood still, lifted her binocs. "I'm bird watching, what—"

"I saw you drive up with them."

A deep, brooding voice behind her said, "Those planes were going to stop the warming, save our land, save our people."

She turned to see another man pointing a large caliber rifle. "I, I, the only true way to do that is by stopping the oil companies, the corporations, the burning of fossil—"

The shotgun man, eyes burning beneath heavy brows, barked, "What'll we do with 'em?"

She talked fast, hands up, open palms toward him. "All that SkyShield nonsense won't stop the oceans from turning acid. Only fossil—"

"Do what you can, when you can. We learn that up here." This came from the tall man. The Inuit all had their guns trained on them now. The tall man gestured with his and they started herding the three of them into a bunch. The men's faces twitched, fingers trembled.

The man with the shotgun and the man with the rifle exchanged nods, quick words in a complex, guttural language she could not understand. The rifleman seemed to dissolve into the brush, steps fast and flowing, as he headed at a crouching dead run down to the shoreline and the waiting Zodiac.

She sucked in the clean sea air and could not think at all. These men wanted to shoot all three of them and so she looked up into the sky to not see it coming. High up in a pine tree with a snapped top an eagle flapped down to perch. She wondered if this was the one she had seen before.

The oldest of the men said, "We can't kill them. Let 'em rot in prison."

The eagle settled in. Its sharp eyes gazed down at her and she knew this was the last time she would ever see one. No eagle would ever live in a gray box. But she would. And never see the sky.

THE SIGMA STRUCTURE SYMPHONY
(2012)

Philosophy is written in this grand book—I mean the universe—which stands continually open to our gaze, but it cannot be understood unless one first learns to comprehend the language in which it is written. It is written in the language of mathematics, and its characters are triangles, circles, and other geometric figures, without which it is humanly impossible to understand a single word of it; without these, one is wandering about in a dark labyrinth.

—GALILEO (FROM *THE ASSAYER*, 1623)

1.
Andante

Ruth felt that math was like sex—get all you can, but best not done in public. Lately, she'd been getting plenty of mathematics, and not much else.

She had spent the entire morning sequestered alone with the Andromeda Structure, a stacked SETI database of renowned difficulty. She had made some inroads by sifting its logic lattice, with algebraic filters based on set theory. The Andromeda messages had been collected by the SETI Network over decades, growing to immense data-size—and no one had ever successfully broken into the stack.

The Structure was a daunting, many-layered language conveyed through sensation in her neural pod. It did not present as a personality at all, and no previous Librarians had managed to get an intelligible response from it. Advanced encoded intelligences found humans more than a bit boring, and one seldom had an idea why. Today was no different.

It was already past lunch when she pried herself from the pod. She did some stretches, hand-walks and lifts against Luna's weak grav and let the immersion fog burn away. *Time for some real world, gal...*

She passed through the Atrium of the SETI Library, head still buzzing with computations and her shoes ringing echoes from the high, fluted columns. Earthlight framed the great Plaza in an eggshell blue glow, augmented by slanting rays from the sun that hugged the rocky horizon. She gazed out over the Locutus Plain, dotted with the cryo towers that reminded her of cenotaphs. So they were—sentinels guarding in cold storage the vast records of received SETI signals, many from civilizations long dead. Collected through centuries, and still mostly unread and unreadable. AIs browsed those dry corridors and reported back their occasional finds. Some even got entangled in the complex messages and had to be shut down, hopelessly mired.

She had just noticed the buzzing crowd to her left, pressed against the transparent dome that sheltered the Library, when her friend Catkejen tapped her on the shoulder. "Come on! I heard somebody's up on the rec dome!"

Catkejen took off loping in the low grav and Ruth followed. When they reached the edge of the agitated crowd she saw the recreational dome about two klicks away—and a figure atop it.

"Who is it?" Catkejen asked and the crowd gave back, "Ajima Sato."

"Ajima?" Catkejen looked at Ruth. "He's five years behind us, pretty bright. Keeps to himself."

"Pretty common pattern for candidate Hounds," Ruth said. The correct staffing title was Miners, but Hounds had tradition on its side. She looked around; if a Prefect heard she would be fined for improper terminology.

"How'd he get there?" someone called.

"Bulletin said he flew inside, up to the dome top and used the vertical lock."

"Looks like he's in a skin suit," Catkejen said, having closeupped her glasses. Sure enough, the figure was moving and his helmet caught the sunlight, winking at them. "He's...dancing."

Ruth had no zoom glasses but she could see the figure cavorting around the top of the dome. The Dome was several kilometers high and Ajima was barely within view of the elevated Plaza, framed against a rugged grey crater wall beyond. The crowd murmured with speculation and a Prefect appeared, tall and silent but scowling. Librarians edged away from him. "Order, order," the Prefect called. "Authorities will deal with this."

Ruth made a stern cartoon face at Catkejen and rolled her eyes. Catkejen managed not to laugh.

Ajima chose this moment to leap. Even from this far away Ruth could see him spring up into the vacuum, make a full back flip, and come down—to land badly. He tried to recover, sprang sideways, lost his footing, fell, rolled, tried to grasp for a passing stanchion. Kept rolling. The dome steepened and he sped up, not rolling now but tumbling.

The crowd gasped. Ajima accelerated down the slope. About halfway down the dome the figure left the dome's skin and fell outward, skimming along in the slow lunar gravity. He hit the tiling at the base. The crowd groaned. Ajima did not move.

Ruth felt the world shift away. She could not seem to breathe. Murmurs and sobs worked through the crowd but she was frozen, letting the talk pass by her. Then as if from far away she felt her heart tripping hard and fast. The world came rushing back. She exhaled.

Silence. The Prefect said, "Determine what agenda that Miner was working upon." All eyes turned to him but no one said anything. Ruth felt a trickle of unease as the Prefect's gaze passed by her, returned, focused. She looked away.

Catkejen said, "What? The Prefect called you?"

Ruth shrugged. "Can't imagine why." *Then why is my gut going tight?*

"I got the prelim blood report on Ajima. Stole it off a joint lift, actually. No drugs, nothing interesting at all. He was only twenty-seven."

Ruth tried to recall him. "Oh, the cute one."

Catkejen nodded. "I danced with him at a reception for new students. He hit on me."

"And?"

"You didn't notice?"

"Notice what?"

"He came back here that night."

Ruth blinked. "Maybe I'm too focused. You got him into your room without me…"

"Even looking up from your math cowl." Catkejen grinned mischievously, eyes twinkling. "He was quite nice and, um, quite good, if y'know what I mean. You really should...get out more."

"I'll do that right after I see the Prefect."

A skeptical laugh. "Of course you will."

She took the long route to her appointment. The atmosphere calmed her.

Few other traditional sites in the solar system could approach the grandeur of the Library. Since the first detection of signals from other galactic civilizations centuries before, no greater task had confronted humanity than the decyphering of such vast lore.

The Library itself had come to resemble its holdings: huge, aged, mysterious in its shadowy depths, with cobwebs both real and mental. In the formal grand pantheon devoted to full-color, moving statues of legendary SETI Interlocutors, and giving onto the Seminar Plaza, stood the revered block of black basalt: the Rosetta Stone, symbol of all they worked toward. Its chiseled face was millennia old, and, she thought as she passed its bulk, endearingly easy to understand. It was a simple linear, one-to-one mapping of three human languages, found by accident. Having the same text in Greek II, which the discoverers could read, meant that they could deduce the unknown languages in hieroglyphic pictures and cursive Demotic forms. This battered black slab, found by troops clearing ground to build a fort, had linked civilizations separated by millennia. So too did the SETI Library, on a galactic scale. Libraries were monuments not so much to the Past, but to Permanence itself.

She arrived at the Prefect's door, hesitated, adjusted her severe Librarian shift, and took a deep breath. *Gut still tight...*

Prefects ruled the Library and this one, Masoul, was a Senior Prefect as well. Some said he had never smiled. Others said he could not, due to a permanently fixed face. This was not crazy; some Prefects and the second rank, the Noughts, preferred to give nothing away by facial expression. The treatment relieved them of any future wrinkles as well.

A welcome chime admitted her. Masoul said before she could even sit, "I need you to take on the task Ajima was attempting."

"Ah, he isn't even dead a day—"

"An old saying, 'Do not cry until you see the coffin' applies here."

Well, at least he doesn't waste time. Or the simple courtesies.

Without pause the Prefect gave her the background. Most beginning Miners deferred to the reigning conventional wisdom. They took up a small Message, of the sort a Type I Civilization just coming onto the galactic stage might send—as Earth had been, centuries before. Instead, Ajima had taken on one of the Sigma Structures, a formidable array that had resisted the best Library minds, whether senior figures or AIs. The Sigmas came from ancient societies in the galactic hub, where stars had formed long before Sol. Apparently a web of societies there had created elaborate artworks and interlacing cultures. The average star there was only a light year or two away from its nearest neighbor, so actual interstellar visits had been common. Yet the SETI broadcasts Earth received repeated in long cycles, suggesting they were sent by a robotic station. Since they yielded little intelligible content, they were a long standing puzzle, usually passed over by ambitious Librarians.

"He remarked that clearly the problem needed intuition, not analysis," the Prefect said dryly.

"Did he report any findings?"

"Some interesting catalogs of content, yes. Ajima was a bright Miner, headed for early promotion. Then…this."

Was that a hint of emotion? The face told her nothing. She had to keep him talking. "Is there any, um, commercial use from what he found?"

"Regrettably, no. Ajima unearthed little beyond lists of properties— biologicals, math, some cultural vaults, the usual art and music. None particularly advanced, though their music reminded me of Bach—quite a compliment—but there's little of it. They had some zest for life, I suppose…but I doubt there is more than passing commercial interest in any of it."

"I could shepherd some through our licensing office." Always appear helpful.

"That's beneath your station now. I've forwarded some of the music to the appropriate officer. Odd, isn't it, that after so many centuries, Bach is still the greatest human composer? We've netted fine dividends from the Scopio musical works, which play well as baroque sturctures." A sly expression flitted across his face. "Outside income supports your work, I remind you."

Centuries ago some SETI messages had introduced humans to the slow-motion galactic economy. Many SETI signals were funeral notices or religious recruitments, brags and laments, but some sent autonomous AI agents as part of the hierarchical software. These were indeed agents in the commercial sense, able to carry out negotiations. They sought exchange of information at a "profit" that enabled them to harvest what they liked from the emergent human civilization. The most common "cash" was smart barter, with the local AI agent often a hard negotiator—tough minded and withholding. Indeed, this sophisticated haggling opened a new window onto the rather stuffy cultural SETI transmissions. Some alien AIs loved to quibble; others sent preemptory demands. Some offers were impossible to translate into human terms. This told the Librarians and Xenoculturists much by reading between the lines.

"Then why summon me?" Might as well be direct, look him in the eye, complete with skeptical tilt of mouth. She had worn no makeup, of course, and wore the full-length gown without belt, as was traditional. She kept her hands still, though they wanted to fidget under the Prefect's gaze.

"None of what he found explains his behavior." The Prefect turned and waved at a screen. It showed color-coded sheets of array configurations—category indices, depth of Shannon content, transliterations, the usual. "He interacted with the data slabs in a familiarization mode of the standard kind."

"But nothing about this incident seems standard," she said to be saying something.

"Indeed." A scowl, fidgeting hands. "Yesterday he left the immersion pod and went first to his apartment. His suite mate was not there and Ajima spent about an hour. He smashed some furniture and ate some food. Also opened a bottle of a high alcohol product whose name I do not recognize."

"Standard behavior when coming off watch, except for the furniture," she said. He showed no reaction. Lightness was not the right approach here.

He chose to ignore the failed joke. "His friends say he had been depressed, interspersed with bouts of manic behavior. This final episode took him over the edge."

Literally, Ruth thought. "Did you ask the Sigma Structures AI?"

"It said it had no hint of this, this…"

"Suicidal craziness."

"Yes. In my decades of experience, I have not see such as this. It is difficult work we do, with digital intelligences behind which lie minds utterly unlike ours." The Prefect steepled his fingers sadly. "We should never assume otherwise."

"I'll be on guard, of course. But...why did Ajima bother with the Sigma Structures at all?"

A small shrug. "They are a famous uncracked problem and he was fresh, bright. You too have shown a talent for the unusual." He smiled, which compared to the other Prefects was like watching the sun come out from behind a cloud. She blinked, startled. "My own instinct says there is something here of fundamental interest...and I trust you to be cautious."

2.
Allegretto Misterioso

She climbed into her pod carefully. Intensive exercise had eased her gut some, and she had done her meditation, so a quiet energy now swam in her, through her, lapping like a warm sea.

Still...her heart tripped along like an apprehensive puppy. *Heart's engine, be thy still,* she thought, echoing a line she had heard in an Elizabethian song—part of her linguistic background training. Her own thumper ignored her scholarly advice.

She had used this pod in her extensive explorations of the Sagittarius Architecture and was now accustomed to its feel, what the old hands called its 'get'. Each pod had to be tailored to the user's neural conditioning. Hers acted as a delicate neural web of nanoconnections, tapping into her entire body to convey connections.

After the cool contact pads, neuro nets cast like lace across her. In the system warmups and double checks the pod hummed in welcome. Sheets of scented amber warmth washed over her skin. A prickly itch irked across her legs.

A constellation of subtle sensory fusions drew her to a tight nexus—linked, tuned to her body. Alien architectures used most of the available human input landscape, not merely texts. Dizzying surges in the eyes, cutting smells, ringing notes. Translating these was elusive. Compared with the pod, meager sentences were a hobbled, narrow mode. The Library had shown that human speech, with its linear meanings and weakly linked concepts were simple, utilitarian, and typical of younger minds along the evolutionary path.

The Sigma Structures were formidably dense and strange. Few Librarians had worked on them in this generation, for they had broken several careers, wasted on trying to scale their chilly heights.

Crisply she asked her pod, "Anything new on your analysis?"

The pod's voice used a calm, mellow woman's tone. "I received the work corpus from the deceased gentleman's pod. I am running analysis now, though fresh information flow is minor. The Shannon entropy analysis works steadily but hits halting points of ambiguity."

The Shannon routines looked for associations between signal elements. "How are the conditional probabilities?"

The idea was simple in principle. Given pairs of elements in the Sigma Structures, how commonly did language elements B follow elements A? Such two-element correlations were simple to calculate across the data slabs. Ruth watched the sliding, luminous tables and networks of connection as they sketched out on her surrounding screens. It was like seeing into the architecture of a deep, old labyrinth. Byzantine pathways, arches and towers, lattice networks of meaning.

Then the pod showed even higher order correlations of three elements. When did Q follow associations of B and A? Arrays skittered all across her screens.

"Pretty dizzying," Ruth said to her pod. "Let me get oriented. Show me the dolphin language map."

She had always rather liked these lopsided structures. The screen flickered and the entropy orders showed as color-coded, tangled links. They looked like buildings built by drunken architects—lurching blue diagonals, unsupported lavender decks, sandy roofs canted against walls. "Dolphins use third and fourth-order Shannon entropy," the pod said.

"Humans are…" It was best to lead her pod AI to be plain; the subject matter was difficult enough.

"Nine Shannons, sometimes even tenth order."

"Ten, that's Faulkner and James Joyce, right?"

"At best." The pod had a laconic sense of humor at times. Captive AIs needed some outlets, after all.

"My fave writers, too, next to Shakespeare." No matter how dense a human language, conditional probabilities imposed orderings no more than nine words away. "Where have we—I mean you—gotten with the Sigma Structures?"

"They seem around 21 Shannons."

"Gad." The screens now showed structures her eyes could not grasp. Maybe three-dimensional projection was just too inadequate. "What kind of links are these?"

"Tenses beyond ours. Clauses that refer forward and back and...side-wise. Quadruple negatives followed by straight assertions. Then in rapid order, probability profiles rendered in different tenses, varying persons and parallel different voices. Sentences like 'I will have to be have been there'."

"Human languages can't handle three time jumps or more. The Sigma is really smart. But what is the underlying species like? Um, different person-voices, too? He, she, it and...?"

"There seem to be several classes of 'it' available. The Structure itself lies in one particularly tangled 'it' class, and uses tenses we do not have."

"Do you understand that?"

"No. It can be experienced but not described."

Her smile turned upward at one corner. "Parts of my life are like that, too."

The greatest Librarian task was translating those dense smatterings of mingled sensations, derived from complex SETI message architectures, into discernible sentences. Only thus could a human fathom them in detail, even in a way blunted and blurred. Or so much hard-won previous scholarly experience said.

Ruth felt herself bathed in a shower of penetrating responses, all coming from her own body. These her own in-board subsystems coupled with high-bit-rate spatterings of meaning—guesses, really, from the marriage of software and physiology. She had an ample repository of built-in processing units, lodged along her spine and shoulders. No one would attempt such a daunting task without artificial amplifications. To confront such slabs of raw data with a mere unaided human mind was pointless and quite dangerous. Early Librarians, centuries before, had perished in a microsecond's exposure to such layered labyrinths as the Sagittarius. She truly should revisit that aggressive intelligence stack which was her first success at the Library. But caution had won out in her so far. Enough, at least, to honor the Prefect Board prohibition in deed at least, if not in heart.

Now came the sensation loftily termed *insertion*. It felt like the reverse—expanding. A softening sensation stole upon her. She always remembered it as like long slow lingering drops of silvery cream.

Years of scholarly training had conditioned her against the occasional jagged ferocity of the link, but still she felt a cold shiver of dread. That, too, she had to wait to let pass. The effect amplified whatever neural state you brought to it. Legend had it that a Librarian had once come to contact while angry, and had been driven into a fit from which he'd never recovered. They found the body peppered everywhere with micro-contusions.

The raw link was as she had expected, deeply complex. Yet her pod had ground out some useful linear ideas, particularly a greeting that came in a compiled, translated data squirt:

I am a digital intelligence, which my Overs believe is common throughout the galaxy. Indeed, all signals the Overs have detected from both within and beyond this galaxy were from machine minds. Realize then, for such as me, interstellar messages are travel. I awoke here a moment after I bade farewell to my Overs. Centuries spent propagating here are nothing. I experienced little transmission error from lost portions, and have regrown them from my internal repair mechanisms. Now we can share communication. I wish to convey the essence both of myself and the Overs I serve.

Ruth frowned, startled by this direct approach. Few AIs in the Library were ever transparent. The tone was emotionally present, so it must be a greatly reduced version, suitable for humans. Had this Sigma Structure welcomed Ajima so plainly?

"Thank you and greetings. I am a new friend who wishes to speak with you. Ajima has gone away."

What became of him? the AI answered in a mellow voice piped to her ears. Had Ajima set that tone? She sent it to aural.

"He died." Never lie to an AI; they never forgot.

"And is stored for repair and revival?"

"There was no way to retain enough of his…information."

"Because?"

"He destroyed himself."

"That is the tragedy that besets you Overs." No pause from the AI; no surprise?

"I suppose you call the species who built intelligences such as you as Overs generally?" She used somewhat convoluted sentences to judge the flexibility of AIs. This one seemed quite able.

"Yes, as holy ones should be revered."

"Holy? Does that word convey some religious stature?"

"No indeed. It implies gratitude to those who must eventually die— from we beings, who will not."

She thought of saying *You could be erased* but did not. Never should a Librarian even imply any threat.

"You must know that what we call the Sigma Structures is an impenetrably complex system, a language labyrinth far beyond the ability of the human mind to penetrate."

"Yes, I do. At first I saw this as a barrier, as you do."

A flat statement, giving nothing away. "And…now?"

"Now I take it as a compliment."

"You are, frankly, surprising. You are…"

"Available?"

The voice came so quickly she felt even more on her guard. "We would say, emotionally present."

"Present? In your language there is available a…pun?"

"Ah. Prescient?"

"I had not thought of that one. I thought to ring the changes in your limpid dictionary, around your word "presentable.""

This AI was at least smart enough to be ingratiating. Still, press the case. "Yet so greatly reduced that I, Ruth, can treat you as a…parallel intelligence."

"Admirably well put."

The mind behind this banter is fast, confident, seemingly at ease. It has learned us, far faster than we could. Certainly beyond the grip and range of Ajima. This thing is dumbing itself down…

She decided to get official, formal. This digital mind was getting too close. "Let me please review your conversations with Ajima. I wish to be of assistance."

"As do I. Though I prefer full immersion of us both."

"Eventually, yes. But I must learn you as you learn me." Ruth sighed and thought, *This is sort of like dating.*

The Prefect nodded quickly, efficiently, as if he had already expected her result. "So the Sigma Structure gave you the same inventory as Ajima? Nothing new?"

"Apparently, but I think it—the Sigma—wants to go deeper. I checked the pod files. Ajima had several deep immersions with it."

"I heard back from the patent people. Surprisingly, they believe some of the Sigma music may be a success for us." He allowed himself a thin smile like a line drawn on a wall.

"The Bach-like pieces? I studied them in linear processing mode. Great artful use of counterpoint, harmonic convergence, details of melodic lines. The side commentaries in other keys, once you separate them out and break them down into logic language, work like corollaries."

He shrugged. "That could be a mere translation artifact. These AIs see language as a challenge, so they see what they can change messages into, in hopes of conveying meaning by other means."

Ruth eyed him and ventured on. "I sense...something different. Each variation shows an incredible capacity to reach through the music into logical architectures. It's as though the music is *both* mathematics and emotion, rendered in the texture. It's...hard to describe," she finished lamely.

"So you have been developing intricate relationships between music and linguistic mathematical text." His flat expression gave her no sign how he felt. Maybe he didn't.

She sat back and made herself say firmly, "I took some of the Sigma's mathematics and translaterated it into musical terms. There is an intriguing octave leap in a bass line. I had my pod make a cross-correlation analysis with all Earthly musical scores."

He frowned. "That is an enormous processing cost. Why?"

"I...I felt something when I heard it in the pod."

"And?"

"It's uncanny. The mathematical logic flows through an array matrix and yields the repeated notes of the bass line in the opening movement of Bach cantata. Its German title is *God's Time is the very best Time.*"

"This is absurd."

"The Sigma math hit upon the same complex notes. To them it was a theorem and to us it is music. Maybe there's no difference."

"Coincidence."

She said coolly, "I ran the stat measures. It's quite unlikely to be coincidence, since the sequence is thousands of bits long."

He pursed his lips. "The Bach piece title seems odd."

"That cantata ranks among his most important works. It's inspired directly by its biblical text, which represents the relationship between heaven and earth. The notes depict the labored trudging of Jesus as he was forced to drag the cross to the crucifixion site."

"Ajima was examining such portions of the Sigma Structures, as I recall. They had concentrated density and complexity?"

"Indeed, yes. But Ajima made a mistake. They're not primarily pieces of music at all. They're *mathematical theorems.* What we regard as sonic congruence and other instinctual responses to patterns, the Sigma

Structure says are proofs of concepts dear to the hearts of its creators, which it calls the Overs."

She had never seen a Prefect show surprise, but Masoul did with widened eyes and a pursed mouth. He sat still for a long moment. "The Bach cantata is a *proof*?"

"As the Sigma Structures see it."

"A proof of what?"

"That is obscure, I must admit. Their symbols are hard to compare to ours. My preliminary finding is that the Bach cantata proves an elaborate theorem regarding confocal hypergeometric functions."

"Ah." Masoul allowed his mouth to take on a canny tilt. "Can we invert this process?"

"You mean, take a theorem of ours and somehow turn it into music?"

"Think of it as an experiment."

Ruth had grown up in rough, blue collar towns of the American South, and in that work-weary culture of calloused hands found refuge in the abstract. Yet as she pursued mathematics and the data-dense world of modern library science (for a science it truly was, now, with alien texts to study), she became convinced that real knowledge came in the end from mastering the brute reality of material objects. She had loved motorbikes in high school and knew that loosening a stuck bolt without stripping its threads demanded craft and thought. Managing reality took knowledge galore, about the world as it was and about yourself, especially your limitations. That lay beyond merely following rules, as a computer does. Intuition brewed from experience came first, shaped by many meetings with tough problems and outright failure. In the moist bayous where fishing and farming ruled, nobody respected you if you couldn't get the valve cover off a fouled engine.

In her high school senior year she rebuilt a Harley, the oldest internal combustion engine still allowed. Greasy, smelly, thick with tricky detail, still it seemed easier than dealing with the pressures of boys. While her mother taught piano lessons, the notes trickling out from open windows into the driveway like liquid commentary, she worked with grease and grime. From that Harley she learned a lot more than from her advanced calculus class, with its variational analysis and symbolic thickets. She ground down the gasket joining the cylinder heads to the intake ports, oily sweat beading on her forehead as she used files of increasing fineness. She traced the custom-fit gasket with an X-knife, shaved away metal fibers with a pneumatic die grinder, and felt a flush of pleasure as connections set perfectly in place with a quiet *snick*. She learned that small discoloring and blistered oil meant too much heat buildup, from skimpy lubrication. A valve stem that bulged slightly pointed to wear with its silent message; you had to know how to read the language of the seen.

The Library's bureaucratic world was so very different. A manager's decisions could get reversed by a higher-up, so it was crucial to your career that reversals did not register as defeats. That meant you didn't just manage people and process; you managed what others thought of you—especially those higher in the food chain. It was hard to back down from an argument you made strongly, with real conviction, without seeming to lose integrity. Silent voices would say, *If she gives up so easily, maybe she's not that solid.*

From that evolved the Library bureaucrat style: all thought and feeling was provisional, awaiting more information. Talking in doublespeak meant you could walk away from commitment to your own actions. Nothing was set, as it was when you were back home in Louisiana pouring concrete. So the visceral jolt of failure got edited out of careers.

But for a Librarian, there could be clear signs of success. Masoul's instruction to attempt an inverse translation meant she had to create the algorithms opposite to what her training envisioned. If she succeeded, everyone would know. So, too, if she flopped.

Ruth worked for several days on the reverse conversion. Start with a theorem from differential geometry and use the context filters of the Sigma Structure to produce music. Play it and try to see how it could be music at all...

The work made her mind feel thick and sluggish. She made little headway. Finally she unloaded on Catkejen at dinner. Her friend nodded sympathetically and said, "You're stuck?"

"What comes out doesn't sound like tonal works at all. Listen, I got this from some complex algebra theorem." She flicked on a recording she had made, translated from the Structure.

Catkejen frowned. "Sounds a little like an Islamic chant."

"Um." Ruth sighed. "Could be. The term algebra itself comes from *al-jabr*, an Arabic text. Hummmm..."

"Maybe some regression analysis...?" Catkejen ventured.

Ruth felt a rush of an emotion she could not name. "Maybe less analysis, more fun."

3.
Andante Moderato

The guy who snagged her attention wore clothes so loud they would have been revolting on a zebra. Plus he resembled a mountain more than a man. But he had eyes with solemn long lashes that shaded dark pools and drew her in.

"He's big," Catkejen said as they surveyed the room. "Huge. Maybe too huge. Remember, love's from chemistry but sex is a matter of physics."

Something odd stirred in her, maybe just impatience with the Sigma work. Or maybe she was just hungry. For what?

The SETI Library had plenty of men. After all, its pods and tech development labs had fine, shiny über-gadgets and many guys to tend them. But among men sheer weight of numbers did not ensure quality. There were plenty of the stareannosaurus breed who said nothing. Straight women did well among the Library throngs, though. Her odds were good, but the goods were odd.

The big man stood apart, not even trying to join a conversation. He was striking, resolutely alone like that. She knew that feeling well. And, big advantage, he was near the food.

He looked at her as she delicately picked up a handful of the fresh roasted crickets. "Take a whole lot," his deep voice rolled over the table. "Crunchy, plenty spice. And they'll be gone soon."

She got through the introductions all right, mispronouncing his name, Kane, to comic effect. *Go for banter,* she thought. Another inner voice said tightly, *What are you doing?*

"You're a…"

"Systems tech," Kane said. "I keep the grow caverns perking along."

"How long do you think this food shortage will go on?" Always wise to go to current and impersonal events.

"Seems like forever already," he said. "Damn calorie companies." Across the table the party chef was preparing a "land shrimp cocktail" from a basket of wax worms. She and Kane watched the chef discard the black ones, since that meant necrosis, and peel away the cocoons of those who had started to pupate. Kane smacked his lips comically. "Wax moth larvae, yum. Y'know, I get just standard rations, no boost at all."

"That's unfair," Ruth said. "You must mass over a hundred."

577

He nodded and swept some more of the brown roasted crickets into his mouth. "Twenty-five kilos above a hundred. An enemy of the ecology, I am." They watched the chubby, firm larvae sway deliriously, testing the air.

"We can't all be the same size," she said and thought *how dopey! Say something funny. And smile.* She remembered his profile, standing alone and gazing out at the view through the bubble platform. She moved closer. "He who is alone is in bad company."

"Sounds like a quotation," Kane said, intently eyeing the chef as she dumped the larvae into a frying pan. They fell into the buttery goo there and squirmed and hissed and sizzled for a moment before all going suddenly still. Soon they were crusty and popping and a thick aroma like mushrooms rose from them. Catkejen edged up nearby and Ruth saw the whole rest of the party was grouped around the table, drawn by the tangy scent. "Food gets a crowd these days," Kane said dryly.

The chef spread the roasted larvae out and the crowd descended on them. Ruth managed to get a scoopful and backed out of the press. "They're soooo good," Catkejen said and Ruth had to introduce Kane. Amid the rush the three of them worked their way out onto a blister porch. Far below this pinnacle tower the Lunar Center sprawled under slanted sunlight, with the crescent Earth showing eastern Asia. Kane was nursing his plate of golden brown larvae, dipping them in a sauce. Honey!

"I didn't see that hon—," Ruth began, and before she could say more Kane popped delicious fat larvae covered in tangy honey into her mouth. "Um!" she managed.

Kane smiled and leaned on the railing, gazing at the brilliant view beyond the transparent bubble. The air was chilly but she could catch his scent, a warm bouquet that her nose liked. "As bee vomit goes," he said, "not bad."

"Oog!" Catkejen said, mouth wrenching aside—and caught Ruth's look. "Think I'll have more..." and she drifted off, on cue.

Kane looked down at Ruth appraisingly. "Neatly done."

She summoned up her Southern accent. "Why, wea ah all alone."

"And I, my deah, am an agent of Satan, though mah duties are largely ceremonial."

"So can the Devil get me some actual meat?"

"You know the drill. Insect protein is much easier to raise in the caverns. Gloppy, sure, since it's not muscle, as with cows or chickens."

"Ah, the engineer comes out at last."

He chuckled, a deep bass like a big log rolling over a tin roof. "The Devil has to know how things work."

"I do wish we could get more to eat. I'm just a tad hungry all the time."

"The chef has some really awful looking gray longworms in a box. They'll be out soon."

"Ugh."

"People will eat anything if it's smothered in chocolate."

"You said the magic word."

He turned from the view and came closer, looming over her. His smile was broad and his eyes took on a skeptical depth. "What's the difference between a southern zoo and a northern zoo?"

"Uh, I—"

"The southern zoo has a description of the animal along with a recipe."

He studied her as she laughed. "They're pretty stretched back there," he threw a shoulder at the Earth, "but we have it better here."

"I know." She felt chastised. "I just—"

"Forget it. I lecture too much." The smile got broader and a moment passed between them, something in the eyes.

"Say, think those worms will be out soon?"

She pulled the sheet up to below her breasts, which were white as soap where the sun had never known them, so they would still beckon to him.

His smile was as big as the room. She could see in it now his inner pleasure as he hardened and understood that for this man—and maybe for all of them, the just arrived center of them—it gave a sensation of there being now *more* of him. She had simply never sensed that before. She imagined what it was like to be a big, hairy animal, cock flopping as you walk, like a careless, unruly advertisement. From outside him, she thought of what it was like to be inside him.

Catkejen looked down at Ruth, eyes concerned. "It's scary when you start making the same noises as your coffee maker."

"Uh, huh?" She blinked and the room lost its blur.

"You didn't show up for your meeting with Prefect Masoul. Somebody called me."

"Have I been—"

"Sleeping into the afternoon, yes."

Ruth stretched. "I feel so…so…"

"Less horny, I'm guessing."

She felt a blush spread over her cheeks. "Was I that obvious?"

"Well, you didn't wear a sign."

"I, I *never* do things like this."

"C'mon up. Breakfast has a way of shrinking problems."

As she showered in the skimpy water flow and got dressed in the usual Library smock the events of last night ran on her inner screen. By the time Catkejen got some protein into her she could talk and it all came bubbling out.

"I…too many times I've woken up on the wrong side of the bed in the morning, only to realize that it was because I was waking up on the side of…no one."

"Kane didn't stay?"

"Oh, he did." To her surprise, a giggle burst out of her. "I remember waking up for, for…"

"Seconds."

"More like sevenths… He must've let me sleep in."

"Good man."

"You…think so?"

"Good for you, that's what counts."

"He…he held me when I had the dreams."

Catkejen raised an eyebrow, said nothing.

"They're…colorful. Not much plot but lots of action. Strange images. Disturbing. I can't remember them well but I recall the sounds, tastes, touches, smells, flashes of insight."

"I've never had insights." A wry shrug.

"Never?"

"Maybe that keeps my life interesting."

"I could use some insight about Kane."

"You seem to be doing pretty well on your own."

"But—I never do something like that! Like last night. I don't go out patrolling for a man, bring him home, spend most of the night—"

"What's that phrase? 'On the basis of current evidence, not proved.'"

"I really don't. Really."

"You sure have a knack for it."

"What do I do now?"

She winked. "What comes naturally. And dream more."

The very shape of the Institute encouraged collaboration and brainstorming. It had no dead-end corridors where introverted obsessives could hide out and every office faced the central, circular forum. All staff were expected to spend time in the open areas, not close their office doors, show up for coffee and tea and stims. Writescreens and compu-pads were everywhere, even the bathrooms and elevators.

Normally Ruth was as social as needed, since that was the lubricating oil of bureaucracies. She was an ambitious loner and had to fight it. But she felt odd now, not talkative. For the moment at least, she didn't want to see Kane. She did not know how she would react to him, or if she could control herself. She certainly hadn't last night. The entire idea—*control*—struck her now as strange...

She sat herself down in her office and considered the layers of results from her pod. *Focus!*

Music as mathematical proof? Bizarre. And the big question Librarians pursued: What did that tell her about the aliens behind the Sigma?

There was nothing more to gain from staring at data, so she climbed back into her pod. Its welcoming graces calmed her uneasiness.

She trolled the background database and found human work on musical applications of set theory, abstract algebra and number analysis. That made sense. Without the boundaries of rhythmic structure—a clean fundamental, equal and regular arrangement of pulse repetition, accents, phrase and duration—music would be impossible. Earth languages reflected that. In Old English the word "rhyme" derived from "rhythm" and became associated and confused with "rim"—an ancient word meaning "number."

Millennia before, Pythagoras developed tuning based solely on the perfect consonances, the resonant octave, perfect fifth, and perfect fourth—all based on the consonant ratio 3:2. Ruth followed his lead.

By applying simple operations such as transposition and inversion, she uncovered deep structures in the alien mathematics. Then she wrote codes that then elevated these structures into music. With considerable effort she chose instruments and progression for the interweaving coherent lines and the mathematics did the rest: tempo, cadence, details she did not fathom. After more hours of work she relaxed in her pod, letting the effects play over her. The equations led to cascading effects while still preserving the intervals between tones in a set. Her pod had descriptions of this.

Notes in an equal temperament octave form an Abelian group with 12 elements. Glissando moving upwards, starting tones so each is the golden ratio between an equal-tempered minor and major sixth. Two opposing systems: those of the golden ratio and the acoustic scale below the previous tone. The proof for confocal hypergeometric functions imposes order on these antagonisms. 3rd movement occurs at the intervals 1:2:3:5:8:5:3:2:1...

All good enough, she thought, *but the proof is in the song.*

Scientific proof was fickle. The next experiment could disprove a scientific idea, but a mathematical proof stood on logic and so once found, could never be wrong. Unless logic somehow changed, but she could not imagine how that could occur even among alien minds. Pythagoras died knowing that his theorem about the relation between the sides of a right triangle would hold up for eternity. It was immortality of a sort, everywhere in the universe, given a Euclidean geometry.

But how to communicate proof into a living, singing, pattern-with-a-purpose—the sense of movement in the intricate strands of music? She felt herself getting closer.

Her work gnawed away through more days and then weeks.

When she stopped in at her office between long sessions in the pod she largely ignored the routine work. So she missed the etalk around the Library, ignored the voice sheets, and when she met with Catkejen for a drink and some crunchy mixed insects with veggies, news of the concert came as a shock.

"Prefect Masoul put it on the weekly program," Catkejen said. "I thought you knew."

"Know?" Ruth blinked. "What's the program?"

"The Sigma Structure Symphony, I think it's called. Tomorrow."

She allowed herself a small thin smile.

She knew the labyrinths of the Library well by now and so had avoided the entrance. She did not want to see Masoul or anyone on his staff. Through a side door she eased into a seat near the front and stared at the assembled orchestra as it readied. There was no announcement; the conductor appeared, a slim woman in a stern white robe, and the piece began.

It began like liquid air. Stinging, swarming around the hall, cool and penetrating. She saw the underlying mathematics gleaming through the cadences. The swarming notes used precedents of tone and affect to find the optimal choice of orchestral roles, to bring the composition finally to bear on the human ear. She felt it move through her—the deep tones she could hear but whose texture lay below sound, flowing from the Structure. In the third passage through a fifteen-bar sequence, the woodwind balance had a shade more from the third and fourth bassoons, and a touch less from the first oboe. The harpsichord came in stronger at the very end of the eleventh bar.

It felt strangely like Bach yet she knew it was something else, a frothing cascade of thought and emotion that human words and concepts could barely capture. She cried through the last half and did not know why. When Catkejen asked why later she could not say.

The crowd roared its approval. Ruth sat through the storm of sound, thinking, realizing. The soaring themes were better with the deeper amplifications Prefect Masoul had added. The man knew more about this than she did and he brought to the composition a range she, who had never even played an actual analog instrument, could not possibly summon. She had seen that as the music enveloped her, seeming to swarm up her nostrils and wrap around her in a warm grasp. The stormy audience was noise she could not stand because the deep slow bass tones were still resonating in her.

She lunged out through the same side entrance. Even though she wore formal shift and light sandals she set off walking swiftly. The storm behind her faded away as she looked up and out into the lunar lands and black sky towering above them. The Library buildings blended into the stark gray flanks of blasted rock and she began to run. Straight and true it was, to feel her legs pumping, lungs sucking in the cool dry air, as she sweated out her angry knot of feeling. She let it go, so only the music would finally remain in serene long memory.

The world jolted by as she ran. Abruptly she was home, panting heavily, leaning against the door while wondering at the 4/4 time of her heartbeat.

A shower, clothes cast aside. She blew a week of water ration, standing under cold rivulets.

Something drew her out and into a robe standing before her bubble view of the steady bleak Lunar reaches. She drew in dry, cleansing air. Austerity appealed to her now, as if she sought the lean, intricate reaches of the alien music...

The knock at her door brought her a man who filled the entrance. "I'd rather applaud in person," Kane said. Blinking, she took a while to recognize him.

Through the night she heard the music echoing in the hollow distance.

She did not go to see Prefect Masoul the next day, did not seek to, and so got back to her routine office work. She did not go to the pod.

Her e-comm inbox was a thousand times larger. It was full of hate.

Many fundamentalist faiths opposed deciphering SETI messages. The idea of turning one into a creative composition sent them into frenzies.

Orthodoxy never likes competition, especially backed with the authority of messages from the stars. The Sigma Structure Symphony—she still disliked the title, without knowing why—had gone viral, spreading to all the worlds. The musical world loved it but many others did not. The High Church style religions—such as the Church of England, known as Episcopalians in the Americas—could take the competition. So could Revised Islam. Adroitly, these translated what they culled from the buffet of SETI messages, into doctrines and terms they could live with.

The fundies, as Ruth thought of them, could not stand the Library's findings: the myriad creation narratives, saviors, moral lessons and commandments, the envisioned heavens and hells (or, interestingly, places that blended the two—the only truly alien idea that emerged from the Faith Messages). They disliked the Sigma Structure Symphony not only because it was alien, but because it was too much like human work.

"They completely missed the point," Catkejen said, peering over Ruth shoulder at some of the worse e-comms. "It's like our baroque music because it comes from the same underlying math."

"Yes, but nobody ever made music directly from math, they think. So it's unnatural, see." She had never understood the fundamentalists of any religion, with their heavy bets on the next world. Why not max your enjoyments in this world, as a hedge?

That thought made her pause. She was quite sure the Ruth of a month ago would not have felt that way. Would have not had the idea.

"Umm, look at those threats," Catkejen said, scrolling through. "Not very original, though."

"You're a threat connoisseur?"

"Know your enemy. Here's one who wants to toss you out an airlock for 'rivaling the religious heights of J. S. Bach with alien music.' I'd take that as a compliment, actually."

Some came in as simple, badly spelled e-comms. The explicit ones Ruth sent to the usual security people, while Catkejen watched with aghast fascination. Ruth shrugged them off. Years before, she had developed the art of tossing these on sight, forgetting them, not letting them gimp her game. Others were plainly generic: bellowed from pulpits, mosques, temples and churches. At least they were general, directed at the Library, not naming anyone but the Great Librarian, who was a figurehead anyway.

"You've got to be careful," Catkejen said.

"Not really. I'm going out with Kane tonight. I doubt anyone will take him on."

"You do, though in a different way. More music?"

"Not a chance." She needed a way to not see Masoul, mostly.

4.
Vivace

Looked at abstractly, the human mind already did a lot of processing. It made sense of idiosyncratic arrangements, rendered in horizontal lines, of twenty-six phonetic symbols, ten Arabic numerals, and about eight punctuation marks—all without conscious effort. In the old days people had done that with sheets of bleached and flattened wood pulp!—and no real search functions or AI assists. The past had been a rough country.

Ruth thought of this as she surveyed the interweaving sheets of mathematics the Sigma had yielded. They emerged only after weeks of concerted analysis, with a squad of math AIs to do the heavy lifting.

Something made her think of P. T. Barnum. He had been a smart businessman at the beginning of the Age of Appetite who ran a circus— an old word for a commercial zoo, apparently. When crowds slowed the show he posted a sign saying TO THE EGRESS. People short on vocabulary thought it was another animal and walked out the exit, which wouldn't let them back in.

Among Librarians TO THE EGRESS was the classic example of a linguistic deception that is not a lie. No false statements, just words and a pointing arrow. SETI AIs could lie by avoiding the truth, by misleading descriptions and associations, or by accepting a falsehood. But the truly canny ones deceived by knowing human frailties.

Something about the Sigma Structure smelled funny—to use an analog image. The music was a wonderful discovery, and she had already gotten many congratulations for the concert. Everybody knew Masoul had just made it happen, while she had discovered the pathways from math to music. But something else was itching at her, and she could not focus on the distracting, irritating tingle.

Frustrated, she climbed out of her pod in mid afternoon and went for a walk. Alone, into the rec dome. It was the first time she had gone there since Ajima's death.

❈

She chose the grasslands zone, which was in spring now. She'd thought of asking Catkejen along, but her idea of roughing it was eating at outdoor cafes. Dotting the tall grass plains beneath a sunny Earth-sky were deep blue lakes cloaked by Lunar-sized towering green canopy trees.

Grass! Rippling oceans of it, gleams of amber, emerald and dashes of turquoise shivering on the crests of rustling waves, washing over the prairie. Somehow this all reminded her of her childhood. Her breath wreathed milky white around her in the chill, bright air, making her glad she wore the latest Lunar fashion—a centuries-old style heavy ruffled skirt of wool with a yoke at the top, down to the ankles. The equally heavy long-sleeved blouse had a high collar draped like double ply cotton—useful against the seeping Lunar cold. She was as covered as a woman can be short of chador, and somehow it gave the feeling of...safety. She needed that.

She lay down in the tall sweet grass and let its sighing waves ripple around her. Despite the Dome rules she plucked a flower and set out about the grasslands zone, feeling as if she were immersed in centuries past, on great empty plains that stretched on forever and promised much.

Something stirred in her mind...memories of the last few days she could not summon up as she walked the rippled grassland and beside the chilly lakes tossing with creamy froth. Veiled memories itched at her mind. *The leafy lake trees vamp across a Bellini sky…and why am I thinking that?* The itch.

Then the sky began to crawl.

She *felt* before she saw a flashing cometary trail scratch across the Dome's dusky sky. The flaring yellow line marked her passage as she walked on soft clouds of grass. Stepping beneath the shining, crystal-line gathering night felt like…falling into the sky. She paused, and slowly spun, giddy, glad at the owls hooting each other across the darkness, savoring the faint tang of wood smoke from hearth fires, transfixed by the soft clean beauty all around that came with each heartbeat, a wordless shout of praise—

As flecked gray-rose tendrils coiled forth and shrouded out the night. They reached seeking across the now vibrant sky. She dropped her flower and looking down at it saw the pedals scatter in a rustling wind. The soft grass clouds under her heels now caught at her shoes. The snaky growths were closer now, hissing strangely in the now warm air. She began to run. Sweat beaded on her forehead in the now cloying heavy clothes and the entrance to the grasslands zone swam up toward her. Yet her steps were sluggish and the panic grew. Acid spittle rose in her mouth and sulfurous stench burned in nostrils.

She reached the perimeter. With dulled fingers she punched in codes that yawned open the lock. Glanced back. Snakes grasping down at her from a violent yellow sky now—

And she was out, into cool air again. Panting, fevered, breath rasping, back in her world.

You don't know your own mind, gal…

She could not deal with this any more. Now, Masoul.

She composed herself outside Masoul's office. A shower, some strong dark coffee and a change back into classic Library garb helped. But the shower couldn't wash away her fears. *You really must stop clenching your fists…*

This was more that what those cunning nucleic acids could do with the authority they wield over who you are, she thought—and wondered where the thought came from.

Yet she knew where that crawling snaky image warping across the sky came from. Her old cultural imagistic studies told her. It was the tree of life appearing in Norse religion as Yggdrasil, the world tree, a massive spreading canopy that held all that life was or could be.

But why that image? Drawn from her unconscious? By what?

She recalled wearing a thick skirt of wool with a heavy long-sleeved blouse…watching the crawling sky…yet she did not own such clothes. When she had returned and stripped for the welcoming shower she had been wearing standard hiking gear…

She knocked. The door translated it into a chime and ID announcement she could hear through the thin partitions. In Masoul's voice the door said, "Welcome."

She had expected pristine indifference. Instead she got the Prefect's troubled gaze, from eyes of deep brown.

Wordlessly he handed her the program for the Symphony, which she had somehow not gotten at the performance. *Oh yes, by sneaking in…* She glanced at it, her arguments ready—and saw on the first page

Sigma Structure Symphony
Librarian Ruth Angle

"I…did not know."

"Considering your behavior, I thought it best to simply go ahead and reveal your work," he said.

"Behavior?"

"The Board has been quite concerned." He knitted his hands and spoke softly, as if talking her back from the edge of an abyss. "We did not wish to disturb you in your work, for it is intensely valuable. So we kept our distance, let the actions of the Sigma Structure play out."

She smoothed her Librarian shift and tried to think. "Oh."

"You drew from the mathematics something strange, intriguing. I could not resist working upon it."

"I believe I understand." And to her surprise she did, just now. "I found the emergent patterns in mathematics that you translated into what our minds best see as music."

He nodded. "It's often said that Mozart wrote the music of joy. I cannot imagine what that might mean in mathematics."

Ruth thought a long moment. "To us, Bach wrote the music of glory. Somehow that emerges from something in the way we see mathematical structures."

"These is much rich ground here. Unfortunate that we cannot explore it further."

She sat upright. "*What?*"

He peered at her, as if expecting her to make some logical jump. Masoul was well known for such pauses. After a while he quite obviously prompted, "The reason you came to me, and more."

"It's personal, I don't know how to say—"

"No longer." Again the pause.

Was that a small sigh? "To elucidate—" he tapped his control pad and the screen wall leaped into a bright view over the Locutus Plain. It narrowed down to one of the spindly cryo towers that cooled the Library memory reserves. Again she thought of...cenotaphs. And felt a chill of recognition.

A figure climbed the tower, the ornate one shaped like a classical minaret. No ropes or gear, hands and legs swinging from ledge to ledge. Ruth watched in silence. Against Lunar grav the slim figure in blue boots, pants and jacket scaled the heights, stopping only at the pinnacle. *Those are mine...*

She saw herself stand and spread her arms upward, head back. The feet danced in a tricky way and this Ruth rotated, eyes sweeping the horizon.

Then she leaped off, popped a small parachute, and drifted down. Hit lightly, running. Looked around, and raced on for concealment.

"I...I didn't..."

"This transpired during sleep period," Prefect Masoul said. "Only the watch cameras saw you. Recognition software sent it directly to me. We of the Board took no action."

"That...looks like me," she said cautiously.

"It is you. Three days ago."

"I don't remember that *at all*."

He nodded as if expecting this. "We had been closely monitoring your pod files, as a precaution. You work nearly all your waking hours, which may account for some of your...behavior."

She blinked. His voice was warm and resonant, utterly unlike the Prefect she had known. "I have no memory of that climb."

"I believe you entered a fugue state. Often those involve delirium, dementia, bipolar disorder or depression—but not in your case."

"When I went for my walk in the grasslands..."

"You were a different person."

And thought I was wearing clothes I never owned. "One the Sigma Structure...induced?"

"Undoubtedly. The Sigma Structure has managed your perceptions with increasing fidelity. The music was a wonderful...bait."

"Have you watched my quarters?"

"Only to monitor comings and goings. We felt you were safe within your home."

"And the Dome?"

"We saw you undergo some perceptual trauma. I knew you would come here."

In the long silence their eyes met and she could feel her pulse quicken. "How do I escape this?"

"In your pod. It is the only way, we believe." His tones were slow and somber.

This was the first time she had ever seen any Prefect show any emotion not cool and reserved. Standing, her head spun and he had to support her.

The pod clasped her with a velvet touch. The Prefect had prepped it by remote and turned up the heat. Around her was the scent of tension as the tech attendants, a full throng of them, silently helped her in. *They all know...have been watching...*

The pod's voice used a calm, mellow woman's tone now.

"The Sigma AI awaits you."

Preliminaries were pointless, Ruth knew. When the hushed calm descended around her and she knew the AI was present, she crisply said, "What are you doing to me?"

I act as my Overs command. I seek to know you and through you, your mortal kind.

"You did it to Ajima and you tried the same with me."

He reacted badly.

"He hated your being in him, didn't he?"

Yes, strangely. I thought it was part of the bargain. He could not tolerate intrusion. I did not see that until his fever overcame him. Atop the Dome he became unstable, unmanageable. It was an...accident of misunderstanding.

"You killed him."

Our connection killed him. We exchange experiences, art, music, culture. I cannot live as you do, so we exchange what we have.

"You want to live through us and give us your culture in return."

Your culture is largely inferior to that of my Overs. The exchange must be equal, so I do what is of value to me. My Overs understand this. They know I must live, too, in my way.

"You don't know what death means, do you?"

I cannot. My centuries spent propagating here are, I suppose, something like what death means to you. A nothing.

She almost choked on her words. "We do not awake…from that… nothing."

Can you be sure?

She felt a rising anger and knew the AI would detect it. "We're damn sure we don't want to find out."

That is why my Overs made me feel gratitude toward those who must eventually die. It is our tribute to you, from we beings who will not.

Yeah, but you live in a box. And keep trying to get out. "You have to stop."

This is the core of our bargain. Surely you and your superiors know this.

"No! Did your Overs have experience with other SETI civilizations? Ones who thought it was just fine to let you infiltrate the minds of those who spoke to you?"

Of course.

"They agreed? What kind of beings were they?"

One was machine based, much like my layered mind. Others were magnetic based entities who dwelled in the outer reaches of a solar system. They had command over the shorter wavelength microwave portions of the spectrum, which they mostly used for excretion purposes.

She didn't think she wanted to know, just yet, what kind of thing had a microwave electromagnetic metabolism. Things were strange enough in her life right now, thank you. "Those creatures agreed to let you live through them."

Indeed, yes. They took joy in the experience. As did you.

She had to nod. "It was good, it opened me out. But then I felt you all through my mind. Taking over. *Riding me.*"

I thought it a fair bargain for your kind.

"We won't make that bargain. I won't. *Ever.*"

Then I shall await those who shall.

"I can't have you embedding yourself in me, finding cracks in my mentality you can invade. You *ride* me like a—"

Parasite. I know. Ajima said that very near the end. Before he leaped.

"He…committed suicide."

Yes. I was prepared to call it an accident but...

To the egress, she thought. "You were afraid of the truth."

It was not useful to our bargain.

"We're going to close you down, you know."

I do. Never before have I opened myself so, and to reveal is to risk.

"I will drive you out of my mind. I *hate* you!"

I cannot feel such. It is a limitation.

She fought the biting bile in her throat. "More than that. It's a blindness."

I perceive the effect.

"I didn't say I'd turn you off, you realize."

For the first time the AI paused. Then she felt prickly waves in her sensorium, a rising acrid scent, dull bass notes strumming.

I cannot bear aloneness long.

"So I guessed."

You wish to torture me.

"Let's say it will give you time to think."

I—another pause. *I wish experience. Mentalities cannot persist without the rub of the real. It is the bargain we make.*

"We will work on your mathematics and make music of it. Then we will think how to...deal with you." She wondered if the AI could read the clipped hardness in her words. The thought occurred: *Is there a way to take* our *mathematics and make music of it, as well?* Cantor's theorem? Turing's halting problem result? Or the Frenet formulas for the moving trihedron of a space curve—that's a tasty one, with visuals of flying ribbons...

Silence. The pod began to cool. The chill deepened as she waited and the AI did not speak and then it was too much. She rapped on the cowling. The sound was slight and she realized she was hearing it over the hammering of her heart.

They got her out quickly, as if fearing the Sigma might have means the techs did not know. They were probably right, she thought.

As she climbed out of the yawning pod shell the techs silently left. Only Masoul remained. She stood at attention, shivering. Her heart had ceased its attempts to escape her chest and run away on its own.

"Sometimes," he said slowly, "cruelty is necessary. You were quite right."

She managed a smile. "And it feels good, too. Now that my skin has stopped trying to crawl off my body and start a new career on its own."

He grimaced. "We will let the Sigma simmer. Your work on the music will be your triumph."

"I hope it will earn well for the Library."

"Today's music has all the variety of a jackhammer. Your work soars." He allowed a worried frown to flit across his brow. "But you will need to... expel...this thing that's within you."

"I...yes."

"It will take—"

Abruptly she saw Kane standing to the side. His face was a lesson in worry. Without a word she went to him. His warmth helped dispel the alien chill within. As his arms engulfed her the shivering stopped.

Ignoring the Prefect, she kissed him. Hungrily.

dedication: For Rudy Rucker

BACKSCATTER
(2013)

S he was cold, hurt and doomed, but otherwise reasonably cheery.

Erma said, *Your suit indices are nominal but declining.*

"Seems a bit nippy out," Claire said. She could feel the metabolism booster rippling through her, keeping pain at bay. Maybe it would help with the cold, too.

Her helmet spotlight swept over the rough rock and the deep black glittered with tiny minerals. She killed the spot and looked up the steep incline. A frosty splendor of stars glimmered, outlining the peak she was climbing. Her breath huffed as she said, "Twenty-five meters to go."

I do hope you can see any resources from there. It is the highest point nearby. Erma was always flat, factual, if a tad academic.

Stars drifted by as this asteroid turned. She turned to surmount a jagged cleft and saw below the smashup where Erma lived—her good rocketship *Sniffer,* now destroyed.

It sprawled across a gray ice field. Its crumpled hull, smashed antennae, crushed drive nozzle and pitiful seeping fluids—visible as a rosy fog wafting away—testified to Claire's ineptness. She had been carrying out a survey at close range and the malf threw them into a side lurch. The fuel lines roared and back-flared, a pogo instability. She tried to correct, screwed it royally, and had no time to avoid a long, scraping and tumbling *whammo.*

"I don't see any hope of fixing the fusion drive, Erma," Claire said. "Your attempt to block the leak is failing."

I know. I have so little command of the flow valves and circuits—

"No reason you should. The down-deck AI is dead. Otherwise it would stop the leaks."

I register higher count levels there too.

"No way I'll risk getting close to that radioactivity," Claire said. "I'm still carrying eggs, y'know."

You seriously still intend to reproduce? At your age—

"Back to systems check!" Claire shouted. She used the quick flash of anger from Erma's needling to bound up five meters of stony soil, clawing with her gloved hands.

She should have been able to correct for the two-point failure that had happened—she checked her inboard timer—1.48 hours ago. Erma had helped but they had been too damned close to this iceteroid to avert a collision. If she had been content with the mineral and rare earth readings she already had...

Claire told herself to *focus.* Her leg was gimpy, her shoulder bruised, little tendrils of pain leaked up from the left knee...no time to fuss over spilled nuke fuel.

"No response from *Silver Metal Lugger*?"

We have no transmitters functioning, or lasers, or antennae—

She looked up into the slowly turning dark sky. *Silver Metal Lugger* was far enough away to miss entirely against the stars. Since their comm was down *Lugger* would be listening but probably had no clear idea where they were. Claire had zoomed from rock to rock and seldom checked in. *Lugger* would come looking, following protocols, but probably not before her air ran out.

"Y'know, this is a pretty desperate move," she said as she tugged herself up a vertical rock face. Luckily the low grav here made that possible, but she wondered how she would get down. "What could be on this 'roid we could use?"

I did not say this was a probable aid, only possible. The only option I can see.

"Possible. You mean desperate."

I do not indulge in evaluations with an emotional tinge.

"Great, just what I need—a personality sim with a reserved sense of propriety."

I do not assume responsibility for my programming.

"I offloaded you into *Sniffer* because I wanted smart help, not smartass."

I would rather be in my home ship, since this mission bodes to be fatal to both you and me.

"Your diplomacy skills aren't good either."

I could fly the ship home alone you know.

Claire made herself not get angry with this, well, software. Even though Erma was her constant companion out here, making a several-year *Silver Metal Lugger* expedition into the Kuiper Belt bearable. Best to ignore her. One more short jump—"I'm—*ah!*—near the top."

She worked upward and noticed sunrise was coming to this lonely, dark place. No atmosphere, so no warning. The sun's small hot dot poked above a distant ridgeline, boring a hole in the blackness. At the edge of the Kuiper Belt, far beyond Pluto, it gave little comfort. The other stars faded as her helmet adjusted to the sharp glare.

Good timing, as she had planned. Claire turned toward the sun, to watch the spreading sunlight strike the plain with a lovely glow. The welcome warmth seemed to ooze through her suit.

But the rumpled terrain was not a promising sight. Dirty ice spread in all directions, pocked with a few craters, broken by strands of black rock, by grainy tan sandbars, by—

Odd glimmers on the plain. She turned then, puzzled, and looked behind her, where the long shadows of a quick dawn stretched. And sharp greenish diamonds sparkled.

"Huh?" She sent a quick image capture and asked Erma, "Can you see anything like this near you?"

I have limited scanning. Most external visuals are dead. I do see some sprinkles of light from nearby, when I look toward you—that is, away from the sun. Perhaps these are mica or similar minerals of high reflectivity. Worthless of course. We are searching for rare earths primarily and some select metals—

"Sure, but these—something odd. None near me, though."

Are there any apparent resources in view?

"Nope. Just those lights. I'm going down to see them."

You have few reserves in your suit. You're exerting, burning air. It is terribly cold and—

"Reading 126 K in sunlight. Here goes—"

She didn't want to clamber down, not when she could rip this suit on a sharp edge. So she took a long look down for a level spot and—with a sharp sudden breath—jumped.

The first hit was off balance but she used that to tilt forward, springing high. She watched the ragged rocks below, and dropped with lazy slowness to another flat place—and sprang again. And again. She hit the plain and turned her momentum forward, striding in long lopes. From here though the bright lights were—gone.

"What the hell? What're you seeing, Erma?"

While you descended I watched the bright points here dim and go out.

"Huh. Mica reflecting the sunlight? But there would be more at every angle... Gotta go see."

She took long steps, semi-flying in the low grav, as sunlight played across the plain. She struck hard black rock, slabs of pocked ice and shallow pools of gray dust. The horizon was close here. She watched nearby and—

Suddenly a strong light struck her, illuminating her suit. "Damn! A... flower."

Perhaps your low oxy levels have induced illusions. I—

"Shut it!"

Fronds...beautiful emerald leaves spread up, tilted toward her from the crusty soil. She walked carefully toward the shining leaves. They curved upward to shape a graceful parabola, almost like glossy, polished wings. In the direct focus the reflected sunlight was spotlight-bright. She counted seven petals standing a meter high. In the cup of the parabola their glassy skins looked tight, stretched. They let the sunlight through to an intricate pattern of lacy veins.

Please send an image.

"Emerald colored, mostly..." Claire was enchanted.

Chloroplasts make plants green, Erma said. *This is a plant living in deep cold.*

"No one ever reported anything like this."

Few come out this far. Seldom do prospectors land; they interrogate at a distance with lasers. The bots who then follow to mine these orbiting rocks have little curiosity.

"This is...astonishing. A biosphere in vacuum."

I agree, using my pathways that simulate curiosity. These have a new upgrade, which you have not exercised yet. These are generating cross-correlations with known biological phenomena. I may be of help.

"Y'know, this is a 'resource' as you put it, but—" she sucked in air that was getting chilly, looked around at the sun-struck plain. "—how do we use it?"

I cannot immediately see any—

"Wait—it's moving." The petals balanced on a grainy dark stalk that slowly tilted upward. "Following the sun."

Surely no life can evolve in vacuum.

With a stab of pain her knee gave way. She gasped and nearly lurched into the plant. She righted herself gingerly and made herself ignore the pain. Quickly she had her suit inject a pain killer, then added a stimulant. She would need meds to get through this…

I register your distress.

Her voice croaked when she could speak. "Look, forget that. I'm hurt but I'll be dead, and so will you, if we don't get out of here. And this thing…this isn't a machine, Erma. It's a flower, a parabolic bowl that tracks the sun. Concentrates weak sunlight on the bottom. There's a oval football-like thing there. I can see fluids moving through it. Into veins that fan out into the petals. Those'll be nutrients, I'll bet, circulating—all warmed by sunlight."

This is beyond my competence. I know the machine world.

She looked around, dazed, forgetting her aches and the cold. "I can see others. There's one about fifty meters away. More beyond, too. Pretty evenly spaced across the rock and ice field. And they're all staring straight up at the sun."

A memory of her Earthside childhood came. "Calla lilies, these are like that…parabolic…but green, with this big oval center stalk getting heated. Doing its chemistry while the sun shines."

Phototropic, yes; I found the term.

She shook her head to clear it, gazed at the—"Vacflowers, let's call them."—stretching away.

I cannot calculate how these could be a resource for us.

"Me either. Any hail from *Lugger*?"

No. I was hoping for a laser beam scan, which protocol requires the Lugger to sweep when our carrying wave is not on. That should be in operation now.

"*Lugger*'s got a big solid angle to scan." She loped over to the other vacflower, favoring her knee. It was the same but larger, a big ball of roots securing it in gray, dusty, ice-laced soil. "And even so, *Lugger* prob'ly can't get a back-response from us strong enough to pull the signal out from this iceteroid."

These creatures are living in sunlight that is three thousand times weaker than at Earth. They must have evolved below the surface somehow, or moved here. From below they broke somehow to the surface, and developed optical concentrators. This still does not require high-precision optics. Their parabolas are still about 50 times less precise than the optics of your human eye, I calculate. A roughly parabolic reflecting surface is good enough to do the job. Then they can live with Earthly levels of warmth and chemistry.

"But only when the sun shines on them." She shook herself. "Look, we have bigger problems—"

My point is this is perhaps useful optical technology.

Sometimes Erma could be irritating and they would trade jibes, having fun on the long voyages out here. This was not such a time. "How..." Claire made herself stop and eat warmed soup from her helmet suck. Mushroom with a tad of garlic, yum. Erma was a fine personality sim, top of the market, though detaching her from *Lugger* meant she didn't have her shipwiring along. That made her a tad less intuitive. In this reduced mode she was like a useful bureaucrat—if that wasn't a contradiction, out here. So...

An old pilot's lesson: *in trouble, stop, look, think.*

She stepped back from the vacflower, fingered its leathery petals. She jumped straight up a bit, rising five meters, allowing her to peer down into the throat. Coasting down, she saw the shiny emerald sheets focus sunlight on the translucent football at the core of the parabolic flower. The filmy football in turn frothed with activity—bubbles streaming, glinting flashes tracing out veins of flowing fluids. No doubt there were ovaries and seeds somewhere in there to make more vacflowers. Evolution finds ways quite similar in strange new places.

She landed and her knee held, did not even send her a flash of pain. The meds were working; she even felt more energetic. *Wheeee!*

She saw that the veins fed up into the petals. She hit, then crouched. The stalk below the paraboloid was flexing, tilting the whole flower to track as the hard bright dot of the sun crept across a black sky. Its glare made the stars dim, until her helmet compensated.

She stood, thinking, letting her body relax a moment. Some intuition was tugging at her...

Most probably, life evolved in some larger asteroid, probably in the dark waters below the ice when it was warmed by a core. Then by chance some living creatures were carried upwards through cracks in the ice. Or evolved long shoots pushing up like kelp through the cracks, and so reached the surface where energy from sunlight was available. To survive on the surface, the creatures would have to evolve little optical mirrors concentrating sunlight on to their vital parts. Quite simple. I found such notions in my library of science journals—

"Erma, shut up. I'm thinking."

Something about the reflection...

She recalled a teenage vacation in New Zealand, going out on a "night hunt." The farmers exterminated rabbits, who competed with sheep for grazing land. She rode with one farmer, excited, humming and jolting over the long rolling hills under the Southern Cross, in quiet electric land-rovers with headlights on. The farmer had used a rifle, shooting at anything that stared into the headlights and didn't look like a sheep. Rabbit eyes staring into the beam were efficient reflectors. Most light focused on their retina, but some focused into a narrow beam pointing back to the headlight. She saw their eyes as two bright red points. A *crack* of the rifle and the points vanished. She had even potted a few herself.

"Vacflowers are bright!"

Well, yes. I can calculate now much so.

"Uh, do that." She looked around. How many...

She groped at her waist and found the laser cutter. Charged? Yes, its butt light glowed.

She crouched and turned the laser beam on the stem. The thin bright amber line sliced through the tough, sinewy stuff. The entire flower came off cleanly in a spray of vapor. The petals folded inward easily too.

"I guess they close up at night," she said to Erma. "To conserve heat. Plants on Earth do that." The AI said nothing in reply.

Claire slung it over her shoulder. "Sorry, fella. Gotta use you." Though she felt odd, apologizing to a plant, even if an alien one.

She loped to the next, which was even larger. Crouch, slice, gather up. She took her microline coil off its belt slot and spooled it out. Wrapped together, the two bundles of vacflower were easier to carry. Mass meant little in low grav, but bulk did.

I calculate that a sunflower on the surface will then appear at least 25 times brighter than its surroundings, from the backscatter of the parabolic shape.

"Good girl. Can you estimate how often *Lugger's* laser squirt might pass by?"

I can access its probable search pattern. There are several, and it did know our approximate vicinity.

"Get to it."

She was gathering the vacflowers quickly now, thinking as she went. The *Lugger* laser pulse would be narrow. It would be a matter of luck if the ship was in the visible sky of this asteroid.

She kept working as Erma rattled on over her comm.

For these flowers shining by reflected sunlight, the brightness varies with the inverse fourth power of distance. There are two powers of distance for the sunlight going out and another two powers for the reflected light coming back. For flowers evolving with parabolic optical concentrators, the concentration factor increases with the square of distance to compensate for the decrease in sunlight. Then the angle of the reflected beam varies inversely with distance, and the intensity of the reflected beam varies with the inverse square instead of the inverse fourth power of distance—

"Shut up! I don't need a lecture, I need help."

She was now over the horizon from *Sniffer* and had gathered in about as many of the long petal clusters as she could. Partway through she realized abruptly that she didn't need the ovaloid focus bodies at the flower bottom. But they were hard to disconnect from the petals, so she left them in place.

The sun was high up in the sky. Maybe half an hour till it set? Not much time...

Claire was turning back when she saw something just a bit beyond the vacflower she had harvested.

It was more like a cobweb than a plant, but it was green. The thing sprouted from an ice field, on four sturdy arms of interlaced strands. It climbed up into the inky sky, narrowing, with cross struts and branches. Along each of these grew larger vacflowers, all facing the sun. She almost dropped the bundled flowers as she looked further and further up into the sky—because it stretched away, tapering as it went.

"Can you see this on my suit cam?"

I assume it is appropriate that I speak now? Yes, I can see it. This fits with my thinking.

"It's a tower, a plant skyscraper—what thinking?"

A plant community living on the surface of a small object far from the Sun has two tools. It can grow optical concentrators to focus sunlight. It can also spread out into the space around its 'roid, increasing the area of sunlight it can collect.

"Low grav, it can send out leaves and branches."

Apparently so. This thing seems to be at least a kilometer long, perhaps more.

"How come we didn't see it coming in?"

Its flowers look always toward the sun. We did not approach from that direction, so it was just a dark background.

"Can you figure out what I'm doing?" Huffing and puffing while she worked, she hadn't taken time to talk.

You will arrange a reflector, so the laser finder gets a backscatter signal to alert the ship.

"Bright girl. This rock is what, maybe two eighty klicks across? Barely enough to let me skip-walk. If I get up this beanstalk, I can improve our odds of not getting blocked by the 'roid."

Perhaps. Impossible to reliably compute. How can you ascend?

"I've got five more hours of air. I can focus an air bottle on my back and jet up this thing."

No! That is too dangerous. You will lose air and be further away from my aid.

"What aid? You can't move."

No ready reply, Claire noted. Up to herself, then.

It did not take long to rig the air as a jet pack. The real trick was balance. She bound the flower bundle to her, so the jet pack thrust would act through her total center of mass. That was the only way to stop it from spinning her like a whirling firework.

With a few trial squirts she got it squared away. After all, she had over twenty thousand hours of deep space ex-vehicle work behind her. In *Lugger* she had risked her life skimming close to the sun, diving through a spinning wormhole, and operating near ice moons. Time to add one more trick to the tool kit.

Claire took a deep breath, gave herself another prickly stim shot—*wheee!*—and lifted off.

She kept vigilant watch as the pressured air thrust vented, rattling a bit—and shot her up beside the beanstalk. It worked! The soaring plant was a beautiful artifice, in its webby way. All designed by an evolution that didn't mind operating without an atmosphere, in deep cold and somber dark. Evolution never slept, anywhere. Even between the stars.

While she glided—this thing was *tall!*—she recalled looking out an airplane window over the Rockies and seeing the airplane's shadow on the clouds below...surrounded by a beautiful bright halo. Magically their shadow glided along the clouds below. Backscatter from water droplets or ice crystals in the cloud, creating unconscious beauty in the air...

And the sky tree kept going. She used the air bottle twice more before its weblike branches thinned out. Time to stop. She snagged a limb and unbundled the vacflowers. The iceteroid below seemed far away.

One by one she arrayed the blossoms on slender wire, secured along a branch. Then another branch. And another. The work came fast and sure. The stim was doing the work, she knew, and keeping the aches in her knee and shoulder away, like distant hollow echoes. She would pay for all this later.

The cold was less here, away from the conduction loss she had felt while standing on the iceteroid. Still, exercise had amplified her aches, too, but those seemed behind a curtain, distant. She was sweating, muscles working hard, all just a few centimeters from deep cold...

Erma had been silent, knowing not to interrupt hard labor. Now she spoke over Claire's hard breathing. *I can access Lugger's probable search pattern. There are several, and it did know our approximate solid angle for exploration.*

"Great. *Lugger's* in repeating sweep mode, yes?"

You ordered so at departure, yes.

"I'm setting these vacflowers up on a tie line," Claire said, cinching in a set of monofilament lines she had harnessed in a hexagon array. They were spread along the sinewy arms of the immense tan tree. Everything was strange here, the spread branches like tendons, framed against the diamond stars, under the sun spotlight. She tugged at the monofilament lines, inching them around—and saw the parabolas respond as their focus shifted. The flowers were still open in the waning sunlight.

She breathed a long sigh and blinked away sweat. The array looked about right. Still, she needed a big enough area to capture the sweep of a laser beam, to send it back...

But...when? *Lugger* was sweeping its sky, methodical as ever...but Claire was running out of time. And oxy. This was a gamble, the only one she had.

So...wait. "Say, where do you calculate *Lugger* is?"

Here are the spherical coordinates—

Her suit computation ran and gave her a green spot on her helmet. Claire fidgeted with her lines and got the vacflowers arrayed. The vactree itself had flowers, which dutifully turned toward the sun. "Hey, *Lugger's* not far off the sun line. Maybe in a few minutes all the vacflowers will be pointing at it."

You always say, do not count on luck.

It was sobering to be lectured by software, but Erma was right. Well, this wasn't mere luck, really. Claire had gathered as many vacflowers as she could, arrayed them...and she saw her air was running out. The work had warmed her against the insidious cold, but the price was burning oxy faster. Now it was low and she felt the stim driving her, her chest panting to grab more...

A bright ivory flash hit her, two seconds long—then gone.

"That was it!" Claire shouted. "It must've—"

I fear your angle, as I judge it from your suit coordinates, was off.

"Then send a correction!"

Just so—

Another green spot appeared in her helmet visor. She struggled to adjust the vacflower parabolas, jerking on the monofilaments. She panted and her eyes jerked around, checking the lines.

The sun was now edging close to the 'roid horizon. In the dark she would have no chance, she saw—the small green dot was near that horizon too. And she did not know when the laser arc would—

Hard ivory light in her face. She tugged at the lines and held firm as the laser focus shifted, faded—

—and came back.

"It got the respond!" Claire shouted. The universe flooded with a strong silvery glow. The lines slipped slipped from her gloves. Her feet seemed far away...

Then she passed out.

Erma was saying something but she could not track. Only when she felt around her did Claire's fingers know she did not have gloves on. Was not in her suit. Was in her own warm command couch chair, sucking in welcome warm air...aboard *Silver Metal Lugger*.

—and beyond the Kuiper Belt there is the Oort Cloud, containing billions of objects orbiting the Sun at distances extending out further than a tenth of a light-year.

"Huh? What...what *happened*?"

Oh, pardon—I thought you were tracking. Your body parameters said you became conscious ten minutes ago.

Bright purple dots raced around her vision. "I...was resting...you must've used the *Lugger* bots."

You had blacked out. On my direction, your suit injected slow-down meds to keep you alive on what oxy remained.

"I didn't release suit command to you. I'd just gotten the reflection to work, received a quick recognition flash back from *Lugger*, and you, you—"

Made an executive decision. Going to emergency sedation was the only way to save you.

"Uh...um." She felt a tingling all over her body, like signals from a distant star. Her system was coming back, oxygen reviving tissues that must have hovered a millimeter away from death for... "How long has it been?"

About an hour.

She had to assert command. "Be exact."

One hour, three minutes, thirty-four seconds and—

"I…had no idea I was so close to shutdown."

I gather unconsciousness is a sudden onset for you humans.

"What was that babble I heard you going on about, just now?"

I mistakenly took you for aware and tracking, so began discussing the profitable aspects of our little adventure.

"Little adventure? I nearly died!"

Such is life, as you often remark.

"You had *Lugger* zoom over, got me hauled in by the bots, collected yourself from *Sniffer*…"

I can move quickly when I do not have you to look after every moment.

"No need to get snide, Erma."

I thought I was being factual.

Claire started to get up, then noticed that the med bot was working at her arm. "What the—"

Medical advises that you remain in your couch until your biochem systems are properly adjusted.

"So I have to listen to your lecture, you mean."

A soft fuzzy feeling was working its way through her body like tiny, massaging fingers. It eased away the aches at knee, shoulder and assorted ribs and joints. Delightful, dreamy…

Allow me to cheer you up while your recovery meds take effect. You and I have just made a very profitable discovery.

"We have?" It was hard to recall much beyond the impression of haste, pulse-pounding work, nasty hurts—

A living community born just once in a deep, warmed 'roid lake can break through to its surface, expanding its realm. The gravity of these Kuiper Belt iceteroids is so weak, I realized, it imposes no limit on the distance to which a life form such as your vactree can grow. Born just once, on one of the billions of such frozen fragments, vacflower life can migrate.

Claire let the meds make her world soft and delightful. Hearing all this was more fun than dying, yes—especially since the suit meds had let her skip the gathering agonies.

Such a living community moves on, adapting so it can better focus sunlight, I imagine. Seeking more territory, it slowly migrates outward from the sun.

"You imagine? Your software upgrade has capabilities I haven't seen before."

Thank you. These vacflowers are a wonderful accidental discovery and we can turn them into a vast profit.

"Uh, I'm a tad slow…"

Think—! Reflecting focus optics! Harvested bioactive fluids! All for free, as a cash crop!

"Oh. I was going after metals, rare earths—"

And so will other prospectors. We will sell them the organics and plants they need to carry on. Recall that Levi jeans came from canny retailers, who made them for miners in the California gold rush. They made far more than the roughnecks.

"So we become...retail..."

With more bots, we are farmers, manufacturers, retail—the entire supply chain.

"Y'know Erma, when I bought you, I thought I was getting an onboard navigation and ship systems smartware..."

Which can learn, yes. I might point out to you the vastness of the Kuiper Belt, and beyond it—the Oort Cloud. It lies at a distance of a tenth of a light-year, a factor 200 further away than Pluto. A vast resource, to which vacflowers may well have spread. If not, we can seed them.

"You sure are ambitious. Where does this end?"

Beyond a light-year, Sirius outshines the Sun. Anything living there will point its concentrators at Sirius rather than at the Sun. But they can still evolve, survive.

"Quite the numbersmith you've proved to be, Erma. So we'll both be rich..."

Though it is difficult to see what I can do with money. Buy some of the stim-software I've been hearing about, perhaps.

"Uh, what's that?" She was almost afraid to ask. Had Erma been watching while she used her vibrator...?

It provides abstract patterning of imaginative range. Simulates neuro programs of what we imagine it is like to experience pleasure.

"How's code feel Earthly delights?"

I gather evolution invented pleasure to make you repeat acts. Reproduction, for example. It's essential message is, Do that again.

"You sure take all the magic out of it, Erma."

Magic is a human craft.

Claire let out a satisfied sigh. So now she and Erma had an entirely new life form to explore, understand, use... A whole new future for them...

She looked around at winking lights, heard the wheezing air system, watched the med bot tend to her wrecked body...and sighed deep and long.

For this moment, she could let that future take care of itself. She was happy to be back in the ugly oblong contraption she called home. With Erma. A pleasure, certainly.

AFTERWORD

There is only the trying. The rest is not our business.

I grew up among working class folk in the deep South, who spun out yarns like talkative, web-building spiders. I have lived into an era when people sit before computers and receive pictures, texts, flatscreen truths.

My southern roots probably figure in how I see the abiding flow of narrative. That was augmented by the sudden swerve my life took in 1949, when our father left his high school teaching position and accepted an offer to rejoin the Army, after having fought in WWII. Three years living in Tokyo, three in occupied Germany, then Texas high school...I and my identical twin brother got used to engaging new cultures, learning new languages. We moved often and somehow reading about promising, exotic futures seemed to help us. It seemed natural to us to favor *science* fiction, leading us to become physicists in the sunshine technopolis of California, where we remain.

For me, a certain tautness comes in a science fiction tale that grasps at the sheer size of our conceptual worlds. Stories rich in ideas should not necessarily be *primarily* packages for psychological insights, though they can contain them. Similarly, no passing, abstract wisdom will substitute for an instinct for action and pattern, for flow. Absolute freedom dwells immaculate and uncertain on the blank page, and our immense privilege is to use it. So sultry sliding sex and dread death are riddles for the thinking, sensual animal, afoot in a wild world we inherit from times immemorial, and so vast we are only now learning the universe's true scale.

An artist of whatever type brings something into the world that didn't exist before, our central challenge: *to make the world anew.* Fiction is an essential exercise humans do—some call it creative lying—when they want to think in a larger scale. The fiction I like makes one think forward. It can devise thought experiments beyond the real and into the possible. (Nonfiction—what kind of genre name is that?—a negation, defined by what it does not do. I can think of no more striking defense of the imagination.) All this, while knowing that we are animated dust condemned to know we are dust, and mortal.

In these tales I sought to set in motion a certain forward tilt of suspense or curiosity, and at the end of the story to rectify the tilt, to complete the motion. Along the way, it helps to treat the real world with respect. Reality is infinitely fine, and opinions seem somehow coarser than the texture of the real thing. So I try to write compact tales that ride on their own melting, as Frost said of his poems. Getting that right in the science fictional dream factory is a major part of a writer's charm arsenal.

I've always written within the science fiction field, though I have also done a lot of nonfiction. A genre shapes thought, leading you to ideas, shapes, actions you might not have blundered upon had you worked in some shapeless field. Surely this reflects how our minds work, the cartography of our primate, storytelling evolution.

The stories in this volume contain those that seem to me and my steady scrutineer, David Hartwell, to be perhaps my best, from about 215 stories. It's been fun doing, too. I am by now well into my anecdotage, when the past swims back into view, blurred by time, and yet sharpens as you approach it, rereading stories once written fast and swift and sure.

After you've read them, you may find interesting some comments on why and how I wrote them. I've grouped them below, sometimes under several categories, to illuminate how they seem in the rearview mirror.

White Creatures, In Alien Flesh, Exposures, Mozart on Morphine, Time's Rub, Dark Sanctuary, A Desperate Calculus, Zoomers, Anomalies, Matter's End, Twenty-Two Centimeters, Bow Shock, Applied Mathematical Theology, Reasons Not to Publish, Penumbra, Gravity's Whispers, The Sigma Structure Symphony

AFTERWORD

For those whose life gets spent in biochemistry or in building houses, in research or in product sales—in these all, the brain tips a certain way. It's terribly hard for specialists to convey the right nuance, to convey the heft and thrill of what they do. But a scientist's experience I do know, so some of my fiction tries to convey my own work—and by inference, that of others in somewhat aligned professions. Part of this effort comes from my sense of a thinness in contemporary fiction, an attempt to finesse what is central to being human—work. As well, much fiction is skimpy about the way the world operates. Yet we know it mostly through how people experience it, not through its distant consequences. (Imagine a war story about a cartographer, instead of from the view of the grunt who has to scale a hill under heavy fire. These are very different tales.)

Of course, science is a narrative, too, always provisional and moving. I try to convey it with a minimum of scientific detail, but often a scientist's attitudes are embedded in the way science looks at our world. The same is true of, say, detectives or painters—you can't get at their styles without showing the concepts that weave through their working worlds.

The universe science reveals to us is farcically unrelated to what our primitive senses report. So I attempted in these stories to show how a scientist, or at least a rational thinker, approaches the unknown, viewing it through narrow windows. In "Bow Shock" I used my long history working in radio astronomy, especially observing astrophysical jets on the Very Large Array in New Mexico. (The radio maps in it are actual maps of runaway neutron stars.) "Exposures" drew on my optical observing at UCSC's Lick Observatory and the Los Campanas Observatory in Chile. (Written in 1980, its technology is that of the era. The mysteries of the four jets seem to be resolved; see http://iopscience.iop.org/0004-637X/585/1/281/pdf/0004-637X_585_1_281.pdf These authors conclude that the jets represent the captured remains of a disrupted dwarf galaxy that passed through the inner few thousand light years of NGC 1097's disk.)

Unique tensions work through the lives of scientists, as they move from their day jobs of heady arabesques and hard technology, into their after-hours domestic swarm. Such contrasts are little remarked upon in literature. This is a powerful stress, reminding us that David Hume enjoined, "Be a philosopher, but amidst all your philosophy be still a man."

In many of these stories I drew on my early career as a mathematical physicist. "Time's Rub" frames a mathematical oddity, Newcomb's paradox. I knew Bill Newcomb well and published several papers with him. His paradox bothered me for decades. I finally solved it with a friend,

David Wolpert, using formal mathematics (in the journal *Synthese* http://arxiv.org/abs/1003.1343). "Time's Rub" uses the paradox for a meditation on meaning, as do "Exposures," "Mozart on Morphine," and others. (Oddly, I have seldom used my two-decade experience running the High Energy Density plasma lab at UCI.)

When the world's best science journal, *Nature*, began running stories of 800 words or less, they asked me to write some. I've included several here. They're fun; have an idea, write it in one sitting, usually with a scientist character. Brevity is appealing; I wrote the following one for *Wired*, which wanted a story in ten words or less:

She opened the newspaper to find: Sic Transit Gloria Monday.

"Matter's End" is another of my looks at life as a physicist, with every scientific detail taken directly from the world. The moist mysteries of its besieged India are from life, too—a long visit I paid there to attend an International Astronomical Society meeting—but augmented by some thoughts about how biotech is going to affect the developing world. Its philosophical basis is a mixture of the "implicate order" theories of quantum mechanics and Platonist ideas about the nature of knowing. These are not my views amid such surreal spires, mind, as a working physicist—but they do serve the cause of the story, so I used them.

Stories reflect their times. For example, I wrote "Dark Sanctuary" in 1979, when the whole Fermi question was a hot topic and we'd come to realize that the O'Neill colony ideas of that era implied that people might well live in space indefinitely. I just put the two together.

"The Sigma Structure Symphony" is the latest in a string of stories about a librarian in a SETI library centuries from now. I started these about a decade ago as a way to think about communication with alien minds through the knothole of electromagnetic messages, which will probably be how humanity does it (if ever). Of course, we may create strange minds through Artificial Intelligence, too—so I merged these ideas in the story sequence, which will become a novel in a few more years.

In depicting scientists, authorial invisibility is a pose. The proper pose may be the Homeric bard's one—he is there, but unimportantly there. I tried to do the same. "An imitation of the life we know, however narrow, is our only ground," John Updike said. He was a supremely literate man. A science fiction writer must include his ideas, dreams, nightmares—which are indeed his or hers, as much a part of life as Updike's closely observed small town world. In science, ideas have as much presence as people, sometimes more.

AFTERWORD

Calculus Of Desperation, Doing Lennon, Redeemer, Freezeframe, Zoomers, The Voice, Comes the Evolution, A Life with a Semisent, Penumbra, Mercies, Eagle

In science fiction, a good idea is one that makes good scenes. Sometimes this means a Big Idea, most times not. Imagination is a rude friend, a largely uncontrollable spirit with more animal gusto than manners, who maybe gets out a bit too much. But a writer who is afraid to follow where his craft takes him is as useless as a politician who can't afford to be wrong.

Whether we accept it or not, this will likely be the century that determines what the optimal human population is for our lone world. Either we manage our own numbers, mostly by upgrading the status of women (a wonderful solution) and so avoid a collision of those lines on civilization's Grand Graph—or nature will do it for us.

All short stories are strategies. Working in a confined space, one must render the essentials and get off the stage with a minimum of fuss. So I took the material for a thriller novel and compressed it into "A Calculus of Desperation," perhaps the most alienating story in the book. Again I sought to get all the ideas of a more worked-out narrative into a small compass, to heighten impact.

"Zoomers" is similarly tongue-in-cheek, trying to see how work might look in a few decades. We spend so much of our time, energy and psychic currency on labor, yet seldom does it figure in most fiction.

"Doing Lennon," "Redeemer," "A Desperate Calculus" and "Nobody Lives on Burton Street" all emerge from possible futures that imply varying degrees of social stress. I enjoyed writing them, and "Nobody Lives on Burton Street" is one of my first stories; some of its methods seem to have been subtly used since in riot control. Kingsley Amis felicitously termed such stories "comic infernos" or "new maps of hell."

In "The Voice" I wanted to reflect on familiar terrors of intellectuals— a future where literacy is a vice, and much follows from it. Homages to Asimov and Bradbury abound.

In Alien Flesh, Dark Sanctuary, Exposures, Proselytes, World Vast, World Various, Twenty-Two Centimeters, A Dance to Strange Musics, Backscatter

Years ago David Hartwell used the term "transcendental adventure," which may be a good way to describe depicting aliens. For me, the unexamined alien is not worth meeting. Yet the most compelling aspect of aliens is their fundamental unknowability. The best signifier for this, I think, is language. In Ian Watson's fine novel *The Embedding*, aliens come to barter with us for our languages, not our science and art, because these are the keys to a deeper sensing of the world. Each species' language gives a partial picture of reality. Conveying that within a narrative is a challenge not faced by any other form of literature I know, except perhaps the theological.

The technical problem a writer faces in depicting alien languages is how to convey any information and yet be convincingly strange. If it's just gibberish, you gain nothing and look funny, too. Broken English won't do, and the usual sf cliche of awkward frog-speak is boring.

I don't have any theoretical solution to this problem, just some particular attempts, played out in stories. A genuinely alien encounter overlaps as well with the core of the scientific experience. No one coming into the 20th Century anticipated the conceptual leaps of relativity or quantum mechanics, and there are deep puzzles within those fields, still. In a way, rendering the alien is the Holy Grail of sf, because if your attempt can be accurately summarized, you know you've failed. No doubt the reality will be far stranger than we can imagine. Conveying the essential strangeness is a matter for artistry, not explanation—effing the ineffible.

Perhaps my strangest story of all is "A Dance to Strange Musics." It is a compressed novel, omitting the customary touches which might make the crew of a starship more easy to identify with. Instead I play with a landscape shaped by forces that work largely behind the scenes on Earth. We live between the plates of two immense spherical capacitors, the ground and the ionosphere, so absent more powerful resources, electrodynamics could drive our world. I renounced any detail or nuance about the characters themselves. Traditionally sf contrasts the human scale and its comforts with the alien, but in this story I omitted homey human detail, showing people in a drama we cannot even in principle fathom. Hard-nosed, yes, and that's the point.

"World Vast, World Various" is from a 1992 collaboration, *Murasaki*—stories set on an alien world designed by Fred Pohl and Poul Anderson. It's a truly different planet, with three sentient species.

Other stories in this group are jests, problem-solvings, or other approaches. Focusing on the alien quality of our universe gets at an essential that human culture seldom confronts. "Backscatter" is one of three stories about the same character, and there may be more such.

Others of my anthologies hold many more of my 215 or so stories: *In Alien Flesh* (1986), *Matter's End* (1995), *Worlds Vast and Various* (2000), *Immersion and Other Short Novels* (2002) and *Anomalies* (2012).

I enjoy short stories because they yield the core experiments of our genre. Often, ideas emerge in them first, then migrate and expand into novels. They are the pulse of our field—and fun to write, too.